CAPE FLATTERY
a novel

by

Lois Arnold

Lois Arnold

Book formatting by
www.pinkcurtainpress.com

This book is dedicated to all my Mennonite ancestors and especially to my great-grandmother, Anna, whose journal of her life in Russia was my inspiration.

LIST OF CHARACTERS

THE MENNONITES:

The Teichroew Family:

Herman Teichroew, Father
Katharina Neufeld-Teichroew
Their children:
Wilhelm and Anna (deceased twins)
Maria and Katharina (deceased twins)
ANNA
Jack
Peter and Jacob (twins)
Katarina (Tina)
Gerda and Alexi, dogs

The Neufeld Family:

Heinrich Neufeld, brother of Katharina Neufeld-Teichroew
Sarah Goosen-Neufeld, wife
Daughters, Judith and Maria (twins)
Helena, daughter

The Klassen Family:

Elder Jacob Klassen
Judith Klassen, his wife
Their daughters:
Agatha, Esther, Martha, Maria, Julia, Sarah, Hannah, Rachel

Others:

Susannah Freizen, Anna's best friend
Frau Freizen, Susannah's mother
Abram Dirks, Susannah's fiancé
Gerhard Yoder, Anna's admirer
Widow Yoder, Gerhard's mother
Hans Loewen, woodcarver
Ivan and Natasha, Russian peasant servants of the Teichroew's

THE SAINT PETERSBURG RUSSIANS

The Bolkonsky Family:

Count Ilya Bolkonsky, Grandfather (deceased)
Countess Elena, Grandmother
Captain-Lieutenant Nikolas Ilyich, Son
Elizabeth Sutton, his wife (deceased)
TATIANA Nikolayevna, their daughter
Count Vasily Ilyich, Son
Countess Irene Mikhailovna, his wife
Mikael, their son
Olga, their daughter

Servants:

Helene, French Governess
Sonya, Tatiana's maid
Madame Frabert, French dressmaker
Colette, Olga's French maid

The Volodin Family:

Baron Ivan Volodin
Baroness Marie Volodina (deceased)
Dmitri, son
Ella, daughter (deceased)

THE SITKA RUSSIANS and INDIANS:

Governor Simeon Yanovski
Irina Alexandrovna, his wife, Alexander Baranov's daughter
Governor Matvei Muraviev
Madame Catherine Grigorevna-Kornilova, housekeeper
Mikhail, valet to the governor

The Bolkonskys:

Captain Nikolas Bolkonsky, Governor's Assistant, Tatiana's father
Sonya Grigorevna, his Aleut mistress (deceased)
Marya Nikolayevna (Tooch), their daughter

Aleuts:

Sergei, (Kauschti) brother of Sonya
Tugidaq, his Aleut wife
Their four daughters
Chignik, Marya's cousin, son of Tugidaq's deceased brother

Others:

Father Aleksei Sokolov, priest
Captain Igor Chernyshov, brig *Suvorov*
Natasha Chernyshov, his wife
Lieutenant Anton Dohktorov

The Volodins:

Lieutenant Dmitri Volodin
TATIANA Nikolayevna, his wife
Keeah, Tlingit maid
Helena, *Creole* cook of Volodins
Maria, Aleut maid of Volodins

The Pushkins:

Captain-Lieutenant Basil Pushkin, brig *Finlandia*
Elizabeth Pushkin, his wife
Anastasia, their daughter, age 12
Twins: Fedor and Nikolai, age 9

The Trotskys:

Captain-Lieutenant Alexis Trotsky, brig *Kuskov*
Irina Trotsky, his wife
Vera Alexisovna, daughter
Sophie Alexisovna, daughter

Others:

Lieutenant Boris Ivanoff, sloop *Kamchatka*
Ivan Putin, aide
Fedor Gorki, sailor on *Alexandria*
Captain-Lieutenant Shekolov from the *Czarina*

THE BRITISH

The Sutton Family:

Lord Henry Sutton (deceased)
Lady Diana Sutton (deceased)
Lord Henry Sutton, their son
Lady Jane Sutton, his wife
Henry, William, Charles, their sons
Elizabeth, sister of Henry (deceased)

Servants:

James, Butler
Molly, Maid

Officers of the British ship, *Elizabeth Ann*:

Captain Matthew Hunter
First Officer Mr. Lennon
Second Officer Mr. Benjamin Todd

THE AMERICANS

The O'Connell Family:

Patrick O'Connell (Paddy)
Kathleen O'Hara O'Connell (deceased)
Their children:
SEAN, son, Rose, daughter
Colum (deceased), Mary and Shannon (deceased twins)

Others:

Father O'Brien, Priest

The Hill Family of Boston:

Thomas Hill, wealthy ship-owner
Priscilla Hill, his wife
John Hill, nephew

The Simpson Family:

Frederick Simpson, banker
Velma Simpson, his wife
Abigail Simpson, their daughter, fiancée of John Hill

Crew of the *Eastern Wind*:

Captain Edward Smythe
First Mate, Arthur Horn
Second Mate, Ethan Campbell
Supercargo, Andrei Leonov
Carpenter/Cooper, Nate Anderson
Armorer (blacksmith), William Carter
Sail maker, Ben Green
Captain's steward, Samuel Washington
Cook, Wang Li,
Apprentices,
Ned Johnson, SEAN O'CONNELL,
Cabin boy, Jake O'Riley
Seaman, Ralph Parsons

Crew of the *Sea Rose*: (First Voyage)

Captain Sean O'Connell
First Mate, Ethan Campbell
Second Mate, Ned Johnson
Third Mate, Jake O'Riley
Supercargo, John Hill
Armorer, Gregory Jones
Sail maker, Tom Harris
Carpenter, Ebenezer Cartwright
Captain's steward, Samuel Washington
Cook, Wang Li
Cabin boys, James (Jimmy) and Robby

Crew of the *Sea Rose*: (2nd Voyage)

Captain Sean O'Connell
First Mate, John Hill
Second Mate, Jake O'Riley
Carpenter, Ebenezer Cartwright
Armorer, Edmund Wilde
Steward, Samuel Washington
Cook, Wang Li
Seamen, Jeb Drake and Nate Tyler
Cabin Boy, Robby
Dog, Jimmy
Cat, Otter

THE MAKAHS

Chief's family:

Chief Utramaka
First Wife, Gray Cloud
Second Wife (deceased)
She-Who-Never-Sleeps, daughter of Second Wife
Laughing Gull, mother of Utramaka

Sons:

1. Black Hawk, firstborn son
First Wife, Soft Fern,
Red Hawk, their son
2. Strong Elk, second son
First Wife, Brown Bird
Daughter, Small Fawn (She-Who-Always-Giggles)
Son, Muddy Feet (He-Who-Has-Muddy-Feet)
Second Wife, Swift Deer

Others:

Utilla, *Shaman*, older cousin of Utramaka
Lightning Eagle, *shaman*'s apprentice
Frog, Utilla's Chinook slave woman
Brave Spear, Black Hawk's friend
Starlight, his widowed daughter

THE QUILEUTES

Chief's family:

Chief Xawishata
First Wife, Many Baskets
Second Wife, Talks A Lot
Hoheeshata, younger brother of Xawishata
First Wife, Hummingbird
Second Wife, Buttercup

Others:

White Panther, *Shaman*

Indian names of the captives:

Sean, Green Eyes, Running Wolf
Anna, Knows Much
Tatiana, Daughter of the Sun
Marya, Whispering Doe
Katya, Little Dawn, She-With-Hair-of-Sunrise
John, Yellow Hair
Samuel, Black Crow
Jake O'Riley, Man With Hair Of Orange
Starfish
Wang Li, Little Man With Big Stories
Robby, Hollow Stomach, Gray Whale
Anton, Canoe Man
Keeah, Tlingit Girl

PROLOGUE

October 1809

The wind blowing across the vast grassy plains of the steppes of southern Russia was a constant presence that each person in the Mennonite farming village of Furstenau became used to shortly after birth. Only in the hottest days of summer or in the icy calm of the coldest nights of winter did it cease to moan around the village houses. In the spring the wind rippled the waist high grass of the steppes into long billowing waves like an ocean of gentle green swells. In the fall it often brought a frosty sharpness that reddened noses and cheeks with a promise of the winter ahead.

One autumn night, on the eve of Anna Teichroew's seventh birthday, the wind carried a new sound, something she had never heard before. It was the deep guttural sound of strange men shouting in anger; then came the pounding of heavy fists on the sturdy oak door of the Teichroew's family home.

Anna and her younger brother Jack were supposed to be asleep in their beds made of straw filled mattresses. The house had four rooms, a kitchen and parlor and two bedrooms. A chimney stood on each end of the house. Between them was built a long brick oven with a door on each side where flax straw was burned for heat and for baking. In the children's snug bedroom the adjacent brick wall radiated steady warmth, seeping into the muscles and limbs of Anna's exhausted little body. It had been another long hard day of numerous and never-ending chores for their family.

Although Anna and Jack were children, they were still expected to help with many of the lighter tasks. In the barn adjoining the rear of the house were the animals, and Anna had already learned to feed the chickens and gather their eggs, help her mama with milking the cows, and help her papa feed the pigs and oxen. Just that day her mama had taught her how to bake rye bread, but trying to knead the dark heavy dough soon tired out her small fingers and she ended up watching Mama expertly pound the dough into fat brown loaves.

Usually the second Anna's head hit her pillow she was sound asleep. But that night she was too excited thinking about her birthday tomorrow. Mama said they would be making sugar *twaback*, a special treat, usually reserved for weddings and other special occasions. And she hoped there would also be a present of some kind for her, perhaps a doll.

Two weeks ago after a church meeting she had seen Papa talking to Hans Loewen, the village wood carver who often made toys for children. When she walked up to them, Papa suddenly stopped speaking, and *Herr* Loewen had winked at her. Mama pulled her away with a few stern words of not bothering her elders when they were in discussion. But Papa hadn't seemed upset with her, and gave her a quick smile that warmed her down to her toes.

As Anna tossed on her mattress, her ears picked up two sounds. One was the normal bedtime fussing of her one-year-old twin brothers, Peter and Jacob, in her parents' bedroom on the other side of the brick wall as Mama settled them down for the night. The other was harsh male voices she heard from outside her window. Before she could reach over to her brother's mattress and poke him to see if he was awake, the tramp of heavy boots and the banging on the front door rolled Jack right out of his bed with a startled cry.

"Anna, what is that?"

Her heart seemed to thump in rhythm with each thud of a fist on the door, and she only managed a croak in reply. "Don't know!"

They heard a note of alarm in Mama's voice as she called out from the twins' bedside, "Herman, Herman--"

Anna's father was not a large man. But at age forty Herman Teichroew had a stocky body with muscles honed by years of long hours working the fields and was considered by most as a man capable of the toughest physical challenges. Anna certainly had felt safe all her young life in her home and village, knowing her papa was there to protect her and her family from the occasional wild animal or snake.

Snakes were a common plague all over the steppes because for centuries the Russian peasants believed in a superstition against killing them. Thus, the earliest Mennonite settlers had encountered snake mounds. Although Anna had never seen a snake mound, she had heard them described as two to three hundred serpents heaped in a writhing mass. Some snakes were as long as sixteen feet, and could knock over a young calf.

Just last summer on washday, her mama had carried in an armload of freshly dried laundry and had placed it in the kitchen for the next day's ironing. Suddenly a big black snake crawled out from among the clothes. Both she and Mama had screamed in unison, bringing her papa and Jack running in from the barn. In a calm voice Papa explained that the snake was not venomous, but warned them to stand still, as he bade Jack to fetch an ax from the shed. The snake was slithering its way toward Anna's bedroom by the time Papa had managed to sever its flat black head with one quick strike of the sharp blade. She still shuddered whenever she thought of it. She was more frightened of snakes than of spiders.

The pounding on the front door grew louder. She and Jack crept into the kitchen and peered into the parlor just as Papa opened the door. Three strange men burst in, angrily shouting in a foreign sounding language. Anna only knew how to speak the Mennonite Low German and a few Russian words of the local peasants. She had no idea what these men were saying.

"They're Tartars, Anna, " whispered Jack.

Anna shivered in dread. Everyone had heard of the Nogai-Tartars, the roving bands of steppe horsemen and fierce warriors who ranged between the Russians to the north and the Turks to the south. They were nomads who saw the settled Mennonite villages as a threat to their way of life, and would make sudden appearances plundering and stealing. The hardworking Mennonites were accumulating grains and stock faster than they could build shelter for all of it, so they were unfortunate enough to occasionally become victims of these thieves. Although a raid on the village itself was rare because of the close proximity of each homestead to the other, the Tartars had learned quickly that the Mennonites believed in nonresistance. Stealing a horse from a pacifist Mennonite farmer was as easy as taking sugar lumps from a child.

The Teichroew house was the last homestead at the end of the village, making it the most vulnerable. Anna could only hope and pray that their next-door neighbors, the Yoders, had heard the commotion. Hans Yoder was a large burly man with four sons who looked just like him. Although Anna had always felt intimidated by the Yoder men, at the moment she would give anything to see them.

All three Tartars had heavy black beards and frowning mustaches that obscured the coarse features of their deeply tanned faces. Their hair was long and greasy and Anna could smell the rank odor of their unwashed bodies mixed with male sweat and blood. She noticed how two of them were bleeding from wounds. One man had a long gash in his right shoulder, the cloth of his coat torn and stained with blood and dirt. Another was limping with what looked like a bullet hole in his left thigh, dark red blood oozing down his leg. He leaned against the wall and uttered something harsh, most likely a curse, while glaring with fierce black eyes at Herman.

Anna's father made a move towards him and gestured at a chair for him to sit down, but the unwounded man took his actions as a threat. He slid a knife out of his belt and quickly grabbed Herman, twisting him around, then pressed the sharp blade against his throat.

Fear shot through Anna's heart at seeing her strong papa reduced to helplessness. Jack made a short lunge as if to go to his aid, but Anna grabbed his arm.

"Let me go," he hissed. "Papa needs me!"

Anna was about to reply when their mother swept passed them with a quick shake of her head. "Stay in the kitchen, children, "she said quietly, "I want you to start boiling some water and get some cheese and bread for our guests."

Katharina Teichroew was a small slim woman with thick hair the color of dark honey, and now at age thirty-four, streaked lightly with gray. She had hazel brown eyes with flecks of gold and a straight nose, and a mouth that smiled often even when exhausted. In her youth she had been considered a beauty, and while the harsh Russian sun and wind had etched lines on her face already, the extra years only added a look of wisdom and quiet strength to her countenance. People said Anna was a younger image of her mother.

Herman gasped, as the knife pressed harder on his skin and a thin line of blood trickled down his throat. He looked at his wife with frightened eyes. He wanted to warn her to flee with the children. His mouth opened to speak, but he could only manage one word, "Tina..."

Anna saw Mama close her eyes briefly and she knew her mother was praying. Then she flashed all three Tartars her warmest smile as if they were her dearest friends instead of dangerous strangers who were threatening her husband. The three men stared at her in surprise. The one holding Herman relaxed his grip slightly.

Later all Anna would remember was that her mama had performed some kind of miracle. One minute it seemed to her the devil himself and his two minions had invaded their house, with the sole intention of killing her papa. The next minute she was slicing bread and cheese to serve them as she would any honored visitors, while Mama bathed wounds with warm water and soap and bandaged them with clean strips of cloth. After being released from the Tartar's knife, her papa handed him and the two wounded men hot cups of tea from the steaming samovar. Little Jack distributed fresh clothing and blankets, but Anna could tell he did so grudgingly. If it weren't for the dark red line on her father's throat, Anna would've thought she dreamt the entire episode.

That night the Tartars slept in the barn, making Anna nervous. She'd heard they weren't the only wounded Tartars in Furstenau. Earlier a small band of them had tried to take over a nearby Russian village. The peasants fought back by shooting several of the Tartars and all their horses. The Tartars fled to Furstenau, knowing the Mennonite reputation of hospitality and were hoping for help, but were uncertain if they would be welcomed or rebuffed.

Anna's family and several others took them in. Two weeks later when the men were well enough to leave, they were sent off with a horse pulling a crude wooden sled with provisions to last them until they reached their homes.

Anna felt nothing but relief at their departure. It was her job to bring them food each day. As she placed their meals before them in the barn, they would stare at her with their narrow slanted black eyes, never speaking. Their roughly bearded faces made her limbs tremble and it was all she could do not to spill anything. When she hurried away, they would erupt into coarse laughter.

These were the last Tartars Anna ever saw. As the years passed, the kindness of the Mennonites paid off and Furstenau was never troubled by Tartars again. However, it was her mother's quiet courage that impressed her the most. Anna had always been taught the Mennonite way of nonviolence and that "A soft answer turneth away wrath," from the Bible.

Yet, she had never quite believed it, until now.

* * *

The young girl with frightened eyes gazed out of her bedchamber window at Saint Petersburg, the Imperial City of Russia. She could see the turrets of the Orthodox cathedrals with gilded spires rising everywhere like golden pyramids. The churches stood on the streets with the proud names of the Admiralty, the Arsenal, the Citadel, and the Academy, as did the Czarina's Winter Palace, which was near her own home, the Count Vasily Ilyich Bolkonsky's palace. The Winter Palace dwarfed all the other structures. It was an immense building of blue-green stucco, massive white pillars, and seemingly endless rows of windows lighting over a thousand rooms. If she squinted, she could even spot some of the statues decorating the roof balustrade.

Her window was open, though the temperature outside was near freezing. Tatiana Nikolayevna Bolkonskaya leaned over the sill, looking down at the river below, the water glittering azure and gold in the dying rays of the setting sun. The Neva River was alive with dozens of sailing ships, their colorful flags and streamers fluttering in the evening breeze.

She longed to board one of those ships and sail away and never come back. Sail around the world to Russian America, the land of Alaska, where her father, Nikolas Ilyich Bolkonsky, was stationed as an important officer in the Imperial Navy. Now that her beloved grandmother, Nana, was dying, there was no one left here in her uncle's palace to care if she was happy or sad; no one to give her hugs and bedtime kisses; no one to protect her from Mikael and Olga.

Ever since she could remember her two older cousins had hated her. She never understood why, unless it had something to do with her mother. The mother she had never seen, who had died when she was born.

Sometimes Mikael and Olga taunted her with the cruel accusation, "Tatiana killed her own mother, her stupid English mother...."

Then she would burst into tears and run to Nana who always comforted her by saying, "What a lot of nonsense! It is impossible for a tiny baby to kill anything. Your mother died only because it was God's will."

"Don't let those two mean spirited children upset you so," she would add, stroking Tatiana's long golden hair. "Remember, I love you the best."

That secret knowledge quickly dried her tears, and the next time she saw Mikael or Olga, she would give them a smug smile. But she would never dare tell them what her grandmother had said, for she knew it would only infuriate them more.

With a meow a small white kitten jumped onto the windowsill next to her, and started to purr. It was her kitten, Snowflake. Although his claws dug into the wood finish for balance, the kitten was only inches away from death if he fell. Tatiana scooped him up into her arms and carried him over to her bed, plopping him onto the soft blankets. If Nana truly did die, she would need Snowflake more than ever. He was the only creature in this cold palace who would give her any affection. And what made him even more special, was that he had been given to her by her father on his last visit a few months before. Russian America was so far away that he came back to Saint Petersburg only once every three or four years. He had been gone when she was born, and had seen her for the first time when she was three years old. This past visit was the second time father and daughter had met, and the next one might not be until she was ten or eleven years old.

She had a vague memory of the first time she saw him. Dressed in a naval lieutenant's uniform, he was a total stranger, a man with a big mustache holding her stiffly on his knees for a few moments, then quickly setting her down with a pat on the head, and turning away to talk to her uncle. Hoping to catch more of his attention she grabbed his pants leg with her sticky fingers and started sniffling.

With a frown he had glanced down at her and said, "I had so hoped Elizabeth would give me a son."

Even at that tender age, Tatiana felt his rejection and immediately let out a wail. Her father only shook his head as her nanny hastily removed her and took her back to the nursery.

Their second meeting last summer had gone much better. Tatiana braced herself to expect nothing from her father, so when he greeted her with a big smile and an armful of gifts, she was pleasantly surprised. This time she didn't try to touch him, although a part of her longed to have him sweep her up into a big hug, the way she had once seen her uncle do to Olga after he had drunk a lot of wine. Instead she politely answered his questions about her studies, and even recited a short poem that her governess had taught her. Her father looked on with much approval then gave her pretty ribbons for her hair, embroidered handkerchiefs, and a small necklace with strange markings on it that he said was made by the savages in Alaska.

"They carved it out of a huge walrus tooth," he said, making her gasp at the thought of a sea creature with teeth that big.

Tatiana knew it was a treasure to keep hidden from the jealous eyes of her cousins. She would never dare to actually wear the necklace in case they snatched it away. She would find a good hiding place in her bedchamber for it. "Thank you, Papa," she said, and then with impulsive delight, added, "I love you!"

He smiled and patted her head and told her she was a good girl. She had never felt so happy.

During the next few weeks she saw very little of her father. He was busy outfitting the ships for the next expedition to Russian America. Finally, the night before he was due to sail, he came up to her bedchamber as she was getting ready for bed and gave her a squirming white bundle of fur.

Stunned, she was speechless. He laughed and said, "Here is someone to keep you company during the long winter nights."

Her French governess, *Mademoiselle* Helene, tightened her thin lips with disapproval, but Nikolas ignored her and added, "Our ship's cat had kittens on the voyage home and I thought you might like one."

Tatiana's joy knew no bounds, and even though her aunt disapproved of the kitten as much as her governess, neither woman would go against her father's wishes by removing him. Dearest Nana also championed her cause by saying, "the kitten is harmless and should stay." But this statement didn't stop Mikael from sneaking into Tatiana's room from time to time and pulling Snowflake's tail or chasing him around the furniture. More than once Tatiana found her kitten cowering under her bed, and she knew immediately that Mikael had been there.

If only she could complain to his mother, Aunt Irene. But Tatiana knew that Mikael would deny all charges and accuse her of lying. His mother always believed him over her and thought her son could do no wrong. Long ago she had learned the hard way how futile it was to complain about anything he or Olga did to her. Aunt Irene would only lose her temper and end up delivering a stinging slap to her face, then order her to be locked up in her bedchamber for the rest of the day without food. Sometimes Nana would find out, but she was intimidated by her formidable daughter-in-law and would never outright confront her. Instead Nana would have a maid sneak Tatiana something to eat.

Now she sighed, wishing it was her Aunt Irene who was terribly ill instead of her beloved Nana. It would serve Mikael and Olga right to be motherless too.

Suddenly it seemed her thoughts had conjured up her aunt for Aunt Irene appeared in the doorway. "Tatiana, your grandmother has requested to speak with you. Come along."

She followed without hesitation, her short legs moving quickly to keep up with Aunt Irene's long strides. "Is Nana better?"

"No. In fact, there isn't much time." Aunt Irene turned and grabbed Tatiana's arm, pinching the skin painfully. "Hurry now."

Her uncle's palace was vast, with multiple wings sprawling out in opulent grandeur, hundreds of rooms furnished with wall coverings of damask and furniture crafted from the rarest woods, mahogany, maple, ash, and rosewood. The floors and the long endless corridors were of smooth marble and plush carpets from Persia, and the windows made of rare Bohemian glass plates. Most seven-year-old girls would be intimidated by such cavernous surroundings, but Tatiana never gave it a thought. She had spent her whole life in the palace and had explored all its secrets, except for the servants' quarters and the dank cellars. To her young mind, it was normal to live in such luxury, and as far as she knew, everyone in the world lived in a palace.

Her grandmother's bedchamber wasn't far from her own, and as she approached the door her feet began to drag. She hadn't seen Nana for a couple weeks, and even then her grandmother had looked so different. She seemed to have shrunk and her skin was as thin as parchment. She wheezed as she struggled to breathe, and Tatiana had been afraid to talk to her. But Nana hadn't known she was there. She was asleep, and Tatiana had left without speaking to her.

Nana, the Countess Elena Bolkonskaya, had been widowed for eight years. In 1801 her husband, Count Ilya Bolkonsky, had been shot and killed when he and other dissatisfied members of the nobility had led a revolt against Czar Paul I, the unstable son of Catherine the Great. During the palace revolution Czar Paul had also been murdered. Count Bolkonsky's fellow revolutionaries placed Paul's son, Alexander, on the throne.

Soon after Czar Alexander I rewarded the personal sacrifice and loyalty of the Bolkonsky family by granting them an iron mine in Siberia and an immense country estate in the Ukraine, plus the ownership of thousands of serfs to operate the mines and work the estate. Then there were the countless servants to take care of the palace in Saint Petersburg and other elegant homes in Moscow. Since the wealth of a great man in Russia was measured by the amount of land and by the number of serfs he possessed, the Bolkonskys were considered to be one of the most powerful families of the nobility.

Yet the Countess Elena had led a hard life. Her and Ilya's firstborn son was Vasily, Tatiana's uncle, now the Count. In the nine years following his birth, Elena had birthed three more babies, but each one died from diphtheria before the age of one year. When Tatiana's father, Nikolas, was born in 1774 and grew to be a healthy handsome boy with a sunny disposition, he easily won all the hearts around him. He became his mother's favorite, much to Vasily's envy. Although Vasily had also inherited the good looks of the Bolkonsky's, he lacked the cheerful smiles and quick sense of humor that Nikolas possessed. Instead he was a quiet brooding child with an eye only for the estates and the title, which would someday be his. As the younger son, Nikolas could not inherit the title of Count or the estates, so he had made a successful career out of the military and now, as a lieutenant in the Imperial Navy, had command of his own ship.

How Tatiana wished her father were here at this very moment. Nana's bedchamber was hot, stuffy, and stank of stale urine mixed with the cloying sweetness of incense. The curtains were pulled and the only light came from several candles, their flames casting dancing shadows across the immense bed where the countess lay gasping her final breaths. Tatiana shrank back in dread. She didn't recognize this shrunken ghastly old woman as her beloved Nana who always looked at Tatiana with sparkling eyes and a bright smile.

Aunt Irene pushed her forwards until she was next to the bed. "I don't know why it was you she wanted to see, and not Mikael or Olga."

"Nana?" Tatiana said in a hesitant voice.

Her grandmother's eyes were opened, staring upwards at the ceiling. With a visible effort, she turned to Tatiana. She opened her shriveled lips to speak, but no words came out, just a rush of air. Her gaze locked on Tatiana and she let out another gasp, then she died. Tatiana froze in disbelief. "Nana?"

Uncle Vasily hurried in the room followed by a Russian Orthodox priest in his robes carrying a golden crucifix and a vial of holy water. "You're too late! She's gone!" Aunt Irene wailed.

The priest shook his head and rushed to the bedside, hastily speaking the Last Rites, and sprinkling holy water on the countess's forehead and face. The monotone words spoken in Latin meant nothing to Tatiana, and she turned and stumbled from the bedchamber. No one noticed her leaving. She fled back towards her own room, tears blurring every step she took.

Nana once said it was God's will that her own mother had died. Now her beloved grandmother was gone. Did that mean that God was taking all the people she loved away from her? Would her father be next? It seemed to her that God didn't care about a little girl's broken heart.

When Tatiana reached her bedchamber she saw Mikael run out the door. With an even greater sense of foreboding, she rushed into the room. "Snowflake...Snowflake," she called looking hastily under her bed and behind the other furniture. Her kitten was nowhere to be found. She walked over to the still open window and glanced down. There far below on the darkening lawn, was a spot of white. It was not moving. And suddenly she knew. There was no God at all. She began to scream.

* * *

It was his sister's screams that woke Sean out of a sound sleep. He knew immediately what was happening. Da was beating Rose again.

Ever since Ma's death four years ago his da had been turning his drunken rages more frequently upon his younger sister. Sean knew his da would rather take his violent fits out on him, but at age fifteen, Sean was now taller and more muscular than his da. Lately whenever Da saw the cold hatred in Sean's eyes, instead of a fist to the jaw, Da only muttered a curse and left him alone.

Sean O'Connell had been born and reared in the filthy tenements and crowded streets of the poorest part of Boston, Massachusetts where the immigrant Irish lived. Ever since he could remember his da had been drunk and angry and his ma, whom he loved with all his heart, had tried to protect Sean and Rose from him.

Raven-haired Kathleen O'Hara had been beautiful once when the handsome young Patrick O'Connell had charmed her back in Dublin, Ireland, and swept her off her feet. After a whirlwind courtship they married and Kathleen found herself on her way to America, convinced by her new husband of the riches waiting for them in the new land of opportunity. She didn't want to leave her family. Although they were poor tenant farmers, they were close-knit. But there was nothing for a newlywed couple in Ireland except to work for brutal English landowners, resulting in poverty, famine and disease. They didn't know there wasn't much for them in America either.

In the late 1700's the Irish immigrants in the young United States were scorned and treated little better than the blacks imported from Africa to be servants in the north and slaves in the south. Since Boston Harbor was the busiest port on the east coast, a lucky Irishman might find steady employment at the docks as a shipyard worker loading and unloading cargo.

At first both Patrick and Kathleen had the fortune of steady jobs. Patrick worked at the docks and Kathleen became a scullery maid in the kitchen of a mansion where a rich ship owner's family resided. Then the babies started coming and Kathleen was let go. A scullery maid was a physically demanding job, and the cook had no time to coddle a pregnant or nursing young mother. Kathleen was easily replaced by another young Irish girl.

Firstborn was Sean, then a year later, Rose. Both were healthy and thrived. Then Patrick's income began to dwindle. He was working as much as ever, but had acquired the bad habit of stopping off at the pub on the way home from the docks, and spending his hard earned coins there. Soon Kathleen began to take in laundry and extra sewing to buy food and pay the rent even as she gave birth to another baby every couple of years.

None of the children born after Sean and Rose lived long. There had been Colum, a sweet-natured boy who had been sickly from birth. At age two years he died one harsh winter from a fever and a horrid cough that never stopped until he gasped his last breath. In 1801 twin girls had been born, Mary and Shannon, but they never reached their first birthdays. Sean couldn't remember why they had died, but it seemed there hadn't been enough milk for them, and they had never grown much. The last baby, an unnamed infant boy, had been stillborn, and Kathleen had never recovered from the birth. As the days passed, she grew weaker and weaker, a look of grief permanently etched on her thin face, not caring how much Patrick yelled at her, and taking little interest in her two remaining children.

Finally one hot summer morning she passed away. Sean always supposed his ma died of a broken heart. Living with a drunken abusive husband and losing four children was more than she could bear. Even her faith hadn't brought any comfort or peace in her last days. She had been a faithful Catholic and rarely missed a Mass, but he never saw any good her religion had brought her. His ma had tried to raise him and Rose as proper Catholics, and sent them to the local parish school, a luxury to which Patrick objected. He didn't know how to read or write and he didn't see why his children needed to either. Rose was forced to quit school after only two years and Sean by age ten.

It was the only time in his life he had agreed with his father. He found school boring and especially disliked the rigid doctrines of the priests. He had no use for religion. He rejected it the day he'd heard the parish priest refer to God as "our Heavenly Father." Instead of seeing God as a kindly loving father figure like the priest implied, all Sean could see was the brutal face of his own father. As far as he was concerned, if God existed, then He was a remote Being who cared nothing for those He created. Otherwise, his beloved mother would be alive today.

It was different for Rose. She believed everything the priests said. She wore their mother's crucifix around her neck day and night and spent many hours sitting on her bed, fingering her rosary beads and softly praying to the Virgin Mary or some saint. Whenever their father came home from the pub and found her like that, it enraged him. He expected her to be cleaning their tiny apartment or using her skills as a seamstress to earn extra income, not lazing around muttering that religious "mumbo-jumbo," as he called it.

"Like mother, like daughter," he'd roar, and then smack her hard enough to make her stop. When she'd burst into tears, he usually left her alone, but lately, her crying had only infuriated him the more.

If it wasn't for Rose, Sean would have run away right after their ma died. He stayed at home only to protect her. She was the only person left in the world he cared about. Yet recently, he had been wondering how much longer he could stay even for her.

Since he was a child his dream was to sail the seas. He'd spent his childhood hanging around the docks where his father worked, often in the way, but accepted by the Irish workers as "Black Paddy's kid." He'd always thought his father's nickname well-suited him. Although he was called Black Paddy because of his black hair and foul temper, Sean thought it was more fitting due to his father's black heart.

Many of the Irishmen were just like his father, hardworking, hard-drinking, frequently getting in brawls. There was much competition at the docks for jobs among the Irish, the Poles, the English, and the Italians. Each ethnic group stayed to themselves and distrusted and disliked anyone not from their own country. Sean had learned at a young age to use his natural intelligence and quickness to stay out of trouble, especially avoiding the port policemen, who had a reputation for arresting Irishmen for the slightest infraction.

When small, he hid himself easily on a dock behind large boxes of cargo, gazing at all the ships and imagining what it would be like to sail away in one of them. He vowed that someday he would be a ship's captain with the sea at his feet and the wind over his head, the elements his to command, to speed his ship and crew to lands and people unknown. In his mind he could hear the surf crash on faraway shores, smell the tangy salt breezes, and feel his ship race through the ocean swells. Never again having to bend his will to his father or anyone, he would be free, the master of his own destiny.

Now he was a dock worker just like his father. In some ways it was torture for him to spend all his days so near to the sailing ships, but not be able to be a part of their crew. He had once hoped to sign on as a cabin boy, but now he was too old and too big. Cabin boys were usually taken at age eleven or twelve, and though he wasn't that much older, all the long hours of lifting heavy barrels and boxes had given him a strong muscular body. He had grown tall, too, almost six feet and still growing. He had also inherited his mother's black hair, green eyes, and high cheekbones, and was considered extremely handsome by the local Irish colleens. He had no interest in them, nor had any intention of getting involved with a girl and being trapped in an early marriage, ending up as miserable as his own parents. He was going to take control of his own life and not let life take control of him.

On this afternoon he had been offered a job as an apprentice seaman on a merchant ship. He had been unloading barrels of rum and molasses from the West Indies off the large three masted bark the *Eastern Wind*, when one of her officers had asked him his name and age. Sean knew most ships were shorthanded after putting into port. After being paid many of the crew went ashore and never returned.

It was a constant struggle to man the ships, especially now with the tensions heating up between the United States and England over British interference in American shipping. With England at war with Napoleon's France, any American ship sailing to Europe ran the risk of being stopped by the British navy. The British claimed the right to remove any sailor of British birth and force him back into British naval service. But whether by design or mistake, Sean had heard horror stories of native-born Americans being impressed along with the British born sailors. In order to replace missing crewmen in port, American officers often resorted to raiding the waterfront pubs and grabbing any man unfortunate enough to be so drunk he passed out. Hours later he would awake and find himself with a pounding headache, a nauseous stomach, and miles out to sea.

The best seaman was made from eager lads like Sean willing to work, and the officer from the *Eastern Wind* knew it. Sean had told him he needed to think about his offer.

"Not too long, "he was told, "We sail first thing in the mornin' with the outgoing tide."

Excitement built in him as he realized how close he was to his dream coming true. Although becoming an apprentice meant being indentured for several years to the ship's owner, performing the most menial jobs onboard, the end result was the opportunity to work up to officer status. After that, Sean hoped it was only a matter of time and experience before being offered the command of a ship.

His excitement waned after coming home. Rose had supper waiting, a thin soup made of potatoes and cabbage, and some dry bread crusts. It was their usual meager fare. Sean gulped the food down quickly to appease the constant gnawing hunger in his stomach. As he ate he looked at her, thinking how small and frail she was for her fourteen years. How could he go off to sea and leave her alone with Black Paddy?

Poor Rose. Not only was she skinny, her face showed the results of their father's abuse. Her nose had been broken twice and was now crooked, and she was missing several teeth, making her look like a little old lady when she smiled, something she rarely did. What did the future have in store for her? He doubted any man would marry such an unattractive girl, although she had a kind heart and an intelligent mind.

It was as if she'd read his thoughts, for Rose turned to him and said, "Sean, I've great news! Father O'Brien told me t'day I can come to the parish in the evenin's an' 'e'd teach me book learnin.' Ain't that grand?"

Unlike Sean, Rose had been devastated years ago when Da forced her to quit school. Since then, she had longed to continue her studies and had confided once that her dream was to be a teacher. They both had dreams, he realized, that might never be fulfilled.

Her dark brown eyes sparkled with happiness, making her look almost pretty. "Father O'Brien said 'e'll teach me for nothin' if I help 'im with the bairns."

"Jus' don't let Da know," he pointed out. "Do it when 'e's out at the pub an' be 'ome before 'e's back."

She nodded uneasily. They both knew their father wasn't working steadily anymore and his hours were unpredictable. His years of heavy drinking were finally taking its toll on him. He was often late for work and slacked off early so he could head to the nearest tavern. Some days he would be turned away at the docks altogether, for there was a work shortage in Boston.

In December, 1807 the US Congress had passed the Embargo Act. It was in response to the British policy of blockading neutral ships in European waters and naval impressments. The act closed all United States ports to foreign ships and American ships were allowed to sail only to other home ports. The result was chaos. Overseas trade had nearly stopped, almost ruining some New England ship owners and putting many sailors out of work. Shipyards closed and goods piled up in warehouses. Most dockworkers were laid off. When Congress realized that the embargo had hurt the United States more than the British or the French, they had repealed it last March, allowing trade with all countries except England and France.

Since then, the docks had returned to activity, but not like before. There was less work and Paddy had discovered that the younger stronger men like Sean were favored over the older men like himself. His pride was stung and he resented his son more than ever. He took to demanding most of Sean's wages, so he could have the means to buy more whiskey. Sean didn't dare refuse to hand over his money. He decided whatever it took to keep Black Paddy out of the house and away from Rose was worth the loss of income.

Soon after their conversation he went to bed and fell asleep. It seemed like minutes, but it was hours later when he was rudely awakened by Rose's screams.

"No, Da, don't!"

Sean shot out of bed. His father's bulky figure seemed to fill the tiny one room apartment. He was leaning over Rose's bed, which was usually partitioned off with a curtain for her privacy. Now the curtain was torn and she was sobbing, huddled over, trying pathetically to ward off the blows from Black Paddy's belt. Sean felt rage building inside of him.

"Leave 'er alone!" He yelled and lunged for his father, his deep anger throwing away all sense of caution.

Paddy looked at him and snarled, "'Tis none of your business, Sean. Leave us be!"

Sean hesitated then saw bright red blood trickling down the side of Rose's head. The sight enraged him further and he grabbed Paddy's thick arm, halting the next blow of the belt in midair. His father turned on him with a growl and a blast of whiskey fumes assaulted his nose. They both grappled for possession of the belt, each man pitting his strength against the other.

Sean managed to grab the end of the belt and yanked hard, pulling his father into him, and they both lost their balance and crashed to the floor. Paddy lost his grip on the belt and Sean flung it away. He didn't see the fist coming until it thudded into his cheek, splitting it open. Blood ran into his mouth and his face felt on fire. With a renewed burst of anger, he pinned his father to the floor with his body and his hands instinctively wrapped themselves around his throat and squeezed tightly. Paddy tried to squirm away, his fists pounding on Sean's back. He only squeezed harder and tighter, the years of frustration and hatred giving him superhuman strength.

Somewhere in the distance he vaguely heard Rose telling him to stop. But he found he couldn't stop. He didn't want to. And he didn't stop choking him until his father's body suddenly went limp.

"Sean, Sean, 'ave ye killed 'im?" Rose cried out.

He released his grip and his father's head thudded backwards onto the floor. Paddy's bloodshot eyes bulged out and his tongue hung over his thick lips. His face was purple and there was a red welt around his neck. Sean wasn't sure if he was breathing or not. He hoped not.

Rose ran over to their father and bent over him. "I think 'e's dead!" She made the sign of the cross then looked up at Sean, her eyes wide with shock. In a shaky voice she said, "May God forgive 'im...an' you."

"I don't believe in forgiveness," he said angrily. "But if there's a hell, I hope Da rots in it!"

Rose clutched the crucifix around in her neck and stared at him like he was a stranger. "Don't say such terrible things, Sean!"

He shrugged, impatient with the religious talk. There was no time for it anyway. He had a more immediate problem to solve. He glanced down at his father's body and he suddenly knew exactly what to do.

Under his bed in what Sean always thought of as his seabag, was an assortment of tools that a sailor needed. He had acquired them over many years of scrounging around the docks. He had a wooden spike called a fid, used in sail making and rope work, a few sail-needles for repairing canvas, a sharp knife, and a goodly length of sturdy rope that he used to practice tying sailor's knots. All this he kept in hopes of someday becoming a sailor.

Now he took the rope out of the bag and said, "Bring that chair over 'ere, Rose."

"Wha---what're ye plannin' to do, Sean?" she asked in a voice filled with dread.

He glanced up at a large hook in the main beam of the ceiling where the old oil lantern used to hang. They had put it away weeks ago since they couldn't afford the price of whale oil anymore. Instead they'd been burning smelly tallow candles for light in the evening.

"We'll make it look like 'e killed 'imself. Hurry, Rose."

With a gasp she shrank back. "Oh, no, Sean, we can't."

He sighed. "Rose, darlin,' if we don't, I'll be the one swingin' off the end of a rope."

Tears sprang into her eyes at the thought of her brother being hung from the city gallows. But it galvanized her into action. She brought him the chair and he jumped up on it and threw the end of the rope through the hook and tied it into a thick knot.

"Help me get 'im on the chair, Rose, and hold 'im steady," he said, grunting with the effort of picking up his father's heavy body from the floor. Rose cringed but she did as he said. Together they managed to lift him onto the chair while Sean adjusted the rope length by tying more knots until it was short enough to draw his father's body up into the air. Then he tied the end of the rope around Paddy's neck and knocked the chair over.

Rose muffled a scream as Da's body dangled a few inches from the floor. Sean looked at his father. He hardly recognized him. His ma once said Paddy O'Connell was the handsomest man she'd ever seen. But the years of drinking had bloated his face and thinned his hair and given him a red bulbous nose and a big pot belly. Death had made him even uglier.

"Rose," he said, "As soon as I'm gone, wash your face an' tidy up the place, an' then get Father O'Brien. Pretend ye jus' woke up an' found Da hangin' like this. Everyone knows Da's a drunk an' been outta work an' I don't think anyone will be surprised 'e'd kill 'imself."

Gently patting the lump on her head, he asked, "Does it 'urt?"

"Aye, but tis nothin,' Sean. I'll wear a scarf over my 'ead. But...but where are ye goin'?"

"I'm signin' on the *Eastern Wind* as 'n apprentice seaman. She's sailin' in a few hours."

Rose choked out a sob and flung herself into his arms. "No, don't leave me...don't leave me, Sean, please..."

He hugged her tightly then said, "I 'ave to, darlin.' You be my brave colleen now, ye hear? Father O'Brien knows how rough yer life's been an' 'e'll help ye. I can't stay, Rose, jus' in case they think I killed Da."

"But won't it look bad if ye leave t'night?"

"Everyone saw me talkin' to the second mate t'day. No one will think anythin' about it. Everyone knows I want t' be a sailor." He smiled down at her. "An' I know ye want t' be a teacher someday. Maybe now ye can." He released her. "I promise I'll write ye whenever I can an' I promise I'll come back."

He grabbed his seabag and stuffed a few extra clothes into it. Then he pried open a loose board underneath his bed, and took out a small leather pouch. He tossed it to Rose. "There's all the money I've hid from Da. It'll tide ye over for awhile, Rose. I don't need it where I'm goin'."

And where was that, he wondered later as he ran through the dark streets towards the harbor. It was raining, an early fall storm with gusty winds. It would be rough out on the open Atlantic, but Sean welcomed the weather.

He lifted his face to the clouds and the rain washed the blood off his face, stinging his cut cheek. If only 'twas that easy to wash away the deed of Da's death. If Ma's religion is true, then I'm on the road to hell an' I'll see Da there when I'm dead an' gone.

He shrugged off the guilty thought and kept running.

PART ONE

1819-1820

CHAPTER ONE

August, 1819

The scorching summer sun beat down on the plain wooden church situated in the center of Furstenau. The heat made the air inside oppressive and Anna struggled to keep from dozing. *Herr* Jacob Klassen was preaching an unusually long sermon this Sunday morning. She should be accustomed to the steady drone of his voice by now. He'd been her teacher at the village school for years. Now he was the Head Elder, a position of great respect and power in their small community.

The congregation was split by gender. The men and boys sat on long wooden benches on the right side of the room. On the left were the women and girls. In the front row was the Klassen family, *Frau* Judith Klassen with their eight daughters. She faced her husband with a rapt look of attention on her round face. The children, ranging in age from five years to twenty-two, had the same rigid look of concentration on their young faces. They better listen closely, Anna thought, with Elder Klassen's reputation for strict discipline and swift harsh punishment. From her own experience at school, she remembered the painful crack of his ruler across her wrists for squirming too much in her chair, or whispering to her best friend, Susannah Friesen.

The Teichroew children were not as well behaved as the Klassen girls. Anna glanced to her right where her three brothers, Jack, and the twins, Peter and Jacob, were sitting. Although Jack appeared to be listening, the toe of one of his boots was tapping softly on the floor, as if keeping in rhythm to one of his melodies he was always composing. Jack had inherited their mother's gift of singing, and his sweet clear voice was a pleasure to hear. Anna, too, was blessed with a low, but lovely voice. She and Jack often were asked to sing duets in church services or at social functions. Lately, however, since he reached puberty, his voice was changing. Without warning during a song it would plunge an octave, much to his mortification and the twins delight.

Peter and Jacob were fidgeting and red-faced, either from the heat or knowing them, suppressed laughter from their endless secret jokes. They seemed oblivious of their father's stern scowls of disapproval. In keeping with her older brothers, Anna's four-year-old sister, Katarina, also could not keep still. Her small sweaty hand kept sliding out from Anna's grasp, as she twisted her head back and forth trying to see around the adults blocking her every view. Did she think there was something interesting to see, wondered Anna, or did she just feel hemmed in like a little sapling in a forest of tall trees?

As a short person herself, she felt sympathy for small children trying to cope with the adult world. Women didn't grow much more than five feet two in their family, so Katarina was probably fated to spend her life like Anna did, struggling to reach items on a high shelf, having to climb on a chair to clean the tops of the windows and walls, or asking one of the busy men for help. She hoped Katarina wouldn't also inherit her fear of heights. Just the thought of climbing a ladder made Anna's heart pound and her stomach sink.

The Klassen women would never have to worry about being too short. They were a family of Amazons. *Frau* Klassen was taller and broader than Elder Klassen, who was a short stocky man with a face like a cruel hawk. Each one of the girls looked just like their mother, except for the eldest, Agatha. She resembled her father in looks and nature. She was one of the few people in the village Anna didn't like, as hard as she tried not to, knowing it was a sin.

It had all started years ago in school. Elder Klassen had given his oldest daughter the privilege of being the teacher's helper. Although Anna could read, write, and do her numbers as well as Agatha, Elder Klassen considered Anna too young to be in any position of authority. Whenever her father had to leave the one-room schoolhouse for other duties, Agatha was left in charge. She relished her role of being the substitute teacher, and bossed Anna and the other children constantly. Because Agatha was built like an ox, none of the boys would dare challenge her, and the younger children were actually afraid of her.

Anna had tried once to make friends with her, but her overtures of friendship had been instantly rebuffed. Anna had always supposed that Agatha felt no need for a friend, because she had so many sisters at home. Either that or she disliked Anna as much as Anna disliked her.

Agatha was sitting a couple of rows ahead of Anna and Katarina. As if sensing her scrutiny, Agatha turned and gave her a smug smile, a smile that never reached her flat gray eyes.

Anna pretended not to notice but she wondered what that was about. And why did they have to go over to the Klassen's house for *faspa* (afternoon lunch) after the service today? It would be the second time this month. She would much rather visit at Susannah's house. The Friesen's household had a happy relaxed atmosphere in comparison to the grim strictness of the Klassen house. Elder Klassen ran his family with the same rigid rules as he had the school and now the church. It wasn't a fun place to spend a Sunday afternoon.

Anna knew she wasn't the only one in her family who dreaded going there. Jack, the twins, and Katarina all put up a fuss yesterday when their father announced he'd accepted *Frau* Klassen's invitation to Sunday afternoon *faspa.*

"Not again," Jack groaned as Peter and Jacob made sounds of disgust.

"But we just went there two Sundays ago, "said Anna.

"Pease, Papa, no go," said Katarina in her little high-pitched voice.

Herman had frowned at all of them. "The Klassens do not invite just anybody to their home for *faspa.* It is an honor and one we should accept with gratitude."

"Mama wouldn't have made us go," muttered Jack.

A look of pain flashed across Herman's face and Anna turned sharply to her brother. "Jack, that's enough! We will do as Papa says and that's the end of it!"

"I wan' Mama," wailed Katarina and burst into tears.

"Now see what you've started," said Anna as she scooped up her sister. Looking ashamed, Jack and the twins made a hasty exit out the front door.

Herman shook his head and sighed, then turned and followed the boys; his broad shoulders slumped slightly as if carrying a heavy burden. He had aged quickly the past few months. Her mother's death from pneumonia last winter had added wrinkles and gray hairs to her father that made him seem much older than his fifty years.

It has aged me, too, she thought, fanning her face with one hand in a hopeless effort to create some sort of breeze to cool her sweating face in the stuffy church. Besides the sharp knife of grief that stabbed her heart whenever she remembered her mother, Anna now had the responsibility of running the Teichroew household and raising her brothers and little sister. In two months she would be turning seventeen, but lately, she felt more like an old woman.

"And so I challenge you, my brothers and sisters, "said Elder Klassen, standing in front of the congregation on a raised platform with low railings, "to turn away from all worldly temptations. Many of you have grown materialistic, obsessed with obtaining possessions and greedy for more land, horses, cattle, and even, "he paused, staring at the women sharply with his black beady eyes, "a desire for the latest fashions from France." His glance fell on his wife and daughters briefly. "But thanks be to the Lord, there are some of us who are so pure in heart that the outward adornment of our earthly shells holds no attraction whatsoever. Let us pray."

As Anna bowed her head, she wondered if Elder Klassen was speaking about her new dress. Last month her Uncle Heinrich and *Tante* (aunt) Sarah Neufeld had come for a short visit. They lived on a grand estate called Silberfeld (silverfield) located near the town of Ekaterineslav. Like Furstenau it was situated in the Dnieper River valley about 66 *versts* away. (100 miles). The estate was where Anna's mother, Katharina Neufeld, had been raised. Her brother, Heinrich, had inherited Silberfeld on their father's death, Anna's Grandpapa Neufeld.

Tante Sarah and the three cousins, the twins Judith and Maria, and their younger sister, Helena, had brought Anna a lovely gown of pale blue silk. All of her aunt's and cousins' clothes either came from Paris or were made by dressmakers who came from Paris to design clothes for the Russian nobility, and were hired by *Tante* Sarah to dress her daughters. Her three younger cousins were also taught by a governess and were learning French, German, Russian, and music. A year ago Uncle Heinrich had imported a pianoforte from Prussia, an instrument Anna had always longed to learn to play. If she had a jealous temperament, she would have been envious of her cousins. But Judith, Maria, and Helena were like *Tante* Sarah, loving, warm, and generous of nature. It was impossible not to love them.

Since her mother's death, the Neufelds had visited as often as possible. They always brought expensive gifts for the children that Herman would protest at first then give in at the looks of joy on their faces. There would be a new leather saddle for Jack's horse, a model of a sailing ship carved expertly out of mahogany for Peter who loved ships, the latest volume of William Shakespeare's plays for Jacob the bookworm, a doll with real hair from Paris for Katarina, and clothes for Anna, from pure linen underwear to shawls, hats, and simple dresses.

The pale blue silk was a wondrous garment. Created in the high-waisted fashion of the French called the Empire style, it had a high-necked lace collar and long sleeves. There was a blue silk sun bonnet to match, decorated with ribbons and lace, and a pair of dainty blue shoes. Once she had tried them all on at home in front of Susannah. Her friend had gasped and said, "Oh, Anna, you look so beautiful and all grown up! But when can you wear it?"

Both girls instinctively knew that Anna could not wear the dress to church or any social function in the village. The Mennonites were known as the "plain people" and to wear anything not made by them was to defy tradition. "Maybe you can wear it someday at a special occasion," Susannah consoled.

The dress, bonnet, and shoes had been packed carefully away in her trunk. Anna was positive Susannah hadn't told anyone except her family. But one of her siblings must have told someone, for somehow news of it must have spread throughout the community. Otherwise, why would Elder Klassen have mentioned the Paris fashions in his sermon? As she filed out of the church with the women and girls, she couldn't help thinking a nasty thought, it would take a lot more than jewelry or fashionable clothes to turn Agatha or her sisters into attractive women. And as for being pure of heart, Elder Klassen must be totally ignorant of the fact that his wife and daughters were the biggest gossips in the village.

It had become a weekly habit of Anna's to walk the short distance to the cemetery after church each Sunday. The village graveyard was situated on a small grassy hill behind the church. Usually Katarina came with her to place a few flowers on their mother's grave, but this Sunday Anna went alone. Katarina had dashed away with several of her playmates as the adults milled around outside conversing with each other before heading to their homes for dinner.

The cemetery was dotted with crude wooden crosses, some with names carved into them, some just with initials or left blank. Anna stood in front of her mother's grave, noting that the violet blue pansies Katarina had left the week before had wilted. All the grass was brown, too, as the summer had been hot and dry.

Her mother was laid to rest next to four tiny graves, the brother and three sisters Anna had never known. There had been the twins Wilhelm and Anna, born two years after her parents were married. Wilhelm had died shortly after birth, but the first Anna had lived to be two years old. She had died in 1797 from a sudden fever, a common malady among young children. Anna had been named after her. Another set of twins had been born that same year, Maria and Katharina, named after their mother. Neither had lived past their third month.

How did Mama and Papa bear such grief, wondered Anna. She had always marveled at how their faith in a loving God never wavered, no matter what tragedy life had dealt them. And life here in Russia was harsh, especially for the women and children. The cemetery held far more graves of women and infants than of men and boys.

Sometimes Anna thought that childbearing was to blame for the high mortality rate of women. Certainly her own mother had never been the same after giving birth when she was forty to Katarina. Most women were considered too old at that age to even have a baby. Anna had never forgotten the terrible day and night it took for her little sister to be born. She had thought her mother was going to die then. She'd spent endless hours listening to the screams and groans coming from her parents' bedroom, watching *Tante* Sarah, *Frau* Friesen, and *Frau* Schroeder, the midwife, running in and out. She had been kept busy boiling water, and bringing clean sheets and cloths, frightened out of her mind the entire time. Her father and brothers had fled to the Yoders' house next door and stayed there until the screams of her mother had turned into the wails of a newborn babe.

Would their lives have been any less hard if her grandparents and relatives had stayed in Prussia where they'd lived before coming to Russia in the 1780's? Or what about Holland where all the Mennonites had originated?

After being raised on all the stories, she knew the answer to those questions. It was a decisive, "No!"

In the sixteenth century, her family ancestors and other Mennonites had lived in Amsterdam near the sea. They prospered as merchants, doctors, teachers, writers, and even artists. They followed the teachings of a Dutch minister named Menno Simons, a former Catholic priest who said that God had called him to preach from the Bible, as the basis of true faith. He stated that infant baptism and confession to priests, who were mere mortals, was contrary to the Holy Scriptures. He preached against carrying weapons and war of any kind. His radical ideas made him and his followers, called Mennonites, unpopular with Catholics and Martin Luther's Protestants alike.

In the late 1500's, the Mennonites were persecuted by the Spanish Inquisition. Anna had never forgotten the story of Annekan Hendriks, a young woman who refused to renounce her faith. After being tortured for days, she was bound to a ladder with ropes and her mouth filled with gunpowder to prevent her from speaking and to hasten her death. Then she was thrown into a huge bonfire. As the flames engulfed her, she was seen to have lifted her hands in prayer.

Had Annekan prayed for her enemies and their souls? Anna pondered. And could she ever be that brave or merciful if faced with such a death? How thankful she was that her ancestors had fled Holland and she would never have to be tested in such a terrible way.

The Mennonites moved to Poland and settled around the city of Danzig on the southern shore of the Baltic Sea. It was there that they learned to farm, turning the coastal swamps into thriving farms. Eventually Poland became a part of the Prussian Empire. But the Mennonites stayed, enjoying peace, prosperity and religious freedom for two hundred more years.

Then in 1786 Frederick the Great died. He had been a freethinking king who was tolerant of all religious groups. During his rule Mennonites were exempt from military service in the Prussian army, and could choose civilian service instead. But after his death, life changed rapidly. Many of their Prussian neighbors who had been envious of the Mennonites prosperity for many years, no longer held back their dislike. If a Mennonite had leased land from them, when the lease expired, the Mennonite farmer found that his Prussian neighbor would not renew it.

Eventually military conscriptions became a threat. Napoleon was rattling the sword of war in Europe, making the Prussians very nervous. Patriotism swept the country, along with an intense military buildup. Many officials in the government protested the special exemption of the Mennonites. It was time for Anna's family to move again.

Like a miracle from God, the steppes of southern Russia opened up to them in the late 1700's. Catherine the Great wished to cultivate all that wild land and she invited the Mennonites to settle there. After hearing about their prosperous farms in Prussia, she wanted the Mennonites to teach her Russian peasants how to farm their land. In return, she granted concessions, which were religious freedom, freedom from military service "for 100 years," lighter taxes, and 165 acres of land to each newcomer plus the opportunity to purchase more. The Mennonites would be allowed to have closed settlements where they could pursue their own culture, education, and social lives.

And here we are today, thought Anna from atop the hill, looking at the neat orderly buildings and plots of Furstenau, which meant "Plains of the Prince." Unlike the scattered farms of the local Russian peasants, the Mennonites lived in communal villages.

Furstenau was a prime example of a Mennonite village, laid out simply with thirty homesteads on each side of one centered broad street. Every homestead was a five-acre plot with three buildings all under one thatched roof. The house faced the street and to the back was an attached barn. At a right angle to the barn was an attached shed for farm tools and wagons. A vegetable garden and an orchard of fruit trees grew in the rear of each plot. The church and the school were in the middle of the village, and on the outskirts of town were small lots with houses for Mennonites who had no land. The farmlands and pastures surrounded the village where crops of wheat and rye and hay grew in the rich black soil. Each farmer had two strips of land, called *streifenfluren*, one near the village and one farther out, involving some traveling for all those seeding or harvesting their crops.

We are a hardworking successful people, Anna continued thinking. *We have passed our methods and ideas on to the local Russian peasants, and many of them also work here in the village, like Ivan and Natasha.*

Just this summer her papa had finally hired a Russian couple to help them at home. The husband Ivan worked in the fields, and his wife Natasha helped Anna with the endless domestic chores.

She should be happy and content for all that she had. But Anna felt restless lately as if she was missing out on something in her life. It was more than missing her mother. It was a yearning for something she didn't have, a longing for something she didn't even know. Sometimes she thought she was losing her mind.

The feeling usually came over her late at night when she couldn't sleep. But she felt it now as she stood on the hill looking at the far horizon. What was beyond the endless sea of grass? What would it be like to travel to other places, a city perhaps like Moscow or even Odessa? She would love to see Odessa, which was located on the Black Sea. Her ancestors had always lived by the sea, in Amsterdam and then in Danzig. But she had never seen any water wider than the river. What would it be like to gaze across a body of water and see no land? What did salt air smell like? What did salt water taste like? What did a beach look like? And how did waves curl into surf?

Peter wanted to be a sea captain. They all teased him about it. He had no more chance of that than she did. It was better for him to settle down and be more like Jack. He was horse crazy and his dreams of raising thoroughbred horses on their farm someday had the stuff of reality.

But at least Peter had a dream. Anna didn't even know what her dream was. She only knew what it was not. She didn't want to get married and keep birthing babies until the day she died. There had to be something more to life.

But what, she wondered, as she left the cemetery and headed back towards the church. As a Mennonite woman her life was practically cast in stone. In the next couple years she would be betrothed to a man of her father's choice, as marriages were always arranged by the parents. Then she would be married, move into her husband's home and start a family of their own. There was nothing else for a girl to do.

It was different for a boy. The firstborn inherited the farm, but the other sons could become a doctor, teacher, church elder, or even a village official who traveled to Moscow to submit the annual taxes and reports for the community. Someday their farm would belong to Jack and his future wife and Jacob, who always had his nose in a book, wanted to go to Moscow and study to be a doctor. She doubted if Peter would ever become a sailor unless he ran away, but he did have a talent for making anything with his hands. He'd recently been spending a lot of time with Hans Loewen, the woodcarver. Their father said Peter had a gift with wood, and he would soon become a carpenter's apprentice. Not as exciting as being a sailor, but at least it was something he loved to do.

There would be no chance for Anna to further her education. She had to quit school when she was thirteen to help her mother at home. And now she was too old for the village school. Her mother always said that God had a special plan for each of their lives, and if they put their trust in Him, it was useless to worry about the future. He would provide for each and every day's needs. She knew her mother was right. Worry was a sin and a waste of time. But yet, she couldn't help wondering what the future had in store for her.

* * *

The Klassens' had a large two story house, one of the nicest in the village. The upstairs was an attic devoted entirely to the girls. Four big beds stood in the room, two girls sleeping in each. Anna always marveled at how tidy and clean the home was. But then of course, with eight daughters, there was no shortage of help for *Frau* Klassen. She had raised them all to be the best housekeepers, cooks, bakers and seamstresses in the village. Her main goal was to make her daughters the most efficient wives Furstenau had ever seen.

It was funny, then, thought Anna, as she helped the girls place dishes on the long wooden tables set outside under a huge oak tree, that none of them had been betrothed yet, much less married off. Agatha was approaching her mid-twenties, and was already considered an old maid. Her next sister, Esther, was nineteen, then there was Martha, a girl Anna's age, then Maria age fifteen, Julia age twelve, Sarah age nine, Hannah age seven, and little Rachel age five.

Anna had to admit that the Lord had blessed *Herr* and *Frau* Klassen. Most couples in the village, including her own parents, had lost infants and young children. But *Frau* Klassen had never miscarried and with every birth had produced a healthy baby. The woman herself was amazing. She'd heard that three days after Rachel's birth, Judith Klassen was seen weeding her garden.

The birth of eight daughters had affected Elder Klassen differently. Each time his wife gave birth, he spent the many hours of her labor in the church, down on his knees, praying loudly. He had been overheard beseeching the Almighty to give him a son. *Frau* Schroeder, the midwife, had the duty of informing him after each birth as to the gender of his child. She said his reactions would turn from hope to anger then to resignation. After Hannah's birth, his seventh daughter, he no longer even reacted. He had given up all hope for a son.

Without any sons it was a good thing *Herr* Klassen was not a farmer. But he did raise pigs and chickens, and had a large orchard of cherry, peach, plum, and apricot trees. An invitation to his home for Sunday *faspa* was highly prized, for his wife and daughters put on a bountiful feast to satisfy every single guest.

This afternoon was no exception. Anna surveyed the checkered cloth-covered tables groaning under the weight of all the food. There were platters of cold meats, mainly smoked ham, sausage, and sliced chicken served with sweet-hot mustard and horseradish alongside plates of buttery yellow wheels of cheese. Baskets of freshly baked *twaback* and *schnetke* (biscuits) were filled to overflowing. Jars of plum and apple jelly to spread on the baked goods sat next to the baskets. There were three kinds of pickles, sweet ones made of little cucumbers, sour dill pickles, and cinnamon and clove spiced beet pickles.

In the center of the table was a huge bowl of cherry *moos*, a thickened sweet fruit soup, which was Anna's contribution to the meal. For dessert, there were peach and apricot *piroshky*, sweetened fruit baked in pockets of dough, and *crullers*, which were long thin crispy fried cookies, served with slices of sweet juicy watermelon. Pots of hot coffee and a samovar of steaming tea rounded out the feast.

A big bowl of sugar lumps sat near the coffee and tea. The adults liked to place a sugar lump between their teeth, and then sip the hot liquids through the sugar, sweetening their drink. The children loved the sugar lumps to pocket and nibble on while running around in the yard.

Katarina and the three youngest Klassen girls, Sarah, Hannah and Rachel, had already helped themselves to the sugar lumps and were happily playing hide and seek. Their shrieks of laughter occasionally punctured the lower drone of adult voices in conversation. Whenever this happened, Elder Klassen looked up from his plate and frowned in irritation, but he said nothing. It was the custom for the adults to eat first, then the children. He knew as well as anyone, that the longer the children had to wait, the hungrier and more restless they became.

Anna's neighbors, the Yoders, were also there. *Herr* Yoder had died three years ago when a horse kicked him in the head. The Widow Yoder, as the village called her, ruled her sons like a haughty queen. The three oldest Yoder boys were now married men with families and they all lived with her. The youngest, Gerhard, was thirty and had shown no interest in getting married until recently. Two days ago Susannah had told Anna that she'd heard from Maria Klassen who had overheard a conversation between her mother and Widow Yoder that Gerhard wanted to marry Anna.

"But I'm too young," Anna had protested. "And Papa has never said a word to me about the Yoders asking him to set a betrothal between us."

"Your family has been in mourning this past year," Susannah pointed out. "And everyone knows how much you are needed at home right now. Perhaps they are waiting until your papa remarries."

Anna had been just as horrified at the thought of her father marrying another woman as she was at the thought of marrying Gerhard Yoder. He was the village blacksmith, a great hulk of a man with massive legs and arms and powerful muscles. His dark hair was always matted with sweat, and his black-bearded face perpetually reddened by the intense heat of the fire in his shop. He had a reputation of being as hot tempered as the hot metal he worked with. He had always reminded Anna of a Tartar. She could not imagine her father ever considering having him for a son-in-law.

She glanced up from her meal to see Gerhard staring at her from across the table. He had the most piercing blue eyes she'd ever seen, and they were fixed on her like a cat watching a mouse. She suddenly lost her appetite. It wasn't that he was an ugly man. In honor of the Sabbath his hair was neatly combed and his beard trimmed into a goatee and he was wearing a crisp white shirt that his mother had washed and ironed. He had a handsome grin with flashing white teeth when he smiled, which wasn't often, for he had a serious nature. He was smiling now. At her.

"Anna," he said in a deep voice, "The cherry *moos* you make is very goot."

"I'm glad you like it," she answered politely.

He blushed and his ruddy face grew even redder. Silence fell between them as Gerhard was a man of few words and being in Anna's presence made his tongue knot up like a ball of yarn in a roomful of kittens. She kept her eyes on her plate, thinking of how none of the Yoder men could read or write well, and Gerhard was no exception. They were all steady hardworking men, but it would be so boring being married to a man who knew nothing more than how to wield a hammer and anvil. She'd grown up next door to him, too, and she knew that as the youngest son, his mother had spoiled him. He was known around the village as a "Mama's boy." Any woman married to Gerhard would be living with his mother until the day she died. And Widow Yoder was as short-tempered as Gerhard. It would not be a marriage made in heaven.

She also sat across the table from Anna next to her son. She was thin with a bony face and a narrow mouth that was usually frowning. Her gray hair was pulled severely back into a knot on the back of her head. She nodded at Anna and her lips cracked into a stiff smile. "Your mother taught you well," she said. "You will make some lucky man a goot wife."

Gerhard blushed again, his face turning almost purple as he mopped the perspiration off his brow. Anna felt panic creeping over her as she caught Agatha's amused glance down the table. "Anna makes the best *pluma moos*, too, Gerhard," she called out. "Maybe Herman will invite you over for *faspa* some Sunday soon, and you can sample some."

Agatha's statement shocked Anna for two reasons. The first was the idea of having to entertain Gerhard in her own home like a beau, and the second was Agatha's improper use of her father's first name. She should have referred to her papa as *Herr* Teichroew not Herman. Didn't anyone notice that besides her?

"Now look what you did, Peter! You ruined my new book!" Jacob suddenly yelled.

"I didn't mean to! It was an accident!" protested Peter. The twins' angry voices diverted everyone's attention away from the uncomfortable conversation, and Anna quickly excused herself, feeling grateful for once for one of their frequent quarrels.

While waiting to eat, Jacob had been sitting on the ground, quietly reading. Peter stood behind him, drinking a glass of water, which he had partially spilled onto the book, William Shakespeare's "Hamlet." Jacob was hopping up and down, trying to shake the water off the pages. Anna brought him a handkerchief to dry off the book and tried to calm him down.

Laughter erupted around the adult table as one of the Yoder men called out, "You better hope young Jacob doesn't turn out to be like one of the Janssen family."

Although Nels Jansson and his family had moved away from Furstenau years ago, no one would ever forget them. *Herr* Jansson had been obsessed by reading, and was a great procrastinator. His wife, and later their children, also enjoyed reading so much that their fields, gardens, and livestock began to suffer. The family was reprimanded by the village fathers and told to clean up their place or they would have to move to another village. Conditions in their home were indescribably filthy and worst of all, to their fastidious neighbors of Dutch descent, their house was infested with bedbugs.

One night when the village was quiet and all were asleep except for the Jansson family, a shout was heard. Everyone ran outside to see their house in flames, the thatched roof burning brightly. The story came out that one of the careless children had knocked over his candle and set fire to his straw ticking. As the fire spread, he walked from bed to bed with his book in his hand, telling each family member to pick up their book and follow him outside. They calmly went out, and kept on reading their books by the light of the burning house until the flames died down. Then they carefully stacked their marked reading materials so they could pick up where they left off, as they all joined hands and made a ring around the ruins of their home and sang, "*Wanna dit nich gote fur da wanskya es dann vate ek nicht vaut bater es*" ("If this isn't good for the bedbugs then I know of nothing better.")

It was fortunate that their house was at the end of the village and the flames didn't spread to any other buildings. Each of their neighbors gave them a portion of their own stores and asked them to go somewhere else to live with their books. The family left, and their land was farmed by their neighbors. They saved all the proceeds for the Janssons, but they were never heard from again. Rumors to this day were that they were trudging along the roads, reading their books, until they ended up in Siberia.

"You did it on purpose, Peter!" Jacob said with an accusing glare.

"No, I didn't, honest!"

The twin's freckled faces under their blond mops of hair mirrored two identical scowls of rage. Although she hushed them sternly, their argument gave Anna an excuse not to return to the table where she'd been eating, and she was secretly glad. She decided to stay with them and keep the peace until the adults were finished with their meal and it was time for the children to eat. It was then that she made her way back.

To her surprise she noticed her father and Agatha walking away from everyone, deep in conversation. As all the children rushed by her to the table, Anna saw *Frau* Klassen glance at her daughter and Anna's father and smile with satisfaction.

Anna's stomach churned. There was something going on here that didn't seem quite right to her. It was unthinkable to quiz her father about it. But tomorrow was the first day of the annual village clothes washing. With all the women gathered in one place, gossip abounded, and she was determined to find out.

* * *

The Mennonites washed clothes only once a year. The wealthier families had at least twenty-six changes of clothing. In the summer after the grain had been planted and the haying done, and before the large vats were needed to make sauerkraut, two weeks were set aside for washing.

The white linens would be soaked in one vat, underwear in another, and colored clothing in a third.

On this Monday, the Russian peasant helpers from each family, including the Teichroew's Ivan and Natasha, were busy going up and down the ladders on the vats, bringing the soaked clothing to huge wooden tubs where about twenty women were scrubbing the articles with homemade soap. Anna, Susannah and her mother, *Frau* Friesen, and *Frau* Loewen, the woodcarver's wife, were bending over one tub, plunging their hands into the hot soapy water, and briskly rubbing clothes.

They had been doing this all morning. It was another hot, almost windless day, and Anna was dripping with perspiration. Her arms and shoulders ached, and her hands were reddened and wrinkled. There seemed no end to the clothing. As soon as she finished scrubbing an item, it was thrown into a huge iron kettle filled with boiling water. There another girl stirred the clothes with a wooden paddle, before lifting them out into a long wooden trough of clean hot water, then into another trough with cold water where the clothes were thoroughly rinsed and hung out to dry.

Everyone was helping with this, including children as young as Katarina. She was considered old enough to be taught to fold the garments carefully and place them in neat piles. During the past hour, Katarina's voice had grown into a complaining whine, and Anna wondered how much longer her little sister would continue working without a break.

They all needed one soon. There were still hours of washing ahead, until evening when the dew fell, and the stacks of clean sweet smelling laundry would be carried into the summer kitchen for ironing. Some of the Russian girls would heat heavy irons inside of the ovens and press the clothes that were wrinkled such as the beautifully embroidered linen shifts the women wore as their main undergarment. The shifts could serve as petticoats and nightgowns both. In the winter their petticoats were made of homespun wool, not as comfortable as linen, but much warmer.

As she worked Anna could not help remembering last year's washing. Her mother had been alive then. She and Anna, and Susannah and *Frau* Friesen, had been a foursome at the tub. They had talked and laughed the hours away, the day passing quickly. How much slower it seemed this year without the bright face of Katharina smiling at her. And there was still another week of washing to go after this one.

A high-pitched scream shattered her thoughts. All the women whirled around and froze.

Five-year-old Rachel Klassen was standing next to the hot iron kettle, clutching her arm and wailing at the top of her lungs. Next to her was Katarina, struggling in the strong arms of Agatha.

"You are a bad, bad girl, Katarina Teichroew," she said in a stern voice.

Tears shot out of Katarina's soft blue eyes. "Didn't mean to---didn't mean to---"

Anna and *Frau* Klassen reached the girls simultaneously. An angry red welt was blistering up on Rachel's right arm as she continued to sob. Nineteen-year-old Esther Klassen, who was the girl in charge of stirring the clothes in the kettle, stood with the wooden paddle in her hands, a horrified look on her face.

"I tried to stop them, "she said, "but they were too quick for me."

Frau Klassen, shaking her bonneted head in disapproval, called out for someone to bring a spoonful of butter from the summer kitchen. "There, there, Rachel," she said soothingly to her daughter, patting her head, trying to get her to stop crying.

"Wouldn't it be better to immerse her arm in the cold water trough?" asked Anna. Her mother had taught her many things about healing, and one of them was that keeping the wound clean was more effective in treating burns than smearing the wound with grease. There was less likelihood of infection that way. Also, the cold water cooled off the pain more quickly than butter.

But *Frau* Klassen ignored her as her other daughter, Martha, brought her the butter. Martha held Rachel's arm while their mother smeared the butter all over the burn, causing the little girl to cry even harder. "Tsch, tsch," clucked *Frau* Klassen. Then she turned to glare at Katarina, still being held by Agatha. "How did this happen, Katarina Teichroew?" she demanded.

Anna's sister was sniffling so hard she couldn't speak. Esther stepped forward, her paddle still in hand, and said, "They started fighting about something while they were folding the clothes, and Katarina started to chase our Rachel. They got too close to the kettle before I could stop them, and Katarina pushed Rachel into it."

"Tina was agoin' to hit me so I ran," sobbed Rachel.

Tina had been Anna's mother's nickname, but since her death, everyone had started to call Katarina, "Tina." Anna often wondered if it bothered Papa, but he never said. He called her that, too.

"She---she hit me fiwst!" yelled Katarina.

"No, I din't!"

"I hate you, Wachael! I glad I pushed you!"

The Klassen women gasped while Anna sighed inwardly. Now her little sister had really gotten herself into trouble. Admitting hatred for someone and being glad of an act of violence were two very big sins to the Mennonites.

But what happened next also got Anna in trouble.

"Take that, you wicked girl!" Agatha's angry voice screeched as she grabbed the large wooden paddle away from Esther and smacked it hard on Katarina's small behind. Tina screamed and Anna lunged for Agatha, taking her by surprise, and knocking her backwards. If Anna had been a larger person, Agatha would have been flattened on the grass. Instead, she recovered her balance quickly and raised the wooden paddle threateningly over Anna's head.

"Stop it, this instant!" roared *Frau* Klassen shoving her huge bulk between the girls. "Agatha, give the paddle back to Esther and Anna, take your sister and calm her down. Enough of all this nonsense! We have work to do!"

Anna and Agatha glared at each other, their mutual dislike for all to see. "You had no right to spank my sister," said Anna in a cold voice.

"Maybe not right now," returned Agatha with a sly smile, "but I will soon, just wait and see."

"And what do you mean by that?"

"Girls---" warned *Frau* Klassen, "I mean it! Back to work now!"

Still smiling strangely, Agatha handed Esther the paddle and walked away. Their mother took the now quiet Rachel and headed her towards the summer kitchen where some of the women were preparing the noon meal. "I'll get you a lump of sugar to suck on, and you'll be feeling as good as new, sweetie," she said. Then she paused and looked back at Anna and Tina.

"Katarina needs a firmer hand to guide her than yours, Anna Teichroew. It is time your father found himself another wife before you and your brothers and sister turn into little Tartars."

Some of the women standing around watching nodded and murmured in agreement while Anna's mouth dropped open. What was *Frau* Klassen implying? It was true that in their community it was the custom for a widower with children to find a bachelor maiden to take over and become his wife and mother to his children. Sometimes the widower would find a comely widow with several children who was willing to become his *hausfrau*. After a few years, they would have a saying in the village, "Your children and my children are quarreling with our children!"

But it was too soon for her Papa to remarry, thought Anna in protest. Mama had been gone only a few months. How could *Frau* Klassen even suggest such a despicable thing?

Katarina whimpered and Anna gave her a quick hug. "Come on, Tina, dry your eyes, and I'll find you some sugar lumps, too."

"I don' like Wachael anymo."

Anna sighed. "You're going to have to tell her you're sorry, Tina. And then, you're going to have to ask God to forgive you for pushing her into the kettle and burning her arm." *As I will have to ask Him to forgive me for attacking Agatha, and for all the hatred I have against her in my heart*, she added silently. *But one thing I won't do. I won't apologize to Agatha after she spanked Tina!*

"I know," muttered Katarina, hanging her head in shame. "I was wong. I'm sowwy."

Anna looked down at her sister's little head of wispy blonde curls and her heart melted. How could she allow any other woman to become this little girl's mother? It wasn't true what *Frau* Klassen said about her being too lax with her siblings. Anna knew she was capable of raising Katarina and the twins properly. As for Jack, he was fifteen and almost a man. There was no reason for her father to ever remarry.

After getting Katarina some food to eat and settling her back among the other children, Anna went back to the huge tub where Susannah was waiting for her. Her mother and *Frau* Loewen had left to help the women with the food. "Are you and Tina all right, Anna?" asked Susannah anxiously. "We saw the whole thing and couldn't believe our eyes. Agatha spanked Tina! And then it looked like she wanted to kill you with that paddle!"

Her friend's freckled face was wreathed in concern. She had reddish brown hair and a nose that was a bit large and a face that was considered by most as plain. But she had the kindest nature and was fiercely loyal to Anna. And when she laughed, which was often, her brown eyes twinkled like two stars. She would make some lucky man a great *hausfrau* someday.

Anna grimaced with distaste. "Who does Agatha think she is, that she dared to spank my little sister?"

"Well, I've overheard something you should know, Anna."

Anna looked at her friend, a feeling of dread beginning inside her. "What is it?"

"I would've told you sooner, but I had to wait until Mama and *Frau* Loewen left us alone." Susannah took a breath and said, "This morning when I first got here, I happened to overhear Martha Klassen telling her sister Maria that she heard their mother and father talking late last night when all the girls were supposed to be asleep. Elder Klassen said that Herman Teichroew, your papa, had asked him for Agatha's hand in marriage."

Anna suddenly felt ill. "No, oh, no..."

"I guess they were arguing about it. Elder Klassen thinks your papa is too old for Agatha. He's almost fifty and she's just twenty-two. Then *Frau* Klassen said she thought only an older man could handle Agatha. So, nothing has been decided yet. Maybe it won't happen. Anna, are you all right? You look awfully pale."

A dizzy feeling spun over her and she sat down on the grass before she fell over. "I don't believe this, Susannah. How could this be true? Why wouldn't Papa tell me if he was thinking of getting married again? And to Agatha? It can't be true!" She wanted to scream, but some of the women nearby were already looking her way. Somehow, she composed herself, but she felt she was teetering on the brink of a nightmare.

"I'm so sorry, Anna," whispered Susannah. "I know you are upset, but I thought you should be warned, just in case. Maybe you should talk to your papa tonight."

"Yes, that's exactly what I'm going to do. I'm not a child anymore, and if he really is planning on getting married again, he should tell me."

Susannah looked at her sadly and said, "If only it was anyone else besides Agatha."

Ah, yes, Agatha. Anna felt a burst of anger and her strength suddenly returned. Now she understood only too well why Agatha looked so smug when she made her comment about having the right to spank Katarina soon, and why there was that conversation between her father and Agatha the day before. Well, it wasn't going to happen. They were not going to get married. For once she was in complete agreement with Elder Klassen.

* * *

That evening in the Teichroew house the atmosphere was strangely subdued. Everyone was tired from the day's washing, including the twins who had worked alongside the women. Only Herman and Jack had been absent since they were busy taking care of the livestock. Anna was impatient to get supper over and the children off to bed since she was anxious to speak with her father.

Natasha had cooked a huge bowl of *borscht* and placed it in the middle of the table for all to eat out of. Each family member had their own wooden spoon for dipping. For the younger children, this meant there was a trail of soup leading to each place from the center bowl. Anna ignored the mess and concentrated on her own meal, but she found she had little appetite. Dark rye bread was served with the *borscht*, and the heavy coarse crumbs stuck in her throat with each bite.

"I hear you got in a fight with Agatha Klassen," said Jack with a grin. His blue eyes sparkled with suppressed laughter, and Anna knew he was probably proud of her.

Herman glowered at both of them. "Your sister and I will speak of this later. Eat your supper, John."

Jack returned to his food, but gave Anna a wink. Peter and Jacob stared at her with a newfound respect. She sighed inwardly. It was obvious all three of her brothers thought she'd done something daring and spectacular, but what a dubious honor it was. She could tell her father thought just the opposite. He was probably humiliated that his own daughter was in a physical altercation with the woman he wanted to marry. And being that they were both pacifist Mennonites, made the situation much worse.

Suddenly she wasn't looking forward to her talk with her father later. She had a bad feeling it was going to be most unpleasant.

Katarina's small head drooped forward and she almost smacked her forehead on the hard wooden table. It was time to put her to bed, and

Anna wished she could crawl in beside her and end this unhappy day. The two shared the same bedroom. Over the years as the three boys had grown, their father had expanded the house and built an upstairs sleeping loft for them. The other downstairs bedroom was her parents. She felt downright ill at the thought of Agatha sleeping in the same bed where her mother had. It would be like her father had betrayed them all.

* * *

Evening twilight lingered late this time of year. In the north of Russia, the summer sun barely brushed the horizon in the middle of the night before rising again. These were called, "White Nights." In the south, darkness finally came, but not before a glorious sunset to the northwest faded into a long gentle dusk. It was Anna's favorite time of day. The heat was gone, most people and animals were asleep after a hard day of work, and it was quiet.

She usually took a short walk in the orchard by herself before retiring, with only their two dogs for company. Being alone was difficult in the closeness of her home and village, so she cherished her moments of solitude. It was a time to collect her thoughts and dream of the future and faraway places. She also liked to talk to Jesus.

Prayer was mostly a formal occasion in church, school, and at mealtimes. She prayed at bedtime, too, but exhaustion usually kept those prayers short. Since she was a small child, she had developed a personal faith in Jesus. Her mother had been a deeply spiritual person, who had taught her children that having Jesus in one's heart and soul made Him your best friend. It was that joy of having a personal Savior as a Friend that had given Katharina Teichroew her spark in life.

The only time Anna had doubted the love of Jesus was when her mother had died so suddenly last winter. But then *Tante* Sarah had told her that illness was a result of sin and evil in the world and not caused by God. "All of us will die someday, Anna," she had said. "But having Jesus in your heart assures you of eternal life. You will see your mama in heaven. Meanwhile, Katharina would want you to keep on trusting God and His son."

Anna wasn't the only one in the family to struggle with this test of their faith. Jack had gone through a brief rebellious period when he talked back to their father and was constantly getting in trouble. Jacob had been depressed for months, burying himself into his books. Peter would disappear for hours at a time, returning only when hungry, his face and clothes muddy from playing by the river. Little Tina had become Anna's shadow.

Time had taken the edge off the family's grief and now life was becoming more pleasant again for all of them, until today.

Her father had joined her outside for her walk. His brow was furrowed in deep thought and he said nothing at first. The two dogs bounded ahead and circled back towards them, sniffing every inch of ground, hoping to find a rodent to chase. They were mutts of mixed breeds, the female was golden in color with floppy ears named Gerda, and the male was black with splashes of white named Alexi.

Because the dogs weren't purebred hounds or collies, both had been abandoned as puppies by the river two years ago. She and Jack had found them, shivering and near starvation. Anna raised them with a mix of love and discipline. As a result, they were the most loyal and well-trained dogs in the village. Somehow she'd even taught them to leave the barn cats alone. She had a deep love and respect for all animals, and nothing flared her temper quicker than an animal hurting another animal, or especially, a person being cruel to an animal.

An evening breeze rustled through the branches of the fruit trees and Anna could smell the sweet scent of overripe plums and peaches and apricots. Most of the fruit had already been picked, but some remained, and perhaps she should have the twins pick the rest tomorrow instead of helping with the washing. In a few more weeks, the apples would be turning rosy red, and the grapes swelling into purple bunches on the vines, a sure sign of autumn.

"I am very disappointed in you, Anna," said her father suddenly in a gruff voice. "Your behavior towards Agatha Klassen today was inexcusable."

'But--" she began.

"You will not interrupt!" He halted and faced her. His features were so much like Jack's with the proud Teichroew nose and bushy eyebrows. Unlike Jack, he had a mustache which drooped over his mouth and now it gave him a grim expression.

"I have never been more humiliated in my life after Elder Klassen told me what happened between you and his daughter this afternoon. It was bad enough that Katarina pushed Rachel into the hot kettle and burned her arm, but I can excuse that as childish mischief. What I cannot condone is you trying to harm Agatha! You are almost a grown woman and you have no excuse to lose control of your senses like that!"

"But she spanked Tina with a huge wooden paddle--"

"Katarina deserved that and more!" he said sharply. "I will not have my daughters behaving like two peasant girls who do not know any better. This isn't how your mother and I brought you up. It makes me think it is time for changes around here."

"What sort of changes, Papa?" she asked hesitantly, dreading the answer.

She stared at him anxiously and he glanced away, not meeting her eyes. "I am going to marry again."

It was the answer she expected, but hearing him say it out loud made her choke. "To---to who?"

He looked her full in the face then. "To Agatha Klassen."

Her choke turned into a gasp, "Oh, no, Papa, oh no!"

He ignored her outburst and went on, "I talked to Elder Klassen and *Frau* Klassen about their daughter some time ago. They weren't in agreement then, but after today, Elder Klassen has given his permission. I have you to thank for it."

Anna gasped again. "What--what do you mean?"

"Elder Klassen had some reservations about the marriage, but after seeing yours and Katarina's unruly behavior today, he is convinced that his daughter is the answer to the obvious lack of motherly discipline in our family. Agatha is a fine strong woman who is capable of turning the most unorderly household into a proper one. She has spent years helping her mother raise her sisters into respectable young girls. I want the same for Peter and Jacob and Katarina, and even Jack, though I know he's almost a man. I believe the Lord will bless all of us with Agatha here as your new stepmother."

Her father finally noticed Anna's stricken face and he added more gently, "I know it will be difficult for all of you at first, especially for you, Anna. But if you give Agatha a chance, she will work hard to make our family the happy one it used to be."

"But, Papa, she can never take Mama's place."

He coughed slightly and patted his chest as if a quick pain had flashed through him. "No one can ever take your mother's place in our hearts, Anna. But she is gone now, and will not come back. My children need a mother."

Tears filled Anna's eyes as she said, "But, Papa, I've been trying so hard all these months to do everything the way Mama did. I thought I was doing a good job. Tina even calls me Mama sometimes."

Her father patted her shoulder awkwardly. "Now, now, Anna, it's not that you aren't working hard to do the right things. I watch you and I know you are doing your best. But you have your whole life in front of you. You will want more someday than just taking care of your father and brothers and little sister. You will want a family of your own."

She wiped her wet cheeks. "And I suppose you have a husband in mind for me, too, already."

He shook his head. "No, Anna, I can't even think about finding you a husband until we have a stable family again."

"But when we do, will you let me make my own choice of a husband?"

He chuckled softly. "You are so headstrong like your mother. She always wanted the last say in everything, too. Come, Anna, let's get some sleep. Tomorrow is another busy day."

Anna knew her father would say nothing more on the subject of marriage, either hers or his. There was no use in questioning him further. They strolled back to the house, the dogs blending into the growing darkness of the coming night.

And in Anna's heart, all hope had ended and a dark depression had fallen.

* * *

Early the next morning she awoke to the furious sounds of dogs barking and men yelling. For one moment she imagined the Tartars had invaded the village. Anna jumped out of bed to find Katarina already up and out, her sharp little voice mingling in with the rest.

She hastily donned her everyday gray dress and apron, and fastened her thick tawny brown hair into a knot at the back of her head. Grabbing a scarf to cover her head, she ran outside to find their end of the village in a slight turmoil. Alexi and Gerda, along with the Yoder dogs and several others, had surrounded a small black buggy drawn by a bony old horse. The horse snorted and flinched as the dogs nipped at its hooves. Two men inside the buggy cursed the dogs and held the reins tightly to control the horse. Her father and Jack tried to grab the dogs while the twins and Katarina jumped up and down in excitement. The Yoder men stood nearby watching, but did nothing to stop their own dogs from snarling and circling the buggy and horse.

Anna understood at once what was happening. The Jewish peddlers had come to the village for their twice yearly visit. And not everyone welcomed them.

"Goot dogs! Goot dogs!" called out Gerhard with a hearty laugh, "let them know we don't like their kind here!"

Anna felt her temper rise, but after yesterday's show of public anger, she managed to bite her tongue. Instead she whistled sharply and her two dogs broke away from the pack and loped over to her. She dropped to her knees and hugged them to her, as they licked her face in greeting with soft whines.

When Gerhard saw Anna call her dogs off, he did likewise, although with a reluctant attitude. "We were just having a little fun," he told her without a hint of shame in his voice.

"I don't think scaring an old horse and two harmless men is what I'd call fun," she said, frowning at him.

"You're right, of course, Anna," he said to placate her, but traded unrepentant grins with his older brothers as they rounded up their dogs and chased them away.

"You and your horse can stay in our straw shed," said Herman to the peddlers, "and my sons will give him some water and feed. Have you eaten this morning?"

The two dark-bearded men in dusty black hats shook their heads. "We thank you, as always, *Herr* Teichroew," said one of them.

Her papa had the reputation of being kind and hospitable to anyone, and Anna recognized the peddlers as the ones they had housed last winter. She didn't understand why Gerhard and some of the other men in their village disliked having the Jews come. Her mama always said that God's word was true: "He has promised good to all who treat His chosen people well but those who abuse the Jews will suffer."

She remembered the day three years before when Hans Yoder, Gerhard's father, was killed. *Herr* Yoder had been the most outspoken against the Jewish peddlers and had taught all four of his sons to make sport of them when they visited the village twice a year. The day he died a traveling Jew had come with his heavy pack on his back. Usually the Jews traveled together in a buggy for safety's sake, but this one old man had come alone.

Hans Yoder had set his dogs on him when Anna's father was still working in the fields and could do nothing to stop him. Although the Yoders said later it was all in jest, one of their dogs, a large brown shaggy beast that Anna never trusted, had mauled the old Jew quite badly before anyone could intervene. His face and arm was bloodied and torn, and Anna's mother had been furious as she cleaned and stitched his wounds.

It was that evening when they heard *Frau* Yoder screaming. *Herr* Yoder's prize horse, a high-spirited mare that Jack had always coveted, had kicked *Herr* Yoder directly in the temple, instantly killing him. "I warned Hans not to buy that horse," said Papa later. "He should stick with oxen like the rest of us do. Horses are nothing but expensive trouble."

The mare was sold to a wealthy Mennonite from another village, much to Jack's dismay. But *Frau* Yoder would not keep the horse, saying it came from the devil. Anna wondered to this day if it had really been just an accident, or a judgment from God. It would be another reason not to ever marry into that family.

Unlike some of the men, all the women and girls welcomed the Jewish peddlers eagerly. While some of the richer Mennonites were able to shop for materials in the larger towns, most of the village *frau*s depended on their semiannual visits to buy goods. It was always a great day when the peddlers spread out their beautiful fabrics and much haggling would go on as to prices. Instead of being sold in bolts, the cloth would be cut in dress lengths, and then there would be lots of comparing along the street the next few days.

Maybe that's why some of the men dislike the peddlers, thought Anna. In the excitement of acquiring new clothes, many of the women neglected their chores. Today was no exception. She wondered how much washing would actually be done by the village women when the peddlers were in town.

She had another reason, more personal, to welcome them. Last night while she struggled to fall asleep, she decided to write a letter to her *Tante* Sarah, telling her about Papa's wish to remarry. Even if her uncle and aunt already knew about it, they did not know what Agatha was really like.

Perhaps if I tell them, they can somehow change Papa's mind. It is worth a try, she thought.

And when the Jewish peddlers left Furstenau and headed in the direction of Silberfeld, they could carry her letter with them.

CHAPTER TWO

Saint Petersburg, August, 1819

The evening was sultry. Not a breath of air stirred in Tatiana's bedchamber. As her maid plaited her hair, tiny beads of perspiration formed underneath the heavy mass and trickled down her neck. Idly she wondered if the moisture would show through the material of her ball gown. Not that she really cared.

As usual, Aunt Irene had ordered the dress sewn without considering Tatiana's coloring, figure, or taste in clothing. The gown was of slightly transparent voile over rose, too heavy and complicated. She would have preferred a simple white silk that molded to her tall slender form instead of hiding every slight curve of her body. Of course, that was Aunt Irene's intention--to make Tatiana look as much like a thin toothpick as possible. She wanted the eyes of every eligible nobleman on the short plump curves of her daughter, Tatiana's cousin Olga. At age seventeen, Olga had yet to snare a serious suitor, even with her dowry worth a fortune.

Aunt Irene blamed Olga's lack of marital success on Tatiana, but she knew it was because of her cousin's failure to curb the sharp words that sprang from her shrewish, mean-tempered nature. While her aunt was blind to this side of Olga, Tatiana had fallen victim to her cruel tongue all her life.

This morning had been a prime example. Olga had awakened her from a sound sleep, a taunting smile upon her round pudding-featured face. "Happy sixteenth birthday, dearest Cousin," she said sarcastically. "Aren't you the luckiest girl in Russia to be celebrating your birthday tonight and also," she paused, a look of malice gleaming from her eyes, "the announcement of your betrothal."

Tatiana had sat up in her bed, not believing what she'd just heard. "My--my betrothal?" she'd croaked out, her throat dry from hours of sleep.

Olga laughed. "I don't know who he is, but I overheard the servants whispering that he is very rich and very old."

Suddenly the night of her sixteenth birthday ball, instead of being an event of great importance that every girl of the Russian aristocracy eagerly anticipated, had become something sinister. The celebration marked the official ending of childhood and the beginning of young womanhood. Tatiana should have been filled with a happy excitement, but now at Olga's words, a feeling of dread overcame her.

She should have been more prepared for this moment. Being betrothed to a total stranger was to be expected in their society. Yet, she had hoped all her young life, it wouldn't happen to her. *Foolish*, she thought, *how stupid I've been.* The world and everything in it, including every advantage and privilege, belonged only to men. Women in Russia, even from the finest families, were considered as possessions of their husbands with little or no power over their own lives and that of their children, duty bound to obey the slightest whim of their spouse.

Her uncle and aunt, the Count and Countess Bolkonsky, had such a marriage. Uncle Vasily had maintained mistresses for years, humiliating her aunt to the point where only a cold politeness remained between them.

Was this to be Tatiana's fate also? The question gnawed inside her as her fears rose anew. "Ah, my dearest Cousin," said Olga, laughing again, "you should see the shock on your face! But you should consider yourself very fortunate that a titled nobleman is asking for your hand in marriage, for after all, you are not a pure Russian aristocrat like the rest of us Bolkonskys. You are half-English, a nothing. You should be groveling at my parents' feet with gratitude for helping your father arrange this marriage."

Tatiana turned a deaf ear to her spiteful words about her background. She had heard it all too many times to care anymore. "It should be you who is having her betrothal announced tonight," she said. "You are the eldest daughter of this family. Is your mother so anxious to have me out of the palace and away from your potential suitors that she is waiving the usual protocol?"

Olga's hearty laughter abruptly stopped. Her face turned pink and she screeched, "How dare you?" As she whirled out the door she had added menacingly, "Just you wait, you half-breed!"

Half-breed? Now there was a new name for her. Tatiana smiled grimly at her reflection in the mirror, as she waited for Sonya, her maid, to finish fixing her hair. Although the blood of one of Russia's most elite families ran through her veins, she was still considered tainted, because her mother was English. If she had been French, that would have been better tolerated, as the French language was spoken by the Russian nobility, and French fashion, furniture and cuisine was in much demand. Even the war with Napoleon, which had ended several years ago at the Battle of Moscow when hunger and the freezing Russian winter had killed 350,000 French troops, hadn't stopped the popularity of anything French.

At least she wasn't half-American, which was the equivalent to being half-barbarian. The young United States of America and all its citizens, who were formerly English anyway, were looked down upon with scorn by all Russians.

But the way Aunt Irene and my cousins have treated me all my life, thought Tatiana, my mother might as well have been an American barbarian instead of the English aristocrat she was.

Seventeen years ago her father's sudden marriage had caused a terrible scandal among Saint Petersburg society. What little Tatiana knew about her mother was told to her as she grew older, by her father during his rare visits to Saint Petersburg in between voyages. No one else in the family would speak of her, unless as an insult from Mikael or Olga.

Her father, Nikolas Bolkonsky, was a lieutenant in the Imperial Navy and his ship often plied the Baltic Sea between Kronstadt, the navy's home port, and England. One fateful night in 1802 when his ship was docked along the Thames River in London, he rescued a young Englishman who was attacked by waterfront thieves. Nikolas ran off the thugs with a loud shot of his pistol. The young man introduced himself as Henry Sutton, the only son of Lord Henry Sutton, and out of gratitude, invited Nikolas to dine the following evening with his family at Sutton Manor in the countryside outside London.

It was there that Nikolas met Elizabeth Sutton, Henry's seventeen-year-old sister. He had told Tatiana it had been love at first sight. He had never seen such a beautiful young woman. She was tall and slender with pale blonde hair and violet blue eyes with long dark lashes, the total opposite of the brown-haired Russian beauties he was used to. Their romance had its beginnings like a story out of a fairy tale. If their marriage had not ended so tragically, Tatiana would have some hope today that a happy marriage could be possible for a woman. But though her father loved her mother very much, they were doomed from the very start.

Lord and Lady Sutton had been so thankful to Nikolas for saving their son from the would-be robbers, and had been so charmed by the dashing young Russian nobleman, that they invited him for dinner each night for the entire week his ship was docked. Soon Nikolas and Elizabeth had eyes only for each other.

One night they had escaped to the manor gardens without a chaperone and carelessly consummated their passion. Henry Sutton discovered them, and in a fit of rage, challenged Nikolas to a duel to avenge his sister's lost virtue. Nikolas talked his way out of the duel by offering to marry Elizabeth, thereby saving her honor. After Henry cooled his temper, he admitted he didn't want to fight to the death the very man who had possibly saved his own life. When Lord and Lady Sutton learned of this, they gave their reluctant consent, knowing of no other way to salvage their daughter's reputation. Nikolas and Elizabeth were given a hasty wedding at the manor church, and then sailed immediately for Russia on Nikolas's naval ship.

When he returned to Saint Petersburg with his English bride, his mother, the Dowager Countess Elena, and his brother and wife, Count Vasily and Countess Irene, were furious. They had already arranged a betrothal for him with the Princess Anastasia, daughter of Count Romanov, a cousin of the new Czar Alexander I. Her large dowry and noble blood lines would have ensured Nikolas and the Bolkonskys added wealth and prestige. His mother insisted on having the marriage annulled, but when it was discovered that Elizabeth was expecting a child, she grudgingly accepted her new daughter-in-law.

A few weeks later Nikolas was ordered to sail for Russian America. The voyage there would take nearly a year as the ship sailed through the Baltic Sea to London, then across the Atlantic and around Cape Horn, the southern tip of South America, and up the coast of North America to New Archangel. After spending a year there he would sail home across the Pacific to China, through the islands of Indonesia and to India, then around the Cape of Good Hope, and north up the coast of Africa and Europe. He could be gone as long as three years.

Since Elizabeth could not accompany him as some of the naval wives did, she begged him to allow her to return to England to have her baby. He refused. However much he loved her, Nikolas was a typical Russian husband. She belonged to him and he would not let her go.

During this time she tried hard to become a part of the Bolkonsky family. Although she was the daughter of English aristocrats, this was ignored. They failed to see the fine breeding and qualities she did possess, and treated her like an inferior creature. Only the Countess Elena was kind to her. Not only was Elizabeth carrying the child of her favorite son, Nikolas, she shared the Countess's devotion to Christianity. The two were diligent in attending church services and often spent time together reading and discussing the Bible, a pastime scorned by Irene as dull.

One hot summer night, such as this one, after an excruciatingly painful birth, Tatiana was born and her mother died, a lonely frightened girl far away from her husband, homeland, and family.

The Bolkonsky family was relieved to be rid of her. They sent all of Elizabeth's possessions back to England to the Suttons, and also cut off any communication with them. To this day, Tatiana had nothing that belonged to her. It was like her mother never existed. And Tatiana supposed by now, her English grandparents had forgotten all about her.

Nikolas's voyage lasted longer than expected, but was a financial and military success for the Russian American Fur Company. The Company had been organized in 1799 after the abundance of sea otter furs were discovered in the Aleutian Islands. Much wealth was to be had through the fur trade, and many of the Russian nobility in Saint Petersburg were investors, including the Bolkonskys. The first governor appointed was a man called Alexander Baranov. Under his stern and capable leadership, several forts had been established, from the Aleutians to Kodiak Island to the protected waters of the southeastern islands where the capitol of Russian America, New Archangel, was located on Sitka Island, now called Baranov Island.

When Nikolas and his ship, the *Catherine*, had arrived, they were just in time to help Baranov and his men reclaim the fort of New Archangel from the local natives who had attacked and captured it months earlier. In so doing, Nikolas and Alexander became friends. Nikolas admired Baranov for his strength of character and unfailing courage in dealing with the warlike natives. Baranov praised Nikolas for his expert handling of his crew and ship's cannon in frightening the natives away. After helping Baranov rebuild the fort, Nikolas and the *Catherine* sailed off with a cargo of rich fox and otter furs. They stopped in Canton, China where they traded for silk and fine porcelain and spices, then returned to Saint Petersburg.

Nikolas's homecoming was bittersweet. He and his officers were rewarded by Czar Alexander I with medals, thousands of rubles, and he was promoted to Captain-Lieutenant. But his beautiful young wife had died giving birth to a daughter in whom he had little interest. At age three she was a small whining child and the visit had been disastrous for both of them. Heartbroken, he left within a month for another voyage to Russian America.

Since then, Tatiana had seen him only two more times in her life, when she was six and he had given her the kitten and the walrus tooth necklace, and when she was ten in 1812. That was the year Napoleon and his French troops had invaded Russia. Her father was sent out to patrol what little coastline Russia possessed in the eastern Gulf of Finland. Her Uncle Vasily was involved in the Battle of Borodino, which resulted in humiliating defeat for the ill-trained Russian troops, and was also seriously wounded in his leg. Tatiana was thankful that her father saw little naval action and was eventually sent back to Russian America.

The last time she had seen him, he had delighted her with his descriptions of the land the natives called Alaska with its majestic snowy mountains and icy blue glaciers and green inland seas. Her father called it the most beautiful place on earth. She always imagined that someday she would live there with him.

Then last month a ship had returned from Russian America with news of two shocking events. The first was of Alexander Baranov's death. At age seventy-two, he was in frail health and had been replaced as governor by young Lieutenant Simeon Yanovski. After reluctantly handing over all his Company records to the new governor, he departed his beloved New Archangel, an old man with a broken heart. By the time the ship reached Java in the tropics, Baranov had succumbed to a fever his advanced age could not fight.

The second surprise was that Captain-Lieutenant Nikolas Bolkonsky would not be returning to Saint Petersburg for many years. He was remaining in New Archangel as the assistant to the new governor, a position of much importance in the Company.

Tatiana was devastated; her dream of living with him lay in ashes. She was consumed by anger and a wound so deep she could barely breathe. She felt like he had rejected her, abandoning her like he had her mother to a lonely miserable existence. And then to discover this morning, that he'd approved her betrothal to an unknown man.

It made her almost hate him.

* * *

"Tatiana Nikolayevna, dismiss your maid at once! Mikael is waiting to escort you downstairs to the ballroom."

Tall and majestic, her aunt stood in the doorway of Tatiana's bedchamber, her eyes flashing with cold dislike, matching the glare of the magnificent necklace gleaming with sapphires and diamonds that encircled her long white neck.

The hard freezing tones of Aunt Irene's voice never failed to chill Tatiana and she obeyed without question, turning to her maid. "Leave us, Sonya!" she ordered. The small Russian girl bowed slightly, then fled out the door, carefully giving the Countess a wide berth.

In slow measured steps as she had been taught, Tatiana walked over to her aunt, so she could examine her appearance from head to toe. Irene's rosebud mouth, which as a young woman held a charming pout, was now clamped together in a critical expression, making her look much older than her forty years. Impatiently she patted the jeweled comb which fastened Tatiana's plaited hair to the back of her head, then checked each pale gold ringlet curling over her ears. Irene's glance swept over Tatiana's gown, lingered scornfully on her small bosom, finally resting on her satin slippers.

"You certainly have big feet for a young woman," she said, seemingly satisfied to have found a flaw somewhere with Tatiana's appearance. "You must have inherited them from your mother. And like her, you have a tendency to walk too quickly. What a shame you don't have small dainty feet like my dear Olga has. It is unfortunate that your large feet betray the uncouth side of your family, but hopefully, no one will notice."

Just in time, Tatiana bit off the retort forming on her lips, *it is true that my feet are larger than Olga's, but then, her feet are the only thing tiny and delicate about her.*

She knew her aunt was trying to find something, anything with which to undermine her confidence before the ball. She wanted her to feel nervous and uncertain. Instead she was making Tatiana angry with her slur against her mother. But Tatiana controlled her temper and managed to give her aunt a slight smile. Irene looked momentarily flustered. It was not the reaction she had hoped for.

As they stepped into the hallway where Mikael waited, Tatiana's smile vanished, and she replaced it with a look of disdain. Irene hurried away from them, rustling down the long corridor in her ball gown of satin, calling over her shoulder, "The guests are arriving, children, so please come at once."

"Tatiana, my sweetest cousin, how utterly enchanting you look tonight." Mikael's full red lips shaped like his mother's, broke open into his usual leer. Tatiana often thought it unfortunate for Olga that her brother had inherited their mother's rosebud mouth while she had the thin lips of their father.

"Thank you, Mikael," she said politely. He did not know how much she detested him.

His dark brown hair was slicked back from his forehead, giving his long Bolkonsky nose a sharp prominence. He reeked of vodka and his face was flushed and sweaty. "You must be nicer to me than that, my sweet, if you want to find out the name of your betrothed."

The Countess had already disappeared down the stairs and Tatiana was alone with Mikael, something she always dreaded, as her childhood tormentor had now become a twenty-year-old man who stared at her often with a strange look in his eyes that she did not understand or trust.

With an effort she kept her voice firm. "How can you possibly know such a thing?"

He laughed softly. "I overheard my parents discussing you in the library last night." He leaned closer, his face bending down towards hers. "If you let me kiss you, I'll tell you everything."

Before his fleshy lips could touch her, she quickly spread out her silk fan in front of her face as a protective shield. "If you so much as breathe on me, I'll scream for your father," she said with a calmness she did not feel.

The mention of Count Vasily stopped him cold. He drew back and hissed, "So, that's how you want to play the game. Fine, I'll tell you anyway. I want to be the first person to see the shock on your face when you find out you're to be the next Baroness Volodin."

Baron Ivan Volodin was a man older than her father. She felt a sense of impending doom as they descended the magnificent double staircase of polished marble sweeping down to the entrance hall below. Mikael had to be lying.

* * *

The palace ballroom blazed with the glow of the great crystal chandeliers, the light from thousands of shimmering candles reflecting off the white marble walls and the marble floor of ash inlaid with huge laurel wreaths. Near the gallery for the musicians and singers was an enormous fireplace, and though this was a warm summer evening, a fire crackled within. Tatiana and Mikael paused in the entryway as the stuffy air from the crowded room greeted them along with the smiles of dozens of richly dressed people, men smart in military uniforms flashing with gold buttons and medals, women sparkling in their finest jewelry and gowns. They were the cream of Saint Petersburg society.

Her emotions were in a turmoil, but Tatiana managed to greet each person with a gracious smile. Her head held high, she nodded and thanked everyone who wished her a Happy Birthday, feeling like a marionette held on a tight string, yanked along by Cousin Mikael. She dutifully danced with him and the many partners who had filled her dance card earlier. The evening went by in a blur of waltzes, Polish *mazurkas*, *anglaises*, and *ecossaises*. The *ecossaises* were especially lively and made her hot and thirsty.

Her only source of satisfaction came when she noted Olga's absence and was told by Aunt Irene that "my poor *dusha moya* (darling) was suffering from one of her beastly headaches and sent her regrets at not attending the ball."

Olga's headaches were always her convenient excuse to escape something she disliked, but her mother had never discovered that fact. Tatiana remembered one afternoon when Olga had been too ill for her pianoforte lesson. She had burst into Olga's bedchamber to see how she was feeling, only to find her cousin sitting up in her mammoth four poster bed, wolfing down French chocolate covered bonbons. Olga's fury at being found out sent Tatiana running out of the room, but not before Olga saw her convulse with laughter. Olga had never forgiven her.

Taking a brief rest from the dancing, Tatiana fluttered her fan against her face to create a slight breeze. She smiled at this memory, and wondered if her cousin might have the right idea after all. Perhaps she should feign illness before the betrothal announcement was made.

"When you smile, Tatiana Nikolayevna, you are easily the most beautiful woman in the room," said a man in a clipped measured voice.

Her smile froze as she stared up into the weathered face of Baron Ivan Volodin. He was holding a glass of champagne. Resplendent in his military uniform, adorned with medals and shiny gold braid, his gray hair and mustache trimmed neatly, he looked every inch the colonel he was. The same Battle of Borodino which had wounded her uncle had made a hero out of the Baron, who had been rewarded with the Cross of Saint George by the Czar.

"Come now, you haven't said one word to me. Is that how you should greet an old Academy friend of your father's?"

Remembering her manners, she dropped a brief curtsy and extended her hand. "I--I'm sorry, Baron. I mean, it's good to see you."

She shivered as his bony fingers closed over her gloved hand. Although he was her father's friend from their Naval Academy days, no two men could be more different.

Tatiana thought the Baron might have befriended her father, because he desired a link with the powerful and influential Bolkonskys. Her grandparents, Ilya and Elena, had ancestors dating back to Peter the Great, making their family one of the oldest and finest of the aristocracy, while the Volodins were of lesser nobility.

She wondered if the Baron knew she was half English. Perhaps he was willing to overlook that fact. Marriage into the Bolkonsky family would help the Baron climb higher into Saint Petersburg society, especially since the scandal associated with her mother seemed to be forgotten.

Not so with the Baron and his family. For years there had been strange rumors about the Volodins. Two years ago his daughter Ella supposedly had committed suicide at age sixteen, then his poor wife Marie had lost her mind and died just last year.

"Why, you are trembling, my dear. Are you chilly? Come, I'll bring you closer to the fire."

The Baron clicked his heels together with military precision and quickly moved her towards the huge fireplace. She was too frightened of him to resist. "Ah," he said, "this warmth should help you to relax."

Russians were notorious for loving overheated homes. Whether it was the warmest day of summer or the coldest of arctic nights, the stoves and fireplaces were always putting out heat. So, it was ironic that the nobility fled Saint Petersburg during the hottest days of summer, preferring the healthier environment of their country estates or *dachas.* Summertime in Saint Petersburg was dry and dusty and full of mosquitoes that bred in the stagnant odorous waters of the city canals.

The Bolkonskys had returned in late August rather than September from their estate in southern Russia only for Tatiana's birthday ball.

How I wish we were still in Ekaterineslav, she thought longingly, remembering all those lovely weeks of riding horses across the hundreds of acres and having picnics by the cool waters of the Dnieper River shaded by oak trees. No lessons and no duties, she and Olga enjoyed a freedom impossible in Saint Petersburg.

With Mikael at the Naval Academy all summer, it was harder for Olga to be her usual bully. Instead she became Tatiana's companion, albeit grudgingly. They picked luscious ripe gooseberries and red currants growing wild in meadows of sweet grass. They explored the farms, orchards, vegetable gardens and entire fields of flowers cultivated for the house, a charming home made of oak, which was smaller and more intimate than the palace.

Towards the end of July on Saint Elias's Day, there was a festival in the serfs' village which lasted three days. Merchants from near and far set up their booths to display their wares. Peasants traveled from great distances in their carts and wagons, and every evening the sounds they made playing their accordions and singing and laughing carried to the house.

It always amazed her how happy they seemed to be. Olga said they were too ignorant to know anything better, and the peasants only appeared to be carefree because of the large amounts of vodka they drank to forget how poor they were.

In stark contrast to the serfs' wooden hovels were the tidy orderly villages of the nearby Mennonites. Tatiana and her cousins thought they were a strange religious sect, but her uncle was impressed by their successful farming methods. Once every summer they would take a tour of the closest Mennonite villages with their vast fields of wheat grown as high as the carriage. She and Olga would poke fun at the drab clothes of the women in their bonnets and the bearded men with their funny black hats.

There were always lots of children in those villages, staring at the gleaming silver and black *droshky*, a carriage drawn by three shiny black horses with tinkling bells in their harness. Their coachman sat proudly on his seat, the reins gathered in one hand, the other tipping his gray felt hat with peacock feathers at the wide-eyed children. When the village dogs yipped at the horses, it would irritate Uncle Vasily. Towards the end of the village he would urge the coachman to full speed. The horse in the middle balancing the great collar would break into a trot, with the other two galloping on each side, their heads down. From the *droshky* she could see their long tails flying in the dust raised by their hooves. It was delightful.

She loved the estate. And next summer, would she be returning there, or would she be the next Baroness Volodina?

A moment of dizziness seized her. The heat from the fire was suffocating. The lack of food, the stress of her birthday and impending betrothal, and her fear of the Baron was increasingly overwhelming any strength she had left. A strange numbness crept up her legs while the roomful of dancers started to swirl around her in a slow circle.

"Tatiana, are you feeling unwell?" The Baron's voice held concern as he looked at her. "Here, try some of my champagne."

He handed her the crystal-stemmed glass and she obediently took a sip. The cool bubbly liquid slid down her parched throat. She had never tasted anything so delicious. Before she could stop herself, she drained the glass.

The Baron chuckled, then glanced behind her, and nodded stiffly to Count Bolkonsky and Mikael who had appeared. "Tatiana," said her uncle, "you look a bit pale and could use some color in your cheeks. Mikael will take you outside for some fresh air."

For once she was glad to see her cousin. She smiled with gratitude at him and her uncle as the room slowly stopped spinning.

Count Vasily Ilyich Bolkonsky was a strongly built and handsome man with black wavy hair, slightly gray at the temples, an imposing black mustache, and piercing black eyes. The dominant Bolkonsky nose gave his face a regal appearance while the same feature looked more comical on his son's fleshy face. Although he walked with a slight limp due to his war wound, an aurora of power surrounded him. He was a close confidant of Czar Alexander and was admired by both men and women alike.

He was the opposite of her father. The two brothers possessed the same nose and dark coloring, but there the family resemblance ended. Her uncle had no interest in people or animals except for their usefulness for his own gain. Her father was the sort of man who could charm the dourest old lady into a smile.

She had a dim memory of a story that Nana had told her about him. As a boy he had a tender heart for any unfortunate creature. He constantly brought home sick or injured dogs, kittens, even birds to nurse back to health. Countess Elena had indulged her favorite son in this interest until the cold winter night he brought home seven children, dressed in rags, which he had seen begging in the snowy streets nearby. They were half-frozen and starving. These she fed and clothed, and sent to an orphanage, then forbade Nikolas to ever bring home stray children again.

Tatiana should have inherited his deep sense of compassion for the poor and the helpless. But her eyes were closed to the spectacle of the starving beggar children of the city, her ears deaf to the sounds of a horse being whipped too hard, or the hungry cries of the skeletal dogs and cats she saw prowling the streets. After the night years ago when her grandmother had died and Mikael had thrown her kitten out the window, she had hardened her heart towards the sufferings of others. She had no wish to ever own another pet or care too deeply about anyone else except her father.

In that regard, she was actually more like her uncle.

She had also come to like him for the first time in her life. When she was a child, he had ignored her existence, but in the past year, he had begun to notice her. He seemed to enjoy talking to her on the rare evenings he was home, and once had told her that she looked just like her mother. "Elizabeth was a beautiful woman," he said. "But don't let your aunt know I ever said that."

Tatiana would never dream of telling Aunt Irene, but she didn't have to. Both her aunt and Olga were aware of Uncle Vasily's interest in her. It made them resent her all the more, but there was nothing they could do to stop his attentions towards her. Count Vasily was a king in his own palace.

"When you two return from your brief walk," he said, "we have an important announcement to make."

He and the Baron exchanged a look that made her heart sink. So, Mikael was telling the truth after all. Once more, feeling like a puppet on a string, she allowed Mikael to take her arm.

He led her outside to the formal gardens which swept out behind the palace for many acres. Darkness had fallen and the night was rich with the fragrance of the moist soil and plants and grass. The cooler air revived Tatiana instantly and she breathed deeply.

To the northwest the sky still glowed with the faint light of the long summer twilight, and to the east the first evening stars were scattered above like diamonds tossed carelessly upon blue-black velvet. Frogs and crickets chirped their songs from their homes among the garden ponds and grasses, their steady drone nature's own lullaby.

Mikael disappeared into the shadowed maze of dark shrubs ahead, and she followed without thinking. She knew every part of these gardens; had played hide-and-seek and other games as a child, and had taken many a stroll in them. So when her foot tripped over a root and she almost fell over, she was taken by surprise.

"Mikael," she called softly, then louder, "Mikael, where are you?"

"Right behind you."

She jumped and spun around. "Were you trying to frighten me?" she demanded.

"Of course not, little cousin. I would never think of such a thing." He snickered quietly.

"We should return to the ball," she said firmly. "We've been gone long enough. I feel much better already."

"As you wish," he said, but instead of taking her arm and guiding her back towards the palace, he put both of his large sweaty hands on her shoulders. "Listen, Tatiana, I need to talk to you about something first. I think I can solve your unhappy problem with the Baron."

It was too dark to see his face clearly and in a suspicious voice she said, "How can you help me?"

"I have a plan."

Surprised by his apparent concern for her happiness, she said, "Thank you, Mikael, but I don't know what you can do to stop the betrothal."

His hands tightened their grip on her shoulders. "When you were a little girl, Tatiana, I thought you were the most beautiful thing I had ever seen, and I knew when you grew up, you had to belong to me."

"What are you talking about? You and Olga hated me."

"No!" His cry rang out in protest. "I was only a confused little boy. Olga made me do all those bad things to frighten you, because she was jealous that you were so pretty. She's still jealous, but that's her problem now." He lowered his voice. "I can't stop your marriage to the mean old Baron, Tatiana. But I know I can make you happy." He took a deep breath. "I can make you happy if you will do me the honor of becoming my mistress..."

His voice ended on a pleading note while she fought the urge to laugh in his face. *Mistress indeed*! The whole idea was disgusting and totally ludicrous.

"Never," she said through clenched teeth. "I don't want anything to do with you, ever, you---you cat murderer!"

Startled, he released his hold on her shoulders slightly and she twisted away. Before he could grab her again, she gathered up her skirts and fled in the direction of the palace. Running was her only hope. It was her athletic ability, probably due to her large feet and long legs. As a child she had outrun Mikael and Olga many a time and now she ran like Napoleon and the entire French army was after her. She knew Mikael's temper when thwarted and he must not catch her alone again.

She could hear him crashing through the shrubs behind her, calling out, "Tatiana, Tatiana, wait, I can explain that, too---"

His voice grew fainter as she neared the immense palace. Every window glowed with light, the sounds of singing violins and laughing people echoing across the lawns. She slipped inside a servants' side entrance and quickly checked her appearance before making her way to the ballroom. She knew her uncle would be furious with Mikael if she told him what he'd said. However, Aunt Irene would try to convince Uncle Vasily into thinking she had tried to seduce Mikael. She always protected Mikael from his father's wrath whether it involved gambling, drinking to excess, or shirking his duties. This situation would be no different.

Mikael was a typical young man of the Russian aristocracy. He avoided every recreation or sport that included exertion. He spurned riding, hunting, and fishing, but had much passion for chess, cards, and billiards. He had little interest in literature, even though her uncle's library was filled with rare and expensive books and manuscripts. Mikael preferred loitering and sleeping away life, and waking up only to selfish pleasures. Although he attended the Naval Academy, the discipline of military life had yet to change his lazy nature.

He was due to graduate next year, with a choice of continuing in the Navy, or pursuing an Army career, which was the quickest route to honor and riches, as their grandfather Ilya, her uncle, and the Baron Volodin had discovered. Her father was the odd man in the family. He had disregarded the traditional call of the Army for the call of the sea. Even so, he had distinguished himself in the Imperial Navy.

Tatiana envied the Bolkonsky men. Women were given the bare minimum of education and while it was enough for Olga, she longed to learn more about the world. She would love to browse through her uncle's library, but the doors remained locked to her. Instead she was given music and dancing lessons, French and English lessons, and embroidery, for which she had no patience.

They'd once had an English governess from London. Besides the English language, she taught geography, history and mathematics, subjects which Olga found so boring she began to complain to her mother. Aunt Irene didn't take much notice of her complaints until the day Olga informed her that Tatiana was continually quizzing Miss Marchant about England and the whereabouts of Sutton Manor where her English grandparents lived. Within a week Miss Marchant had been sent back to London, and in another week, they'd had a French governess, *Mademoiselle* Helene, a cold thin woman with a quick temper. She taught only French fashion, language and embroidery, which involved hours of fine needlework. How Tatiana had loathed her.

"Do you think to escape from me so easily, little cousin?"

She stiffened as Mikael fell into step beside her. "Leave me alone, Mikael!"

"I'll never leave you alone as long as I live. No matter whom you are married to."

She looked at him then and saw the vicious threat veiled in his eyes and the unpleasant twist to his thick lips under his bushy mustache. Her temper flared quickly. "If you don't stop harassing me, I'll tell your father."

"And I'll deny everything. I'll say you made everything up because you are hopelessly in love with me."

"He'll never believe that!"

"Won't he?" Mikael snickered. "You think because my father is paying you so much attention lately, that he will take your word over mine? He doesn't really care about you. You are only a toy to him, a beautiful toy I'll grant you, but a toy just like all women are to him. I've seen the way he looks at you. If you weren't his niece, you'd be his mistress by now. No wonder my mother resents your presence in this family. She is probably the one who pushed for your betrothal to the old Baron just to get rid of you."

Before she could respond, he added more gently. "Remember, Tatiana, I'm the only Bolkonsky who really loves you."

"What about my father?" she shot back, thinking that Mikael must be deranged to believe that he loved her. He didn't know the meaning of the word. And it couldn't be true what he implied about her uncle's lack of genuine feelings for her.

"Ah, yes, the great but absent Captain-Lieutenant Nikolas Bolkonsky," he said sarcastically. "Where has he been all your life if he really loved you?"

Without giving her a chance to answer that tormenting question, he whisked her into the ballroom, both of their faces pasted into polite expressions. There was a lull in the dancing at that moment, and the guests ceased their conversations when she and Mikael appeared.

Count Vasily motioned them to his side in the center of the great room, his white teeth flashing under his black mustache into a smile as he faced the crowd of glittering people. To his right was Aunt Irene with her mouth primly set in her artificial social smile. On his left Baron Volodin stood in an erect military bearing. His expression was impassive, yet his cold gray eyes never left Tatiana's face.

His close scrutiny added to her discomfort as icy fingers of dread crept around her heart. She wondered if this was how the French prisoners of war had felt as they waited for sentencing in front of the Russian generals during the war with Napoleon. At this moment, she could not imagine despair greater than hers.

"Honorable Friends and Guests," said Count Vasily in his deep authoritative voice, "the Countess and myself are pleased that all of you can be a part of this special evening. As you know, tonight is the sixteenth birthday celebration of our niece, Tatiana Nikolayevna. But even more importantly, tonight we are here to announce her betrothal. It is usual for a young woman's father to have the honor of announcing her betrothal, but my brother, Nikolas, is stationed in Russian America as assistant to the new governor. Instead he sent his written permission for the Countess and me to act in his behalf."

He cleared his throat. "I am delighted to announce the betrothal of Tatiana Nikolayevna Bolkonskaya to the future Baron Dmitri Ivanovich Volodin, the son of our good friend, Baron Ivan Volodin."

There was a hush and then the sound of hundreds of hands clapping. The words were a tiny trickle of warmth invading the frozen numbness of Tatiana's mind. Had she really heard her uncle say, "The future Baron Volodin?" Or were her ears playing a trick on her? But no---she had heard correctly and there was more...

"Of course, this means," continued Uncle Vasily, "that our beloved Tatiana will be leaving Saint Petersburg in the next year to undertake the long voyage to Russian America. Dmitri Ivanovich is a lieutenant in the Imperial Navy and he and his ship are presently stationed in New Archangel. The wedding will take place there in compliance with the wishes of my brother, Nikolas, who will give the bride away as a father's right."

The ice around her heart melted in a flood of joy at his words. Russian America! Alaska! She was going to New Archangel to be with her father! He had sent for her at last! Her dreams were to become true after all...

In the midst of her euphoria it didn't matter that he wanted her to marry a total stranger. She was certain she could change her father's mind about Lieutenant Volodin when he realized all the lost years of not knowing each other which they needed to catch up on. Right now all she could think of was being freed of the strict confines of the palace and her unloving family.

And Mikael....at last she could be free of his dangerous and unwanted attentions. She glanced at him and almost laughed to see the shock her betrothal had given him. His normally ruddy complexion was a pasty gray color and he stared at her with a desperate anger like a frustrated cat whose prey had just escaped.

She gave him a quick triumphant smile then turned to smile at everyone else. The betrothal ring was presented next. As Baron Volodin slipped the exquisite diamond and gold ring over her finger, he leaned closer and whispered, "My son is indeed a fortunate man to have so lovely a woman as his wife."

Tatiana nodded graciously while thinking, *indeed, I am most fortunate to have escaped being your wife. I only hope your son is not a chip off the old block.*

* * *

Near midnight dinner was served in the enormous banquet hall. Everyone was seated at an immense table in the shape of a horseshoe. Count Vasily and Countess Irene were placed at the head, with Tatiana and the Baron on the Count's right and Mikael to the left of his mother. The other side of the table inside the horseshoe was not occupied, so the guests could see their host and hostess more easily.

First were the toasts, the chamberlains presenting each guest with a tall champagne glass on a golden plate. Count Vasily began with a toast to the Baron, "I am proud to welcome your son into our family." The Baron countered with. "And I am proud to welcome your niece into my family."

There were several more toasts with caviar, the salty sturgeon eggs, which were considered a delicacy. Then the first course arrived, turtle soup. By that time Tatiana was feeling quite tipsy. This was the first time in her life she had been allowed champagne and she realized that she liked it. The alcohol relaxed her enough to make even the Baron seem like a friendly dinner companion. She certainly preferred sitting next to him over Mikael.

The dinner seemed endless with too much food. After the turtle soup there was the asparagus, then the veal, the wild duck, venison, haunches of beef, and fillets of sturgeon and salmon. All this was eaten with oceans of wine and vodka. Her linen napkin had a gold embroidered "B" in one corner, and kept sliding on the slippery surface of her dress and falling to the floor. Each time the page behind her chair disappeared under the table to retrieve the napkin, she giggled like an idiot.

Finally Aunt Irene turned to frown at her and she immediately tried to sober up. Conversations swirled around her. She had no interest in any of it until the topic switched to how a young woman like herself would be able to adjust to the primitive conditions in New Archangel after being accustomed to luxury all her life.

On Tatiana's right sat a heavyset woman, the Countess Trotskaya, who was a distant cousin of Aunt Irene. She turned to Tatiana and said, "My dear girl, you have no idea what you're letting yourself in for. My brother, Alexis, and his wife and two daughters live in New Archangel. My sister-in-law, Irina, has written me much about the place. I shudder every time I read one of her letters, knowing my two nieces, Vera and Sophie, are living in such a barbaric town. They are surrounded by terrible influences. Why, except for several officers' wives, there is an appalling lack of aristocratic women there."

Tatiana was disappointed to hear that the Trotsky's were living in New Archangel. Irina was a good friend of Aunt Irene, and was a person who had not forgotten the scandal about Tatiana's mother. Whenever she and her daughters came to visit, they snubbed Tatiana quite openly, and the oldest daughter, Vera, always joined Olga in making fun of her.

The Countess Trotskaya leaned over and touched Tatiana's arm with her short pudgy bejeweled fingers and said, "My dear girl, I must warn you of something else. Most of the women you will encounter in New Archangel are heathenish Indians or half-Indian and half-Russian women who are called *Creoles*. It is a terrible disgrace to Russia that some of our men have married Indian women and have fathered their children!"

Mikael, who had been guzzling wine faster than his food, said in a slight slur, "I heard the great Alexander Baranov himself had an Aleut wife an' two half breed brats."

Several of the ladies sitting nearby murmured in disapproval. Tatiana was surprised at this news about a man her father respected, but obviously not the Baron, who said in a scornful voice, "Baranov, for all his achievements in Russian America, was little more than a peasant, the son of a storekeeper."

"The Company is aware of these problems," said Uncle Vasily. "But it is mainly the *promyshlenniki*, the fur hunters, who are common peasants or criminals from Siberia that consort with the native women. Tatiana will have nothing to do with these men whatsoever. She will be staying in the governor's mansion with her father until the wedding."

His answer satisfied most of the ladies. Count Bolkonsky was on the Russian American Company Board of Directors. He was also a major stockholder, as was Baron Volodin, and the profits from the fur trade were making these rich men even richer. Tatiana's father owned stock in the Company as well, but was not the sort of man who cared about obtaining wealth just for the love of money.

Tatiana could hardly believe that by next summer she would be sailing around the world to see him. Nothing the Countess Trotskaya said could possibly dim her joy at the prospect of living in New Archangel near her father. And the Countess would be horrified if she knew that her warnings about half-breeds intrigued Tatiana all the more. After all, hadn't Olga just called her one that very morning?

"But what about the wild Indians?" Countess Trotskaya persisted. "Just the thought of them terrify me. Don't they frighten you too, Tatiana, darling?"

"I don't know. I've never seen one." She giggled.

Her feeble attempt at a jest brought frowns of disapproval from everyone except Mikael, who gave a brief snort of laughter. Baron Volodin raised his eyebrows at her and said, "You will see plenty of natives in New Archangel, Tatiana. We call them the *Kolosh*. They call themselves the Tlingits. They are a proud, warlike tribe, but we have subdued them, just as we have conquered the Aleuts from the Aleutian Islands. You have nothing to fret your beautiful head about."

Tatiana opened her mouth to say she wasn't fretting at all when he added, "However, it was different years ago. One terrible day in 1803 the *Kolosh* attacked the fort of New Archangel and massacred its inhabitants. At the time Alexander Baranov was at Kodiak Island. If he had been in New Archangel, it is probable that the *Kolosh* would not have dared the attack, because they feared him so."

"Why did the Indians hate us so much?" Tatiana asked, curious about this event which her father had referred to as the Sitka Massacre, but never told her any details. It wasn't for tender young ears, he had said.

The Baron shrugged as her uncle replied, "There is a story that we built our fort upon the natives' sacred rock hill, and they swore to never rest until we were driven away. However, I believe they were incited to rebel by a certain English sea captain whose ship was anchored nearby. The Englishmen encouraged the *Kolosh* to attack our fort by giving them advice and by providing guns and powder. The English captain remained aloof during the attack and took action only when everything was burnt and destroyed. Then he rescued the few survivors, three Russians and a handful of Aleut slaves."

The Baron shook his head in disgust. "Altogether, several hundred Russians and Aleuts died, plus three thousand sea otter and other prized pelts were stolen. A terrible waste."

Tatiana was not certain if he meant the tragic loss of human life or the stolen pelts as a terrible waste. The tipsy effect of the champagne was disappearing as she focused on hearing about this long ago tragedy. She took a bite of salmon and listened as her uncle continued the story.

"After the *Kolosh* took control of what was left of the fort, they rebuilt it into a village. But we had our revenge. My brother Nikolas's ship reached Kodiak in November, 1803. He wintered there then in the spring he and Baranov sailed across the Gulf of Alaska to Baranov Island. Their first attack to recapture the fort was repelled by the *Kolosh*. Several Russian sailors were killed and many were wounded, including Baranov. Finally, my brother's ship bombarded the *Kolosh* village with cannon shot until they withdrew."

Uncle Vasily took a deep drink of his wine, then smiled grimly at the Baron and Tatiana. "The last part of this story was told to me years later by Nikolas himself. It is horrible indeed, but it shows how depraved the heathenish natives can be. To expedite their flight from the village, the *Kolosh* warriors killed all their children. It devastated Nikolas and Baranov to see such a monstrous sight."

"Oh, Vasily," exclaimed Aunt Irene, "those Indians are inhuman!"

He patted her hand absently. "Those days are long over with, my dear. Most of the *Kolosh* have moved far away from New Archangel, and the ones who remain are well-controlled." He looked at Tatiana. "You also have nothing to fear from the Aleuts. Many of our Russian Orthodox priests have converted them to Christianity, and the men hunt for us while the women are our servants."

Christianity? She thought scornfully, how could wild Indians believe in a God that didn't exist? The priests must have forced their beliefs down their ignorant throats.

But with all the information she was learning that night, she realized she too was ignorant when it came to the history and people of Russian America. For one thing, she was puzzled that the English provoked the Indians to attack the Russians.

She turned to the Baron and asked, "Why did the English incite the *Kolosh* against us?"

He swallowed the large piece of beef he was chewing then wiped his thin lips and mustache with a napkin. Clearing his throat, he said, "England, the United States, and Russia are competitors in a land of diminishing resources, Tatiana. Sea otters, fur seals, and other fur bearing animals are disappearing from too many years of hunting.

"Many years ago it was different. The Americans actually helped our Russians survive at New Archangel. We continually suffered shortages of supplies, particularly food. The American shipmasters had surplus goods and welcomed the chance to turn them into a profit. So, they frequently called at New Archangel to exchange bread, flour, rice, and molasses for otter and beaver furs. Baranov actually welcomed each Yankee captain with lavish banquets and musical entertainment's.

"But now the English and Americans, especially, do not want us Russians in the land they call Alaska. So, they trade guns, powder, and ammunition to the natives for pelts then they urge them to use the firearms against us. This has been going on for so long, that our blessed Czar has requested the United States government to prohibit American citizens from trade with the natives in our North American colonies."

"And so, have the American sea captains stopped their trading there?" she asked.

Her uncle frowned. "Indeed, they have not. They also run contraband to the people of California whose Spanish government has forbidden trade relations to all foreigners. This has brought complications to our settlement at Fort Ross on the coast north of San Francisco. At times the Spanish have turned hostile towards our Russians as if we were the ones there illegally. And we need Fort Ross for the rich grain it produces for Russian America.

"We should ex-exterminate 'em all, those nasty interferin' Yanks!" Mikael suddenly blurted out drunkenly. "Including the stupid English!" He sneered at Tatiana.

"Now, now, my dearest," clucked Aunt Irene as Uncle Vasily scowled at Mikael. He didn't seem to notice his father's disapproval, and slammed his heavy fist down on the table so hard, the plates and silverware rattled and his wine glass tipped over. Dark red liquid poured out, like pools of blood, staining the cream colored linen tablecloth.

The Baron glanced at Mikael with distaste. "The boy doesn't seem to hold his liquor very well."

Both his parents looked embarrassed as the nearest servant hastily blotted up the mess with a towel. Mikael, not at all ashamed by his clumsy outburst, laughed. "I am more of a man than your Dmitri will ever be."

The Baron stiffened and he said in a terse voice filled with barely controlled rage, "Count Bolkonsky, your son owes me an immediate apology for his insult against my son."

"Mikael Vasilyich," growled his father. "Apologize to our guest at once!"

The massive hall had grown silent. All eyes were on Count Bolkonsky and his son. The Countess looked faint as she clutched her sapphire and diamond necklace nervously.

The Baron rose and faced Mikael. "I do not wish to challenge you to a duel, young man, but you have tarnished the name of Volodin in public."

"Mikael---" said his father in warning.

"The Volodin name ish already tarnished, Baron," said Mikael, standing up with some difficulty as his chair crashed to the floor. "Your crazy wife an' daughter saw t' that years ago."

An outraged hum ran through the hall as the Baron's face blanched white. A look of deadly hate sprang into his icy gray eyes and he said, "Very well then. I challenge you to a duel, Mikael Vasilyich Bolkonsky. Pistols. Tomorrow morning at dawn."

He strode over to Mikael, took off his gray gloves, and struck him in the face. "I shall look forward to it." Nodding briskly to the horrified Count and Countess Bolkonsky, he marched out, leaving the hall full of stunned guests.

It was a fitting end to an evening Tatiana would never forget. As her aunt swooned into her uncle's arms and the hall burst into a babble of excited voices, she wondered if Mikael would be sober enough by dawn to shoot a pistol straight. Then again, it probably didn't matter. The

Baron was an expert huntsman and military marksman. And poor Mikael was an expert only at drinking, womanizing, and cards.

She didn't expect her cousin would survive the duel.

CHAPTER THREE

Vancouver Island, August, 1819

Thick fog shrouded the shores of Nootka Sound from Sean O'Connell's view off the starboard rail. The sky, water, hills and trees had blended into a solid gray mass as if someone had tossed a blanket of finely spun cotton over everything. He decided the fog could be a problem. The Nootkas could be approaching the ship in their canoes at this very moment and they wouldn't see them until the last second.

Their rescue mission here was important and dangerous. It was critical that each crew member of the *Eastern Wind* had a knife and a pistol concealed under his coat. If they were lucky and the natives were in a generous mood, none of the weapons would be needed. If the natives refused the ransom and turned hostile, then it was best to be ready for action. Captain Smythe had made one thing very clear. They were not leaving without the two men.

A couple years ago the captain and crew of the Boston brig, *Lydia*, had been ambushed and massacred by the Nootka Indians. Only two men survived. One was the ship's armorer or blacksmith, and the other was the ship's carpenter. Both men possessed skills the Indians valued, so they had been captured. John Hill the carpenter was the nephew of the *Eastern Wind's* owner, Thomas Hill. Rumors from other British and American ships trading up and down the west coast were that John Hill and Gregory Jones the armorer were alive and well.

The primary purpose of this voyage was to rescue Hill and Jones. Secondary was the accumulation of furs to trade in China. The Chinese valued the exquisite purple-black fur of the sea otter most of all. The mandarins and their ladies were greedy for otter skin robes, pearl-trimmed otter sashes, and luxuriant otter capes. They would pay an ounce of gold for a skin, and a cargo of them was a gold mine. In the 1790's the coastal natives traded a pelt for a few beads. Now they demanded much more for one otter skin, two yards of broadcloth, a gun with ten cartridges, or four pounds of lead and powder. But there was still much profit to be made.

If all went as planned, this voyage would be providing Captain Smythe and his three officers, including Sean, a comfortable income. Not only would they earn a share of the profits in the sale of the furs, but Thomas Hill had promised them all extra money if they brought his nephew home safe and sound.

Nothing made Sean happier than the secure feeling of gold or silver coins in his pockets. Unlike the other sailors who spent their earnings on rum, gambling, and women the minute the ship docked in a port, Sean hoarded his money. He still had the dream of having his own ship someday. It wasn't out of the realm of possibility anymore. After years of saving every cent he'd earned, he'd built up a nice little nest egg. The money was stored in a Boston bank, growing yearly with interest. One day he would have his ship.

It wasn't like he had any family to spend his money on. Ten years before when he had run off to sea, his plan was to provide for his sister, Rose.

Poor little Rose. The thought of his sister still made him wince inside. She hadn't survived the first winter he'd been gone. But he hadn't known that. He left Boston in the fall of 1809 and didn't return until the summer of 1811.

During that time the tough life onboard the *Eastern Wind* had turned him from an ignorant boy of fifteen years into a hardened sailor. And somewhere between the brutal treatments he'd received from the ship's crew as his initiation into their brotherhood of sailors, and the frightening gales off Cape Horn, to the heat and thirst of the equator, Sean had lost his romantic view of life at sea.

The first month had been the worst, he remembered, especially the first week. The *Eastern Wind* sailed out of Boston into the Atlantic during a fall storm. The waves were near twenty feet high, and though the ship's bow spliced over each crest and down through each trough in a steady motion, Sean thought he was going to die.

At least he wasn't alone in his misery. There were two other newcomers besides him, Ned Johnson, fourteen years old, and Jake O'Riley, about thirteen. Jake was the new cabin boy. All three boys curled up in their narrow hammocks swinging below decks in the gloomy dank crew quarters, full of fear that the ship would founder as she groaned and pitched. They also couldn't stop retching, and puked their guts into a bucket hour after hour, soon becoming objects of ridicule.

The other sailors laughed at them, even though they must have recalled their first days at sea. Some of the men took delight in eating their dinner near Sean, and jeered as the strong aroma of fish stew and onions turned his face green. By the second day, when the wind and waves had calmed, the ship's cook, a Chinese by the name of Wang Li, fed them some dry biscuits and a bit of whiskey and water. The biscuits settled Sean's stomach somewhat, but the taste of the whiskey reminded him of his alcoholic father, and he spit it out in disgust. He blamed alcohol for all the evils that had possessed his father and destroyed his family. He wouldn't mind the occasional glass of ale, but he'd sworn an oath to himself to never be a drinker of strong spirits.

He and Ned were soon on their feet, but young Jake couldn't keep any food down, his thin face growing paler each day, his eyes sinking into purple shadows. Sometimes his muffled cries could be heard as he called out for his mother.

One evening, after their fifth day at sea, the first mate Arthur Horn, stepped into the crew quarters. Since the officers kept to their own quarters, his appearance startled Sean, Ned, and a handful of men who were resting after being on watch all day.

If the captain was like God on this ship, the officers were demigods, especially the fearsome first mate. Horn was a tall thin man with cruel eyes and a face pitted with smallpox scars. He was known for his pleasure in flogging a lazy or insolent sailor with a long leather whip. Sean had already witnessed one unfortunate man being punished for sleeping on duty. When he was whipped his screams and the bloody welts on the torn skin of his back made Sean determined to stay alert, no matter how sore or weary he felt.

The quarters were dimly lit by a swinging oil lantern, which smoked a foul odor. Horn ignored the smell and the stares of the men and marched straight to Jake's hammock. In one hand he held a chunk of salt pork attached to a piece of string. With the other he grabbed the boy by the scruff of his neck and hauled him upright. Jake's curly carrot red hair seemed to spring straight up in alarm and his blue eyes bulged out in fear.

"You were hired on t' work, not lay 'round an' cry fer yer mammy all day," Horn growled, as he forced Jimmy's mouth open, and with his dirty tobacco-stained finger, shoved the salt pork way down the boy's throat.

Sean watched in horror as Jake gagged and choked, his eyeballs rolling backwards. Just when Sean thought the boy was going to faint, Horn pulled the salt pork out and stepped back quickly, as a stream of vomit spurted out of Jake's mouth.

"Now," said the first mate with an evil sounding chuckle, "you'll be so sick you'll never be sick again."

To Sean and Ned's amazement, the brutal cure for seasickness worked. Jake lay in his hammock all night, but he ate breakfast the next morning and weakly went about doing some small chores. Then his appetite returned to normal and he soon acquired his sea legs. Although still homesick, he never cried for his mother again.

The days and nights blended into a blur of endless work and exhaustion for all of them. Up each morning at four, Jake would empty the vile smelling slop buckets over the side while Sean and Ned scrubbed the cabin floors, then the decks. They polished medal and painted wood. They learned how to overhaul the gear, grease down the masts and how to furl and unfurl sails. They gathered coal for the galley stove and eggs from the hen coop for Wang Li. They cleaned the pig sty and fed the poor pigs that had to endure the roaring seas and winds while waiting to be slaughtered. They were always cold and wet.

To Sean and Ned, learning about the cobweb of ropes was a nightmare. There were three hundred different ones, each with its own name and special function, and woe to the hand that pulled the wrong one. Sean would never forget the first time he had to climb the forward mast to shorten a sail. It was during a roaring wind with sideways rain pelting like icy needles against his face inside the hood of his oilskins. The motion of the ship was exaggerated aloft, and Sean felt like he was going to be tossed overboard, his stomach threatening to heave his breakfast of bacon and biscuits with each sickening roll. Shivering from fear and the numbing cold, he somehow managed to cling to the mast and rigging and finish the job, and scamper down to the deck again.

The second mate, Ethan Campbell, a big red-haired Scotsman, clapped him on the back with approval, and roared, "Good laddie!"

They were the first words of praise he had heard, and Sean treasured them. Everyone liked Mr. Campbell as much as they hated Mr. Horn. The second mate was as tough as nails, but treated all the men equally. He was also a strict Protestant who spent much of his spare time reading his well worn Bible. Although most of the men looked askance at that, he still held their respect.

Captain Edward Smythe was a stern taskmaster who was merciless when angered and swift to punish any man for the slightest infraction of his rules; but he was fair-minded too, and he believed that rewarding the men for good work was just as important as punishing them for shirking their duty. He knew that the success of any voyage was in the hands of the crew. He made sure that they were fed well and that their quarters were as dry as possible, even providing a clothesline to hang their oilskins and wet clothing. His belief was, if you take care of your crew, they will take care of the ship.

Sean knew that sailors swore by the good ships and cursed the poor ships. A half-starved crew treated like dogs would be sullen and unresponsive, even in the nastiest weather, caring less than nothing for their own lives or that of the ship. But sailors treated like men were the most loyal, active, brave bunch in the world. They would put up a terrific battle to save a ship in which they got decent food and fair treatment. Such a ship was the *Eastern Wind*, and Sean felt fortunate to be a part of her crew.

As the weeks and miles of ocean passed, Sean, Ned and even Jake were finally accepted as part of the crew. They found their biggest challenges to face were the unpredictable weather and waves, the monotonous diet of salt pork, beans and hard bread, the constant presence of rats down below, and the boring routines that rarely varied. Yet, they thrived in life aboard ship and the three boys became fast friends.

Their voyage was the popular Boston-London-Sitka-Canton-Boston route, sailing across the Atlantic to London, to take on a cargo of textiles and goods to trade for furs, then back across the Atlantic again to the east coast of South America, turning west at Cape Horn, and sailing up the western coasts of the continents to Alaska. There they traded with the natives and the Russians for furs, and then headed across the Pacific to China to sell them for huge profits.

On the trip eastward through the southern Pacific they encountered the edge of a fierce typhoon, and the three boys had been frightened speechless by mountainous seas that thundered across the decks, washing anything overboard that hadn't been tied down, including one unlucky sailor who had been careless with his harness. The man had never been found.

"If 'e was lucky 'e drowned, if not, the sharks got 'em," said Horn with little sympathy. The vision of a man being torn apart by sharks made Sean and his friends shudder. They had all seen the huge sharks with their gaping jaws and rows of giant sharp teeth. Once Sean was leaning over the rail watching a shark, and the monster jumped high out of the water. For a brief second the boy and shark looked at each other, before the shark plummeted back into the sea. Sean had never forgotten the cold lifeless look in the shark's eye. It was like staring death in the face.

In September of 1811 the *Eastern Wind* docked in Boston. The voyage had been a financial success for the ship's owner, and thus, for the captain and crew alike. The first thing Sean did after going ashore was to find his sister, Rose. He intended to give all of his wages to her. But she was nowhere to be found. To his shock the old tenement building where he had grown up had burned down the year before, and in its place stood an Irish pub.

A fitting memorial to Da, he thought. After asking around as to the whereabouts of a Rose O'Connell and getting no answers, Sean finally went to see Father O'Brien.

The gray haired priest had aged greatly in the past two years, his shoulders more stooped, his thin face deeply lined, his hands wrinkled and spotted. But his blue eyes were brighter than ever, and he greeted Sean warmly. The smile faded from his face when Sean asked about Rose.

"She had the coughing sickness, Sean," Father O'Brien said. "Sister Constance and I nursed her the best we could, but she couldn't fight it. She died on Christmas Eve. I had no way of letting ye know."

Grief and guilt seized Sean with a fierce pain. "I shouldna left 'er," he cried out.

"Ye staying wouldn't have changed it, lad," he said. "Twas God's will."

God, he'd thought bitterly. *The same God who'd taken Ma 'ad taken Rose. An' they both believed in 'im with all their hearts. Look where it got 'em---dead and buried.*

"If tis any comfort to ye, Sean, I know Rose is in heaven with your ma. As for your da, well," Father O'Brien hesitated, "ye know what the church teaches about suicide. 'Tis the same as murder."

The priest's eyes burrowed into Sean sharply and he had a sudden fear. Did Father O'Brien know what really happened to his da? Had Rose said anything to him before she died?

"When was the last time ye had confession, Sean?"

Sean hung his head and mumbled, "I'm not sure, Father."

"We can do it now, if ye like."

Sean stared at his boots in a moment of panic. What in the world would he say?

Bless me, Father for I 'ave sinned. I killed me own da with me bare 'ands. An' I've ne'er regretted it since. I hated 'im an' 'e deserved to die for what 'e did to me ma an' Rose.

He wondered how many rosaries and Hail Marys it would take to be forgiven of such a sin. For some sins there could be no forgiveness, especially if there was no repenting of the sin. If there was a God, only judgment and eternal damnation and his father awaited him.

He once had a dream where his father was in a deep pit with flames dancing around him. He was standing on the edge, looking down on his father moaning in torment. Da glanced up and saw him and stretched out his arms, as if in loving welcome. "My son," he cried out, "save me. Save me."

In the dream Sean said, "No, I cannot, Da, even if I wanted to."

"A wee drop of water, then. Me tongue is burning."

Only his tongue? "No, Da, I cannot."

His father groaned and said, "Then forgive me, Sean, please forgive me."

"No, Da, I cannot."

At that his father had bowed his head and sobbed, "If ye cannot forgive, Sean, ye will never be forgiven."

He remembered feeling an evil presence behind him, but when he whirled around, he had seen only pitch blackness. He awakened, bathed in sweat and trembling. *Twas only a nightmare*, he'd thought. *Nothing more.*

But the dream had haunted him for days until its dark memory faded. Seeing Father O'Brien now brought it back. "I don't 'ave time for confession, Father," he said. "I must get back to me ship."

The priest shook his head. "Ye don't have a few minutes to save your immortal soul?"

As Sean remained stubbornly silent, Father O'Brien sighed and said, "All right then, lad, but remember this, no matter how far ye run from God, He can always find ye."

Sean left quickly after that, clutching an envelope that Father O'Brien had given him. It contained Rose's personal possessions, a pathetic collection of rosary beads, some girlish trinkets and ribbons, their mother's crucifix, and a folded up piece of paper. Later onboard the ship, he opened the paper and read,

"*Der Sean, I nevr told Nobode abowt Da. I Love Yu. Yer sistr, Rose.*"

* * *

Standing at the ship's rail as he stared blankly into the fog of Nootka Sound, Sean sighed with regret. He remembered how he had tossed all of Rose's things overboard and now had not one keepsake from his family. Perhaps it was just as well.

The flood of memories continued. During the summer of 1812 war broke out between the United States and England. The *Eastern Wind*, along with many other American ships trading in the waters off the west coast of North America, fled to the Sandwich Islands, where they were out of reach of British warships. The English seized Fort Astoria, near the mouth of the Columbia River, bringing the fur trade to a virtual halt. Other Yankee ships were docked in Canton, China, rather than run the gauntlet of the British across the Pacific. The rest of the American merchant fleet was unable to leave New York or Boston or any of the ports of the East Coast.

King Kamehameha, the ruler of what the natives called Hawaii, welcomed the Americans. Here, in the warm breezes of the tropical islands, Sean flourished. He had never seen such a beautiful place with its white sandy beaches, emerald green palm trees, surrounded by turquoise blue water. The crew called it Paradise, and Sean believed it was as close to heaven as one could get and still be on earth.

The natives were kind and generous, the food plentiful and nutritious. Fruits he had never heard of, but was delicious to eat, such as pineapple, banana, mango, papaya, and guavas, cured the men of their continual battle with scurvy. There were plantations of coconut and sugar cane, and huge acres of sandalwood trees. The Chinese prized sandalwood just as highly as otter furs, and Captain Smythe knew there were added profits to be made after the war.

They stayed in Honolulu for three years until the war ended in 1815. During this time some of the crew deserted and went "native," living with the attractive Polynesian women. The rest kept the ship in order for the day they would set sail again.

Sean was tempted, as all the young men were, to spend his leisure time with a native girl. But when eighteen-year-old Ned contracted a venereal disease and had to be treated by the American missionary doctor in

Honolulu, enduring a strong religious lecture on sexual immorality at the same time, Sean decided to put this period of his life to better use.

He asked Ben Green the ship's sail maker to show him how to sew sails and mend canvas; he asked Nate Anderson the carpenter to show him how to carve the wooden spikes used in sail making and rope work, how to make and repair barrels and caskets; he watched William Carter the armorer how he forged daggers, knives, and small hatchets for trade to the Indians and how he repaired weapons. Of all these skills, Sean found he was the most adept at carpentry. Sometimes he'd carve crude toy ships for the ever present Hawaiian children.

One day he asked the second mate Ethan Campbell if he would teach him the art of navigation. In Sean's mind, navigation was the most essential skill at sea. It was also the most mysterious. Although hauling lines and setting the proper sails to keep the ship moving was important, along with the physical intimidation of the crew to keep order, a captain needed to know more than that. Unless someone aboard knew the ship's exact location and how to plot a course to its destination, no amount of hauling lines or cursing sailors would prevent disaster.

The books and charts on navigation were in Captain Smythe's cabin. When Sean said he could read the big Scotsman was surprised since most of the common sailors were illiterate.

"I'll have to ask Cap'n Smythe's permission, laddie," he told Sean.

It hadn't gone unnoticed by Campbell that Sean had been working hard at learning new skills all these months when the majority of the men were lulled into idleness by the temptations of their lush tropical surroundings. He'd even mentioned it to the captain and first mate at dinner one night.

Arthur Horn had snorted his disbelief that a common sailor, an apprentice no less, was as industrious and intelligent as Campbell had made Sean out to be. Captain Smythe was more curious. "I'd like to talk to the boy sometime," he said.

The second mate arranged an appointment for Sean to meet with the captain in his cabin one afternoon when the trade winds were blowing the morning rain clouds off Diamond Head. The air had a salty tang, such a refreshing change from the sultry heat of the sewage infested harbor of Canton. It made Sean glad they were waiting out the war in Hawaii, and he pitied the unlucky American ships and crews stuck in China.

He had never been inside Captain Smythe's cabin. Even Jake, who cleaned the officer's cabins, was not allowed in there. It was the special domain of the steward, a tall muscular black man named Samuel Washington. He belonged to the captain, and although a slave, he had the haughty manner of a nobleman as if he was the son of an African tribal chief.

"Don't make no matter what his daddy was," said Ned with scorn, "a nigra's a nigra."

Ned was born and raised in South Carolina. Like most southerners, rich or poor, he considered Africans as something between humans and animals. His family owned a small pig farm on the outskirts of Charleston. He was the third son in a family of eleven children. They were always struggling to make a living, and he had known nothing but hunger and despair all his life. His family was considered poor white trash by their wealthier neighbors who owned cotton plantations. When Ned turned fourteen, he ran away to Charleston, then hopped on a small coastal sloop sailing north to Boston where he signed on the *Eastern Wind* around the same time Sean had.

"Ahm never goin' back to that pig farm," he'd say in his soft drawl, then chuckle, as he and Sean fed the ship's pigs their daily slop.

At least now all the pigs had been eaten, but Sean knew when they sailed again, more would be onboard. The islands were full of pigs, as the natives loved to eat pork, usually roasting the whole pig as is, and devouring the animal in its entirety.

When Sean knocked on the captain's cabin door, the steward opened it and nodded at him silently to enter. The black man's face was a closed mask under his head of graying curly hair, his dark eyes inscrutable as he studied Sean.

Sean decided that Jake was right and Ned was wrong. There was a regal air about Samuel and a sense of dignity that no common slave could have, unless he was a prince descended from a line of kings. It made Sean wonder how Samuel could tolerate slavery, but then, he had little choice in the matter. Whereas he and Ned ran away from their homes without fear of punishment, a slave faced possible death if he fled his master.

Stepping into Captain Smythe's cabin was like stepping into another world, a world Sean never knew existed on board the ship. His scuffed boots sank into a thick burgundy red carpet as he looked around the spacious cabin with his mouth hanging open. A matching maroon-colored leather bench, handsomely carved in mahogany, sat under the stern windows from end to end. There was a custom built shelf in the bulkhead, full of intricately carved crystal port decanters. And more shelves held navigational books, protected from falling out in rough seas by a fastened rope. A chart cabinet and a table stood to one side, while the captain himself sat at his polished mahogany desk in the center of the room, writing intently in his logbook with a quill pen.

At Sean's entrance, he put down the pen and glanced up. Sean had always imagined the typical sailing master as a surly harsh mannered man, but Captain Smythe was the total opposite. He was calm and soft spoken, a natural gentleman with the look of a man accustomed to authority. In his late thirties, he was close to retirement, since being a captain of a ship was no job for a man over forty. He was short and on the plump side, with a rounded belly that gave proof for his fondness for fine wines and rich foods. His face was as brown as tanned leather due to his years in the tropical sun and his eyes set in a permanent squint under two bushy gray eyebrows. He had a receding hairline that extended back from his broad forehead, and what was left of his graying brown hair was tied in a queue behind his neck.

Sean was dressed in his best clothes for the meeting, the double-breasted brass-buttoned suit of an apprentice with a small peaked cap on his thick black hair, tied back in a similar fashion as the captain's. He had shaved that morning. At age nineteen his beard grew in as dark as any man's, making him look older and tougher. But that wasn't the appearance he was striving for in front of the captain. He wanted to look like an intelligent ambitious lad, not a brawny sailor.

Captain Smythe was also dressed well, in a coat of blue broadcloth with flat pearl buttons and fitted dove-gray pants. He wore shiny black patent leather boots and on his desk laid his tall beaver hat, more suited to the cool climate of Alaska than that of warm Hawaii.

"Mister Campbell here," said the captain, nodding towards the second mate who was standing next to the desk, "told me you would like to learn how to navigate. Is that correct, lad?"

Sean nervously cleared his throat and said, "Aye, sir."

"And why is that? Why do you want to spend all your free time while we are here in these lovely islands with your nose stuck in a book and learning to read a navigational chart, and having to concentrate on plotting courses and drawing maps, when you could be drinking rum and sleeping with those luscious native girls like everyone else does?"

Before Sean could stop himself, he blurted out the truth, "Because I don't like rum an' the girls 'ere 'ave the clap an'...and someday I want t' be a ship's Cap'n, Sir."

Captain Smythe looked startled, then smiled slowly, showing two front teeth capped in gold. "How old are you, O'Connell, isn't it?"

"Just turned nineteen, sir."

"Well, well, you are amazingly wise for being such a young age. You remind me of someone I used to know," he laughed softly, "myself, I think." He glanced up at the second mate.

"Mister Campbell, you may allow O'Connell here access to this cabin when I'm elsewhere and begin teaching him navigation, and Samuel," he motioned to the steward, "could you bring us some of that fine tea from Ceylon we have on board? And perhaps some of those delicate meat pastries that Wang Li is making." He sniffed appreciatively as a delicious smell wafted in from the galley. "We can't let this young man begin his studies on an empty stomach, can we."

Sean smiled broadly. "Thank you, Sir, thank you!"

"Don't thank me yet, O'Connell," said the captain, "you will still be expected to perform all your regular duties aboard ship and you will be studying on your own time." He gestured towards a shiny object sitting on his desk. "Do you know what this is?"

"I think it's a sextant, Sir."

"That's right, O'Connell, it's an expensive British-made Dent sextant, and its arc is fashioned out of pure ivory. I hope you put it to good use."

In the weeks that followed Sean applied himself diligently to Mr. Campbell's instructions. He discovered that he had a thirst for knowledge he never knew at the parish school. He devoured the *Nautical Almanac* and Nathaniel Bowditch's *American Practical Navigator*, and learned how to use the sextant to find a star and measure the angle of the star's position to the horizon, then using the *Nautical Almanac* to figure lines of position and draw them on a chart until getting an accurate fix on the ship's exact location.

The second mate was pleased at how quickly his pupil learned, but warned him, "Tis a bit harder out at sea when the ship is heavin' to and fro and the horizon along with her."

The two had developed a friendship. This irritated some of the men, including the first mate Arthur Horn. He glared at them with obvious dislike whenever he saw them together. It made Sean nervous, but Mr.Campbell just laughed.

"Don't mind him, laddie. He's the one who should be learnin' navigation, but he dinna ken how to read."

This shocked Sean. "Then how can Mister Horn be the first mate?"

"The Captain needs him to put fear in the hearts of the men so they work hard. And he knows the sea and how to sail this ship better than anyone, maybe even better than the captain himself. Ye don't need book learnin' for that. Ye need years of experience. I've seen Horn figure the speed of the ship within a half knot and sense a change of wind even when he was half asleep in his bunk. And he can smell land long before we ever see it over the horizon."

"Do ye want to be a master of your own ship someday, Mister Campbell?" asked Sean curiously.

The Scotsman shrugged. "Aye, if the Lord wills it. If not, then He has something else in mind for me."

Sean never knew what to say when Mr. Campbell started any religious talk. He was the only son of a Scottish Protestant minister and had run away to sea to get away from his strict upbringing. His father wanted him to study to be a minister, but at age fourteen he had different plans. Born in the port city of Edinburgh, Scotland, the lure of the sea and adventure had always called him. Without much thought for his parents, he turned his back on them and their faith. He signed on an American merchant ship, and began a life of drinking, gambling, brawling, and loose women.

If he had continued on that path, he once told Sean, he would've died long ago, probably from a knife in the back or from a diseased liver.

"Have ye ever heard of tarantula juice, laddie?"

Nodding his head, Sean frowned in disgust. Tarantula juice was a nickname for an alcoholic beverage that many sailors drank when in certain ports. It was a combination of strong spirits, cooked peaches, and tobacco juice, diluted with a little water. He'd seen it almost kill the strongest of men.

"I used to drink it like it was just a cuppa tea, then pick a fight with anyone who looked cross-eyed at me. Once I even jumped an officer. It got me fifty lashes. Couldn't walk for two weeks after."

Sean had seen the white lines of puckered scars on Ethan Campbell's back many times, and had always wondered what foul deed had instigated such punishment. Now he knew.

"Then God stepped in and changed everything," said the second mate, explaining how his ship foundered off the coast of Florida during a hurricane when he was twenty years old. By some miracle he and the captain made it to shore, clinging to a large wooden hatch cover as a raft. Twice the captain had slipped off and almost drowned, but Ethan lashed the two together with a piece of rope he'd found floating after the ship sunk. They were rescued by some friendly Seminole natives who took them north to a cotton plantation. When they returned to Boston, he was rewarded with the position of second mate on the *Eastern Wind*.

Even so, he might have continued in his former vices, if not for a letter from his parents, dated the day after the shipwreck. They wrote how the night before, they had felt danger surrounding him. They prayed for him the entire night, imploring God to send an angel to guard him.

"Suddenly it was like my eyes were opened, laddie, and I knew I was a wretched sinner. I fell down on my knees and asked God to forgive me. And ever since then, I've become a changed man. Have ye ever heard the story of the prodigal son?"

"No sir," said Sean, finding it hard to believe that God, if there was a God, would care enough about some Scottish boy anymore than he would an Irish boy, to intervene in his life and save him from drowning by sending an angel. He'd always thought angels and demons were as unproven as God himself. And as for Mister Campbell's parents praying for him the night of the shipwreck, well, it was just one of life's strange coincidences that happen to people from time to time.

"It's a story that Jesus told. Here, I'll show ye." Campbell pulled out a small well-worn black Bible from his shirt pocket and thumbed through some pages.

The sight of the holy book made Sean's pulse quicken. He opened his mouth to tell Campbell to put it away, that he didn't want to hear the story. He thought the second mate's entire story hard to swallow much less someone else's called a prodigal son. And as for the Bible, he'd always believed it was just a bunch of old myths and had nothing to do with modern day life. It certainly had never made sense to him when he was a lad at the parish school.

But Mr. Campbell was already reading a passage in the Book of Luke in the New Testament and Sean knew it would be impolite to refuse to listen.

A wealthy man had two sons and the youngest demanded his inheritance immediately. So the father divided it all up between them. The younger son left home and traveled far away to another country where he wasted all his money on riotous living. When he had nothing left, a great famine came upon the land and he began to grow hungry.

Finally he found a menial job feeding pigs. The farmer refused to feed him except for the same corn husks the pigs ate. One day he realized his own father's servants had plenty to eat while he was starving. He decided to return home and throw himself upon his father's mercy.

So he left the pig farm and went back home. While he was still in the distance his father saw him and had great compassion on him and ran to greet him. After they embraced the son said he had sinned against his father and was not worthy to be called his son any longer.

But the father was so filled with joy at his son's return that he told his servants to bring the best robe and a ring for his son's hand and shoes for his feet. They were going to celebrate with a feast because he'd believed his son was dead, but now was alive again, that he was lost, but now was found.

After Ethan finished, Sean had to admit it was a fascinating story, one he had never heard before. He thought the younger son was a fool to have spurned the love and wealth he was born into. But he couldn't help envying him at the same time.

What would his own life been like if he'd had a father who loved him that deeply?"

"I was the prodigal son," said Mr. Campbell. "I left two loving Christian parents an' the faith of my childhood in exchange for an empty life of debauchery."

"An' did you ever go home again?" asked Sean, wondering why Ethan ever left it in the first place.

Sadness washed over Ethan's face. "Aye, laddie, I did, but 'twas too late to see me da. He'd passed away from a fever a month before. My poor ma was a widow and sickly, too. But she was glad to see me and hear that I'd changed my life. She wanted me to stay and study to be a preacher. I promised her I'd try, but when she died, I felt God calling me back to the sea. He told me I could be a preacher without a church."

He looked at Sean. "And here I am."

Sean felt uncomfortable under his steady searching gaze. It didn't help matters that two nights ago he'd had the same old nightmare of his father in hell begging for forgiveness. And now all this talk about fathers and sins was making him break out into a sweat. All the sins Mr. Campbell said he'd committed were nothing as compared to killing your own father. Even the prodigal son hadn't murdered anyone.

From his way of thinking, if sin did exist, then his was unforgivable.

* * *

The sound of paddles splashing in the water of Nootka Sound caught Sean's attention, jolting him back to the present.

"They're here, Mister Horn," he called out softly to the first mate. "Tell the captain."

Arthur Horn scowled as if insulted to take any type of order from Sean, but he marched off without a word. Weeks before Nate Anderson, the ship's carpenter, had died from a tropical fever. Remembering Sean's skills in carpentry, Captain Smythe promoted him to the position and Sean was now a respected member of the crew.

It was at that moment the fog began to lift, rays of sun streaming through the mist, turning their gray world into a golden bright blue. Sean blinked in the sudden glare then stared towards the shore.

The *Eastern Wind* was anchored in a small inlet of calm water as clear and flat as a mirror. On one side thickly wooded forests of dark green grew to the rocky shore. The other side had a wide sandy beach, and on a hill sloping gently from the beach was a cluster of about twenty houses, the Nootka village. Each wooden house was a different size, depending on the rank of the family. The chief's house was the largest and Sean estimated it to be at least 150 feet long.

Three canoes were approaching the *Eastern Wind*. Captain Smythe and his officers stood on deck watching as the crew stood to attention, each man looking nervous and tense. The Indians circled the ship several times, then dropped their paddles into the water and waited.

Earlier on this voyage they had stopped at the Russian settlement of Fort Ross, California where Captain Smythe had hired on a supercargo, a man skilled in trading with the coastal natives. Andrei Leonov was a half-breed, the son of a Russian fur hunter and an Aleut slave. He was a short silent man who kept to himself, sleeping on the deck away from the crew each night, often staring out at sea with a dark brooding expression in his slanted eyes.

It startled everyone when Leonov raised his hand in greeting to the Indians, then spoke loudly in English, his voice carrying through the still morning air,

"Friends, we have come in peace to trade with you. Your chief and a few of his men are welcome aboard." Then he repeated the words in the Nootka language.

The Indians murmured among themselves, raised their paddles in greeting then dipped them back into the water and turned the canoes around, speeding back to the shore.

"Now we wait," said Leonov.

After a two hour delay that seemed interminable to Sean, several canoes shot out from the beach to the ship. In the largest was King Maquina of the Nootkas. He and five of his warriors climbed up the ladder to the deck where they were welcomed by Captain Smythe and Leonov.

The king was a magnificent savage. standing over six feet tall, he was finely dressed in a large mantle of black sea otter skin which reached to his knees and was tied around his waist by a broad belt of cloth painted with figures in several colors. His face, legs and arms were covered with red paint and his eyebrows were painted black in two broad stripes. His long black hair glistened with oil and was fastened in a bunch on the top of his head.

The other Indians were just as fierce looking, but their clothes were plain. They wore *kutsacks*, or mantles, which resembled straw matting. The *kutsacks* were nearly square with two holes in the upper part large enough for arms, reaching down to the knees and tied around their bodies with a wide belt of the same material.

Sean had never seen such coarse and ugly clothing, but he supposed it might be practical in shedding the rain of this damp climate. All five warriors had to remove their *kutsacks* when boarding, to be certain that each one had no weapon hidden underneath.

Captain Smythe smiled at Maquina and the two shook hands. The king gave the captain a gift of smoked salmon and they spoke briefly. Sean was surprised to hear the Nootka king speak in English. But then he remembered that the captain had told them earlier how intelligent he was, and that he had learned some English from all the British and American ships his village had traded with over the years.

Maquina and his warriors were invited to go below to the captain's cabin where they would be served their favorite food from the "Boston men," as the Americans were called. Leonov, Horn, Campbell and Sean also accompanied the group, making the cabin a bit crowded. The air soon became ripe with the mixed smells of the perspiring white men and the Indians greasy painted bodies.

Samuel served each native freshly baked biscuits, molasses and a small shot of rum. The Indians stared at the big black man with unabashed curiosity and fascination. At one point, Maquina scratched his fingernails over Samuel's right hand, as if to see whether the black color could be rubbed off. When it didn't, Maquina pointed his chin at Samuel and spoke rapidly.

Leonov translated, "The king said he wants the black man to come and visit his village for his wives to see."

There was a moment of silence in the cabin as the captain and his men all glanced at each other in amusement, but no one dared laugh. To insult the king of the Nootkas would be unforgivable and ruin their chances in rescuing John Hill and Gregory Jones.

Captain Smythe raised his bushy gray eyebrows, but only said mildly, "Tell him perhaps later, after we finish our trading."

It was time to get to the real business at hand. The Nootkas thought the Americans wanted to trade for furs, but Captain Smythe shook his head. "No furs. We have come to ransom the white men you captured two years ago."

As Leonov spoke, the king's black eyes narrowed thoughtfully and he said in Nootka, "They are worth much to me. The one who works with metal makes copper bracelets for my wives and he repairs our weapons. The other one took my youngest daughter for wife."

When Leonov explained this, Sean knew it complicated the whole process. Gregory Jones, the armorer, had become a valuable asset to the king, and John Hill, the owner's nephew, had married an Indian princess. But at least the two men were still alive, and probably in good health if they were such important members of the tribe.

"We are willing to offer many goods for their release," said Captain Smythe, then hesitating slightly as he added with reluctance, "even guns and powder."

Sean knew that trading guns and ammunition was a last resort. If the Russians found out about it, the *Eastern Wind* would be banned from west coast trading in the future, risking capture or being fired upon by the Russian navy patrols. Yet, it looked like Captain Smythe had little choice.

Maquina's eyes lit up greedily with the promise of guns. Nothing was more precious to the natives than the white man's powerful weapon that could shoot farther than any arrow to bring down a deer or a hated enemy.

"How many guns?" asked Maquina in English.

"One musket and shot for each man," said the captain, "and also blankets, a looking glass, beads of different colors, several knives, a barrel of molasses and a hogshead of rum."

Maquina shook his head and spoke to Leonov who said, "He wants three looking glasses, one for each of his wives, and more beads and pretty cloth for his daughter as compensation for losing her husband."

As Captain Smythe nodded in agreement, Maquina said in English, "One more rum. One more molasses." Then he added with a sly smile, holding up three fingers on each hand, "three guns, more powder for each man."

Captain Smythe sighed as if the price was too great then said grudgingly, "Agreed."

The king stood up and shook Captain Smythe's hand to seal their bargain. Maquina turned to Leonov and said a few words.

"The king said to bring the goods and guns to beach before sunset. Then they will bring the two men."

"We would rather do the trading here on board ship," said Captain Smythe, knowing that to go ashore was to leave the safety of the ship and put them at the mercy of the natives.

Leonov translated to Maquina and he scowled and a hard look came over his face. "No" he said stubbornly, "you bring guns. You bring black man. We trade."

The captain and his officers all exchanged frowns of dismay, but it looked like they had no choice. The Nootkas held the captured men, thus, all the power in the trade was on their side. But Sean knew they would be going ashore later with plenty of weapons hidden under their coats, just in case. Not a man aboard ship trusted the Nootkas after what happened to the doomed crew of the Lydia two years ago.

Captain Smythe looked at the king and said, "We will come. And to show our good faith, we will give you one musket now before you leave."

Appearing satisfied, the Nootkas left, the king clutching his musket, a rather ancient double barreled fowling piece.

A brisk northerly breeze was blowing that evening as the longboat of the *Eastern Wind* put ashore on the sandy beach. Two seamen stayed in the boat to row it back when the trading business concluded. Stepping out was Captain Smythe, followed by Mr. Campbell, Leonov, Sean, Samuel and one muscular seaman named Ralph Parson in the rear. Mr. Horn, the first mate, was left on board to prepare the ship for sailing as soon as they returned with the ransomed men.

"Keep an eye out for trickery," Leonov cautioned everyone.

As Sean helped Samuel carry the boxes and barrels unto the beach, he was glad to have his pistol under his coat and his long knife hidden down his boot. He knew the others were mentally checking their weapons, too, since they had to be prepared for anything.

It looked like the entire village had arrived for the trade. Dozens of natives milled about, including the elderly, the women and many small children, all peering curiously with huge eyes the color of molasses from behind their mothers. Most of the stares were aimed at Samuel, who ignored them by keeping his expression impassive.

Maquina approached with ten ferocious looking warriors, followed by two white men dressed in *kutsacks*. Captain Smythe gave the king a brief bow out of courtesy, then gestured towards the boxes of goods, the barrels of rum and molasses, and the six muskets. Maquina and his warriors examined everything meticulously, especially the guns and ammunition. While they were busily doing so, the two white men, John Hill and Gregory Jones, ran over to the longboat and jumped inside.

A sudden cry from the crowd rang out and a young woman rushed towards the longboat. An older woman hurried after her and caught her, wrapping her arms around her in restraint.

It was the princess. She looked about seventeen years old, slim and petite, with long soft black hair and small even white teeth, that flashed brightly as she called out to John Hill in English, "John, my John."

Her voice held heartbreak and all the white men glanced around uneasily as the some of the Nootkas muttered in disapproval. John Hill refused to look at his young wife, and he buried his face in his hands. Maquina appeared irritated and spoke sharply to the older woman and his daughter. The princess was sobbing quietly as she was led back to the village, and Sean felt a moment of compassion for her.

Then Maquina turned to Captain Smythe and frowned, "Gun you give--bad---*peshak*!" He motioned to one of his warriors who handed over the old fowling piece. The chief pointed to one of the locks. "Broken," he said, and spit, "*Peshak*!"

Although the fowling piece was old, it had been intact when the king took it with him earlier in the day. Before Captain Smythe could reply, Ralph Parson sneered in contempt, "He's a liar! There wasn't a thing wrong with that gun before he took it!"

Maquina glared at him in sudden fury, understanding the white man's words enough to realize he had been given a great insult. With one swift motion he unleashed a knife, raised it and brought it down towards Parson's thick chest. But the seaman saw it coming and jumped backwards just as Captain Smythe stepped towards Maquina and cried out, "stop--No--" his words ending abruptly in a shriek as Maquina plunged the knife into his chest.

Everyone froze, including Maquina who was startled momentarily that he had missed his intended target. Captain Smythe crumpled to the ground, mortally wounded, his blood draining out over the sand like long crimson fingers.

Parson drew his pistol out and aimed it at Maquina and fired just as one of his warriors shoved the king aside, taking the bullet right in his face. His head exploded, spraying the king with splashes of blood and blobs of gray matter, the warrior's brains. In the next second, Parson gurgled strangely. Another warrior had thrown his knife directly at the man, striking him in the neck. A scarlet geyser spurted out of his throat and he collapsed, drenching the already red sand with his life's blood.

At once Sean and Mr. Campbell and Leonov drew their pistols, all three weapons pointing threateningly at Maquina. "Hold your fire, lads," ordered the second mate. "Leonov, tell the king he's a dead man if he doesn't stop the killing right now and let us go."

Leonov barked out a few words, but they weren't necessary. Maquina and his warriors, their faces full of frustrated menace, understood the situation well.

"Go!" said Maquina with a snarl, his face a thundercloud of hate.

Leonov and Mr. Campbell kept their pistols trained on the king, as Sean grabbed Captain Smythe and Samuel took Parson, and they half dragged, half carried them back to the longboat. Hill and Jones, waiting in the boat, were horrified at the sudden turn of events.

Gregory Jones, a huge bald man with a scar running down one cheek, cursed when he saw the bloodied bodies of the captain and the sailor. "How did all this happen?" he demanded in a deep baritone of a voice, "What stupid thing did your captain say to rile up Maquina?"

"He didn't," Sean replied sharply. "It was Ralph Parson here who insulted the king. And now they're both dead because of it."

"Two of Maquina's best warriors are dead," said John Hill calmly, "and one of them was his brother."

"They'll be hell to pay, then," said Sean, "if we don't get outta here fast!"

"Not if we don't shoot any more of them," said Hill. "The Nootkas believe in an eye for an eye. We have two dead men, and they have two dead men. Maquina will think that the death of a ship's captain is equal to that of his brother's."

The high keening wail of women in mourning carried over to the men in the longboat. John Hill looked towards the village with a sad expression on his handsome face. He was a fair skinned man in his mid-twenties with blond curly hair and dark blue eyes, of average height and a wiry build. He had a kind and sensitive manner about him, the type of man women were attracted to.

After comparing him with the brusque behavior of Maquina, Sean could see why the princess loathed letting her young white husband go.

"The dead men's wives and mothers will be hacking their hair off and cutting their skin with sharp knives as a sign of love and respect," said Hill, "and the mourning will go on for days." He sighed bitterly. "I wish I could have brought her with me."

Before Sean could answer, a yell rang out. Mr. Campbell and Mr. Leonov were running towards the boat when one of the Indians fired an arrow at Campbell, hitting him in the lower leg. The big Scotsman stumbled and would have fallen if Leonov hadn't thrown his arm around the second mate in support. The two managed to make it safely back to the boat as Sean and Samuel leaped out and pushed it off towards deeper water, all the while darting fearful glances back towards the group of warriors rushing at them, screaming out bloodcurdling war cries.

The two crewmen rowed fast and furiously. Sean fired his pistol in the direction of the shore, as a warning to some of the Nootkas who were attempting to follow them in their canoes. The longboat pulled away quickly in a shower of arrows, most of which fell short. One thudded into Parson's shoulder, but since he was already dead, nobody cared. Sean decided luck and the tide were with them.

Mr. Horn had heard the gunshots and seen the commotion on the beach. The crew was already setting sail as they reached the *Eastern Wind*. When all the men and the longboat were back on board, he ordered the anchor hauled up. The ship quivered like a horse in a race stall waiting for the start, then the sails billowed out with the wind, the timbers creaked, and she took off eagerly, racing towards the open sea. The Nootkas and their canoes were soon left behind.

The sun was sinking into the horizon, streaking slivers of rose pink, lavender and gold across the western sky. The calm waters of Nootka Sound mirrored the same vivid colors in a beautiful rippling pattern of waves. It was a wondrous sight Sean normally enjoyed. But tonight he had no eyes for sunsets and scenery.

All he could think of was that they were in big trouble. The captain was dead and the second mate suffered a grievous wound.

That left Arthur Horn in sole command of the *Eastern Wind*.

CHAPTER FOUR

One week after her seventeenth birthday in October Anna finally heard a reply to her letter from *Tante* Sarah. A small parcel had come for her, brought by a family in their village who had been visiting relatives near Silberfeld. With excitement she opened the birthday present first. It was a shiny new tortoiseshell comb. Anna was grateful for the gift since her old comb was missing most of its teeth and no longer did a good job at combing the snarls out of her waist-length hair.

But it was the letter that interested her the most. In recent weeks her father had been spending more time at the Klassen house visiting Agatha and her parents. Anna knew it was inevitable that their engagement would be announced soon. She slipped the letter in her apron pocket to be read later when she could find a time alone. That evening after her family had gone to bed, she read it quickly. Her aunt had written:

"My dear Anna,

Your Uncle Heinrich and our girls, Judith, Maria, and Helena, all send you their fondest birthday wishes. We hope you will enjoy our small gift to you.

In regards to your letter from last August concerning your Papa's remarriage. Anna, my dear, there is nothing we can do to stop him from marrying the Klassen girl. In July when we last visited with you and your family, your Papa told us about his plans. Your uncle and I appreciate your reservations about Agatha Klassen, but you must trust your Papa on this. He would not marry anyone who is not suitable to be his wife.

However, if your concerns about her are true, and life with Agatha as your stepmother becomes intolerable for you, your uncle and I want you to know that we would welcome you to live with us. At any time if you need us, please send a message, and we will come for you."

Her aunt and uncle were her last hope. The marriage would take place after all. With despair Anna threw the letter in the brick oven, not wanting to share it with anyone.

* * *

During the first week of November another letter of great importance to Anna and her siblings was passed around in Furstenau.

"On Sunday, November 14, 1819 there will occur the marriage of Herman Teichroew to his promised bride, Agatha Klassen. You and your family are invited to be present at the home of Herr and Frau Klassen at one o'clock in the afternoon. Please carry this invitation to the home of the neighbor whose name appears under your name as rapidly as possible."

The list of neighbors included every name in the village.

The letter caused a gigantic upheaval in the Teichroew household. Except for the one conversation with Anna in August, Herman had foolishly delayed talking to the rest of his children about his impending marriage to Agatha. As a result, the news sent a terrible shock wave rippling through his family.

For weeks Anna had respected her father's silence and said nothing. Jack had asked her a couple of times why their Papa had been spending so much time at the Klassen house, and she had only told him that Papa had personal business with Elder Klassen. She longed to confide in Jack. Only one year of age separated them and they had always been close. But she knew Jack disliked Agatha as much as she did, and he had a fearful temper. No telling what he would say or do if he knew their Papa's plans.

Peter and Jacob and Katarina were oblivious to any of the tension between Anna and their father. They were still at the young age when the world revolved around them. Now their familiar little world was about to come crashing down upon them.

The day began innocently enough. It was a Friday, a school day for the three boys. Peter and Jacob were in their fifth year while Jack was taking the required course in the Bible in the *Oberschule* or Upper School for young men. Herman hoped his oldest son would someday be a minister. Anna wasn't sure Jack had the spiritual calling or temperament for that. But it wasn't her place to say anything.

Next year when Katarina was six she would start school. Besides learning to read, write and do arithmetic, all the children were expected to learn their catechism before they were sixteen and then be baptized and join the church.

The Mennonites did not practice infant baptism. Anna had been baptized a year ago and Jack was baptized the past spring. They both were now official members of the church.

Anna cherished her baptismal experience. She looked upon it as an opportunity to declare her faith in public. Joy filled her heart as she was immersed in the river, knowing that her life was now committed to God. She was also glad that her Mama had still been alive then.

Her mother questioned her deeply the night before she was to be baptized, to make sure Anna understood that true meaning of baptism. Katharina said she feared that too often baptism had become a custom among the Mennonites rather than a result of heart conviction. Anyone who wished to join the church could just memorize the catechism and recite it without any of the doctrines their ancestors died for penetrating their heart.

She used to say, "There is an eternal difference between head knowledge and heart knowledge."

This morning had started out sunny and cool, but as the afternoon wore on clouds built in from the south, a sure sign of rain. Natasha and Anna scrubbed floors, wiped windows and dusted the furniture as Friday was the usual cleaning day. Natasha and her husband Ivan had been married nearly one year, and they were expecting a baby in three months. During the week they slept in a room Herman built for them off the kitchen. On Saturdays after all the baking was done for Sunday's meals, they went back to their own village, which was on the other side of the Dnieper River, to stay with their family until Monday.

The two Russian peasants were a superstitious pair, especially Natasha. Anna wished she could share her faith with them. The couple was respectful towards the family when they prayed or read the Bible, but Ivan and Natasha had no interest in the Mennonites' religion. They preferred their own. Their foremost belief was that they worshiped the Czar as their God, and the Father of all the peasants. They could not comprehend the Mennonites' God of the Bible, but believed in fate, and good and bad luck.

The result was that their beliefs were so full of omens and superstitions, that Anna sometimes thought the only way a typical Russian peasant could avoid bad luck was to stay in bed all day. Whistling indoors, shaking hands over a threshold, returning something borrowed after nightfall, and mending a hem or button while wearing the garment were just a few activities shunned in the belief they tempted misfortune. Even stricter rituals were involved in the more serious matters of traveling, marriage, and death.

Sometimes Natasha would blurt out one of her superstitions. Just that morning during breakfast, while buttering a slice of toast, Anna had accidentally dropped her knife onto the floor. Natasha gave her a sly wink and said in her thick Russian accent, "Anna have man visit her sometime today, *da*?"

The twins erupted in laughter, bread crumbs spewing out of their mouths. Jack, who was gulping down a glass of milk, snorted loudly, then choked as air and liquid combined to pour down his throat. His face turned red and he sneezed, spraying Katarina with droplets of milk. She let out a cry and smacked him hard enough in the shoulder, so that what milk was left in his glass spilled down the front of his shirt.

Anna was thankful her father had already eaten and he and Ivan had left to check on one of the oxen which was ailing. The way things were between them lately, he would likely blame her for the messy behavior of the children at breakfast.

"Jack, go change your shirt and be quick about it, or you'll be late for school," she said, thinking that her act of dropping the knife had only triggered a chain of clumsiness among them, rather than the ridiculous superstition that she would have a male visitor later.

Cleaning the house from top to bottom was hard work, and kept Anna and Natasha busy all afternoon. Katarina helped with the dusting then was excused to play until the boys came home from school. Without asking permission she went to the barn and fetched two kittens and put them in her and Anna's bedroom to entertain her. Their mother had disapproved of having cats in the house, but Anna was not so strict about it. Since Katarina had no little brother or sister to play with, Anna allowed the kittens inside for short periods of time.

Dark gray clouds soon obscured the sun, making the November day shorter than usual. The light was waning by the time Anna decided the housework was finished. Natasha looked tired, her broad face reddened by the effort of bending over and scrubbing floors. It was obvious that her pregnancy was draining her energy as much as it was increasing her girth. Not a small person to begin with, Natasha was looking plumper with each passing day. It wasn't unattractive on her, however. She was a big-boned woman and the extra weight filled out her large frame and gave her skin a healthy glow. Ivan was always grinning at her with a proud sparkle in his dark eyes, and she was always fussing over him, making sure he had plenty to eat. He was a tall powerfully built man of little words and brusque manners, but he treated his wife as carefully as if she was made of fragile eggshells. The couple never ceased to amuse Anna.

"Natasha," she said, "why don't you take a short rest before we make the *keelke* for supper." *Keelke* was a type of flat noodles that Anna's father loved, particularly served with onion gravy. Fried ham, stewed cabbage and raisins, and beet pickles would round out the rest of the meal.

Natasha nodded wearily, but before she could move, Jack, Peter and Jacob returned from school, bursting into the house with Alexi and Gerda right behind them, the dogs' paws tracking mud across the freshly washed floor. "Gerhard Yoder is coming this way, Anna," said Jack.

"He said he has a letter for us," Peter added with a knowing grin at his brothers. "But maybe it's just for you."

Anna started in surprise as Natasha turned and smiled at her, showing her red gums and yellow teeth. "Just what I speak this morning, *da*?"

Two polite knocks resounded at the door. Jack chuckled and quickly opened it, inviting Gerhard Yoder to come in.

In an instant his massive bulk seemed to fill the parlor, dwarfing everyone else. Both dogs started to growl. Gerhard had obviously just washed up after working in his blacksmith's shop all day. His black hair was still damp and shiny, his face scrubbed to a ruddy glow and his blue-eyed gaze fastened on Anna like a bull watching a cow.

"Good day, *Herr* Yoder," she said with a stiff smile then looked at Jack. "Take the dogs outside, could you, please?"

Jack turned to obey as Katarina walked out of the bedroom with the two kittens, both gray and white-striped tabbies, in her arms. The kittens took one look at the dogs and hissed, digging their sharp claws into

Katarina's chubby little arms. She shrieked as they leaped off her, leaving bloody streaks across her tender white skin.

Gerda and Alexi immediately lost interest in Gerhard and jumped after the kittens as the two cats fled back into the bedroom. Although Anna had taught the dogs not to chase their own cats, the temptation was too great and they ran past everyone, barking in excitement. Gerhard was momentarily forgotten as Anna tried to console a crying Katarina and the boys, hooting with laughter, went to round up the dogs and kittens

Gerhard seemed bewildered by all the noise and activity. He was not used to the antics of children and pets. He lived in a quiet household where his mother reigned like a strict queen over her sons, their wives and their well-behaved children.

Standing in the middle of the parlor with a strained smile on his face, he clutched a piece of paper.

It was this scene of utter chaos that greeted Herman when he walked in after a hard day of work. He was expecting a spotless house and the mouthwatering smell of his dinner beginning to cook, not the muddy floors, the barking dogs, the yowling kittens and the sobbing child with bloody arms.

"What is happening here in my house?" he demanded.

Gerhard looked embarrassed. "Mama asked me to pass this letter on to your family, *Herr* Teichroew," he began in explanation as if all the commotion was his fault. "She thought it only proper, even though your family already knows you are marrying Agatha Klassen one week from this Sunday."

Gerhard's words fell into a moment of silence. Katarina had halted her crying briefly to take a breath of air, the twins had quieted the dogs down and were pulling them to the door, and Jack had grabbed the kittens by the scruff of their necks. All the children froze, their eyes widening in horror as the meaning of Gerhard's words sunk into their brains.

Then it was sheer bedlam again. Jack dropped the kittens in shock, the twins lost their grips on the dogs, and Katarina started to cry even louder. "No, no," she wailed. "Not 'Gatha..."

The kittens flew off once more and the dogs gave chase, barking and whining. Anna glared at Gerhard who had the sense to realize that maybe he should make a hasty exit before he made things worse. He placed the letter on the table, nodded at Anna, then backed towards the door.

"My apologies, *Herr* Teichroew," he murmured then was gone.

Now it was Herman's turn to feel helpless. He stood in the midst of his family, his sons angrily shouting, "Papa, it can't be true! Tell us it isn't true!" His youngest daughter was shrieking, "No 'Gatha! No 'Gatha!" His oldest daughter was looking at him with a sad expression while his dogs and cats ran uncontrolled through the house.

Somehow Natasha restored the order. With one motion she swooped up the kittens as they tried to run past her, chased the dogs out the door, deposited the spitting kittens in a startled Ivan's arms as he was just coming in, told him to take them back to the barn, and picked up Katarina, whose screams were dwindling into hiccups.

"*Moya devochka*, (my little girl)," she said, making comforting clucking noises like a mother hen, "I wash arm. You get sugar lump."

Katarina whimpered, but was otherwise quiet as Natasha pocketed a sugar lump from a jar in the kitchen, then took her outside to the well to draw a bucket of water for washing.

Jack grabbed the letter off the table and shushed his brothers, reading the wedding invitation out loud. Then all three boys stared at their father with pain and accusations written all over their faces. They erupted again.

"Papa, how could you do this to us?"

"Papa, why didn't you tell us?"

"Papa, we don't like Agatha Klassen!"

"Quiet!" He roared. He looked at Anna as if for help, but she shrugged. Her father should have explained about Agatha weeks ago. Like Ivan, he'd always been a man who spoke little, but now he was paying the price for his stubborn silence. His family was in danger of fracturing and only he could keep them together.

Herman sighed deeply and said, "I know I should have told you about my intention of getting married again. I kept delaying because I knew all of you would be unhappy about it. But the truth is out now, and all you children have to accept my decision."

"But we don't need another mother," said Jack in a low angry voice. "Especially someone like Agatha Klassen."

"That's enough, John!" Herman growled. "I don't ever want to hear any of you speak against the woman I've chosen to marry. She is a good woman and she will make us a better family. All I ask of you children is to give her a chance to prove that."

"Do we have to call her Mama?" asked Peter. "I can't do that, ever."

"Neither can I," said Jacob.

"Nor I," echoed Jack.

"You children can call her Agatha for now. Maybe later you might change your minds and start calling her Mama," said Herman.

"Not likely," sneered Jack.

Herman raised his hand as if to strike Jack across the face, and Jack flinched, "Sorry, Papa," he muttered.

Although she felt the same about Agatha as her brothers did, Anna realized her feelings were not as important as supporting her father and keeping their family together. Somehow she knew it would be what her mother wanted. Whether she would have approved of Agatha as a stepmother or not, Anna knew her mother would expect her as the eldest child to help keep the peace.

"We must do as Papa asks," she said gently, looking at her three brothers with a reassuring smile. "We must give Agatha the chance to prove that she will be a good stepmother to all of us. I think it is what Mama would want."

Jack frowned and the twins' freckled faces still looked mutinous, but they were listening. Herman gave her a grateful smile. "Yes," he said, "Your Mama did tell me last winter before she passed away that she would give me her blessing to marry again someday. She said she didn't want you children to grow up motherless."

His eyes grew moist and the boys glanced away, suddenly feeling awkward. The anger in the room had disappeared, but Anna could tell it was replaced by a deep unhappiness in all of them. "I will only say this once," said Herman quietly, "and never again. I loved your Mama with all my heart. No one can ever truly take her place. But she is gone now. So, we go on with our lives the way she would want."

It was later that night, after Katarina had fallen asleep next to her, soothed into slumber by Anna's soft voice singing a lullaby, that Anna realized something important. Her father had never once said he loved Agatha.

* * *

The Teichroew-Klassen wedding was considered the grandest occasion in Furstenau of the entire year. On the day before all the women and girls of the village gathered together at the Klassen house to bake the special *twaback.* Each woman brought her own previously prepared yeast, lard, milk, and flour to the big wooden bowls or dough troughs, placed in a central location near the ovens. *Frau* Klassen supervised the mixing of all the ingredients. The stronger women mixed the larger batches of dough, while the younger ones who were learning mixed smaller amounts.

It was strenuous work. All the dough had to be continually kneaded, adding enough flour gradually, until the dough left the side of the bowl and none of it stuck to the hands. The women were so expert at this, the troughs or bowls never had to be washed afterwards, as every speck of flour or dough was gone from them by the time the *twaback* were put on the iron pans.

They had specially made iron pans to put into the ovens so the *twaback* baked evenly. A rack with legs stood right on the glowing ashes and the pan would be slid onto this rack. A long sort of rake was used to pull the pans out or push them in. The dough was mixed at intervals so it would come out just right, that when the first pans were barely cool enough, the *twaback* could be set on them to rise while the other pans were baking.

The delicious yeasty smell of freshly baked *twaback* usually made Anna incredibly hungry. Not this Saturday afternoon, however. As she and Susannah were busily kneading dough, Anna wished she never had to look at a *twaback* again, and here she was, surrounded by hundreds of the little golden brown buns.

Her friend kept glancing at her in sympathy. Susannah knew how depressed Anna was by her father's wedding and there wasn't much left to say.

If only Uncle Heinrich and *Tante* Sarah and her cousins could have come, thought Anna. Having their cheerful loving faces around would have been lots of comfort for her and her siblings. But the twins, Judith and Maria, had come down with chest colds, and *Tante* Sarah sent their regrets along with a wedding gift for the newlyweds, delivered by one of their Russian helpers on horseback.

Jack was excited about having a horse to take care of for a night or two, and he'd talked the Neufeld's servant into letting him ride the horse before he returned to Silberfeld. All three boys had seemingly resigned themselves to their father's remarriage. Though a sense of gloom still pervaded the household, there were no more outbursts of anger, at least not from them.

Katarina was another problem.

She was furious about the wedding and at first, refused to attend. Anna tried everything she could to coax the little girl, even promising her she could eat all the special sugar *twaback* she wanted. But to no avail.

Finally, this morning, Herman sternly told Katarina that if she didn't go and behave, she would be spanked. With tears running down her face, she agreed to be a good girl, but Anna knew her little heart was broken. To lose her own mother, then to have her father whom she adored be so harsh was almost more than the child could bear.

"Didn't you tell me, Anna," said Susannah, "that your *Tante* Sarah wrote you a letter and said you could live with them if you can't stand living with Agatha?"

She nodded. "But I don't think I could do that, no matter how awful it might be. I couldn't ever leave Tina. She's afraid of Agatha, especially after what happened last summer when Agatha hit her with the paddle."

"I don't blame her for being scared," said Susannah. "I think she'll have to be on her best behavior all the time after tomorrow. I think all of you will."

"I know there will be big changes," sighed Anna. "I just pray that Papa doesn't expect me to obey her like the younger ones. I'm not sure I can do that, especially if Agatha turns out to be as hard a stepmother as I'm afraid she might be."

Susannah lowered her voice and glanced around at the other women. "Do you think she and your Papa are in love with each other?"

Anna smiled slightly. "She may think my Papa loves her, but I know that he still loves only my Mama."

"Then maybe she's to be pitied," said Susannah. "She's an old maid who's grabbing the first man who looks her way."

"I would rather never marry than marry someone who does not love me."

"Me, too," answered her friend, "except that we girls don't have much say in who we marry, do we? It's all up to our parents."

"That's true," said Anna, thinking of Gerhard Yoder. "But I will never marry unless it is for love."

Susannah giggled softly. "You are a hopeless romantic, Anna."

Anna punched the mound of dough in the bowl, wishing for a second it was Agatha's face. But that was no solution, she thought. The real answer was to live one day at a time, praying for God's help each morning, to face whatever the future had in store for her and her family.

Starting tomorrow, the wedding day.

* * *

It was not a healthy autumn for the Bolkonsky family. First there was Cousin Mikael's duel with Baron Volodin. The duel took place outside of Saint Petersburg in the thick gloomy forest, which was a popular location for such dubious matters. Later everyone decided it was nothing short of a miracle that saved Mikael.

At the very moment the Baron turned and fired on him, a large acorn tumbled down on the Baron's head, thrown by a screeching squirrel sitting on a tree branch right above him. The distraction caused the Baron to jerk his arm, knocking his aim off slightly, and Mikael was struck in the right shoulder just as he fired off his pistol. His own shot went wild, shooting over the Baron's head, and hitting the unfortunate little squirrel, who fell off the branch and landed on the ground with a soft thud.

The shoulder wound took two months to heal. The lead ball had shattered muscle and bone and was extracted by the Czar Alexander's own surgeon, but fever and infection set in. Mikael tossed in his bed for days, delirious and full of pain.

When the fever finally broke, it left him feeling weak and listless. He whined and complained incessantly, demanding attention day and night from the servants, his mother and sister, and even Tatiana. Nothing irritated her more than being told to keep him company. When he began to recover, Aunt Irene ordered her to relieve his boredom by playing endless games of cards with him, a duty she loathed. There were many times she wished her future father-in-law's aim had been right on the mark.

Baron Volodin's pride appeared to have been appeased by the outcome of the duel. He seemed to harbor no grudge against the Bolkonsky family. Although he never inquired after Mikael's health, he visited Tatiana occasionally, bringing her gifts of French chocolates, pearl earrings, or a diamond bracelet.

"These are the little things Dmitri would give you if he was here to court you properly," he would say with a small smile when she exclaimed in delight over each present.

Tatiana always thanked the Baron with a warm hug, noticing how his cold demeanor melted slightly each time she did so. She was soon losing her fear of him. The more time she spent in his presence, the more she realized he was actually to be pitied rather than feared. The image of the terrifying Baron was giving way to a lonely old man whose main wish in life was to see his son carry on the family name. He wanted a grandson more than anything.

Since Tatiana held all his hopes to make his dream come true, he fawned over her. It gave her a sense of power, similar to the feeling she had whenever Uncle Vasily lavished all of his attention upon her at dinnertime instead of talking to Aunt Irene or Olga. They obviously resented his attentiveness to her, but at the same time, they had no choice but to defer to Tatiana's new status in the family.

And now that she was betrothed to Dmitri Volodin, she was no longer afraid of Mikael either. Instead his infatuation with her only made her scornful of him. He would never dare touch her again with the Baron as her constant protector. She was certain his fear of Baron Volodin was greater than his so-called love for her.

Each autumn day brought her more contentment. Her life had never been better, and her feelings of happiness spilled over in her relationships with others. When Olga was finally betrothed Tatiana managed to congratulate her cousin with a superficial display of affection, even though she privately thought the betrothment was a miracle given her cousin's dowdy looks and prickly temperament.

The prospective groom was Count Vladimir Kornilov, a wealthy widower with four young daughters. He was rumored to be over forty, overweight and overbearing. Tatiana didn't know who to pity more, Count Kornilov or Cousin Olga.

Then one icy November evening Aunt Irene suddenly toppled out of her chair at dinner, a surprised look on her face, and was dead before she hit the priceless Persian carpet. The doctor declared the cause as a heart attack. Olga was inconsolable.

"Mama wasn't ailing even the slightest," she moaned, as Tatiana tried to comfort her after the Countess Bolkonsky had been laid to rest in the immense family vault. "Why did this happen to her?"

"It was God's will," answered Tatiana automatically, echoing Aunt Irene's own words to her from long ago when her beloved grandmother, Nana, had died.

Olga rubbed her swollen eyes and glared at her. "You don't seem very sad about losing the only mother you've ever known," she said accusingly.

"She wasn't my mother."

"Of course she was. She brought you up."

"My real mother was the woman who gave birth to me, not Aunt Irene."

Olga frowned, wrinkling her forehead, making her homely face even less attractive. "You never loved my mother, did you?"

Tatiana shrugged. "She never loved me."

It was the truth and Olga knew it. She glanced away from Tatiana looking a bit ashamed, not wishing to speak about the painful memories of their childhood.

"What do I do now, Tatiana?" she asked in a pathetic voice.

Tatiana tried to feel pity for the cousin she used to hate and fear, but found that she could not. It was about time Olga knew what it was like to be motherless.

"The same as I do," she said coldly. "You look forward to the day you are married and can start living your own life as you please."

CHAPTER FIVE

Soon after leaving Nootka Sound, Captain Smythe and Ralph Parson were stitched in their shrouds by Ben Green the sail maker, and buried at sea. A few days later an argument developed between Captain Arthur Horn and John Hill. The condition of Ethan Campbell was critical and he needed medical help. The Indian arrow had broken the bone of his left leg and infection had set in. The leg soon swelled with gangrene and Campbell developed a raging fever. John Hill told Captain Horn to head for Sitka where they could find a doctor.

At first Horn refused. He wanted to do some trading at other friendlier Indian villages before returning to Boston. He didn't care to waste time sailing north to Sitka. But Mr. Hill insisted, saying if the first mate died because of Horn's neglect, his uncle would be furious.

Horn resented the younger man giving him orders, but knew he had no choice. He also was angry that he was forced to share the plush captain's cabin with Hill, which Horn figured belonged to him alone. If it wasn't for the fact that Thomas Hill would pay a handsome bonus to the captain of the *Eastern Wind* for delivering his nephew safe and sound, Horn would've had the man flogged, just so he'd realize who was the real master of this ship. He decided he would bide his time, and perhaps an opportunity would arise when he could put the upstart Mr. Hill in his proper place.

Another thing bothered Captain Horn greatly. Since the first mate Campbell was incapacitated by his infected leg, the only other man on board who could navigate the ship was Sean O'Connell. With great reluctance Horn was forced to promote him to second mate.

In less than a fortnight the *Eastern Wind* reached Sitka, or what the Russians called New Archangel. The only doctor there was a ship's surgeon off a Russian naval vessel. He was like most ship's surgeons, a butcher. He took one look at Campbell's leg and said it had to come off.

"Pray for me, laddie," Campbell begged Sean before the operation. Sean nodded, pretending to comply, knowing he was the last person on earth God would ever listen to.

Before the operation started, Campbell was forced to drink rum until he gagged in order to render him as senseless as possible. Then he was tied down, and with Sean and the steward, Samuel, holding him steady, the surgeon sawed off the leg right above the knee. Poor Ethan's screams were earsplitting, ending only when he finally passed out.

The surgeon said he had done all he could. "Keep the wound clean, and change the bandage frequently," he ordered. "His life is now in your hands and God's."

During the next few days Ethan became delirious with a high fever. Sean doubted he would survive. Both day and night the first mate thrashed about on his bunk inside the cabin the two men shared. Most nights Sean lay awake, listening to Ethan call out for his mother and for God to help him, and then the poor man dozed off, mumbling incoherent words in his fitful sleep.

Meanwhile, the Americans traded supplies to the Russians for furs. The crew was sworn to silence about the guns they had exchanged to the Nootkas for the freedom of Mr. Hill and Mr. Jones. Captain Horn did not want himself and the crew to be arrested and the ship and their cargo seized if the Russians found out.

Sean wondered if they could trust Andrei Leonov to keep his mouth shut. The Russian supercargo had taken his pay and left the ship to join the other fur hunter half-breeds living in Sitka. He supposed Leonov had some family nearby.

In the absence of Alexander Baranov, who had died the previous April enroute to Saint Petersburg, a new governor was in control. He was a naval lieutenant by the name of Simeon Ivanich Yanovski and he was married to Baranov's daughter Irina.

Captain Horn, John Hill and Gregory Jones spent the evenings dining with Governor Yanovski and his wife at the governor's mansion. All the Russians were interested in hearing about Hill's and Jones's two years with the Nootka Indians. The story of their capture and rescue made a fascinating adventure, one that would be told up and down the coast for many years to come. As second mate and a ship's officer, Sean was also invited to the governor's residence to dine. But he chose to stay on board ship and help take care of Ethan.

As the days grew shorter and darker Captain Horn became impatient for Campbell to recover enough so they could depart. He wanted to be long gone before the dreaded winter storms of the Pacific set in, making their voyage to China even more dangerous.

"If he's not better in two days," he announced one morning, "we leave him here."

Sean and Samuel exchanged looks of disapproval, not unnoticed by Horn. He slapped Samuel in the face and said, "Don't give me that uppity look of yers, you big dumb slave. I'm yer master now that Captain Smythe's dead, you hear?"

"I belong to Cap'n Smythe's family now," said Samuel, touching his stung cheek.

"Not till we get to Boston," snarled Horn, raising his fist threateningly as if to strike another blow.

A flash of anger lit up Samuel's dark eyes, but he quickly hid his rage by lowering his gaze as if in defeat, and whined like a typical slave, "Yessah, massah, Cap'n Horn."

Luckily, Horn didn't realize that Samuel was being sarcastic and said, "That's more like it. Now get me some real hot coffee, and none of that Chink tea Wang Li makes that tastes like pig swill!"

As Samuel left to fetch the coffee, Sean felt a strong sympathy for him. He despised slavery and considered it a great evil. Samuel had told him that he'd been born on the Ivory Coast of Africa, the only son of his tribe's chief. When he was five years old, he and his older sister, age ten, and their mother had been stolen by warriors from a neighboring tribe, and sold to slave dealers. During the hellish voyage to America on the disease ridden slave ship, his mother had died from the brutal treatment, and her body thrown overboard in the Atlantic to feed the sharks. When he and his sister arrived in New York in 1789, they were sold to different masters. He had not seen his sister since.

Now thirty five years old, he'd spent almost all his life as a slave in the Smythe household. He'd grown up with Captain Edward Smythe and though master and slave, the two had been close companions, and the captain's death upset Samuel greatly.

Sean sensed the resentment and hatred burning inside Samuel towards their new captain. He felt the African's rage as his own, yet, the two of them dared not express it. They did not want to provoke Horn's anger. Unlike Captain Smythe, Horn ordered men whipped for the slightest infractions, and fed the crew meager rations while he dined with the finest foods and wines from Captain Smythe's private stores. With each passing day Horn was becoming more feared and hated. The *Eastern Wind* had now become one of those ships men cursed to sail on.

An hour later Sean walked into his and Ethan's cabin with a bowl of watery meat broth. The first mate startled him by giving him a lopsided grin and saying, "Sean, be a good laddie and fetch me some real food. I dinna want any more of that babbie's brew ye been giving me."

Amazed, Sean stared at him. The fever had melted away much of the flesh off the big Scotsman's bones and he appeared like a gaunt skeleton with a long red beard. But now it was obvious his fever was gone. Ethan's blue eyes sparkled with life again and Sean gave a relieved laugh. "'Bout time ye woke up, Ethan. I'll have Samuel fix some oatmeal an' molasses for breakfast."

"An' a big cuppa tea," said Campbell. "I'm verra thirsty."

Sean's spirits immediately lifted with Campbell's miraculous recovery. That evening he agreed to accompany Horn, Hill, and Jones to dine with Governor Yanovski. The governor's residence was built on a huge rocky cliff above the harbor. It was two stories high and had a beacon tower on the roof to guide ships entering Sitka Sound. Once inside the Americans were greeted by Yanovski himself, a tall handsome man about thirty years old with wavy dark hair and an imposing mustache. He wore a gold braided naval uniform and polished black boots, which gave him the appearance of a military governor.

Before dinner he ushered them into his library where they were offered glasses of chilled vodka and trays of *zakuska*, salty hor d'oeuvres of pickled fish, pickled mushrooms and pickled cabbage. Sean gazed in awe at the shelves of hundreds of finely bound books.

Yanovski noticed his interest and said in perfect English, "All the books in this library are from Alexander Baranov's collection, about twelve hundred in all. There are volumes on astronomy, navigation, mathematics, theology, metallurgy, Russian Orthodox Church history, grammar, and literature. Half are in Russian, three hundred in French, one hundred and thirty in German, thirty in Latin, and the rest in Spanish and Italian."

"I am most impressed, Your Excellency," said Sean, meaning every word. He noticed that Horn ignored everything but the vodka. Remembering that the captain was illiterate, he wasn't surprised.

Then a young woman entered the library. With pride Yanovski presented his wife, the daughter of Alexander Baranov. Sean had heard of Baranov's marriage to an Aleut woman, taken place after his Russian wife died. The native woman still lived on Kodiak Island. In following the Russian custom of bestowing titles on conquered people, the Czar had issued a *ukase* recognizing her as "The Princess of Kenai." This meant her children were legitimate and could enter the schools of the nobility in Saint Petersburg.

About twenty years old Irina Baranova had the bearing of a queen, her mother's blood casting a warm dark glow to her beautiful face. She had a vivacious manner and a captivating smile as she welcomed their visitors with grace and style. When she glanced at Sean, he thought he would drown in her flashing brown eyes.

"Would you play the piano for our guests, my dear?" Yanovski asked in a tender voice.

With a soft laugh she sat down and bowed her raven-haired head over the ivory keys of the mahogany pianoforte placed in the corner of the library. In a moment the room was filled with the lively sound of a song she called the "*Pyesnya Baranova*." When it was over they all applauded loudly.

"Now for my favorite song of the Russian peasants," she said. "Its name is Dark Eyes."

The music from this piece began slow and softly in a minor key, then swelled to a passionate climax whihch evoked images of dancing gypsies, before gradually fading to a final note. As she stood up and gave a quick curtsey, none of the men clapped more enthusiastically in appreciation than Sean.

Then dinner was announced and she excused herself with a smile. "As in the days of my father, we are an old fashioned family. The banqueting is for the men."

With keenly felt disappointment, Sean watched Irina glide from the library. He had never seen such a stunning creature. She was like the brightest star shining in the night sky as compared to all the dull girls he'd known, especially the loose coarse women who frequented the docks in every port. He wished there was a way to see her again.

Then he felt like laughing at himself. Besides the fact she was another man's wife, he had no use for women in general. As far as he was concerned, they were to be used only for pleasure, then discarded. Now at age twenty six, except for Irina Baranova, he had never met a woman who made him feel any differently.

Dinner was served in the large banquet hall by Aleut servants, short quiet women who never looked anyone in the face. There was a big fireplace and a dais at one end of the room for the musicians. A quartet of men in Russian naval uniforms softly played violins while Sean and everyone else enjoyed an enormous dinner of roast wild geese and duck, venison, salmon, halibut and Russian dark bread and pickles. He had never seen so much delicious food in his entire life. He noticed that Hill and Jones tried hard not to be gluttons, but after living with the Nootkas, they couldn't help stuffing their mouths so full they almost choked on every swallow.

Governor Yanovski allowed them enough time to satisfy their appetites before asking, "Gentlemen, did either of you ever despair of being rescued, especially after the first year of your captivity passed?"

"Aye, Your Excellency, we soon lost hope," answered John, placing his fork down on his plate. "We then decided if we were doomed to live the rest of our lives with the Nootkas, we had to change our previously held ideas about them as total savages. Gregory soon pointed out to me how similar their society is structured to ours. They are ruled by a chief, who is descended directly from the previous chief, like an English king and his heirs. The chief's closest relatives are the noble class, and his most distant, the commoners. Their slaves are either bought or taken in war. The first months we were abused by the common people. Then Gregory made a steel harpoon for Chief Maquina. Not only was it the finest he ever saw, he used it to harpoon a huge whale that fed the village all spring. After that the ill treatment ceased and we became honored members of the tribe."

"Did you ever find out why they attacked your captain and crew in the first place?" asked the governor.

"A few weeks before our ship the *Lydia*, had come to Nootka Sound, a British ship had stopped to trade. Their captain had deceived the Nootkas by pretending to offer many goods for their furs, then when the Indians came on board to receive their payment, their furs were stolen by the crew, and all ten Nootkas were slaughtered. Nothing is more sacred to the Nootkas than revenge. They swore to kill all the white men on the next ship that came to trade, which was the unfortunate *Lydia*. The Nootkas think nothing of making the innocent suffer for the sins of the guilty. Most of them can't tell the difference between the Americans and English anyway. They say all white men look alike to them, especially since we speak the same language."

John paused then glanced around the table with a stern look before adding, "Maquina once told me he never would have harmed any white man if they hadn't first insulted the Nootkas by stealing from them, and then killing his people for no reason."

Sean was sitting next to him and he leaned over and muttered, "It seems we white men have given the natives just cause for their bloodthirsty reputation."

John nodded in agreement as the servants brought in sweet cakes for dessert and placed a huge glass bowl in the center of the table. It was the infamous hot punch, a tradition begun by Alexander Baranov. The mixture contained raw rum and boiling punch as strong as sulfur. It didn't take long for the governor, his naval officers, and the Americans to drink an astonishing amount.

Two Russian officers sitting together caught Sean's eye. The first was Lieutenant Dmitri Volodin, a young man with a cold arrogant manner and sharp eyes which appeared to study everyone at the table. Although Yanovski didn't seem to notice that Sean avoided drinking the punch, he was sure Volodin had.

Not a man I'd like as an enemy, he thought.

The other officer was Captain-Lieutenant Nikolas Bolkonsky. He was distinguished looking with gray hair and aristocratic features. Sean noticed how he was Volodin's opposite, warm, friendly, with an engaging smile.

The conversation around the table was boisterous and mainly good-natured. After a few glasses John became half drunk and began to speak of his Indian wife.

"She was sweet tempered, intelligent, and pretty besides. If it wasn't for her, I would've gone mad. It hurt like the dickens to leave her." Then he added sadly, "But she's best forgotten. I have a fiancé waiting for me in Boston, unless Miss Abigail Simpson has given up on me by now and married some other fellow. Can't blame her if she has."

"*Da*," blurted the governor a bit drunkenly, "there's nothing like a beautiful native wife. Someday when I take Irina back to Russia with me, there will be a revolt in New Archangel."

"And why is that, Your Excellency?" John asked with a laugh.

"She is so beloved here by more than just me. She visits the old Russian fur hunters in their cabins and listens to their stories. She's learned all the native languages and has befriended our Aleut hunters.

She knows the names of their wives and children who live as far away as Unalaska, Atkha Island, Kodiak, and Cook's Inlet, and asks about their health. She even moves freely among the *Kolosh* in their village near here. Their old crones greet her and so do their men returning from hunting and fishing. And she is as devoted to God as she is devoted to New Archangel."

Yanovski shook his head. "When I first met Irina, I was afraid I was not religious enough for her. My wife's faith is so real that she does not understand any man who has religious doubts or a lack of faith. She is like her mother when it comes to the church."

"They say your wife knows everything that goes on in the Pacific, Your Excellency," said Captain-Lieutenant Bolkonsky. "She can tell the duty a skipper must pay at Canton, and she knows the time it takes to sail from Cape Horn to the Sandwich Islands. I once saw her estimate in one glance, the tonnage of a Yankee brig anchored in the sound."

If she wasn't already taken, Irina Baranova would be the perfect wife for the ship's captain I'll be someday, thought Sean.

Pleased at the praise, the governor said graciously, "And I hear you have a beautiful daughter, Nikolas, who is much like my wife."

Bolkonsky grinned. "Indeed I do, Your Excellency. I am looking forward to the day when Tatiana arrives in New Archangel to wed Lieutenant Volodin."

Yanovski nodded at Volodin. "Yes, the lieutenant is fortunate to be betrothed to the beautiful Tatiana. But it is your other daughter, Marya Nikolayevna, whom I was referring to. She is also so lovely you will have no trouble finding her a husband."

Bolkonsky frowned slightly and said, "She is still a child."

"Irina was not much older when I first met her."

"True," Bolkonsky acknowledged, "but Marya is more Aleut than Russian. She needs more education before I would consider a betrothal for her."

"Does Tatiana know of her existence?" Volodin asked with a curious look on his face.

A pained expression crossed Bolkonskys face and he hesitated. Then he said quietly, "*Nyet.* I will tell her when she arrives."

Sean sensed a tension between the two men, but decided it was none of his business. Unfortunately, Horn, who was deep in his cups, blurted, "Sounds like a heap o' trouble to me when the white lady finds out she has a half breed sister!"

A dead silence followed. Then Governor Yanovski rose and said, "Gentlemen, thank you for your presence at dinner this evening. Good night." He gave Horn a curt nod and abruptly exited the banquet hall. Dinner was over.

Minutes later as Sean and the Americans were leaving the governor's house, he thought he saw Andrei Leonov waiting in the shadows by the entrance. He hoped he was mistaken, but it gave him an uneasy feeling.

* * *

Sean spent a restless night as thoughts of Irina Baranov danced in his head. He kept wondering what it would be like to fall in love with a decent woman, get married and have a real family of his own. Then reality set in. No lady in her right mind, especially if she was religious, would ever consider him good enough for a husband. Finally, he fell into a deep sleep.

Near dawn he awoke to hear the ship creaking and the clank of the thick metal chains pulling up the anchor. Above deck came the familiar sounds of men shouting as they hauled lines and hastily unfurled sails. No one had informed him they were departing this morning. There must be something wrong.

He glanced over at Ethan, who was snoring soundly in a peaceful slumber. Sean donned his coat and quickly left the cabin. Climbing the ladder to the hatch, he arrived on deck to see Captain Horn shouting orders to the sailors and the helmsman to make way at once. Dark gray clouds hung over the water spitting out intermittent rain showers, obscuring the buildings of Sitka, as the *Eastern Wind* began to move, making her way gingerly towards the string of treacherous rocky islands dotting the choppy waters of Sitka Sound. They were slipping away like a guilty thief.

"That dirty no good Leonov opened his yap," growled a blurry-eyed, hung over Captain Horn. "The gov'nor knows we traded guns to the Nootkas for Hill and Jones, so we're gettin' outta here."

Sean instantly remembered his suspicion of seeing Leonov the night before. It seemed he was right. "How did ye find this out?"

"From the little red squaw I had on board last night," said Horn, coughing after a drag on his pipe. "She said she heard the gov'nor was gonna bring me an' you in for questioning sometime today."

"I hope ye thanked her for that information," said Sean. "She saved our hides."

Horn gave a harsh laugh. "I sent her back to shore with her face intact. That's the thanks she got from me."

Sean wished he could spit in the man's vile face. Horn was known for his brutality to the women he slept with. If they didn't please him perfectly, he would break their nose or slit their earlobes or lips, marring any beauty they might have left. It was even rumored that once Horn had strangled a whore in Canton, a young Chinese girl caged up in one of those tiny filthy boxes of prostitution near the docks. Horn said he wanted to put the poor girl out of her misery, to free her from a life of never-ending hell. Somehow Sean didn't believe Horn had killed her out of mercy, but more like out of the pleasure it gave him.

He felt the familiar hatred for the man building inside him, and he tried to quell it as Horn, oblivious to his anger, added, "We're not out o' the brink, yet, O'Connell." He peered at the thick clouds and rain surrounding the ship. "If we don't pile up on a rock, those bloody Russkies might come after us with one o' their cursed navy brigs."

"They were all friendly enough last night at dinner. 'Tis hard to believe we're in danger now."

Horn leered at him. "May be the Gov'nor noticed yer makin' sheep's eyes at his wife when she was playin' that pi-ano."

Sean flushed. "I don't know what you're talkin' about!"

Horn snorted in derision. "Just 'cause she's married to the gov'nor don't make her no different from the rest of those redskin half-breeds."

A sudden roaring shot through Sean's head at the same time his fist smashed Arthur Horn in the nose. Sean heard a crunch and a pop, and Horn bellowed in pain. Instead of retaliating, he yelled to the nearest sailors, who were staring, mouths agape. "Johnson, O'Riley, get some rope and tie Mr. O'Connell to the mast. He's got a floggin' a comin'!"

The urge to fight left Sean as quickly as it began. He realized he was in deep trouble. Not that he regretted punching Horn in the face. It was something he'd wanted to do for years, ever since he stuffed rancid pork down poor Jake's throat. He hoped the captain's nose was broken.

With a mutter of apology his friend Ned told him to strip to the waist. Sean shivered as the cold wet rain spattered on his bare chest and back. After his wrists were fastened to the mast and his arms stretched over his head, Sean looked at Ned and Jake. There were expressions of anger, sympathy and respect etched on their faces.

He gave them a halfhearted smile of bravery he did not feel. "Lighten' up lads," he called out, "I expect I'll survive this."

"Not if I can help it, you won't!" Horn shouted, brandishing a long black leather whip. "You get a hundred lashes for strikin' me, 'cause I'm the cap'n!"

"A hundred?" Ned repeated. "He won't live t' see fifty!"

"Shut yer mouth, Johnson, or yer next!" Horn growled then spit out a mouthful of blood which had trickled down from his damaged nose.

He raised his arm and brought the whip down with a loud crack across Sean's back. He jerked involuntarily, feeling his skin split open like a ripe plum. He closed his eyes and fought the waves of pain as the whip continued to rise and fall in a deadly rhythm, cutting his back into bright red ribbons of blood. His body convulsed at each stroke, pressing into the rough wooden mast and causing dozens of splinters to slice into his naked chest.

Suddenly John Hill rushed up to them, a look of horror on his face. "Have you lost your mind, Horn?" he demanded. "First, you order the ship to sail without consulting me then I find you beating your finest officer senseless! Stop this outrageous whipping at once!"

Gregory Jones, always John's giant shadow, loomed up behind him. He looked like a huge sea lion in his glistening wet oilskins, frowning whiskers and all. No one seemed to notice him tense his muscles as if waiting to spring into action.

Horn scowled at both of them and said, "The gov'nor found out we traded guns for yer ransom an' we're not gonna stay here an' be arrested. An' as for me floggin' O'Connell, he hit me in the face! Now he's gettin' the punishment he deserves!"

"Poppycock!" John exclaimed. "Knowing you, I doubt that Mr. O'Connell struck you without provocation. Untie him now, Captain Horn, or you'll regret it!"

Horn gave an evil laugh. "I'm the cap'n, not you, an' there's nothin' you can do about it!"

"You're not the captain my uncle hired for this ship! Once we get to Boston he'll dismiss you and hire someone else more qualified. Someone who can at least read a cargo list!"

Horn's illiteracy had always been a sore point to his ego. Having it shoved in his face in front of the crew totally enraged him. "O'Riley," he snapped, "put Mr. Hill under arrest fer questionin' orders. Lock 'im up below in the hold. Tis time he an' everyone else knows who's the real master of this ship!"

Jake hesitated as John shouted, "That's ridiculous! I'm not one of your crew! You can't arrest me, you stupid imbecile!"

Horn snarled like an attack dog. He flicked the whip towards John's face, cutting a red line at the corner of his mouth. "Take that, you young puppy!" he exploded then screamed a string of curses.

As John staggered backwards, holding his hands protectively in front of his bleeding face, Horn aimed the whip towards him again. In an instant Jones jumped forward and caught the whip in mid air. It wrapped harmlessly around Jones's thick right arm like a coiling snake. Before Horn could react the big man yanked the whip out of his grip, then took his left fist and crashed a powerful blow to Horn's temple. The captain toppled over, unconscious before he hit the deck.

Sean was immediately untied from the mast. He staggered, feeling his back on fire, but managed to keep his balance. A wave of dizziness rushed over him and he struggled to fight it off. Suddenly he realized he was the sole officer in charge. All the crewmen nearby were staring at him, waiting for him to do something. Recently Ned and Jake had warned him about the discontentment of the sailors and Sean knew a firm hand of authority was needed at once.

With a tremendous effort he forced himself to ignore the fiery pain shooting across his bloodied back with each move he took. "Mr. Johnson, Mr. O'Riley," he called out to his old pals, "take Mr. Horn and lock him up in the brig. Mr. Jones, help Mr. Hill to his cabin and take care of his injury. The rest of ye," he turned to the crew standing by, "make haste with those sails, and Mr. Scott," he yelled over to the helmsman struggling with the great wheel, "keep her steady as she goes. We head for the Pacific."

For one brief terrifying second, he wondered if everyone would obey. Then a sailor shouted, "Aye, aye, Cap'n O'Connell!"

With that they all jumped to their tasks. Ned and Jake dragged the unresponsive Horn away and Gregory carefully helped John down the hatch. The crew sprang to their duties with grins on their faces. Much laughter echoed topsides as the wind hummed through the rigging and snapped the canvas sails taut. It was obvious they were delighted with the unexpected change of command.

Minutes later Sean stumbled down the hatch to his cabin where he collapsed onto his bunk face down with a groan. Ethan woke up and when he saw the torn flesh on Sean's back, he let out a startled cry. "Laddie, what's happened to ye? Did ye run afoul of Horn?"

"Ye can say that again," Sean moaned, then quickly told him the recent turn of events.

"I dinna know whether to say yer a fool or just a verra brave lad, Sean," said Ethan, shaking his head in disbelief.

At that moment Samuel and Wang Li rushed in. The Chinese cook, who also had some knowledge of medicine, took one glance at Sean and clucked in dismay. He hurried out to fetch water and cloths to clean the wounds.

Samuel eyed Sean with an expression of admiration. "Looks like you took care of Horn once an' for all, Cap'n. Me an' the rest o' the crew say a big thank you. But we sorry 'bout the whippin'. I expect when yer back heals, you'll have some mighty fine scars to show the ladies."

Sean almost chuckled, but his back hurt too much. Instead he said, "I just hope it heals quickly. With me an' Ethan feelin' poorly, the ship's shorthanded in officers."

"Ye need to promote a man to second mate," said Ethan. "How about Ned Johnson?"

Sean thought quickly. "Jake's a better man, but Ned is older an' more experienced. The crew will listen to him. Samuel, tell Ned we want to see him."

Samuel frowned in disapproval, but neither man noticed. "Yessah, Cap'n O'Connell," he said, then immediately left the cabin.

Sean sighed as he realized all the work waiting for him. As soon as his wounds were bandaged, no matter how weak he felt, he needed to study the navigational charts. Their position had to be plotted and their course set for China. If luck was with them they would survive the autumn gales of the north Pacific and reach Canton safely. After selling all their furs to the Chinese, they would load up the ship with tea, silk, spices and the handsomely carved oriental tables and screens so fashionable in New

England homes. Then the *Eastern Wind* would sail eastward back across the Pacific and around Cape Horn to Boston.

Samuel had called him Captain O'Connell. In the midst of all his pain Sean managed a satisfied smile. His dream of becoming a sea captain was now a reality.

CHAPTER SIX

Summer, 1820

The soft June breeze rustled her skirts and carried the refreshing scent of the nearby Dnieper River as Anna walked through the fruit orchard towards the grand two story house that belonged to her uncle and aunt. She had been living in Silberfeld with Uncle Heinrich and *Tante* Sarah and her cousins, Judith, Maria and Helena for the past six months. Although she missed her brothers immensely, it was her little sister she missed the most. *Poor Tina.* Would she ever stop feeling such a terrible guilt about leaving her?

She would never forget the bitter January day she left: Jack's face set in a false smile, masking his feelings of betrayal; the twins Peter and Jacob, waving good-bye as they struggled to control their tears, and Tina, crying so hysterically, Natasha had to take her back into the house. Papa looked sad and relieved at the same time, and then there was Agatha, an expression of triumph written all over her sharp featured face as she slyly patted her rounded belly. The new baby was due in October.

Anna sighed wearily as she remembered how intolerable life in the Teichroew household became soon after Papa's marriage to Agatha last November. Just as she'd feared, Agatha took over the family and ruled them like the wicked queen Jezebel in the Old Testament.

The first thing Agatha did was to forbid the whole family to eat together at mealtime. It was a Mennonite custom for the parents of a large family to eat alone while the children had to stand and eat at a special table near the main kitchen, fed by the oldest girl or a house servant.

The Teichroew family followed this practice only when they had company. Otherwise Herman and Katharina had loved having their children eat with them as a time to enjoy each other. They encouraged each child to talk about their day, giving them a feeling of being special and well loved.

All that family closeness vanished when Agatha became their new stepmother. She ordered Anna, Jack, Peter, Jacob and Katarina to eat in the kitchen, served by Natasha, while she and Herman ate alone at the big table. Anna and Jack both protested to their father at first, saying they were adults also, but Herman could not disallow his young bride anything. They were both banished to the kitchen along with the younger ones.

"Maybe it's just as well," said Jack later, "If I had to look at Agatha's mean face all through dinner I'd lose my appetite."

Anna didn't mind eating with her young siblings, and if that was the only change she would still be living at home. But Agatha was a harsh disciplinarian and when she gave an order she expected to be obeyed immediately. If not she was quick to merit out punishments, such as going to bed without supper, a particular cruelty for the three growing boys of the house.

Skipping a meal as punishment didn't faze little Katarina at all, and one evening in December Anna discovered that Agatha was using a different type of discipline on her.

Anna noticed all during supper how Katarina was squirming around uncomfortably. Her blue eyes were puffy and reddened as if she had been crying a lot. She suspected something was bothering her little sister, but when she quizzed Katarina about it, she said she was all right.

There was no one else to ask except Agatha. That morning the family went their usual separate ways after breakfast, Herman to the church to help Elder Klassen and some of the other men repair leaks in the roof, the boys to school, and Anna to the Freizens to help Susannah care for her mother who was ailing with a fever and a nagging cough. After Natasha left for her village late in the afternoon, Agatha and Katarina were home alone for a short time.

"Did something happen to Tina today?" Anna asked Agatha as they washed up the dishes after supper.

Agatha glanced sharply at Anna. "No, nothing, why do you ask?"

"Chicken soup is one of her favorite foods and she hardly ate a thing."

Agatha sniffed disdainfully. "She pretends to act like she's getting sick so you'll give her extra attention. You should stop falling for such spoiled pranks."

"I don't think she's pretending, Agatha. She looks unwell."

Agatha shrugged indifferently. "Send her to bed early, then. It doesn't matter to me."

Her stepmother's cold indifference towards Katarina made Anna angry, but she kept silent, remembering her promise to her papa to give Agatha a chance to be a part of the family. But later when her little sister was changing into her nightgown for bed, Anna saw a vivid purple welt across her tiny buttocks.

"What's that on your behind, Tina?"

Katarina hastily brushed her white linen shift down to her ankles and quickly climbed into bed, pulling the covers up to her chin. She looked like a porcelain doll with her big blue eyes and golden curls spilling over the pillow. But unlike the placid expression of a doll, Katarina's face was full of fear and her tiny mouth quivered.

"I fell on the floor," she said.

Anna frowned, not quite believing her. "You must have fallen really hard to get such a bad bruise. How did that happen?"

"I dunno."

Anna knelt by Katarina's side and stroked her head softly. "Tina, did something happen between you and Agatha this afternoon? You can tell me."

Katarina twisted her head away. "Can't tell."

"Of course you can. I'm your big sister. You can tell me anything, sweetheart."

Tears spurted down her cheek as she said, "I was a bad girl. 'Gatha said so."

"Oh, Tina, you're not a bad girl. You're a good girl. Tell me why you think you're bad."

"'Gatha said so 'cause I hurt Rachel."

"But that was months ago when you accidentally burned her sister's arm. Why would she bring that up again?"

Katarina sniffled. "She asked me to bring her tea an' when I did, somehow I dropped it on her hand. An' then she got mad and said I was a bad girl an' liked to hurt people like I did Rachel." She looked imploringly at Anna. "I didn't mean to, Anna, I didn't."

"I believe you, Tina," said Anna with a sympathetic smile. "We all spill things from time to time. But then what did Agatha do? Did she spank you?"

Katarina nodded slowly, looking frightened again. "She said not to tell or I'd get worse next time."

"What did she hit you with? Her hands wouldn't leave such a big bruise, Tina."

"She took one of Papa's belts, an'---an'" she couldn't finish as she burst into sobs, reliving her terrifying ordeal.

Anna stood up with a grim expression on her face. "You go to sleep, Tina, and don't worry about it. I'll take care of Agatha. She won't hurt you again."

She found Agatha sitting by the stove, reading the Bible to Herman. He was watching her with a satisfied look on his face that irritated Anna greatly. As hard as she tried to accept Agatha as her papa's new wife, she still couldn't stand to see him touch her in any affectionate manner or speak to her in a loving, submissive voice that reminded her of how he used to treat her mama. It probably bothered Jack and the twins, too, because they were spending the evening upstairs in their attic bedroom. She could hear their deepening male voices as they discussed the days' events, something they used to do every night with their papa and her.

How things had changed lately, she thought, and not for the better.

"Agatha, I need to talk to you," she said, interrupting her reading of the Book of Ruth. Anna had noticed how much Agatha enjoyed the books of the Bible that were centered on strong women, like Ruth and Esther. Too bad she didn't realize those powerful women of long ago had a loving, gentle side to their natures as well.

"What about?" asked Agatha, looking irritated.

Anna hesitated, wondering how her papa was going to react to the criticism of his new wife, but then her memory of Tina's bruised flesh spurred her on. "You had no right to hit Tina this afternoon with a belt! It was cruel and unnecessary punishment for such a trivial matter as spilling some tea!"

Agatha jumped up, the Bible falling to the floor as Herman stared at Anna with startled eyes. "I had every right, Anna!" she said in a terse voice. "Katarina burned my hand, just like she did my Rachel last summer! It's time your little sister realizes that when she hurts someone, she's going to be hurt, too. Spare the rod and spoil the child," she ended primly.

"Tina did not burn Rachel or you on purpose," said Anna, glaring at her. "You don't spank a child for being clumsy!"

"How do you know she didn't do it on purpose?" asked Agatha sarcastically. "Were you here today or even watching the girls last summer on washday? Well, were you?"

As Anna shook her head, Agatha crowed, "So, you don't know, do you?"

"I know Tina, Agatha. I know that little girl inside and out. I've practically raised her since Mama died, and I know there's not a mean bone inside her whole body."

"Well, that's not what the Scriptures say, Anna. We've all sinned and come short of the glory of God, and that includes Katarina, too!" said Agatha in a smug voice. "Isn't that true, Herman, dearest?"

Her papa cleared his throat and said reluctantly, "Anna, calm down. Agatha would not spank Tina without good cause. You are making too much of the matter."

Anna whirled on him, outraged. "You didn't see the huge welt on her, Papa! It looks horrible and the poor little girl can't even sit down!"

Her papa's face whitened at that, for Anna knew he did love Tina dearly. "Wife," he said to Agatha in a gentle voice, "perhaps you did get a bit carried away. Maybe you should find another way to discipline Tina from now on when she misbehaves, like making her stand still in a corner for an hour or so. She's such a restless child that should be punishment enough."

Agatha's pale gray eyes turned icy with fury, but she kept her voice level. "Whatever you say, Herman."

He smiled at her tenderly and patted her on the knee. "Now where were we, my dear?" he said, pointing at the Bible on the floor.

Anna knew she was dismissed, her papa already forgetting she was there. She hoped Agatha understood she was never to hit Tina again, but as she turned to go, she was dismayed to see the venomous glare Agatha hurled at her. Had her papa noticed? No, Anna realized, he had his eyes closed, listening happily to Agatha's well-moderated voice as she started reading again.

She instinctively knew Agatha was not to be trusted. And here she had promised Tina that Agatha would never hurt her again. Uneasily, she made her way back to her room where her sister was finally asleep, her small rounded cheeks streaked with her drying tears.

And I was right to be worried, thought Anna now, as she paused for a moment under the shady branches of a peach tree. Christmas that year was hard enough as the first one without their mama, who had always made it such a joyous occasion. But when Agatha refused to let Tina have even one present, because she said the little girl had been so bad she didn't deserve one, Anna lost her temper. They'd quarreled on Christmas morning and said things to each other that made even Jack and the twins blanch. Herman had intervened, taking Agatha's side, of course, and said that he'd had enough of their constant bickering. When Uncle Heinrich and *Tante* Sarah came to visit for New Year's Day, he'd asked them to take Anna back with them.

Anna was shocked when she realized she had to leave the only home she'd ever known. Her papa had told her without any warning, and hurt her further by saying, "My house is too small to hold two grown women who continue to fight like a couple of tomcats! By your own behavior, Anna, you are forcing me to choose between the two of you. Although you are my daughter, my primary duty is to my wife. As your father, I am ordering you to live with the Neufelds until the day you are to be married."

"And when is that, Papa?" she'd asked with dread.

"As soon as I can make arrangements with the right man."

He didn't elaborate any further, and she had no intention of asking if he had anyone in mind. In her heart she'd already known---Gerhard Yoder.

And she had been right. Yesterday Uncle Heinrich had received a letter from her papa. He'd written that he'd found a suitable husband for Anna, and wished her to return immediately. On the fifteenth of July she was to become *Frau* Yoder. That was only one month away.

Tears of frustration threatened to spill down her face as she pondered her dilemma. If only she could continue to live here at Silberfeld. Instead of being a place of loneliness and exile, the huge estate where her mama was raised had become a warm and loving home. Her uncle and aunt were kind to her, *Tante* Sarah always welcoming her with open arms and ears to any problem she had. Her fourteen-year-old cousins, the twins Judith and Maria, were a lively and generous pair, and Helena, age ten, had a sparkling personality that reminded her much of Tina, at least the way Tina used to be.

Their sister had changed, Jack wrote recently. Tina was no longer the happy little girl with the sunny smile. Instead she had become withdrawn and subdued, obeying Agatha's slightest wish instantly without a bit of back talk. Their papa didn't seem to notice. He was proud of his young wife and looking forward to the new baby expected in the fall. Now that Agatha had established her authority, Jack and the twins also found it easier to do as she asked instead of defying her. "I still don't like her," Jack wrote, "and we miss you terribly, but I have to admit Agatha does run the household well."

So, they were all getting along without her, Anna realized. All except poor Tina who had finally discovered that the key to peaceful coexistence with Agatha was to become the perfect little girl. Anna wondered what long lasting emotional harm her sister might suffer. But at least she wasn't being spanked anymore, which Jack made clear in his letter.

It was a small consolation, Anna thought, as she remembered how worried she was about Tina when she arrived at Silberfeld last winter. She was homesick, too, with a heart that felt broken. Perhaps *Tante* Sarah sensed her misery, for she told Anna that though she and Uncle Heinrich considered her as part of the family, they believed it would be best for her to stay busy.

She was given the job of housekeeper. Besides keeping the house servants in order, her duties included the dividing of the tons of food for the peasant workers. Each week the wives of the workers would come for their allotment of dark flour, *sauerkraut*, beets, potatoes, meat, and cabbage.

At the beginning Anna had been nervous, being in charge of such an important task as giving out food to these strange women. But she was careful to be fair to all of them, and she tried to get know them by asking about their children and families. Soon they responded to her kindness with trust and even affection.

Today was sauerkraut making day, an immense process involving all the workers. First, under Anna's supervision, they gathered in a large room and cut up all the cabbage with knives. After salting the cabbage chunks, they carried the cabbage in wooden pails up a ladder to the top of a huge vat and emptied them. The cabbage then was crushed down by a group of barefooted men who sang as they trampled on the salted vegetable to the rhythm of their songs until the juice covered the kraut. They also had a vat full of cooked beets with leaves that another group of men trampled down to be used for their *borscht*.

It was a day of hard work, but also one of camaraderie as everyone worked happily together to provide food for all. They were tired, including Anna, but she never minded the weariness that came from work well done. It gave her a feeling of accomplishment, and the hours flew by so quickly, she hadn't time to worry about marrying Gerhard Yoder.

But now as she continued her way through the orchard toward the house, the thought depressed her deeply. Spending the rest of her life with him was like spending the rest of her life in prison. There had to be a way out.

She wiped her eyes and considered. If she outright refused to marry him, she was afraid of what might happen. Both her papa and Gerhard would be furious; her papa because of her disobedience and Gerhard because of the humiliation. If only there was a way to make Gerhard change his mind about her. In the past she'd never encouraged his attentions and had treated him as distantly as possible, but nothing seemed to discourage him. So now she doubted there was anything she could do to make him dislike her.

Last night she'd prayed about this problem, begging God for His divine help. She knew the Scriptures taught children to obey their parents, something she had done all her life without question. But now a feeling of rebellion was forming in her heart. When her wedding day came, she didn't think she would be able to go through with it. But what else could she do?

Supper that evening was the usual noisy affair. The Neufeld family and Anna sat at the long polished oak table in the dining room, the food served by two smiling Russian peasant women. Uncle Heinrich presided over the meal at his end of the table, his weathered face with its gray mustache and neatly trimmed beard set in an indulgent expression as he watched his wife and daughters eat heartily of fried ham and sausage with fresh sauerkraut and *schnetke* (biscuits) and plum jam.

Tante Sarah sat at the opposite end of the table. She looked like the typical Mennonite matron, dressed conservatively in a dark gray dress with a tight black collar, her gray hair pulled back into a bun. But her perpetual smiling face and intelligent eyes belied her severe appearance.

Now her gaze was centered on her twin daughters. Judith was short and plump like her mother with brown hair and hazel eyes. She had a nose too large for her face, but she was a girl so full of laughter and wit that people only noticed her smilingly curved lips and perfect white teeth. Maria was much quieter by comparison. She was several inches taller than Judith and slim, though she had the same coloring of hair and eyes as her twin and a similar large nose. Her face always wore a dreamy expression as she spent hours reading books and imagining stories. Both girls were competent musicians, having taken years of piano lessons.

The youngest girl Helena was very pretty. She had gleaming dark brown hair and soft blue eyes and a small petite nose. Like her mother and Judith she was short and would probably struggle with her weight as she grew older. But at age ten she was a restless young girl, running all over the estate, curious about every animal and person who lived and worked at Silberfeld.

Today she had been in the midst of all the activity making the sauerkraut. She had a pleasant soprano voice, and Anna heard Helena singing along with the peasant workers who were trampling the kraut, their deep baritone voices harmonizing delightfully with her lilting one. Anna tried to join in once with her alto voice, but her spirits were so low, she couldn't bring herself to sing.

Helena ate heartily as she told her sisters about her busy active day. They in turn, described the visit that afternoon of the French dressmaker from the nearby Bolkonsky estate. Their mother had hired her to make new gowns for all of them.

"*Madame* Frabert is from Paris," said Judith excitedly, "and she knows all the latest fashions."

"Did she say anything about the Bolkonsky family?" asked Helena curiously. "Is the whole family staying here this summer again?"

The arrival of the aristocratic Count and Countess Bolkonsky and their children and servants was an annual event in their area each summer for years. Not that they ever socialized with them, of course, but the Neufeld girls saw glimpses of the richly dressed family occasionally when they rode in their fancy carriage through the villages and fields. Now the Bolkonsky children were grown adults, but the Neufeld girls were still highly interested in the happenings of such a noble Russian family. Luckily for them, the French woman was a gossip.

"*Madame* Frabert said the Countess died of a heart attack last fall," said Judith, "so only the Count himself and his daughter, Olga, and niece, Tatiana are here for the summer. The son, Mikael, is at the Naval Academy in Kronstadt. She said he had been shot in a duel last year and now has a meaner temper than ever."

"A duel?" Helena's blue eyes glowed with delight. "How romantic!"

Judith giggled. "It wasn't over a woman, you little idiot. He was shot by Tatiana's future father-in-law for insulting his family. It caused quite a scandal in Saint Petersburg."

"Yes, the beautiful Tatiana is finally getting married," said Maria with a note of envy. "*Madame* Frabert said she is betrothed to a handsome naval lieutenant stationed in Russian America and will be sailing to New Archangel sometime in July."

Anna, who was eating little and only half listening to the conversation perked up at this. "She must be very brave to sail around the world to such a faraway place."

"Brave, or foolhardy," said Uncle Heinrich. "It is a dangerous voyage to an even more dangerous place. There are savage Indians still living there."

Helena shuddered with excitement as she and Maria both imagined what an adventure such a journey would be. Judith looked at her sisters and grinned. "Maybe one of you should go along as her new lady's maid," she laughed teasingly. "*Madame* Frabert said that Tatiana needs another maid since her last one ran off after Tatiana had her severely punished for spilling ink on her favorite gown. It seems the lovely Tatiana is not as beautiful inside as she is outside."

"*Favour is deceitful, and beauty is vain: but a woman that feareth the Lord, she shall be praised,*" said Uncle Heinrich, quoting Proverbs 31:30 from the Bible. He glanced at his wife and winked.

She gave him a quick smile then turned to Anna, "Child, I've noticed you aren't hungry, even with all the hard work you did today. I hope you aren't ailing?"

Her uncle and cousins glanced at her with concern. She tried to brush it aside. "I'm fine, *Tante* Sarah, really, I am. Just a bit tired, that's all."

Her aunt hesitated, not entirely convinced. "You've been so quiet since Herman wrote us yesterday. I thought you would be overjoyed at the news of your wedding, although," she paused and narrowed her eyes thoughtfully, "you've never mentioned this Gerhard Yoder. Don't you wish to be his wife, Anna?"

Anna dropped her fork on her plate with a clatter. "No, I don't!" she blurted out. "I've always despised Gerhard Yoder and if Papa makes me marry him, I don't know what I'll do!"

She was as shocked at her outburst as the Neufelds were at this sudden revelation. There was a moment of silence, then *Tante* Sarah exclaimed, "You poor girl! First your mama's death, then your papa's remarriage, and now this!'

"Oh, Anna," Judith said worriedly, "we can't let you go back to Furstenau now. We didn't want you to leave anyway, but we can't let you be married off to a man you dislike."

Maria and Helena echoed that statement as Anna said, "I appreciate your concern, but how can any of you stop it? Papa's coming here next week to bring me home, and if I refuse to go with him, he'll become very angry. I don't think I could bear that."

She felt the hot rush of tears as Uncle Heinrich cleared his throat and said, "I'm sure Herman means well with his choice of husband for you, Anna, but if he knew how you really felt about the man, I'm sure he wouldn't force you to marry him. I would never make any of my girls marry someone that they didn't wish to."

All three of his daughters smiled gratefully at him. Anna shook her head, choking back the tears.

"Papa knows how I feel, Uncle Heinrich. But I think Agatha is pushing him to make this marriage. She won't be happy until she sees me totally miserable."

Tante Sarah clucked sympathetically. "There must be something we can do to change Herman's mind, Heinrich. When he arrives we should have a talk with him and tell him we aren't in favor of this marriage."

Her husband frowned. "Anna isn't our daughter, Sarah, and we have no right to oppose Herman's choice of husband. I would resent anyone who interfered with our choice of husbands for Judith, Maria or Helena. If Herman only listens to his wife and not to Anna, I'm afraid there is nothing we can do."

Anna bowed her head in defeat as the tears ran down her cheeks. Uncle Heinrich and *Tante* Sarah looked at her sadly as Judith and Maria started to sniffle in sympathy. Suddenly Helena gave a little squeal and announced, "I know what I'd do if Papa made me marry a man I hated. I'd run away!"

Her sisters started to scoff at her remark when Helena added, "Mama, why don't you ask *Madame* Frabert if Anna could apply to the Bolkonskys for the position of Tatiana's new maid? Gerhard Yoder would never find her in Russian America!"

Uncle Heinrich and Judith and Maria chuckled weakly at Helena's attempted jest, but Anna noticed that instead of smiling with them, *Tante* Sarah shot her a speculative look.

* * *

Three days later in an upstairs bedchamber of the Bolkonsky country house in Ekaterineslav, Tatiana Nikolayevna tossed on her bed, feeling the beginnings of a pounding headache. A new day and she was in a bad temper already. Lately she found fault with almost everything in her world, starting with when she left Saint Petersburg to each day here on the estate. In the past she'd always loved every minute spent in the country, but now she was so anxious to leave for Russian America to see her Papa and begin her life with Lieutenant Dmitri Volodin, each second in this dreary old place seemed endless.

To make matters worse, her maid Sonya ran off just because Tatiana had the clumsy girl beaten slightly for ruining a new frock. She'd only ordered two strokes of the lash, and then allowed the sobbing girl to be taken care of by the local healer, a peasant woman. Soon after that Sonya was gone. The old woman denied all knowledge of her disappearance, but Tatiana and Uncle Vasily weren't convinced. He'd had the woman tied up underneath the house in a corner of the dark wine cellar for the past week, but they'd learned nothing new.

Tatiana rubbed her forehead and sighed. Perhaps she'd been too harsh on the girl when she accidentally spilled the bottle of ink on her latest gown. But the dress was a beautiful creamy silk creation from Paris, made especially by *Madame* Frabert, and the sight of the large black splotch destroying its loveliness was more than Tatiana could bear. She had planned to take it to New Archangel as a part of her wedding trousseau.

Maybe she was well rid of the girl. She'd always considered Sonya too pretty to be her maid, and lately she'd been getting more and more careless. Just the other night she yanked Tatiana's hair so hard when she was brushing it, Tatiana had to whirl around and slap her in the face as a reminder to be more efficient.

Sonya had been her maid longer than any of the others, almost two years now. Except for her recent clumsiness, she was the perfect lady's maid. It was going to be difficult to find another decent maid in this backwoods part of the Ukraine. So she'd asked Uncle Vasily to keep looking for the girl. She had to be somewhere among the villages.

Yesterday Olga pointed out that if Sonya was forced to return, she would make an even poorer maid than before. Tatiana knew that was true, but it was the principle of the thing. She was furious that the girl dared to defy the Bolkonsky family, and most importantly, herself. She needed to be found if only to be punished even harder. Perhaps twenty lashes would send a clearer message to Sonya and all the other servants of the severe consequences if they ran away.

Her aunt always declared one must let the servants know who was in control. There wasn't much Aunt Irene said that Tatiana ever listened to, but the woman did know how to strike fear into the heart of her servants.

In contrast, her grandmother, the dead Countess Elena, had dealt with her servants far differently. She vaguely recalled Nana once saying, "Servants are people, too, just like us, with feelings and lives of their own."

But Nana was too lenient on the palace servants. She and Aunt Irene were always at odds at how to get the most work out of them. Her aunt believed ruling by fear was more effective than by kindness, and in Tatiana's experience, she had to agree.

However, now she was forced to share Olga's French maid until a new one could be found. And that might take awhile since all the young girls nearby were country peasants who were ignorant of any type of fashion sense. It took time to train a good maid. They didn't just grow on trees.

Meanwhile Olga held the upper hand when it came to borrowing her maid. That was already causing trouble between them. After a week without her own personal maid, Tatiana was getting desperate.

I'd even take some stupid serf at this point, thought Tatiana, pressing a hand against her throbbing forehead. *Where is that big nosed maid of Olga's? I need someone to empty the stinking chamber pot, and then bring me a basin of clean water so I can wash. Then I need her to help me dress and arrange my hair, and...*

Her thoughts trailed off as a sharp pain stabbed at her temples. Perhaps she should ask her uncle to release the healing woman so she could make some concoction to soothe her headache. If the old crone was going to tell them anything about the whereabouts of Sonya, she would have spoken by now. She probably knew nothing.

A knock rapped sharply on Tatiana's bedchamber door, adding to the painful throbs in her head. She groaned as the door opened and *Madame* Frabert entered, her black silk dress rustling as she moved. The French woman had been widowed twenty years before at age twenty five and still wore nothing but black. Her husband had been the one love of her life, was her explanation, and she never wished to marry again.

"*Madame* Frabert," croaked out Tatiana, "tell Olga to fetch me Colette. I need her at once."

"*Bon jour, Mademoiselle* Tatiana," spoke the dressmaker, her heavily powdered face and rouged mouth set in a cheerful expression, "I have someone even better for you, your very own maid."

Tatiana struggled to sit up straight in her plush four posted bed with the burgundy red velvet drapes hanging on the sides. She opened her eyes wide as a slender petite young woman walked in behind *Madame* Frabert. "Who is this?" she asked with a note of irritation.

"This is your new maid that Count Bolkonsky hired just this morning. Her name is Anna and she is eager to serve you."

Tatiana was surprised at the sight of the girl, her headache temporarily forgotten. She didn't look like one of the slovenly local peasant girls, yet, there was something familiar about her. She had a neat appearance, wearing a plain gray dress with a white apron and a white scarf tied around her hair. Unlike most serfs who never dared look an aristocrat in the face, this girl was staring quite boldly at her, curious and unafraid. She had the most remarkable eyes, a hazel brown speckled with gold.

How dare she? Tatiana thought. Doesn't she know any better?

"Where did she come from?" she demanded. "And what are her qualifications to be a lady's maid?"

Madame Frabert motioned Anna forward. "I met her a few days ago. She is the niece of the wealthy Mennonite farmer, Heinrich Neufeld, who has his estate a few *versts* away from here. She's almost eighteen years old, can speak German, English, Russian and French, and is knowledgeable in cooking, cleaning, laundry, sewing and I'm told, has a lovely singing voice. She doesn't know much about fashion obviously, from looking at her, but her aunt says she is very intelligent and quick to learn. She's been employed as their housekeeper the past six months."

Of course, she's a Mennonite girl. Now Tatiana remembered why she looked so familiar. All those summers spent sightseeing through their villages, the women dressed plainly like this girl. How she and Olga used to laugh at their drab clothing.

Her mouth twitched in a slight smile as *Madame* Frabert added, "But if she isn't suitable, Count Bolkonsky said we can always hire one of the serfs from the village instead."

"She'll do," said Tatiana, "for now. Perhaps after I return to Saint Petersburg next month, I can find a French maid like Colette for my voyage to Russian America."

The young Mennonite girl looked startled. Tatiana smirked. "You wouldn't want to go with me, now would you, Anna? It's a long way from your family. You'd probably never see them again."

"Perhaps, that would be best for me," said Anna softly, "the way things are between me and my papa at present."

"And how would that be?" asked Tatiana curiously.

"He wishes me to marry a man in my village that I dislike. I cannot go home."

Madame Frabert raised her painted eyebrows in admiration. "Ah, a *mademoiselle* with spirit. You defy your *pere*."

"By coming here, I defy more than my papa. I defy my whole Mennonite village. I am now considered an outsider. I cannot go home again," she repeated, this time with a deep despair in her voice.

Tatiana studied the girl with more interest than she'd felt in anything the past couple of weeks. She wasn't as pretty as Sonya, or as beautiful as herself, which Tatiana was relieved to see, but there was something attractive about her. Perhaps it was the haunting sadness in those lovely eyes or the fresh healthy glow to her face. She didn't look like a servant or even a person who would be easily cowed. But she was a Mennonite. And from what she'd understood about that strange religion, they refused to fight for anything.

Tatiana decided the girl's spirit could be easily broken if it hadn't been already by her mean papa. She would make the perfect maid.

"Anna," she said in an imperious tone, "I want you to see to my needs at once. The chamber pot must be emptied and cleaned, I want water for washing, and--" she broke off as her headache came roaring back.

"Is *Mademoiselle* feeling unwell?" asked Anna hesitantly, noticing the pinched look of pain around the extraordinary blue-violet eyes. She had never seen such a beautiful girl before. Her light blond hair shimmered like the pale golden tops of fully ripened wheat, surrounding a face with features so perfect she could have stepped out of an artist's painting.

"I have a beastly headache," Tatiana snapped.

Madame Frabert flashed Anna a sympathetic look and on her way out, murmured, "*Au revoir*, *Mademoiselle*. Good luck."

With a forced smile Anna approached her new mistress. "Would you like some willow bark tea for your headache, *Mademoiselle*? It will ease the pain."

Tatiana looked at her in surprise. "Do you know how to make it?"

"Yes, my mama taught me years ago. Would there be a supply of willow bark in the kitchen, perhaps?"

"You can ask the cook. Tell her I ordered it."

Anna nodded and stepped over to the reeking chamber pot. "First I will empty this and when I return, I'll bring you water for bathing and the tea."

Tatiana smiled her approval and as Anna turned to leave, holding the chamber pot gingerly at arm's length, Tatiana said, "Is your mama your village's healing woman?"

Anna stopped short, almost spilling the pot's foul contents. "No, my mama was just a *hausfrau.* She died last year," she said quietly.

Tatiana said nothing as Anna exited the room. She felt a faint twinge of sympathy for her new maid then brushed it aside. She had survived all her life without a mother; at least the Mennonite girl had known hers.

* * *

Anna was given a small room adjoining Tatiana's spacious bedchamber. It held nothing more than a plain bed with a real feather mattress, a stand with a washbasin, a trunk in the corner for her possessions and a tiny window that overlooked the green rolling fields and the Dnieper River in the distance. By a wealthy person's standard, it was nothing more than a box. To Anna, who had never had a room to herself before, it was a luxury. At Silberfeld she'd shared a room with ten-year-old Helena, and at home she'd shared a room with Tina, and when she was younger, her brother Jack.

That night at she prepared for bed, she wondered if she would be able to sleep without listening to someone else breathe. She had never spent a night alone before. A pang of homesickness washed over her, first for Silberfeld and her noisy cousins, and then for Furstenau and her beloved family.

She told herself she wasn't going to cry. She'd made her decision and now she was going to stick to it, no matter how difficult her life became. She remembered how two days before *Tante* Sarah had approached her with little Helena's idea of applying as a maid to the Bolkonskys.

"My youngest daughter can be such an imp sometimes," her aunt said, "but she might have found a solution for your problem, at least temporarily. When your papa hears about you going to work for the Russian nobility, he will realize how deeply you feel about not marrying *Herr* Yoder. Herman will be forced to change his mind and call off the wedding. He is a reasonable man or your mama, Heinrich's sister, would never have married him!" She tried to laugh.

Anna was stunned by the proposal and told *Tante* Sarah she needed time to think about it. "Not too much time, child," she warned her. "You need to be gone before your papa arrives."

Anna was afraid if she went to work for the Bolkonskys she would be shunned by the Mennonite community and not be allowed to ever return to Furstenau. When she voiced this concern to her uncle, he said, "You only need to work for them until the girl, Tatiana, leaves next month. By then, both your papa and *Herr* Yoder will have calmed their tempers, and you will be free to move home, if that is your wish. Otherwise, you are always welcome to stay here with us. We do consider you a part of our family, Anna."

Now she hoped she could last here an entire month. The first day had been hard enough, satisfying every whim of that spoiled Tatiana. And the interview early this morning with her uncle, Count Vasily Bolkonsky, had been almost terrifying.

At least she hadn't felt intimidated by the Bolkonsky's house. Square and made of old oak, it wasn't much larger than the Neufeld's home, boasting only one more story on top and an extra wing for the servant's quarters and the kitchen. Cottages for guests were scattered throughout a lovely park, which bordered the river for some distance.

On the ride over, Uncle Heinrich gave her some general information about the estate. It was about 2400 acres, a modest property in comparison to the more magnificent country estates which most families of the nobility possessed. The place brought no profit and cost the Bolkonskys a great deal of money to maintain. The count raised fine horses, had a magnificent herd of Holstein cattle, and there were elaborate poultry houses in which he took a special interest. Anna was amazed at all the orchards of fruit trees, vegetable gardens, and greenhouses and fields, growing nothing but flowers.

When they arrived in the Neufeld's carriage, Uncle Heinrich walked her to the rear entrance of the house near the kitchen where *Madame* Frabert met them. After Anna said farewell to her uncle, she took her to see the Count who was eating his breakfast alone in the dining room.

She had been extremely nervous, as she had never met or spoken to a real Russian count in her life. Her expectations were of an impressive figure of a man and Count Bolkonsky didn't disappoint her. He was strongly built with thick wavy dark hair and an elegant gray mustache. She would have thought him handsome if not for his fierce black eyes and prominent nose, even larger than what she and Jack jokingly referred to as the Teichroew nose in their family.

She could tell he was a man who did not smile much. Perhaps it was because he lost his wife recently. When *Madame* Frabert announced her, he took a sip of his tea and gave her a swift cursory glance. Anna hoped he didn't notice her trembling.

He listened to *Madame* Flaubert's recitation of all her skills with a slightly bored look, then said, "A Mennonite girl, eh? Tatiana will carve her up and spit her out for the buzzards. Well, no matter. Send her upstairs at once."

With that frightening comment ringing in her ears, Anna steeled herself to meet some sort of monster. And after the first ten minutes, she realized why Count Bolkonsky had said such an unflattering thing about his beautiful, but self centered niece. The girl was indeed a trial.

But she was no meaner than her stepmother, Agatha. As Anna finally fell asleep in her strange bed, she felt certain she could manage to serve Tatiana Nikolayevna Bolkonsky without a problem for the next few weeks.

CHAPTER SEVEN

Several hours after the *Eastern Wind* docked in Boston one muggy June morning, her officers and crew were met with great fanfare. Dozens of horse drawn carriages lined the street near the pier where the ship was tied, and throngs of well dressed people, including several reporters from the Boston and New York City newspapers were eagerly waiting. Sean was amazed at the attention generated, but John Hill wasn't surprised.

"My uncle is a prominent citizen and the rescue of his nephew from bloodthirsty savages isn't an every day occurrence," he remarked with a tinge of sarcasm.

His facial injuries inflicted months ago by Arthur Horn had finally healed, leaving a slight scar at the corner of his mouth. Instead of marring his handsome boyish looks, the scar only enhanced them. John now had a rather dangerous cast to his smile that Sean supposed the ladies might find appealing, a situation similar to his own face. Women often made comments about the pale jagged scar that ran across his left cheekbone, a grim reminder of a long ago night he would rather forget.

It would be hard not to remember now that he was back in Boston, the city of his childhood; his mother, his sister Rose and his father. Sometimes it seemed like they had belonged to another boy's life, not his. So much time had passed. He hadn't even had the bad dreams about his father for years.

He hoped being in Boston for a few weeks wouldn't bring back the memories and dreams. The shorter the stay here, the better, he decided. He would collect his pay from Thomas Hill, deposit it in his growing bank account, and sign on another ship as soon as possible. There was nothing for him in Boston anymore.

Not so for his friend, John. Sean watched as he ran down the gangplank into the crowd and was immediately embraced by a short rotund man wearing a powdered wig and gold rimmed spectacles, obviously his uncle Thomas Hill. A tall slender young woman with auburn hair stood a few feet away, dressed in a fetching gown of pale blue linen with frothy white lace at the throat and wrists. She held a matching pale blue parasol to shield her face from the harsh rays of the summer sun. One foot tapped impatiently as she stared at the two men, and Sean guessed her to be John's fiancé.

As John finally turned to the young woman and she fell into his arms with a small cry, Sean wondered how she would take the news that her husband-to-be had married an Indian princess during his captivity.

"Do ye think he'll ever tell the lass about his Nootka wife, then?" asked Ethan Campbell who had been leaning on his cane at Sean's side.

Sean shrugged, giving the big Scotsman a sidelong glance. "How did ye know I was just thinkin' that meself?"

"Tis a fair question, laddie, I mean, Captain," Ethan hastily corrected the form of address as he was in earshot of several seamen who were busily stowing away sails, ropes and other gear to make the ship presentable for visitors.

The two men had developed a peculiar relationship over the past months, a public one and a private one. In public, Ethan, as first mate, treated Sean with all the respect due his captain. In private, they were just close friends, with Sean still looking up at Ethan as the older and more experienced officer. If it hadn't been for Ethan's leg wound and the long recovery following the amputation, Sean knew that Ethan would have been the captain of the *Eastern Wind* after Arthur Horn's imprisonment.

Most men would have resented the promotion of a younger, more inexperienced man, but Ethan was not like most men. He could have turned bitter over the loss of his leg and the chance at the command of a ship, but instead he was full of praise and thanksgiving to his God for having spared his life. The rest of the voyage found Ethan taking any opportunity to share his faith with anyone who cared to listen, dubbing him the nickname, "Preacher Campbell." It would have made his Presbyterian minister father proud.

Sean wasn't sure if Ethan had been "saved from death" by God or was just lucky, but he wasn't about to argue the point. It was a great relief to him to have the first mate back to health to help him run the ship. Ned was an experienced sailor, but not at being an officer, and some of the crew had a hard time getting used to him as second mate.

Since all the men respected the big Scotsman, it was vital to have the first mate on his "feet" as quickly as possible. A skilled carpenter was needed to make a pair of crutches, but when Sean had become the second mate last fall, the *Eastern Wind* had gone without one.

It was fortunate John had been the carpenter on the doomed ship *Lydia*. When Sean asked him to become their carpenter for the remainder of the voyage, John was more than happy to use his craft. Not only did he make crutches for Ethan, he also carved a crude wooden leg. Using leather strips he fastened the leg to Ethan's stump and by the time they left Canton, Ethan was able to limp around the ship with the help of a cane, also carved by John.

"Now that we're in Boston," Sean said to him, "we'll find ye someone who can make ye an even better leg, Ethan."

"Aye, I could use something with a wee bit more padding that won't rub me sore flesh so hard and perhaps a bit of a foot as well."

Both men glanced down at his peg leg then straightened up to attention as John and Thomas Hill and the attractive young woman came aboard.

"Uncle," said John, smiling broadly, "I'd like you to meet two of the brave men who rescued me, Captain Sean O'Connell and First Mate Mr. Ethan Campbell. Gentlemen, may I introduce my uncle Mr. Thomas Hill and my betrothed Miss Abigail Simpson."

Tears glistened behind the thick spectacles of Mr. Hill and he shook hands with both Sean and Ethan firmly. "My family and I are forever grateful for how you men saved John and Mr. Jones from the savages in Nootka Sound. We're especially grateful for the personal sacrifices made by the terrible death of Captain Smythe and the loss of your leg, Mister Campbell. And then to have the two of you sail my ship successfully back home with a cargo hold full of treasures from Canton, well," he cleared his throat, "how can I ever repay you men?"

"Yes,"said Abigail, smiling, her soft brown eyes brimming with unshed tears, "my heart is overflowing with joy at having my beloved John home safe and sound. I cannot thank you enough for what you did."

Ethan blushed, his face turning a shade of red almost matching his hair and beard, as Sean grinned at her and said, "Yer welcome, ma'am."

Thomas Hill chuckled and said, "You'll get more than just our thanks, young man. Come to dinner tonight, both of you. I have a proposition I think you might find very interesting."

* * *

The Hill residence stood in the finest section of Boston nestled amongst the homes of the wealthy shipping families. Made of red brick, the stately mansion had a magnificent view of Boston harbor dotted with sailing ships of all kinds. Sean and Ethan were welcomed by Thomas and his wife Priscilla, a plump gray-haired woman near sixty, and introduced to the other guests, Abigail's parents Frederick and Velma Simpson. Simpson was a banker and a big investor in Thomas's ships. They were friends and had known each other for many years. When John and Abigail married the two families would be joined, which would make his uncle extremely happy, John had told Sean a few days before they reached Boston.

"It's a match made in capitalistic heaven, the bank heiress and me, the heir to a shipping fortune. You see, Uncle Thomas and Aunt Priscilla never had any children of their own. Why they didn't, I'm not sure, but when I was young, and both of my parents drowned in a boating accident, they raised me as their son."

"So ye never knew your ma and da, then?" Sean had asked.

"No. And it's a strange twist of fate that my father, the younger of the two Hill brothers, had sailed all around the world without mishap, then one summer day he took my mother sailing on a small sloop for a picnic at Martha's Vineyard and they were caught in a sudden squall on the way back. Their boat overturned and they drowned. Luckily for me my mother insisted I stay at home with Aunt Priscilla since at two years of age I was given to sudden tantrums, and she didn't think I would be safe in a small boat. How right she was."

"I'm surprised that ye, the heir to all of this, woulda been a mere carpenter on the *Lydia*."

John had laughed slightly. "My uncle is from the old school. Learn the business from the ground up. He sent me off on his ships when I was just a lad still wet behind the ears, much to my aunt's dismay, and I worked my way up to the position of carpenter. If I hadn't been captured by those cursed Indians, I'd be an officer by now. Instead, when I return home, my family and fiancé will never let me out of their sight again. Uncle Thomas will probably have me chained to a desk for the rest of my days, and I'll be envying the likes of you as you sail off in our ships."

Sean remembered that conversation at the dinner table as he watched Abigail, seated next to John, chatter incessantly to him. He answered her politely whenever she took a breath or a bite of food, but it seemed to Sean, that he wasn't as excited about being with her again as she was with him. Perhaps he was just overwhelmed by all the food, more than they had seen since leaving Sitka.

Served by two black-haired Irish maidservants, who couldn't take their eyes off him, the dinner was a rich multi-course affair of thick, creamy clam chowder, fresh baked bread, succulent roast beef and brown sugar glazed ham, broiled cod, smoked salmon, baby carrots and potatoes, fruit salad and cheeses, served with expensive wines and a fancy chocolate mousse for dessert. Afterwards when they could hardly move Sean, Ethan, John and Frederick Simpson were ushered into Thomas's study for brandy and a smoke, leaving the three women to their tea in the drawing room.

The study was a man's room, smelling of stale tobacco, with burnished walnut paneled walls and shelves full of books, and heavy black leather chairs. As Sean stepped inside his gaze was drawn to an intricately carved wooden model of a type of ship he'd never seen before, sitting on top of the large mahogany desk. Before he could inquire about it, he and Ethan were each handed a glass of brandy. They sipped the amber liquid slowly, masking their dislike of the strong alcohol taste, not wanting to offend their host and employer.

John drained his glass in one swallow then sighed, "I've waited years to drink a glass of fine brandy like a civilized gentleman, Uncle, and my regards to Aunt Priscilla for such a delicious dinner."

"I noticed you didn't touch the fish or the clam chowder, John."

He grimaced slightly. "I spent two years in a village where I mainly ate salmon and clams, surrounded by the constant odor of rotting fish, especially whale meat, which had the most appalling stench of all. The

Nootkas prized whale meat and blubber, but I found it tasted like rancid fat." He shuddered. "Gregory and I used to fantasize about meals like the one we just ate."

Thomas poured another shot of brandy into John's glass. "Now that you are home, my boy, you can start putting all that behind you."

Frederick Simpson, a large man with a beefy face and small squinty eyes, lit his pipe and took a puff, then looked at John thoughtfully. "I say, John, I did hear rumors about you and some Indian woman. For my daughter's sake, I hope there isn't any truth to it."

John swirled the brandy around inside his glass then glanced up and met Simpson's curious gaze boldly. "If the rumors say I married an Indian princess, then they are true."

The mottled veins on Simpson's bulbous nose immediately turned a deep purple as he barked, "Explain yourself, young man, before I cancel your engagement to Abigail!"

Thomas opened his mouth to defend his nephew, but John silenced him with a shake of his head. "There's little to explain, sir. If I had refused the offer of Maquina, the King of the Nootkas, to marry his daughter, he would have considered that a major insult and I would have been immediately killed. I really had no choice in the matter."

"Well, well, then," Simpson blustered, "in that case, perhaps, everyone will understand, including Abigail."

"If she doesn't, sir, then I will be the one to call off the engagement," John replied firmly.

Simpson tugged uneasily at the tight collar of his shirt pressing against the rolls of fat around his neck and said, "Now, now, John, let's not be too hasty here. I apologize. If you were to call off the betrothal, Abigail would be heartbroken. You have no idea of what she went through all that time you were declared missing, perhaps dead. After a few weeks of weeping, she pulled herself together and instead of turning to other young men like many empty-headed young women would do she immersed herself in her Abolitionist work. You know, the Quaker movement to abolish slavery. Her mother and I really didn't approve, but her work took her mind off you, so we didn't stop her from going to their meetings and some such. Now that you are back, she can forget all that silly Quaker nonsense."

Thomas cleared his throat. "Gentleman, perhaps this subject is best left alone for the moment. If you will, I'd like to draw everyone's attention to this fine ship's model on my desk."

About time, thought Sean impatiently. "What sort of ship is that, sir?" he asked eagerly.

"It's a new design called a clipper ship, O'Connell. It was developed in Baltimore by naval architects during the war with the British. These new ships will be faster than any British brig. Notice her sleek hull, gentlemen. It's long, low, and broad with a sharper bottom. She's built with a greater draft aft and a raked stern that produces this overhanging bow, which will provide a sharp entry into the water, making her swift under any conditions. The masts are higher and also raked, and can carry huge fore-and-aft sails. She's armed with eight small guns on the open deck, four on each side. Note her hatches and skylights to the accommodations below."

"She makes the *Eastern Wind* look like a fat slug," said John.

"What's a slug?" asked Simpson, as he poured himself a drink.

"A slimy creature, several inches long, which crawls without legs through the forests of Vancouver Island and leaves a trail of sticky goo. Some are brown, or black, or even yellow and green with black spots. Not something you want to step on in your bare feet."

Simpson snorted with disbelief as Sean and Ethan laughed. Thomas smiled and went on, "John is correct in saying that the *Eastern Wind* and others like her will be a thing of the past. This ship is the first of a fleet of clippers I'm having built. She was launched last fall, and is docked in Baltimore, waiting for her new captain and crew to take her on her first voyage to Alaska." He looked at Sean. "I am hoping you will be that captain, O'Connell."

Speechless with shock, Sean could only stare at him. Thomas chuckled and turned to Ethan. "Mister Campbell, originally I was intending to give you the command of my new ship, but I wasn't certain of your health, sir. You do have seniority over O'Connell here, yet, he did such a fine job of bringing the *Eastern Wind* home, I realize he has the leadership qualities and the knowledge I require in a captain, although he does need more experience. And there's only one way to get that, of course. However, I'd like to have my doctor examine you, and if he gives you a clean bill of health, I would like to offer you the job as first mate."

"Aye, I accept of course," said Ethan, "but what about Arthur Horn? What are ye plannin' to do with him?"

John and his uncle exchanged frowns, then Thomas said, "The man should be charged with assault and locked up. But John feels he's had his punishment after all those months in the brig. Instead I'm sending out letters to every ship owner and reputable captain on the east coast describing Horn's irrational and violent behavior. I expect that Horn will find it impossible to ever find a berth on a ship as an officer again. He'll be lucky to even be hired on as an ordinary seaman."

"He'll be blackballed in the maritime community forever," said John. "He'll have to retire from the sea and live on land. For a life long sailor like Horn, that's punishment enough."

"The man could join the crew of a privateer," said Ethan. "Might be more fittin' for the likes o' him."

"Either way, this family is finished with Horn." Thomas smiled at Sean and gestured towards the ship model. "Well, O'Connell, what do you say to my proposal? Are you willing to become the first captain of the *Sea Rose*?"

The *Sea Rose*. Sean stared at the tiny carved figurehead of a young woman on the prow, staring boldly out to sea. Her large nose and flowing hair reminded him of his sister.

"It would be my honor, sir."

* * *

Arthur Horn had led a miserable life. Born in Hamburg, Germany, he'd immigrated with his parents to New York City at age six. Two years later he and his parents fell sick with smallpox. He survived but both of his parents had died. With no older siblings or other family to help him, the young orphan had grown up in harsh world of the muddy, dusty streets of New York, spending most of his time as a pickpocket to survive. Finally caught by the police, he was sent to an orphanage, a damp smelly cold house where he and the other children were frequently beaten and never had enough to eat. It was funded by charity and the headmaster was a brutal man who took an instant dislike to Arthur, making fun of his German accent and pointing at the smallpox scars on his face, and telling him he was the ugliest boy he'd ever seen.

Of course, his name wasn't Arthur Horn then. It was Wilhelm Kruger.

All the other boys taunted young Wilhelm too. It made him full of hate. He hated them; he hated being German and he hated his parents for dying and leaving him pitted with scars; he hated schoolwork and refused to learn how to read and write and do his numbers. He kept running away and getting caught and sent back. Each time the headmaster punished him through pain and humiliation. He made Wilhelm drop his pants in front of the class as he struck his bare buttocks soundly with a large wooden ruler. Then he was locked in the damp cellar for twenty four hours without anything but water.

Wilhelm was tall for his age, and wiry, and one day when he was eleven, he'd had enough. During another beating, he whirled around, grabbed the end of the ruler and twisted it free. In a rage, he smashed it across the headmaster's surprised face, then ran out of the house, and climbed over the iron fence that surrounded the grounds of the orphanage.

He would always remember the cheers and applause from the boys he left behind. Although they never liked him, he had won their admiration that day.

He headed for the waterfront. Ever since he could remember, he wanted to be a sailor. He ran up the gangplank of the first ship he saw and asked if he could sign on as a cabin boy. By that time he had lost his German accent, and since he had already discovered that Germans, along with the Irish, the Poles, the Italians, the Indians and the black Africans were considered subhuman in America, it was best to start his new life as an English boy.

Wilhelm decided to change his name. He remembered a story he'd liked from the orphanage, the story of King Arthur and the Roundtable. So, he chose the first name of Arthur. Since he'd always wanted to sail around Cape Horn, he decided that Horn would be a suitable surname for a sailor. Thus, he became Arthur Horn.

Although life at sea was hard, it wasn't as bad as the orphanage. In the years that followed, he became a seasoned sailor, fearing neither God nor man, nor any storm that blew his direction. By the time he was thirty, he had worked his way up to first mate on the *Eastern Wind*. His only goal left in life, was to be a captain of a ship.

When Captain Smythe had been slaughtered by the Nootkas, it had become a dream come true for Horn, but a dream that soon turned into a nightmare.

The day after the *Eastern Wind* docked in Boston, Horn was finally set free of his months of imprisonment below decks. He had lost a great deal of weight, his bony pockmarked face grown even more skeletal, his eyes sunken into their sockets, their stare full of a burning hatred for the two men he considered responsible for destroying his once promising career at sea, John Hill and Sean O'Connell.

As he walked away from the ship he'd once commanded, practically penniless instead of rewarded with a captain's pay, all he could think of was revenge. He didn't know how long it would take, or what he'd have to do, but he vowed there was going to come a day when he made both of those men wish they had never been born.

It didn't take him long to find out where the Hill family lived, with all the other rich nobs that owned ships. The next week he divided his time by watching the activities of the family during the day, and by frequenting the waterfront taverns at night, looking for possible work. He soon discovered that no honest captain wanted to hire the likes of him.

His anger grew deeper, more intense. It was there every morning when he awoke in his dirty lice ridden cot in the rat-infested sailors boardinghouse, and it was there at night in his dreams, haunting him like a dark demon. He found he could barely choke down a bite of food without wishing it was Hill or O'Connell choking to death.

By the end of the week he was down to just a few coins in his pocket. Then he got lucky. One night, drinking a pint of ale in the Sea Hag Tavern, he heard that the first mate of the *Jupiter* had been stabbed to death in a knife fight, and the captain was searching for a replacement. He remembered seeing the *Jupiter* once, somewhere off the Maryland coast. She was a sleek black-hulled schooner, rumored to be a privateer, running illegal rum and slaves from the West Indies to hidden coves off Florida and the Carolinas where the contraband was sold for rich profit.

Horn knew smuggling was dangerous. If caught, it was the hangman's noose around your neck. Yet, it was quicker, easier money than the long voyages of a Boston fur trader, and Horn wanted to get rich as fast as he could.

Finishing off his pint, he glanced around the dim smoky tavern, reeking of salt, sweat, rotten fish, and beer. The young tavern wench caught his eye. She looked about sixteen, with long stringy brown hair and a pimply face. She had a nice figure though, he noticed, unlike that beanpole of a haughty young woman he'd seen visiting the Hill mansion the day before, the one that John Hill was going to marry.

He was hoping to find out where she lived and luck had been with him once again. Yesterday evening Hill had walked her home instead of calling for the carriage. He had followed them at a discreet distance, thanking his lucky stars that Hill's former companion, the huge Gregory Jones, had disappeared into the taverns and brothels of Boston to spend his pay instead of accompanying Hill everywhere.

After a half mile the couple turned into a long driveway shaded by enormous oak trees. He hid himself easily in the shadows of the trees, watching them disappear inside the three story mansion. The next couple of hours he spent walking around the perfectly landscaped grounds, staring into the windows, trying to discover which room might be hers, hoping it wasn't on the upper floor.

He was amazed at the lack of security on the premises, no guard dogs, and no servants keeping an eye on things. Windows were wide open to catch the evening breeze off the harbor after the heat of the day, like an invitation welcoming intruders.

Around midnight, a light went on in a second story room in the rear of the house. Standing in the pitch blackness, under a large oak tree, Horn could easily look through the window and see the young woman undressing. When she was down to her thin white chemise she began to unfasten her hair. A cascade of rich auburn curls tumbled across her bare shoulders and down to her waist.

Beads of sweat broke out on Horn's brow and he trembled slightly. *Not yet*, he'd told himself. *Patience*.

Her window opened onto a small balcony. Horn noticed one of the thick branches of the oak tree extended past the balcony. It would be so easy to climb the tree and use the branch to get to the balcony. After that.... he fingered the sharp knife he always carried in a sheath attached to his belt, and licked his lips in anticipation.

Her name was Abigail Simpson. He remembered that from a conversation he'd overheard on the *Eastern Wind* after they had rescued Hill from the Nootkas.

"Hey, Mistah, do ya want another pint?"

The young tavern maid was standing next to his table, her mouth pulled back in a polite smile, showing her crooked yellow teeth. As he hesitated, she lowered her eyes in a flirtatious manner and wiggled her ample hips and bosom in his face. "Or tis somethin' else ya might be wantin'?"

He stood up and flung a coin down on the greasy rough hewn wooden table in disgust. "I got me somethin' better'n you, ya ugly wench."

She drew back in surprise then snarled an obscenity at him as he exited the tavern. That angered him, and if he didn't have plans he would have waited until she was off work, then taught her a lesson she'd never forget. But he had two important visits to make that night.

First, he was going to find the captain of the *Jupiter* and sign on as the first mate. Then he was going to pay Miss Abigail Simpson a visit and teach her and John Hill a lesson they would never forget.

CHAPTER EIGHT

Two weeks before Tatiana was to leave for Saint Petersburg and her voyage to Russian America, the maid Sonya was found. It was a sultry evening and Anna was helping Tatiana prepare for bed. They were in the midst of their nightly ritual, Anna brushing Tatiana's waist-length hair one hundred strokes before twisting the heavy strands into a long golden braid, when Olga came bursting in the room.

"I have news, Cousin!" she exclaimed.

"Don't you ever knock?" demanded Tatiana irritably. "What's so important that it can't wait until morning?"

"Papa said to tell you that they have your maid Sonya locked up in the cellar. He wants you to decide the proper punishment for her and tell him tomorrow at breakfast."

Tatiana jerked her head away from the hairbrush in Anna's hand and laughed delightedly. "That is wonderful news indeed! Wherever did they find her?"

"In the serfs' village where we first suspected. It seems the old healing woman had hidden Sonya behind her hovel in some bushes when Papa had his men search her place. And that's why they didn't find her then. Eventually Sonya had grown careless, thinking we had given up the search. One of the kitchen maids saw her walking in the village yesterday and told Cook."

Anna didn't like the excited predatory gleam in Tatiana's eyes and she said, "What are you going to do to the girl, *Mademoiselle*?"

"You should have her whipped again," said Olga.

Tatiana considered. "How many times?"

"At least ten, perhaps twenty lashes."

Anna gasped. "But that could kill her!"

Olga shot her a threatening look. "Who are you to question us, anyway? Just another maid like Sonya, dispensable and stupid."

Tatiana laughed slightly. "Oh, Anna, isn't stupid, Olga. She's actually a well educated girl who is working for me only temporarily. When I leave for Saint Petersburg in two weeks, she'll be sent home to her Mennonite village."

"How dull!" exclaimed Olga then shrugged her broad shoulders.

For once Anna agreed with Olga. Life in Furstenau or at Silberfeld would be dull indeed, but much more peaceful after working for the Bolkonskys. The past two weeks had been like living in another world entirely; the bewildering array of rich foods she'd never seen or tasted, the heavy drinking of wine and vodka by both the family and the servants, and the strict hierarchy of the servants themselves. Count Bolkonsky had three personal valets to attend to his needs alone. Then there were the footmen, dishwashers, lamplighters, laundry women and housekeeping maids, all under the watchful eye of the chief steward. There was Cook and two lesser cooks under her besides numerous kitchen maids. Outdoors there were more gardeners than she could count, and in the stable, coachmen, grooms and stable boys.

There were so many new faces and names to put together, and since most of them viewed Anna as that "odd Mennonite girl," she kept herself aloof from them, staying mostly in the house on the upper floors with Tatiana, Olga and her snooty French maid, Colette, and *Madame* Frabert, who was always kind to her.

All of the male servants were splendidly dressed in white livery and the female servants wore black dresses with white aprons and caps, similar to the style of clothing Anna was used to as a Mennonite girl. However, nothing in her life had prepared her for the excesses of clothing Tatiana had. Countless gowns and frocks hung in immense wardrobes with row after row of dainty shoes and slippers. In chests with drawers there were pairs of gloves by the dozens in boxes lined with white satin, endless pairs of stockings and white petticoats, delicate muslin under things and chemises, laces, feathers, ribbons, fine handkerchiefs in rose-scented sachets and Chinese silk fans. On Tatiana's dressing table were hairpins, combs, soaps, perfumes and a beautiful crystal bottle of expensive eau-de-Cologne from Paris.

Anna was kept busy from sunrise to late at night, making certain every item of clothing was clean and pressed in preparation for whenever Tatiana might wish to wear them. It was a tremendous responsibility. No wonder she changed maids as frequently as she did her gowns and shoes, Anna often thought. As it was, she drew on all her experience in managing the Teichroew household and her duties as housekeeper at Silberfeld to keep herself so organized and efficient that Tatiana rarely found fault with her.

"Perhaps I shall bring Anna with me," said Tatiana, a smile playing around the sweet curve of her lips. "So far, she has been the best maid I've ever had."

Olga glanced at Anna and barked an obnoxious laugh. "Just be careful she doesn't convert you to her strange religion," she said, then added, "Good night, Cousin. See you in the morning at breakfast."

After Olga left, leaving a sour taste in Anna's mouth, she went to turn down the covers of Tatiana's bed. Her mistress seemed in good spirits, humming tunelessly as Anna then helped her into her fine linen nightgown, edged in soft lace.

When Tatiana wished her goodnight Anna hesitated then said, "*Mademoiselle*, are you really going to have Sonya whipped tomorrow?"

"Yes, what of it?" she said flippantly then bit her lip gently as she studied Anna's face. "Don't worry, Anna. I'd never do that to you. Like I told Olga, you are the best maid I've had in a long time."

"It's not that, *Mademoiselle*, it's just--it's just that Jesus teaches us to forgive those who wronged us and-- "

"I don't want to hear it, Anna!" Tatiana spoke sharply. "I don't care what your Jesus teaches. You might as well know right here and now that I don't believe in God. When I attend church it's for appearance's sake and my duty as a Bolkonsky and for no other reason."

Anna appeared stunned at this confession. In her whole life she had never met or heard of anyone who didn't believe in God.

"And furthermore, Anna, if I don't punish Sonya as she rightly deserves for running away, the other servants and serfs will think they are free to leave without fear of reprisal. And that would not do at all."

"Perhaps if you showed the girl some mercy, *Mademoiselle*, all your serfs and servants would learn to love you instead of fear you."

Tatiana made an unladylike snort. "Love! What does that mean anyway? It's just a stupid emotion that makes you vulnerable to others. I don't care if they love me or hate me. All I ask is that they obey me, and that includes you, too, Anna."

"Yes, *Mademoiselle*, I understand that. Jesus also teaches that slaves should obey their masters and--"

"Anna," interrupted Tatiana, "if that is true, then I order you to cease telling me anything which your God teaches, is that understood?"

Anna nodded sadly and turned to leave. "Good night then, *Mademoiselle*. I hope you sleep well, and I will pray that you have a change of heart concerning Sonya."

She blew out the candles, plunging the bedchamber into darkness as Tatiana muttered, "Anna, you are trying my patience."

Alone in her small room adjacent to Tatiana's room, Anna knelt at her bedside and said her usual bedtime prayers, remembering each of her family by name, then added in a whisper, "Dear Lord, if it is Your will, please intervene tomorrow and spare poor Sonya any further harm."

* * *

The next morning dawned bright and sunny, a fine day for a whipping, or a picnic, Tatiana told Anna as she was helping her get dressed.

"After this business with Sonya is taken care of, Anna, I will ask Olga to bring Colette and we can have a nice picnic lunch down by the river this afternoon, just the four of us."

Nodding nervously, Anna swallowed, a thick lump of dread sticking in her throat as she marveled at her mistress's hard heart. It would be nothing short of a miracle to get her to change her mind about punishing the poor maid.

The Count summoned all the house and outdoor servants to watch, a group of near one hundred people. They crowded behind the stable where the punishment was to take place. Some of them looked angry, some frightened, but most had no expression at all, just empty looks of resignation.

Anna stood near Tatiana, Olga, and Colette, her gaze riveted on the trembling, sobbing young girl whose hands and wrists were tied around a fence post. She was begging in Russian, "*Nyet, Nyet*----"

The girl was about fifteen, small-boned and slender with long blond braids, and would have been considered very pretty if not for her swollen red eyes and dirty clothes and face. One of the grooms, a burly fellow with meaty arms, held a long black whip in his big hands. As the girl cried louder he grinned in anticipation, his mouth missing several front teeth.

The Count looked at Tatiana. "You may give the order to begin whenever you wish, and it is your decision as to when she's had enough." He stirred impatiently, obviously wishing the spectacle over and done with, so he could get on with his day.

All eyes turned to Tatiana, who in her white muslin gown with her pale golden hair, appeared as beautiful and gentle as an angel. A dark angel with a deadly power, thought Anna, sending a quick prayer of desperation heavenward.

Tatiana glanced at Anna and saw the pleading in her eyes, as if she was silently begging her to call a halt to the distasteful proceedings. For a moment it caught her off balance then she raised her head and stared coldly at the groom. "Begin!" she called out.

The groom raised his arm and brought it down with a crack. Horrified, Anna saw a thin red line slice through the back of Sonya's dress as the girl let out an ear splitting scream. She jerked against the fence post as another crack resounded and a second line appeared. If it was possible, she screamed even louder.

Anna wanted to close her eyes, but found her eyelids wouldn't obey, and when the whip snaked down the third time, there was nothing she could do to block out the sound coming from the girl's mouth, like an animal in terrible pain.

At this point Tatiana felt her stomach roll in a spasm of nausea. She looked at Olga to see how she was reacting. To her disgust Olga was smiling, the same sort of cruel smile that she saw on Mikael's face when they were children and he was mercilessly teasing her; probably the same cruel smile on his face when he'd tossed her kitten out the window. Was that what she had become? Exactly like Mikael? She shuddered, her head beginning to ache.

Then she saw the old woman, the village healer. She was hunched over by a group of serfs who were holding her up, a tiny wrinkled elf, so frail it looked like a breeze would knock her over. The old crone was staring at her, her eyes like two shining black buttons that seemed to pierce right into her heart. She reminded Tatiana of someone. Someone she knew a long long time ago, her grandmother. And she was wearing the same expression of sad disapproval that Nana had when she'd misbehaved as a child.

Her grandmother would despise what she was doing. And maybe her father would as well. Nana always said what a kind man he was. Tatiana looked at Anna. Her maid was as pale as the full moon and there were tears running down her cheeks. Then their eyes met, and Tatiana saw the compassion and pity in her maid's face. Not just for Sonya, but also for her, Tatiana Nikolayevna Bolkonsky.

She suddenly saw herself as they must, a hard cruel young woman. But she wasn't like that, really. She knew she wasn't, but how to convince them?

"Stop it!" she heard herself shout. "That's enough!"

The whip halted in midair and the groom whirled around in surprise. The Count also seemed startled. "Are you sure, Tatiana? That was only five lashes."

The girl's cries had subsided to deep guttural moans as Tatiana said, "She's learned her lesson, Uncle. Please have them untie her and take her away."

Olga frowned in disappointment. "But she deserves at least ten more lashes, Tatiana."

"Perhaps, but I am coming down with one of my beastly headaches, and I can't stand out here any longer." She glanced at the Count. "Uncle Vasily, you said I was to determine her punishment. So, I ask that instead of anymore of this--this whipping, you just send her out to work in the wheat fields. Digging in the dirt in the heat the rest of the summer should be punishment enough for a former chambermaid."

The Count shook his head then shrugged. "Whatever you wish, my dear."

Anna smiled at her mistress as they returned to the house. "Do you want me to make you some of my special tea for your headache, *Mademoiselle*?"

Tatiana pressed her hands to her temples and nodded. "Yes, Anna."

"I am so proud of you, *Mademoiselle*."

Tatiana halted and stared at her. "What do you mean?"

"I think you showed strength of character by stopping such inhumane punishment and granting mercy to poor Sonya."

"Is that what it was?" asked Olga rushing up behind them, "strength of character? If you ask me, I think it showed a weakness of character, a certain squeamishness that a true Bolkonsky wouldn't have."

"Nobody asked you Olga, "retorted Tatiana. "Now if you want to stay in my good graces, you will drop this entire subject. Otherwise, I will not invite you and Colette to accompany me and Anna on a picnic this afternoon."

Olga scowled but fell silent as the prospect of a picnic, however childish, was more interesting then spending the rest of the day having *Madame* Frabert making her stand still for hours while she measured her for another new dress for her wedding trousseau. Just a couple more weeks, she kept telling herself, until Tatiana left for Russian America. Then her papa would be devoting all his attention to her the rest of the summer instead of to Tatiana.

After her mama died, it seemed her papa could never say no to her cousin. Olga assumed that was because her papa had a weakness for pretty women. But the way Tatiana had her papa wrapped around her little finger, it was like she was the daughter of Count Vasily Bolkonsky, instead of herself.

When September came Olga would be married to Count Vladimir Kornilov, the beginning of a brand new life where she would not be living in the shadow of her beautiful cousin. She could hardly wait.

Three hours later after Tatiana's headache finally ebbed away, the four girls strolled through the lush green lawns and forested park surrounding the house to the Dnieper River. Both Anna and Colette each carried a wicker basket, one containing food, the other bottles of lemonade and white wine.

Anna spread a blue and white checkered tablecloth on the grass near the riverbank shaded by oak and chestnut trees. Olga told Colette to take the bottles down to the river and let them cool in the water before drinking.

The two made an incongruous pair, the heavy dark haired Olga and her dainty blond maid. Colette had wide set blue eyes and would have been pretty if not for her long pointed nose and her lips that were usually pursed in an expression of perpetual disapproval. With a pained look on her face, she made her way gingerly down the muddy bank to the river to place the bottles of lemonade and wine in the water to chill. As it was midsummer the river was running low and murky, and there was a tiny pool near a small sandy beach edge where the bottles would not float away.

The French maid returned with a frown of dismay as she wiped at the mud clinging to her thin slippers. She was always fussing about everything, being a totally fastidious person. "Peekneeks are so bourgeois," she said, rolling her eyes in an exaggerated motion.

Tatiana giggled at her. "If you don't like the mud, Colette, have Anna fetch the bottles later. She grew up on a farm and she's used to it."

"*Oui*, *Mademoiselle*, that is a fine idea. I'll serve the luncheon."

Tatiana and Olga wore simple frocks, so they could sit on the ground and not be concerned about grass stains and dirt. As if they would anyway, Anna thought dryly. When they dirtied a gown it was easily replaced by another.

She helped Colette slice cold chicken and ham and set out the golden crusted bread with strawberry preserves, pastries, cheese, fresh peaches, and for Olga, some French chocolates, which were melting slightly.

As Anna ate she breathed deeply of the sweet smelling grass dotted with wild daisies and bellflowers and the fresh watery scent of the river. "My brothers and I used to swim in the river on hot days," she said, looking longingly at the water. A pang of sudden homesickness swept over her as she remembered those carefree summer days as a child. Thank goodness she would be going back to Silberfeld soon.

A letter had arrived for her two days ago from Uncle Heinrich and *Tante* Sarah. They'd written that when her papa and Jack had come to fetch her home, and were told she'd gone to work for the nobility, they'd both reacted differently. Her papa was very angry, saying she'd disobeyed him and had humiliated the family name. He said it was likely Gerhard might change his mind about the marriage. Jack wasn't upset at all, but had asked many questions about the Bolkonskys. When he'd mentioned he'd like to pay her a visit, her papa refused to allow it. He also said he thought it best she stay in Silberfeld after her employment with the Bolkonskys had terminated, unless Gerhard still wished to marry her. Then they both departed for Furstenau.

"Anna," said Colette as she neatly bit into a piece of chicken and wiped her thin lips with a blue and white checkered napkin. "Did you not catch your death of a cold swimming in the river?"

"No, but we used to get quite muddy. Mama didn't appreciate that."

Tatiana looked at her with a hint of admiration. "So can you really swim, Anna?"

"My brother Jack and I learned together when we were children. Then we taught my two younger twin brothers, Jacob and Peter. Have you never tried swimming, *Mademoiselle*?"

Olga let out a guffaw as she chomped down on a chicken leg, spraying bits of chicken onto the tablecloth. "Can you imagine my mama's face if we had gone swimming, Tatiana?"

"I think it would have given Aunt Irene a heart attack."

Olga almost choked on her chicken. "How dare you make fun of how Mama died! What a terrible thing to say!"

For the first time since Anna had come to the Bolkonskys, she saw Tatiana look ashamed. "I apologize, Olga. I spoke without thinking, truly."

Olga turned her face away, but not before Tatiana saw a glimmer of tears in them. Knowing that her cousin needed a moment to get her emotions under control she motioned to Anna. "I think we could all use a drink."

Anna jumped up and made her way down the path towards the river bank to the bit of sandy beach. The two bottles were still in the tiny pool, now well chilled. As she carried them back she suddenly noticed that the three girls had gone very still, their faces drained of all color. They were staring at the tablecloth like it had suddenly sprouted horns and a tail.

"Is something wrong?" she asked as she approached. No one answered her, but Colette made a funny gurgle in her throat.

Anna glanced down and froze in horror. A long thick black snake was crawling onto the tablecloth, its flat head moving back and forth, its tongue flickering, as it smelled the scent of the chicken and ham.

"Don't anyone move," she said softly, her lifelong fear of snakes striking terror into her heart, making her pulse race as sweat broke out in her armpits. What should they do? she thought, her limbs beginning to tremble. If she started screaming, if any of them started screaming to get the attention of someone nearby, they would startle the snake and it might bite one of them. Was it poisonous? She knew some of the black snakes were and some not. As she studied it, a memory came rushing back, her papa chopping off the head of a big black snake with an ax.

Frantically she glanced around. They had no ax. Yet there was a large knife in the one of the wicker baskets they used to slice the meat. When the snake wasn't looking in her direction, she began to back away, very, very slowly.

Three pairs of frightened eyes watched her as she cautiously edged the several yards to the wicker basket and found the knife. Meanwhile, the snake began to coil up in a black circle, deciding it had found the perfect place to eat and take a nap.

Creeping ever so quietly, she came closer, holding the knife in her hand. She knew she had one chance and one chance only. If she missed, she didn't know what would happen.

Anna took a deep breath, praying silently, "Jesus, please help me."

The snake looked at her for a second with its black opaque eyes then its empty gaze slid away. With one quick decisive motion she flung the knife straight at its face. The sharp point of the blade hit the snake right behind its head, went through the tablecloth, and pinned it to the ground. Red blood spurted out of the wound as the snake began to thrash its long shining dark body all over the food, trying to free itself from the knife point.

Tatiana, Olga, and Colette all let out one gigantic scream simultaneously as they sprang to their feet and fled from the death throes of the snake. Colette managed to get only a few yards before swooning into a faint.

Anna couldn't believe what she had just done. Paralyzed with shock and a sick fascination, she was unable to tear her gaze away. The snake was barely moving now, and she could tell it was nearly dead.

She had never killed any living creature larger than a spider before. How had she done it? But she hadn't. Not on her own. She was convinced God had helped her, just like He had softened Tatiana's heart towards poor Sonya earlier that day. Two answers to prayer in just a few short hours. How she wished she could share all this with her mama! Her heart filled with gratitude to the Lord, and she closed her eyes briefly and thanked Him.

Later that same evening, Count Bolkonsky took Tatiana aside and said, "My dear, your little maid is quite the brave heroine. I think you should seriously consider taking her with you to Russian America. Anyone who is that skilled with a knife could come in quite handy in a foreign land *Frau*ght with wild savages and beasts."

Tatiana shivered, remembering the nightmarish picnic that afternoon. "I still can't believe Anna killed such a huge snake. When you first sent her to me I thought what a timid little mouse she was. And her religious talk can be so wearisome I was looking forward to finding a French maid like Colette when we return to Saint Petersburg. But after today I think you are right, Uncle Vasily. Where I'm going I might need a maid like Anna. So how can I persuade her to come? She is determined to return to her family."

With one finger he stroked his gray mustache thoughtfully then a slight sinister smile broke across his aristocratic face. "You can leave that little problem to me, my dear. I promise you, when we leave here in two weeks time, Anna will be coming with us."

* * *

John Hill collapsed his head into his hands and wept, trying Sean's patience for the hundredth time in the past week. It wasn't that he didn't feel for the man. It's just that there wasn't anything more to be done, and crying in his beer wasn't going to change a thing. What's done was done.

He and John, Ethan, and Gregory Jones were all having one last night out before the *Sea Rose* sailed at first light. The tavern, the Lucky Clover, was a favorite haunt of theirs, serving better food than most for a good price. As with all taverns the atmosphere was ripe with smoke from pipes and the ill-kept lanterns, ale fumes and the raucous laughter of drunken sailors. Often a quarrel broke out, but before any real damage could be done, the proprietor, a giant of an Irishman who always kept a pistol tucked in his belt, would put a stop to it by throwing out the instigator, or if that wasn't easily determined, all the offending parties. He was called One Eyed Mike because he'd lost an eye years ago when a malfunctioning musket had exploded in his face.

One Eye had known Sean's father. "A 'ard worker yer da was," he told Sean once, "till the drink got to 'im. Right sorry shame bout 'im killin' 'imself. Wouldn't 'ave thought it o' Black Paddy, but too much whisky can make a man lose 'is mind. Sorry lad."

Sean had grunted in reply, and changed the subject. To his great relief One Eye never mentioned his da again. So far Sean had spent his time in

Boston without thinking about his family or dreaming about them, and he wanted to keep it that way.

Of course it helped to have someone else's tragedy to dwell on rather than his own life. John had been inconsolable ever since the night Abigail had been attacked when she was sleeping in her own bed. Someone had climbed into her room through the open window and tied her up and gagged her, then slashed her nose with a knife, slitting both of her nostrils wide open. The instant he'd heard the terrible news Sean knew it was Arthur Horn. It was his favorite method of dealing with women.

"Tis my fault," John was moaning, "all my fault. If I'd pressed assault charges on Horn when we docked, he'd be locked up in jail and it never would've happened."

The four men looked at John sympathetically, having heard it all many times the past days. There wasn't much left for any of them to say. The police had been searching for Horn all over the city, but there wasn't a trace of him anywhere. Rumors on the docks said he'd signed on the privateer, *Jupiter*, and if that was true, then he was long gone from Boston.

Meanwhile Abigail had been cloistered in the Simpson's home and refused to see anyone except her parents and her doctor. She especially refused to see John. Finally that very morning a letter from Abigail was delivered to him.

"She said she was breaking off our engagement. She said her face was ruined forever and she never wanted me to see her again."

"The lass needs time to heal, man," said Ethan.

"How much time?" John demanded angrily, gulping another glass of whisky. "If I ever see Horn's ugly face again I'm going to kill him!"

"Not unless any of us lads get our 'ands on 'im first," said Jones, his broad face flushing in suppressed rage.

All the men said, "Aye, aye" to that, as One Eyed Mike brought another round of drinks. Sean and Ethan exchanged glances of mutual pity for John over their mugs of tea then Ethan mouthed the word, "Supercargo."

Sean stared blankly at his friend for a moment before realization hit. He smiled at John. "Hey, mate, what do ye say to signin' on the *Sea Rose* as supercargo and sailin' with us first thing in the mornin'?"

John raised his weary bloodshot eyes to Sean's face. "But you already have a supercargo."

"I had a man in mind, but he told me this mornin' that his wife was so sick he couldn't leave her with five bairns to look after."

"I don't know. What about Abby? Even though she doesn't want to see me, I wouldn't feel right to leave her in such a state."

Ethan looked at him thoughtfully. "Puttin' some time an' miles between the lass an' ye might be good, John. When we get back, she might be thinkin' different 'bout things."

John fell silent, considering, while Sean wondered if any amount of time could heal a woman damaged as physically and emotionally as Abigail. Some wounds time could heal; some wounds never healed. Wincing inside, Sean thought of his father and how he died.

John tapped himself on his head, like he was trying to clear out the cobwebs. "I should know this, Sean, but lately I haven't been able to think about anything but Abby. So, besides you and Ethan, who are the officers and crew of the *Sea Rose*?"

"Besides the usual motley assortment of ordinary seamen, our second mate is Ned Johnson, an' Jake O'Riley is the third. Wang Li is the cook of course, an' we 'ave two new cabin boys, twin brothers Jimmy an' Robby, both thirteen years old. An' then you won't believe this, but Edward Smythe's former slave, Samuel, has signed on to be me steward. It seems that when Captain Smythe's will was read to his widow, instructions were that if Samuel should outlive Smythe, he was to be given his manumission papers, his freedom. After Mistress Smythe set Samuel free, the first thing he did was find me an' ask to go to sea again. He said there was nothin' for him on land since he had no idea where his sister was. I told him I would hire a private investigator to try an' find her. I'm hopin' that when we return, he'll have some news for us."

"An' I'm the ship's armorer," said Jones with a big grin. "Ol' Ben Green retired. He said the *Eastern Wind* 'ad been 'is ship as long as he could remember, an' since she was being scrapped, he'd 'ad enough of the sea. Said he doesn't trust these newfangled clipper ships. It'll be like old times, exceptin' we won't be captured by Injuns."

The anguish in John's blue eyes lessened slightly and he looked more alive than he had in days. "Count me in, men," he said firmly.

Hours later on board the *Sea Rose* as John was stowing his gear away in the cabin he was sharing with Jones, Sean asked him how it went with his uncle and aunt.

"Aunt Priscilla started to cry, but my uncle shook my hand and wished me well. He said I was making the right decision, that it was best for me to leave Boston under the circumstances. He said he hoped when I returned, Abigail will have recovered enough to want to see me. I know they are both bitterly disappointed that the engagement is off."

John hung his head briefly then looked up and met Sean's gaze, "But I have to tell you the truth, there's a part of me that is relieved we aren't getting married."

"I'd guessed that the first time I saw the two of ye together, John."

"Was it that obvious?"

"To me it was. I don't know about anyone else."

"I've known Abby all my life; we practically grew up together. It was always understood that someday we would get married. But after being with the Nootkas, something changed inside me. I believe I actually fell in love with my young wife there. You might think I'm crazy, but sometimes I think I can still hear her crying out for me." He gave a deep sigh.

"I like Abby and admire her strong convictions and work with the Quaker abolitionists, but to be honest, I don't love her like she loves me. Now after what happened to her, I feel so guilty. You must think I'm a stupid man."

Sean smiled slightly. "I'm the last person to judge you about women, John. I prefer to love em' and leave 'em."

"So now I'm consumed with guilt," he said with a frown. "And guilt is a heavy burden for a man to carry around."

As I know well, thought Sean soberly.

CHAPTER NINE

The relationship had altered between Anna and her mistress. No longer did Tatiana order her around so imperiously, but rather her commands were punctuated by surprising terms such as, "please" and "thank you." If Anna hadn't seen her still treating the rest of the servants with her usual haughty coldness, she would have thought Tatiana was becoming a softer, kinder person.

It was the same with the rest of the family. Olga stopped making snide remarks about her religious beliefs and the Count even smiled and nodded at her once when they'd passed in the hallway. Some of the servants changed their attitude towards her, as well. Colette, who'd previously stuck her nose up in the air and ignored Anna whenever they met, often chatted away as if they were old friends. It was totally mystifying.

Now that her time with the Bolkonskys was nearing its end, she was surprised to find herself feeling a bit sad about it. She knew she would not miss the decadent ungodly world of theirs but she thought perhaps God had placed her in their household for a reason. She had never seen a family that needed Him more than they.

It wasn't that they weren't religious. Each Sunday they attended the service in the small but beautiful church on the estate. The family sat in the front pew with the servants in the back ones, Anna included. The first time she'd attended she could not help noticing the ornate beauty of the Russian Orthodox Church as compared to the plain structure of her village Mennonite church.

She admired the stained glass windows, creating a colorful glow inside the sanctuary. There were shining icons on the walls and Eucharist vessels made from Spanish silver. The altar was intricately carved and covered with a cloth of gold and Chinese silks, and the vestments were made of the same rich materials.

The parish priest was an elderly white haired man with a beard and solemn dark eyes which always had a faraway look in them as if he was seeing something off in the distance. He recited the liturgy and prayers in a monotonous tone that often put to sleep some of the servants. After two hours of this even Anna had to fight the temptation to doze. He read mainly from the works of the church fathers, and on occasion a few words from the Bible.

Towards the end of each service the priest encouraged everyone to partake of Holy Communion, blessing each one who did by sprinkling a few drops of holy water on their foreheads while making the sign of the cross over them.

After confessing her sins privately, Anna went forward to receive communion with the rest. Tatiana accompanied her with a bored face, and Anna knew she was just going through the motions to please her uncle and to present a good example of piety to the servants and common peasants.

One morning before church she told Anna, "Church is such a waste of time. I can think of a million things I'd rather be doing."

"If you believed in God, you'd feel differently," Anna pointed out.

"When I was a little girl, there was a time I believed in God, and I still hated church. I'll never forget the first time I was forced to make confession to a priest. I was about six or seven, and Aunt Irene brought me to the big church in Saint Petersburg. It was cold and empty, except for the priest waiting for me. I was so terrified of him. The only sin I could think of to confess was that I'd taken a few pieces of chocolate candy. After crying an abundant amount of repentant tears, the priest absolved me of my horrible sin." She shook her head in disgust. "If I had my way, I'd never step foot inside a church again."

"But, *Mademoiselle*, don't you ever worry about dying and what happens after?"

"No, why should I? I was baptized as a baby, so if all this religious nonsense is true, I'll go to heaven, if it exists."

"I was baptized last year when I was sixteen, when I understood what I was doing."

Tatiana looked at her in surprise. "I've never heard of that before. Your odd Mennonite teachings, I suppose?"

"No, actually the Holy Scriptures teach baptism as a public declaration of believing in Jesus. The first example in the Gospels was our Lord Himself when John the Baptist baptized Him in the Jordan River, and the Holy Spirit came down from heaven in the form of a dove and--"

"That's enough, Anna," Tatiana interrupted hastily. "I should know better by now than to ask you a question about your religion. It's like opening the gate to a stampede of horses, something almost impossible to stop."

Anna bowed her head in sudden embarrassment, murmuring her apologies while Tatiana awkwardly patted her shoulder. "No harm done, Anna."

The affectionate gesture surprised her and now as Anna followed Colette and the Bolkonsky family out of the church, she realized why Tatiana was treating her so kindly. The family was leaving for Saint Petersburg in two days. It was obvious that Tatiana wanted her to go with them as her maid.

In a way it was tempting. To be able to travel across Russia to the Imperial City would be an exciting dream come true. But in her heart, all she longed for was to return to Silberfeld. She was anxious to see Uncle Heinrich, *Tante* Sarah, Judith, Maria and lively Helena again, and to hear all the latest news in the family. How were Jack, Peter and Jacob, and little Tina faring this summer? And how was her best friend Susannah?

The last she'd heard Susannah was betrothed and very excited about it. Her beau was Abram Dirkson, a pleasant young man from Furstenau who was training to be a doctor. Anna thought that Susannah would make the perfect doctor's wife. She was happy for her friend, and was looking forward to the wedding in October, the same month Agatha's baby was expected to be born. Somehow that blessed event didn't make Anna as happy even though she knew she should be.

Perhaps having a baby of her own might soften Agatha a bit. One could always hope and pray it would be so, for Tina's and the boys' sakes.

After church the Bolkonsky family, the servants and the villagers all went their separate ways. Anna thought wistfully of how this was the time that her family would gather at someone's house for *faspa* and eat and socialize the afternoon away. At least next Sunday she would be at Silberfeld enjoying the traditional Mennonite feast.

Anna was so engrossed in her memories of home that she wasn't watching where she was going and almost ran into Tatiana and her uncle who were deep in a conversation. They both fell silent when she approached but not before she overheard Tatiana say, "So the die is cast, and now we wait for the cards to be played."

The statement puzzled Anna, but she knew better than to ask questions of the nobility. Perhaps they were just discussing a game of cards, an activity along with dancing and drinking that was forbidden to a Mennonite girl. Yet the times she'd watched Tatiana, Olga and Colette play cards, often shrieking with laughter, she thought it seemed harmless enough.

Later that afternoon Anna was busily setting out the gown Tatiana was to wear for dinner when a kitchen maid came upstairs to tell her she had a visitor waiting outside by the servants' entrance. Surprised, Anna asked to be excused, and Tatiana graciously told her to take all the time she needed. Thanking her, she hurried out, missing the satisfied smile on Tatiana's face.

It was her Uncle Heinrich. He was clearly agitated, pacing restlessly outside the door, his bushy eyebrows furrowed in anxiety.

She greeted him happily, but her smile quickly faded when he said they needed to talk in private. The late afternoon sun was casting long shadows across the lawns as they strolled away from the house toward a grove of trees.

"What is the matter, Uncle?" Anna asked. "I can tell you are troubled. Has something happened to Papa, or the boys, or to Katarina?"

"No, no, child, not to worry. Your family is fine and so are your *Tante* Sarah and the girls. They all send you their love."

He hesitated then frowned. "But your brother Jack arrived a couple hours ago with word from your papa. He needed to warn us."

"A warning?" Anna was startled, but also excited to hear that Jack was close by. She hoped he would stay at Silberfeld for a couple more days so she could see him when she moved back there.

"There is trouble with that young man of yours, Gerhard Yoder."

A feeling of dread came over Anna as she heard the name. "What has happened? What has he done?"

"Jack said your papa recently received a letter from someone on the Bolkonsky estate informing him that you had fallen in love with another man, one of the servants here, and that the two of you are to be married soon. Is this true, Anna?"

Shocked, Anna could only stare at him. Then she said, "Of course not! In the past month I've hardly spoken to any of the men here. Perhaps just a few words now and then. How could he have believed such a thing? I shall write Papa at once and tell him that it is all a lie and---"

"It's too late for that, Anna. Jack said your stepmother, Agatha, showed the letter to *Herr* Yoder, because she knew he was still planning to marry you. He went into a terrible rage, and kicked one of his dogs in the head so hard it died. He has threatened to kill you both, and now he has disappeared from the village. We are afraid he may be hiding hereabouts looking for you."

She was stunned to silence, wondering how Gerhard could be a true Mennonite. She had always thought him a bit cruel-natured, remembering how he laughed when he set his dogs on the defenseless Jewish peddlers. And now he had killed his own dog. But was he capable of cold blooded murder? Her papa seemed to think so, or he wouldn't have let Jack ride a horse all the way from Furstenau with a warning.

"In two days the Bolkonskys are leaving, Uncle Heinrich, and I'll be returning to Silberfeld with you. Surely, nothing bad can happen to me there."

He shook his head, worry shining out of his normally placid eyes. "Anna, I love you. You're my niece. But with this Gerhard, this madman after you, I can't have you staying at my home. It endangers my family. If he can take out his anger against a defenseless animal, what is there to stop him from hurting one of my own daughters?"

Anna thought of sweet little Helena and the twins, Judith and Maria, and found she couldn't bear it if any harm came to them because of her. "If I can't return to Silberfeld or Furstenau, then what can I do?"

He took a deep breath. "You must leave with the Bolkonsky family and go with them to Saint Petersburg. Gerhard will never follow you there."

"But---but---but Uncle Heinrich," Anna stammered in sudden confusion, "if---if I leave with them, that means I might have to accompany Tatiana to Russian America. Then, how can I ever come home again?"

He was silent, and the awful realization slammed into Anna that maybe she could never go home again. A sharp pain seized her heart. "Are you sure there is no other way, Uncle Heinrich?"

"God will watch over you wherever you go, Anna. He will guide your path and keep His angels around you. And when the time is right, if it is His will, you will return safely to us and your home." He embraced her, smiling sadly. "I'll send Jack over here tomorrow morning to see you before he returns to Furstenau. Good-bye, my dearest Anna. May God be with you."

"And you, dearest Uncle," she called after him, sobs choking her throat, wondering if she would ever see him again, wondering how her whole life had turned upside down into this sudden nightmare.

She stumbled back inside the kitchen, not noticing how the cooks and kitchen maids paused briefly in the midst of preparing dinner to stare at her curiously. The smell of the roasting meats and simmering sauces nauseated her and she fled toward the haven of her tiny room, hoping for solitude.

She was thankful to find Tatiana out of her bedchamber, and when she reached her room, she flung herself onto her bed, letting the tears flow freely. Despair filled her entire being, and she felt that her life was truly over.

When the truth came out, that she had never been involved with a Russian servant, she was certain there were those of her village who would not believe it. Agatha and Elder Klassen were two of them, not counting the entire Yoder family. She wouldn't be surprised if Elder Klassen had already condemned her and cast her out of the church. And where was Papa in the midst of all this? Why hadn't he come himself, instead of sending Jack? She knew the answer to that question. Agatha wouldn't allow it.

What would her mama say to all of this? Anna rubbed the tears from her eyes and looked towards her small leather bound black Bible sitting on top of her trunk.

Her mama would tell her to turn to the Bible and read the verse, "*And we know that all things work together for good to them that love God, to them who are called according to his purpose.*"

The words meant that out of the mess her life had become, God had a plan and a purpose. All she had to do was trust Him. It sounded simple, but Anna knew it wasn't. Right now, she was full of hurt, anger, and fear of the future.

How she wished she could feel her mama's comforting arms around her right now. She had never felt so alone in her life.

Time passed as she lay on her bed, sobbing and crying out to God for help. It was in the midst of her pain and tears when suddenly, she heard a quiet voice inside her head say, "*Anna, peace I leave with you, my peace I give unto you...Anna, let not your heart be troubled, neither let it be afraid.*"

She sat up in surprise, her sobs stilled. A gradual feeling of peace began to steal over her and she knew she wasn't alone anymore. Thank you, Jesus, she prayed. Thank you for being here with me.

She rose and poured some water from the pitcher into the basin and washed her face. She could hear Tatiana in the adjoining room, calling out for her to come help her dress for dinner. It was time to quit feeling sorry for herself She had duties to perform.

Yet, one thing puzzled her, the mysterious letter from the Bolkonsky estate. Who had sent it and why?

* * *

Tatiana noticed the red-rimmed swollen eyes of her little maid, and she felt a twinge of guilt. Earlier she had come into her bedchamber and heard the sounds of muffled sobbing coming from Anna's room. At first she felt elated, thinking that Uncle Vasily's plan of ostracizing Anna from her family and village was working.

"There's nothing those Mennonites dislike more than intermarriage with outsiders," he had told her. "If Anna's father believes she's contaminated herself with a Russian man, she will never be welcomed home again. She will have no choice but to stay with us as your maid."

Her uncle was such a clever man, Tatiana was impressed. But now, seeing the anguish in Anna's lovely eyes, she found herself feeling pity for the girl.

"You look a bit peaked, Anna. Who was your visitor? Is everything all right with your family?" she asked in an innocent tone.

"It was my Uncle Heinrich from Silberfeld," Anna answered. "He came to warn me about some trouble I seem to have found myself in, through no fault of my own."

"What kind of trouble? Is it something I can help you with?"

Anna hesitated, not wanting to burden her mistress with all the sordid details about Gerhard Yoder, but then, seeing the unusually concerned look on Tatiana's face, she burst out with the entire story.

Tatiana's surprise was half-pretense, half-genuine. She had expected Anna's family to reject her after receiving the letter, but she hadn't expected this Gerhard Yoder to react in such a violent fashion.

"I will tell Uncle Vasily at once, and he'll set out guards on the estate. *Monsieur* Yoder will never get near you, I promise." Then she added with enthusiasm, "There is one bright spot in all of this, though, Anna."

"And what is that, *Mademoiselle*?"

"You can come with us to Saint Petersburg the day after tomorrow, and then to Russian America. What an exciting adventure it will be!" Tatiana gave her a big smile of encouragement.

Anna struggled to return the smile, though her heart wasn't in it. As she fastened the row of tiny buttons down the back of her mistress's blue silk dinner gown, she said, "I do need to ask you something, *Mademoiselle*. Do you have any idea who might have sent my papa that letter?"

Tatiana felt her ears beginning to burn and was thankful she had her back to Anna, so she could not see her face when she lied, "I don't have a clue, Anna."

* * *

Saint Petersburg nearly took Anna's breath away. Never in her life did she dream of such a splendid city. She had thought Moscow with its stone houses and churches, shop-windows piled high with glittering treasures and crowds of carriages and people was impressive. But nothing had prepared her for the Imperial City of the Czar. Her eyes saw the churches first, the Admiralty with its golden spire, the Cathedral of Saint Isaac with its golden dome, the gold-roofed cathedral in the Peter-Paul fortress on an island in the middle of the Neva River. When Tatiana told her that was where prisoners of the state were kept, the traitors and the spies, and those whose views differed from the czar, the beauty of the cathedral immediately dimmed.

In Senate Square she saw a huge bronze statue of Peter the Great on a rearing horse, trampling a serpent beneath its hooves. She remembered her papa telling her how Czar Peter's obsession with building a city on the swamps by the Neva River had led to the deaths of the thousands of serfs who constructed it.

Tatiana proudly pointed out the Academy of the Arts, considered by many to be the second finest building in the capital next to the Czarina's extravagant Winter Palace. The Academy was situated on the right bank of the Neva opposite the English Quay. It contained a fine collection of foreign and Russian masterpieces exhibited in light, spacious galleries, and an art school boarding two hundred students.

The streets were wide thoroughfares lined with the classical palaces of the nobility. One of them was the Bolkonsky's palatial home located on the English Quay in the Admiralty Quarter, a stone's throw from the Winter Palace. At first sight Anna thought it was the Winter Palace, for she could not imagine a building more magnificent. Six huge white columns were centered in the portico of the palace, its exterior painted a pale rose and white stucco. On the immaculate green lawn in front, stood an eighteenth-century Italian statue of Apollo Belvedere, which to Anna, looked more like an indecent statue of a naked man holding a cloak over his arm than an artwork of sculpture.

Whereas Anna was not intimidated by the Bolkonsky's summer estate, nor even their grand house in Moscow, she was totally cowed by their palace. It was constructed of immense rectangular wings which surrounded a spacious inner courtyard. Marble statues of Greek mythology were placed among the emerald grass of the courtyard, making Anna think of an ancient Greek palace.

Once inside, she would have been lost immediately if not for Colette taking her in hand to Tatiana's lavish apartments upstairs. On the way, she was bewildered by the endless corridors and drawing rooms, which Colette referred to as the Blue Room, the Gold Room, the Crimson Room and so on. On floors of smooth gleaming parquet they walked past richly carved doors, rooms where chandeliers glittered and were furnished with gilded chairs and marble-topped tables. They passed an art gallery of priceless oil paintings by Rubens, Rembrandt and Titian. And everywhere were endless servants, dressed in white, gliding silently about their duties.

It had been a long exhausting trip of hundreds of *versts* to Saint Petersburg. They traveled by *droshky*, a carriage drawn by three horses, in an immense train of wagons with armed escorts. For night they stayed at wayside inns, some clean and decent, some dirty and flea ridden. Instead of the latter, they erected tents, and slept in the fresh air of the outdoors. If Anna's heart had not been so heavy, she would have enjoyed seeing places she had never been before. But as each *verst* passed, she was further away from home, away from her family.

The farewell meeting with Jack had been heartbreaking. He'd met her early, before breakfast, outside near the stable. He was sixteen now and many inches taller than she. His voice had deepened and he was growing a soft beard and slight mustache. With a slight shock she realized he was almost a man.

"I've brought you gifts from Silberfeld," he'd said, his eyes straying past her to the stable where the grooms were feeding oats to the handsome Bolkonsky horses. "*Tante* Sarah said to tell you the workers miss you and here are some tokens of their affections."

She was pleasantly surprised when he gave her several colorful handkerchiefs, painstakingly embroidered by the peasant women she had once helped to feed. There was also a package from her aunt that included a bag of freshly baked *twaback* and a jar of peach preserves.

"For the journey," he said with a sad smile.

"Oh, Jack, I shall miss you so much," she exclaimed and hugged him tightly. "I wish I didn't have to go. I wish none of this had happened."

"Me, too, Anna, but Papa and Uncle Heinrich are right. You are in danger from Gerhard."

"Who brought that letter to Papa?"

"We found the letter in an envelope two days ago at first light, by the front door where someone had placed it. We never saw who brought it, although Tina said the dogs woke her up during the night, growling, and when she got up, she heard a horse trotting out of the yard."

"Did anyone sign the letter?"

"It was signed, 'from a friend.' There was no name."

"Was the letter written in feminine hand writing?" Anna could not help a suspicion that Tatiana or Olga could have written it.

"I saw it only briefly, but the writing looked more like the bold strokes of a man. It was written on a thick cream colored paper of a higher quality than any we have in the village. Do you have any idea who might have sent it?"

She shook her head. "No, but it seems someone here wants to cause trouble for me."

Jack frowned, glancing around the stable yard. "I thought it was suspicious from the very beginning and Papa did, too. He told Agatha that it could all be a falsehood, but Agatha kept saying she thought it could be true and Gerhard should know. After Papa went to work in the fields, she walked over to the Yoders. First she showed the letter to *Frau* Yoder, who immediately started to screech for Gerhard. He hadn't left for the blacksmith shop yet, and when he read the letter, he threw it into the fire and went into such a terrible rage, Agatha said she ran out of their house in fright. Later we heard that he had taken his anger out on one of his dogs, and no one has seen him since. When Papa found out what Agatha did, he became so angry with her, she started to cry."

Then he added with a satisfied tone, "I think it was their first quarrel."

"Oh, Jack, what trouble this is for everyone," sighed Anna. "So, it's probably best that I leave with the Bolkonsky family. But I will miss all of you more than you know. Please tell Papa, and Jacob and Peter, and little Tina that I love them with all my heart, and I will come back someday."

* * *

They left Ekaterineslav the next morning. Anna shared a *droshky* with Tatiana, Olga, and Colette. As the days passed, she remembered how her Mennonite ancestors from Prussia had traveled these same great distances in their crude wagon trains pulled by plodding oxen. They didn't have swift horses like the Bolkonskys nor armed men to ward off wild animals, thieves or bands of marauding Tartars. But God had watched over them all, and brought them to their new homes in southern Russia near the Black Sea. The thought brought her some comfort in her grief.

Anna had never been off the steppes. Putting her emotions aside, she was fascinated as the vast grasslands gradually disappeared and forests of beech, elms, oaks and other deciduous trees took their place. The further north they went the forests deepened into thick evergreens and pines, and finally as they reached Saint Petersburg, the land became full of swamps and murky bogs. The city itself was built upon several islands on low and marshy ground in the middle of an immense forest.

Rainfall was much heavier in the north, and Anna was hardly prepared for the sticky humidity of Saint Petersburg after living her whole life in the drier climate of the south. She noticed the city had a foul odor, wafting from the stagnant sewage infested water in the many canals, and there were dark clouds of mosquitoes each evening that descended like an avenging horde on anyone caught outside.

Tatiana told her Saint Petersburg was the most beautiful in the winter when the Neva River froze and snow covered the streets. The nobility would parade the river daily in their handsome sledges, highly decorated in red, green, gold, and silver. The sledges could carry two people and were warmly lined with rich furs and velvet. Then there were the horses, the pride of each sledge occupant. Of Arabic descent, they were light and graceful, with a peculiar looseness of pace like an Italian greyhound. Their tails and manes were always of an enormous length, a beauty so admired some of them had false ones, which Tatiana thought was ridiculous.

She described the scene with enthusiasm, making Anna see the picturesque sledges and their beautiful horses, the scattered groups of the watching multitudes, the superb dress of the nobility, their fur cloaks and caps, adorned with colored velvets and gold. In the perpetual night of the northern winter, ten thousand torches would line the Neva, making it glow like an exquisite painting.

Then Tatiana fell silent, thinking how she wouldn't be here this coming winter to enjoy such activities, nor would she be able to attend her usual amusements, such as the opera, or a masquerade, a popular pastime for Petersburg High Society. She could only hope New Archangel had something similar, or it would be a dull place to live.

In one week's time the naval ship, *Suvorov*, was to sail. In the meantime there wasn't a moment to rest with all the preparations for the voyage. Anna was in charge of packing all of Tatiana's possessions carefully in the many trunks, including her beautiful bridal gown and her entire wedding trousseau. Then there were her new frocks, made of warm materials, such as wool, muslin, and wadded silk with fur trim. At times she despaired of getting everything organized.

The night before they sailed the Count gave a grand reception in Tatiana's honor. Anna was relieved she wasn't allowed to attend. She felt especially fatigued after helping Tatiana dress that evening. Dinner attire at the palace was a bit more complicated than dinner at the country estate. And with tonight's reception, it was even more demanding.

First there was the bath. In Tatiana's dressing room stood a white marble bathing tub, filled with endless pitchers of hot water scented with verbena. Rose petals floated in the water.

When Tatiana finished bathing she dried herself with cambric linen towels bordered with lace, then she slipped on stockings, petticoats, and the gown itself, a lovely violet silk creation which matched her eyes. After Anna swept her long thick hair up into a mass of pale gold ringlets, she fastened a necklace of flashing diamonds around Tatiana's slender neck, with diamond earrings to match.

Her mistress had never looked so beautiful and Anna thought what a lucky man her future husband was. Tatiana never talked about him, only that he was a naval lieutenant by the name of Dmitri. She did mention his father, the Baron Ivan Volodin, however, and seemed to look forward to seeing him again at the dinner and reception.

Count Bolkonsky was resplendent in his gold braided military uniform, and on his arm was the lovely *Madame* Maria Petrovna, his latest mistress, also rumored to be the next Countess after the one year of mourning was over in the autumn. Colette told Anna that Olga despised *Madame* Petrovna, and was hoping that her father would lose interest in her like he did with his other women. Colette doubted it, however. *Madame* Petrovna was a young widow in her late twenties with an enormous fortune, and one of the Czarina's closest friends. Marriage to her would be a great social and financial advantage to the Count.

It made Anna feel quite sympathetic towards Olga. She knew exactly what it was like to have one's father marry a young woman too soon after losing one's mother. At least Olga had her marriage to Count Vladimir Kornilov to look forward to, in case her father did replace her mother with *Madame* Petrovna.

Anna watched Olga leave for the reception, dressed in an elegant gown of red silk, which "only enhances her dowdy figure," Colette whispered cattily in her ear. "My mistress is too fond of the chocolates and the cream sauces, I theenk," she added, shrugging her shoulders in her usual dramatic French fashion.

"What have we here?" said a deep masculine voice. "The two loveliest maids in the palace, I presume."

Colette immediately sank to her knees in a deep curtsy and Anna reluctantly followed, as the French maid simpered, "Oh, *Monsieur* Bolkonsky."

It was Olga's brother, Mikael Bolkonsky. This was the first time she had seen him, since he resided in Kronstadt where he was due to soon graduate from the Naval Academy as a lieutenant. Anna had heard Tatiana speak of him in a desultory manner, as if he was someone she despised, rather than a beloved cousin. Anna wasn't certain of the reason, but as she tilted her head up and met his appraising gaze, she felt like something slimy had just slithered over her entire body.

He looked remarkably like a younger version of his father, complete with the noble Bolkonsky nose, dark hair and mustache. She thought he could be considered handsome if not for the dissipated look on his face, the slight cruel twist to his thick lips, and his hooded black eyes, already showing the glaze of inebriation. He smelled strongly of vodka and Anna could not help a grimace of distaste.

"Colette, you may go," he said, dismissing her with a jerk of his head.

She glanced at Anna worriedly, then gathered her skirts and rushed down the hall towards Olga's apartments. Mikael bent over Anna and grabbed her arm, lifting her upright. "Anna, is that your name, maid?"

His grip was like iron and Anna tensed, feeling like a rabbit caught in a snare. "Yes, *Monsieur* Bolkonsky."

"I hear you killed a big snake and saved my sister and my cousin from possible harm. Is that true?" His eyes were like two dark fathomless pits and Anna tried to tear her gaze from them.

"Yes," she said softly. "but only with the help of God."

He suddenly released her and stepped backwards slightly. "Oh, yes," he sneered, "now I remember. You belong to some weird religious sect. What is it called?"

"Mennonite, *Monsieur*."

"Ah, yes, Mennonite." He studied her briefly. "You are much too pretty to be so religious, Anna. Religion is for old people. Not for a young girl like you." He smiled his most charmingly. "It would be my pleasure if you would allow me to show you the enjoyments of life here in Saint Petersburg. As long as you keep it a secret from my dear cousin, of course."

He winked at her, making Anna feel slightly nauseated. "It wouldn't be proper, *Monsieur*. You are the son of the Count and I am only a lowly maid."

"That makes no difference. Ask any of the maids here in the palace, ask Colette. They will tell you that I am their champion, their friend." He pressed his full lips together in a slight smirk that made Anna shiver with revulsion.

Unfortunately, he saw her tremble, and misread her signals. "So you do understand, my dear. I shall see you later."

Before Anna could answer, he stepped past her and vanished down the long corridor.

* * *

By midnight Tatiana was weary of the endless courses of food, the endless farewell speeches and best wishes for a safe voyage, and especially, was weary of having to keep a polite smile pasted on her tired face. Would all these guests never leave, she wondered for the hundredth time, as she nodded and murmured her gratitude for all the little gifts and kind parting words from people she didn't care if she ever saw again.

Only a fraction of Saint Petersburg high society attended, as most families of the nobility were still enjoying the pleasures of their summer estates, including Czar Alexander and Czarina Elizabeth. However, even if their Imperial Majesties had returned to Saint Petersburg, they would not have come to her reception this evening.

Unlike Mikael and Olga who had been presented to their majesties as young children, Tatiana had never been allowed in their royal presence. Her father had done the unforgivable, he had married an Englishwoman without the Czar's permission. If Nikolas had not been a Bolkonsky, he would have been deprived of all his rights, had his rank in the Navy revoked, and been banished from Russia forever. Such severe punishments, though not common, had happened to other unfortunate members of the lesser nobility.

However, Nikolas had not totally escaped the Czar's wrath. While his brother Vasily was granted all the wealth, land and family titles, Nikolas remained land poor and held no title except for his naval rank. Czar Alexander could have changed that, but he chose not to, even after Nikolas had represented the Russian America Fur Company so well, and had helped to defeat the natives at Fort Archangel. Tatiana believed the real reason her father didn't succeed Alexander Baranov as governor of Russian America was because of the scandal of his marriage.

All through her childhood, Tatiana had the stigma of being the product of that union attached to her. When Mikael and Olga were invited to the Great Palace at Tsarskoie-Selo to play with the children of the Czar, the invitation never included her. Her cousins would return with glorious stories of the private garden, which had been built like an enchanted playground. The garden sloped gently towards a pond with many small islands. On these islands playhouses were constructed. One was a farmstead in the peasant Russian style, complete with two rooms, a dining room and a kitchen, equipped with dishes and cooking utensils. To Mikael's delight, there was also a play fortress of red bricks with a small bridge in the center.

How Tatiana had envied them their royal acceptance, but she refused to let her cousins know. Instead she turned a deaf ear to their description of the wonders of the Great Palace and pretended she wasn't interested. Yet, in her heart she longed to be acknowledged by Czar Alexander and Czarina Elizabeth.

When her betrothal to Dmitri Volodin was announced last summer, she hoped it meant that she would finally be able to meet their Imperial Majesties. But her uncle had obtained the necessary permission for her marriage without her being present.

Soon he would be asking the Czar for his permission to marry *Madame* Maria Petrovna. It was obvious to her that Uncle Vasily was besotted with the woman and all of poor Olga's hopes for more attention from her father before her own marriage were in vain. Tonight her uncle had fawned over *Madame* Petrovna the entire evening with nary a glance in his daughter's direction.

On the contrary, her cousin Mikael never seemed to take his gaze off her, watching her every move. It made her thankful the Baron Volodin was at her side during dinner and afterwards. Mikael would not dare approach her with the Baron's formidable presence nearby. Although their duel was never mentioned, it was also not forgotten. His eyes smoldered with hatred each time they lit upon the Baron.

Olga spent the evening on the arm of her fiancé, Count Vladimir Kornilov. He was a tall lean man, balding, with somber dark eyes and a mouth that never smiled. Olga had met his four daughters only once, and said they were like four little mice, all large eyed with squeaky voices. The first thing she intended to do after the wedding was hire a bevy of nursemaids and a strict governess. "I don't know one thing about raising children," she said with a shudder, "and I don't wish to know until Vladimir and I have our own. I shall give his daughters some attention, of course, but not a bit more than I must."

With those words, Olga reminded Tatiana of the cold unloving manner in which Aunt Irene had raised her. Tatiana couldn't help feeling slightly sorry for the motherless Kornilov girls with Olga as their future stepmother.

When the long evening was nearly over, and some of the guests were departing, she noticed that Mikael had finally left as well. She was relieved for a part of her was afraid he was going to make some sort of farewell scene. She would never forget his sickening declaration of love at her birthday ball the summer before.

The Baron embraced her tightly before his departure, giving her another beautiful piece of jewelry as a bon voyage gift, a pearl and gold bracelet. There were actual tears in his usually cold gray eyes when she assured him that she had every intention of making his son the best wife possible.

"And a grandson," he murmured. "You must give the Volodins an heir."

"Of course," she said in a placating voice, knowing that motherhood was not a state she intended to find herself in for a very long time. She had too much living to do first. Babies could wait. Forever, if she had her way, remembering what happened to her own mother. Childbirth was something to be avoided at all costs.

After the final guest departed, Tatiana made her way back upstairs, looking forward to a few hours sleep before leaving for Kronstadt in the morning. As she neared her apartments she saw Mikael hurrying out her door. It gave her an eerie feeling of *deja vu*, of the night he had thrown her kitten out the window.

"Mikael," she demanded, "What were you doing in there?"

Surprised, he glanced over his shoulder at her then halted in his tracks. "Looking for you, my dearest cousin. What else?"

What else indeed, she thought, not believing him for an instant. "I'm here now. What do you want?"

He came closer, swaying slightly in his drunkenness. "To bid you a fond farewell, Tatiana. I have missed your beautiful face all summer and now I shall miss seeing you for years, perhaps. Whatever shall I do without you?"

"I think you will survive nicely, Mikael," she answered in a wry tone. "Now leave me be. I must get my beauty rest for the morrow comes quickly."

"First a good-bye kiss, my love." He swooped over her as quickly as an eagle finding its prey and pressed his thick mouth over hers before she could stop him. His thick lips felt like warm gelatin and she jerked her head back.

Wiping his saliva off, she raised her hand as if to slap his face, but he caught her wrist in midair. "Say you love me just a little," he pleaded.

"Never," she hissed. "And let me go at once or I'll scream so loud I'll wake the entire palace."

The desire in his eyes instantly faded, replaced by a dark gleam of malice. "You witch," he snarled, "you are just like your stupid maid. I wish you both a cursed voyage. May your ship sink and the two of you follow it to the bottom of the sea."

He released her wrist and stalked away, his evil words striking a note of unease inside her. What did he mean that I am just like Anna? With a sudden pang of fear, she rushed into her sitting room, calling out for her maid.

* * *

Anna had been in a deep sleep for some time, dreaming of the rolling wheat fields of Furstenau with their golden tops gracefully bending in the summer breezes when she was rudely awakened by rough hands. Their grip on her shoulders brought her to full alert, as the strong alcohol fumes of the man's breath seared her nostrils. She knew immediately it was Mikael.

"Let me go," she said firmly, hoping he could not hear the frantic pounding of her heart. "At once."

"Now aren't you the coy one, little Anna," he said in a surprised voice. "Say you want me. I know you do."

"No, *Monsieur*, I do not. You have misunderstood. I wish you to leave me, now."

"But I've been thinking of you all night, Anna. You don't know how tiresome these infernal dinner receptions are, and the thought of you waiting here for me was the only thing that kept me going all night," his voice ending on a childish whine.

"If you touch me, I shall scream," she warned him, not showing her fear. *Please, God, help me*, she prayed.

He uttered a nasty sounding chuckle. "Go ahead. There's no one about. No one to come to your rescue."

"There is God," she said.

In the semi darkness of her small room, located next to Tatiana's, she could barely make out the form of his head as he reared back and laughed again. "Where? I don't see him."

"He sees you, *Monsieur* Bolkonsky. He sees everything you do and hears everything you say and knows your every thought. Someday He will be your eternal Judge if you don't allow His son to be your Savior first."

Mikael tried to laugh again, but it came out more strangled. "You sure know how to kill a man's appetite, Anna," he said, suddenly releasing her. "I think you should be a nun, not a lady's maid."

With those words, he was gone, and Anna rolled out of her bed, any desire for sleep disappearing with him. She found she was shaking almost uncontrollably, so she went into Tatiana's luxurious bedchamber, her bare feet sinking into the plush Persian carpet. She was standing there in a daze, when Tatiana rushed in, a perfumed cloud of diamonds and violet silk.

"I saw my cousin leaving, Anna. Did he hurt you?" Her voice was full of anxiety, especially as she saw Anna robed in her nightgown, with a frightened look on her pale face.

Anna shook her head, wondering if she was feeling like her mama had, the night the Tartars came, when her mama had stopped them from harming her papa. She had thought her mama so brave, but perhaps, she had been as terrified as she was tonight with Mikael bending over her, threatening her with some unspeakable harm.

But God had helped her mama then, and Anna knew He had saved her from Mikael's evil desires as well. And just like that night, it was true that a soft answer turned away anger. "God saved me from him, *Mademoiselle*."

Tatiana flinched. "What do you mean? What did Mikael try to do?"

When Anna told her what happened, Tatiana grew extremely angry. "I should have known he would try something like this. He has the morals of an alley cat. Olga told me how she had to tell Mikael to stay away from Colette, and I should have realized he might try to harm you, too. I am very sorry, Anna."

Tatiana looked so distressed, Anna found herself comforting her mistress when she should be comforting her. Patting her on the shoulder, Anna said, "I'm fine, *Mademoiselle*, really I am. Let me help you out of this dress. We both need some sleep tonight since tomorrow morning we are leaving."

"Yes, we are leaving, aren't we?" Tatiana said almost fiercely. "And not too soon either. After we are gone, I hope we never see my horrible cousin again."

Anna couldn't help but agree with her on that score. When Tatiana was finally undressed and her hair brushed and braided for bed, she said, "Anna, what did you mean when you said that God saved you from Mikael?"

"He gave me just the right words to say to stop him from hurting me."

"And what were those words?"

Anna repeated exactly what she'd said to Mikael. Tatiana listened carefully then gave a hollow laugh. "Yes, I can see why that would cool off even the most ardent man in pursuing a woman. Goodnight, Anna."

Minutes later, as Tatiana tried to fall asleep, she thought about what Anna had said. If God really existed like Anna believed, then Mikael wasn't the only one who God was watching every second. As a child it would have given her comfort to believe in a personal God who cared that much about anyone. Now it just made her feel uneasy, imagining a supernatural being knowing everything she did.

But I don't believe in God, heaven or hell, or any of it, she thought defiantly. *The priests are all hypocrites and the Bible is just a book of myths and fairy tales. Those who believe it are fools.*

CHAPTER TEN

Early the next morning Anna and Tatiana left for the naval base of Kronstadt located on the eastern Gulf of Finland, a fat finger of the Baltic where the naval ship, the *Suvorov*, awaited them for the voyage to Russian America. To reach Kronstadt, they sailed north on the Neva River on a small bark, a half-day's journey past gloomy forests of wild poplar trees which grew on both sides of the river.

Anna would never forget her first sight and smell of the sea. Where the river spilled out into the sparkling blue waters of the Gulf, she was greeted by the sharp tangy scents of salt and seaweed, the pungent reek of ship tar and bilge water, all a medley of odors she'd never breathed before. The summer sun reflected bright gold flecks in the white foam of the waves, dancing before the stiff afternoon breeze. When they climbed aboard the *Suvorov*, it seemed to Anna that the great ship was straining against her lines, anxious to cast off from the land and set herself free to face the far horizon.

The sight filled her with half-fear and half-excitement. She wondered if she was brave enough to endure such a long treacherous voyage; just that morning she'd asked Tatiana if there was another route to Russian America besides sailing half way around the world.

"Yes, there is an overland route across eastern Russia," Tatiana had said. "Baron Volodin mentioned it to me during dinner last night. He said the first part is easy, sailing down the Lena River. But when the river turns north, all freight and passengers have to be transported on Yakut pack horses through the enormous wasteland of Siberia, a trip which is grueling and dangerous. He'd heard how in the more impassable parts of the tundra and marshes, the weariness of the horses, dogs and reindeer often compelled the travelers to march on foot until all were exhausted, some even to the point of death. Then when they reached the eastern seaport of Okhotsk, there still was the brutal voyage across the Bering Sea to be faced. It is ludicrous to suppose that either one of us could survive such an ordeal, Anna."

"Yes, *Mademoiselle*," she'd agreed, "it is far better to be confined on a ship for almost a year, however claustrophobic, in comparison with the overland route across Siberia."

But now, standing on the deck, watching the sailors weigh anchor and hoist canvas to catch the sharp gulf wind, with the gray and white seagulls screeching as they circled overhead, her heart plummeted in despair as she realized she was leaving Russia, the land of her birth, the only country she knew. She was leaving her beloved family as well. How she had hoped against hope that she would have a reprieve at the last moment, that Gerhard would come forth, apologizing for his violent behavior so she would be able to return home.

In contrast to Anna's sadness Tatiana stood with her eyes closed in joyful bliss. This was the special moment Tatiana had dreamed of for so long. She was finally to be rid of Olga, Mikael and Uncle Vasily. How tired she was of them! Her true family, her father and future husband, were waiting for her in Russian America. At last she would find where she truly belonged in this world.

Both girls were clothed in warm cloaks, for though it was still summer, the wind blew from the north and they were thankful for the added protection. Tatiana's cloak was of thick velvet with a soft fur-lined hood and lavish fur trimmings at the hem and wrists. Its hue was of a deep rich purple, a color that complimented her violet eyes and blonde hair.

Anna's cloak was also of warm velvet, a greenish-gold color that brought out the golden highlights in her hair and hazel eyes. It was a surprise gift from Tatiana, along with several other pretty gowns, given to her just that morning. Anna was speechless, never owning such wondrous clothing in her life.

When she finally found her voice she thanked Tatiana over and over until her mistress laughed and said, "It's nothing, Anna. I've had that cloak for ages and never wore it, because the color is all wrong for me, and it's too small and too short. It looks perfect on you, however." She laughed again. "And I want you to wear normal gowns on this voyage instead of that tiresome maid's uniform. I don't want my maid looking like a drab little hen anymore."

The commander of the *Suvorov* was Captain-Lieutenant Igor Chernyshov, a close friend of Tatiana's father. His wife, Natasha, was making her first voyage with him, thereby solving the problem of a suitable chaperone for the two girls. Chernyshov had already noticed the admiring glances of the rough looking sailors aimed in their direction, and he sent his wife to bring Tatiana and her maid below decks.

When the couple first welcomed them aboard earlier, Tatiana had to suppress a giggle. They reminded her of a walrus and a skinny ostrich. The lieutenant was short and stocky, a bald, round-headed man with a thick black mustache and two large front teeth which protruded slightly from his mouth. He was continually barking out orders to his crew.

Natasha was the complete opposite of her husband. She was several inches taller than he and extremely bony. Her lips were two straight thin lines and she had a pointed nose like a large beak. Her long skinny white neck supported a head of dark brown hair, on top of which perched a stylish hat richly decorated with ostrich feathers.

Now that the ship was under way, the hat was replaced by a more practical bonnet, tied firmly under her jutting chin. She herded the two girls below to the main salon in the stern, where they could rest in privacy. Tatiana's and Anna's cabin was on one side of the large room, and Igor and Natasha's on the other.

It didn't take long for Anna to realize that Natasha was the type of person who talked continually without letting anyone else speak. In short order, she told them her entire life story, which thankfully, was short and uneventful. She was the only daughter of a highly respected physician of Moscow, and had married at age twenty five, almost a spinster. Fifteen years later after several miscarriages, she and Igor remained childless and had spent most of that time apart. Natasha obviously adored her husband and longed to be with him, but only recently when he was given command of his own ship, the *Suvorov*, was she allowed to accompany him. This was her first sea voyage and she confided that she was quite nervous about it.

Captain-Lieutenant Chernyshov was a man of many responsibilities in command of the ship. The crew consisted of three officers under him, a navigator and his two assistants, a ship's surgeon, a supercargo, who was a man experienced in trading with the Indians, forty-two naval ranks, or common sailors, and twenty-eight *promyshlenniki*, the rough looking fur hunters.

"You two girls must stay away from the *promyshlenniki*," Natasha warned. "Whenever you wish to take a stroll above decks, you must have Igor or one of the officers to escort you."

Tatiana looked a bit downcast at that, but she nodded in understanding. Natasha chuckled then and said, "Don't look so forlorn, *Mademoiselle* Tatiana, I have some news which should cheer you. Although we are well-supplied with provisions for our voyage, we need to stop in London for a few days to obtain goods for trading with the natives. Igor says if our business there is concluded in time, we may be allowed to go ashore and see some of the sights. After all, who knows when we will be able to see the world's largest city again."

London, England! Excitement rushed through Tatiana and she broke into a smile of delight. Immediately she thought of her English relatives, her mother's family. Were her grandparents still alive? If she could find where they lived, would they know who she was?

"Will there be time for me to visit my mother's family?" she asked. "They are of the English nobility and live outside of London on an estate called Sutton Manor."

Natasha appeared intrigued by the thought of visiting English aristocracy. "I shall ask Igor at dinner tonight."

But when evening came none of the three ladies were hungry. By dinnertime the *Suvorov* had left the more sheltered waters of the eastern Gulf of Finland and entered the Baltic Sea where the seas grew rougher. Natasha disliked the rolling motion of the ship and soon complained of feeling ill. Tatiana and Anna also felt queasy, but they forced themselves to sit with her and her husband and the officers and other men of rank at the large table in the forward cabin.

Chernyshov and his men ate heartily of the overcooked beef, swimming in a greasy gravy with biscuits as heavy as lead. It was the worst meal Anna and Tatiana had ever seen, and they used the excuse of having a touch of seasickness to just pick at it. Both girls had the same thought, if the ship's cook was this bad, it was going to be a very long, insufferable voyage.

Tatiana perked up a bit when Chernyshov began telling her how much he admired her father. He had served under Captain-Lieutenant Nikolas Bolkonsky's command in New Archangel when Alexander Baranov resigned as governor.

"I always suspected that Baranov wished your father to succeed him as governor, and was bitterly disappointed when Lieutenant Hagemeister replaced him by order of the Company Board of Directors." He gave an exasperated sigh then added, "So, *Mademoiselle*, your father remained as the new governor's assistant. When the job became too much for Hagemeister eight months later, Nikolas became assistant to the next governor, Lieutenant Yanovski. I have heard that Yanovski will also be replaced soon, even though he married Baranov's daughter. It seems none of the young naval officers who have succeeded Baranov have been able to fill his shoes very well, so to speak."

"Perhaps they will choose my father," Tatiana said eagerly.

"It would be fitting, *Mademoiselle*. Perhaps when we arrive in New Archangel, Nikolas will be the new governor."

Natasha took a dainty peck of a biscuit, then said, "Dearest husband, will we have time when we are in London for *Mademoiselle* Tatiana to visit her English relatives? They are of the aristocracy."

"I will have to think about it," he said, frowning slightly, his walrus mustache drooping over his mouth. "You are my personal responsibility to your father and I cannot risk anything improper happening to you. As it is, the streets of London are very dangerous for women as beautiful as you three, and you will need armed escorts to go anywhere in the city. Isn't that correct, Natasha, darling?"

"Oh, yes," she said, fluttering her eyelids adoringly at her husband. "We must listen to Igor, and do whatever he says. He always knows best."

Anna and Tatiana exchanged amused glances. As much as Tatiana admired their close relationship, she could not help feeling irritated at Natasha's blind worship of her husband and his assumption that all women were helpless creatures to be protected. She decided to drop the matter of visiting her English family for now, but she was determined to bring up the subject later when they docked in London.

During the next few days the *Suvorov* passed Copenhagen, leaving the Baltic Sea behind, and sailed into the North Sea. There they encountered what Chernyshov said was a small gale. The waves rose over ten feet high and Natasha took to her bunk in the vicious throes of seasickness. The steep pitching and rolling of the ship made Tatiana and Anna feel ill as well, but whenever Chernyshov allowed them on deck, they both felt much better.

It gave Tatiana a sense of exhilaration to watch the gray and white crested waves as they broke and slid by the ship's wooden hull. Laughing, she told Anna, "I think we're discovering our 'sea legs' as my papa once said."

"Now if only Natasha could find her sea legs," Anna answered, as they returned below to face the stuffy air reeking of stale vomit. Tatiana did not have any patience with illness and refused to enter Natasha's cabin. But Anna pitied the poor woman and spent many hours trying to make her as comfortable as possible by sponging her pale sweating face with tepid water and offering her small sips of brandy weakened with water, her husband's remedy for seasickness.

Nothing seemed to help. Natasha continually complained in her high whining voice. Between bouts of sickness, she pestered Anna with questions concerning the Bolkonskys and the Volodins. Because her background was middle-class bourgeois, the nobility seemed to fascinate her and she even considered herself to be an authority on Russian aristocracy.

She especially enjoyed dwelling on the darker side of human nature. Anna supposed Natasha's life had been so dull, waiting all those years for her husband's brief furloughs from the sea, that other people's lives were her chief source of entertainment.

She loved to speculate on the Volodins. "I wonder why Ella, the daughter, committed suicide. I heard that she hung herself in her bedchamber from the top post of the tall canopied bed using a long scarlet-colored silk nightgown that some say her father, the Baron, gave her. It's an odd present for a father to give his daughter, wouldn't you say, Anna?"

"I wouldn't know, Natasha," she answered, wishing the woman would stop her gossiping about Tatiana's future husband's family.

Natasha smiled, her illness momentarily forgotten. "And did you know that Baron Volodin used to beat his wife, Marie? She was terrified of him."

"How can you know such things?" Anna asked, growing increasingly irritated.

"Many years ago my father, who was a doctor you know, was visiting a colleague in Saint Petersburg, the Baroness Volodina's private physician. One day my father's friend was called to the Volodin's home. He asked my father to accompany him. He told me later that the Baroness was covered with bruises and welts, all in places that wouldn't show when she was fully dressed. She explained the bruises away by saying her husband was too amorous in their intimate moments. My father and his friend did not believe a word of it, but they could do nothing since her wounds were not life-threatening."

Anna had a dreadful feeling that this time she was telling the truth. Horrified, she kept listening as Natasha went on, "They say the Baron despises women and considers them stupid inferior creatures. He married Marie only for her rich dowry. A year after their marriage her wealthy parents died in an accident, conveniently for the Baron. Being an only child, Marie inherited a huge fortune which immediately became her husband's. The first thing he did was pay off all his gambling debts, then he invested in the Russian-American Fur Company and other profitable ventures."

She paused and looked at Anna, her eyes narrowing into slits. "Just imagine, if the Baron mistreated his wife, he probably mistreated his children, too. Did you know that Ella and Dmitri were twins?"

"No, I didn't know," said Anna, "and I don't care to hear---"

"They say the Baron's servants are terrified of him," she interrupted, oblivious to Anna's look of disgust. "He has a vile temper when drunk." She smiled, showing her small pointed teeth. "What if Dmitri Ivanich is just like his father?"

Anna decided she had heard enough. She turned to leave the cabin, only to find Tatiana standing at the door, a shocked look on her face.

"How much did you hear, *Mademoiselle*?" Anna asked worriedly.

"Most of it," she snapped, glaring at Natasha with dislike. "What a pack of lies! How dare you slander the Volodins who are my future family!"

The woman refused to be intimidated. She shrugged. "It is the truth, *Mademoiselle* Tatiana. I believe you should be warned about the family you are marrying into, that's all."

"Come, Anna," Tatiana ordered, her eyes gleaming with anger. "Let's leave Natasha to her sick ravings. She is obviously a very ill woman."

"There's one other thing you should know, *Mademoiselle*," Natasha called out.

Anna shook her head at Tatiana. "Don't listen to her," she advised, but Tatiana hesitated long enough to hear Natasha say, "When we arrive in New Archangel, you should ask your father about a girl named Marya."

* * *

The path from the governor's house to where Marya Nikolayevna's Aleut family lived was called the Governor's Walk, in honor of Alexander Baranov. He used to follow this trail to the end of the crescent-shaped beach where a natural rock promontory stood, his favorite spot for meditating. It was named Baranov's stone and overlooked the middle channel of Sitka Sound and the eastern roads. It was also Marya's favorite spot to sit and think.

But she had no time for idle thought today. She hurried along the path, passing by Governor Yanovski's vegetable garden, which was situated near the marsh. A large drainage ditch was being dug; hopefully to solve the problem of the stench of rotten vegetation from the malodorous swamp by the time the governor's wife's lovely tea garden nearby was finished. Marya could see where new paths were in the process of being laid out, a summerhouse was under construction, and shrubs, various trees and flowers were to be planted before winter.

After the marsh was behind her, the air became a mixture of the salty perfume of the sea and the pungent spice of the nearby pine forests. She breathed in the scents with delight, the freshness a welcome change from the stuffy overheated rooms of the governor's house.

Her people, the Aleuts, lived just beyond the stockade, past the bridge across Swan Creek. Behind their settlement or *kashim* was the cattle barn where the few head of cattle brought in from Fort Ross, California, were reduced to eating seaweed by spring because of the scarcity of hayfields and dry weather. Due to the same lack of fodder, there were no horses kept in New Archangel, but they were not necessary for transportation in such a small place where one could reach any destination by foot or by boat.

Of livestock in general, there were pigs, but they often dug up clams from the beach for food, which made their flesh almost inedible. Marya remembered when the Russians tried raising goats once, but the pesky little creatures had a bad habit of knocking down the poles on which the Aleuts and *Kolosh* dried their fish, and the goats soon lost their popularity. Chickens were raised, in spite of the troubles with the large rats which ran rampant through the warehouses and storehouse along the docks. A few cats were brought in from the naval ships to combat the problem. She thought the furry whiskered little animals were so cute and amusing to watch, but her mother wouldn't let her have one as a pet.

Beyond the barn along the beach were the vegetable gardens belonging to the Company and private citizens. There were potatoes, turnips, Brussel sprouts, lettuce, parsnips, carrots, beets, peas, radishes and cabbages. Yet, the quantities grown were never enough to supply the town, so the Russians had to supplement with vegetables from California.

For all its pride in being the capital of Russian America, New Archangel was not a self-sufficient town.

Unlike the *Kolosh* houses made of logs and standing above ground level, her people dug their homes, called *ulaqs*, partially underground. It was a custom carried over from their life spent on the violent wind-swept Aleutian Islands.

Marya halted in front of a house a bit larger than the others where a group of black-haired children, plainly dressed but with clean faces, played near the door. With a smile she greeted her four young girl cousins, and then scooted them away. They scampered in all directions, screeching and hollering like a flock of seagulls being chased by a dog.

The door was opened by her Aunt Tugidaq, which in Aleut meant the moon. Tugidaq had a full round face and once was an attractive girl, tiny and slender. But now she was short and squat with cheeks of lined leather and a sullen twist to her mouth from too many years of hard work and childbearing. The weary expression in her black eyes fled when she saw Marya, and her dark-skinned face creased into a smile of welcome.

"Come in, come in, Tooch," she said in the language of the Aleuts, reminding Marya that her real name among her people was Tooch, meaning Little Duck.

"I need your help, Aunt," Marya said, stepping down into the warm, comfortable interior of the *ulaq*. It was well finished with windows, walls, and a ceiling covered by planks painted with white clay. A wooden floor was built in the center of the house and along the walls, planked beds were constructed. Glancing around, she noticed the familiar feeling of orderliness and cleanliness of the dwelling where she was raised.

On top of an ancient stove, a shiny samovar was boiling water for tea. Marya recognized it as once belonging to her mother, a gift from her Russian father. Her aunt bade her to sit as she busily prepared two mugs of tea. No matter how much of a hurry she was in, it would not be polite of her to refuse the offered tea.

There were two old wooden chairs at the small table. Marya sat down and waited patiently for the ritual of the tea drinking. Tugidaq placed a dish of crow berries mixed with fat on the table and urged her to eat.

"You are much too skinny, Tooch," she chided. "Are they not feeding you enough at the big house?"

"I eat well," she assured her, thinking of all the rich heavy foods the Russians preferred over the simpler diet of fish and vegetables she had eaten as a child.

"You are almost a woman," Tugidaq said, narrowing her eyes as she studied Marya, noting the glossy black hair in startling contrast to her paler skin, the amber brown eyes above her high cheekbones, the small nose, delicate chin and mouth. She noted with disapproval her Russian clothes, the dress of blue linen with a white apron and blue flowered shawl, and a scarf partially covering her long black braid. Since living at the castle, Marya had spurned traditional Aleut clothing, such as the skin parkas. "When is your father finding you a husband?"

"I just turned fourteen, Aunt," she laughed. "I'm not ready to marry yet."

"Your mother met your father at that age," she said, "You are not too young to think about a husband."

Who wishes for a husband when there is still so much living to do? She had no desire to tie herself down to a man for a very long time. What had marriage done for her aunt? She had borne her uncle a brood of children and was old before her time. As for her mother, she had spent her life longing to marry her father, praying each day that he would make their union legal in the eyes of God and the church, but he had refused to do so, even when she lay on her deathbed begging him.

A sharp pang of grief pierced her briefly. Her beloved mother had died less than a year ago, taken by a fever and an infection in her lungs that the doctor called pneumonia.

"The last thing your mother told me, please find Tooch a good husband. Don't let her end up like me."

Resentment towards her father flared up inside her. It wasn't as if he had another wife living in Russia so he couldn't have married her mother. He was a widower, and his wife had been dead for many years.

Her mother had been such a beautiful and loving woman, never allowing one negative word against her father no matter how deeply he'd hurt her. Marya knew that was because of her mother's strong faith. She had tried to pass on that faith to Marya, and although she attended church faithfully, she struggled inwardly to believe in the Russian God who allowed the Russians to inflict so much suffering on her people.

Many of the Aleuts living here in New Archangel were baptized Christians. Her mother, who was born on Kodiak Island, told her how many years ago when the fierce Russian fur hunters had come to enslave her people, the Orthodox monks had come also

The Aleuts were fascinated with the priests whom they called the Russian *shamans*. They paddled their skin covered *bidarkas* from as far away as the mainland to watch these Russian *shamans* perform in their church with their robes, hats, candles, incense, altar and singing such as they had never heard before.

The priests kept the main tents of their faith simple. They preached the one God, the Creation, the Fall, the Redemption by the blood of Christ and Life Everlasting.

This God of whom they spoke was familiar to the Aleuts. They also knew of a supreme being called *El*, who was all-powerful and had created everything. They believed he had a son, too, who sometimes interceded for people when his father punished them. As for the words about st.s and guardian angels, the Aleut *shamans* taught that everyone has a *yeik* who follows him at all times, guarding him from evil.

Sometimes she found religion so confusing. She was by nature a girl of a sunny disposition. She preferred to live her life one day at a time, enjoying the moment, and not worrying about such depressing matters such as death and one's soul. But when her mother had passed away, some of the spark had vanished from her eyes, and she began to look at life more seriously.

She always hoped her father would take a more personal interest in her. Everyone said she looked so much like her mother. But after her death, he seemed to withdraw even further and seemed content to leave her at her uncle's home while he immersed himself in his duties as assistant to Governor Yanovski. It was Irina Baranova, the governor's wife, who took pity on her, and installed her in the nursery to look after her infant son, Alexander, named after his famous grandfather.

At first it was strange to live in what everyone called "Baranov's Castle" after growing up in its shadow. But soon Marya not only adored little Alexander, she admired his mother greatly. She was a lovely and warm person, talented and brave, and a devout Christian. And she understood the difficulty of being a *Creole*, a half-Russian, half-Aleut.

"The child Alexander is sick, Aunt. He cries much and eats little." Irina had sent Marya to her aunt, who was skilled with healing herbs. The doctor, a gruff Russian, had examined the boy and insisted it was nothing, just the cutting of teeth, and recommended a rum soaked cloth for the baby to bite on. The cloth had not soothed him.

As Marya explained this, Tugidaq pulled a basket off a shelf and gave her a packet of salmonberry leaves, roots, and bark. She instructed her how to make a leaf infusion to treat the baby's stomach upset, a tea from the roots to stop any diarrhea, and that a poultice made from the pounded bark rubbed on the baby's gums would relieve his toothaches.

"Thank you, Aunt," said Marya, smiling with gratitude.

The door flung open and the room was filled with giggling, chattering children, her cousins. Marya greeted each one by name, thinking how sweet they looked with their shining eyes like brilliant black pearls set into their eager young faces. Then as they suddenly fell silent, hanging their heads shyly, she noticed the man standing in the doorway. Andrei Leonov.

Tugidaq immediately broke into a big grin, showing the gaps in her teeth where she had ground them to nubs after all the years of gnawing skins to soften them to make clothing and boots. "You come for Tooch, yes?" she said.

He nodded, his dark eyes fastening on her with a soft glow. "I will walk you back to the castle, Marya, if you wish."

She sighed. He had been following her then. It wasn't the first time, and without a doubt it wouldn't be the last. Since his return last year from his successful voyage on the American ship, the *Eastern Wind*, as their supercargo, he had become a man of means. He'd earned enough to invest in the Company and was now making some profits on his own out of the fur trade. He had come a long way from his childhood spent with his illiterate, drunk *promyshlenniki* father and his mother, a pox scarred Aleut slave.

He now had a house of his own and a bit of land, and was thought of as a good catch as a potential husband. Although he was more than ten years older than she, Marya saw the delight on her aunt's face, and she knew it would do her no good to refuse Andrei's offer. She nodded her acquiescence then murmured her farewells to her family.

They walked in silence for a few minutes, and after leaving the settlement behind, Leonov said, "It is not safe for you to come here alone."

She tried to keep the irritation out of her voice as she answered, "No one has ever bothered me before."

"Not yet, but your father should send a guard to escort you."

"Papa does not concern himself with what I do or where I go. He is a busy man."

Leonov snorted with disdain. "Too busy to take care of his own daughter?"

"He forgets he has a daughter most of the time." Marya was unable to keep the pain out of her voice and she was surprised to see the sympathetic, tender smile Andrei bestowed upon her.

When he smiled like that, especially in his black-green frock coat, woolen trousers and polished black boots, she thought he was almost handsome. He had inherited his short stocky body from his mother, but his facial features were from his father, the slanted dark eyes, the proud nose and bearing of his Cossack ancestors. She'd heard that his father had been sent to Siberia years ago for disobeying his military officer, then was recruited by the Company as a fur hunter. The fierceness of a Cossack warrior made Andrei's father a typical *promyshlenniki*, skilled with the club and too fond of vodka.

His son was totally different. He was highly intelligent, and learned to speak a dozen native dialects up and down the coast, making him an invaluable Indian trader, or supercargo. However, no American sea captain would hire him now. Not after he'd informed the Governor last autumn that the crew of the *Eastern Wind* had sold guns and powder to the Nootka Indians.

Governor Yanovski had been livid, and would've pursued them after they left port until Irina reminded him that the Americans had done so only as a last resort to free the captives, John Hill and Gregory Jones. But he did issue a command, that none of the officers of the *Eastern Wind* would ever be welcome in Russian American waters again. If they returned, they would be arrested at once.

"Does he forget about his other daughter who lives in Saint Petersburg?" Leonov asked her.

"Ah, yes, the beautiful Tatiana. Papa and Lieutenant Volodin speak of her often, like she is a goddess among mere mortals," she said enviously.

"Is it true she will be arriving here soon?"

"Papa said Tatiana will be here next spring, and then she and the lieutenant will be married." A look of dislike crossed her face, partly for the half-sister she'd never met, and partly for the aristocratic naval lieutenant with his mean eyes and his arrogant nature. As far as she was concerned, the two deserved each other.

"He will never make her happy," said Leonov. "He loves only himself."

Marya shrugged. "It doesn't matter to me if she is happy or not. I don't intend to have anything to do with her. Except for *Madame* Yanovskiaya and her brother, Antipatr, we *Creole*s don't mix well with the nobility."

Her voice held a note of ancient bitterness that Leonov immediately understood. *Creole*s were welcomed by the native people in a way the Russians never did. He wondered if Irina's brother, who left New Archangel a few months ago for the Imperial Cadet School in Saint Petersburg would discover racial prejudice there.

As they neared the steps leading up to the castle, which was perched on a high hill overlooking Sitka Sound, Leonov put his hand possessively on her shoulder. "I'll leave you here, Marya, but I want you to know, that if you ever need me for anything, I'll come."

The warmth of his hand through her thin dress made her uneasy, but she smiled up at him and said, "Thank you, Andrei, I'll remember that."

It was the first time she'd ever called him by his first name, and he broke into an engaging grin. She smiled again and with her natural grace, danced up the stairs, immediately forgetting him as she thought of Irina and baby Alexander waiting in the nursery.

So, she was totally unaware of how long Andrei Leonov stood, staring up after her, his face set in a determined expression. *If I have anything to say about it,* he thought, *by this time next spring, Captain-Lieutenant Bolkonsky will be marrying off both his daughters.*

CHAPTER ELEVEN

It was the morning of the fifth day since their arrival in London. Tatiana stood on the deck as usual and stared longingly at the stone and brick buildings of the city. Hundreds of chimneys belched out black smoke like dirty fingers reaching up into the gray sky. The air smelled of soot and the murky Thames River. Occasionally the breeze wafting over the city streets brought the raw stench of open sewers. Yet, she was fascinated by the sounds and the sights of everything she saw from the waterfront, and she yearned to see the rest.

There were dozens of ships from all over the world docked nearby on the riverside quays. For the past few days all of them, including the *Suvorov*, had been swarming with activity. Endless boxes of cargo was loaded: English fabrics, Dutch blankets, looking glasses, colorful beads, sugar, molasses and hogsheads of rum from the West Indies, knives, razors, ammunition, cutlasses, pistols, muskets and fowling pieces. Except for the guns and powder, the rest of the goods were to be used in trading with natives for furs.

The crew was also doing repair work about the ship. They painted whatever needed painting, replaced any poor wood with solid planks, and made certain all the spars and sails were in good condition. The frenzied pace of constant work was in sharp contrast to the idleness of the three women on board.

This morning at breakfast Chernyshov announced that they were departing with tomorrow's evening tide. When Natasha pleaded with him to let them have this last day to sight see around London, he finally agreed. It wasn't a bit too soon. There was an uncomfortable strain between all three ever since Natasha's tirade against the Volodin family and her even stranger comment about some girl named Marya in New Archangel.

Tatiana's curiosity had been aroused, but Anna convinced her to ignore Natasha. "The more interested you appear, *Mademoiselle*, the more she will gossip. We need to stop paying her any attention."

When Natasha saw that Tatiana and Anna would no longer take notice of her malicious tales, she became resentful, and spent more time in her cabin alone, pouting. The break from the older woman's incessant chatter was a relief, especially as Anna found herself feeling extra tired since the ship had docked in London. The past two days her throat had been sore and now her head ached something fierce. She wondered if the dirty air from the city was disagreeing with her.

So, it took all the strength she had to appear enthusiastic at the day's outing in London. One of the ship's officers, Lieutenant Anton Dohktorov, was to accompany them in the rented carriage. He was a fine looking man in his early twenties. Anna remembered him from the ship as the only officer of the three on board who blushed whenever she or Tatiana looked at him. Like an overgrown puppy with his warm brown eyes and anxious expression, he was eager to please his commander's wife and their aristocratic passenger and her maid.

Grinning broadly, he made certain the three women were seated comfortably inside the rented carriage on cushioned seats, each with a view out the window. Natasha's thin hands flopped in nervous excitement. "There's so much I want to see," she said.

Tatiana glanced at her with barely hidden disdain. Natasha was a colorful sight with her brightly checkered frock and cloak and her hat with the ostrich feathers. It was true that checked and striped materials were in fashion, but the effect was not flattering to a forty-year-old woman.

In contrast, Tatiana and Anna were dressed in attractive gowns with matching bonnets, Tatiana in lavender silk and Anna in dark green muslin. Tatiana carried a reticule and Anna was in charge of their cloaks in case the evening grew cool before they returned to the ship.

"After we finish sightseeing," said Tatiana, "I would like to visit my English family, Lord and Lady Sutton. I've already spoken to the driver, and he said he knows where Sutton Manor is located, only an hour's drive outside London."

Lieutenant Dohktorov frowned slightly. "We may not have time for that, *Mademoiselle.* Captain-Lieutenant Chernyshov insisted we return before dark."

Tatiana bestowed her most brilliant smile upon him, and said, "Of course, Lieutenant, whatever you say. But I want you to know how deeply I've longed to see my grandparents my entire life, and if you grant me this one favor, I shall be forever grateful."

He blushed so hard his ears turned red. "Then I shall tell the driver to make haste, so we will have the time, *Mademoiselle*."

Anna sighed inwardly as she watched Tatiana use her beauty to get the Lieutenant to do what she wanted, even if it went against his better judgment. The motion of the carriage made her slightly dizzy and she could feel her own face flushing hotly, too, as the inside of the carriage grew increasingly stuffy with the four of them seated so close together.

The pounding of her head was growing stronger and she wished she had made herself some willow bark tea from her supply for Tatiana's occasional headache. But she had been too busy this morning and now she hoped she would be able to survive the day's outing. Tatiana would never forgive her if she became so ill they had to return to the ship without meeting her English grandparents.

The carriage drawn by two matching gray horses clattered down the maze of cobblestone streets. After leaving the waterfront area with its narrow twisting alleyways and shabbily dressed men and women, they soon reached the broad avenues of historical London. They drove past London Bridge, Hyde Park, Buckingham Palace, Westminster Abbey and Saint Paul's Cathedral, an immense cathedral with a magnificent dome. By early afternoon they came to Bond Street where all day long the highest level of London society paraded up and down the street in the latest fashions.

"I've heard that many of these people of the English aristocracy appear in new creations of clothing several times a day. Can you imagine anything more exciting?" asked Natasha eagerly, staring out her window with fascination.

Tatiana could not imagine anything more decadent and boring as watching pompous English dandies and conceited ladies flaunting their wealth. Bond Street was so choked with crowds of people that the carriage could go no further. Natasha wanted to get out and do some shopping, but Tatiana shook her head.

"Lieutenant, tell the driver to turn the carriage around and drive to Sutton Manor at once."

He obeyed her immediately as Natasha darted an angry look at both of them. She opened her mouth to protest, but then closed it again as she realized the young lieutenant was infatuated with the beautiful niece of Count Bolkonsky, and it was futile to argue with either of them. She consoled herself with the thought that meeting actual members of the English aristocracy was decidedly more interesting than spending time watching them on Bond Street.

The drive to Sutton Manor seemed endless to Anna. The streets of London and the noise of the city eventually gave way to the rolling green hills of the country where meadows of purple asters and wild daisies grew among herds of cows and sheep. If she hadn't felt so poorly, she would have enjoyed the peaceful sight, reminding her of the livestock grazing contentedly in pastures at home in Furstenau. Right now, in the warm days of late summer, would be the annual village washing. Had it already been a year since that day her papa announced his attention to marry Agatha? So much had happened since then, and none of it had been good for her.

When the carriage finally turned down a long drive, bordered with rows of poplar trees, Anna was feeling so lightheaded and nauseous she imagined for a moment that it was Ekaterinoslav, the Bolkonsky's country estate. But the house looming ahead was much larger, a stately brick mansion three stories high with long windows overlooking the lovely gardens filled with late summer flowers. The carriage pulled up in front of the two massive doors at the entrance.

Lieutenant Dohktorov stepped out first then helped each lady, starting with Natasha, the eldest. Tatiana turned to Anna and whispered, "I'm frightfully nervous."

Anna barely heard her. She was concentrating solely on where to put each foot, so she wouldn't swoon. It wouldn't do to mar this long sought reunion for Tatiana and her grandparents.

The lieutenant escorted them to the entrance and rang the bell. An elderly white-haired man dressed in a black coat with white gloves, opened the doors and peered down his long patrician nose at them, before saying in a clipped voice, "May I help you?"

"I am Lieutenant Dohktorov of His Majesty, Czar Alexander's, Imperial Navy," he said in heavily accented English. "I am escorting Tatiana Nikolayevna Bolkonskaya, the niece of His Excellence, Count Vasily Ilyich Bolkonsky, to meet with Lord and Lady Sutton. Accompanying her is her maid, Anna, and Natasha Chernyshovaya, the wife of Captain-Lieutenant Igor Chernyshov, the commander of my ship, the Russian Imperial Naval vessel, the *Suvorov*."

The butler shifted his gaze from the lieutenant and fastened upon Tatiana. His eyes under two fuzzy white eyebrows, squinted at her sharply and a look of astonishment spread across his austere features. "Can it be?" he muttered, then stepped aside to let them in.

"You are most fortunate," he added, "Lord and Lady Sutton are both in the drawing room having their afternoon tea. I will announce you."

He left them standing in a great hall with a grand mahogany staircase leading upwards past the Sutton family coat-of arms and gilt framed family portraits. In a few moments he returned, ushering them through another set of doors into a large beautiful drawing room filled with richly upholstered chairs and sofas, a plush French carpet and a gleaming white marble fireplace on one end. The room was lined with tall windows of plated glass, through which Tatiana could see bushes of blooming blue and rose colored hydrangea flowers.

"Lord Henry Sutton and Lady Jane Sutton," said the butler in an imperious voice, "may I present Tatiana Nikolayevna Bolkonskaya and her maid, Anna, and Lieutenant Dohktorov and Natasha Chernyshovaya of the Russian naval ship, the *Suvorov*."

A man and a woman were seated on one of the sofas, each holding a cup of tea. A plate of buttered scones with strawberry preserves and tiny cakes with cream stood on a nearby table. The woman took a dainty sip then placed her blue and gold china cup down, giving them all a puzzled smile of welcome. But it was the man who caught Tatiana's attention. When they were announced, he jumped up, nearly dropping his tea into his lap, and uttered an explosive curse.

Tatiana's first thought was that they were far too young to be her grandparents. Lord Sutton looked about forty and Lady Sutton many years younger. She shot her husband a look of disapproval then said, "James, send Molly in with more tea for our guests, please."

The butler bowed and with another quick glance at Tatiana departed the room. Lord Sutton, a tall lean man with thinning fair hair and eyes as blue as the hydrangeas, was also staring at her. Lady Sutton didn't seem to notice. She stood and graciously gestured towards several chairs and invited them to sit down.

She was an attractive woman with dark brown hair swept back into a chignon, brown eyes that sparkled, and two small dimples on each side of her mouth when she smiled, displaying perfect white teeth. "My, the four of you have come a long way from Russia to see us."

"Actually, your Ladyship, we are on our way to New Archangel in Russian America, and we are presently in London to load supplies for the voyage," explained the lieutenant. "*Mademoiselle* Bolkonskaya said she wished to visit her English grandparents and--"

"Yes," interrupted Tatiana glancing around somewhat wildly, "my mother was Elizabeth Sutton, and I was hoping to meet her parents, my maternal grandparents. Where are they?"

Lady Sutton's smile instantly vanished and she looked at her husband in amazement. "Can this be true, Henry?" she asked doubtfully.

Lord Sutton crossed the room in quick strides and took Tatiana's hand, gazing intently into her face. "Tatiana---Tatiana---I can't believe it! After all the years I've tried to contact you and they wouldn't let me. And here you are, standing in front of me, the spitting image of dear Elizabeth!" A joyous grin broke over his face and he threw his arms around her, crushing her to him. "I'm your Uncle Henry!"

Dazed, all Tatiana could think of was, she had another uncle, her mother's brother. But where were her grandparents?

As if reading her mind, her uncle released her and his smile dimmed. "I know you were hoping to meet my father, the first Lord Henry, and my mother, Lady Diana, but they both passed away years ago. My father went first from a weak heart and my mother soon after. They were never the same after Elizabeth left home. And when the news came that she had died after you were born, well, they were so stricken with grief, their health declined. My father, your grandfather, wrote letters first to Nikolas Bolkonsky, then to his brother, the Count, asking to see you. Your father never replied, but your uncle sent a letter, refusing to allow us any contact with you. After my parents were gone, I began to write you every year on your birthday and send you a gift, but I never knew if you received them."

"You sent me birthday gifts?" asked Tatiana, startled. "But I never saw even one."

Lord Sutton frowned. "I am not surprised, my dear. But I kept hoping year after year, that perhaps, when you grew older, they would change their minds and let me come visit you. Isn't it ironic that in a few days, you will be turning seventeen, and I've already sent you a gift, one that you'll never receive."

"Meeting you is the best gift of all, Uncle Henry," she said, and turning to Lady Sutton, added, "and Aunt Jane."

Lady Sutton laughed then, a delighted tinkle that made even the serious expression of Lieutenant Dohktorov relax. She walked over to Tatiana and kissed her on both cheeks and said, "We must celebrate this wondrous reunion, dearest niece. Please stay for dinner this evening, and meet your younger cousins, our three sons, Henry, William, and baby Charles."

"Oh, I would love, too, but we must return to the ship before dark. Captain's orders. We sail tomorrow evening," she added with great disappointment.

Lord Sutton looked at the lieutenant. "If your ship isn't due to sail until tomorrow, then perhaps, Tatiana and her maid could stay the night. I give you my word that they will be delivered safely to the *Suvorov* first thing in the morning."

"It is not my decision to make your Lordship," Lieutenant Dohktorov said, scowling. "Only Captain-Lieutenant Chernyshov can decide."

Lady Sutton smiled her sweetest at Natasha. "Since you are his wife, certainly you can persuade him that no harm is done if Tatiana and her maid spend one night with us. Surely, you can understand how all of us have years of catching up to do."

Natasha pursed her lips worriedly. "I don't know," she began, "my husband was most insistent we return this evening. He does not like to be disobeyed."

During this conversation no one seemed to notice Anna, who was sitting on a chair, feeling happy for her mistress that her meeting with her new family was going so well. As she studied the large oil painting in front of her on the wall above the fireplace, of a lovely young woman with golden hair, dressed in a sapphire blue gown, she began to feel hot and cold all at the same time. Intense pain suddenly streaked down her throat, making it impossible to swallow, and her head hurt so intensely, it seemed it might explode. At the same time the voices in the room started to fade away in the distance and a strange buzzing sounded in her ears.

The young woman in the painting continued to smile down at her, unconcerned at her distress. How had the Suttons managed to have a painting of Tatiana if they had never seen her before, was her last confused thought before she toppled off her chair and lost consciousness.

* * *

Time had no meaning for Anna in her new world of fantasy where she could forget her sufferings and pretend she was a child living in Furstenau again. In front of her eyes she always saw the loving face of her mother and the stern, but kind face of her father. Their mouths were always moving as they spoke to her, but she couldn't hear their words, because of the continual buzzing in her ears, like a swarm of angry bees. The teasing face of Jack sometimes replaced her parents, and she tried to speak to him, but found her lips wouldn't move. Then her whole family would disappear, and she saw the houses in the village, and her friend Susannah walking with a young man, laughing and talking together. She tried to call out to them, but they took no notice.

When the village vanished, she saw glittering palaces floating on a sea of turquoise, and gardens of beautiful flowers growing profusely to the water's edge. Was it heaven, she wondered. Was she dying?

All these visions disappeared whenever any person came near her. After such wonderful daydreams her moments of lucidity were full of pain, in her head, her throat, and her entire body, especially her throat. It was so full of mucous she couldn't swallow and sometimes she struggled to breathe, feeling as if she might suffocate or choke to death. Once she heard a man say the word, "diphtheria," and she hoped he was talking about someone else.

The nights were the worst when she slept fitfully, and the dreams changed, turned darker, more menacing: images of Gerhard kicking his dog then laughing wickedly, Agatha running after a shrieking Tina with a large stick, the lustful, sneering face of Mikael Bolkonsky. It was no surprise that she often awoke, screaming.

Once after such a nightmare, a white shadow bent over her, and she saw the kind concerned face of Lady Jane Sutton. A cool wet cloth was in her hand and as she wiped Anna's burning face, she said, "*The Lord is my shepherd. I shall not want. He maketh me to lie down in green pastures. He leadeth me beside the still waters. He restoreth my soul...yea, though I walk through the valley of the shadow of death, I will fear no evil, for thou art with me...*Peace, my child. The Lord Jesus is watching over you. Sleep and be at rest."

Anna knew enough to recognize Psalm 23 in the Bible, one of her favorite Psalms. The familiar words brought comfort to her soul, and soon the frightening dreams faded away. Then came one morning when she opened her eyes and discovered she no longer hurt anywhere. Even more surprising she was hungry and very thirsty.

"Water," she called out weakly.

The rustling at her bedside turned into Lady Sutton again. Her face wreathed in her dimpled smile as she bent over and helped Anna sip a glass of cool water. "You are an answer to my prayers, dear Anna," she said.

The water felt delicious in her parched mouth, and the best of all, she could swallow it all the way down, soothing the delicate tissues of her ravaged throat. "How long have I been ill?" she asked in a raspy voice.

"You've been here at Sutton Manor for ten days now."

Ten days? That meant Tatiana and the *Suvorov* were long gone, leaving her all alone in England where she didn't know a soul. Panic seized her and she struggled to rise, gasping, "Tatiana....the *Suvorov*..."

Lady Sutton laid a restraining hand on her shoulder and gently pushed her back onto the bed. "Yes, your ship sailed days ago, but your mistress is still here. Tatiana refused to leave you behind. You obviously mean more to her than just a mere maid."

Relief flooded through Anna, then she stammered, "But---but how are we to get to New Archangel if---if---"

"You are not to worry, Anna. Lord Sutton has arranged passage for the two of you on another ship, leaving in one week's time. That gives you some time to recover and get your strength back, something we shall start at once. I will tell Molly to bring you some hearty meat broth."

The servant girl carrying a tray and Tatiana both arrived at the same time. As Molly held the bowl of steaming broth in front of her, and gave her several spoonfuls, Tatiana was all relieved smiles. "Oh, Anna, you have no idea how worried I've been about you. You were so dreadfully ill, there were several times, I was afraid you might never get well again."

"Frankly, *Mademoiselle*, I thought I might die, too," she answered, "but Lady Sutton took such good care of me, and she told me how she prayed. God heard her, I know."

"Perhaps He did," she said. "If your God exists, you would be the first person he would look after."

"He loves you, too," blurted Anna without thinking.

Instead of chastising her maid, Tatiana burst into laughter. "Oh, Anna, I never thought I'd say this, but you don't know how good it makes me feel to hear your religious talk again. It means you must be feeling better."

She was better, but her recovery was slow, as she found in the next few days. Everything exhausted her, sitting up in bed then trying to stand up, walking, the simplest tasks left her weak and trembling. She worried that she wouldn't be strong enough to face the voyage.

"Perhaps you should go without me, *Mademoiselle*," she told Tatiana one evening two days before they were due to sail.

They were sitting downstairs in the drawing room with Lady Sutton. It had taken all of Anna's strength to manage the many stairs, her first attempt at leaving the warm security of her bedchamber. The three were looking at the portrait of Tatiana's mother hanging over the fireplace. It had been painted when Elizabeth was seventeen, the fateful summer she met Nikolas Bolkonsky. Anna thought the likeness between mother and daughter was startling. And now Tatiana had turned seventeen, her birthday celebrated with the Suttons while Anna lay in her feverish deliriums.

They had presented her with an enormous cake, frosted with icing and decorated with flowers. Her cousins, Henry the third and William, ages ten and eight, nearly bounced out of their chairs with excitement at the sight of the cake. Tatiana told Anna how the two impish boys with mops of chestnut hair and bright blue eyes, stuffed themselves almost to the point of being ill. The youngest, baby Charles, not quite two years, insisted on feeding himself, and smeared more icing all over his sweet face and into his dark brown curls than into his mouth.

The scene reminded Anna of a typical meal at the Teichroew household when her siblings were younger, but Tatiana described it with such wonder, that she realized how little her mistress knew of ordinary family life.

"Nonsense!" said Tatiana. "I'm not going anywhere without you, especially after the big quarrel I had with Natasha and Lieutenant Dohktorov the day you fainted in this very room."

"I remember little of that afternoon," said Anna. "How did you persuade Captain-Lieutenant Chernyshov to allow you to stay behind with me?"

"It took all of us to fight that particular battle," said Lady Sutton. "After you fainted, it was obvious to the lieutenant and the captain's wife that you had to spend the night here. Tatiana insisted on staying with you, even though they both became quite angry. Finally, the two of them returned to the ship. The next morning when it was apparent you were extremely ill and in no position to be moved, we sent a message to the *Suvorov*, informing the captain. He and his officers came here immediately and ordered Tatiana to leave."

"He said it was of no consequence if you stayed behind, Anna," said Tatiana. "You were only a maid and easily replaced."

"That is true," said Anna. "You should have left with them."

"You are more than a maid to me, Anna," said Tatiana in a serious voice. "You have become my friend. I need you with me. And when I told Captain-Lieutenant Chernyshov those exact words, he was furious. But I refused to go with him."

A smile danced around the lips of Lady Sutton as she looked at the surprised expression on Anna's face. "Your mother would be proud of you, Tatiana. According to my husband, she was always kind to her servants. They loved her greatly."

Thinking of poor Sonya and the other Russian servants who feared and disliked her, Tatiana knew she wasn't at all like her mother. She had been brought up to view servants as inferior creatures and all foreigners as barbarians, especially the English and Americans. But here she was, staying with her English family, who had opened their arms and hearts to her, a perfect stranger.

Her uncle, Lord Henry, had spent the past week trying to change her mind about leaving. Although he was careful not to say anything derogatory about her father, she sensed his hostility against Nikolas Bolkonsky and the entire Bolkonsky family. She couldn't blame him. It piqued her no end that Uncle Vasily and Aunt Irene had kept secret the fact that her English family had sent her letters and gifts every birthday. And here she had believed they had totally forgotten her.

She couldn't deny it was tempting to stay at Sutton Manor. For the first time in her life, she felt as if she belonged to a family who really cared about her. Uncle Henry doted on her every word like she was her mother reincarnated. Aunt Jane surrounded her with warmth and love, the same as her own children. Tatiana thought she was the most amazing woman, reminding her of Anna in many ways. They both had their deep religious faith and both actually lived it. All those days and nights when Anna was so sick, her aunt had tenderly cared for her, resting finally when the doctor insisted she do so or fall ill herself.

Then there were her rowdy cousins, young Henry and William. They were in awe of her at first, but after their initial shyness now asked her to play games with them, such as lawn croquet, and acted like she was their big sister. What a startling difference from her Russian cousins, Mikael and Olga! Baby Charles had also charmed his way into her heart. She had never been around an infant before and found his gap toothed grins and the way he chuckled when tickled, a constant delight.

Even the staid old butler, James, had taken her aside one day and told her how much she reminded him of her mother, whom he'd known since she was a little girl. He said her visit had brought a sense of healing to Lord Sutton after the terrible loss of his sister, and he hoped she would stay.

She was going to miss them all desperately. If it wasn't for her deep love for her father and the anticipation of marrying Dmitri, she would postpone the trip to Russian America.

And then there was Anna. For some reason she didn't understand, Tatiana had become extremely fond of her maid. It had started before that infamous day of the picnic. There was something special about her, something she couldn't quite explain. At first the dowdy little Mennonite maid had irritated her no end with her pious Jesus talk, but as the days passed, and it became apparent that Anna wasn't easily cowed like the others, she grew to admire her strong spirit. She saw something of herself in her, or perhaps, if she could admit it, something in her she wished she had.

Life would be easier explained and dealt with, she often thought, if she had a religious faith like Anna's, or like Aunt Jane's. But she didn't have their faith, still didn't believe in God. When Aunt Jane insisted that God had healed Anna, it did seem that she had made a miraculous recovery from diphtheria, a disease that was usually fatal.

Whatever had happened, all Tatiana knew now was that she couldn't leave Anna behind.

"But we will arrive in New Archangel much later than planned, and your wedding will be delayed. All because of me," Anna said sorrowfully. "I am so sorry, *Mademoiselle*."

"Anna, there is nothing to forgive," said Tatiana with a smile. "Uncle Henry booked us on a new type of ship built in America called a Baltimore clipper. It is very fast and we should overtake the slower *Suvorov* enroute somewhere. Even if we don't, we should still arrive in New Archangel nearly the same time."

"Yes," said Lady Sutton, nodding her head. "Henry told me that even though the captain of the American ship is rather young, he sailed this new ship in record time across the Atlantic from Boston. The *Sea Rose* has become quite the rage in London."

* * *

Captain Sean O'Connell was chafing at the delay. If he wasn't a man of his word, he would have hoisted the anchor yesterday and sailed down the dirty stinking Thames River and away from the foul air of London into the fresh breezes and waters of the English Channel. Each day spent tied up at the quay increased the risk of encountering early fall storms in the Atlantic. He cursed himself for being so greedy at the sight of all that gold the English lord, Henry Sutton, offered him for the fare of the two passengers, who were unfortunately, women. The men were already grumbling about the presence of women on board being bad luck. He knew it was nonsense, but sailors were a superstitious lot, and a good captain respected their beliefs.

For instance it was bad luck to leave port on a Friday, and here it was Thursday afternoon. If the two women weren't on board by tonight's high tide, he was sailing without them. No way on earth was he going to wait until Saturday, another two days hence, to set sail.

His officers were also displeased with having women passengers, but for more practical reasons. First Mate Ethan Campbell had to move out of his spacious cabin to make room for them, and squeeze into the smaller cabin occupied by the second and third mates, Ned Johnson and Jake O'Riley. The only other alternative was for him to give up his own cabin, and that was unthinkable. He was the captain and he deserved the best accommodations the *Sea Rose* had to offer.

Now all the cargo was fastened below, the supplies loaded, the sails repaired, woodwork painted, ropes oiled and coiled, the decks scrubbed until they gleamed and there was nothing left to do except wait. He sighed with impatience.

A commotion on the quay caught his attention. A shiny silver and black carriage piled high with a dozen trunks or more, clattered to the gangplank and halted. The two horses, one silvery gray and the other midnight black, snorted and rolled their eyes fearfully at the ship creaking against the ropes holding her fast.

Ethan strode up to him and glanced down. "Cuttin' it a bit close, aren't they, Captain?" he commented in his Scottish burr.

Sean grunted irritably and watched as two footmen unloaded the trunks, and gestured to several of the sailors to fetch them on board. The coachman opened the carriage door and Lord Sutton debarked first then turned to help the women out. One wore a rich looking cloak of purple, the other a cloak of green and gold, their heads covered with matching silk bonnets. Their clothing might be suitable here in London on this misty afternoon, but in a storm out at sea Sean knew it was worthless.

However, to greet their illustrious passengers, he and his three officers were dressed in their best coats as well, with shiny brass buttons down the front and on the cuffs, tailored breeches and silk stockings in polished black shoes with brass buckles. But as soon as the ship left the quay, they would all change their attire into the more practical shirts and dungarees and boots of a sailor.

"Looks like one of 'em is no more than a wee bairn," said Ethan, peering down. "One puff of wind, an' she's a goner."

"The tall one's a looker though, ain't she, O'Riley," broke in Ned. The third mate, his curly carrot colored hair only partly contained under his cap, grinned and nodded in agreement.

Inwardly Sean groaned as the pair walked up the plank and stepped gracefully onto the deck. Ned was correct. One of the women was incredibly beautiful, and that was going to make this voyage even more difficult. The other, well, Ethan was right, she was so small and thin, she was either still a young girl, or after seeing the extremely pale face, was in poor health. *Great. A sickly type.*

He pasted a smile on his face and welcomed them to the *Sea Rose*. Lord Sutton shook his hand and introduced his niece, Tatiana Nikolayevna Bolkonskaya and her maid, Anna Teichroew.

He had never been a man who believed in love at first sight. To him, it was a bunch of poppycock that belonged in second rate novels. But when he gazed down into the lovely face of the Russian woman named Tatiana, he found himself falling into the depths of the most enchanting violet blue eyes he had ever seen. They were framed by thick dark lashes which fluttered artfully against her rosy cheeks. Pale golden hair, the color of the full moon, peeked out from underneath her bonnet, and when she bestowed on him her exquisite smile, he knew he had entered unchartered seas and if he wasn't careful, he was going to sink and drown.

"Pleased to meet ye, Miss Bolkonsky," he mumbled, then nodded at her maid, "And ye as well, Miss Teichroew." In a stronger voice he added, "My first mate, Mister Campbell, will see ye both safely to your cabin, and my steward, Samuel, will help ye unpack your trunks and settle in before we sail."

Lord Sutton embraced his niece in farewell, and as Ethan led the women down below, Sean said to the man, "If the wind is with us, we will catch the Russian ship before she reaches the southern latitudes and the storms of Cape Horn. If not, I promise I'll deliver your niece and her maid safely to New Archangel."

"I'm certain her father, Captain-Lieutenant Nikolas Ilyich Bolkonsky, will reward you for the safe return of his daughter."

The name sounded familiar to Sean, but he couldn't place where he'd heard it. No matter. It would come to him in time. As Lord Sutton turned to leave, Sean called out, "One question, Lord Sutton, about your niece's maid, has she been ill? She looks poorly."

Lord Sutton gave him a dismissive wave. "Not to worry, Captain. She's recovering from a bout with diphtheria, but the doctor said she is not contagious, and should manage the voyage well. She's a bit on the weak side at present."

"Jus' a bit weak, eh?" echoed Ned worriedly, "Ah don't like the sound o' that much."

Sean shrugged. He didn't like it either, but it was done now. "I'll tell Samuel to keep an extra eye on her."

"Wang Li will put some meat on 'er bones," said Jake confidently. "She'd be a right fine lookin' woman then, like the Russian Countess."

Sean gave both of his officers a stern glare. "Just a reminder, men, both ladies are off limits to all of the crew for the entire voyage."

"Aye, aye, Cap'n," chorused the two mates together, grinning unabashed.

It was going to be a long voyage, indeed, thought Sean grimly. The sooner they overtook the Russian ship, the better, as far as he was concerned. Heaven help them if they somehow missed the *Suvorov* and were stuck with the two women on board all the way to Alaska. While warning his men to stay away from them, it was himself he was most worried about.

And the lovely Tatiana.

PART TWO

Autumn, 1821-Spring, 1822

CHAPTER TWELVE

Anna was dreaming that she was a prisoner on a pirate ship. The pirate captain was standing over her as she was chained in the dim, rank hold. He had a face that repelled and attracted her all at once. Darkened by constant exposure to the wind and sun, it was face of a devilishly handsome man. His long black unruly hair gleamed in the lantern light and there was dark stubble on his square jaw. His firm, well molded lips were curled into an expression of contempt while a muscle twitched slightly under the thin one inch scar on his left cheek.

His eyes, as green and hard as polished jade, gazed into hers and held her transfixed while another part of her mind took in the rest of the man, his towering height, his wide shoulders and broad chest, his arrogant stance, and the commanding air of authority surrounding him as someone who demanded instant obedience to his orders. He reminded her of ...

She awoke with a jolt, momentarily disoriented. The morning sun streamed through the small cabin window. The bright rays struck her eyes and she winced. Now she remembered where she was and who she was dreaming about.

Sometime during the night the *Sea Rose* had ceased her uneven pitching from the choppy waters of the English Channel as she encountered the smooth rollers of the north Atlantic and now rode the ocean swells with a steady rhythm. It was her captain, the American, who she had been dreaming of.

Shame flooded through her. How could she be dreaming of a man she had just met? The illness must have weakened her more than she imagined. Glancing up at the narrow bunk above her, she noted it was empty. Tatiana must have risen, washed and dressed herself while she slumbered on, dreaming forbidden dreams. What sort of lady's maid was she?

Irritated, she quickly stepped out of her bunk, balancing herself carefully to the motion of the ship. At least she wasn't seasick but her legs trembled. As she washed and dressed she asked God for the strength to face the day. Each morning she awoke with a bit more energy than the day before, and for that she was grateful. But she was a long way from total recovery.

A sharp knock rapped on the cabin door and her heart gave a sudden lurch. She opened it and almost laughed at herself. Instead of the captain she was half hoping, half dreading to see, stood one of the young cabin boys, either Jimmy or Robby. They were twin brothers, both freckle faced with curly brown hair. They reminded her of Jacob and Peter so much it almost took her breath away.

"Good mornin,' Miss," he said, holding a tray of food in his hands. "The Countess said to bring yer breakfast."

"You mean *Mademoiselle* Tatiana Nikolayevna Bolk---"

"None of us lads can say 'er fancy name, Miss, so we jus' call 'er the Countess. Tis easier all around."

His cheerful face made her smile in return. "Of course, then, is it Jimmy or Robby?"

"Tis Robby. The cook, Wang Li, made yer tea. We lads like coffee best, but 'im bein' a Chinaman an' a tea drinker like you Russkies, oh, pardon, Miss, I mean---"

"It's quite all right, Robby," she said, smiling. "Please thank Wang Li for the tea and food for me. And when I feel a bit stronger, I'll come to the kitchen and thank him myself."

"That's the galley, Miss, an' I think he'd be 'appy to see you." Robby placed the tray on the small table bolted to the cabin floor. The table had raised edges to keep items from rolling off, and Anna thought that very clever. She didn't recall the *Suvorov* having such practical furniture.

After Robby left, she sat down and ate hungrily. The cook had prepared bacon, eggs, oatmeal and toast with butter and marmalade, and a pot of hot tea. There were even two lumps of sugar to sweeten it, just like she preferred. For a moment, she remembered her papa sipping his tea through sugar lumps held between his teeth, an old Mennonite custom.

She was almost finished eating when Tatiana swirled through the door, humming gaily. "Oh, Anna, I see you're up and having breakfast. How are you this beautiful morning?"

"I'm feeling stronger today, *Mademoiselle*. But I wish you had awakened me to help you with your toilette this morning. Forgive me for sleeping so soundly I didn't hear you."

Tatiana brushed her apologies aside. "I didn't want to wake you. You need your sleep, Anna, so you will get your strength back soon. And besides, being up early on this ship has its advantages."

"Such as?" Anna shot her a questioning look.

"An invitation to dine with the very good-looking captain for breakfast. He and I got along famously. I think I'm going to enjoy this voyage, Anna, with such a delightful charming man for company. I hope we don't catch the *Suvorov* for a very long time!"

A tiny knot of envy twisted inside Anna at her flirtatious words then she was ashamed of herself. What was it to her if the captain liked her mistress? What man wouldn't desire a beautiful woman like Tatiana? As long as she remembered she was betrothed, there was no harm done.

"Now, now, Anna, don't look at me like that. I know I'm almost a married woman. But it's only an innocent flirtation. After all, what else is there to do for the next few months?"

"Captain O'Connell doesn't look like the type of man who would indulge in only a flirtation, *Mademoiselle*," she answered, remembering the dangerous man in her dream.

Tatiana shrugged. "Flirting is all he'll ever get from me. Even if I wasn't betrothed to Lieutenant Volodin, Captain O'Connell would be the last man on earth I'd ever fall in love with. He's an American, an uncouth, uncultured, uncivilized barbarian. If he wasn't the captain of this ship, I'd have nothing to do with him, absolutely nothing."

"I think the lady doth protest too much," Anna replied, quoting a statement from one of the books her brother Jacob was always reading.

Tatiana looked at her thoughtfully. "You're not jealous, are you, Anna? Do you have an interest in the handsome captain yourself?"

A blush warmed her pale cheeks as she said, "Nonsense, *Mademoiselle*. And even if I did, what man would look twice at the skinny scarecrow of a girl that I am?"

"That first mate, what was his name, Mister Campbell? He certainly hovered over you most attentively yesterday afternoon when he showed us to our cabin. I don't think he even looked at me twice," she added in a surprised note.

"He was only being kind, doing his duty," protested Anna. But she had noticed the big Scotsman with his long russet colored hair tied in a queue down his back. He had watched her with concern in his warm brown eyes, and once flashed her a handsome grin under his dark red mustache. She had been too weary to respond to him, except for a polite thank you.

"No man is kind to a lady unless he wants something from her, my dear," Tatiana sighed in a worldly manner. "You could do worse on this voyage. Next to the captain, he is the second most important man on the ship. Too bad about that bad limp he has though. It takes away from his physical attractiveness, I fear."

Anna disagreed but said nothing as Tatiana rattled on, "Captain O'Connell introduced me to the nephew of the owner of this ship. His name is John Hill and he is the supercargo. You should meet him, Anna. He's quite handsome with blonde curly hair and bright blue eyes. He seems well educated and even more interesting he was captured by savages and lived with them for two whole years! Imagine! And then he was rescued by none other than Captain O'Connell himself, along with the first mate, Mr. Campbell. That's how he became a cripple. His leg was wounded by an arrow and it had to be amputated. What a story!"

"*Mademoiselle*, you need to be careful around all of these American men. You have your reputation to consider. Here we are, without a chaperone and without permission from your father to even be on this ship. Your behavior from now on must be above reproach."

"Thank you for the warning, my pious little maid, but I do remind you that my English uncle gave me permission to sail on the *Sea Rose*." A flash of determination lit her eyes as she added, "And for once in my life, I am on my own, without any family or society rules to restrict me. I shall do as I please, and you, my dear, must swear to secrecy anything that happens while we are on this ship. Do you swear, Anna?"

"I do not swear, *Mademoiselle*, but I give you my solemn word that I will tell no one, unless you give me permission otherwise."

"That will do, Anna." She smiled then, a strange catlike smile, which made Anna extremely uneasy. She realized she needed to start praying they would catch up to the *Suvorov* as soon as possible, before her mistress did something she might regret.

* * *

Sean was enjoying the sunny morning on deck, remembering with a smile his delightful breakfast with Miss Bolkonsky earlier. She had surprised him by being as intelligent as she was beautiful. Unlike most women, she'd expressed interest in his ship, even asking if he would take her on a tour sometime.

He was impressed by her ability to speak English with only a trace of a Russian accent. She could speak French, too, she'd told him, which was actually the language preferred by the Russian nobility. Her sophisticated background made him glad he had learned years ago how to speak proper English, though when he was very angry or very tired, he still slipped back into the Irish brogue of his childhood.

"A letter for you, Cap'n," said Ned, explaining how it had been delivered right before they'd sailed the night before, given by mistake to one of the common sailors, who had forgotten it until now.

"Looks to be important," he said, frowning. "Say the word, Cap'n, an' I'll 'ave the fool flogged."

"We whip the men for outright defiance, Ned, not for stupidity," sighed Sean, opening the cream-colored envelope stamped with the heavily embossed seal of the United States of America. The letter inside was short and to the point:

"To Captain O'Connell of the Sea Rose out of Boston,

This letter of warning is being sent to all captains of American merchant vessels here in London. There is a heightened state of tension between our country and Russia over the fur trade in Alaska. With Alexander Baranov gone and the Russian Imperial Navy now in charge of the Russian American Fur Company, there is increased danger to Americans trading with the natives in Alaska.

First, I need to inform you of a few facts: As of last year, 1819, the financial worth of the Russian American Fur Company was seven million gold rubles. They have twenty-four establishments, ranging in size from simple hunting stations in the Pribylov Islands to Sitka (New Archangel), which is estimated to be worth two million, five hundred thousand rubles alone. The census that year showed 391 men and 13 women of pure Russian blood, and 244 Creole men and 111 women. They have 8,384 male natives (Aleut and Tlingit) available for command. 198 of the Russians are at Sitka, twenty seven at Fort Ross, California. Others are stationed elsewhere from Kodiak to the Pribylovs.

With such a great enterprise as this, we believe the Russian Imperial Navy will do anything, and we mean anything, to safeguard their interests. We have had reports of Russian spies in London, searching American ships to discover what type of cargo is on board, mainly guns and ammunition to be sold to the natives, which the Russians claim to be illegal. The spies also wish to discover our trading routes in Alaska, so their Imperial Navy warships can seize our ships for illegal searches, and perhaps make arrests if any evidence is found.

There is a strong rumor that Czar Alexander will issue a Ukase in the coming year, forbidding Americans to trade at all in Alaskan waters. Beware of any Russians you come in contact with. Do not trust them.

Your obedient servant,

Richard Rush, American Foreign Minister to Britain"

His gut clenched as the food in his stomach from this morning's breakfast with the inquisitive Miss Bolkonsky suddenly turned sour. Sean folded up the paper with a grim face and said, "Ned, tell Campbell, O'Riley, Hill, and Jones that I wish to meet with them in my cabin at once."

Ten minutes later the men were grouped inside the captain's large cabin with the door locked and Samuel standing guard outside. Sean read Mr. Rush's letter out loud, then waited impatiently as all the men exploded in curses, except for Ethan, who stood dumbfounded and silent.

"I say we bring them women in 'ere and threaten' 'em if they don't tell us the truth," said Jake, his face almost purple with rage.

"Threaten them with what?" asked John. "We have no proof they are spies, just because of their nationality."

"Threaten' 'em with a sound floggin' by Jones 'ere," Ned answered, nodding at the giant hulk of a man. "One look at 'im an' they'll be tellin' us everythin.'"

Jones shook his shiny bald head. "Ain't got no wish to hit ladies, Mister Johnson."

"Ya' all will if the Cap'n says so," Ned retorted. "Back where I come from in Carolina, the slave gals got whipped jus' like the boys if they misbehaved like. Made no difference."

"This ship isn't a cotton plantation, Ned," said Sean with a look of disgust, "and our passengers are not slaves. I don't want to hear another word about harming so much as a hair on either one of the ladies' heads."

"I'm relieved to hear ye say that, Captain," said Ethan with relief. "The wee lassie, Anna, is nae well yet an'---"

"I find it hard to believe they are Russian spies," John interrupted. "If they were, then that would mean the Englishman, Lord Sutton, is one too. He's the one who arranged for their passage. And he also said one of them is his niece. The Suttons are an old established shipping family of the aristocracy with a fortune greater than my uncle's. It's ludicrous to think they could be in league with the Russians."

"Far-fetched, but not impossible," said Sean thoughtfully. "Not too many years ago we were at war with the British, and now we compete with them on the west coast of North America in a fur trade that is quickly disappearing. It would be to England's advantage to have any of our ships impounded by the Russians. It would mean more furs for the British shipping fortunes." He looked at each man in the room and added, "I'm not sure we can trust the Brits anymore than the Russians."

"Do ye have any proof Miss Bolkonsky is really Lord Sutton's niece?" asked Ethan.

"Only the word of an English gentleman," said Sean.

"Not good enough fer the likes of me," commented Jake. "Nor that cock n' bull story 'bout the maid bein' so sick the Russkies sailed off wi' out 'em."

"The maid was ill with diphtheria, men," said Sean. "One look at her and I know that part of the story is true. But it's Miss Bolkonsky I'm most concerned about, and the fact that Lord Sutton told me yesterday her father is Captain-Lieutenant Nikolas Bolkonsky, stationed in Sitka.

At the time, it meant little to me, but then I remembered he is the Governor's assistant there."

"I have a plausible theory," said John with a grim expression. "Perhaps Miss Bolkonsky wasn't originally a spy, but when her maid took ill in London, she was approached by Russian officials, who arranged through Lord Sutton to have her placed on board our ship. Meanwhile, the Russian ship sails off, and Miss Bolkonsky uses her feminine wiles to search for any guns we're carrying, and to discover our trading routes to the native villages. When we eventually catch up to the Russian ship and hand her over to them, she carries that information to her father, who will have an Imperial Navy ship waiting for us when we arrive in Alaskan waters."

A dead silence enveloped the cabin until Sean said, "If 'tis any chance of what ye said is the truth, 'twould be in our best interests if we never find the *Suvorov*. Then Miss Bolkonsky wouldn't have any opportunity to pass on the information."

"If we took the ladies all the way to Alaska with us," said John, "we could use them as hostages if we're threatened by an Imperial Navy ship."

"Or we can dump 'em off at Fort Ross on our way up the California coast," said Jake.

"We need to steer clear of California," said Sean. "The Spanish don't take kindly to us Americans anymore than the Russians do."

"What should we do then?" asked Ethan, and all the men started talking at once, voicing their many opinions until Sean raised his hand to quiet them.

"First of all, we do not let either of our passengers know we suspect them. I'll allow the ladies to stroll the deck in fair weather and to enjoy the comforts of their cabin and the main salon. Every other part of the ship is off limits to them. Ethan, since ye seem to have your eye on the maid already, I want ye to keep it on her whenever she is feeling well enough to leave her cabin. I will take the responsibility of keeping my eye on Miss Bolkonsky. Meanwhile, not a word of this to any member of the crew. Understand, men?"

They all nodded in agreement, and Sean dismissed them, then sat down at his desk, deep in thought. The angry look in Ned's eyes when he left made him uneasy. He hoped his second mate would keep his wits about him, what little he had. He had promoted him to an officer for old times' sake, and sometimes he regretted it. Ned was hot-tempered and didn't look beyond the color of a man's skin. The crew didn't like him, but they did obey his orders, however reluctantly. At least Ned wasn't as sadistic as Arthur Horn.

Making Jake O'Riley the third mate was possibly another error in judgment. Younger than Ned, he'd always looked up to him, and blindly followed Ned no matter what. He believed Jake was a good lad at heart, but lately, he was beginning to think neither man was officer material. Thomas Hill had questioned his promotion of the two men back in Boston, and Sean had quite a time convincing him they were capable leaders. Ultimately, Mr. Hill had allowed him to make the final decision.

Then there was the problem of what to do with the Russian women. At least now that he suspected Tatiana Bolkonsky to be a spy it was going to be easier to resist her charms. If there was one thing he despised in a woman it was deceit. He remembered how after breakfast she'd had the audacity to ask him to show her around the ship. Luckily, he'd had some duties to attend to, and said he would another time. No chance of that in the future.

Up on deck, it was a troubled Ethan Campbell who busied himself taking the ship's position at noon with the sextant. He had a hard time keeping his mind on it, however. American law stated that a person was innocent until proven guilty. But the captain and the rest of the men had already judged the women and decided they were guilty. As for himself, he thought it more likely that neither of the women was a spy, especially the little maid. There was something about her that attracted him, but as yet, he wasn't sure what it was.

Meanwhile, as the captain ordered, he would keep his eye on her, a duty he was looking forward to.

* * *

The *Sea Rose* was built in two sections below decks. The forward cabin was a long narrow room lighted by a skylight. The galley and pantry and several small cabins opened off the sides. In the center was a long dining table, designed with racks to keep dishes from sliding off. A revolving armchair was fastened at the head of the table, reserved for the captain. On each side of the room were settees made of teak that were screwed to the floor.

The smaller cabins were for the steward, the cook, the carpenter Ebenezer Cartwright, the supercargo John Hill and the armorer Mr. Jones, all who were privileged members of the crew. The common sailors were berthed near the bow in rows of tiered wooden bunks.

The stern of the *Sea Rose* housed a large area known in most ships as the after cabin. The Captain's cabin or quarters was in one corner; the remaining corners held three other cabins, one used as a chart room, the other two, quarters for the first mate, now occupied by Tatiana and Anna, and quarters for the three officers, Misters' Campbell, Johnson and O'Riley.

A cross-shaped space left in the center of the after cabin was called the main salon. The alcoves at the sides were fitted with built-in sofas, ornately carved and upholstered in royal blue damask. The rest of the room was furnished with several easy chairs and a teak table, all bolted down to the floor.

During the day the salon was well-lit and cheerful even in the gloomiest weather with a large raised skylight in the center of the ceiling. In the stern were small square windows that were protected from bad weather by heavy shutters which could be closed. At night, light was provided by swinging whale-oil lanterns.

After several days at sea Tatiana and Anna both agreed that the accommodations of the *Sea Rose* were far superior to those of the older *Suvorov*. They also agreed they didn't miss the company of whining Natasha or her stuffy husband. This afternoon Anna was seated in the salon reading her Bible while Tatiana paced restlessly around the room, glancing out a window periodically. There was nothing to see except the endless march of gray-green waves and the constant up and down motion of the distant horizon.

Irritated, Tatiana looked at her. "Don't you ever tire of reading that old book? You should have it memorized by now."

Anna smiled patiently. "Each day I find something new in God's word that He wishes me to know. If you ever care to listen, I'd love to share His promises with you."

She shuddered. "I would have to be bored out of my mind to ever read that dull book, although if I don't find something interesting to do soon, I just might take you up on your offer."

"Have you ever read the Bible?"

"I've heard enough of its words touted from the lips of priests to last me a lifetime."

She sighed so heavily Anna looked at her curiously. "Whatever is the matter, *Mademoiselle*? You are so restless perhaps you should go up on deck for a short walk."

"What is the point of that when he will be too busy to talk to me?"

"Do you mean Captain O'Connell?"

"Of course," she snapped, "haven't you noticed how he is hardly civil to me anymore? At first, he was so attentive, but now he treats me like I'm some sort of leper. He politely brushes aside any of my questions, refuses to take me on a tour of his ship, and at dinner, he talks mainly to his officers, and not to me. Americans!" she spat out the word. "Uncle Vasily was right, they are barbarians!"

"Tis it how ye truly see me, Miss Bolkonsky?" asked Captain O'Connell, standing in the open doorway of his cabin.

Anna froze, aware of the open hostility emanating from him, and he suddenly looked too much like the dangerous pirate captain in her dream. Tatiana didn't seem to notice the quiet anger in his voice, and she tossed her head and faced him, "So, you were eavesdropping on our conversation, Captain? How uncouth!"

"What else would ye expect from a Yankee barbarian?"

Tatiana curved her lips into a haughty smile, reminiscent of her Aunt Irene, and said, "I expect you to respect a lady's privacy like a proper gentleman, Sir."

His expression darkened and he said, "What little game are ye playing, anyway, Countess?"

"Countess? Game?" Tatiana started to laugh, but he cut her off, saying, "My crew calls ye the Countess and now I see how fitting it is. So, who are ye really?"

"What an absurd question, Captain, as if you don't already know, but I'll tell you again. I'm Tatiana Nikolayevna Bolkonsky, born in Saint Petersburg. My father is Captain-Lieutenant Nikolas Ilyich Bolkonsky, the younger brother of Count Vasily Ilyich Bolkonsky, and my mother was Elizabeth Sutton, daughter of Lord Henry and Lady Diana Sutton. I have no brothers or sisters, and only two cousins, Mikael and Olga." She fluttered her eyelashes and added, "When I reach New Archangel, I shall be married to Lieutenant Dmitri Ivanich Volodin, the son of Baron Ivan Volodin. So, one day I shall be a Baroness, not a Countess."

As she rattled off all her aristocratic Russian and English family names, Sean felt his own lowborn Irish roots keenly, and the comparison between them only deepened his anger. Her arrogance in flaunting her betrothal to an Imperial Navy lieutenant was the final catalyst to losing his composure.

Before he could stop himself, he snapped, "I have it on good authority that ye may be a Russian spy, placed on my ship to discover our trading routes in Alaska and what cargo we carry in our hold."

Anna gasped and Tatiana's mouth fell open in shock, then she laughed. "What sort of game are you playing, Captain?"

"This is not a game, Miss Bolkonsky. Your presence on my ship has become a danger to me and my crew. Whether ye are a spy of the Russian government or a young woman of Russian nobility who has fallen into an unfortunate experience remains to be seen."

All traces of frivolity vanished as Tatiana demanded, "How dare you even suggest such a ridiculous thing?" She thrust out her left hand, on which diamonds and sapphires sparkled in a gold band. "Look at this ring, Captain. It is my betrothal ring, the family heirloom of the Volodins. Do you suppose that a common spy could possess such a priceless piece of jewelry?"

"Tis true that your ring is not something the average Russian woman would possess. But your expensive jewelry and fine clothes could have been given to ye for your disguise as a member of the nobility."

"So, you believe I am posing as Tatiana Nikolayevna Bolkonsky? You are impossible! You are determined to think me a spy regardless of my answers. I am very weary of playing this game, Captain. Think what you like. I don't care anymore."

She whirled away towards her cabin door, but Sean was too quick and grabbed her arm before she could leave. "Ye are either the best little actress I have ever met, or ye are telling the truth."

As the two stood in the middle of the salon, glaring at each other like two pugilists before their fight, Anna said quietly, "Captain O'Connell, I will swear on the Bible I'm holding, that my mistress is exactly who she says she is, and that she is not a spy of the Russian government."

Sean had forgotten the maid was even in the room. He'd had eyes only for Tatiana, who was the most maddening, bewitching woman he'd ever met. Holding her arm, feeling the warmth of her delicate skin under the silk material of her gown, gazing into those extraordinary violet blue eyes, made him long to crush her into his arms.

The maid's voice saying the word, Bible, was like throwing a pitcher of ice cold water on a flaming ember.

He dropped Tatiana's arm as if it burned him, and turned to Anna, seeing her clearly for the first time since she arrived on the ship. She was small and too slender, almost childlike with wide hazel eyes set over high cheekbones. Her hair was the color of rich honey and it was swept back except for a few girlish curls around her face. She had a calm, almost regal air about her and her expression was direct and unafraid.

"Anna never lies, Captain," said Tatiana hurriedly. "It's impossible for her. She is a Mennonite and the most religious person I've ever known."

All anger suddenly left him. With the Bible in her lap, the sweet faced maid reminded him of his mother and his sister, Rose.

He bowed his head to her and said, "I believe ye are telling the truth, Miss Teichroew, or as much as ye know the truth to be."

At that moment, Samuel walked in the salon and said, "Cap'n suh, yo' wanted up on deck."

Sean gave a brusque nod to both women. "Ladies, we will continue this conversation another time. G'day."

As he and the tall black steward left, Tatiana looked at Anna, "You rescued me once again, Anna. How can I ever thank you?"

"Perhaps by not antagonizing the captain. You seem to infuriate him."

Anger colored her eyes to a dark purple. "He's the most obstinate man I've ever met! How ludicrous to think that I am a spy!"

Then a crafty look stole over her face. "You know, Anna, his outrageous accusations have given me an idea. Since he already thinks I might be a spy, why don't I just become one? Here we are, in a perfect position to find out if the Americans have guns on board to trade to the Indians. And if I can find out where he does his trading in Russian America, when we reach New Archangel, I could tell my father and the new governor."

She paused, thinking, "Hopefully, my father will be the new governor by then."

Anna felt a terrible foreboding at Tatiana's reckless words. "I don't think that is such a good idea, *Mademoiselle*. Captain O'Connell might be arrested."

"That's the idea," said Tatiana, laughing softly. She imagined how proud of her Lieutenant Volodin and her papa would be if she helped the Imperial Navy catch one of their enemies violating the rules of the Czar. Someday when Captain O'Connell was safely in a Russian prison, she would actually tell him he was the one who put the idea in her head to become a spy. What perfect revenge for the insulting manner in which he was treating her!

* * *

The *Sea Rose* was blessed with fair weather. The clipper flew over the ocean mile after mile as gracefully as the porpoises who escorted her. One afternoon Anna and Tatiana stood on deck, watching in fascination as the elegant gray sea creatures darted back and forth in front of the ship, avoiding the sharp bow with their speed and agility.

With little to do except eat and rest, Anna's strength had returned. The daily chores of cleaning the cabin and emptying chamber pots were taken care of by Jimmy and Robby, and once a week, Samuel instructed them to bring in a tub of water for bathing and laundry. Her job as lady's maid was mainly to help Tatiana with her hair and dress, neither of which was a complicated affair with no dinner parties or balls for her to attend.

It was sunny with a brisk cool wind blowing across the deck. The fresh salty breeze was a refreshing change for the two women from the stale air below. Anna squinted at the bright sunshine sparkling over the dark blue water dotted with creamy whitecaps.

Many of the crew was about. They kept the sails spread high and the braces taut so the *Sea Rose* could sustain her speed. The first mate was at the helm, a big open wheel so heavy that on many ships it took more than one man to control it. Ethan Campbell steered the ship through the waves easily, his arm muscles under his long shirt sleeves, contracting and bulging into massive knots. His face was ruddy with the strain and the wind, his cap pulled low over his forehead, his dark red hair tied back. He saw Anna watching him and gave her a friendly nod.

She smiled at him and turned away, not noticing the extra redness staining his cheeks in a blush. Tatiana nudged her and said, "Don't you think the crude carving of that woman quite scandalous?"

Tatiana was referring to the figurehead, a wooden sculpture of a bare-breasted maiden with long flowing hair. When Anna had first laid eyes on it, she was properly shocked, thinking how horrified Elder Klassen or Papa would be to see such a thing. "Perhaps she is the Rose the ship is named after, and the sailors believe she brings them good luck," Anna commented.

"Your assumption is correct, Miss Teichroew," said Captain O'Connell strolling up behind them. "While most sailors believe a woman onboard a ship brings bad luck, they also believe a figurehead of a woman on a ship's prow does just the opposite. To them the sea is like a woman, capricious, mysterious and unforgiving." He looked directly at Tatiana as he stressed the last three words.

She stiffened and said, "When do you expect us to find the *Suvorov*, Captain?"

"Hopefully before we reach Brazil and Cape Horn. Are ye anxious to rejoin your countrymen?"

"Of course, especially since you made it so very clear that my maid and I are not wanted on your ship."

He bowed slightly. "My apologies for my outburst the other day concerning my suspicions." Inwardly he was still angry at himself for losing his control and accusing Tatiana of being a spy without any solid proof. He had told only Ethan and John of that debacle. Since then, he had tried to avoid her, something difficult to do under such close quarters.

She looked at him coldly. "By now I hope you have come to your senses, Captain, and realize that we are innocent of any charges of being spies."

He nodded towards Anna. "Your maid has convinced me ye are who ye say ye are, Miss Bolkonsky. Once again, please accept my sincerest apologies."

She hesitated, fighting the urge to slap the smirk off his handsome face. But she knew it would do no good to continue behaving in a hostile manner towards him. The only way to discover the information she sought was to pretend to be friendly.

She held out her gloved hand. "A truce, Captain?"

He took her hand in his large one and shook it lightly. "Perhaps ye and your maid might join me and my officers for dinner this evening."

"Perhaps," she said, then withdrew her hand from his grasp and pressed it to her forehead. "Anna, I feel one of my headaches coming on. I think I shall retire for awhile."

"I'll come with you and tell Samuel to have Wang Li boil some willow bark tea."

Tatiana shook her head. "No, Anna, stay here and enjoy the fresh air. It has put some color back into your cheeks. All I want to do is take a nap." She glanced at Sean. "Until dinner then, Captain."

She smiled and made her way aft, past the mounted guns, four on each side, to the main hatch near the mainmast. Anna and the captain watched her graceful willowy form recede, then he said, "Does she really have a headache or is she still angry with me?"

"*Mademoiselle* is plagued by headaches at---at certain times of the month," said Anna, then she blushed in embarrassment at her improper words. What was she thinking to mention such a private feminine function to a man, a near stranger?

When he realized what she was referring to, he hastily changed the subject. "Well, Miss Teichroew, she is right. Yer looking much better these days."

He couldn't help noticing that the maid was almost pretty with her cheeks rosy from the wind and the sun highlighting the gold in her hair, reflecting the golden flecks in her hazel eyes. She had gained a few pounds, too, and wasn't as thin as before. If he hadn't been so dazzled by her mistress, he would have to admit little Anna had a beauty all her own.

"I must tell you, Captain, that I admire your ship greatly. In comparison to the bulky, slow *Suvorov*, she is like a swift seagull winging its way over the water."

The compliment, delivered so sincerely without a drop of guile, suddenly warmed him and he grinned at her. "Thank you, Miss Teichroew."

"The man who designed this ship must be a creative genius," she said. "It seems that the Americans are always inventing new things. The Czar needs to encourage the people of Russia to do the same."

"Your country is hardly a breeding ground for inventors. What I've heard is that most Russians are closed to any new ideas, especially foreign ones."

"That's not true, Captain. Czar Alexander has encouraged foreigners to travel in Russia, and he is a firm supporter of education. Our flourishing universities are proof of that. He has even formed the Russian Bible Society which works in connection with the British and Foreign Bible study. *Mademoiselle* says he is a man of remarkable understanding and information."

"I beg your pardon, Miss Teichroew. I didn't mean to slight your country or your Czar."

"I'm not insulted," she said with a smile. "I'm a Russian by birth, but not by blood."

"What do ye mean?" he asked, his curiosity aroused.

"My people, the Mennonites, are from Holland originally. My ancestors fled the Lowlands to Prussia to escape persecution for our faith, and when life in Prussia became dangerous for them, they finally settled in southern Russia by the invitation of Catherine the Great several decades ago. My family owns a farm in the village of Furstenau near the Dnieper River, which flows into the Black Sea."

"Who persecuted your people?"

"In Holland it was the Catholic Church and the French Huguenots, and in Prussia, the Prussians themselves, jealous of the successful farmers we had become."

At the mention of the Catholics, Sean winced, remembering stories he'd heard as a boy of the Spanish Inquisition and other long ago atrocities committed by the Church against those who dared defy their doctrines.

"Since I was raised a Catholic," he said, "I'm afraid my Irish ancestors and your Dutch ancestors would not have liked each other much."

She laughed lightly. "It wouldn't matter to a Mennonite. My people believe in total nonviolence. They would have forgiven any insults your ancestors gave them then welcomed them into their homes for *faspa*."

At his look of confusion, she explained, "*Faspa* is the traditional afternoon meal we serve after church."

"The Mennonites sound like good, kind people," he said, and thought, just like you, Anna.

"Most of them are," she said, thinking, *except for Gerhard Yoder and Agatha.*

"Ye are a long long way from your village," he said. "Ye must miss your family."

She sighed. "More than you know, Captain. Sometimes I wonder if I'll ever see them again, my papa, my younger brothers and my little sister. And you? Do you miss your wife and family on these long voyages?"

During this conversation Anna had forgotten to be afraid of the Captain, as he kept smiling at her in such a friendly manner. But now after she asked that question, it was like a shutter closed in her face. His smile vanished and he said brusquely, "I have no wife or family."

At that he turned and gestured to the first mate. "Mister Campbell," he called out over the wind, "Have one of the men take over the helm. I need ye to keep Miss Teichroew company while she is up on deck."

He nodded at her and politely excused himself, once more the dark brooding captain. As he walked away, Anna knew that for a few seconds she had caught a glimpse of the real Captain O'Connell. He was a man who seemed haunted by some deep sadness.

"Tis a fine day for a bit of air," said the first mate, standing at the rail. He was almost as tall as the captain, and looked to be a few years older, in his early thirties. He had warm brown eyes that crinkled at the corners when he smiled, and she felt more at ease in his company in one second than she could ever feel in the Captain's presence.

"I don't mean to keep you from your duties, Mister Campbell," she said, conscious of the sailors glancing in her direction, some with shy smiles, some with frowns. She wondered if the crew resented her and Tatiana's presence on board, and the extra work they were causing for the increased speed of the *Sea Rose* to catch up to the *Suvorov*.

When she voiced her worry to the first mate, he shrugged his broad shoulders. "Tis no concern of the men to question the cap'n's order for extra speed. Ye needn't trouble yer bonny head about them, lassie."

"I'm afraid it's in my nature to think about other people, Mister Campbell. All those days resting in my cabin I had little else to do except wonder at the stories behind some of your crew, like your Chinese cook, and Samuel, the steward, and the young cabin boys. They remind me much of my own twin brothers back in Russia."

"The Cap'n found Jimmy an' Robby in Boston. They picked his pocket an' he caught 'em right in the act. He dinna want to turn 'em in, 'cause he said they reminded him of himself when he was twelve. 'Tis a sad story fer the poor lads. They were orphaned when young, then an older fellow, a thief by trade, was teachin' em' how to steal for 'im. The Cap'n took pity on the lads an' hired 'em on afore we sailed."

Anna was astounded to learn that the Captain had such a charitable nature. She wondered if he had been orphaned too, as he mentioned how he had no family waiting for him in Boston. It wasn't something she dared ask him, however.

"The boys seem to be adjusting well to ship life," she said. "I hear them whistling as they work and they smile frequently." She had noticed that though Jimmy and Robby did the work the most menial servant would do in the Bolkonsky palace, they performed their duties without the sullen attitudes of the serfs.

"We dinna work 'em any harder than the men. They're up at five an' in their bunks by eight at night. They do all the odd jobs on board ship, all the scrubbin,' sweepin,' helpin' Wang Li in the galley, an' takin' care of our fresh meat supply, the pigs, chickens, an' goats in the hold."

"The steward is an interesting man," she said. "I've never met an African slave before."

"Samuel's a free man, lassie."

Surprised, she said, "Did the Captain set him free?"

"Nay, Samuel was owned by Cap'n Smythe of the *Eastern Wind*. When Smythe was killed by Indians, his widow set Samuel free. Now Samuel is paid crew like the rest of us."

"I don't believe in slavery," said Anna. "It is an evil in the sight of God and man."

He nodded his agreement. "Tis a cruel fate for the blacks. Families are torn apart forever. Our Samuel here has not seen his sister since the day they were sold as bairns in New York thirty years ago. Afore we sailed, the Cap'n hired a man to find Samuel's sister, but I don't hold out much hope for that after all this time."

"The slaves of America remind me of the serfs of Russia. They also have to obey their masters without question or suffer the consequences." She glanced up at him. "Did Wang Li leave China on his own accord, or was he forced, too?"

"The wee Chinaman has a verra interestin' story. He used to be the chief cook in the Empress of China's royal household. But he fell in love with one of the Empress's maids, named Lily Flower, an' married her without the Empress's permission. When she found out, she was so angry, she ordered him executed. With the help of Lily Flower, he managed to escape to Canton where our old ship, the *Eastern Wind*, was docked. He stowed away an' we dinna find 'im until we sailed. Horn, our first mate, wanted to throw 'im to the sharks, but Cap'n Smythe put 'im to work scrubbin' decks and so on. Halfway 'cross the Pacific one night, our cook fell overboard. Horn thought Wang Li pushed 'im. Wang Li said it was fate. Either way we needed a cook. After the first meal, the tastiest chicken stew we'd ever ate, Horn never said another word agin 'im."

"Whatever happened to his wife back in China?"

"Wang Li said she was likely killed. Every night afore he goes to sleep, he burns incense or what he calls joss sticks to her spirit. Sometimes you can hear 'im talkin' to her in his cabin; sounds like a lot of mumbo jumbo."

"That's one of the saddest stories I've ever heard," said Anna. "He needs to find himself another Chinese wife."

"Wang Li can't go back to China, ever, an' Chinese ladies don't just grow on trees in Boston."

Anna giggled. "I shouldn't laugh, but you have such a funny way of speaking, Mister Campbell."

"No offense taken, lass. I'm a born an' bred Scotsman, an' we all talk funny." He grinned down at her, and she laughed again.

"And how about you? Do you have family back in Scotland?" She was a bit hesitant to ask the first mate about his family after the captain's bizarre reaction to a similar question, but she needn't have worried. He was very open about his life, relating to her briefly how his father was a Presbyterian minister in Edinburgh, his subsequent rebellion, and how he ended up shipwrecked off Florida, the very night his parents were praying for him.

She was fascinated by his story and when he finished she said softly, "God did answer your parents' prayers, I believe, Mister Campbell."

"The Cap'n told me you have a Bible," said Ethan, "so now there are two of us on board. An' your religion, what's it called---"

"Mennonite. Our beliefs are similar to the Quakers in America. Have you heard of them?"

"Aye, they are a people I've always admired. They speak out against slavery an' they have schools for the Indian bairns. They are also laughed at for refusin' to fight when attacked."

"Most people consider a creed of nonresistance foolishness in this violent world. But we follow words of Jesus who tells us to love our enemies and to do good to them who hate us. We are to bless those who curse us and pray for them. And if someone strikes us on one cheek we are to offer the other cheek as well."

She smiled. "As for me, I prefer to trust God rather than relying on a sword or a gun."

She's a brave wee lass, he thought, looking at her with admiration. And she was intelligent, educated, beautiful and most importantly, a person of faith. He felt a deep attraction to her that he had never felt for any woman. But she was so young, so innocent, so unaware of the effect she had on him. Was this how Wang Li felt when he fell in love with the Empress of China's maid?

"Would it be too forward of me to ask when you lost your leg, Mister Campbell?" she asked with a gentle smile.

He had forgotten about his wooden leg. Most women pretended they didn't see it by averting their eyes. He admired Anna even more for her directness. "Nay, lass, I appreciate your concern. 'Twas 'bout a year ago that I was shot in the leg with a poisoned arrow by a bunch of crazy Nootka Indians on Vancouver Island." He proceeded to explain how gangrene had set in, and that a Russian doctor at Sitka had removed the infected leg to above the knee.

"So, now I have a wooden leg an' foot. Not a sight for a fine lass as yerself to see," he added, waiting for the expected look of disgust to cross her face.

Instead she glanced down thoughtfully at his legs. "It looks like God saved you once again, Mister Campbell. He must have something special for you to do someday."

It wasn't the reaction he expected and he must have looked startled, for she added, "Everything happens to a child of God for a reason."

"Well, well, lookee 'ere," drawled Ned Johnson, shifting his close-set eyes back and forth between Anna and Ethan. "Don't you both look jus' like a cozy lil twosome. Don't min' my interruptin' now. I'm jus' passin' by."

He tipped his cap to Anna then strutted off. She felt a shiver run through her at the insolent way he had stared at her, a slight leer playing at his mouth. She had noticed the second mate watching her before and thought him a fierce looking man with his heavy dark beard and mustache. He reminded her of a Tartar.

"I'll walk you back to yer cabin, lass," said Ethan, with a sharp glance of dislike at Ned's retreating back. She nodded, her enjoyment on deck suddenly gone. They were silent as he escorted her down the hatch ladder to the main salon. She smiled her thanks, and he left her reluctantly, hoping he might see her at dinner later that evening.

Anna walked through the empty salon to their cabin. She opened the door and peered in, expecting to see her mistress resting, but there was no one inside. Alarmed, she whirled around in confusion and was about to call out her name when Tatiana stepped out from the captain's quarters.

She was smiling triumphantly when she caught sight of Anna. "Come with me to our cabin, Anna, I have something to show you."

* * *

Earlier Tatiana had faked the headache. When she realized Captain O'Connell and his first and second mates were all up on deck, she thought it finally might be her chance to search the captain's cabin. During the past week she'd studied the shipboard routine, and she noted that in the middle of every afternoon, there was a kind of lull in activity below decks. The morning cleaning by the cabin boys was finished, and they were busy elsewhere in the ship, and though the steward was unpredictable in his routine, this afternoon she'd seen him disappear towards the galley, presumably to discuss the evening meal with the cook. The third mate, Mister O'Riley, was sound asleep, as he was every day at this time since he was in command of the night watch.

When she went below she hurried past his cabin, hearing his deep snores. She glanced furtively all around, then pushed open the captain's door, and felt relieved it wasn't locked. The cabin was spacious, furnished with a wide bunk, a mahogany desk and table, and the walls were lined with bookshelves upon which were rows of leather-bound volumes. She was surprised that the captain was educated enough to enjoy reading good literature. She noted the names of American and

English authors, Benjamin Franklin, Thomas Jefferson, Thomas Paine, plays by William Shakespeare and many others.

But it was the desk that held her interest. She didn't know quite what she was looking for, but finding the ship's log would be a good start. There were two drawers on each side of the desk and one in the middle. They were all locked except for the bottom right hand drawer. She pulled it open and saw it was filled with important looking papers.

Quickly she scanned them, feeling grateful for the years of English lessons from her childhood. One of the papers was a letter to the captain from the ship's owner, Thomas Hill. He had written that if this voyage yielded high profits in the fur trade, Captain O'Connell was allowed a certain percentage, making him a wealthy man.

Good for him, the black-hearted rogue, she thought, but this information was not what she was looking for. Then she found it---the cargo manifest. It was a sheet of paper with the list of everything the Captain had bought in London, including, she saw with a quickening of her pulse, dozens upon dozens of boxes of muskets, fowling pieces, powder, and ammunition.

She clutched the paper to her chest and smiled with glee. It was exactly the proof she needed to show her father and her betrothed, Lieutenant Volodin, that Captain O'Connell had every intention of trading guns illegally with the natives in Russian America.

CHAPTER THIRTEEN

Late summer and early autumn was the hurricane season in the Atlantic. The monster storms were born off the west coast of Africa as tropical depressions, growing in strength as they fed off the warm waters. It could be a tricky time of year to sail from England to Brazil.

But the *Sea Rose* was lucky and did not encounter such a storm. Instead she was blessed with the brisk trade winds, blowing her quickly towards the equator. When the ship entered the Horse Latitudes, or the doldrums as the sailors called them, the steady breezes died. The sea became flat and glassy, rolling the ship uneasily about. The air below decks grew unbearably hot during the day and not much cooler at night. Sleep in the cabins was nearly impossible. Most of the crew slept topside, including the captain.

For propriety's sake, Anna and Tatiana were not allowed that privilege. They struggled to survive the smothering tropical heat by ripping the long sleeves off their heavy wadded silk gowns, or when alone in their cabin, just wearing a chemise and a petticoat.

"I keep dreaming of the frozen Neva River," said Tatiana one evening. "All that lovely cold ice."

The two women leaned wearily against the stern rail, waiting for the blazing sun to set in hopes that a breeze of any kind might spring up to banish the sticky heat. Although they were forbidden to be on deck by themselves, they had long ceased to care. Their usual escorts, the captain and the first mate, were eating dinner below in the forward cabin.

They'd invited Tatiana and Anna to join them, but tonight neither girl felt hungry. The heat had spoiled the fresh fruits and vegetables, and the chickens and pigs had long since been slaughtered and eaten. Now their food consisted of salted beef, hard biscuits, beans and pea soup. There was a superstition about the pea soup among the sailors. "If you cook up pea soup you're cooking up a storm," they said. Wang Li shrugged and muttered in broken English that they needed a storm with a good wind to blow them out of the doldrums.

Still, some of the men threw their soup overboard rather than eat it.

Earlier that day there'd been a sudden squall to get their hopes up. The captain's skill was put to the test to set the proper sails to use any favorable wind from the squall to push the ship as quickly as possible. The men also put out buckets, barrels, jars, anything to catch the precious raindrops for fresh drinking water.

But the wind died as abruptly as it started, and the sails soon hung as limply as before. The monotonous sound of the lifeless canvas continually banging against the masts was getting on everyone's nerves. The captain ordered the oldest sails hoisted and tried to keep the crew occupied with repairing the best sails, the hard weather sails which would be needed at Cape Horn.

The doldrums climate of sudden rain and blinding hot sun was hard on canvas and men alike, and increasingly, was turning many of the crew into surly cross-tempered morons who picked fights with each other over nothing at all.

"I dreamt it was late spring, and the Neva was waking up from its long winter sleep." Tatiana looked at Anna. "That's a sight and sound you would never believe. The air is filled with a continual grating noise, and immense pieces of ice break apart and crash together in the current. I wonder if I will ever see such a marvelous thing again."

The sound of laughter made both women turn, and they noticed a group of crewmen gathered near the forward mast. They were drinking their evening's share of rum and telling stories, and one was singing a sea chantey loudly in an off-key voice to the accompaniment of an old tarnished fiddle.

"At least we have this beautiful sunset to watch," said Anna. Sunset was her favorite time of the day. She never tired of seeing the western sky glow in a stunning display of coral pink, fiery orange and gilded yellow as the sun slowly sank into the stagnant sea. The flat calm waters reflected each vibrant color in glassy hues more striking than any artist's painting.

She waited with abated breath, hoping to see what the sailors referred to as the "green flash." It was a phenomenon most common in the tropics, an extraordinary flash of brilliant green at the exact moment when the sun disappeared over the horizon. Each night she waited expectantly, but as yet, had never witnessed the beautiful sight, and tonight was no exception.

Sighing with disappointment, she glanced down at the ocean, wondering what it would be like to jump into the warm waters as many of the sailors did each night. Even the threat of sharks did not deter the men, for the water on board was now being rationed carefully and they had lost the luxury of bathing. Both women were finding their own body odors harder to bear.

"Can you imagine the hue and cry if I were to dive into the sea and take a swim right now?" said Anna, laughing.

"The captain would order someone to jump in and fish you out," said Tatiana with a wry smile, "and then he would be very angry with you."

"It would be almost worth it to feel clean again, even if a bit salty."

"It's too dark now to see in the water. You might bump into a shark," she shuddered.

In the tropics there was no twilight, only a swift descent into darkness after the sun was gone. The stars appeared, one by one, then in a mass of twinkling lights. "Look," said Anna, "there's the Southern Cross. It always reminds me of Jesus and His sacrifice for us."

Smiling, she lifted her face upwards at the four bright stars of the constellation, a familiar sight in the southern hemisphere, but alien to those from the north that were used to seeing the North Star and the Big Dipper in the night sky.

"The Bible says God calls the stars by their names," she whispered. "If they are that important to Him, then think of how much more precious we are as His children."

Tatiana pretended not to hear her words. "We better go below, Anna, before the captain catches us up here without his permission."

In the darkness the deck of the ship had become unfamiliar territory. The starlight coated the masts, sails, riggings, coils of ropes and hatches in black and gray shadows, making both women feel uneasy as they picked their way gingerly forward to the main hatch. As they reached the aft mast, several of the shadows moved towards them.

"Good evenin' ladies," said a voice in a lazy drawl. "Out a bit late, ain't ya?"

"If you'll excuse us, Mr. Johnson," said Tatiana haughtily, "we are on our way below."

The second mate quickly grabbed her arm. "Not so fast, Countess. Me an' Jeb an' Nate 'ere 'ave some questions fer ya all."

"I can't imagine what we have to discuss. Take your hand off me at once."

He let out a sinister chuckle that echoed among the other men. "Now don't go gettin' so uppity on me, Countess. We all got some business wi' you an' the maid."

"If you don't leave us be this instant, I shall scream for the captain," she said in an angry tone to mask her growing fear.

In a flash a filthy hand clamped over her mouth, and she felt the sharp tip of a knife at her throat. Tatiana heard Anna gasp and the second mate said to her, "Keep yer yap shut, miss, or I'll slice 'er throat."

Two sweaty seamen grasped Anna by her arms, one on each side, and shoved her forward to the darker privacy of the bow, away from the dim glow of the forward and after cabin skylights and open hatches. The second mate followed with Tatiana, who was whimpering with fright.

"What do you want with us?" asked Anna as calmly as possible.

The men holding her didn't answer, but looked expectantly at Ned. He was the officer in charge and they waited for his orders.

"Now Countess," he said, still holding the knife to Tatiana, "me and the lads believe you are a Russkie spy. But we'll give you one chance to explain yerself. But ya better not scream or I'll slit yer purty white throat. Understand?"

Tatiana glared at him as a deep rage built up inside her. Throwing caution aside, she bit one of his fingers as hard as she could. Warm salty blood spurted between her teeth.

Ned shouted in pain and jerked his hand away from her mouth. In the next second she shrieked a high pitched scream which resounded all over the ship. At the same time some basic instinct Anna didn't know she possessed caused her to kick the second mate directly in his shinbone.

Ned cursed and jumped backwards, but not before he slashed his knife across Tatiana's throat. Her scream ended abruptly in a strange gurgle and she crumpled to the deck. The men holding Anna quickly released her and scattered as angry shouts and pounding footsteps came towards them. When Anna dropped down beside Tatiana a pistol shot thundered over her head. The second mate howled in pain then he pitched forward and fell down with a mighty thud.

It was all over in a matter of seconds. But Anna had no time to feel relief, for she saw with horror that Tatiana's neck and bodice was covered in dark sticky blood.

"Help us," she cried, "please help us, someone!"

With an oath the captain was at her side, gently lifting up the injured Tatiana and carrying her swiftly below decks. Anna hurried after them, nearly tripping over her skirts. Ethan helped her down the hatch ladder, saying, "Steady now, lass."

She was so relieved to see his kindly face that she almost threw herself into his arms. Instead she straightened her shoulders and marched into the salon where Captain O'Connell had laid Tatiana on one of the sofas. Blood drenched the left side of her neck and shoulder, and her face was as white as the belly of a seagull. She was limp and unconscious.

The captain barked orders to Robby and Jimmy to bring basins of hot water. The boys, nearly as pale as Tatiana, raced to the galley to find Wang Li. Samuel handed the captain a wad of cloth and he pressed it against the cut on Tatiana's neck.

Anna hovered anxiously next to him. "What can I do to help, Captain?"

"Are ye handy with a needle and thread, Miss Teichroew?"

At her nod, he added, "After I get the bleeding to stop I'll need ye to stitch up her wound as neatly as ye can. Luckily, he missed her throat and just sliced her across the collarbone. It's messy, but not life threatening, unless infection sets in. After ye finish sewing it up, we'll wash the wound and pour some rum on it."

"Wouldn't it do her more good to drink the rum after she wakes?" asked Anna. "She's going to be in a lot of pain."

"'Tis an old sailor's remedy, Miss Teichroew. Alcohol is known to stop wounds from festerin'."

Anna went to the cabin to fetch her sewing kit, and when she returned, she saw with relief that the bleeding had almost stopped. Taking a deep breath and steadying her trembling fingers, she began to neatly stitch the two sliced pieces of skin together that crossed over the collarbone. As she did so, she was thankful for all the years of training in tiny needlework and embroidery that her mama had taught her. But she never imagined that someday she would use her skills in sewing skin instead of cloth.

Samuel and the captain were watching her closely, and when she was about done, the captain said, “Fine work, Anna. No surgeon could have done better.”

His compliment and the familiar use of her name made her flush, and she hoped if the two men noticed, they would just think she was red from the oppressive heat in the salon. “Thank you, Captain,” she murmured.

The boys had returned with a large basin of warm water then made a hasty retreat. Tatiana started to moan and flutter her eyelids as Anna cleansed the swelling wound and the surrounding area with a clean wet cloth. When she doused the four inch long cut with a liberal splash of rum, Tatiana jerked and opened her eyes and let out a slight screech.

“Don’t move, *Mademoiselle*,” she said in a soothing tone as she covered the wound with a clean cloth for a dressing, “you have a cut near your neck, and you must lie still.”

“What happened?” she said in a faint voice.

“You were attacked by Mister Johnson,” answered the captain.

“I remember,” she said. “Horrible man.”

After Anna helped her mistress drink several large swallows of rum, Tatiana closed her eyes and fell asleep. “Can we leave her here tonight?” she asked the captain. “I’m afraid if you move her into our cabin, her wound will start to bleed again. I don’t mind staying with her.”

He nodded his agreement as Ethan, Jake, John and Gregory Jones came into the salon. “How is the lass doin’ then?” inquired the first mate.

Sean glanced down at Tatiana, still lovely in her disheveled state in her blood encrusted gown. Her hair had come undone from its chignon and the long golden strands tumbled around her shoulders. Her dark eyelashes fanned out over the pale delicate skin of her cheekbones, and her full lips were slightly parted as she breathed deeply in her sleep.

A mixture of desire and concern made his voice rough as he said, “She’ll live, I think.”

“That’s more than we can say about Ned,” said John flatly, his eyes appraising Tatiana with admiration. “He’s dead.”

Sean turned to him in surprise. “I thought I only wounded him.”

“Yer shot hit ‘im right in the heart,” said Ethan. “Poor lad.”

Sean sighed heavily. “I don’t understand what he and the others were trying to do with the women. They must have been out of their minds. Where are the other two men anyway?”

“We got Nate Tyler and Jeb Drake locked up below, Cap’n,” said Jones in his deep voice. “They says twas all Johnson’s idea, to scare the women into confessin' they're spies. I beg yer pardon, ma'am," he nodded to Anna.

He was the biggest man she'd ever seen, towering over even the Captain who stood well above six feet. With his shiny bald head and long black mustache, he reminded her of a huge Russian from a band of gypsies that traveled through Furstenau years ago. The man was famous for challenging others to fist fights, if anyone was foolish enough to try.

At sixteen years of age Gerhard Yoder was just such a man. He had tried to fight the gypsy, and was knocked unconscious in a matter of seconds. To add to his humiliation, the following Sunday Gerhard had been publicly chastised in church by *Herr* Yoder and Elder Klassen for disobeying the Mennonite doctrine of nonviolence.

"Keep them both chained up for a week in the hold," said Sean. "If they survive this hellish heat, they'll have learned their lesson. Meantime, O'Riley here is promoted to second mate to replace Johnson."

He looked at Jake, whose freckled face ~~under his unruly mop of carrot colored hair~~ broke into a delighted grin. "Ye won't be sorry, Cap'n. I can be just as hard on the lads as Ned was."

Anna hid a smile, thinking how young Mr. O'Riley appeared with his unruly mop of carrot colored hair springing out from his hat and the impish sparkle in his vivid blue eyes. He glanced at her and blushed in sudden embarrassment.

"Now I need a third mate," said Sean, turning towards John. "Mr. Hill, here's your chance at being an officer. I'm pleased to offer ye the position, if ye don't mind the double duty of still bein' our supercargo."

John flashed his white teeth in a wide smile and he shook Sean's hand. "Thank you, Captain, I'm delighted to perform both duties."

"I believe ye'll make your uncle proud," said Sean. "We'll gather the crew in the mornin' to bury Johnson at sea, and then announce the change in officers."

After that the four men left the salon, Ethan casting a lingering glance at Anna. Sean told Samuel to help Miss Teichroew as needed with Miss Bolkonsky during the night then he retired to his quarters.

Anna noticed the troubled look on his weary face as he wished her goodnight, and she said to Samuel, "It must be devastating for a man as fine as the captain to face the fact that he killed a man, especially one of his own officers."

The steward was carrying the basin of dirty water out and paused. "Yes, Missy, the Cap'n's the finest man on this 'ere ship, an' the one he killed, well, he was jus' plain scum."

At her surprised expression, he added, "Me an' Wang Li are mighty happy that man's gone for good. May he rot in hell, pardon, Missy."

With no further explanation than that, Samuel went up on deck to throw the filthy water overboard. He knew he shouldn't have spoken those harsh words to the little maid, but he couldn't help himself. The second mate had made his life and Wang Li's life miserable ever since they left Boston. He was one of those white men, like Arthur Horn, who believed their race and gender were superior to any other and treated Africans, Chinese, and women accordingly.

It was no surprise to him that Ned Johnson had tried to harm the Russian women. As he stood at the rail, breathing deeply of the slightly cooler night air, he almost wished the second mate had finished the job he'd started on the snooty Countess. She was cut from the same cloth as Ned, maybe even worse.

She treated him as if he was one of her serfs. She never looked him in the eye or smiled or asked him politely when she wanted something. Instead she demanded, ordered, and never thanked him afterwards. The little maid, Anna, was just the opposite. She was a sweet tempered, warm hearted young woman, and whatever man ended up with her someday was fortunate indeed.

He had noticed the way Ethan Campbell looked at Anna, and Samuel suspected the first mate was falling in love with her. Too bad it wasn't the Cap'n, he thought. But the Cap'n had eyes only for the beautiful Miss Bolkonsky. And therein was the problem. For Samuel was convinced the Russian woman was a spy.

He recalled one afternoon a few weeks ago when he went into the captain's quarters. Although everything seemed to be in order, he sensed something not quite right. Later he realized it was the fragrance he smelled in the cabin. Lavender. The same perfume he always smelled on Miss Bolkonsky.

At the time he didn't say anything to the captain. Nothing seemed to be missing from his cabin and he didn't want to accuse a white woman of spying when he had no proof of it. For that matter, a black man didn't accuse a white woman of anything, unless he wanted his head to roll. Even though the captain was the fairest white man he'd ever known, he couldn't take that chance.

Samuel hated all white men except for Captain Edward Smythe who had freed him in his will, Captain Sean O'Connell and Ethan Campbell, who lived what he preached and never saw the color of Samuel's skin.

Anna reminded him of Mister Campbell. She didn't see him as a black man either. She treated him as kindly as she treated anyone else. He'd watched her reading her Bible and knew she was a Christian like Mr. Campbell. Samuel thought they were different from the other so-called Christians he'd seen who were cruel and abusive to their slaves. The religion of Christianity had always bewildered him, because it seemed so divided between the rare ones who actually followed Jesus' teachings and the ones who only gave it lip-service.

As a young slave boy, he grew up in the strict Puritan household of the Smythe family, and was familiar with the Bible's teachings of love and forgiveness. But they were virtues he rarely saw in the white man's world and he decided long ago, Christianity was not for him. Not as long as he held such hatred and bitterness in his own heart against the white men who'd torn him away from his own family and killed his mother and enslaved his sister.

Sometimes he tried to remember the religion of his African village. All he had were the impressions of a child; the fear in his parents' faces when cautioning him about the dark spirits of the forest, the blood of a slaughtered chicken splattered on the threshold of a neighbor's hut, the frightening mask of the witch doctor when he danced around his sick baby brother, all to no avail. The infant had died regardless. To this day, he felt sorrow for his father, losing his wife and his only son and daughter to the slavers.

He sighed and shook his head. He had no interest in the beliefs of his ancestors. None of it had saved his family. But the way Ethan Campbell and Anna Teichroew lived the white man's religion intrigued him. He would continue to observe them.

Below in the stifling heat of the captain's cabin, Sean was wrestling with his own inner demons. His friends and officers on board thought he had just killed his first man, ever. They couldn't know that he had killed once before. And tonight he was afraid to fall asleep, for he was afraid of the dreams he might dream.

Instead of sleeping, he sat down at his desk and wrote down the tumultuous events of the day in the log. He didn't understand what had possessed the two women to wander around the deck in the dark, especially after he had forbidden them to do so. Tomorrow he was going to try to convince the crew that having women on board was not bad luck. But with the second mate dead, two men imprisoned in the hold, and the ship drifting aimlessly with the lack of wind, he wasn't certain he could.

Muttering to himself about sailors' superstitions, he remembered he'd promised Ethan earlier to double check the cargo manifest to see if they had bought enough cloth in London to trade to the natives. If not, when they stopped at Rio de Janeiro on the coast of Brazil to take on fresh water and food, they could also buy more bolts of fabric. Frowning, he opened the bottom right hand drawer where he kept the cargo manifest.

Strange, he thought. *It's not here.*

He quickly rifled through all the papers then examined the other drawers. In frustration he realized he couldn't find it anywhere. He glanced around his cabin. No, he wouldn't have put it anywhere else. He was more organized than that. Someone must have taken it.

Out in the salon, Anna kept one of the lanterns lit. Although she felt very hot and tired and drained, she was determined to stay awake in case Tatiana needed her. She was worried her mistress might be feverish, for she was muttering restlessly in her sleep and her forehead felt quite warm to the touch. When Samuel returned she was going to ask him for more water to cool her down.

And perhaps for herself as well. The heat was stifling in her gown and petticoat. She had loosened her plaits and slipped off her stockings and slippers, but nothing would stop the perspiration running down her neck unless a cool breeze wafted through the stern windows. Here it was, like the hottest day of summer, but at home it would be autumn. In fact, if she counted the days correctly, tomorrow wouldn't be just any day. It was her eighteenth birthday.

"Happy Birthday, Anna," she said, as she struggled to keep her eyes open.

But she must have dozed off for suddenly she saw a big man standing over her. In the dim light she gave a start and a small cry. "Samuel?"

"Nay, Miss Teichroew," said the captain in a deadly serious voice. "I think it's about time you an' I had a nice long talk."

She rubbed the sleep from her eyes and stared at him. Gone was the friendly smile and manner of the man she'd known the past weeks. In his place was the hostile face of the pirate captain of her nightmare.

Instinctively she shrank back from him. He didn't seem to notice her reaction, for he was clearly in a rage. His green eyes smoldered with fury as he said in his Irish lilt, "There's a paper missin' from me desk. Tis the manifest, the list o' cargo we bought 'n London. Where is it?"

She had dreaded this moment, had feared it would come. A few weeks ago when Tatiana showed her the cargo manifest she'd taken from the captain's desk, Anna had tried her best to persuade her mistress to return it at once. But Tatiana refused, saying she finally had evidence of illegal contraband on the *Sea Rose*. She intended to give it to Captain-Lieutenant Chernyshov when they reached the *Suvorov*. After that, Captain O'Connell would be arrested and the ship seized as soon as they sailed into the Imperial Navy patrolled waters of Russian America.

Now Anna was in a dilemma. If she confessed knowing that her mistress had stolen the cargo manifest and Anna knew where it was hidden, the captain would have proof that they were spies. And then what would happen? Imprisonment? Perhaps even death?

The only way out would be to feign innocence. But how could she tell a lie and live with herself and God? She would have to tell the truth and leave the consequences in God's hands.

"The paper is in our cabin, Captain," she said quietly.

Her quick admission startled him and for a moment took the edge off his anger. Then it came roaring back. "So, the two of ye are spies after all! So much for your takin' an oath on your Bible!"

"It was the truth when I said that *Mademoiselle* was not a spy." *At least at that time before she stole the document.*

He was taken aback once again. "So, are ye saying that ye are the one who stole the manifest instead of her?"

Anna was silent. She couldn't confess to being a spy when that would also be an untruth. He shook his head in confusion, his long black curly hair undone from his usual queue grazing his shoulders. He grabbed her shoulders and lifted her up like she was a porcelain doll that he wanted to shake.

She gazed into his face, partly shadowed in the dimly lit salon. He was the handsomest man she'd ever seen and she knew with a sinking feeling in her heart, that she was attracted to him in a way she'd never felt before.

They were inches apart and Sean saw an odd mixture of fear and warmth in her lovely hazel eyes. His gaze dropped to the sweet curve of her gentle mouth and he fought the sudden impulse to kiss her.

What was wrong with him, he asked himself in disgust. How could he even think of such a thing? Perhaps he had been without a woman for too long. It was one thing to desire a shallow beauty like her mistress, quite another to force his attentions on an innocent girl with a deep faith in God. It would be like kissing his sister, Rose.

He gently lowered her down and released her, then said in a quieter tone, "Anna, I don't believe yer a thief and a spy. But I do believe ye are the kind of person who would protect your mistress, even if it would hurt ye. I commend ye for your loyalty to her, but I must know, which one of ye stole the manifest?"

She hung her head, unable to look at him and unable to answer. He uttered a curse as he ran a hand through his unruly hair. "Have it your way for now, but I'll get to the truth of it no matter if it takes me the rest of the voyage. Now fetch me the manifest and we'll continue this conversation when your mistress is feeling stronger."

She fled into her cabin and found the document in one of Tatiana's trunks where she kept her under things. When she handed it to him, Sean noticed the scent of lavender attached to the paper.

"No harm done, Captain," said Anna, trying to smile. "Here it is, safe and sound."

"Unfortunately, there's much harm done already. If word of this got to the crew there's some of the men who'd throw the two of ye overboard as soon as my back is turned some dark night. First thing in the mornin' ye both will be locked in your cabin for your own safety."

"But it's so hot in there and *Mademoiselle* is already burning up with fever." She gave him an anxious look. "What do you intend to do with us?"

A slight moan escaped from Tatiana's lips and Sean glanced down at her with pity then tried to harden his heart as he reminded himself that she was most likely a scheming spy.

"Haven't decided, yet, Miss Teichroew," he said coldly. "But if I were ye, I'd start prayin' to the Almighty. G' night."

In her fevered half-conscious state, Tatiana had heard enough of the conversation to curse herself for not managing to return the cargo manifest to the captain's desk before he discovered it was missing. But she'd never had the chance.

Now as she drifted back into the pain filled haze of sleep, she remembered with relief the duplicate document hidden behind a loose board in the bulkhead of their cabin. One afternoon when Anna was taking some exercise topside, she'd quickly copied the manifest, word for word. After seeing how easily Anna had given the captain what he wanted, Tatiana was determined that her maid would stay ignorant of its existence.

CHAPTER FOURTEEN

During the next few days Tatiana's fever finally broke, bathing her in sweat. Anna hardly noticed the extra perspiration soaking the bedding in her bunk, for the tropical heat was sweltering in their small cabin. The one window stayed open, day and night, but with the door closed and locked, there was no circulation of air. It was like being in a hellish prison.

Each morning and evening Jimmy and Robby brought them food and water, and emptied their soiled buckets, but otherwise they were left alone. At least her prayer for Tatiana's recovery was answered. Her neck wound was slowly healing and the fever was gone, thanks to the willow bark tea Wang Li was considerate enough to boil for her.

One morning they awoke with the sound of the crew calling out excitedly to one another and footsteps thundering overhead on the deck. At first Anna was afraid they had formed a mutiny and were coming to seize her and Tatiana. Then she felt the ship, which had drifted dormant for so long, suddenly vibrate with new energy. She heard the familiar sounds of creaking timbers and wind singing through rigging as sails were hoisted and furled.

Both women looked out their window and saw whitecaps frothing on the ocean. A stiff wind was picking up. They hoped it would be steady, unlike the brief savage winds of the tropical rain squalls, which died as soon as they were born.

"We picked up the southeast trades!" shouted Robby, racing past their door.

"We're outta the doldrums!" yelled Jimmy.

Already they could feel a breeze rushing in the window, bringing fresh cooler air into the torrid heat of the cabin. Tatiana smiled at Anna and said, "At last! Soon we'll be finding the *Suvorov*. Perhaps when we reach Brazil."

Their good luck continued. An hour later it began to rain in a steady downpour which quickly replenished the ship's fresh water supply. Tatiana bribed the boys with a silver coin to bring in a large wooden barrel filled with water, and the two enjoyed their first real bath in weeks.

After the clouds cleared that afternoon, many of the crew caught a goodly number of fish and Wang Li fried them, their delicate crispy flavor a delicious change from salted beef and cold beans.

Samuel delivered some of the fish to their cabin with the news that the captain wished to see them in the salon after dinner. Both Tatiana and Anna heard this with mixed feelings, relief to finally be out of the confines of their little cabin, and foreboding as to what the captain had in store for them.

"We must look our best," stated Tatiana, rummaging through her trunks and tossing Anna a champagne colored silk gown. "Put this on, Anna. Then help me with my lilac gown. If only I didn't have such an ugly wound by my neck." She sighed. "What if it leaves a terrible scar? I'll never be able to wear low necked gowns again."

"If there is a scar we can hide it under some powder and no one will notice," said Anna slightly irritated. How could her mistress fuss over a little scar when Ned Johnson could have ended her life? "At least he didn't cut your face, *Mademoiselle*."

Tatiana shuddered. "Horrors!" she exclaimed. "What a terrible thought! My face disfigured and my beauty ruined? I would rather die."

"Surely you don't mean that, *Mademoiselle*."

"Of course I do. All my life men have paid attention to me only because of my face, whether it was my uncle, my father, my cousin Mikael or Baron Ivan Volodin. And now there is Lieutenant Volodin waiting for me. I plan on wrapping him around my little finger after we're married. But I can't do that if I'm scarred or ugly."

Anna thought of her sweet-natured friend, Susannah. Although plain of face, she had attracted a man who saw her inner beauty and wished to marry her if he hadn't already.

"What is today's date?" she asked Tatiana.

"By the American calendar probably around the second of November."

Anna thought quickly. Russia still used the old style Julian calendar which was thirteen days behind everyone else. That meant it was around October 20th back home. By now Agatha was probably a new mother and Susannah a new wife. Life in Furstenau was going on without her. A feeling of sadness swept over her. Every day she prayed for each one of her family, even Agatha. Anna hoped the newest member of the Teichroew's was a little sister for Tina to enjoy.

"Time to wrap Captain O'Connell around my little finger," smiled Tatiana as they finished their preparations. Anna had arranged her mistress's newly washed hair into a shiny flaxen cascade of ringlets, a charming contrast to her silky lilac gown. The dressing over the wound on her delicate skin was the only flaw to her otherwise perfect appearance.

Anna's creamy complexion and tawny colored hair also glowed with cleanliness and her pale gold gown shimmered around her as she moved with an elegance that belied her status of lady's maid.

When Samuel ushered them into the forward salon to dine, the five men waiting were immediately struck by the sight of the two Russian women. Each man had a different reaction.

To Second Officer O'Riley, they looked as unattainable as any high society woman he'd seen in Boston.

To Third Officer John Hill, they reminded him of the two lost loves of his life. The proud beauty of the Bolkonsky woman was Abigail before Horn destroyed her, and the little maid's fresh loveliness was his Indian princess, both gone forever. He prayed to God that they both were innocent of the captain's charges.

To Mister Jones, his massive bulk looming over them, they were like two delicate flowers. As the master of the whip, he fervently hoped he wouldn't be asked to crush the life out of them if execution was their fate.

Ethan had eyes only for Anna. He'd long since dismissed the gorgeous Miss Bolkonsky as a superficial strumpet. Even knowing that Anna had nearly confessed to being a spy was not enough to stop himself from falling in love with her. If the captain was determined to bring her to justice, he had already decided how he was going to save her.

After days and nights of agonizing and discussing the matter with his officers, Sean had come to his decision concerning the two women. Now the enchanting vision they presented nearly took his breath away. For a moment he wavered, his resolve weakening.

Then he summoned up all his strength and determination and faced them with a stern expression. "Miss Bolkonsky, Miss Teichroew, I charge you both with spying and treason on the high seas against the United States of America. The sentence for such an act is death, but," he paused as the women gasped in shock and his officers gaped at him with horror, "as the commander of this ship, the *Sea Rose*, I am your sole judge and jury. With that authority, I am commuting your sentence to exile as soon as we reach land."

Tatiana looked like she was going to faint and Anna reached out a hand to steady her. "And what land might that be, Captain?" she asked calmly, her heart racing with dread.

"Rio de Janeiro on the coast of Brazil. We should arrive there soon."

"But we don't know a soul in Brazil," said Tatiana in a panic, "nor do we speak Portuguese. How would we survive?"

"I'm sure a woman of your beauty and intelligence will think of something," he said coldly.

"Perhaps the *Suvorov* will be there, *Mademoiselle*," said Anna.

Sean glanced at Anna and softened his voice slightly, "Miss Bolkonsky, ye can spare your maid from having to follow ye into exile if ye would confess that ye alone stole the manifest from my desk with the intention of passing on the information to the Russian Imperial Navy."

She arched one lovely eyebrow. "And why should I confess such an outrageous lie?"

"Because I have a witness."

This information clearly startled everyone in the room, except for Samuel who stared impassively at the captain. Hours earlier he had finally told him how he'd suspected Miss Bolkonsky of searching the captain's cabin one afternoon weeks ago. Samuel's loathing for the haughty woman and his admiration for the maid made him decide to take the risk of accusing a white woman of thievery.

To his relief the captain had believed him. Sean was the first to admit that the lingering trace of lavender scent was thin evidence, yet, he wasn't above twisting the truth a bit.

"My witness says he saw ye creeping out of my cabin one day several weeks ago. Do ye deny this, Miss Bolkonsky?"

Tatiana seemed at a loss for words. "Who---who---" she began.

"It is I, Samuel," said the steward, glaring at her.

With the realization that a former slave was her accuser, Tatiana quickly regained her composure. "How dare you take the word of an illiterate savage over mine?"

Anna winced inside at the arrogant words, remembering the first mate's story of the captain's fondness for his steward.

"I've known Samuel for many years as a trustworthy servant, and I believe anything he says over the likes of ye, Miss Bolkonsky, who has done nothing but lie and play your silly games since ye boarded my ship."

Tatiana glanced around the salon. Everyone was staring at her without pity and even Anna had an expression of dismay on her usually loyal face. She suddenly realized it would do her no good to continue to protest her guilt. Perhaps it was time to admit part of the truth and hope she could change the captain's mind about abandoning her in Brazil.

She bowed her head in pretended submission and said softly, "All right then, Captain, I confess, I did take the manifest from your desk. But I am not a spy for the Russian government. I am just a young foolish woman who wished to impress the father I haven't seen since I was a child and my fiancé as well, by giving them the information about the guns on board your ship. I realize now what a stupid and dangerous thing it was to do. I apologize from the bottom of my heart, and I promise that if you allow us to continue our voyage until we reach the *Suvorov*, I will not say or do another thing that will be harmful to you, your crew or your ship."

She raised her head and looked directly into Sean's eyes, her gaze as honest and unflinching as she could muster. He was torn. A part of him still didn't trust her, but she was so utterly beautiful even with the reddened gash on her neck, which gave her a look of vulnerability. And she was young, probably no more than eighteen, almost a child herself.

"My maid has returned the document, Captain," she continued, "and without the manifest as evidence of your cargo, there's nothing I can do to prove to Captain-Lieutenant Chernyshov or my father you are carrying guns illegally. After all, I haven't seen any guns on board your ship except for the pistols you and your officers carry."

"And what about your fiancé?" questioned Sean. "If ye tell him about the cargo manifest ye saw on board this ship, he might believe ye."

"You are in no danger from Lieutenant Volodin, Captain, I can assure you of that."

"But how well do ye know him? If he is like most of the other Imperial Naval officers stationed in Sitka, he would leap at the chance to seize this ship. Since Alexander Baranov was dismissed from the office of governor, the naval lieutenants have taken over the Russian American Fur Company. Unlike Baranov who welcomed us Yanks and Brits, the aristocratic officers now in charge hate and fear us."

"That can't be so," Tatiana protested thinly, knowing full well he spoke the truth.

"Not only is it true, Miss Bolkonsky," said John, his blue eyes snapping underneath his thick head of curly blond hair, "but your naval officers have created problems they don't know how to solve, problems born from their own ignorance and arrogance."

"What sort of problems?" she asked, tilting her head in his direction.

He paused momentarily as he felt the full impact of her violet eyed gaze, then answered, "Because we are no longer allowed to trade freely in Alaska, there are major shortages of grains and other goods vital to your growing settlements, staples we Yankee traders used to bring to Sitka frequently, but if we did now, we'd be seized, arrested, imprisoned and lashed with the *knout*!"

Jones gave a mighty grunt and growled, "Those threats won't stop us! Tis the maiden voyage of the *Sea Rose* an' no Russkie warship's gonna hunt us down!"

"Aye, aye, Mister Jones," agreed Jake.

The captain nodded with a grim smile then said, "Miss Bolkonsky, whether ye are an actual spy or just a victim of your own impulsive behavior, the results are the same. You and your maid have a dangerous knowledge about my ship which cannot fall into the hands of the Russians. Therefore, my original verdict and sentence still stands. We are putting ye both ashore as soon as we reach Rio de Janeiro."

* * *

The first mate was in a terrible state. As time passed and the *Sea Rose* sliced through the waves closer towards the coast of Brazil, Ethan knew he couldn't wait any longer. One morning when they were about two days away from the coast, he walked into the chart room where Sean was plotting their course from Brazil to Cape Horn on a large navigational map. The captain was sipping from a mug of hot coffee and muttering under his breath about the tricky route that lay ahead of them.

"Sean, I need to speak with ye," said Ethan.

The first mate rarely called him by his name these days, and when he did, Sean knew it meant that he was talking to him as a friend, not his captain.

"What is it, Ethan?" He noted the dark circles under the Scotsman's eyes and the worried frown underneath his red mustache.

"Tis the lass, Anna." He sighed heavily then said, "I aim to marry her, if she'll have me. An' if she will, ye mustn't leave her behind in Brazil."

"Ye can't be serious, man," said Sean in surprise. "When did all this come about?"

"The first time I saw the lass, I knew she was for me. Since then, I've come to love her."

"Does Anna know this?"

Ethan shook his head. "Nay, not yet. I aim to ask her this evenin.'"

"Well," said Sean, thinking rapidly, trying not to let the first mate know how dismayed he felt at the thought of Anna marrying him or anyone else. He didn't understand why he felt like this, because there were many times lately he'd thought that Anna would make some lucky man the ideal wife. If he was the marrying sort, he would ask her himself. But he wasn't, and he also didn't think he was good enough for the likes of her, anymore than he was good enough for Irina Baranova.

But Ethan now, that was a different story. He was a fine man who believed much the same things Anna believed. He probably could make her very happy. At the very least, if she married him, he could save her from spending the rest of her life waiting hand and foot on that imperious mistress of hers.

"If she agrees to be your wife, Ethan, she is welcome to stay on board wherever we sail. Ye have my word on it." They two men shook hands, as the first mate broke into a wide grin of relieved gratitude.

"Don't thank me yet," warned Sean. "Ye still have to convince the lady."

* * *

Tatiana also had plans that evening, desperate plans which involved herself and the captain. She wasn't about to tell Anna about them. Later when her maid and most of the crew were sound asleep, she would put her plan into action.

She ate dinner with little appetite, toying with the tasty stew that Wang Li had prepared using the special tins of meat and vegetables, a new kind of way to store food for a long time without spoilage that was invented in England. The tins were the only nutritious food left on the ship until they could restock at Rio de Janeiro.

Anna, on the other hand, enjoyed her meal, trying not to worry about their fate when the *Sea Rose* sailed away, leaving them stranded in a strange city in a foreign country. After all she had experienced the past months she was convinced God was watching over her. She knew He would be taking care of her when they went ashore as well, she just wished she knew how He would be doing it.

A knock on the cabin door made her call out automatically, "Come in," thinking it was Samuel or one of the boys to fetch the dinner plates.

Instead it was the first mate, looking quite presentable in a freshly washed ivory colored linen shirt tucked into the belted waistband of his black breeches. He was wearing shiny black boots on his feet and his dark red hair was neatly combed and tied back with a black band.

Although he was smiling, there was an air of nervousness about him as he restlessly clenched and unclenched his long fingers. "Miss Anna," he said softly in his Scotch accent, "would ye do me the honor of a walk topside this fair evenin'?"

She looked at Tatiana for permission. "The fresh air will do you good, Anna," she urged. "Stay as long as you like."

Anna nodded and slipped on her green and gold cloak, knowing the wind would be stiff outside on the deck. Ethan helped her up the hatch ladder. The second mate, Jake O'Riley, was at the helm, his carrot hair flying around under his cap in the wind.

He gave Ethan and Anna a shy smile as they walked by him to the stern rail. A frothy wake of cream and blue waves followed the *Sea Rose*, like a long undulating road leading to nowhere.

"I'm still uncomfortable around the crew," said Anna. "It's hard for me to trust any of them after those two men attacked us."

"Nate an' Jeb won't trouble ye again, lass. They sat in the brig for a week an' if they ever so much as speak to ye again, the Cap'n will have their hides."

"I'm sure the crew is somewhat afraid of Captain O'Connell after what he did to Mister Johnson."

"Tis true. None o' them will be forgettin' that night."

"Nor will I," she shuddered. "Do you know that I actually kicked Mister Johnson in the shin when he was about to cut *Mademoiselle*'s throat? It made his knife slip, or he might have killed her. Yet, the way I was taught as a Mennonite, it would be considered wrong for me to have kicked him. Sometimes I feel so confused."

"Tis a strange world, lass, but don't be gettin' hard on yerself. The Bible also says there's a time for war an' a time for peace."

"And a time for love and a time for hate," she added then looked up into his smiling face. "I need to tell you how grateful I am for your kindness, Mister Campbell, and your trust in me after all that has happened. In a couple days when I have left this ship, I will always remember you as the one true friend I had aboard her."

"Anna," he said, enfolding his large warm hands around her gloved fingers, "I would like to be more than a friend to ye."

An uncertain frown crossed over her face as he swallowed nervously then bent closer to her. "Anna, I must confess I love ye with all of me heart, an' I wish to marry ye, if ye'll have me."

His proposal came as a total surprise to her. For a few seconds she was speechless then she said, "I don't know what to say, Mister Campbell."

"Ethan. Please call me Ethan."

"Yes, Ethan. I---I----"

"Ye don't have to give me yer answer now, lass. If ye canna say aye, then please think upon it. I've already spoken to the Cap'n an' he gave us his blessing."

Anna was silent, her mind whirling rapidly. If it was Captain O'Connell standing in front of her, asking that very same question, would she have already said yes? He made her heart race and her pulse pound in a way that no man had ever done. But was that enough for marriage? She didn't believe so.

A true marriage was between two people who worshipped the same God and had respect for each other. That's what her papa said when he married Agatha. But what about when he had married her mama? Had there been a romantic love between them? Or did that happen after the wedding? Among the Mennonites all marriages were arranged between the parents, and very few young people married for love. She did remember her mama once saying that real love was something that grew between a man and a woman.

She looked at Ethan. He was a gentle kind man who was a strong Christian, even if he didn't follow the doctrine of the Mennonites. Somehow she felt that her mama would have approved of him. And to be honest, she liked the man very much. She also admired him and thought he was quite good looking.

He was as opposite to Gerhard Yoder as sunlight was to darkness. She could do so much worse for a husband.

"I am honored by your proposal, Ethan," she said with a smile. "I do need some time to think about it, because there is much to consider. *Mademoiselle*, for instance. I am her maid and she needs me, especially when the captain leaves us in Rio de Janeiro."

"If you marry me, Anna, the Cap'n would change his mind. He told me so."

"Even for *Mademoiselle*? He would allow her to stay on board?"

Ethan hesitated, and Anna knew with a sinking feeling what the answer was. "I gave her my word that I would be her maid on this voyage. If I agree to be your wife, what then?"

He thought quickly. "I have no problem with ye bein' her maid an' me wife at the same time, Anna. Till we reach Alaska, of course. But she has her da an' a new husband waitin' for her there. Where would ye fit in with them?"

She sighed. “It is something I’ve been troubled about. I could continue as her maid even when she’s married, but....” her voice trailed off and she sighed again. “I don’t wish to be a lady’s maid the rest of my life.”

“Well then,” he said, pressing her hand lightly, his brown eyes sparkling with hope, “I mean to offer ye a life of your own, Anna Teichroew, a good life blessed by the Lord Jesus. When the *Sea Rose* returns to Boston, I intend to ask Thomas Hill for a ship of me own. How would ye like to be a cap’n’s wife someday, lass?”

Her eyes widened at the thought. He noticed and went on eagerly, “If ye like, ye can sail with me on our ship, or when the bairns come,” he flushed slightly, “I might retire an’ build us a nice big house in Boston. Ye can have yer own maid then.”

It was on the tip of Anna’s tongue to say yes. Only the thought of Tatiana held her back. “Ethan, I need to talk to *Mademoiselle* tonight. Then I will give you my answer in the morning.”

She gave him a heartfelt smile that brought a big grin to his face. As they stood together by the rail, Sean happened to come up on deck. They didn’t see him. But he saw them quite clearly, Ethan’s tall form bending protectively over Anna’s small slender body. They were holding hands, gazing into each other’s eyes.

She’s going to marry him, he thought, surprising himself with a sickening lurch deep inside his gut. He turned away and went back down the ladder, heading for his quarters. He wasn’t a drinking man and he despised anything stronger than ale, but for the first time in his life, he longed for a stiff swig of something.

“Samuel,” he called out to the steward as he passed him in the salon, “fetch me a bottle of that French brandy from Mister Hill’s private stock, an’” he paused, “tell John I want to see him.”

The odd request for strong drink made Samuel start in surprise, but he obeyed without question. Minutes later both the third mate and two bottles of fine brandy were closeted in the Captain’s cabin with him.

Curiosity overcame the steward and he ventured up on deck. Something up here had set the Cap'n off. The sun had already set behind a bank of angry looking clouds to the west and the wind was increasing. They were probably in for a small gale later, but that couldn’t have upset the Cap'n so.

He almost ran head first into the couple in the deepening gloom of the approaching night.

“Evenin,’ Samuel,” greeted the first mate with a jaunty grin. He was holding the arm of Anna, who gave him a bright smile. Samuel immediately sensed an aura of expectant happiness around the two. He watched how carefully Ethan helped the maid down the main hatch ladder as if she was made of fragile glass.

After their heads disappeared below he let out his breath. So, dat's how it is, he mused. No wonder the Cap'n was in a mood fit only fo' the devil.

He made his way to the forward hatch and went down to the galley to seek out Wang Li. It was about that time of evening when Jimmy and Robby were done with the dinner dishes. He and Wang Li had the galley to themselves and they had a habit of sharing a pipe of opium and talking until bedtime. His friend was going to be very interested in this latest news about what he saw as a love triangle taking shape on board.

* * *

"The man is a barbaric Scots with a wooden leg!" said Tatiana in an angry voice. "I can't believe you'd even consider such a proposal, Anna!"

"He is a wonderful man who loves me, and most importantly, we both believe in Jesus as our Lord and Savior."

Tatiana rolled her eyes in frustration. "So, you have your religion in common, but you also did with that other nasty man from your village, what was his name, Gunther Yaeger?"

"Gerhard Yoder disgusted me, *Mademoiselle*," said Anna, raising her voice. "I like and admire Ethan very much. He will make me a fine husband. And if I agree to be his wife, he said the captain will not put me ashore in Brazil. I will be allowed to stay on board the *Sea Rose* with Ethan."

"And me? Am I allowed to stay, also, or will the captain abandon me to my lonesome fate?"

Anna lowered her eyes, unable to look Tatiana in the face. "He didn't say."

Tatiana opened her mouth then snapped it shut as she suppressed a furious retort. None of this was Anna's fault, she realized, and yelling at the maid would not change a thing. In fact if she pondered the situation further, she had to admit there was an advantage to her if Anna agreed to marry the first mate. Between the two of them, they could help persuade the captain to change his mind. And just to make sure he did, she still had to continue her plans for tonight.

"Anna, I apologize for every unflattering thing I said about Mister Campbell," she said suddenly in a contrite voice. "You are right. He will make you a respectable husband. I think you should accept his proposal. Now, tonight. Why wait until morning?"

Anna's mouth dropped open in shock. She couldn't believe what she was hearing. "But are you certain?"

"Yes, Anna, and don't worry about the captain separating us. I've thought of a way to change his mind about leaving me behind. I can't tell you what is it yet, but the best thing you can do for me is become betrothed to Mister Campbell. I give you my blessing, dearest Anna."

Tatiana gave her a quick hug, surprising Anna again. "Now, why don't you tell your handsome Scotsman that you're happy to become his wife."

She gently shoved Anna out the door and into the salon, where Anna spied Ethan heading for the captain's cabin.

"Ethan," she called out softly, not noticing that Tatiana had left the cabin door cracked open.

He paused in mid stride and turned around, a look of part expectation and part fear flashing over his face. "Ethan, I have your answer for you," she said, and smiled so sweetly at him he felt a burst of joy swelling upwards through his entire being.

In a moment he reached her side as she said, "Yes, Ethan, I will gladly marry you."

His eyes misted over as he bent down and crushed her to him, murmuring tenderly, "Ah, my wee bonnie lass," over and over.

Tatiana quietly closed the door. She had never seen a man so besotted and so in love. And with little Anna of all people! A part of her resented the fact that Ethan Campbell had never looked at her once in all the weeks spent on this ship. She wasn't used to being ignored by a man. Another part of her felt a twinge of envy. How did her maid inspire such devotion in a man when Anna hadn't even tried? And here she, Tatiana, one of the most beautiful women in Saint Petersburg, had tried over and over to bewitch Captain O'Connell and failed miserably each time.

Not anymore. Tonight was going to be different. By morning, he was going to be begging her to stay on board.

* * *

The winds were near gale force by the time Ethan left the captain's cabin after sharing the glad news of his impending marriage with him and John Hill. He had been shocked to see Sean on the edge of drunkenness, a condition he'd never seen the captain in before. The two men were drinking brandy, lots of it, by the looks of the half empty bottles.

John was handling the liquor just fine, but the captain, who never drank the strong stuff, was near to passing out from what he could see.

"Congratulations, Ethan," said John. "Anna's going to make you a beautiful wife. Just make sure you take better care of her than I did with poor Abigail. You don't want anything happening to her."

"Not bloody likely," said Sean, slurring his words slightly. "Lil' Anna has God to take care of her an' now she's got Ethan as well." He held up a glass of brandy like a toast and added, "Cheers."

The ship pitched into a large wave at that moment and the jolt knocked the brandy out of his glass, splashing onto the floor. Ethan looked at John. "Time for me to get on the oilskins. I'll take over the wheel from O'Riley, while you get the crew on watch to shorten the sail. She's runnin' a bit hard. Anythin' else, Cap'n?"

Sean waved them away. "No, the two of ye can manage this little storm jus' fine. I'm a bit weary meself. Think I'll take a nap. Wake me if it gets any rougher," he yawned.

After the men left, he dimmed the lantern and curled up on his bunk, expecting to fall asleep in an instant. But even with all the brandy inside him, making him feel slightly queasy as the ship fought through the choppy waves, sleep was elusive.

Why did he care if Ethan married Anna? Why should it bother him so? Had the little wench somehow stole her way into his heart without him noticing? It wouldn't be that she had ever tried. Lovely Anna went about her ways with a sweet innocence, unaware that all the men on board stared at her with as much longing as they did with her flamboyant mistress, himself included.

Tatiana. Now there was the woman for him, Russian spy or not. She was the type he deserved, gorgeous, but shallow. He sometimes pitied the naval lieutenant. He didn't have a clue what he was marrying. More than likely he was as arrogant and calculating as she. They belonged together.

He was finally dozing off, the feelings of self-pity waning, when the rustle of silk and the scent of lavender stole over his senses. Before he could rouse himself she slipped in besides him, all softness and warmth.

"Anna," he murmured in his alcoholic stupor, reaching towards the woman on his bunk.

Tatiana couldn't believe her ears. The captain loved her maid, too? Who else did on this cursed ship? She thought with sudden fury.

Anna, he called silently, hope flaring up as instantly as it died. No, she wasn't Anna and would never be Anna. Anna was soon to be his best friend's wife.

The ship rolled sharply to port, and he found himself sprawled across Tatiana Bolkonsky. In the dim light her hair was a glinting mass of silver tendrils tumbling down to her waist, her eyes a bottomless pool of purple velvet, her lips a luscious red, parted in a half-smile of invitation.

He leaned over to kiss her, and as he did, all thoughts of Anna Teichroew fled his mind.

* * *

Rio de Janeiro was a picturesque world of its own. The weather was warm and sunny and the busy harbor waters a turquoise blue. The capital of Brazil was a teeming city of hillside villas and crowded waterfront buildings. Outside the city there were lush coffee plantations and groves of lemon, banana and orange trees. The crew of the *Sea Rose* quickly restocked their provisions with the fresh fruits to battle scurvy, vegetables, meats and barrels of fresh water. After the long haul around the tip of South America and Cape Horn, the next port of call would be Valparaiso, Chile.

When *Sea Rose* was preparing to depart several ships sailed into the bay. Two were American whalers bound for Boston, one was a British trader laden with cargo from China and the other was the Russian naval ship, the *Suvorov*. The British and American ships all had torn canvas sails and shabbily repaired rigging. The British ship the *Elizabeth Ann*, even had her forward mast braced as if it had cracked during a storm. Sean knew he needn't ask her captain how it happened. Two words explained it all---Cape Horn.

Captain Matthew Hunter of the *Elizabeth Ann* was a well-respected and seasoned sailor. To see his ship with such storm damage made Sean and his officers tense at what lay ahead for them in the Roaring Forties of the south Atlantic latitudes.

Yet, he had another, more immediate predicament to solve, also with two words---Tatiana Bolkonsky. She was still on board the ship. His plan to be rid of her had gone awry the moment he took that first sip of brandy. He awoke the following morning with a dreadful headache and very little memory of what had transpired inside the rumpled sheets of his bunk the night before. At first he hoped it was only a dream, even if a rather bawdy one at that.

But later that day Tatiana sought him out with an uncertain gleam in her eyes. "You can't be putting me off your ship now, Captain," she said boldly. "Not after last night."

She tensed, waiting for his reaction. The truth of the matter was that nothing had happened at all. After a few kisses Captain O'Connell had passed out. At first she'd been frustrated then realized she could still get what she wanted without having to give him anything. She'd slipped out his door, leaving him snoring like an old man, as virginal as the day she was born. But she wasn't about to let him know that.

"What exactly did happen last night?"

She arched one eyebrow. "Even if you don't remember, Captain, I do."

"I recall ye bein' in my bunk and acting like a common tramp, but that's about it," he said bluntly.

Her cheeks flushed a rosy pink. "Which you were happy to oblige, including your promise that I could stay aboard until we find the *Suvorov*."

He scratched the dark stubble on his chin thoughtfully. "I don't remember saying that."

"Oh, but you did and a gentleman never goes back on his word to a lady."

He glared at her, his green eyes as sharp and cold as shards of jade. "I'm no gentleman and ye, Miss Bolkonsky, are no lady."

She tossed her head a bit nervously, wondering for a moment if she'd pushed him too far. Then she decided to throw all caution aside and blurted out, "You can't leave me alone in a foreign country. What if I'm carrying your child?"

This was an entanglement he had never thought of. She had taken him for quite the fool. He was silent for a few moments, weighing the odds. He had made a lot of mistakes in his life, but one thing he was determined he'd never do and that was abandon his own child. If he ever had a son or daughter someday, he would be the kind of father his own da had never been.

"Ye can stay until we come across the *Suvorov*. Then ye will agree to leave without your maid. I'm sure the Russian captain can find you a native girl to take her place."

She frowned. "No one can take Anna's place."

How true that is, he thought, wishing it had been Anna in his arms last night; as his wife.

* * *

Now Tatiana was safely tucked away in her cabin aboard the *Suvorov* with Natasha clucking over her like a mother hen. As soon as Tatiana and all her trunks and possessions had been transferred over, the *Sea Rose* had sailed away. She should have been delirious with joy as the American ship disappeared over the horizon. Instead she'd experienced a lump in her throat and an urge to weep.

Perhaps it was the loss of Anna. Even though she'd been jealous of her maid and irritated by all the undue attention she'd attracted from Captain O'Connell and Ethan Campbell, she couldn't stay angry with her for long.

Their parting was emotional, at least for Anna. She hadn't been too proud to shed a few tears and embrace Tatiana with a sincere display of affection. "I will be praying for a safe voyage for you, *Mademoiselle*," she said. "And I hope to see you again someday."

"Thank you, Anna," she'd replied, hugging her back. "I wish you well with your Ethan."

"And I wish you much happiness with Lieutenant Volodin."

The two girls smiled at each other then it was time for Tatiana to leave. Her last memory of Anna was watching her stand on the deck, her small hand waving back and forth until she was a dot on the vanishing ship.

"Tell your husband to find me a maid, Natasha," she demanded.

The captain's wife was outraged that Tatiana's maid had left her employ for marriage to an American sailor. When she asked why Tatiana hadn't forbidden her, she'd reminded Natasha that Anna was a free woman, not a slave or a serf.

So, it was no surprise to Tatiana the day before they sailed from Rio de Janeiro, that Captain-Lieutenant Chernyshov bought a young African slave girl about fourteen years old, to be her new maid on the rest of the voyage.

The girl was chocolate colored with kinky black hair and could only speak Portuguese. She flinched each time Tatiana spoke to her and cowered in fright if Tatiana raised her voice or showed any displeasure.

Her name was Isabella and she was terrified of every male she saw, a real annoyance on a navy ship full of men. But she was intelligent and soon understood her duties as a maid. She made certain Tatiana had clean clothing, water for bathing, and learned quickly how to arrange her hair and help her dress each day.

But Isabella wasn't Anna. As the *Suvorov* headed back out to sea, Tatiana realized how lonely she was without her constant companionship. Their relationship was more than mistress and maid, more like close friends. She never thought she'd admit it, but she even missed Anna reading her Bible and bowing her head in prayer. At first the sight had annoyed her no end, but eventually, it brought a strange sort of comfort. The thought that she might never see her again filled her with sadness.

So one morning after breakfast she decided she had to do something to bring Anna back into her life. She took a deep breath and presented Chernyshov with the duplicate of the cargo manifest she'd copied on the *Sea Rose*.

At first he was speechless with surprise, but after scanning the document he gave her an approving smile and said, "Good work, *Mademoiselle*! As soon as we reach New Archangel I will give this manifest to the governor. You can mark my words that he will send out a navy ship or two to intercept the *Sea Rose* before she can trade her guns to the natives. Her captain and her officers will be arrested, perhaps imprisoned. Your father will be so proud of his daughter! You will be the heroine of New Archangel!"

His praise warmed her and gave her hope. Perhaps when the *Sea Rose* was caught and Ethan Campbell imprisoned in New Archangel, Anna would have no choice but to return to her as her maid.

Then there was Captain O'Connell. It amused her no end how she tricked him into keeping her on the *Sea Rose* with the pretense of their night together. She couldn't wait to see him in a Russian prison.

CHAPTER FIFTEEN

Clutching the sides of her bunk, Anna moaned with a mixture of nausea and fear as the ship slid down yet another gigantic wave into the trough. The *Sea Rose* hesitated for one sickening moment before beginning her climb up the face of the next huge swell.

Welcome to Cape Horn, she thought miserably, except that they hadn't come even close to the infamous tip of South America. It was ironic how December was the beginning of summer in the southern hemisphere, but in the past fortnight as they approached Cape Horn, the ship encountered the same freezing temperatures, savage weather and treacherous seas that any winter storm could create.

Ethan told her it was called the "Cape Horn problem." All the wind, waves and current came from the west when west was where they wanted to sail. This resulted in the ship being pushed backward more than forward.

It was enough to drive any sailor mad. Certainly Captain O'Connell and Ethan had become driven men, shouting orders day and night to the frustrated exhausted crew. They spent forty-eight hours at a time on deck in their oilskins, which offered little protection from the freezing spray, as they anxiously watched for the exact moment when it would be safe to raise some sail.

The wind was a sailing nightmare, gusting to gale force then suddenly dying out. The crew worked in a continual routine of going aloft to shorten sail quickly before the violent winds could shred the canvas, then watching in dismay as the wind died two hours later, making the ship wallow in the heaving waves, so they had to go aloft to release the gaskets, haul the yards around and sheet the sails, over and over again.

A mixture of snow, sleet and rain froze in the rigging. The men were soaked and numbed with cold, and their hands bloody from grabbing frozen canvas. Yet Sean and Ethan refused to let them give up. They shouted commands through a speaking trumpet while two men at the wheel kept the ship's bow heading into the seas.

Anna closed her eyes and shivered under her blankets. She could imagine the chaos topside as the ship bucked and pitched on the enormous waves, snarling grayish green monsters topped with hissing foam that thundered across the deck, drenching everything and everyone in their path, leaving a coating of ice in the subfreezing temperatures on masts, railings and deck.

How many days had she spent tossing in her bunk, praying for their safety, and unable to eat a thing? Her constant seasickness reminded her of Natasha and how impatient she and Tatiana were with her. Anna decided if she ever saw her again, she would treat her with more understanding.

Early this morning Ethan had checked on her, but he was so weak with exhaustion himself, he could offer little except a hug and a prayer. "We'll be out of this soon, lass," he'd said with encouragement. "Then we'll be round the Horn and into the calmer Pacific. Keep your thoughts on our weddin' day."

They had decided to be married as soon as they could find a reputable ship's captain to perform the ceremony, preferably an American or British navy captain. Anna remembered how they'd first asked Captain O'Connell to marry them. To their surprise he'd refused without an explanation. Anna thought it was rather odd, but Ethan told her later that perhaps the captain was too worried about reaching Cape Horn safely, and the thought of a wedding on board was the least of his concerns.

Now she shoved all thoughts of her coming marriage away as the ship suddenly shuddered like a live rabbit being shaken in the jaws of a wolf. Were they about to sink? Frightened, Anna crawled carefully out of her bunk, already fully clothed in her warmest wool gown. With haste she donned her oilskins and boots and staggered into the salon just as the skylight cracked overhead and icy water spattered about the room.

She ran from the salon and flung herself onto the ladder leading to the deck. Halfway up she collided in the semi-darkness with a man in wet oilskins coming down. She gasped as she practically fell backwards to the floor. The man let out a curse, then dropped down and seized her roughly about the shoulders.

"Why aren't ye in your cabin?" Sean demanded.

"We're sinking!" she cried out. "Water is coming into the salon!"

With a grunt of exasperation he said, "We're in no danger, Miss Teichroew, but ye will be if ye go up there right now."

He tried to push her into the salon, but she refused to budge. "I won't go back in there."

He glanced into the darkened wet salon, noticing the cracked skylight and the water trickling across the floor.

"We shipped a heavy sea and we have a bit of damage, but we're not sinking. I'll have some men board up the skylight at once and get Samuel to bail out the water."

"Please let me go up on deck," she begged. "I can't stay down here by myself any longer. I promise I won't be any trouble. You can tie me to something so I won't be swept overboard."

He hesitated, then she heard amusement in his voice when he answered, "Aye, little sailor, ye can come up, but it won't be long until ye wish ye were back down here agin."

A minute later Anna realized how right the captain was. It was a scene out of a watery hell. The waves were an endless march of white capped, black mountains rolling out of the west. The wind gusted continually to a high-pitched scream, blowing stinging sleet and spray in horizontal sheets across the slippery deck.

The captain tied her to the aft mast with a good strong rope. She tried not to notice the astonished look of dismay on Ethan's bearded face as he and Gregory Jones struggled with the big wheel at the helm. The ship was running heavily and it took two strong men to steer.

The steep rolling and pitching of the *Sea Rose* was alarming, but strangely, out here the movement had no nauseating effects on her stomach. Her seasickness vanished in the face of the wild elements around her.

She didn't know whether to join the wind in shrieking with fright, or to trust God and the captain with his knowledge of the sea, his ship and his crew, and give in to the exhilaration of the untamed southern ocean in a gale. There was an awesome beauty about the dangerous scene Anna knew she would never forget, if she survived.

At that moment she heard a sharp cry above the roaring wind, "Man overboard!"

The captain, still at her side, jerked to attention. "Where?" he shouted. "And who?"

"Robby fell off the bow on ice watch," said John, peering at the two of them from underneath his hooded oilskins. His blond mustache was covered with tiny white icicles.

"Did the little fool forget to tie himself tight to the forward mast?" The captain sounded angry at the boy as if it was his own fault.

Anna was horrified. "Turn the ship around and find him, or he'll die!"

The two men shook their heads as John said, "He's dead already in these freezing seas. There's nothing we can do."

Anna knew he was right, though every nerve in her being cried out at the injustice of it. Hot tears of grief sprang into her eyes and froze into white drops halfway down her cheeks. She was going to miss his freckled smiling face, his cheery helpfulness in performing the most mundane tasks. And poor Jimmy was going to be devastated.

The captain stayed at her side while she continued to cry her freezing tears. Once she thought she saw a few streaks of white down his cheeks, but she could have been mistaken with all the ice frozen onto his mustache and beard. He looked like a ghostly snowman, as all the men did. The only thing alive in his face were his green eyes, the lashes coated white, staring at her with a sad weariness.

Perhaps she was wrong. Perhaps he blamed himself and not Robby for his death.

The ice watch was the most feared job rounding Cape Horn. It usually fell to the lowliest sailors on board, cabin boys or apprentices. They tied themselves to the forward mast in the lookout perch, the most precarious part of the ship in a gale, but also the best place possible to watch for floating icebergs. High winds and waves were not the only dangers to threaten and sink ships rounding Cape Horn. Glaciers from the Andean fjords lurked nearby, sending tons of broken ice into the ocean, creating deadly ice floes which could slice a careless ship in two.

The shock of Robby's drowning and the bitter cold was overwhelming to Anna. She began to tremble so violently that Sean untied the rope around her and pulled her into his arms. He turned towards the helm and yelled at Ethan, "I'll take her below and get her warmed up. Not to worry."

He helped Anna down the ladder and brought her into the forward cabin which was relatively dry and warm from the galley stove. They removed their drenched oilskins and boots and wrapped themselves up in dry blankets. She slumped into a chair at the table, her face so numb it was a struggle to force her lips into a smile of thanks as Wang Li placed a bowl of steaming soup in front of her.

The Chinaman was short with a round belly. His clean-shaven face was sallow-skinned and he had a thin black mustache drooping over his mouth. His hair was one long black braid, reaching past his waist. He bowed his head briefly to her and smiled, showing brown stained teeth from all the years of smoking opium.

"Missy want tea?" he questioned kindly.

As she nodded her assent, he went to fetch the teapot, almost bumping into the wild eyed boy bursting into the room.

"Robby? What the---" exploded the captain in surprise.

Anna gave a small cry of delight. "We thought you had fallen overboard."

"It weren't me. It shoulda been, but it weren't!"

He gasped the words out over and over between sobs, not making any sense. Sean forced him to sit down at the table and gave him his mug of tea.

"Easy now, lad. Just have a sip of this and take a hold of yourself."

Robby slumped dejectedly over the table and sniffled. He swallowed two large gulps then took a deep breath. "It was me turn to take the ice watch, but I was so tired I couldn't get up. So---so Jimmy took it for me. He's the one who's dead. Not me, but it shoulda been me---"

He started to wail again as Sean and Anna exchanged helpless looks. The ice on Sean's face had melted into water and he wiped his hand across his eyes. "Robby," he began.

"Yesterday Jimmy saw a snow petrel," he babbled. "Ye never see those birds in a storm. He shoulda been more careful today."

Anna glanced questioningly at Sean, who sighed and said, "The snow petrel is a very large bird from Antarctica. Sailors believe it to be a sign of ill omen," he explained. "Usually we see them before storms, not during storms. But they're common enough around here along with many other kinds of birds."

Sean shrugged as if to deny his belief in the superstition. Feeling pity for the poor boy, Anna reached out a hand across the table and patted Robby on his arm.

"It's not your fault," she said. "Don't blame yourself."

He shrank back from her touch and stared at her with fright. Grief gave him a crazed look. "Maybe the men 'r' right about you an' the other Russian lady. Maybe you do bring bad luck."

"Enough, Robby!" said Sean in a stern voice. "I know yer distraught over the loss of your brother, but I won't allow any of that kind of nonsense about Miss Teichroew. I suggest ye apologize. Then make your way to your quarters. Ye are relieved from any further duty on the ice watch today."

As Robby bolted from the room he mumbled a halfhearted apology in Anna's direction, but refused to look at her. She sighed, feeling a heavy sadness weighing down on her spirit.

"Captain, do you think he really believes his brother drowned because of my presence on board is bringing him bad luck?" And you, she added silently, do you believe that too?

Frowning, he scratched at the two weeks growth of dark scrubby beard on his face and muttered, "Ah, to shave and sleep for a week; to feel like a human being again."

He was to the point of utter exhaustion and seemed unable or unwilling to answer her question. She waited patiently, sipping her tea, noticing the dark circles under his eyes. How much longer could he go on before he dropped, she wondered with compassion.

The sudden warmth in her lovely eyes startled him. Feeling uneasy, he looked away and said, "Robby wants to believe ye are bringing bad luck to this ship so he can appease his own conscience about letting his brother take his place on the ice watch. He'll be better able to cope with Jimmy's death if he believes someone else is responsible for it."

"Do you believe I'm bad luck, Captain?"

"No." His mouth twitched in amusement for a brief moment, then he shrugged wearily. "It's common enough to lose a hand or two rounding the Horn, sometimes more. If Jimmy had been tied properly to the mast he'd still be alive. We make our choices. Luck has nothing to do with life. But many of the crew is superstitious and that's why most ships have a female figurehead."

"What does a figurehead have to do with luck?"

"Figureheads became popular in the last century as a way to bring the female presence aboard a ship without insulting the sea. Sailors believe that the um--um," he hesitated, "the bare breasts of a carved figurehead have the power to quiet storms."

Anna felt herself flushing in embarrassment then noticed his lips tilting upwards in a mischievous quirk. She knew she should be insulted by his immodest words, but instead she shocked herself by blurting, "Then to make everyone on this ship feel better about me, I suppose I should strip to the waist and have someone tie me to the bow."

He choked on a mouthful of tea. "If you did that," he let out with a strangled laugh, "we'd have to rename the ship."

Anna surprised herself again by bursting into a giggle. "And why would that be?"

"Figureheads are often directly related to the name of the ship, so we'd have to call the *Sea Rose* the--the *Sea Anna*."

"If that is true, then who is Rose?"

His humor ended abruptly. "I didn't name this ship, but I once had a sister named Rose."

Instinctively, Anna knew she was treading dangerous waters. "You said, 'had.' Does that mean she died?"

"Aye. She was only fourteen and she had weak lungs. She died when I was at sea."

"I am so sorry. That must have a shock for you when you returned. And it must have been so hard for your parents, too."

"They both died afore Rose," he said, unconsciously slipping into his Irish lilt. "Ma was a good Catholic, but Da was, well, let's say I'm not sad 'bout him bein' gone."

There was a belligerent tone in his voice as if he was daring her to question him further. She decided not to. "My mama passed away almost two years ago when I was sixteen. I still miss her, too."

Her voice was as soft and sweet as honey and it flowed around him like a soothing blanket. Their eyes locked together in a shared understanding of sorrow.

She smiled at him. "To what you said before about luck versus choice in life, I agree with you that it is our own choices that help or hinder us. Long ago as a child I chose to follow Jesus Christ, and ever since then, I have the security that my life and my future are in God's hands."

So, that was the secret of her serenity, he thought. Why worry about life and death if the Almighty Himself was taking care of you?

"I've never believed in a God that cared whether I lived or died," he said.

"But He does," said Anna firmly. "Jesus said that His Father sees when a tiny sparrow falls. And if God can notice a bird, how much more precious are we to Him? He even numbers the hairs on our very heads."

"I wish that was true," he said, wishing even more that it was she who cared that much about him. His fingers twitched as he longed to reach over and touch hers.

"Good news, Cap'n! " Ethan stood in the doorway, dripping sea water all over the floor. He grinned excitedly at both Anna and Sean. "The wind's droppin' an' the glass is risin.' We've spotted a clearing to the west."

The intimate moment was shattered. If the gale had finally blown itself out, now they could round the Horn. Sean shot up from the table, dropped his blanket and grabbed his oilskins. He rushed for the door without a backwards glance. Ethan gave Anna a wink and followed him.

After both men had left, Wang Li padded silently into the room in his cloth slippers. As he refilled her mug he said in his pidgin English, "Missy, tell me about this Jesus."

* * *

After all the weeks of unending struggle to reach the southernmost tip of South America in the foulest weather imaginable, the actual rounding of Cape Horn took place under fair skies and in relatively calm seas.

It was as if the jagged stone face of the Horn was laughing at them, "You foolish sailors tremble at the very thought of me, but look, there's nothing to be afraid of after all."

To make the day even more memorable, it was Christmas morning. Anna and Ethan stood on the deck enjoying the bright sunshine and watching the antics of the sea lions and brown fur seals. Near Horn Island dozens of the creatures frolicked in the short choppy waves, sometimes swimming close to the ship's hull and staring curiously up at them. It was obvious they hadn't encountered fur hunters as yet so far south. The males were massive, thick necked and full of blubber, weighing as much as 700 pounds, while the females were half their size, streamlined and graceful. Anna found them adorable with their long whiskers and large glistening dark eyes.

The air was alive with the cries and calls of many different types of birds, swirling, diving, and gliding all around the ship. Black-browed albatross, swooping black and white checkered cape petrels, and great brown skuas with four foot wingspans circled above the gulls and terns as they waited to steal any fish the smaller birds caught.

Anna's breath caught as she admired the magnificent scenery. An infinite array of unnamed, unexplored snow topped mountains marched northward among heavily wooded islands and icy blue-green glacier fed fjords.

"Alaska looks as bonny as this," said Ethan, smiling down at her.

She returned his smile, feeling happier than she had in a long while. On her ears was a pair of pearl drop earrings, set in gold, a present from Ethan, given to her after breakfast in the forward cabin. Ever since Tatiana left the ship, Anna had been allowed to eat with the captain and his officers. She spent many an amusing meal watching someone's plate being thrown in their lap by the excessive rolling of the ship. She had learned quickly the necessity of holding onto her mug with one hand and her plate with the other, occasionally snatching a mouthful of food between the rolls.

This morning Christmas breakfast had been a relaxing meal with the captain and his mates in a good mood. The worst of the weather was behind them and everyone felt like celebrating. In the galley Wang Li clattered pots and pans, contentedly humming his odd Chinese melodies.

After everyone finished eating and the two were alone, Ethan placed the earrings on the table in front of Anna with a shy smile. "Merry Christmas, me bonnie lass," he said.

She had never owned a pair of earrings before. Jewelry was frowned upon by the Mennonites. But Anna didn't give it a thought. She was so overcome she rose from her chair and threw her arms around Ethan, giving him a big hug of thanks. He took quick advantage of her closeness by giving her a lingering kiss.

His beard scratched her chin and she withdrew, rubbing the skin of her face and smiling. "Where did you find such beautiful earrings?" she asked.

"In a market in Rio de Janeiro. I meant to give them to ye for a weddin' gift, but I dinna want to wait that long."

Now on deck, watching the sea lions, with the warmth of the sun overhead, the sky so blue and cloudless, wearing a surprise gift from the man she was to marry, Anna felt this was the best Christmas since her mama had died.

"Cape Horn isn't such a bad place," she said.

"The Horn is deceitful in this type of weather," said the captain, who had approached them from behind. He stood tall and masculine in his heavy buttoned up captain's coat with his cap tucked over his unruly black hair. Ethan was wearing a similar coat and cap, and Anna was dressed like a civilized lady, chemise, petticoat, a frock, and her velvet cloak. No need for the ugly oilskins on such a beautiful day.

"Those jagged peaks over there are the grave markers for a burial ground of thousands of brave souls who have perished in these waters since the time of Magellan and will continue to do so in the years ahead."

His depressing words had an immediate dampening effect on the couple. Ethan cleared his throat and said, "Aye, Cap'n, time for me to take our noon position, is it?"

At Sean's curt nod, Ethan excused himself from Anna by giving her arm a gentle squeeze then he hurried off to fetch the sextant.

"I'd like to learn navigation, Captain," said Anna. "Would you allow Ethan to teach me sometime?"

He hesitated then said abruptly, "Wouldn't hurt to have a third person on board knowing how to plot a course. In case something happened to me or your betrothed," he added, looking at her shiny earrings with a sour expression.

Anna sensed he was in one of his dark moods. She had noticed how easily the captain could swing from light-heartedness to a brooding unhappiness when he withdrew into a silence only punctured by abrupt, often rude replies. Once again, she felt a deep compassion for him that she didn't understand.

"Look!" she cried, pointing upwards to the blue sky. "There's one of those giant snow petrels! What a graceful bird!"

He squinted into the sun. "Aye, they are, but I hope the crew doesn't spot the creature. There's been enough superstitious talk already."

"But you don't believe in all that nonsense about those birds being bad luck."

"No, I don't believe in anything except myself."

The arrogant statement made her feel sad somehow. A man's pride was his biggest stumbling block between him and God. And if she ever saw a man who needed God, it was the captain. "If you were raised in the Catholic Church, why don't you believe in God?"

He gave a harsh laugh. "I believed when I was a little boy. But I stopped believing after watching my father beat my mother all the years I was growing up. My mother was the kindest, most devout woman imaginable. Where did her faith get her? She died after too many babies because my father wouldn't leave her be. Then there was my sister. Rose loved God, too. But she took sick and died. How did God help them any?"

She saw the lines of bitterness around his eyes and her heart ached for him though she didn't know why. She wished she could say something to ease his pain. Instead she took his hand in hers, startling both of them by the instant warmth between them.

"My mama was also the kindest, most loving Christian woman I've known," she said softly. "But God took her, too. Perhaps our mothers and your sister are together in heaven right now, talking about us."

He was silent, staring out over the water, the sharp peaks of Cape Horn fading in the distance behind the ship. Anna chewed nervously on her lower lip waiting for his reaction. She never knew what to expect from him. He was as unpredictable as the weather around the Horn.

The wind tugged at a few black curls that had escaped from underneath his cap. She raised her eyes to find him watching her with a curious intensity.

"Ye never cease to amaze me, Anna," he said, then broke into a smile so handsome, it nearly took her breath away.

She returned the smile, and his hand tightened around hers. He edged closer to her, his eyes glinting in a strange way that made her pulse quicken. When he bent his head over her face like he was going to kiss her, Anna knew she should step backwards, but she felt frozen in her place.

A loud cough broke them apart. Sean dropped Anna's hand like it had branded him.

Samuel stood in front of them, his expression stoic but his eyes dancing merrily.

"Cap'n, Miss Anna," he politely nodded to each of them, "Christmas dinner's served in an hour. It'll be mighty special." He suddenly grinned, a rare event, his teeth flashing a brilliant white in his dark face.

"Tell Wang Li we're looking forward to it, Samuel," said Sean, stepping quickly away from Anna, his face falling into a dark expression once again.

As Anna watched him walk aft towards the helmsman, she felt relieved he was gone. The captain stirred up feelings inside her she didn't welcome, especially since she was a betrothed woman. Her gaze fastened on Ethan standing near the forward mast as he aimed the sextant towards the sky. He reminded her so much of Papa, solid, dependable and comforting. He was going to make her a wonderful husband. Smiling, she made her way over to him, pushing all thoughts of the captain aside.

That evening the forward cabin was crowded with men, the three officers, Mister Jones the blacksmith, Mister Harris the sail maker, and Mister Cartwright the carpenter. Samuel served the food to each person, starting with the captain, then Anna. The meal was the best they'd seen in weeks, the last of the good beef which had been bought in Brazil, plenty of vegetables, such as carrots and beets and potatoes, fresh baked bread and a treat made of rice and molasses, a stiff flour pudding liberally seeded with raisins and citron called duff.

When Wang Li brought the Christmas duff into the cabin, the men cheered and toasted each other with mugs filled with brandy and rum while Sean, Ethan and Anna sipped tea.

Sean sat at the head of the table in the captain's chair. Anna was placed at his left, Ethan across from her on his right. Spirits were high and laughter grew louder. After the meal was finished Samuel cleared the table and Wang Li came in to receive a round of applause from the slightly intoxicated men.

He bowed gracefully then made a quick exit. Ethan leaned over and whispered into Anna's ear, "He's in a hurry to retire to his cabin so he can smoke his daily pipe of opium."

"But opium is a harmful addiction. How can it be allowed?" she asked with concern. Tatiana had once told her of the Chinese opium dens where the rich and poor alike smoked their lives away in an oblivion of drug induced dreams.

Sean heard her question and replied, "A good cook is worth his weight in gold. His job is the hardest one on the ship. Opium smoking is a conventional addiction for a Chinese cook and I allow it because I'm not about to lose Wang Li by denying him his little habit."

She remembered the empty sadness in the cook's oriental eyes the day he was asking her questions about Jesus. He seemed quite eager to know more about a God and His son who loved him. Anna wished she had a Bible in the Chinese language to give him. It was difficult trying to explain her faith to a man who spoke little English.

Everywhere she looked on this ship there was someone else who needed God, from the captain to the cook and to the lowly cabin boy. Poor Robby wasn't the same since Jimmy had died. He performed his tasks with a downcast face, rarely smiling. Her heart ached for him and she wished she could comfort him somehow. But he continued to rebuff any of her attempts at friendliness.

Sean watched the play of emotions across her sweet face. He had never met anyone who cared so much for other people. How different she was from her former mistress whose main concern in life was herself. Thinking of Tatiana Bolkonsky made him wonder where the *Suvorov* was. The Russian brig had left Brazil before them, but if she had encountered the same contrary winds around the Horn, she could be anywhere about.

Now that the calmer waters of the Pacific lay ahead, it was time to let the *Sea Rose* fly like the swift clipper she was born to be. It was important to reach Alaska before the *Suvorov*, just in case Miss Bolkonsky had found a way to convince the Russians that the *Sea Rose* was carrying guns to trade to the natives. The last thing Sean planned on this voyage was to have his ship and cargo seized and himself and the crew arrested.

If such a disaster happened, he feared Thomas Hill would never allow him to command another vessel again.

CHAPTER SIXTEEN

Anna kept her attention fixed on the British naval captain as she and Ethan stood together on the poop deck of the *H.M.S. Victoria,* listening to him recite the words of the wedding ceremony. He was a tall gaunt man with a thin gray beard and kindly blue eyes. In one hand he held a Bible and after a few words about marriage in general, he read the thirteenth chapter of I Corinthians in a deep gruff voice.

For a second she closed her eyes and it was like hearing the verses being read by Elder Klassen. If she kept them shut, she could pretend she was back in Furstenau, surrounded by her family and friends as she spoke her wedding vows. But with the breeze tugging at her hair, the cries of the gulls circling overhead, the muted creaking of the ship in the swells, and the soft slap of the water against the hull, it was impossible to imagine she was anywhere but on the ocean, a few miles off the coast of Chile.

This wasn't how she always dreamed her wedding would be. With a touch of sadness in her heart she promised to trust, honor and obey Ethan until death parted them. When it was his turn he smiled down at her in such love, that her spirits lifted, reminding her that it was God's will that she marry this man.

And she believed He had sent the British ship for just that purpose.

Early that morning after the *Sea Rose* sailed out of Valparaiso harbor, fully provisioned with fresh food and water, they had met the *H.M.S. Victoria* sailing towards the city. The British navy brig was returning to England, heading eastward around the Horn after taking on supplies in Valparaiso.

Ethan asked Captain O'Connell to hoist the signal flag for the ship to heave to. At first the captain had refused and protested the delay, citing the threat of the *Suvorov* as an excuse to keep sailing. John had taken Ethan's side and said a brief wedding wouldn't make any difference. Finally he relented, and reluctantly launched the ship's longboat to row the couple over to the navy vessel. He and John accompanied Ethan and Anna to act as witnesses.

The weather was perfect, sunny with a warm breeze, and the ocean was a series of gently rolling deep blue swells. Ten miles to the east the snowcapped peaks of the Andes Mountains rose majestically from the Chilean shoreline.

Anna was dressed in her most becoming gown from Tatiana, a cream-colored muslin with a high waist and a satin sash of pastel green. A lacy white silk scarf covered her hair while the pearl drop earrings dangled from her ears, her only jewelry.

Clean shaven with a neatly trimmed mustache, his long russet hair tied behind him with a black ribbon, Ethan looked quite handsome. He also wore his best clothes, black breeches tucked into shiny black boots and a white shirt with a black belt. The tall Scotsman towered over Anna as he took her small trembling hands in his large warm fingers and drew her closer to his side.

"And now I pronounce you man and wife," said the British commander. "You, sir, may kiss the bride."

As Ethan bent over to kiss her, a mighty shout rose from all the British crew watching. They broke apart quickly, laughing with self-consciousness.

The first person to congratulate them was Sean. He forced himself to shake Ethan's hand and then he kissed Anna chastely on her cheek, breathing in her fresh scent of vanilla and roses. Somehow he managed to bare his teeth in a grin, but it felt false and tight on his face. She had never looked lovelier, and he cursed inwardly at the fool he was for wishing he was standing in his best friend's place.

The wedding put him in a foul mood, a mood that stayed with him as the days went by. Seeing the newlyweds so happy in each other's company grated on Sean's nerves. Ethan soon taught his new wife how to navigate and they made a fine team, one taking the reading on deck with the sextant, the other plotting the ship's position in the chart room. Sean couldn't bear to watch if Ethan held Anna's hand, or even worse, when she smilingly returned his affections. He was often tempted to place Ethan on night watch, just so he wouldn't have to think of what went on in the private intimacy of their cabin at night.

On their wedding night any doubts Anna had about the marriage was banished. At first both of them had faced each other with nervousness, Anna as a virgin bride, and Ethan, ashamed of offering Anna a husband who was not physically whole.

But the love between them calmed all their fears. Before going to bed when Ethan moved to blow out the lantern so Anna would not be repulsed by seeing his leg stump, she'd said, "No, Ethan, I'm your wife now and there's nothing you need to hide from me."

And to Ethan's pleased surprise she had not turned her face away from his unsightly appendage, but had lightly touched his puckered shriveled flesh and with tears in her eyes, said, "Your leg is a testimony to God's healing power, Ethan, and is something to be proud of."

He had never thought of his handicap as a blessing from God. Joy flooded his soul as he realized what a precious jewel of a woman he had married. With great love and gratitude beating steadfastly inside his heart, he opened his arms to her and tenderly showed her his deep devotion.

Later they fell asleep entwined together face-to-face in the narrow bunk. In the morning Anna awoke thinking of her parents, and wondered if her mama had felt so cherished and loved by her papa. Then she thought of Agatha and an expression of sadness flickered across her features.

At that moment Ethan opened his eyes and saw the flash of pain in her eyes. "Did I hurt ye last night, Anna?" he asked anxiously.

She saw his worry and quickly answered, "Oh, no, Ethan, I just was thinking of my family and how much I miss them. I wish Papa and my brothers and little sister and uncle and aunt and cousins could've been at our wedding yesterday."

Ethan kissed the tip of her nose. "I promise ye that someday when I have a ship of me own, I will take ye back to Russia to visit them."

"What if we have children by then?" she asked, blushing, as she remembered their love making of the night before.

He gave her another kiss, this time on the mouth, and murmured huskily, "We'll take the bairns with us, *m' leannan*."

She pulled back slightly. "What did you call me?"

He chuckled. "In Gaelic it means 'my darling.'"

Smiling, she felt a new feeling of happiness flood through her. Truly, God was blessing her with a fine husband and a new life, she thought, returning Ethan's kiss with one of her own.

* * *

By the middle of February the *Sea Rose* reached the southwestern coast of Mexico. For two weeks they drifted in circles without wind or current. Similar to the doldrums, the hot sun beat mercilessly down upon the ship, melting the tar from between the deck boards like black sticky blood. The water supply grew low and most of the food bought in Chile spoiled. They were back to eating salted meat, dry biscuits and pickled cabbage. Fishing off the deck was the only source of variety in their diet, but only if it netted something edible. Sharks were plentiful but Anna didn't care for their tough dry flesh.

There was much grumbling among the crew. Some wanted to find a hidden cove on the Mexican coast and search the jungle for fresh water and food. Sean reminded them that Spanish Mexico was a grim, inhospitable place for Americans to be and claimed their plan as a foolhardy and dangerous one.

As each day passed without a breeze he became more irritable and cross-tempered. Like the crew, Anna was careful to stay out of his way, for he had become impossible to please. Everything anyone said or did he took wrong. His curses were heard all over the ship.

Finally by the first of March, the wind returned, steady and fair, and the *Sea Rose* lifted up her bow with joy and skimmed northward. After passing southern California and the Russian settlement of Fort Ross near San Francisco, heavy bands of clouds appeared, bringing much needed rain. Fresh water soon overflowed the barrels again and there was plenty for drinking and washing.

It didn't take long for the novelty of the rain to wear off. As they neared the Columbia River the sea and sky blended together into one hazy gray mist of unending drizzle. No horizon could be seen and the ship threaded her way cautiously through the gray waters. The wind had a cold bite. Though spring was coming, winter still had its icy clutches on the northwestern coast.

At dinner one evening Anna said that this part of the world was the most depressing she had seen thus far. Her hands were wrapped around a steaming mug of tea, its heat the fastest way to warm her fingers on such a damp cold night.

"Southwestern Alaska suffers from the same miserable climate," said John, "especially Sitka, which is notorious for its never-ending rain."

"I wonder how *Mademoiselle* Bolkonsky will manage to live in New Archangel, then," she answered. "She never did care for the rain."

Sean quirked his eyebrows. "I'm sure she will do just fine. Women like her always find a way to survive."

A trace of bitterness edged his voice and Anna sensed the hostility he felt for her former mistress. Was it because the captain had fallen in love with Tatiana and she had spurned him? The sparks flying between the two whenever they were near each other had been obvious to all but the most dimwitted. Even Ethan once told her, "Me and the lads always thought the Cap'n had a soft spot for the Baroness. More n' once, I spied him watchin' her like he dinna know if he wanted to kiss her or hang her from the yardarms."

She remembered how suddenly the captain had changed his mind about leaving Tatiana in Brazil months ago. Anna always suspected it had something to do with that one night when she awoke to use the chamber pot, and found Tatiana's bunk empty. Alarmed, she was thinking of looking for her when Tatiana crept in, reeking of brandy with her hair disheveled and her gown wrinkled.

Anna was immediately suspicious. "Where have you been, *Mademoiselle*?"

"None of your business!" Tatiana had snapped, "but if you must know, the captain invited me to have a nightcap with him."

"But he doesn't drink liquor." It was something Anna always admired about him.

Tatiana gave a sarcastic laugh. "Well, he certainly put it away tonight..." Her voice trailed off as she noticed her maid's expression of shocked disapproval. "And don't look at me like that, Anna! I know it was wrong of me to go to his cabin alone, but nothing happened between us. Absolutely nothing!"

She sounded more disappointed than contrite and Anna didn't believe her. If nothing improper had taken place, then why were some of the hooks on the back of her gown still unfastened?

At the time Anna had bit her tongue and returned to bed, knowing that to question Tatiana further would only provoke her temper. The very next day Tatiana told her the captain was allowing her to stay on board the *Sea Rose* until they found the *Suvorov*. Anna never thought it was a coincidence, but Tatiana refused to speak of that night again.

Now Anna wondered if the reason the captain had been so ill-natured lately was because he missed Tatiana. As irritating as she was, Anna missed her as well, and prayed daily for her welfare and that of the crew of the *Suvorov*.

"Do you suppose we are still ahead of the *Suvorov*?" she asked the captain.

"I assume so," he said curtly, then fell silent.

Ethan and Anna exchanged glances, as John mentioned, "Soon we'll be nearing Vancouver Island and we can start trading with the natives for furs, but I suggest we pass by Nootka Sound."

"Agreed," said Sean. "And then the further north we sail, the more we need to keep a sharp lookout for the Russian Imperial Navy brigs."

Ethan set down his fork and frowned. "The greed of the Russian American Fur Company is a blight on the North American continent. 'Tis a crime the way they've abused the Aleut Indians and even their own Russian fur hunters. Remember that *Creole* supercargo on the *Eastern Wind*, Andrei Leonov? He told me that the *promyshlenniki* are underpaid, ill-treated, and kept at their work 'til they are past exhaustion. Their food and housing are wretched. After years of hard work they often find themselves owing the Company money for clothes and other necessities. Many return to Russia with empty pockets and broken minds."

"*Mademoiselle* always said that the *promyshlenniki* are mostly criminals fleeing Siberia or common adventurers who had made their choice to sign on with the Company," said Anna, remembering how Tatiana had scorned them.

"Too bad the Russians didn't give the Aleuts a choice whether to work for them or not," said Sean. "Their harsh treatment is well known among us traders. Entire Aleut families labor under oppression equal to that of the black slaves in the American South. They can't own their boats or clothes, an' everything they have is considered Company property. The men are forced to hunt and fish for the Russians while the women prepare skins to make Russian clothes, to clean and dry their fish and to warm their beds."

He glanced at Anna when he said the latter and she felt her cheeks burn in embarrassment. With a touch of anger that the captain could so easily irritate her, she blurted, "The prevailing belief in Saint Petersburg among the nobility is that the Russians have civilized the Aleuts and brought them Christianity, an act to be applauded, not belittled."

Some of the men at the table reacted to her statement with snorts of derision while others shook their heads and frowned. Even Ethan gave her a condescending smile as he said, "Sorry, lass, 'tis a well known fact the Russians have destroyed most of the Aleut Indian nation.

"If that is so," she said sadly, "then the truth has not been told in Saint Petersburg."

"That shouldn't be a surprise to anyone who has ever dealt with the Russian government," said Sean in a sarcastic tone.

His statement started a heated discussion about governments in general and as the men argued and talked, Anna finished her meal in silence, feeling humiliated and chastened. Later as they prepared for bed Ethan apologized.

"Some husband I am," he said, "sidin' against my own wife in front of all the lads. Can ye forgive me, Anna?"

As she brushed and braided her long hair, she sighed and said, "There's nothing to forgive, Ethan. If anything, I should be asking you to forgive me for shaming you by talking about things I knew nothing about. I only showed everyone my own ignorance. From now on, I promise to keep my opinions to myself. Women should be seen and not heard, you know," she added grumpily.

Ethan chuckled and reached over to tweak one of her braids. "I was always told 'twas bairns that should be seen and not heard. Not the bonny lasses."

His warm brown eyes danced and twinkled teasingly and she felt her anger slipping away. Ethan always knew what to say or do to make her feel better. She broke into a big smile and laughed.

* * *

The next morning Anna went up on deck and was greeted by a surprise. The gray clouds had disappeared and the sun shone warm and bright with a promise of spring. A breathtaking view of snow-peaked mountains loomed to the east, the Olympics. At their base ran smaller hills of emerald green forests. When the hills reached the sea, some flattened out into wide sandy beaches, others ended abruptly into jagged cliffs. It was a scene of wild beauty and utter desolation.

Hearing someone walk up behind her she spoke, assuming it was Ethan, "Except for Cape Horn, it is the loneliest stretch of land I have yet seen. Has any man ever stepped foot there?"

"No white man, 'less he was the unfortunate survivor of a shipwreck off these cursed rocks," said the captain, leaning against the starboard rail, peering intently at the shore. The clear weather had enabled the *Sea Rose* to sail closer in without worry of impaling the ship on one of the sharp stacks of rocks clustered menacingly along the coast.

"Why would it be unfortunate to survive a shipwreck?"

"Because these seemingly empty beaches and forests are, in fact, full of Indians, the Quileutes and the Makahs."

"I've never heard of them."

His lips stretched into a grim line. "When John was a captive among the Nootkas on Vancouver Island, a bit north of here, he heard many stories about them. The two tribes are either making war or trading with each other. But they both fear and hate white men. I've never heard of a white man surviving captivity among them."

"*Mademoiselle* told me once that the Americans and the British are much to blame for the natives' hatred of white men. You trade their furs for firearms, ammunition, knives and liquor, and bring them diseases. Is it not true that the very Tlingits who burned New Archangel years ago were eventually rearmed by American traders?"

He glanced at her. "Ye shouldn't believe everything Miss Bolkonsky told you." Then he looked away and gave a harsh laugh. "We do arm the natives, but for their own protection against Russian imperialism. I, for one, don't care to see the Tlingits, Nootkas, Haidas, or even those fierce tribes over there go the terrible way of the Aleuts."

"Nor do I," she said, remembering the conversation of the previous evening, then she added, "but you Americans and the British don't live in Russian America in permanent settlements like New Archangel. You can come and go as you please. It seems to me that the Russians are the ones in danger of the Indians if they have guns. Perhaps that is why the Imperial Navy is so determined to keep you away."

"These waters do not belong to the Russians," he said, anger darkening his words. "I'll trade what and where I please."

The ship suddenly pitched upwards on a large swell and Anna slid backward into Sean. Instinctively he caught her as she glanced up into his scowling face.

"And I? Do you wish me back in Russia as well?" she asked, her heart pounding.

"Of course not!" he growled, quickly releasing her. An emotion that Anna didn't understand, but Sean did all too well, charged between them.

To cover the awkwardness, Anna stepped away then asked, "Do you trade liquor to the Indians along with the firearms?"

"Sometimes it can't be helped, Anna, even though I have seen with my own eyes what rum does to an Indian. 'Tisn't a pleasant sight." He frowned. "Sort of like what too much whiskey does to an Irishman."

"Not you. I never see you drink liquor." Except for that night with Tatiana, she thought.

He hesitated, then said, "Me Da was a drunk an' the last thing I aim to be is like him."

"Was it the drink that killed him?" she asked in an innocent voice.

He turned and looked at her, his green eyes frozen into glacial ice. "Nay. I killed him."

As Anna choked in disbelief, he tipped his cap to her and strolled off.

* * *

The *Suvorov* reached New Archangel in early April. It was evening and Tatiana and Natasha were both on deck to watch their approach to the capital of Russian America.

The thick cloud cover which had plagued the ship for days had miraculously vanished as they sailed on the west side of Baranov Island. Golden rays of the sun glistened off the snowy cone of Mount Edgecumbe and the sharp peak of Mount Verstovia to the east. On their lower slopes the mountains were luxuriant with verdant forests, now lightly dusted with a powdery fresh snow. It had been a very cold spring.

The harbor was sprinkled with tiny islands on which grew trees of pine, fir and cedar. Frothy white surf swirled around the rocky base of each island, seemingly to block every route to the town. A cannon boom thundered through the air, announcing the arrival of the *Suvorov*. Soon after, bonfires were lit on Signal Island, their blazing fires a beacon to guide ships into the harbor. Suddenly the bow swung sharply to starboard then to port as Captain-Lieutenant Chernyshov stood at the wheel, gingerly navigating the *Suvorov* past the jagged rocks.

Dusk already covered the native village on the beach with a dark shadow from the adjoining forest. A short distance away stood the high walls of the palisade, extending from the shore on both sides to surround New Archangel. The main fort was built on a high pinnacle of rock emerging straight up from the sea.

One wooden structure, more imposing than the others, Tatiana surmised to be the governor's residence. A bright light was beaming across the water from a cupola on top the roof. Next to the house stood a flagpole from which the Russian flag with the double headed eagle of the Imperial Crest, snapped smartly in the breeze.

As the ship nudged closer in and dropped anchor, she could see a big wharf jutting out into the harbor with a large warehouse attached near the shore. Beyond were many buildings and houses, some of which looked weather-beaten and rather dilapidated. In the midst of this dreary cluster of buildings rose a tall spire from a church belfry. It was the Russian Orthodox Church; the place where she would be married.

She studied the general appearance of New Archangel with dismay. This was the "Paris of the Pacific," the jewel of Russian America that her father had spoken so proudly? It was more of a well-armed fortress than a city.

Where the palisade began on the seashore a warship with guns was anchored. On each corner of the stockade was a three-story high blockhouse armed with soldiers. In the harbor stood a battery of twelve cannons aimed directly at the Indian village.

It looked like they were prepared for any act of aggression whether by land or sea. She shivered in the cold air. It had been eighteen years since the *Kolosh* had massacred the fort's inhabitants, but obviously, the Russians had not forgotten and would never trust the Indians again.

"And what do you ladies think of our fair capital?" asked Chernyshov.

"After all the months at sea, Igor," said Natasha, "it looks marvelous to me."

"The town is much smaller than I imagined, but the mountains are beautiful," Tatiana said tactfully. "I can understand why my father chose to live here. I should like to see him as soon as possible."

"The harbor is shallow and rocky, so we must anchor out. Several small boats are approaching and one will take us to the landing. From there I shall escort you to the governor's house where your father is."

And Dmitri? she wondered with increasing excitement. Will he be there as well?

The small boat was barely seaworthy and had several inches of cold water in the bottom. The hem of her velvet cloak and gown soon became soaked and when they docked, she was grateful to have dry land under her feet.

A crowd of people stood watching, husky bearded *promyshlenniki*, dark-skinned Indians, uniformed soldiers and sailors. She turned her face away from all the men and their inquisitive stares. Chernyshov barked a command and the crowd retreated slightly.

"We will walk up the hill for a short distance."

As soon as they left the wooden landing their boots sank into thick black mud. Obviously the sun did not shine in New Archangel all that frequently. Everywhere Tatiana looked the ground oozed a soft muck. She wrinkled her nose in disgust.

Walking remained difficult, and not only due to the mud. The ground seemed to sway slightly, as if she was still aboard the ship. She and Natasha both found themselves clutching each arm of the captain to keep their balance.

"You ladies need to find your land legs," he chuckled, imagining the debonair picture he must make with two women clinging to him.

They walked past several large buildings, more warehouses, a shop and store, a storehouse for goods, and a rank smelling fur tannery. Near the two story barracks they came to a series of high wooden boardwalks which led to the base of the hill. A steep flight of stairs reached to the summit, about eighty feet high, where the governor's house was perched. As they climbed they passed several sentinels which Chernyshov said were kept posted day and night.

Halfway up they came to a building that was obviously used as a military prison. A light battery of brass cannon, loaded and ready for any emergency, stood in front of the door. Here Tatiana slowed her steps and smiled briefly as she pictured Captain O'Connell and his officers soon languishing within.

At the top of the stairs was a terrace leading to a broad verandah which commanded a fine view of the settlement below, the harbor dotted with islands and Mount Edgecumbe in the distance. The governor's house was two stories high and built of thick wooden logs. Except for the beacon tower crowning the roof, it reminded her more of a large barn on her Uncle Vasily's country estate than a proper residence for a governor.

They were admitted by a stocky uniformed soldier who saluted Chernyshov respectfully. He ushered them into a waiting room which Tatiana found to be a startling contrast to the building's drab exterior. It was tastefully decorated with colorful oil paintings of navy sea battles, and statues that could only have come from the drawing rooms of Saint Petersburg.

Moments later the soldier returned. "Captain-Lieutenant Chernyshov, Sir," he said, "His Excellency Governor Muraviev is not here at present. But his assistant will receive you and the ladies in the governor's office."

As they followed him Tatiana felt a great disappointment that her father was not the new governor. Perhaps he was the assistant. With anticipation she straightened her shoulders, hoping no one would notice her soiled cloak and gown.

The governor's office was a spacious room with a wide view of Sitka Sound, now a darkening blur in the distance. A blond haired man was seated in a plush armchair at the large mahogany desk, partly gilded and inlaid with ebony and pewter in the French style of the late eighteenth century. Tatiana was certain it was the great Alexander Baranov's desk. How many times had her father been in this room to talk to the man whose name was legend up and down the west coast of America?

The soldier announced them in a loud voice and the man rose as they entered. He was dressed in an officer's uniform with brass buttons and gold braid at the shoulders. In his late twenties, he was tall and lean, his strong Russian features set in an impassive expression. His eyes fastened on Tatiana and glittered strangely of an undetermined color, similar to the ever-changing hues of the glaciers.

She realized he was the perfect image of a Russian aristocrat, proud, elegant, with an air of superiority. He reminded her of a dashing young Baron Ivan Volodin.

"*Mademoiselle* Tatiana Nikolayevna, I presume," he said in a clipped voice, glancing down at her muddied clothing with a hint of disapproval.

"Yes," she breathed, "and you must be Lieutenant Dmitri Ivanich Volodin."

He swiftly crossed the room and took Tatiana's gloved right hand and pressed it to his mouth as his eyes noted the jeweled betrothal ring on her left. "You are more beautiful than I ever imagined. Your father has described you to me countless times, but nothing he said has done you justice."

She broke into a smile of delight. This was the man her father had selected to be her husband, the man she had traveled halfway around the world to marry, the man who had set her free from the confining walls of her uncle's palace. Already she felt like she was falling in love with him.

They gazed at each other until Chernyshov cleared his throat and said, "Lieutenant Volodin, I would like to speak to Governor Muraviev as soon as he returns."

With a frown, the lieutenant turned his attention toward Chernyshov. "I'm afraid that won't be possible for some time, Sir. Two weeks ago he left to visit the other settlements in Russian America. As the new governor, it is most important that he keeps a firm control of all our colonies in this wilderness. He went to Kodiak first, and from there to the forts on Cook Inlet and Prince William Sound, and if the weather holds fair, to Unalaska. We don't expect him to return until the end of summer."

"So then, you are the man in charge, Lieutenant Volodin?"

"I am the one in complete authority during Governor Muraviev's absence," said Dmitri stiffly.

Tatiana made a quiet sound of dismay. "I thought my father would be the governor's assistant. I am most anxious to see him. It has been many years." *Since I was ten years old, to be exact*, she thought.

"Your father is the governor's chief assistant, but he has been quite ill lately, and so, I have been left in command."

Tatiana looked alarmed. "He is ill? Please, I must see him at once."

Chernyshov was startled as well. "What is the matter with my good friend Nikolas?"

"During the winter Captain-Lieutenant Bolkonsky took sick with a severe chest cold. He seemed to recover, though he still had a bad cough. A few weeks ago the cough worsened and he began to suffer chest pains. At first they were mild and he was able to perform his duties. But now all his strength has left him. He can barely eat and he lies in excruciating pain that only the strongest doses of laudanum can alleviate."

Tatiana gasped as Chernyshov asked in a gruff voice, "Has a doctor examined him?"

"Doctor-Surgeon Behrs from the *Buldakov* believes that Captain-Lieutenant Bolkonsky has a sort of growth in his lungs, a cancerous tumor."

"Then there is no hope?"

Lieutenant Volodin shook his head. "The doctor gives him a month, perhaps less." He looked at Tatiana. "I am so sorry, *Mademoiselle*."

A heavy feeling of despair clutched her and she pressed both hands over her face. There was a painful lump in her throat. She swallowed convulsively and struggled to control the tears threatening to spill down her cheeks. She did not want Dmitri to think she was a weak woman.

"My father is such a good man," she said. "It's not fair for this to have happened to him."

"Nothing in life is fair, *Mademoiselle*," said Dmitri with a shrug. "The good and the bad both have their time to die. Your father has led a full life. He has been very happy here in Russian America. Come, I'll take you to him."

The Chernyshovs stepped aside, looking at her with sad pity, as Dmitri led her out of the room, a slight smile of satisfaction creasing his thin lips.

He was pleased at the hand life had just dealt him. His betrothed was the loveliest woman he'd ever seen. Soon they would be married and she would belong to him, heart, mind and body, and more importantly, he would have a permanent bond to one of Russia's most powerful, aristocratic families. The fact that his father-in-law was dying was of no consequence. If anything, after Nikolas Bolkonsky was dead, he would have even more control over his daughter.

Now his only wish was for his own father to die soon. Then he would become the Baron Volodin and Tatiana, his beautiful Baroness.

The future was bright, indeed, he thought, as he helped Tatiana up the staircase leading to the second floor.

She could have sworn each step moved under the heel of her boots and she clung to his arm and the polished banister to help restore her sense of balance. Once she'd heard that dastardly Captain O'Connell joke about a sailor feeling land-sick, and now she knew what he meant.

"His Excellency has his living quarters up here," said Dmitri, "and there are several guest chambers as well. When your father became so ill last month, he was removed from his house, the residence of the Assistant Governor. We do not have a hospital or even a regular physician here in New Archangel. We have to depend on a doctor from whichever ship has arrived from Russia. Hopefully, the Company Board of Directors will be rectifying that soon and send us a full-time physician."

He opened a door into a small darkened sitting room. "You must prepare yourself, *Mademoiselle*. Your father has lost a great deal of weight, and due to the large doses of laudanum, he is not always coherent. He rambles in his speech and sometimes is not aware of who we are or where he is. He may not even know you."

It was an added blow and Tatiana was too full of grief to answer. Dmitri stepped through the doorway into the bedchamber and spoke sternly to someone inside the room.

"Captain-Lieutenant Bolkonsky's daughter, *Mademoiselle* Tatiana Nikolayevna, has just arrived. She wishes to see her father, preferably alone."

As Tatiana moved towards the doorway, a young girl burst out, almost knocking her off her feet. The girl muttered something unintelligible, then glared at her with a look of such hatred that Tatiana's breath caught in her throat.

"Come back here, you idiot girl!" Dmitri snapped. "You must apologize at once!"

The girl paid him no heed and fled, her long black hair streaming behind her.

"Who is she and whatever is the matter with her?" Tatiana asked in confusion.

"Her name is Marya. She's a *Creole* and they are known for their unpredictable behavior," he said with obvious irritation. "But she is a servant in this house and I will have her apologize to you later."

"If she is a *Creole*, then she must have an Aleut mother and a Russian father."

Dmitri hesitated then said, "This is true."

"She doesn't appear to be dependable enough to be taking care of Papa. But now that I am here, she won't be needed."

Dmitri frowned slightly. "The girl is quite fond of him and has spent most of her waking moments, and even many nights, at your father's bedside. She might become extremely agitated to be excused from nursing him."

"I appreciate her care of my father and her devotion to him will be well rewarded. But she is only a servant, a young one at that. As his only daughter, my place is with my father. Surely, she will understand that."

Dmitri's right eyelid twitched slightly, betraying a possible nervousness. "Yes, well...." he began when they both heard the words, "Water...water."

Hearing her father's weak voice, she immediately forgot about the strange *Creole* girl. Tatiana ran into the bedchamber and halted, her heart beating so loud her eardrums throbbed.

The small room was dimly lit by one oil lamp sitting on a dark walnut dresser. Heavy brocade curtains hung over a tall window. The large four-poster bed was the dominating piece of furniture. Half-buried beneath a heavy quilt, Nikolas Bolkonsky twisted uncomfortably and moaned.

Dmitri had tactfully withdrawn, leaving them alone. Tatiana poured a glass of water from the pitcher on the washstand and brought it to him.

"Papa, here is your water," she said softly. "It's me, your daughter, Tatiana."

She was dismayed at his emaciated appearance. His once luxuriant black hair had disappeared, now reduced to a few strands of gray. His skin was as pale and thin as parchment, and in his shrunken state, his cheekbones and the Bolkonsky nose protruded sharply. He had the look of death already upon him.

Where was her handsome father with the flashing dark eyes and sunny smile? Memories flooded through her, his strong arms holding her, his voice deep with laughter and full of stories, his uniquely charming way of banishing all her fears and pointing out the good in everyone, even in her uncle, aunt, and Mikael and Olga. For a moment she was blind to the reality which lay before her.

Then he muttered, "Elizabeth? Is it really you?" He was looking at her in confusion, his eyes dull with pain.

He thinks I'm Mama, she thought with shock as she slid her arm under the pillow and supported his head while he sipped the water in between loud rasping gulps of air.

"Papa, it is Tatiana, your daughter. I arrived in New Archangel about one hour ago and I came to see you immediately. I didn't know you are ill. If only I could have come earlier."

A few drops of water trickled down his chin onto his sparse gray beard. She took the glass away and set it down carefully on the small night stand next to the bed.

His eyes fastened on her in sudden recognition. He struggled to speak, his mouth opening and closing, his breathing ragged and painful. Finally he said, "Ah, Tatiana, my child. You are here at last. I'm so sorry you have to see me like this, but don't distress yourself. You have come as quickly as you could. I know Igor and the *Suvorov* well. He takes his time on a voyage and refuses to push his ship."

He paused, taking a tortured breath then his dark eyes lightened briefly with a ghost of the old spark she had known. "My little girl has grown into such a beautiful young woman, so like your mother. When I first saw you, I thought you were my beloved Elizabeth."

His eyes glazed over with a faraway look. Then with a visible effort he focused on Tatiana again. "Have you met Lieutenant Dmitri Volodin yet?"

"Yes, Papa. I have met him."

"You must marry him as soon as possible. I don't have much time left and my last desire in this life is to see you safely wed. Dmitri is a good boy and I've known his father since my Naval Academy days. The Volodins are a wealthy family. You will be well taken care of. That's all I ask."

An obvious pain tore through his chest and he winced. Tatiana shuddered, feeling the same pain piercing her heart. "I will marry Dmitri as soon as you wish, Papa."

A look of satisfaction flickered across his face and he sighed heavily. Then he asked, "What day is this?"

"Tuesday, Papa."

"Have the wedding on this Sunday. I know it doesn't give you much time, but I want you to be married on a Sunday as Elizabeth and I once were."

He coughed and wheezed, his face twisting into a painful grimace. "I need my medicine, Tatiana. Where is my other girl? She gives me my medicine..." His voice trailed away and his eyes closed as he fought the gnawing torment of the cancer within.

"The other girl?" she repeated with puzzlement. "Do you mean the young girl who has been taking care of you?"

"Yes, Marya, I need her. She knows what to do..."

The last thing Tatiana wanted now was another confrontation with the wild-eyed *Creole* girl. "I can help you, Papa. Do you know where she keeps your medicine?"

"No," he murmured, "she hides the bottle from me, because she knows I'd take it constantly if I could---"

He broke off as a tall graceful woman wearing a dark blue linen gown with a white apron hurried into the room, a small brown bottle in her plump hand. "Here's your medicine, Captain. Marya gave it to me."

He groaned with relief and eagerly gulped down the dosage of laudanum she administered to him with a large spoon. Then he said, "*Madame* Kornilova, have you met my daughter, Tatiana Nikolayevna? If it is possible, I wish her wedding to take place this Sunday. Could you speak to Father Sokolov, please?"

She smiled at him. "With pleasure, Captain. I will make all the arrangements." She motioned for Tatiana to follow her out. "He'll be asleep soon."

Her father had closed his eyes and was already drifting off into a drugged sleep, his features relaxing as his breathing steadied.

"I am Catherine Grigorevna, His Excellency's housekeeper," *Madame* Kornilova said to Tatiana. "I have worked here for many years, first as a governess for the children of His Excellency, the great Alexander Baranov himself, and then after he was replaced by Governor Yanovski, I was asked to be in charge of the household and the servants. I am one of the first Russian women to ever arrive on Baranov Island," she added with a proud expression on her round face. "I came with my husband, Mikhail Kornilov, who was sent by the Company board of directors to help Governor Baranov establish New Archangel. My husband was an architect and builder. He died from lung consumption one year after we arrived. At first I thought about returning to Russia, but I didn't wish to be a burden to my elderly widowed mother or to my sister who is married with six children. Governor Baranov graciously allowed me to stay. Now I cannot imagine living anywhere else."

She studied Tatiana with sincere compassion. "I am sorry about your papa, *Mademoiselle*. It must be quite a shock for you to find him like this."

Tatiana nodded at her, having heard little of the housekeeper's chatter. "I still cannot comprehend that Papa is so terribly ill. I keep thinking it must all be a bad dream, *Madame* Kornilova."

"Call me Catherine," she said, giving Tatiana a sympathetic pat on her shoulder.

Tatiana smiled slightly, seeing the housekeeper for the first time. She was at least forty with streaks of gray in her dull brown hair, and she had an air of faded elegance about her as if she had been well brought up. But what Tatiana noticed the most was the kind expression of motherly concern on her face. *Mama would be almost her age if she had lived*, Tatiana thought with a pang.

The *Creole* girl was waiting for them in the sitting room. Tatiana was surprised once again to note the avid dislike in her eyes. Why? What had she done to provoke such spitefulness? They were total strangers.

Tatiana took a moment to study the girl. She was almost her own height, an oddity for someone of her race since Aleut women were short. *Her Russian father must have been tall indeed*, Tatiana decided.

From him, she also must have inherited her delicate light skin, a striking contrast with her straight black hair worn with thick bangs across the forehead. She had the high cheekbones of an Indian, but her eyes were not as dark. They were light amber brown, slanting upwards slightly, giving her an exotic look. Otherwise, Marya's small straight nose and gently curving lips were little different from her own. She was a pretty young girl who would one day be a beautiful woman.

In a firm voice *Madame* Kornilova ordered Marya to apologize for her previous rude behavior. Marya smiled and dutifully obeyed, but her words of apology sounded insincere and Tatiana noted that the haughty look never left her eyes. After Marya was dismissed, the housekeeper showed Tatiana to the bedchamber next to her father's. There was an adjoining door between them. A dozen of her trunks off the *Suvorov* crowded the floor.

Madame Kornilova motioned to them. "Do you have a maid or shall I find you one?"

"I had two maids on our voyage," said Tatiana, smiling wryly. "They both deserted me. My Russian maid ran off with an American sailor, the other, a Portuguese slave named Isabella, ran away when we docked at Valparaiso, Chile to resupply the ship. She was practically useless anyway, frightened of everything and everyone. However, I do miss my Russian maid, Anna."

Tatiana yawned tiredly and *Madame* Kornilova gestured towards the four-posted bed.

"Why don't you rest before dinner? I'll send a maid in with water for washing, and she can unpack your trunks and lay out some clean clothes. Keeah is one of our most dependable *Kolosh* girls. We employ many of them from the *Kolosh* village outside the fort as chambermaids and kitchen maids. They are hardworking and eager to please, for their wages help out their families."

After the housekeeper left, Tatiana glanced around the room. The walls were hung with silken tapestries and the furniture was expertly carved and upholstered in blue satin and damask. The high ceiling was painted in little cupids and sun gods playing hide and seek between delicate clouds. She walked over to the bed, hung with silk curtains of a pastel shade of blue, matching the color of the carpet and chairs.

She smiled and stretched. It was almost like being back in the luxury of her uncle's palace. If it wasn't for her father's illness, she would be as happy as a fairy princess in a castle.

In the bedchamber next to Tatiana's, Marya Nikolayevna sat on a chair at their father's bedside, sobbing quietly, allowing the suppressed anger inside her to slowly drain away. It was obvious to her Tatiana had no idea they were sisters. She had almost blurted it out, but Marya knew that wasn't the right way to tell her. If only their father was well enough to explain the situation.

But soon he would be gone, and then what was going to happen to her? Marriage to Andrei Leonov would make her uncle and aunt happy, but not herself. Ever since former Governor Yanovski and his wife, Irina, and baby Alexis had sailed away for Russia last winter, her life had changed for the worst.

Through her tears, she looked at her beloved papa, and suddenly wished it was her half-sister lying there, ill, and waiting to die.

CHAPTER SEVENTEEN

Tatiana spent her first evening in New Archangel at a lavish dinner in the banquet hall of the governor's residence. It was her chance to be introduced to New Archangel's small circle of nobility, made up of the other naval officers and their families.

There was Elizabeth, the wife of Captain-Lieutenant Basil Pushkin. His ship, the *Finlandia*, was the pride of the Russian fleet, and was currently taking Governor Muraviev on his voyage to visit the other colonies. Both husband and wife came from wealthy aristocratic families. Their two oldest sons, Sergei and Gregory, attended the Naval Academy in Saint Petersburg. A daughter, Anastasia, age twelve, and twin sons, Fedor and Nikolai, age nine, lived in New Archangel with their parents.

Elizabeth Pushkina had a perpetually bored expression on her face and spent the evening drinking too much and saying little. Tatiana thought she had lovely facial bone structure and must have been pretty once, but now her looks had faded. Her once rich auburn hair was dull and limp, her fair complexion was mottled and lined, her dark gray eyes had a vacant look to them, and her mouth was set in a petulant frown.

Madame Pushkina had no interest in any of the newcomers. Her total focus was on making sure her wine glass was refilled promptly, as she ignored the obnoxious behavior of her two sons seated next to her. Both rosy-cheeked, plump-faced boys had poor table manners and Tatiana watched with distaste as they burped loudly after shoveling food into their mouths. She wondered why they were allowed to eat with the grown-ups instead of with a governess or nanny.

Seated next to the Pushkins was Lieutenant Boris Ivanoff, in command of the sloop, *Kamchatka*. He was a grossly overweight man with a pug nose and squinty eyes and the manners of a peasant. His father was a count on the Company Board of Directors and no one dared cross either father or son. To Tatiana's dismay, when Dmitri introduced him to her as one of his dearest friends, the man seemed to salivate as if seeing a tasty morsel of food.

The Trotsky family needed no introductions to her. Tatiana remembered them very well as childhood visitors to her uncle's palace. Lieutenant Alexis Trotsky was a friend of Uncle Vasily's and a distant cousin to Aunt Irene. He was the commander of the brig, *Kuskov* and was a tall elegant man with grayish blond hair and mustache. After nodding politely to Tatiana, he was more interested in conversing with Captain-Lieutenant Chernyshov.

His wife, Irina, was as arrogant as he, but lacked his fine aristocratic features. Her hair and eyes were of a nondescript brown and she was horse-faced, toothy and as bony as a starving wolf. She was a gossip, a woman who was critical of everyone and everything. Irina and Aunt Irene had been like twin sisters, a formidable duo who struck terror in the heart of every servant.

The Trotskys had two daughters, Vera and Sophie. Vera had inherited her fair beauty from her father, but Tatiana remembered well how her charm concealed a heart as selfish and sarcastic as her mother's. On many a visit, Vera and Olga had teased and ridiculed her to tears in plain sight of both of their unconcerned mothers.

The only member of the Trotsky family Tatiana had found tolerable was Sophie. At age sixteen she was a year younger than Vera and as sweet as her older sister was sour. She had always refused to join in the cruel taunts with Vera and Olga against her. Unfortunately, she had inherited her mother's long nose and toothy smile, and was as plain as a brown mouse.

Both Irina and her daughter Vera acknowledged Tatiana with forced smiles, their eyes cold and hostile, while Sophie told her most sincerely how happy she was to see her again.

Tatiana was also introduced to several more officers of lesser rank and their wives, but she promptly forgot their names. Only the last two men at the far end of the table registered with her. One was the current priest, Father Aleksei Sokolov of the Church of Saint Michael.

Tatiana remembered a letter her father had written her years ago, describing Father Aleksei Sokolov's arrival in 1816 when he had been sent by the Company to Russian America to minister to both the Russians and the Indians. He had brought with him a beautifully decorated icon of the Archangel Michael, patron saint of the colonies, to be placed in the church built by Governor Baranov out of a reconstructed old ship. A bell fashioned in New Archangel's own foundry was hung in the steeple. When the building was finished and dedicated, old Baranov had declared it the happiest day of his life, his advancing age turning him to religion for the first time ever.

Tatiana wondered if the same thing was happening to her own father. Just before dinner she had peeked in to visit him and had found the *Creole* girl, Marya, reading to him from a Bible. Her father was so engrossed in listening to her he didn't notice Tatiana hovering in the doorway. Feeling like an intruder, she made a hasty exit, her heart troubled at how much her father seemed to depend on that girl.

Sitting next to the priest was Lieutenant Anton Dohktorov, who had escorted her and Anna and Natasha to Sutton Manor near London to meet her Uncle Henry and Aunt Jane. How long ago and far away all that seemed now. Yet, the lieutenant obviously remembered her. Handsomer than she recalled, he gave her a wide smile of greeting, his teeth flashing in the light of the candelabras positioned about the room. She nodded at him then noticed with amusement during dinner, how Sophie's eyes continually gravitated in the young officer's direction.

Madame Kornilova had set a beautiful table. All the dishes were of fine blue and white Wedgwood china from England, the tablecloth of delicate white lace, service of gleaming silver, and the best wine sparkled in costly crystal goblets. The steaming food had a delicious aroma that tempted even the poorest of appetites. Tatiana had not seen such a feast since leaving Saint Petersburg.

There was a variety of meats, roast wild geese and duck, baked salmon and halibut, roasted chevreuil which was a type of wild deer, and vegetable dishes of peas, carrots, potatoes and cauliflower. Sweet and sour pickles, a number of freshly-baked breads and cakes also were served by the Aleut female servants. Dressed in European clothing, with their round faces and expressionless black eyes, they went about their duties quietly and efficiently.

Dmitri dominated the conversation in his authoritative voice. "Lieutenant Trotsky," he said, "I hear you will be sailing to California soon. I hope there will be a substantial crop of wheat waiting for you in Fort Ross this summer, enough to last us through the coming winter."

"I wouldn't count on it," said Alexis Trotsky darkly. "The interminably damp climate is damaging the crops at Fort Ross. Last summer when we were there we had hoped to take on grain. But the entire crop of wheat had been wiped out by stem rust, a disease caused by the frequent fogs and moist sea air. Even their vegetable yield was barely enough to feed their own population, much less that of New Archangel. We had to stop at Santa Cruz and Monterey and buy wheat from the Spaniards on our return."

"Fort Ross needs better management," said Dmitri. "The original purpose of the fort was to provide the colonies here with tons of wheat, barley, fresh vegetables and beef. But in the past ten years, what have the Russians there accomplished? Nothing! Instead of farming they hunted sea otters nearly to extinction, then forced the local Pomo Indians to work the fields for them. The Pomos stole our wheat and rustled our cattle. And the Aleuts," he frowned scornfully, "were not any better. They only know sea hunting, not raising cattle."

Alexis Trotsky agreed with an elegant laugh. "Last summer I saw with my own eyes a group of Aleuts trying to drive cattle. Instead of driving the animals to the fort, the Aleuts were chased by wild bulls and steers. It was quite humorous!"

Most of the men broke into amused laughter and many of the ladies tittered into their napkins. Tatiana could not help wondering if the serving women had heard and understood the insult to their race, but they continued to pour the wine and serve the food, their heads bobbing politely, their manners docile and meek. The Aleuts truly were a conquered people, she thought.

Then she remembered the wild behavior of Marya, the half-Aleut girl. Most likely she inherited her rebellious streak from her father, probably some rough *promyshlennik*, who was a criminal from Siberia.

"How is the shipbuilding progressing at Fort Ross, Lieutenant Trotsky?" asked Lieutenant Dohktorov in a cool tone. He had not even smiled at Trotsky's humiliating description of the Aleuts. His serious question instantly quieted the laughter.

"Not very well, Anton. The two barks being built at present are made of unseasoned oak." He shook his head in disgust. "Any fool knows to use seasoned wood in shipbuilding. Those vessels will rot in a few short years."

Boris Ivanoff scowled heavily and with a mouthful of food sputtered, "You are right, Dmitri. Fort Ross needs a new manager, and a new climate." He bit into a large piece of meat then smacked his thick lips together with satisfaction as the grease dribbled down his chin.

Ignoring it, he continued, "But we also could use better weather. Nowhere else does it rain more than here. We have two seasons in New Archangel, the long rainy season and the short rainy season. In the long rainy season it pours nine months of the year. In the short rainy season the other three. Rain! Rain! Rain!" He laughed, spewing bits of half-chewed food on his plate. "Baranov Island is a paradise fit only for ducks and the seagulls."

Tatiana was thankful she was sitting far away from him. She looked at Dmitri, who was placed on her right. "As we sailed north on the *Suvorov*, I noticed how it was rarely sunny longer than a day or two at a time. I'm looking forward to winter when we can go ice skating."

"It rarely stays cold enough for snow," Dmitri told her with an amused expression. "The average winter temperature here is just above freezing, so when it does snow, it soon melts into slush. A cold snap is a godsend for it hardens the mud and slush, but it is possible only about two months of the year when the wind blows from the northeast across the snow-covered mountains. Only then is there a perceptible dryness in the air."

Young Sophie Alexisovna looked at Tatiana and sighed. "We all miss our cold, dry winters in Saint Petersburg when we could go skating and sledding on the frozen Neva."

Everyone around the table murmured their agreement then suddenly quieted, as the plates and silverware began to rattle, and the wine in the glasses sloshed back and forth. Tatiana felt the floor trembling slightly as the table creaked and she cried out, "Whatever is happening?"

"Just an earthquake," said Dmitri calmly, and as quickly as it had begun, it stopped.

"We have them quite often," he added with a slight laugh at the shocked look on her face.

"Not to worry, *Mademoiselle*," said Boris with a slight leer, "most of them are so small, you will hardly notice them."

As if nothing had happened, Captain-Lieutenant Chernyshov attacked a piece of salmon on his plate with relish and said, "There is one thing to be said for New Archangel. It abounds in fresh seafood. I've heard there are streams nearby where salmon is so plentiful they impede the movements of a canoe."

"Bah, fish!" said Boris. "I prefer the hearty flavor of moose meat and chevreuil! As long as we can hunt those animals, we won't need the beef from Fort Ross." He grinned at no one in particular and helped himself to another slab of venison.

Lieutenant Dohktorov looked in Tatiana's direction and said quietly, "Doctor-Surgeon Behrs was telling me yesterday that an inhabitant of New Archangel can be compared to an amphibian. His body is continually submerged in a mass of air akin to a cold steam bath. He believes this condition is harmful to the natives who are inclined to have weak lungs, and also to Europeans who have not become acclimatized. Your father, *Mademoiselle*, is an example of what happens to a man who stays too long in this accursed climate."

A look of sadness crossed Tatiana's face, and she said, "Yes, I am shocked that he is so ill. I was hoping to spend years more with him."

The Trotsky sisters, Vera and Sophie, were sitting nearby and Sophie, a shy smile on her plain face, said, "It must have been difficult for you to grow up without him."

Tatiana gave her a warm smile. "Yes, it was, Sophie. You and Vera are most fortunate to be able to live here with both of your parents."

"Have you met little Marya yet?" Vera asked with an innocent air.

"Marya?" Tatiana questioned. "You mean that strange *Creole* girl? Why do you ask?"

"Well," Vera began, but at that moment, her mother leaned across the table and gave her oldest daughter a stern glance of warning. "Hush, Vera," Irina said with a frown.

Vera flushed and fell silent, looking mortified and angry.

Confused, Tatiana glanced at Dmitri, who was also staring at Vera with a cold expression. The girl seemed to wither under his icy gaze. Tatiana sensed a mystery surrounding the girl Marya and she puzzled over it. The solution seemed tantalizingly close, yet was just out of reach.

Then her head began to pound. She could feel another one of her headaches was coming on and the sight of all the rich food suddenly nauseated her. "Excuse me," she said, "It has been a long day and I must retire."

With an exclamation of concern, Dmitri immediately helped her up and sent for a servant to escort her back to her bedchamber. A few minutes later as she reached the tranquil privacy of her room, she sank onto the bed, closed her eyes, and decided she would solve the secret of Marya some other day.

* * *

During that first week in New Archangel Tatiana saw little of her betrothed. Besides filling in for the governor, he was the commander of the brig, the *Buldakov*, and his duties kept him occupied from early morning to late at night. He also lived on board the *Buldakov*, preferring the comforts of his captain's cabin rather than a room in the unmarried officers' quarters in town.

All married officers and their families, such as the Pushkins and the Trotskys resided in a two story building in furnished apartments, waited on by native servants. The Chernyshovs lived on board the *Suvorov*, and Natasha came ashore daily to socialize at the governor's house, the center of New Archangel society.

The governor's residence was also referred to as "Baranov's Castle" by some. In comparison to her uncle's palace, Tatiana thought it more like a guest cottage. Still, she had to admit the building had a charm and quiet elegance all its own. Full of costly ornaments and furniture from Saint Petersburg and England, she remembered how her father told her once that Ivan Kuskov, the founder of Fort Ross, had built the house for Alexander Baranov during a time when he had been in Kodiak. On his return to New Archangel, Baranov had been delighted with his new home.

Kuskov had constructed it well. The upper floor had several comfortable apartments with bedchambers and sitting rooms, and the lower floor had an office, a library for Baranov's fine collection of books and paintings, including a rare pianoforte which Baranov had imported through Yankee friends for his daughter. Downstairs also boasted reception rooms, a billiard room, a large kitchen and a banquet hall for entertaining.

Two days after Tatiana arrived she was summoned to the office where Captain-Lieutenant Chernyshov was already waiting. Dmitri had the copy of the cargo manifest document of the *Sea Rose* on the desk.

"Good work, *Mademoiselle*," he said, smiling with approval. "Because you have provided us with the proof of the *Sea Rose* trading guns to the natives, we will be sending out extra patrols this summer to catch them."

"And what will happen to the captain and crew when you do?" she asked anxiously.

He misinterpreted her expression for concern and scowled. "They will be arrested at once, any guns and furs confiscated, and when His Excellency returns, he will decide their fate." He paused and studied her curiously. "You spent many weeks on board with the Americans. Do you have any other information we could use against them?"

Tatiana remembered the night she was attacked by Ned Johnson and the other men. "Yes," she said, a certain hardness creeping into her voice, "I was brutally attacked by one of their officers and two sailors. I could have died if not for the bravery of my maid, Anna." She slipped off her silk shawl, exposing the thin puckered scar across her collarbone, instantly shocking both men.

A sudden fury suffused Dmitri's face and he snapped, "How dare anyone put his hands on you! I shall have the men whipped and hung as soon as we find the ship!"

"One of them is already dead. Captain O'Connell shot him with his own pistol."

"Well then," he said, his right eyelid twitching in a nervous tic, "as grateful as I am to the good captain, he is still breaking our laws, and unfortunately will have to pay the price." He gave her a hard stare. "Women have a tendency to become fond of their rescuers in a time of crisis. You wouldn't have any such feelings for the American captain, would you, my dear?"

With a slight flush, she remembered her night in the captain's bed, something Dmitri must never know. "Of course not," she answered without hesitation. "I found him to be a most uncouth barbarian." She flashed him one of her loveliest smiles. "Dmitri, I may call you Dmitri? I do have a request to ask of you."

He reddened, momentarily dazzled by her beauty. "Of course you can call me Dmitri and I will call you Tatiana. Any wish you desire I will grant, if it is in my power to do so."

"My former maid, Anna, is married to their chief officer, Ethan Campbell. I do not wish any harm to come to her. In fact, I would like her to be returned to me as my maid after her husband is arrested."

"That should present no problem unless the crew of the *Sea Rose* resists us and a sea battle ensues. We couldn't guarantee your maid's safety then, of course."

Seeing Tatiana's worried frown, he hastily added, "But the chances of a battle are slim. Most merchant vessels are no match for one of our Imperial warships, and no rational captain ever attempts to challenge us."

"Captain O'Connell is not always a rational man," Tatiana said.

"That's because he is little more than a peasant," said Chernyshov in a scornful voice. "Our navy intelligence reports that he is the son of poor Irish immigrants. This is his first command of a ship and if we have anything to say about it, most likely his last."

Dmitri nodded. "If we haven't caught them by the time His Excellency returns, I shall set out in the *Buldakov* myself to find the *Sea Rose* and her ill-bred captain."

A few minutes later after Tatiana and Chernyshov left the office he allowed himself a moment of unrestrained fury as he threw the blotter of ink across the room to splatter a black smear on the wall. He was outraged that his betrothed's perfect beauty was scarred by some Yankee officer. He wished the man was not dead, so he could personally squeeze the life out of him. Yet, revenge was still to be had. A captain was responsible for his officer's actions, and as far as he was concerned, that made Captain O'Connell liable for Tatiana's hideous scar.

* * *

The wedding of Lieutenant Dmitri Ivanich Volodin to *Mademoiselle* Tatiana Nikolayevna Bolkonskaya was the social event of the year in New Archangel.

That Sunday afternoon Tatiana dressed in her bridal gown, fussed over by Natasha, who twittered and fluttered around her like an excited wren. The dress was high-waisted in the Empire fashion, a popular style made famous years ago by Napoleon's wife, the Empress Josephine. Since blue was the color of a Russian bride, the gown itself was a silvery blue gauze with an under dress of pale blue satin and had long full sleeves. Beneath the dress was a chemisette with a frilled neck. As she moved, a shimmering effect was produced in the skirt and sleeves, causing Natasha and Tatiana's new maid, to gasp with admiration.

The *Kolosh* girl with the Tlingit name of Keeah was about sixteen years old, black haired and dark eyed, with an unattractive scar on her lower lip that marred an otherwise pleasant face. Her demeanor was quiet and respectful, but she wasn't much more competent than the unfortunate Isabella in helping Tatiana with her clothing, hair, and other personal needs. At least she could speak passable French and also some basic Russian. If Tatiana had not been so engrossed in her own problems, she might have noticed an air of sadness about the girl.

It was the Russian custom that on the day of the wedding the betrothed couple could not see each other until they met to go to the church. A sense of unreality surrounded Tatiana as she entered the sitting room where Dmitri awaited. He was in his full-dress uniform with golden epaulets on the shoulders, white gloves in hand and his sword at his side. He stood rigidly in a military bearing, so like his father the Baron Volodin.

When she appeared he flashed a brilliant smile. "You are exquisite, my dear."

A tremor of nervousness passed through her. For one brief second she was possessed by a sudden impulse to flee. She was marrying a total stranger and the thought was terrifying. With difficulty she controlled herself and instead, meekly followed Dmitri into her father's bedchamber.

Doctor-Surgeon Behrs said he was in too critical a condition to be moved to the church. This saddened her greatly. All her life she had imagined her father being present at her wedding someday.

Inside the room the doctor stood near the bed wearing an anxious expression. Nikolas was propped up against several pillows in a sitting position. His face was gray and drawn, looking more fragile and delicate than the gauze net on her bridal gown. The room was hot and stuffy, and reeked of stale urine and vomit. For a moment it reminded Tatiana of another room in another place and time when Nana lay ill on her deathbed. Shivering from the unwanted memory, she hurried to her father's bedside and took one of his thin cold hands into her gloved hand.

"I am so proud of you, Tatiana," he said, his eyes sparkling with the first sign of life she had yet seen.

With a smile, she knelt at his side to begin the old custom of the ceremony at the bride's home before the wedding. First she asked his forgiveness of all her sins. In a trembling hand he gave her the traditional piece of bread and a grain of salt as a symbol that he would never let her go hungry, even though she was leaving his house for another's. Then Dmitri also knelt, and she gave him a tiny whip braided from her own hair in token of her complete submission to his will. Finally, Nikolas, in a shaky voice, read the ordained prayers.

After he finished Nikolas said, "When I hear the cannon boom, I will know that you are truly married, my dearest daughter."

Tears filled her eyes as Tatiana kissed him farewell. Then they walked out, leaving the door to her father's apartment left ajar as customary, meaning that his "home" would always be open to receive her if her husband was not kind. For her, she thought this tradition quite meaningless. She expected her husband to give her the love and respect that her father showed to her mother. And if Dmitri ever treated her harshly, an unthinkable thought, her dying father would not be alive to protect her.

The sun was setting in streaks of gold and rose in the sky beyond the island dotted harbor when she and Dmitri walked out of the governor's house onto the terrace. It seemed the entire garrison of New Archangel had turned out to watch them march down the stairs and across the little square to the church. As the bridal procession neared the church Tatiana noticed a large crowd of *Kolosh* Indians on top of a huge rock. They watched silently, curiously, crouching inside their blankets.

"Why are they there?" Tatiana asked.

"They think the rock belongs to them," said Dmitri in a scornful voice. "They are such a strange people. Even though they do not care for Christianity, they like to be passive spectators of our religious ceremonies. Every Sunday during the service they will be there on that rock, dressed in their own ceremonial clothes, staring at the church. If I was governor, I would forbid it."

The Church of Saint Mikael was tiny compared to the great cathedrals of Saint Petersburg. But like all Russian Orthodox churches, it was comprised of the three main rooms, the vestibule, where the worshippers gathered in the entryway, the knave, which was the main room were the people stood to worship, and the sanctuary, where only the priest was allowed.

The gold and white interior was richly decorated with brass candelabras, priceless icons, Eucharist vessels of Spanish silver, and chalices with exquisitely embroidered covers. There was a strikingly beautiful *ikonostas*, or gate to the altar. The priestly vestments and the altar cloth were sewn from the rich cloth of gold and Chinese silks. The delicate beadwork of the altar cloth, expertly sewn by Aleut women in Baranov's time, was an intricate mosaic of thousands of tiny beads blended together to create a resplendent painting on the heavy cloth.

The rich ornaments of the church faded into the background as Father Sokolov, wearing his stiff chasuble of gold cloth, placed the two wedding crowns on Tatiana's and Dmitri's heads. Then he moved around them, performing the various rites of the Russian Orthodox marriage ceremony.

When they knelt in front of the priest, Tatiana's knees began to tremble almost uncontrollably. Somehow she managed to keep still while Father Sokolov blessed their union by making a large sign of the cross over their bowed heads with the icon he held.

The rest of the service blurred together to Tatiana in the religious talk she always found so empty and meaningless. Like a wooden statue she watched as the earthen vessel was broken, the symbol of the submission of the wife to her husband, even to the extent of dying for him. Her lips curled contemptuously at that idea then she gave a start as Dmitri tapped her shoulder with a small whip, a reminder of the punishment which was hers if she failed to completely submit her will to his.

To Dmitri, the whip was more than just a token. He was a man who had no inhibitions of wielding the *knout* to a hapless sailor for punishment, although striking a beautiful wife was another matter entirely. But after today Russian law stated she was his possession, and he knew he could chasten her as he saw fit. As long as she remained a dutiful, obedient wife, he wouldn't dream of hurting her, but if she ever disobeyed him or heaven forbid, ever looked at another man...

She felt Dmitri's gaze burning into her and she shuddered briefly with a twinge of fear. Who was this man she was pledging the rest of her life to? Although he was incredibly handsome and elegant, and he seemed to be madly in love with her, sometimes a cold dark look crept into his gray eyes that made her squirm with uneasiness.

When the mass was finally over and a Te Deum was sung, they rose, and Dmitri slipped a possessive arm around her waist. As they left the church the assembly cheered as a cannon saluted, making the windows rattle.

It was done. She was no longer a free woman, but a future Baroness.

* * *

Captain-Lieutenant Nikolas Ilyich Bolkonsky died in the wee hours of the morning two days later. Both Dmitri and Tatiana were awakened by a loud pounding on the door of their bedchamber. A frightened looking Keeah announced that *Madame* Kornilova had sent her to fetch them at once.

They both dressed hastily. Dmitri was irritated that his night of pleasure with his new bride was interrupted while Tatiana was immediately grief-stricken. The housekeeper and Doctor-Surgeon Behrs were waiting for them.

Her father lay as immobile as a waxed statue, his face and skin a colorless hue, his hands crossed over his chest, and his eyes closed over sunken sockets. The stench of death hung heavily in the darkened room and Tatiana almost gagged. She stood by his side and wept silent tears. Oh, my papa, my beloved Papa, why did you have to leave me again? Where are you?

If there was a heaven, she hoped he was there. He seemed to find so much comfort in the Bible and religion the past weeks. In fact, the last thing he said to her the day before was something about how she should read his Bible. Of course, she had no intention of doing that.

"He's at peace now, *Mademoiselle*," said *Madame* Kornilova, giving her a sympathetic smile. "He's free at last from his prison of pain. It's a miracle that he lasted this long. Doctor-Surgeon Behrs believes he fought to stay alive just long enough to see you married. Marya said he died with a smile on his face."

"Marya was with him when he died?" She lifted her head and wiped the tears from her eyes, suddenly aware that the *Creole* girl was in a corner of the room wailing in a strange soft voice.

"Marya," she said loudly, "Did my father speak before he died?"

The girl continued moaning as if she could not hear. The doctor, a portly kind-faced man with gray sideburns and whiskers, shook his head. "*Madame*, it is no use asking her that question. When I came in this morning for my routine check on your father, I discovered he had died some time before. The girl was already weeping over his body."

Tatiana looked at *Madame* Kornilova. "Catherine, her constant wailing is upsetting me. I wish her to leave."

The housekeeper frowned. "I don't think we should force her to go."

"I said I want her out of here!" Tatiana's voice bordered on hysteria as anger and a feeling of guilt flooded through her. She should have been the one at her father's side when he died, instead of lying in her husband's arms all night performing a duty she found repugnant.

"Out, girl! Let my wife mourn her father in peace!"

Dmitri's sharp voice cut through Marya's wails as effectively as a dagger slicing through an artery. She choked off her cries and stared at him with puffy, bloodshot eyes full of deep distress. Without a word she brushed past them, a strange dignity in her bearing.

Tatiana's brief anger disappeared with her. Shaking, she began to cry again. This time Dmitri held her in an awkward attempt to offer some comfort. *Madame* Kornilova and Doctor-Surgeon Behrs withdrew, leaving them their privacy.

"Nikolas was a fine officer and a dedicated Russian," Dmitri said stiffly. "My father will be saddened to hear of his death. They were the best of friends. Did you know they discussed the possibility of our marriage years ago when you were still a baby?"

As Tatiana shook her head, he said, "It should prove to you that our marriage was destined. We belong together, Tatiana."

She heard his words as if in a distance. Sorrow weighed like a heavy stone upon her chest.

"He is with Mama now. He loved her so much, but their happiness together was too brief."

"Our happiness will last forever," Dmitri murmured in her ear.

She slumped against him, despair making her feel weak all over. Even though she had told herself to expect her father's death at any time, she was still unprepared for the intense emotions of grief which surged through her. There was a bitter sense of loss, followed by the feeling that she was all alone in the world, except for the man she had married, a man she still didn't know.

Dmitri held her tightly, acting the part of the sympathetic husband, even though her grief for her father was an enigma he could not understand. If it was his own father lying dead a few feet away, he knew he would be overjoyed.

The only two emotions he'd ever felt for his father were fear and hatred. As a young boy growing up in the Volodin family, he had witnessed the verbal and physical abuse his father had dealt to his mother, Marie, and his twin sister, Ella, too many times. The day he found his sister hanging from the bed post was the day he left home for the Naval Academy. He had hardly spoken to his father since.

His mother died soon after, and now the only family left to him was the one he could create himself. Tatiana was extremely precious to him as the woman through which he would found a new Volodin dynasty, free of the sordid past. In the veins of their children would run the supreme bloodlines of Russian and English nobility.

Someday he planned on being governor of Russian America, expanding the territory southward to include the entire west coast of North America. He and Tatiana would rule like a king and queen. After that, they would return to Saint Petersburg and become a part of the intimate circle surrounding the Czar. He was quite excited about his future possibilities.

As for his father-in-law, Dmitri felt nothing but contempt. Nikolas Bolkonsky could have risen so much higher in the Company and the Navy, but he was content to remain an assistant. Years ago he should have remarried, perhaps a daughter of some powerful noble, instead of having an affair with a mere native woman. He hoped Tatiana would never discover that sordid fact about her father.

In the dark days that followed she leaned on Dmitri utterly, especially to help her survive the endless funeral service. According to the Orthodox religion the coffin of the deceased was to remain open until burial. Draped in black, Nikolas Bolkonsky's casket rested on a platform inside the Church of Saint Mikael. Officers with drawn swords stood at attention at the four corners. During the all day service, Tatiana tried not to stare at her father's corpse, but again and again her eyes were drawn towards him, filling her anew with grief each time.

The prayers and liturgy readings were interminable, and the church so hot and crowded that towards the end of the day she almost fainted. When Dmitri noticed her extreme pallor and felt her swaying against him, he immediately grabbed her arm to take her outside. As they exited the church, she was aware of Marya standing in the back. When they walked past her, the girl looked at Tatiana with a strange imploring expression, as if she wanted something.

Tatiana could not imagine what it could be unless she wished a reward for all the weeks of unselfish care she had given her father. She decided she would speak to Dmitri soon about giving Marya a gift of appreciation for all her devotion. They certainly could afford it. Her father's death had left her a tidy investment into the Company. His shares had now become hers, or rather, Dmitri's. As his wife, she could not own any property or investments, so her father's stocks in the Company were now under Dmitri's control.

A tangy salt breeze was blowing off the harbor and the fresh sea air revived her in a matter of minutes. "Thank you, Dmitri," she said. "I feel much better now. We can go back inside."

"Very good, my dear," he said with relief. "For a moment in there I was afraid you were about to faint."

They turned toward the church entrance then halted as Marya stumbled out, her cheeks streaked with tears and her face full of sorrow. She appeared to be grieving as deeply as Tatiana.

Impossible! Tatiana thought with irritation. *No one on earth could've loved Papa more than I did. Unless...*came the nagging thought, *unless she was more than just a servant girl to him...*

Something inside Tatiana snapped. It was time she found out the truth no matter what the cost. She hurried over to the girl and confronted her. "Marya," she hissed angrily, "I demand to know immediately, who is your father?"

Marya's face drained of all color and she cowered like a trapped rabbit. Dmitri strode over to them and said, "Tatiana, what is all this nonsense?"

She ignored him and said in a louder voice, "Tell me, Marya. Who are you?"

Suddenly the girl underwent a transformation. Her chin popped up and her eyes, dewy wet with tears, sharpened their pupils. She stared straight at Tatiana and said in a calm tone, "My papa was Captain-Lieutenant Nikolas Ilyich Bolkonsky."

A proud defiant expression crept into her face. "I am Marya Nikolayevna, your half-sister."

With those words, she whirled around and flew past Tatiana away from the church in the direction of the Aleut village outside the stockade. Tatiana stood frozen, looking stunned, her mouth open with shock.

"It can't be true," she whispered. "It can't be true."

Dmitri took her gloved hand in his and squeezed gently. "It is true, Tatiana. She is your half-sister."

"No, it is a lie. How dare she speak such slander about my father!"

"It is not a lie," said Dmitri, giving her a look of pity. "It is common knowledge in New Archangel that your father had an Aleut mistress for fifteen years."

The words exploded into Tatiana's brain with such volcanic force that her mind fragmented into a thousand disjointed thoughts. She pressed both her hands to her temples and uttered a slight moan as pain flashed throughout her entire body. Her father had betrayed her mother's memory and had betrayed her as well. How could he have done such an abominable thing?

With a supreme effort she gathered her wits and glared at her husband in accusation. "Since you knew, why didn't you tell me, Dmitri?"

"I was hoping your father would tell you before he died. When he didn't," he shrugged his shoulders carelessly. "I thought it would be best if you never found out. I didn't want your memory of your father to be tarnished by such a sordid incident, even though most of our men here consort with the native women. Why do you think there are so many *Creole*s?"

"I thought only the *promyshlenniki* lowered themselves with Indian women, not officers like my father." Then a sudden thought struck her. "What about you, Dmitri? Do you have an Aleut mistress too?"

"Indeed not!" A look of revulsion flashed across his aristocratic face. "I've always found the thought of creating some half-breed child perfectly revolting. As long as you remain my loving wife, Tatiana, you need never fear me going astray."

He took her firmly by one arm. "Come, my dear, compose yourself. We must return to the church before our absence starts tongues wagging."

CHAPTER EIGHTEEN

As the *Sea Rose* sailed along the western coast of Vancouver Island they passed by Nootka Sound without incident. Some of the crew thought they should've stopped to trade with the fur rich Nootkas, but others said the skins of the sea otter were not worth losing their own hides over. And there were many Indian villages ahead of them, such as the Kwakiutl, the Bellabella, the Haidas of the Queen Charlotte Islands, and the Tlingits who welcomed Yankee traders.

"I daresay 'tis a good thing we didna stop there," said Ethan to Anna in their cabin one night as they readied for bed. "Poor John doesna need to be reminded of his time with the Nootkas an' the wee lass he married an' left. Nor does Gregory want to think of it."

"What an adventure they must have had," said Anna. "Two years as captives among Indians. It is amazing they survived. God was watching out for them."

Ethan nodded in agreement. "He loves us all, believers and nonbelievers. The Almighty doesna wish that any of us should perish. During each man or woman's lifetime He tries to draw them to Him, so at the Day of Judgment, no one shall have an excuse. All those years I was runnin' away from God, me da an' ma never stopped prayin' for me. I'm a thankful man they an' the Almighty never gave up."

"I think the captain needs God," she said, remembering his startling confession about killing his father. Had she really heard correctly? It was something she'd never told Ethan.

"Ach, Sean," said Ethan with a shrug. "He's a lad who's been runnin' all his life, an' still is, from God an' who knows what else."

Anna was tempted to share the captain's shocking words, but found she could not. The two men were such close friends. If Sean wished Ethan to know about his father, he would have told him by now. Perhaps she had misunderstood. Either way, it was best forgotten.

"I think Robby and I are finally friends," she said, changing the subject. Ever since last Christmas, the day his brother drowned, she had tried to win him over. It hadn't been easy, but two things were in her favor.

First, marrying Ethan had halted all the rumors of her being bad luck. The men trusted the first mate, and if she was worthy of being his wife, who were they to argue? And secondly, the fact that she helped him each day with navigating the ship made her an important part of the crew.

With Robby she had taken a step further. One day off the coast of Mexico when they were becalmed in the broiling heat with little to do, she asked him if he'd like to learn how to read. Knowing he was an illiterate orphan had always tugged at her heart. She wasn't certain of his response, but to her surprise, he brightened up and agreed.

Since then, each night when he had finished cleaning up after dinner, the two of them sat down in the forward cabin at the big table. She had begun by teaching him his letters, then simple words, using her Bible as the main textbook. Robby was a bright boy and learned quickly. Often when he was reading, Wang Li and Samuel would linger nearby, listening, instead of rushing off to share the opium pipe.

"Tonight all three of them were asking me questions about Jesus and eternal life," she told Ethan. "I had just started explaining the way of salvation when Captain O'Connell marched in and ordered everyone out, including me. He said teaching the boy how to read was one thing, but spreading my Mennonite drivel to his crew was another." She sighed, remembering the angry scowl on the captain's face.

After the others had left the cabin, she told him she wasn't spouting her own beliefs, but that of Jesus Himself, written in the word of God. Then she added, "Believing in Jesus will make them better sailors, not worse, Captain."

He ignored her comments and said, "'Tis time ye let the boy read something other than your Bible. I've a number of books in my cabin, such as the plays of William Shakespeare. Ye are welcome to use any of them."

"Thank you, Captain," she said, frustration lacing her voice.

He raised his dark eyebrows and his mouth twitched as he said, "I do believe I've actually made ye angry, Missus Campbell."

She could feel her face burning. He was right. She was angry. Although he was the captain, she resented his interference in what she considered God's work. If he hadn't come bursting into the cabin at that moment, perhaps Robby, or even Samuel or Wang Li, might have become more interested in learning about God.

The rosy color in her cheeks and the flash of righteous indignation in her eyes made her look like a lovely avenging angel, and he felt an unholy temptation to kiss her. Then he felt furious with himself. She was his best friend's wife. What was he thinking?

And even worse, what did she now think of him since that day he'd stupidly blurted out that he had killed his father? What had possessed him at the time?

It was a secret from his past that his own sister had carried with her to the grave. He couldn't believe he had said such a thing. Thankfully, Anna had not mentioned it since. He could only hope she would forget about it.

Abruptly he turned away and growled, "Leave me be, Anna."

She was tempted to lash out at him, but held her tongue. Instead she stomped out, feeling confused as to how he always stirred such strong emotions inside her. If she wasn't already happily married, she would think she was feeling things toward the captain she shouldn't.

"Ye are an amazin' lass, Anna," said Ethan, nuzzling her hair with his mouth. "Ye spend so much time helpin' others. Now 'tis time ye spend some of your attentions on me."

"Gladly," she said, turning towards her brawny husband with a loving smile as she tried to forget the mocking smirk on the lean sun-darkened face of the captain.

During the next few days they entered the inland seas. After all the months on the open ocean Anna was amazed at the tranquility of the water. On a cloudy day the sea was as smooth as gray satin. On a clear day with a slight breeze the water appeared like blue rippled glass. As they sailed further north sometimes the sea turned into a crystal clear green, caused by the silt from the many mountain glaciers.

The beauty and power of the glaciers were truly awe-inspiring. Rivers of blue-gray ice flowed out of the mountains to the water's edge, ending in spectacular ice cliffs, dangerous places where icebergs were born. In many ways, the fjords of Alaska were like the Andean fjords near Cape Horn.

Now the business of trading began in earnest. They sailed from one Indian village to another, each one tucked away in a forest shrouded inlet or rocky bay. The first time they approached a village, Ethan told Anna to stay below and out of sight.

"But I am very curious about the natives and wish to see them," she protested.

He silenced her quickly when he said, "The Indians on this part of the coast have never seen a white woman. If they see ye on board, Anna, some chief will want to add ye to his collection of wives, either by trading for ye, or by attackin' us."

The anxiety in his eyes convinced her he was telling the truth. After that, whenever they dropped anchor to trade, Anna found herself spending hours on end in her cabin or in the salon, restlessly peering out the stern windows to view glimpses of copper skinned natives shooting past the ship in long cedar canoes, or hearing the strange babble of their language as they boarded the ship for trading.

The captain and his officers entertained the Indians in the forward cabin, after making certain none of them were carrying weapons. Wang Li served what they liked to eat and drink, fresh biscuits, molasses and a small shot of rum. While the captain and the chief discussed the bargaining, part of the crew went ashore with the water casks and barrels and also cut timber for Nate Anderson the carpenter-cooper to make yards, spars and wooden barrels for the furs. The rest of the crew busied themselves with refitting the rigging and repairing sails. There was never an end to the work on board.

Sometimes when they were near a village, she would look out the window and see women and children on the beach. There were young mothers with infants strapped on their backs and elderly gray haired women with stooped shoulders. Smaller children stared at the ship with mouths agape and eyes wide. They all looked so interesting to her. She thought how exciting it would be to communicate with them, but with Ethan's warning ringing in her ears, she knew that was impossible.

These were the moments when Anna missed Tatiana's company. It had been many months since she had another woman to talk to. Even though her former mistress could be a trial, Anna had come to care deeply for her, and she often wondered how she was. Had the *Suvorov* reached New Archangel yet? Was she married to her Dmitri by now? Anna hoped she was happy in her new life with her husband and father.

She also wrote long letters to her Uncle Heinrich, *Tante* Sarah and her cousins, her papa and Jack, the twins, Tina, and Susannah. Even if she could never find a ship to carry them back to Russia, she decided the letters would be a sort of journal of her voyage to Alaska. Someday when she had children, they would be able to read about her adventures.

* * *

The summer passed quickly in a haze of busy trading. One afternoon in early September, the *Sea Rose* was anchored in the shadow of a great glacier in a small inlet near the Chilkat mountain range, many miles northeast of Baranov Island. The inlet was lined with dark forests and craggy mountain peaks. Soon the fall storms would be blanketing the mountains with blizzards of snow, but now in late summer, they were a patchwork of brown rock and dirty white spots.

The sun was shining, bursting through the heavy clouds, casting a path of gold dust across the water. Anna was up on deck, wrapped warmly in her cloak, enjoying the splendid view. It was even more precious, because tomorrow at dawn they were leaving for China, and she didn't know when she would see this beautiful part of God's world again.

During the past weeks Alaska had overwhelmed her with its pristine grandeur. She had never dreamed of such beauty and wildness as in the islands, forests, mountains and creatures surrounding them at every turn of the head. Black and white porpoises were a constant escort, their graceful bodies swimming next to the hull then darting ahead of the bow, narrowly escaping collision each time. She'd seen glistening black humpback whales hurtling skyward, only to thunder back into the water with a mighty splash. Majestic bald eagles soared overhead, then with breathtaking speed dove into the water, emerging moments later with a fish grasped tightly in their sharp talons. Often near the shore of some uninhabited island, there were graceful deer feeding in the brush, brown and black bears in the water catching fish, and gray wolves slinking in the trees.

Alaska was the land of untamed dreams, a land of great wealth and natural resources, a land of much mystery, danger, and raw violence. She was going to miss it and the carefree summer they had spent here.

The trading was over. Most of the tribes had left their summer villages at the beaches to travel inland to their fall and winter camps. Anna sighed. The thought of the coming voyage across the Pacific filled her with nervous trepidation.

The ship wasn't the only one carrying an extra load. Without a doubt she knew she was to have a child.

Lately she had been nauseated each morning, sometimes the entire day. She remembered her mama suffering such an affliction when she carried her little sister. And she also would never forget the hard time her mama had birthing Katarina, and how long it took for her to recover. The thought of having a baby on a ship with only men, without the support of any knowledgeable woman, was frightening. And how was Ethan going to react when she told him? She worried that he would disapprove, saying it was too soon and too dangerous to start a family now.

A hand gripped her shoulder and she gave a small start. Bundled snugly into a heavy wool coat and cap, he smiled down at her. The crisp cool air had reddened his nose and cheeks and his brown eyes sparkled with anticipation.

"Yer as jumpy as a salmon goin' upriver to spawn, lass."

She tried to laugh at his attempt at humor, but failed miserably. A wave of nausea rolled over her and she clutched the rail so tightly with her hands the knuckles turned white.

"Anna, what's the matter? Are ye ill?" He looked at her with a worried frown and added, "I've not seen ye eatin' much lately an' ye stay abed longer than ye used to."

She swallowed, then said softly, "I think I'm going to have a child."

His red-bearded face showed a fleeting array of emotions--surprise, uncertainty, and something else, a deep tenderness. He bent down and gently brushed his lips across her forehead, his mustache tickling her sensitive skin.

"Ach, me bonnie lass, I should've known. I'm such an idiot!"

"Are you pleased?" she asked uncertainly.

"I'm so proud an' happy I feel like tellin' the whole world!" He threw his arms around her and hugged her, then seeing Sean talking to John and Jake nearby, he lifted his head and yelled, "Hey Cap'n, hey, Hill an' O'Riley, I'm to be a da!"

John and Jake immediately broke into wide grins and shouted their congratulations while some of the common seamen who overheard cracked a few ribald jokes. Only Sean was quiet. The announcement was something he'd hoped to never hear.

All summer he had been too busy to worry about such a thing. Trading was brisk and successful and the cargo hold was now filled with pelts, fox skins of black, reddish, or silver-gray, beaver, lynx, marten, and the most prized, the glossy purple-black fur of the sea otter.

His only concern had been how the price for the rapidly disappearing sea otter skins had increased. Years ago a few beads or trinkets would buy one pelt. Now with the otter being in danger of over hunting by the Russians, British, and Americans, the Indians wanted several blankets per otter, with some demanding a bonus of knives, guns, powder, or ammunition.

The future looked grim for the fur trade. Not only were the best pelts becoming scarce, but he'd heard the market in Canton, China was becoming glutted by the immense quantities of furs shipped in. Perhaps with a couple more summers like this one, he could buy Thomas Hill out, and still make enough profit to branch into other trades, such as tea or opium.

Recently Ethan had shared with him his own hopes of owning a ship someday, and also his plans to build a fine house in Boston for Anna and any children they might have. Sean had responded with a few noncommittal grunts, remembering Captain Edward Smythe of the *Eastern Wind.* The man had a wife and six children in Boston, and like most captains who left their wives at home, he saw them only once every few years. The crew used to joke how each of his children were spaced three years apart. Sean had laughed, too, but now, he didn't think it was so hilarious if it was Anna stuck by herself raising a brood of children. He knew if she was his wife, he'd never leave her alone while he sailed off.

He felt a stab of envy. Anna should be having his baby, he thought then he angrily shoved that ridiculous idea aside as a moment of fear clutched him. Birthing a child on a ship out at sea without a doctor on board was dangerous. What was Ethan thinking? The anger returned, only this time it was aimed at his friend.

He stepped forward to give the man a piece of his mind, then checked himself, just as Robby, perched high in the crow's nest on the forward mast shouted, "Ship ahoy! Ship ahoy!"

There was a few seconds pause then Robby called down, his voice breaking in fright, "Sir, she's carryin' a Russian flag!"

Anna was immediately forgotten as he rushed aft to the helm, yelling at the startled crew, "Men, weigh the anchor! Hoist the sails!" He turned to his three ashen faced officers. "Campbell, Hill, O'Riley, make haste! We must head for the open sea afore there's no way out!"

The men scrambled to do his bidding. Anna moved out of the way, her heart racing as a terrible foreboding clutched her. This situation was Ethan's worst fear come to reality. All summer he and the captain had been on edge, constantly looking out for Russian ships. Until now, they had seen none, only a few British and American traders like themselves.

Sailing the inland waters was both an advantage and a possible curse. There were many places to hide from the Russians, but also many places to be trapped. Navigational charts of the area were incomplete. At times it was anyone's guess in the maze of inlets and narrow channels, as to which one led to another or ended abruptly against the side of a sheer mountain. All of the clipper's superior design for speed and maneuverability would be for nothing if they were caught in an inlet like this one, by a Russian warship blocking the only exit.

Suddenly Ethan bellowed, "Cap'n, she's comin' too fast for us to get past her!"

"Then we prepare to fight!" Sean shouted. "Man the guns!"

The *Sea Rose* swung around to port and turned broadside to the Russian ship in a fighting position. Men leaped to the four starboard guns and readied them for firing, waiting anxiously for the signal from Sean. While he hesitated there was a loud boom from the Russian ship and a black cannonball shot towards them and splashed harmlessly into the water near the bow.

The urge to return fire was instinctively overwhelming even though he knew their eight guns were not a match for the heavy cannon of the Imperial warship. He opened his mouth to tell the sailors to light the fuses, then clamped it shut as his gaze found Anna standing on the deck in the open, a likely target for any Russian gun. Her face was gray with fright and her eyes two enormous pools of fear. Both of her arms were crossed protectively over her abdomen.

He knew he could not give the order to fire. Not with a pregnant woman on board, a woman he loved. No cargo of furs, however precious, was worth saving by putting her life in jeopardy.

With the foul taste of defeat in his mouth he turned to the crew and yelled, "'Tis suicide to fight, men. We have to surrender. Mister O'Riley, hoist the white flag."

Most of the men saw the sense in his words and stepped back from the guns while others grumbled to each other, giving the Russian ship angry looks. Ethan limped over to Anna and put his arm around her protectively. Both of them watched as the warship edged closer. She read in Russian the name of the ship painted on the bow, the *Buldakov*.

Sean was in a helpless fury at the financial disaster staring them in the face. He was afraid the Russians were going to seize all the precious furs on board, thereby ruining their profits on this voyage. But if he and his men kept their tempers, perhaps, the loss of the furs would be the end of it. Hopefully, the Russians would allow the ship and crew to depart, even if it meant they would escort them south to international waters.

Lines and grappling hooks shot out from the brig to secure the *Sea Rose* to herself like a black spider snaring a butterfly in its web. Armed sailors lined the deck, waiting to jump onto the clipper. Shouting orders to them, stood the Russian captain, a tall fair-haired man wearing a gold braided uniform and a gilded hat surmounted with the double crest of the Imperial Eagle.

"Pray, Anna," said Ethan, "Pray as hard as ye can."

* * *

Governor Matvei Muraviev rustled a stack of papers on his desk and frowned. Until this morning he'd had no complaints with his life here in New Archangel. Now unexpected circumstances threatened to undermine his smoothly running administration of Russian America.

He'd always thought of himself as a man who had everything in perfect control. Born into a famous and brilliant family in Russia, he was an intelligent scholarly man who became one of the Navy's most able captains. It was no surprise to anyone, least of all to Muraviev, when he was appointed by the board of the Russian American Fur Company to his present position of supreme power over this immense land. One year ago in September of 1820, he arrived in the colony, leaving without regret, his complaining childless wife in Saint Petersburg. At once he made changes, inspecting all the posts, ordering new construction and reorganizing the administration. He was determined to earn his 40,000 rubles a year, eight times Baranov's salary.

His recent voyage around Russian America had been a great success. Now all the colonies knew without question who was in power. Baranov and then his son-in-law, Yanovski, had both been popular governors. It was imperative that as their successor, he instilled the same sort of respect as they had among the Russian colonists, the Aleuts and the *Kolosh* Indians.

But trouble was looming in the immediate future with the arrival yesterday of the American vessel, the *Sea Rose*. The seizure of the ship by Lieutenant Volodin had thrown his neat orderly world into immediate disarray. At first he thought it would only be a simple matter of confiscating all the furs and any contraband cargo, such as guns and ammunition, and sending the Americans away after a stern warning to never return.

But earlier this morning a *Creole* by the name of Andrei Leonov had come to see him. The man had once been hired by the American crew of the *Eastern Wind* as a supercargo, the same ship which the previous governor, Yanovski, had declared all her officers as wanted criminals by the Imperial Crown for trading arms to the natives. Leonov claimed that the American captain, O'Connell, and the chief officer, Campbell, had been two of the officers on board the *Eastern Wind*. If so, then they were subject to any sentence he deemed appropriate for their crimes, whether whipping, imprisonment, or hanging.

Lieutenant Volodin was putting pressure on him to have the two men whipped with the *knout* and then hanged as just punishment. He claimed that the Americans needed to learn the consequences of defying Russian authority and supremacy in Alaska.

Perhaps Volodin was right, he mused. He certainly was a splendid naval officer. He had done a superb job as temporary governor in his absence the past months, and he had impeccable connections to the Company. Both his wife's uncle, Count Vasily Bolkonsky, along with his own father, Baron Ivan Volodin, were on the Board of Directors. But the one thing Muraviev disliked about the aristocratic young lieutenant was his fondness for unnecessary brutality.

At the moment, as a courtesy to their rank, the Yankee captain and his officers were under armed guard on board their ship, waited on by their own Chinese cook, the steward and the cabin boy. The common sailors were all locked up in the prison, protesting their lot with loud and profane language. Thank goodness hardly a soul in town understood English.

There was also some fuss about the Russian wife of the chief officer, who was the former maid of Lieutenant Volodin's wife. She was still on board the American ship as well. Later after he interviewed the captain and his officers, he would decide what to do about all of them.

Meanwhile, he had another matter to contend with. A few weeks earlier when he was in Kodiak, he had met with a messenger from Saint Petersburg. The man had traveled thousands of miles, overland through Siberia to Okhotsk, a port city located on the eastern shore of Siberia. There he'd crossed the Gulf of Alaska with his important news.

The Board of Directors, including Baron Volodin and Count Bolkonsky, had petitioned Czar Alexander for permission to forbid foreigners to trade with the natives along the coasts of Russian America. The Czar agreed and recently published an imperial decree, or *ukase*, banning the transaction of commerce and the pursuit of whaling and fishing, or any other industry along the northwest coast of America from the Bering Sea to the fifty-first parallel. It also prohibited any foreign vessel putting ashore or approaching the coast within one hundred miles.

To help insure these new policies, a number of warships had sailed recently from Kronstadt. Unfortunately, the armed cruisers were the only ships that would be arriving in New Archangel in the near future. Governor Muraviev was also told that after next year, no supply ships would be coming in 1823 or 1824.

He was afraid that in another year New Archangel would be in for a serious food shortage. And if no supply ships arrived for another three years or more, they could be in danger of starvation.

Fort Ross in California was supposed to send them a steady supply of wheat and cattle each summer, but a report from the company commissioner there stated that due to crop failure and other circumstances, fewer provisions would be sent this year.

The Czar's *ukase* could not have come at more inopportune time. When Alexander Baranov was faced with the same problem years ago, he obtained goods from the Americans and British. Now that was impossible. And there was another complication. The *Kolosh* were used to trading with foreigners and they already resented the Czar's *ukase*. He predicted there was going to be problems with the natives at any time. And that made him uneasy.

He had not yet shared these concerns with his officers. The announcement of the *ukase* had brought cheers from them, especially Lieutenant Volodin. It had made his seizure of the American ship perfectly legal, unfortunately.

"Everyone awaits you for dinner, Your Excellency," said Mikhail, his valet, standing in the doorway of his office. "The capture of the American ship has given us a cause to celebrate, *da*?"

"*Da*," Muraviev sighed heavily. "We can always use their rich cargo of furs to add to our supply, Mikhail, but sometimes I think it would be better to send the *Sea Rose* to the Sandwich Islands for provisions and upon their return, give them back their furs or their equivalent in rubles."

"Unless we are in dire need of supplies immediately, Your Excellency, I don't think your idea would be a popular one among our men or among His Imperial Majesty, the Czar himself."

Mikhail's gentle warning brought him up short. His valet was right. He must not speak openly of trading with foreigners, even though in his heart Muraviev felt the Czar had made a mistake, a belief that bordered on treason in Imperialistic Russia.

* * *

Their small group of nobility was already seated around the long table in the banquet hall. The governor sat at one end in a plush armchair. The Volodins, Trotskys, Pushkins, the Chernyshovs, Igor and Natasha, Father Sokolov, and Lieutenants Dohktorov and Ivanoff were all placed on either side, facing each other. As usual, Tatiana Nikolayevna outshone all the ladies, even dressed in her black mourning gown.

What a terrible shame about Nikolas Bolkonsky, thought the Governor. He missed the man's intelligence and insight already. Nikolas was one who would have wholeheartedly agreed with his opinion of the Czar's *ukase*.

Tatiana noted the governor's serious expression and assumed he was thinking of how he was planning on punishing the captain of the *Sea Rose*. She had almost fainted with joy that morning when the *Buldakov* and the *Sea Rose* had been sighted in the harbor.

At breakfast she'd heard the batteries blasting their charges in welcome. The sound was deafening as boom after boom thundered and echoed in the gorges of the surrounding mountains. Startling her maid Keeah, she dashed out the front door of her house, located at the base of the "Hill." She looked up at the governor's residence and saw the Imperial flag being raised high on the ninety foot native pine flag staff in honor of the approaching ships.

The Volodins' home was a square two story house with a roof made of spruce bark. As private homes went in New Archangel, it was second only to the Governor's. When Tatiana had first seen the house where her father had lived, she was dismayed at its plain, unpainted exterior. The inside smelled of damp, rain-soaked timber which the heat from the brick stoves struggled daily to dissipate. However, her father had furnished the house well, with plush wall hangings, oriental carpets, ornate framed paintings, heavy furniture, and numerous mirrors and windows to catch whatever sunlight could be had in the dreary climate.

Her father's interest in religion was evident across an upper corner of each room, where a small painting of either the Savior, the Virgin, or the heads of various Saints was placed, framed by gold or silver filigree. It hadn't taken Dmitri long to order them all put away, except for one of the Virgin Mary in the downstairs parlor.

They had three servants, Keeah as Tatiana's lady's maid, a young Aleut girl named Maria to clean and do laundry, and the cook Helena, a heavyset, middle-aged *Creole* woman. She was married to a Russian carpenter who worked in the shipyard, and she came in early each morning to prepare breakfast and any other meals, if needed. Their small kitchen was a rarity for a home in New Archangel. Meals were usually eaten in the communal dining halls with one for the common sailors and soldiers, another for the workmen, and the other for the officers and their families. The nobility dined as often as possible with Governor Muraviev, including Dmitri and Tatiana.

Tatiana glanced around the table at all the men. Ever since she had discovered the heartbreaking knowledge about her father's Aleut woman, she could not help wondering which of them possibly had native mistresses. Perhaps all of them did, even the governor. If so, could she really blame them? They were all married to a bunch of shrews, alcoholic Elizabeth, irritating Natasha, and cold Irina. Soon she could include Vera Alexisovna in that dubious list. Just yesterday she'd heard that she and Lieutenant Anton Dohktorov were betrothed. The nice lieutenant had no idea what he was getting into by marrying that mean-spirited girl. And poor little Sophie,; she was probably heartbroken.

Dmitri squeezed her knee under the table and she jumped slightly. "My dear," he said, "the governor has asked you a question."

"I beg your pardon, Your Excellency," she said, blushing.

Muraviev was smiling at her. "*Madame* Volodina, would you be willing to meet with me in my office after dinner this evening concerning your experiences on the *Sea Rose*?"

"Certainly, Your Excellency," she answered.

"Splendid." He smiled and nodded at Dmitri. "With your husband's permission, of course."

Tatiana thought Matvei Muraviev was a rather ordinary looking man to be such a powerful governor. Of average height with a robust build, he had a sparse gray mustache and his thinning gray hair was covered by an outdated powdered wig. Yet, when he spoke in his deep rich voice, he commanded an air of shrewdness and strength that demanded respect from all his subordinates, even Dmitri.

Her husband had been gone the past month on patrol duty, and she hadn't missed him as much as a newly wedded bride should. After a summer of trying to be the perfect wife, she found a certain freedom in his absence. Now all that would change. Once again, at the end of each day, he would demand to know every single thing she did and with whom. She had to be careful how she described her daily routines, for he was quick to criticize whatever he deemed as inappropriate. Sometimes it seemed to her that he was jealous of any person, man or woman that she spoke to.

Tatiana wondered if Ethan Campbell was as domineering with Anna. Now that her former maid was in New Archangel, she was anxious to see her and share their experiences about married life. She expected Anna to be unhappy at first about being separated from her husband. But she would do everything in her power to make Anna comfortable, no matter what Ethan's fate may be.

Dmitri laid a possessive hand on her arm. "If you wish, I shall accompany Tatiana. We have been apart too long as it is."

"I wouldn't have it otherwise, Lieutenant," said the governor, smiling broadly. "That's what husbands are for; to take care of their wives."

She returned his smile with a forced laugh, thinking if that was true, then why was his own wife back in Russia instead of living here with him? Dmitri had said she refused to leave her parents who were in poor health, and Tatiana could not help feeling envious of the woman. With her husband always gone, *Madame* Muravieva could live as she pleased instead playing the role of a typical Russian trophy wife, a piece of property to be shown off. Tatiana remembered once telling her cousin, Olga, that when they were married, they would be free to live their own lives.

How wrong she was! There were times when she thought she had left the confines and restrictions of her uncle's prison only for another.

* * *

As the sole woman to attend the meeting in the governor's office after dinner, Tatiana was seated in an armchair across the big desk from Governor Muraviev. Dmitri and the other officers, Pushkin, Chernyshov, Ivanoff and Trotsky, stood around the room congratulating themselves on the seizure of the American ship.

Noticing her nervousness, Muraviev smiled at her, trying to put her at ease. "*Madame* Volodina, I've asked you here for your help. My officers and I have been discussing the fate of the captain, crew, and the *Sea Rose* herself. We would appreciate any knowledge you have that might help us decide. For instance, if we release them with their promise to cease trading in Russian America, do you believe that Captain O'Connell is a man who will honor his word and never return?"

Tatiana thought quickly. For all his uncouth manners and their mutual dislike, she knew the captain was an honest man. Yet, if she said he would keep his promises, it would mean all her plans for Anna to stay in New Archangel would come to naught. The *Sea Rose* would sail away, taking her with them.

"He is a devious man, not to be trusted," she replied. "He is greedy as well, and if he has command of his ship again, I believe he would trade guns to the natives."

"And not only that," said Dmitri quickly, "but the captain needs to be held accountable for what happened to my wife when she was a passenger on board his ship. She was attacked by one of his officers and wounded."

"I heard of that incident." Muraviev shuddered. "It was a most dreadful business. Only a barbarian would attack a defenseless woman. You have my deepest sympathy, *Madame* Volodina, for such a frightful experience. But didn't the captain shoot and kill the officer involved?"

"Well, yes," Tatiana began, thinking that she should say something truthful about Captain O'Connell when Dmitri interrupted her, "Whether he did or did not, the captain of a ship is still responsible for the actions of his officers, and he must be held accountable."

"Perhaps, we should hang him and all the officers," said Boris Ivanoff with a hearty chuckle. "And then, we should put the crew to work here in the garrison."

As Chernyshov, Trotsky, and Pushkin nodded in agreement, Dmitri said, "Boris is right. Executing them will serve as a warning to all the other American and British ships which are trading illegally here to respect our boundaries, or else prepare to suffer the same consequence."

"We have already accomplished this by seizing the ship and her cargo," said Muraviev sternly. "The United States government might consider it an act of war if we also execute any American citizens. However," he added, noticing the disappointed looks of the men, "Lieutenant Ivanoff's idea of putting the common sailors to work is commendable. After enough time in prison to sufficiently subdue them, I shall order their release. There are many new buildings in town under construction and we can use the extra hands. As for the captain and his officers, I will have them brought here first thing in the morning to be questioned. I will also summon the *Creole* Andrei Leonov. I need him to identify which of the Americans were the actual officers of the *Eastern Wind*. After I have weighed all the facts concerning this case, I will pass sentence on the captain and his officers. And if I find enough evidence to hang them, I will do so, no matter what the international consequences."

As the meeting adjourned, Tatiana felt a sickening dread in the pit of her stomach. This was not what she had in mind when she lied about

Captain O'Connell's character. But now it was too late. She didn't dare change her story and risk angering Dmitri. He and all his friends wanted the American captain and his officers hanged. As much as she despised the captain, she had never wished him dead, only imprisoned as revenge for all the humiliations he'd given her on board his ship.

Then there was Anna. If her husband was harmed or heaven forbid, executed, Anna might suspect she had something to do with it, and would never forgive her. Ever.

CHAPTER NINETEEN

The mood in the salon of the *Sea Rose* was grim the next morning. All night two armed Russian sailors had stood at the main door of the salon, guarding their important prisoners. Inside the room, Sean, Ethan and Anna, John and Jake were finishing their meager breakfast of oatmeal and the last of the bacon, cooked by Wang Li in the galley under the watchful eyes of another Russian guard. Samuel was allowed to serve the meal, and Robby, to clean up afterwards.

He usually performed his job whistling cheerfully, but this morning he cast looks of resentment towards the Russians whenever he had to brush by them with the plates and bowls. Samuel pretended they didn't exist. When one of the young Russians said in broken English that he was an uppity black slave, he ignored the comment and continued his duties in a dignified manner.

Anna found it harder to ignore them. The shininess of their polished boots and neatly pressed uniforms of white cotton trousers, black *kurtkas* (sailors' jacket), and their black visor less caps, were a startling contrast to their coarse-features faces. They reminded her of the peasant workers at Silberfeld. Only instead of lowering their dark eyes respectfully in her presence, the men stared with bold gazes that made her feel uneasy.

Sean prowled restlessly around the salon like a caged panther, berating himself for putting his ship and crew into such a predicament. "Perhaps we should've tried fightin' after all," he muttered angrily to Ethan, John, and Jake.

"Then the *Sea Rose* would be sunk for sure, and most of us at the bottom of the sea," said John. "Uncle Thomas would say you made the wise choice in saving his prize ship. Hopefully, the Governor is a reasonable man and will let us go. He has our cargo now and detaining us will only make relations between our countries strained."

"That Lieutenant Volodin didn't seem like a reasonable man to me," said Sean, frowning. "I've never seen such a pompous arrogant---"

"He's the man who married *Mademoiselle* Tatiana," interrupted Anna.

Sean spewed out a couple more colorful insults before saying, "I'm sure we have her to thank for our arrest. He knew way too much about me, the ship, the crew, and what sort of cargo we had to just be happenstance. I certainly regret the day in London I allowed her to step foot on my ship."

"Not me, Cap'n," said Ethan with a tense smile, "that day brought me the love o' me life."

Sean glanced at Anna and his face softened slightly. "I beg your pardon, Anna," he said, noticing how pretty she looked in her soft green muslin frock as a few dark golden strands of hair escaped her scarf, framing her pale face.

She smiled at him. "I understand your frustration, Captain. I do hope *Mademoiselle* Tatiana did not betray us, but if she did, then our fate will be on her conscience."

"I don't think the woman or her husband has one," he growled, remembering the cold haughty manner of the Russian lieutenant. "The two of them is a match made in hell."

All the men glanced at Anna to see if she was shocked by Sean's comment, but she pretended not to have heard. Privately, she agreed with him about Lieutenant Volodin.

Yesterday after he had boarded the *Sea Rose*, he had made a point of calling her "his wife's maid," and smiled at her with such malice, she had sensed a feeling of evil around him.

It made her concerned for Tatiana. Somehow she didn't think her former mistress was as happy and content with her husband as she was with Ethan. She glanced at him lovingly, thinking what a wonderful father he was going to make.

The door burst open and several Russian sailors marched in followed by a fat man in a lieutenant's uniform. His reddened jowls were moist with sweat as he explained in guttural English, "I am Lieutenant Ivanoff. All of you to come with me now. His Excellency's orders."

The sailors carried ropes and one by one, they fastened them around each man's wrists. "What's the meaning of this?" Sean demanded as his arms were twisted behind him and bound so tight he felt his hands growing numb. "There's no need for these ropes."

"*Da*, there is, Captain," Ivanoff grunted. "You are not guests, but prisoners of the Imperial Navy now."

Ethan, seeing Anna's anxious expression, said, "Be brave, lass, remember I love ye." He looked at Samuel, who was frozen in place, holding a half empty bowl of oatmeal. "Samuel, take care of Anna, will ye?"

"Yessuh," he muttered, giving all the Russians a black scowl of loathing.

Ivanoff chuckled and then sneered at Ethan. "The woman is not staying here. His Excellency has other plans for her." He looked at Anna, thinking how he envied his friend, Dmitri, to have such a pretty Russian woman living in his house as maid to his wife. If she wasn't already married to one of the Americans, she would be courted by many a Russian in town, since there was such a shortage of eligible Russian women in New Archangel.

But then, he thought, *if His Excellency decides to hang them all, she will be a widow soon.*

The thought gave him a feeling of satisfaction, as he knew he would be the first one to offer *Madame* Campbell his condolences. With a smug expression, he turned to one of the sailors and barked an order in Russian.

Ethan gave her a frantic look. “What did he say, Anna?”

“I’m to be taken to Lieutenant Volodin’s house,” she answered as the young guard acknowledged the order by clicking his heels together, then rattled off some words to her.

Anna nodded to him, and quickly went to her cabin to gather a few personal belongings. A few minutes later she stepped out with a small satchel. “He will come for the rest tomorrow,” she said to Ethan, who was now bound tightly along with the other three men.

He frowned, his dark red mustache drooping over his upper lip. “If ye go back to that woman, I will worry about ye something fierce, lass.”

She tried to give him a reassuring smile. “Ethan, I shall come to no harm there. Tatiana will look after me. It’s you and the captain and Mr. Hill and Mr. O’Riley who will need my prayers.”

“We will do whatever they ask so no one is harmed,” said Sean, staring at her with the same sort of worried intensity she saw in Ethan’s eyes. “Take care of yourself, Anna,” he added softly.

“Silence!” Ivanoff shouted. “No more talk!” With a curt motion of his head he ordered the prisoners out of the salon.

Anna’s arm was gripped by the young Russian guard. As they followed the men, her brief attempt at courage faded and was replaced by a deep feeling of dread. It didn’t help that the last she saw of Samuel, Robby, and Wang Li, they were looking at her with miserable expressions of despair.

Mama would tell me not to give up hope, she told herself. And she would also say that God will work everything out according to His purposes.

I can only hope that is true, she thought, stumbling up the hatchway ladder.

* * *

Governor Muraviev studied the faces of the four Americans standing in front of his desk. He had just finished questioning them for the past hour and now Andrei Leonov was giving his testimony. In particular his gaze rested on the proud defiant expression of Captain O’Connell. He was a dangerous looking man and he remembered how *Madame* Volodina said the captain was devious and greedy and not to be trusted.

Somehow her words didn’t quite ring true with the open manner in which the captain had spoken with him, answering all his questions with apparently honest answers while looking him directly in the eyes instead of shifting his gaze like a man with something to hide. *Rather a handsome devil, too*, he thought, *with the charisma of a ladies’ man*. No wonder Volodin was eager to have him hanged after spending so much time with his wife before they were married.

Muraviev looked at the first officer, Ethan Campbell. A cripple, he'd noticed, seeing the man limp in on a wooden leg. But he sensed a strength and integrity about the big Scotsman and an aura of competent leadership that he wished he had in more of his own naval officers. He was the man married to *Madame* Volodina's Russian maid, he'd heard.

The second officer, Jake O'Riley, had the sullen angry look of a common seaman except for his carroty orange hair and freckled face which made it hard to take his seething temper seriously. Yet, Muraviev recognized the glint of hatred in the man's blue eyed gaze and knew he was not as comical as he appeared.

The third officer and supercargo, John Hill, was the nephew of the ship's owner, Thomas Hill. He had the elegant mannerisms and speech of an aristocrat, and it was difficult for Muraviev to imagine the man spending two years of captivity with the Nootka Indians and surviving that dreadful experience as well as he had. Obviously, Hill was made of an inner strength as hard as nails.

"And so, Your Excellency," continued Andrei Leonov in English, "while Captain O'Connell and Mr. Campbell and Mr. O'Riley were a part of the crew of the *Eastern Wind*, only Mr. Campbell was actually an officer, the chief mate. The captain, Edward Smythe, and the third officer, Ralph Parsons, were both killed by the Nootkas."

"And who was the responsible for the decision to trade arms to the Nootkas, *Monsieur* Leonov?" Muraviev asked the *Creole*.

The stocky black haired man hesitated before answering. He was an office supervisor in one of the warehouses, and was dressed appropriately for his position in a dark green frock coat, tan trousers with an olive green waistcoat, and a black-green visor.

"Captain Edward Smythe, Your Excellency."

"Anyone else, such as the first officer Campbell here?"

Leonov glanced at Ethan and was about to answer when Sean said, "As supercargo, Leonov, you were also responsible for what was traded to the natives. In fact, that was your primary job, keeping control of the trade goods, and knowing when and which items the natives wished."

Leonov's dark swarthy face blanched as Muraviev shot him an appraising stare. "Is this true, *Monsieur* Leonov?"

"*Da*, Your Excellency," Leonov blurted nervously, "except the final decision was always Captain Smythe's, not mine or Mr. Campbell's, especially if arms were considered as trade goods."

Muraviev wiped the perspiration off his forehead, his wig smothering his scalp like a hot itchy blanket. The brick stove radiated heat in the corner, adding to the already stuffy atmosphere in the crowded room. Between the American prisoners and himself and Leonov, the presence of five of his naval officers along with several guards, made his office swelter with the suffocating heat of a blacksmith's shop.

He could see by one glance at his own officers that they were bitterly disappointed in Andrei Leonov's testimony. The *Creole* had said nothing incriminating against any of the Americans. In fact, he had almost incriminated himself by confessing as supercargo for the *Eastern Wind*, he had also taken part in trading guns to the natives.

However, there still remained the problem of Ethan Campbell. Because he had been the first officer of the *Eastern Wind*, he was still considered a wanted criminal by the Imperial Crown and thus, subject to the most severe punishment Muraviev could invoke. Yet, the man was a cripple and Muraviev had no taste for hanging or whipping a man with a wooden leg unless he was guilty of a foul deed such as murder. And Ethan Campbell was no murderer.

He sighed and mopped his brow again, feeling the stare of every man in the room, waiting for him to pass judgment. Clearing his throat, he finally said, "Captain O'Connell, First Officer Ethan Campbell, Second Officer Jake O'Riley, and Third Officer John Hill of the American vessel, the *Sea Rose* out of Boston, I find all four of you guilty in committing the crime against the Imperial Crown of trading arms to the natives in Russian American waters. I also find First Officer Ethan Campbell guilty of an earlier crime, that of being an officer of the *Eastern Wind*, forbidden to ever return to Russian America."

Muraviev gave each man a grim look. "Gentlemen, I hereby sentence all four of you to six months in prison, with an extra six months for Chief Officer Ethan Campbell. Furthermore, the vessel the *Sea Rose* and all her cargo are now the property of the Imperial Crown. Your incarceration starts today, September 15. Guards, take them away."

None of the prisoners looked surprised. They'd all expected to be imprisoned at least through the winter months. But Ethan felt an extra measure of despair with his longer sentence, as he realized he would not be able to be with Anna when their child was born in the spring. He and Sean exchanged glances of mutual unhappiness.

It was going to be a very long miserable winter ahead for all of them.

* * *

The front parlor of the Volodins' house was brightly lit by a silver candelabrum containing three burning wax tapers placed on a mantel. The room was small by the standards of the nobility, but artfully decorated with green and gold upholstered sofas and chairs sitting by polished walnut tables. A Belgian brick stove at one end of the room gave off a comforting heat.

The glowing warmth in the room was in direct contrast with Dmitri's dark mood. He had been in a fury every since the meeting at the governor's office that morning.

"I can't believe His Excellency refused to order at least a whipping for the Yankee captain as punishment for what you endured on board his ship last year!" he told Tatiana, who was sitting in a plush armchair sipping amber colored tea out of a dainty floral china cup. "Even the *knout* is too good for the likes of him!"

A short time ago she would have agreed with him, but now her old antagonism against Captain O'Connell was fading after seeing the torment in Anna's eyes because she was facing the next year without her beloved Ethan. Tatiana looked at Dmitri, watching his rage contort his handsome features into a face that was almost ugly.

At the moment she wished it was her husband who was to be imprisoned for the next twelve months. Her high hopes at their wedding last spring had now turned into the frightening realization that she had married a man with a violent temper, a man she could never love. So far, he had not turned his anger upon her, but she lived with the fear that someday he might. As it was, his ardor in their bedchamber at night brought her more pain than pleasure, but perhaps, that was normal between husbands and wives. It was something she was eager to ask Anna when the time was right.

She sighed and said, "There is nothing more to be done about it, Dmitri. I'm sure spending the winter in the damp and drafty cells of the unheated prison will be punishment enough for him and his officers."

"Bah!" Dmitri said as he paced restlessly around the parlor. "I must find a way around His Excellency's authority and order the whipping myself."

"But wouldn't that get you in trouble?" she asked feeling alarmed, not for him, but for how his actions could affect her own position in town.

He saw the anxiety in her face and gave her a pompous smile. "I appreciate your wifely concern for me, Tatiana, but there's nothing for you to worry your beautiful head about. I always have everything under control." He stroked his blond mustache and suddenly eyed her in a lasciviousness manner. "It's late, my dear. Time for us to retire. Why don't you fetch your new maid to prepare you for bed?"

"She was so exhausted after all the emotional proceedings of the day that I sent her to bed already. Remember, I've told you that Anna's more like a companion to me than just an ordinary maid. She has always helped me through the hardships we've experienced together, and now it's my turn to help her."

Tatiana had put Anna in a small room with Keeah off the kitchen, as far from her and Dmitri's upstairs bedchamber as possible. After spending the day introducing Anna to the other household servants and her new responsibilities, they had managed to spend only a half hour alone. Anna had not been able to stop yawning and she looked so close to tears, Tatiana finally bid her goodnight.

Dmitri frowned in irritation. "I don't care what she has done for you in the past," he said coldly. "As long as she lives with us, I expect her to work as hard as our other servants."

"Yes, Dmitri."

Tatiana pretended to agree with him, but she knew she would not force Anna to do little other than light lady's maid duties. There was something different about Anna, she'd noticed, a certain air of fragility as if she wasn't well. She'd eaten practically nothing since setting foot in the house, and Tatiana was very concerned about her. Anna must be worried sick about Ethan. Even she was sincerely distressed that Ethan was sentenced to a year in prison. Of all the men on the *Sea Rose*, the only man she held no grudge against was the first mate. During her stay on board, he had always behaved towards her with politeness and respect.

Otherwise, Tatiana was looking forward to having Anna with her to relieve the monotony of her days. As *Madame* Volodina there was little or nothing for her to do. Dmitri's position of assistant governor entitled them to more servants than they needed. The cook and housekeeper, Helena, kept the small household running smoothly as she oversaw the chores of the native girls, Keeah and Maria.

This past summer, especially when Dmitri was gone on patrol, Tatiana's daily routine was the same as the other officers' wives. They slept in late each morning, then spent the afternoon together either in her own house, or at the Governor's residence, drinking enormous amounts of tea, embroidering, and gossiping.

Tatiana thought their company extremely boring. The ladies' chief concerns were what to eat, what to wear, and who knew the most scandals. They enjoyed berating the women of the lower ranks, complaining how they allowed their children to run around half-naked and unwashed, even in the rain. Then when the children returned home, the mothers were too lazy to take off their wet clothing. Many of the children sickened afterwards.

In contrast, the few young children of the nobility were well cared for. They had a French governess, a Russian tutor, and Father Sokolov to teach them their catechism. But Tatiana found their presence irritating. The Pushkin children were a handful. Twelve-year-old Anastasia was as snooty as her mother, Elizabeth. Nikolai was a whining overweight child who continually pestered his inebriated mother for attention. Only Fedor Pushkin ever brought a smile to her face. He was a mischievous imp who reminded her a bit of her young English cousins, Henry and William.

The ladies of the nobility complained endlessly about how New Archangel had little entertainment to offer. Once the past summer when the weather permitted, they had taken a boat excursion on Sitka Sound, and another time had a picnic at Indian River, until the biting mosquitoes drove them back to town. Tatiana was warned that in winter there was even less to do. They spent the dark afternoons and evenings putting on mimes and pageants, and dancing and visiting with each other. The most exciting thing to do was to build an ice mountain out at Swan Lake.

Life was not much better for the officers and their men. If not on duty, there was only gambling, billiards, and drinking. The Company dispensed up to twelve bottles of strong spirits per month to each ranking officer. Irina Trotskaya once remarked maliciously behind Elizabeth's back, that in the Pushkin household, much of the liquor ended up in her own cups, starting with her breakfast tea.

"If you have dismissed your maid already," said Dmitri breaking into her thoughts, "then I shall have the pleasure of undressing you tonight."

"Yes, Dmitri."

* * *

The next morning Anna awoke, feeling disoriented at first. She had been so used to the rocking motion of the ship, the creaking of the timbers, and the slap of waves against the hull when she slept, that the stillness of her bed and the sound of barking dogs in the distance was as if she had slipped back in time to Furstenau.

She sat up and flung the quilt aside and slid out of the narrow bed, noticing that Keeah's bed on the opposite wall was empty. The girl must have risen very early and left quietly so as not to wake her.

The room wasn't much to look at. It had bare white walls, a hardwood floor, and meager furnishings consisting of an old wooden chest of drawers and a chipped porcelain jug and basin for washing. One small window covered in oilcloth allowed some light to enter. It was as simple and plain as a ship's cabin, but at least it was clean and fairly warm. She could feel the heat from the kitchen through the wall.

Compared to Ethan and the rest of the men languishing in the filthy cold prison cells, her room was the lap of luxury. A sudden depression sank down upon her at the thought. She closed her eyes and tried to pray, but the words wouldn't come. Had God forsaken her, or had she forsaken Him by her feelings of despair and anxiety, robbing her of her usual inner peace, she wondered sadly.

She took a deep breath as she decided to try and forget about her problems for awhile. It was time to begin her duties as Tatiana's maid. She quickly washed, dressed, and braided and pinned her hair up under her scarf. Then she went into the kitchen and asked Helena for a mug of honey sweetened tea and a dry biscuit to relieve her morning sickness. The large round-faced woman had a gruff manner and a bosom like the prow of a ship, but her eyes were kind.

"That's not enough food to keep a kitten alive," she said with disapproval.

Anna almost told her she was with child and could hardly bear to look upon even that much food, but instead she smiled and said, "I'll eat more later, Helena. Right now I should prepare the mistress's breakfast tray."

"*Madame* doesn't usually eat much before noon."

"She will today. She and I have much catching up to do after all the time we've been apart. Is the Lieutenant still at home?"

Helena gave a snort of disbelief at the thought of the mistress eating breakfast then said, "No, he's always up at the crack of dawn and off to his ship or the castle to work with the governor."

Anna felt relieved knowing she wouldn't have to see Lieutenant Volodin this morning. She preferred to keep out of the man's way as much as possible. Helena helped her arrange a tray with a pastry, a boiled egg, and a thick slice of ham that the cook fried quickly in a pan on the brick cook stove, made from a unique Finnish and Russian design. Anna thought it a marvel. The stove was built with a central fire tube which circulated superheated air and gases to the exterior brick shell. After the wood was burned, dampers to the flue were closed and the stove radiated heat for cooking and warmth for twelve to twenty-four hours. Her mama would have loved it.

"If *Madame* won't eat any of this food, you eat it, Anna," said Helena with a slight smile, showing a gap between her two front teeth. "You look as if a slight breeze would knock you over. I'll send one of the girls up with the samovar shortly."

Anna thanked her and carefully balanced the tray of food as she walked upstairs and entered the bedchamber. It was a spacious well furnished room with a window facing east to the mountains. After setting the tray on the nightstand, Anna opened the curtains and let the sun stream in, always a rare sight in New Archangel. The sunlight forced Tatiana to open her eyes and she groaned as she struggled upright to see who had dared invade her bedchamber when she was still asleep.

"Who is it? Keeah, is that you?"

"Good morning, *Madame*. I trust you slept well?"

Tatiana rubbed the remains of sleep from her eyes and laughed slightly. "Anna, you don't have to be so formal with me. And no, I didn't sleep well. How about you?"

"I barely slept a wink."

"Yes, I can see how tired you look. You should've stayed abed longer." Tatiana noticed the dark shadows under Anna's eyes and the pinched expression on her thin pale face.

"I brought you some breakfast."

Tatiana glanced at the food and grimaced. "I'm not hungry yet."

Someone rapped lightly on her door and the native girl, Keeah, stepped in with the steaming samovar. She placed it carefully on a small table near the window. Anna looked at her. The girl was a *Kolosh*, or a Tlingit, as Ethan would have called her. She looked to be about sixteen and had shiny black hair tied back with a ribbon. She had a nice slender figure and Anna thought she would be pretty if it wasn't for the ugly disfigurement of her lower lip.

Keeah smiled at them shyly then quickly left before Anna could initiate a conversation.

Anna turned to Tatiana. "Whatever happened to Keeah's mouth?"

"The *Kolosh* have a custom when a girl reaches puberty, a hole is cut into her lower lip to insert a *kaluga,* or a lip plug," said Tatiana, shuddering. "Eventually, a labret six inches in diameter is inserted. This ornament is believed to honor and beautify the girl. Their Indian slaves, for instance, never have the right to adornments like that.

"Thankfully, since they moved here from their village, Keeah and other young *Kolosh* servant girls like her are not allowed to wear their lip plugs. Now her lip is scarred and she cannot wear one even if she wanted to."

"Do you think Keeah is bothered by having to give up her native custom?" asked Anna.

She remembered Ethan mentioning something about native women with strangely stretched lips among the Tlingits when they were trading with them a few weeks earlier.

Tatiana shrugged. "Who cares if they are? She and the other *Kolosh* servant girls should be grateful for their work here. Most of them were traded to us because their parents died, which left them in the care of other relatives who did not want them.

"For example, I was told that Keeah's parents were killed by Russians in 1805 when New Archangel was retaken after the massacre. She was only a tiny babe then and her uncle and aunt raised her. Four years ago when she was twelve, they traded her for some cloth and beads."

Anna felt a sudden compassion for the girl, but she also wondered how Keeah truly felt about living with the people who had killed her parents. Ethan once said the Tlingits hated all Russians and were not to be trusted.

"Why do you think the Russians allow such a large number of the Tlingits, I mean the *Kolosh*, to camp so close to New Archangel?"

"Dmitri says it is Governor Muraviev's idea to allow any *Kolosh* who wishes, to build a large camp close to the fort. He believes he can have much better control of them when they have their wives, children, and possessions all under the reach of the cannons. This way he can more easily discover any evil intentions they might have."

She paused. "But the best way of obtaining knowledge of their actions is to encourage the intermixing of the Russians with the *Kolosh* women."

Anna looked startled and Tatiana laughed lightly.

"There is a shortage of true Russian women here. The sailors and *promyshlenniki* have little choice except to marry an Aleut, *Kolosh* or *Creole* woman. In the past, because of the Russians' relationships with the *Kolosh* women, the fort has had fair warnings of attack. Dmitri says the *Kolosh* are a proud, treacherous war-loving people and we have by no means conquered them as we have the Aleuts. He's warned me to not let the apparent docility of maids like Keeah fool me."

Anna handed Tatiana a cup of tea. "But Keeah seems so meek natured," she said.

"She has been so far," Tatiana agreed, taking a small sip. "Dmitri says that the *Creole*s, the half Aleuts and half Russians, are more irritable and high strung than the *Kolosh*." *Like Marya, my wild little half-sister*, she thought.

"I know so little about *Creole*s," said Anna, remembering how strict the Mennonites were about never marrying outside their own people. A *Creole* in Furstenau would be as common as an alien from the moon.

"Basically, the *Creole*s in New Archangel have formed a class of their own, which is similar to that of the *meshchanstvo* (lower middle class) of Russia. Dmitri says our *Creole*s here have little to complain about. They are exempt from taxes. They are raised and educated at the Company's expense, and given all the necessities for their households and families. The only thing asked of them, is that they remain in the Company employment for ten years. After that they are free to do as they please.

"Dmitri says that the *Creole*s try to avoid the occupations of hunting and trapping unless they are given authority over the natives, because they are ashamed of their native descents. Yet, I've also been told some of them are intelligent and make resourceful citizens. Many work in the Company offices, and if they die while employed, their families receive a yearly pension."

Tatiana remembered that after her father's death, as an orphan of a Company employee, she was offered the pension. She had dismissed it as mere pittance but in a moment of generosity, told Dmitri they should give it to Marya.

He had refused, saying, "The pension is only for legitimate children, so she is not entitled to receive it."

"Then what will she live on?" Tatiana had asked.

"She's not our concern," Dmitri answered firmly, "and I do not wish to ever hear the girl's name again."

Tatiana knew it was a great humiliation to him that his aristocratic wife should have a half-breed sister.

"Anna," she said hesitantly, "I need to ask you a personal question."

Anna gave her a smile. "Ask. I have little to hide," she added, thinking of the child growing inside her.

Tatiana's creamy complexion darkened in a blush as she said, "Does--does Ethan hurt you when you and he are in bed at night and he, well, you know..." Her voice trailed off in embarrassment.

Anna's cheeks turned a bit pink. "Only the first time, but never after that. He is a very kind gentle man."

It was then that Anna noticed how puffy Tatiana's lips were and the faint purple bruising on her upper arms. Were there more bruises concealed under her nightgown, she wondered with concern.

"Has your husband harmed you?"

"Oh, not on purpose," Tatiana said quickly, too quickly. "I think he just forgets sometimes how delicate a woman is made." She glanced towards the window. "Look, it's a rare dry day. After I eat and you help me dress, I would like to show you the town, Anna."

Anna sensed there was more Tatiana was not telling her, or could not tell her. She remembered how uncomfortable she felt in Lieutenant Volodin's presence, as if the man was possessed by some dark malignant force. Poor Tatiana, she thought, feeling a rush of pity. With her father dead, who was able to protect her from an abusive husband?

"That sounds wonderful. I would like to take a walk later."

Early in the afternoon they set out, wrapped warmly in their hooded cloaks and wearing fur-lined boots and gloves. Although the sun shone brightly, there was a cold breeze blowing off the water as the two women and the maid Keeah accompanied them.

Anna's spirits rose immediately after leaving the house, but then plummeted when they passed under the shadow of the hill, where half way up the prison was perched. She immediately thought of Ethan and wondered how he and the others fared. She worried that he might catch a cold or worse, the lung disease so rampant in this cold damp climate. What was he eating? Did he have enough blankets to keep himself reasonably warm? And what was going to happen to Robby, Samuel, Wang Li, and the rest of the crew?

"Tatiana," she said, "does your husband know what the governor plans to do with all of the Americans in the prison?"

"Dmitri told me last night that the governor intends on releasing the common sailors as soon as they settle down and behave themselves. The town is growing and needs the labor of strong men. They will be given work to do on the several large buildings under construction right now, the two-story Company Office House, a school for the Russian and *Creole* children, a hospital, and a two-story house for Father Sokolov near the church. The governor also plans to build a meteorological observatory on nearby Yaponsky Island, and bath houses for us of the aristocracy to enjoy at the Mineral Hot Springs, about ten *versts* outside New Archangel."

At least the crew will all be fed and kept busy, Anna thought, as Tatiana pointed out the various buildings. Already completed were the two-storied married officers building and a three-storied timber barracks for the garrison troops, which were made up of Siberian infantry regiments and sailors from the Navy. There were also several shops and stores, a foul smelling fur tannery, a bakery, a foundry, a flour mill, ropery, fish stores, and coal sheds. A large shipyard was under construction, so New Archangel could soon build its own vessels. Further away from the businesses were many small houses, which were homes for the Russian workmen and their families. One belonged to the cook Helena and her husband and their children.

"Most of the large buildings have roofs covered in red-painted iron," commented Anna. "But why are they so flat? You'd think with all the rain you have here, the roofs should be steeper."

"Dmitri said the governor recently received a notice from the Company Main Office in Saint Petersburg about the roofs here in New Archangel," said Tatiana. "They want him to build flatter roofs, because the steep roofs are more liable to destruction from the strong gales we often have."

She laughed slightly. "But you are right, Anna. Dmitri says the flat roofs do not drain the rainwater as well. Still, we must do as they order."

"Is there a problem with rats in the town?" Anna asked, noticing all the stray dogs roaming about, but she hadn't seen any cats.

Tatiana nodded. "Rats are such a problem that Dmitri said the governor had to ask for thousands of pounds of flattened lead to sheath all the lower walls and floors of the warehouses to repel them. I suggested to him that we import more cats for the town, but he didn't take kindly to it. He doesn't like cats."

"Helena say she see rat in the pantry the other day," said Keeah, who had been listening to their conversation. "She say you ask *Madame* Kornilova for some kittens from the big house soon. They have a new litter."

"It would be nice to have some kittens around," said Anna, as she noticed the magnificent view spread out before them.

The mountains glistened in the sunshine, their jagged peaks thrusting into the clear blue sky like sentinels guarding the valley of New Archangel from the bitter temperatures of the Arctic Circle. These mountains and the mountain range of Saint Elias to the north were the partition between the treeless north and the icy Bering Sea, and the wooded coast and the milder southern ocean.

The mountains were the sole reason for New Archangel's mild climate, and they were the most beautiful sight Anna had seen since coming here. She sighed, feeling guilty at enjoying the view when Ethan and the others were trapped in the ugly confines of prison.

The three women soon reached a curving sandy beach called Crescent Beach. Bordering the beach were dozens of vegetable gardens belonging to the Company and private citizens.

At the end of the beach stood the large rock promontory named "Baranov's stone." It overlooked the channel islands, and Anna could see why this spot was the old governor's favorite place to meditate.

They watched as a number of Aleut men dressed in their gut skin parkas and caps propelled their *baidarkas* skillfully through the choppy blue waters of the harbor. The paddles and the bows of their boats were richly ornamented. As they came closer to shore, Anna could see their Mongol featured faces, the narrow black eyes, low foreheads, high cheekbones, and straight stiff black hair.

"Ethan once told me that the Russians destroyed the Aleuts as a race by slaughtering them, then enslaving them. Is that true?"

Before Tatiana could answer, Keeah surprised both of them by saying in a sad voice, "*Da*, that is true. My people say that in the beginning when the Russians first come, thousands of Aleuts were killed by the *promyshlenniki* on Kodiak and Unalaska."

Tatiana frowned at Keeah, then turned to Anna and said, "But now, Anna, you can see for yourself how content the Aleuts are in New Archangel. They have been converted to Christianity and I've seen these past months how almost all of the Aleuts eagerly perform church duties. They buy candles and frankincense for the services and take part in the singing. They seem to be a meek obedient people who rarely quarrel with anyone or among themselves. Instead they share their food and worldly goods with each other, even to the point of their own impoverishment."

She gave Anna a quick smile. "Don't they sound as religious as your own Mennonite people, Anna?"

"Yes, they do," she had to agree, thinking that if Tatiana was right, the life and faith of the Christian Aleuts were the most impressive examples of Christianity she'd ever heard of.

Leaving the beach they came to the stockade walls, about twenty-five feet high. Next to one of the blockhouses, the palisade was broken by a portcullis gate which led to the Indian marketplace within the walls. An elevated gun battery stood nearby, a favorite sightseeing point for visitors curious about the doings of the *Kolosh* or the Aleuts. As they climbed up to it, the two soldiers on duty saluted the women respectfully.

Tatiana gestured beyond the *Kolosh* village to a cluster of Aleut dwellings. "The two groups of natives live so close together, Dmitri says it indicates how well our relations are with the *Kolosh* at this time."

Anna could see the many families working busily around their small houses, drying fish and making their crafts, which Keeah said were quite beautiful. She seemed to lose her shyness even more as she explained, "They make wooden hats decorated with sea lion bristles, colored stones, and feathers. They also make amulets, charms, masks, baskets, parkas, and festive dance costumes."

As most of the natives and the Russians themselves, the Aleuts were great lovers of bathing. Keeah pointed out the hot steam baths which were located at each house.

"Their homes are clean and neat inside," she said, "and they have good family life. Like my people, the Tlingit, the men teach the little boys to hunt, trap, and provide food for the family, and the little girls help their mothers with the housework and drying fish."

"Ethan once told me that the Aleuts are called the Cossacks of the Sea, because they are the most skillful of sea hunters," said Anna. "While they are bobbing up and down on the choppy ocean in their lightweight *baidarkas*, an Aleut takes only a few seconds to aim and throw his harpoon before his prey can get away by diving beneath the water.'

"They also catch most of the fish we eat," said Tatiana, staring intently at the Aleut village with a peculiar expression.

Anna glanced at her and wondered if she was looking for someone in particular. She opened her mouth to ask when a commotion at the gate of the palisades caught their attention.

A large group of *Kolosh* Indians were approaching the gate and singing loudly in ceremonial voices. Anna climbed down a few stairs to obtain a better view, with Tatiana and Keeah quickly following her.

"During the day the gate is left open," said Tatiana, "so the *Kolosh* from the village outside the palisade can come into New Archangel to trade. But they must leave before nightfall."

Keeah nodded toward the group of Indians. "They come from my village on Chatham Strait."

"That is the *Kolosh*'s main settlement," Tatiana explained to Anna. "It is where their chief, Dichatin, moved his people after they were forced out of New Archangel in 1805. I understand their village is placed on a steep cliff which hangs several hundred feet above the water. They have built an earth wall around their houses, so it is actually a hidden fort and cannot be seen by an approaching ship."

"What are they here for?" Anna asked, nervously eyeing the man who looked to be the leader of the group. He spoke forcefully in a strange mixture of Russian and Indian dialect.

"They come to visit relatives and trade fresh game for cloth, rice, and other goods," Tatiana answered. "The chief is beginning an oration about friendship, trying to persuade us of their honorable intentions."

"Some of them are wrapped in beautiful blankets." Anna stared appreciatively at their white woolen blankets embroidered with square figures and fringed in black and yellow tassels.

"Only the wealthiest *Kolosh* have those," said Tatiana. "They are made of the wool of wild sheep, or mountain goats, and are as soft as Spanish merino. The *Kolosh* are as talented with their hands as the Aleuts."

Feeling a deep sadness, Keeah gazed at her people, standing about a hundred yards away. She knew her rightful place was with them, but they did not want her anymore. Without marriage to a *Kolosh* man, her future held only two possibilities, a lifetime of servitude to the Russians, or becoming some crude *promyshlennik*'s woman and the mother of his half-breeds brats.

Anna saw the longing flicker across the *Kolosh* maid's face. She felt a moment of compassion for her, then heard the urgency of Tatiana's voice, "Come, Anna, we must return to the house before we are seen. For all their offers of friendship, they can be quite hostile. We dare not trust them."

They began to walk away, but not before their quick movement caught the attention of the *Kolosh* chief. He ceased his speech and stared intently at the women, especially at Keeah, who he recognized from his village. He saw the subservient manner in which she meekly followed the Russian women. He shot her a scowl of disapproval then turned away, dismissing her as a slave.

By this time a crowd of local *Kolosh*, Aleuts, and *promyshlenniki* had gathered to trade with the newly arrived *Kolosh*. Tatiana hastened past them, looking at their many faces, wondering if Marya was among the group of people. As much as she'd tried the past months, she hadn't been able to stop thinking about her half-sister and what had become of her. She hadn't told Anna yet about her. She was afraid if Anna found out that her father had a native mistress, his noble image would be tarnished.

Their quick pace soon exhausted Anna. Between the lack of sleep, the nausea always gnawing at the pit of her stomach, and the recent trauma of the past two days, Anna began to feel quite weak and dizzy. As they passed the harbor, she stopped to catch her breath. She could see the familiar lines of the *Sea Rose* a few hundred yards out, riding high and empty at anchor.

The ship was as imprisoned as her captain and crew and as eager to be free.

Suddenly her legs lost all their strength and she swayed. Tatiana grabbed her arm. "You look ill, Anna," she said with concern.

"I am not ill." She paused then added, "But I am with child."

* * *

Marya had watched Tatiana looking for her in the crowd. The proud tilt of her half-sister's head as she searched the native faces brought back memories of the callous and arrogant manner in which Tatiana had treated her when their father died. It was the same haughty attitude of the Russian officers and their ladies towards her kind. With pity she saw the Tlingit maid, Keeah, and knew her life to be one of humiliation and drudgery, continually enduring Tatiana's imperious orders.

"Come, Marya," said Andrei at her side. "Your Uncle Sergei invited me to dinner at his house, and we mustn't be late."

Nodding in agreement, Marya followed the man who was soon to be her husband. By marrying him, she knew she was trading one type of subservience for another. But with her father dead, and her uncle anxious to be rid of another mouth to feed in his large household, she had no other choice.

Andrei Leonov was almost twice her age, about thirty years old, but according to her aunt, his maturity only made him more responsible, a better husband. Marya wished she loved him. It would make the marriage a joy to look forward to, instead of something she dreaded.

Once she had mentioned this to her Aunt Tugidaq. The weary-faced woman had cackled, “Love? A father loves his sons. A mother loves her daughters. But a wife obeys her husband, and he takes care of her. That is all there is between a man and a woman.”

It was true there was little affection to be seen between her uncle and aunt, or among the other couples she knew in their village. But she had grown up with the romantic image of her own parents, the noble Russian officer falling in love with the shy Aleut princess after saving her from a bunch of drunken *promyshlenniki*.

Her mother, Sonya, had told her the story many times. In 1804 when she was seventeen, living on Kodiak Island as the daughter of an Aleut chief, she met Captain-Lieutenant Nikolas Bolkonsky. He was the commanding officer of an expedition of Russians to Kodiak. After rescuing the pretty, but terrified young girl from the fur hunters who killed her parents, Nikolas had felt a strong sense of compassion. He gave her the Christian name of Sonya, and brought her and her little orphaned brother, whom he named Sergei, back to New Archangel. He had a small house built for them and she became his mistress. Marya was born nine months later.

She always imagined someday she would fall in love with a dashing young Russian officer, one as handsome and kind as her father. Instead she had to settle for a *Creole* man.

She had recently sought Father Sokolov’s advice about the marriage. The priest had been a daily visitor at her father’s bedside the weeks before he died, talking to him about preparing his soul for eternity. Her father had never seemed a religious man, but as his life neared its end, he asked Marya to read passages of the Holy Scriptures to him. His favorite was the Twenty-third Psalm. The words brought him comfort in the dark days of his approaching death.

As she watched him during that time, she was reminded of her mother, who also turned to that very same Psalm in the Bible. Marya had felt much bitterness after her mother’s death. But when her father died, it occurred to her that perhaps the two of them were now in heaven together. Then the question struck her, would she be there with them someday after she died?

To make certain, she attended Sunday Mass diligently, and had become devoted to Father Sokolov. He was the one who counseled her to marry Andrei Leonov.

“It was your father’s wish to see both of his daughters married well, Marya,” he said kindly. “Although Andrei doesn’t attend church regularly, I believe he was baptized in the faith as an infant. Perhaps, with your influence, he will find his way back to God.”

Marya didn't care much about Andrei's soul, but she was very concerned about her own. After her father died she had taken his Bible, knowing that all his possessions legally belonged to Tatiana, his legitimate daughter. At the time, she only wanted something of his to remember him by. She had hid it away, feeling guilty since stealing anything, even a Bible, was a sin.

Last Sunday she had gone to see Father Sokolov again, saying, "I have a confession to make, Father. I have taken something that doesn't belong to me."

The priest had gazed down at her and said gently, "If you can, my daughter, you must return it to the owner and ask for forgiveness."

Now as she and Andrei walked towards the Aleut village, Marya agonized over having to bring the Bible back to Tatiana. Most likely, her sister didn't know it existed. But that wasn't the point. She had to obey Father Sokolov, and cleanse her conscience of this sin.

Beside her, Andrei was oblivious to her inner conflict. He considered himself the luckiest man in the world. After avoiding his attempts at courtship the past year, the lovely Marya had finally accepted his proposal of marriage. Her change in attitude towards him had happened after her father's death. Whatever the reason, it made no difference to him.

By Christmas she would be his wife, installed in his small house. They would have a good life with many children. He had a respectable position as overseer in one of the Company's warehouses, where he was responsible for the collection and storage of bales of skins and furs from the Aleuts and *promyshlenniki*. Except for that uncomfortable meeting in the governor's office the day before, when he'd feared he might be going to prison along with the Americans, his life was in perfect order.

He smiled down at her, his serious features softening. If only he could dispel the haunting sadness from her beautiful eyes. Ever since her father sickened and died, she rarely smiled. He wondered if that was because she spent so much time with that priest. She had become almost as religious as her mother. After they were married, he would forbid her to attend church. He had no patience for priests or the white man's religion.

CHAPTER TWENTY

The small prison cell held four narrow wooden cots filled with musty flea ridden straw pallets and a stinking slop pail. Slimy moisture constantly dripped down the wooden walls, turning the dirt floor into filthy slick ooze. Up high on the outside wall, there was a tiny barred window, which admitted a faint light during the day. It was how Sean knew if it was day or night. Not that it mattered to any of them anymore.

Their main focus in life was not the passage of time. He and John and Ethan and Jake shivered on their cots, each wrapped in a thin blanket, trying to stay warm, an impossible feat in the cold dank cell. Ethan coughed a harsh sound deep in his chest which sounded ominous.

If they weren't released soon, or housed in a warm dry place, Sean figured the Russian governor might lose all of his prisoners before winter's end. John and Jake were also coughing and just this morning, Sean had awakened to a raw throat and a tight painful feeling in his own chest whenever he breathed deeply.

A rat squeaked in the corner, shuffling about in the dirt, looking for any crumbs from their usual dinner, some boiled cabbage and moldy bread. Once a week, probably on Sunday, they were given two salted *Herr*ings each. At least there was plenty of water to drink, but it sat in a dirty bucket, with a coating of greenish scum on top. They drank it anyway.

John was muttering in a feverish dream, calling out for Abigail then lapsing into a few words of Nootka, as if he was dreaming of his Indian wife who by now had long forgotten him.

When Sean fell asleep he dreamed of sailing the *Sea Rose*, or of Anna. When he was awake he thought about her, and wondered how she fared. He knew Ethan was tormented by the same thoughts. He kept saying how he'd failed as a husband to take care of her. The thought of her having their child among strangers while he was still in prison drove him into deep despair. He spent much of his time muttering prayers to God.

At least the rest of the crew had been released weeks ago. Only the four of them were left in the prison. Some time past Gregory Jones had managed to bribe the guard with a bottle of vodka to allow him a brief visit, but he couldn't come any closer than speaking through the slot in the thick wooden door.

Jones had said that all the crew was working in the town, helping in the construction of several buildings except for Wang Li, who was cooking in the bakery. Even Robby was learning how to pound nails, hoist beams, and saw timber. And at night they were housed in a type of barracks.

"'Tis not such a bad life, Cap'n. We git Sundays off, an' we earn enough to put food in our bellies an' have our rum in the evenin.' Sometimes one of us gets in a fight with one of them feisty *Creole*s or one of them dirty *promyshlennik*s. They stay clear of me, though. 'Tis Robby I'm always lookin' out fer. The lad's got a temper of his own lately."

"Do ye ever see or hear of Anna?" Ethan had asked eagerly.

"I heard yer wife is lady's maid to Missus Volodin, but I ain't seen her. 'Tis rainin' everyday an' the ladies don't leave their houses much, except to hobnob up at the Guvnor's castle. An' that ain't for the likes of us Yankees."

The guard had ordered Jones to leave then, and they'd not had another visitor since. Now Sean reckoned it must November already, but he wasn't sure. That meant they'd spent almost two months in this hellhole with four more months to go, except for Ethan, who had ten more.

His friend coughed again, then choked as he started coughing flecks of bloody spittle down his tangled dark red beard now streaked with gray. Sean looked at him grimly. He saw the feverish glitter in Ethan's eyes and the flush on his face. The man was very sick. He needed to see a doctor, or at the very least, be moved to a warmer drier cell, if there was such a thing in this cursed Russian prison. He rolled off his cot and walked to the door, keeping himself wrapped in the thin moth-eaten blanket.

"Guard," he called out in Russian, rapping on the thick heavy wood, "we need a doctor in here. We've got a sick man!"

There was no answer, so Sean pounded the door harder and yelled. Finally the soldier came, a big burly man with a thick black beard and a ruddy face like a meaty hog. He opened the slot in the door and peered through at Sean.

When Sean repeated his demands, the guard laughed mockingly, "*Nyet*, *Nyet*, Yankee!"

His breath wafted through the opening, reeking of vodka and onions. He closed the hole and turned away from the door, still laughing drunkenly.

"Ain't no use, Cap'n," said Jake weakly, his blue eyes dulled and sunken into his pale freckled face. "Them Russkies don't care if we live or die."

Sean knew he was right. With frustration and anger boiling inside him, he slammed his fist against the door, splitting his knuckles. He swore loudly and hit it again and again, wishing the door was the guard's ugly face. It was only when he felt the pain and the blood dripping from his hand that he finally stopped.

Wearily, he returned to his bunk, feeling a black depression sinking down upon him. By the time their sentences were up next spring, he wondered if they would still be alive, and if so, would they be sane?

* * *

At the same time, in early November, Dmitri sailed away in the *Buldakov* on a routine patrol of the inland waters along the coast. The night before he left they quarreled about Anna.

"She doesn't do much of anything around here except fix your hair and pick out what gown you should wear!" he complained.

"That is what a proper lady's maid is supposed to do, Dmitri," Tatiana said, feeling worried about her husband's recently increasing hostility towards Anna. Was it because he was jealous of all the time they spent together? Many evenings he would come home and find the two of them playing chess cozily by the stove or laughing together over some ladies' gossip.

"*Madame* Campbell is the wife of a Yankee criminal, and she should be treated as such. If I had my way, she would be locked up with the rest of them instead of being coddled in my own home!"

"But she is with child!" Tatiana gasped. "You cannot put her in the prison!"

Dmitri gave her a harsh laugh. "No, you're right. His Excellency would never allow it." He walked across the bedchamber and stood in front of her. She was already in her nightgown and ready for bed. Anna had left minutes ago after plaiting her hair into one long golden braid that snaked down her back. Her maid had brushed past her husband in the doorway as she left, murmuring goodnight, but refusing to curtsy to him. Anna's barely concealed dislike of Dmitri was what had set off his temper.

Now he grasped one of her delicate wrists and squeezed until she grimaced in pain. "Why aren't you with child, Tatiana? Do you have any idea how seeing your common little maid with a Yankee brat growing inside her while my own aristocratic wife is barren drives me insane?"

So that's what was really bothering him, she realized. He was just like his father; her only worth to him was for her to produce the next heir to the Volodins.

The thought angered her and she retorted without thinking, "The last thing I wish to do in this Godforsaken wilderness is have your baby!"

Her words shocked both herself and Dmitri. But he reacted first. With a curse, he slapped her across the mouth, splitting open her lower lip.

The droplets of blood on her lovely mouth horrified him. Instantly contrite, Dmitri fell to his knees, begging her to forgive him. "I will never hurt you again," he cried out. "I promise, Tatiana, my dearest."

Holding a lace embroidered handkerchief to her throbbing lip, she accepted his apologies, but in her heart, she felt a deep anger. The next morning after he carefully kissed her farewell, promising to return by Christmas, she had a brief vision of his ship being caught in one of the vicious storms around Cape Decision, the entrance to the inland Straits of the Alexander Archipelago islands, and never seen again.

The next ship to sail away was the *Suvorov*. Natasha cried and hugged Tatiana, much to her hidden disgust, while Captain-Lieutenant Chernyshov kindly assured her that he would deliver the sad news of her father's death personally to her uncle in Saint Petersburg. She thanked him for his consideration, although she doubted Uncle Vasily would take much time away from his new wife to mourn his younger brother's passing.

Doctor Behrs also left in the *Suvorov*, as his tour of duty was up. His departure left the town without a physician once again, a concern for Anna whenever she thought about the delivery of her baby, due to be born in early spring. It was her only worry so far. Since the daily nausea had finally disappeared, she was gaining weight and feeling quite healthy.

One morning she awoke noticing a light flutter deep inside her. The child was moving! It brought her a mixture of joy and sadness as she wished Ethan could be with her to feel his son's or daughter's first movements.

If only she could see him! She had tried to visit him once by first asking Tatiana for permission, but when Tatiana passed on her request to Dmitri, the lieutenant refused, saying the American officers were not allowed any visitors by the order of His Excellency.

Without giving up hope, Anna tried another way to communicate with him. She wrote Ethan a letter and sent Keeah to deliver it, but the prison commander just laughed in her face and threw the letter back at her. In despair, Anna realized she had no way of knowing how Ethan was, nor could he know how she was. It was the only dark cloud in an otherwise tolerable existence.

Their household soon acquired two more inhabitants, a couple of kittens, a male and a female. Anna found them adorable, and they quickly became her two shadows, following her everywhere, and even sleeping in her and Keeah's room at night. The Tlingit girl was in awe of the kittens since domestic cats were not found among her people. After watching their mischievous antics, from chasing a paper ball across the floor, to climbing curtains and racing so fast through the house, they sometimes couldn't stop until they bashed their heads against the wall, she declared the animals were touched by the spirits. She named the male, a black cat with golden yellow eyes, Raven, and the gray and white female, Otter.

* * *

November slid into December, another dark month of incessant cold rains and winds and streets full of thick black mire. Days went by when the sun never shone, not even for a moment. The wooden houses suffered from the constant moisture, and fires roared day and night in the brick stoves of each room in the house. As hot as they were, the steady heat could not completely dispel the high humidity.

One December morning the town's inhabitants awoke to a hard freeze. During the night the wind had shifted from the southeast to the northeast, and was blowing cold dry Arctic air over the coastal mountain ranges into New Archangel, freezing the muddy streets and bringing clear skies. It was a welcome change that brought a smile to the face of even the most dour citizen.

On this crisp winter day, Anna was helping Tatiana dress for the afternoon's habitual visit at the castle with the other ladies when Keeah announced a visitor.

"Who is it?" asked Tatiana with irritation, as Anna wound her thick golden hair into a plait behind her head. "I would rather not see anyone now, perhaps later."

"It is Marya Nikolayevna, *Madame*," said Keeah with a quick curtsy.

Anna glanced at the *Kolosh* maid. The two girls had developed a mutual understanding of one another in their service to Tatiana, and Anna could see at once that Keeah had lost her usual composure by the nervous way her black eyes darted to and fro. Whoever this visitor was, she was not someone their mistress expected.

Tatiana jerked her head away from Anna's fingers. "What in heaven's name does she want?"

When Keeah shook her head in an expression of ignorance, Anna asked, "Who is she?"

Tatiana hesitated then said, "She is my father's illegitimate daughter by his Aleut mistress. The woman died about a year before Papa did."

Anna's eyes widened in surprise as Tatiana briefly explained what little she knew about Marya, then added, "You can understand how humiliated and angry I felt, Anna, and betrayed. All those years as a child growing up, I thought of my father as the perfect man, mourning the loss of my mother just as I did. How stupid and naive of me to think he had remained faithful to my mother's memory when he was no different from any other ordinary man."

"But you have a sister," said Anna with a trace of excitement, "blood kin closer than your cousins, Mikael and Olga. You once told me you wished you had a brother or a sister. After the initial shock passed, weren't you anxious to become acquainted with her?"

"It wasn't as simple as that. The moment we met, we could not stand the sight of each other. Later, when I found out who she was, she had already moved back to her uncle's house in the Aleut village. Dmitri has forbidden me to have any contact with her."

Anna and Keeah exchanged glances, thinking the same thing. He would be furious to know Marya was here. They both were aware of his violent temper. A few weeks ago, the morning after he left on patrol duty, they'd noticed Tatiana had a swollen lip, and suspected Lieutenant

Volodin had hit her, though she explained it away as a slight mishap with the bedpost in the dark the night before. They would have to keep Marya's visit a secret.

"The girl had no say in her birth, *Madame*," Anna pointed out sensibly. "And it seems she has suffered much recently by losing both mother and father in a relatively short time."

Tatiana tilted her head to one side as she considered Anna's words then uttered a nervous sigh. "You are right as always, Anna."

Minutes later, she entered the downstairs parlor where Marya waited. Tatiana was wearing her best mourning gown, a black silk with white lace at the wrists and throat. A pair of gold and diamond earrings dangled from her ears, a gift from Dmitri for her eighteenth birthday last August. Dainty black slippers were on her feet, and a warm woolen shawl edged in soft mink was wrapped around her shoulders.

The *Creole* girl made a shabby comparison to Tatiana's glittering appearance. Her cloak was an odd patchwork of skins and furs, and her dress a threadbare gray woolen gown with a calico apron. On her feet was a pair of muddy black boots. But it was her face that Anna saw, an interesting mix of the high cheekbones of the Bolkonsky's and the large expressive eyes of the Aleuts. She was strikingly beautiful just like her half-sister.

"I've brought you our father's Bible," Marya said, clutching a black leather-bound book to her chest.

Tatiana's eyes narrowed. "I didn't know he had one."

She remembered the day she went through the contents of his trunks. They contained his clothing, uniforms, boots, hats, a handsomely carved scabbard and sword and a pearl-handled pistol. He had saved her letters, written in a childish scrawl, and a few books, but no Bible. She had been disappointed there was not one memento of her mother, Elizabeth, not even a letter she might have written to him.

There hadn't been any keepsakes from his affair with Marya's mother either, and for that, she was grateful. It had been appalling to realize that her illegitimate half-breed half-sister had a closer relationship to her father than she, his true daughter. At least he had left Marya nothing. Or so she thought.

"Did my father give you his Bible, Marya?" she asked, stressing the word, "my."

Her gaze fell as she said quietly, "No, *Madame*. I took it after he died."

Silence thundered throughout the room as Tatiana flushed in anger. "You mean you stole my father's Bible?"

Marya hung her head. "Yes, *Madame* Tatiana, and I beg your forgiveness. I know it was a bad thing to do. I have confessed my sin to Father Sokolov." She rushed forward and placed the large Bible on the table next to the silver candelabra. "You see it is not harmed."

Her anger dissolved slightly as Tatiana realized Marya was not the same hostile girl she had first met. There was a tranquility about her, a humbleness of manner that reminded her of Anna, of all people.

She picked up her father's Bible and noticed how well worn it looked, similar to Anna's Bible. Strange. Except for the last weeks of his life, she'd never thought of her father as religious. It was a heavy book and she rested it on her lap as she opened the cover and turned the pages at random, suddenly recalling her father's last words to her, telling her to read his Bible. She had forgotten all about it.

A small sealed envelope slid out of the Book of Esther, with her name written on the front in her father's handwriting. Tatiana looked at Marya. "Did you know this was inside?"

She shook her head and said, "After I took it, I put it away and never opened it once."

With trembling fingers, Tatiana opened the envelope then hesitated, knowing there were three pairs of curious eyes watching her. "Anna, serve Marya some tea, please. Keeah, you are dismissed for now. I will take this letter to my bedchamber."

As soon as she was upstairs, she unfolded the thick paper and read:

"My dearest daughter, Tatiana,

I expect your arrival any day now. I cannot tell you how much I am looking forward to seeing you again. If only I was feeling better. But I fear there is little time left for me in this world, and before I go, there is something I must confess.

First of all, you know how deeply I loved your mother, my beautiful Elizabeth. I love her still. There is no other woman I have ever loved as much. But a man becomes lonely without the woman he loves. Fifteen years ago I saved an Aleut girl from the promyshlenniki. I must confess that she became my mistress. Her Christian name was Sonya. She bore me a daughter, Marya Nikolayevna, who is now fourteen years of age.

I cannot tell you how much Sonya and Marya have eased my anguish over your mother's death these years. They have made life bearable again. More than bearable. They gave me life again.

I hope you will not despise me too much, but you must understand that I am not like my brother Vasily. He cares nothing for people, only for what wealth and power he can acquire. As hard as I tried, I could not be like him. Without someone to love, or love me, life is meaningless.

And now I must beg your forgiveness, Tatiana, for leaving you to be reared in a household where you were so unhappy. Yes, I was aware of the misery haunting your little face. I knew you wanted to sail away with me to Alaska. My heart broke anew each time I left you.

Many times I wished to bring you here to live. I know our life would not be as safe and luxurious, but we would have had each other. Yet, I was a coward, and could not go against my family's wishes. They were insistent that the barbaric land of Alaska was no place to raise a young girl. At the time I agreed with them, but now, I am not so certain.

Last year Sonya died. After my death Marya will be quite alone. She is a good girl, and quite intelligent. I saw to it that she received a decent education, but she needs a strong hand to guide her. After I am gone, I hope you and your husband can give her your support. I have put aside a sizable trust fund for her, one thousand shares of the RA Company stocks. Governor Muraviev has the deed in his safe. You may use it for a dowry when you find her a suitable husband. I do not wish her to marry a native or a promyshlennik.

Please understand that I love both of my daughters. And also, please grant me one final request, give Marya this Bible for her own to keep.

Forgive me.

Your loving father, Nikolas Ilyich Bolkonsky"

His familiar signature blurred through the veil of her tears. Different unexplainable emotions coursed through her veins, as Tatiana reread the letter until she could not see the words any longer. Sobbing quietly, she knew it was a letter she would treasure always. It was first time her father had referred to any regret for the brief part he had played in her life.

Then there was Marya. She had to face the fact that she was his daughter, too. It was clear enough in the letter that he expected her to take care of her younger half-sister. He had more of a belief in the goodness of her character than was actually true. But then, that was how her father was---he saw good in people when there was none, and was kind to everyone. She remembered her grandmother once told her how he was always rescuing abused animals as a boy. She shouldn't be surprised he had done the same thing with a native girl.

An unfamiliar sense of guilt assailed her at the months of bitter feelings she had felt towards Marya. In all honesty, she had to admit, Marya's grief for their father was likely deeper than hers. She had lived mostly without him, whereas, Marya had grown up used to his constant presence. Her loss was by far, greater than hers.

Tatiana brushed all traces of tears from her cheeks. She decided to hide the letter in one of her jewelry boxes and give the Bible to Marya. With a wry smile, she had to admit her father did know one thing about her, she had little use for a Bible.

She took a deep breath. For the sake of their father's dying wish, it was time to make peace between Marya and herself.

When she entered the parlor, she saw her half-sister sipping tea daintily from a crystal glass. Marya looked like any highborn Russian who preferred drinking tea in glasses rather than cups, so that its lovely amber color could be enjoyed as well as its aroma and flavor.

For the first time, Tatiana saw her without anger.

Her nose and mouth is similar to mine, she thought with surprise, *and also the oval shape of her face. Except for the blackness of her hair, she looks remarkably like me.*

She walked over to Marya, holding out the Bible, and said, "It is our father's last wish for you to have this."

Marya stared at the Bible then glanced up at Tatiana, a look of wonder flickering across her face. She seemed unable to speak and her eyes began to fill with tears.

"Do---do you wish me to have his Bible, too?" she finally asked.

"Yes, Marya Nikolayevna. You are Nikolas Ilyich Bolkonsky's daughter, too. I am sorry that it took so long for me to realize that fact."

Marya reached for the Bible and stroked the leather binding lovingly. "Thank you, *Madame*."

Tatiana sighed and said, "Please call me Tatiana. I am your sister, after all."

At those words Marya's face took on an amazing transformation. She burst into a beautiful smile so like Tatiana's that Anna was shocked. It was like looking at opposite twins, one dark and one fair.

"My sister, at last," Marya laughed with a sound of pure joy.

Tatiana laughed too, infected by her happiness. And when she did, she felt something strange happen inside her. She realized that she had feelings of affection for this strange girl, a feeling of kinship, a bond of blood that she did not share with anyone else on earth. Suddenly it didn't matter that they hadn't grown up together, or that they shared only a father rather than both parents.

She truly was her sister and Tatiana was glad of it.

With a sudden impulse, she said, "Marya, why don't you come here to the house to live? Can your uncle and aunt spare you?"

As quickly as her laughter began it ended and Marya frowned uncertainly. "My aunt would miss me, but Uncle Sergei considers me an extra burden. Most of his furs go to the Company and he has little to feed his family. He has arranged a marriage for me with Andrei Leonov."

"Is he one of those *promyshlennik*'s?" asked Tatiana worriedly, remembering her father saying in his letter that he forbid Marya to marry a fur hunter.

"Oh, no, I wouldn't think of marrying one of those men," she said with a look of disgust. "I find their business of clubbing animals, skinning them, and drying the furs revolting. My aunt is half-blind from all the sewing she does for the Russians, and much of her teeth have fallen out from using them to soften the skins. That would be my fate, also, if I married a fur hunter like Uncle Sergei."

"This Andrei Leonov, then, what does he do?"

"He is a Company man in charge of overseeing warehouses of furs. My aunt and Father Sokolov say he will make me a fine husband."

"And you, what do you say?"

"He is well established in New Archangel with a house, but---"

"You do not really wish to marry him," Tatiana finished for her.

"No, I do not love him."

"I didn't even know my husband when I married him," said Tatiana. "But he takes good care of me. That is all a woman can ask for, I think."

Anna thought of Tatiana's swollen lip, but said nothing. She looked at both young women with pity, thinking how grateful she was to have the love of a wonderful man like Ethan, even though their happiness together had been cut short. She could only pray that God would bless them with many wonderful years ahead, after Ethan was released from prison.

"When is the marriage to take place, Marya?" Tatiana asked as a plan formed in her head.

"Two days before Christmas."

"Then there is time to break off the betrothal. But first, you must move in here with me and Dmitri."

Marya looked stunned. "But your husband hates the sight of me. He would never allow me to live with you."

"He won't be back yet for a fortnight, and when he does, I shall inform him and everyone else that I have acknowledged you as my sister, as a Bolkonsky, in accordance with my father's dying wish for you to achieve your proper station in life. I have his letter as proof."

"There are many who will never forget I am only a *Creole*."

"So were the great Alexander Baranov's son and daughter, and look how they were respected. It will be the same for you, Marya."

Tatiana's eyes glowed with excitement, but Anna saw the skepticism in Marya's face. "I was once a servant at the governor's house, and the ladies will never accept me as anything else."

"Perhaps they will if we find you a better husband such as a naval officer."

Marya's pretty eyes widened. "But I'm already promised to Andrei Leonov."

Tatiana waved her hand carelessly. "A betrothal between two *Creole*s is easily broken unless you would rather marry this man."

"No," she said firmly, "I don't wish to."

Tatiana smiled happily, as she always did when she got her way. "Then it is settled, sister dear. I will send a guard to escort you here tomorrow with your personal belongings."

* * *

Anna had reservations concerning Marya becoming a part of their household, but she kept her feelings to herself. The next day the *Creole* girl moved into the small guest apartment down the corridor from Dmitri and Tatiana's sitting room and bedchamber. She welcomed Marya by helping her arrange her few possessions.

"*Madame* will be sending a seamstress tomorrow to measure you for a new wardrobe," she said. "Until then, you won't be expected to socialize with the officers' wives."

Marya made a grimace. "That is not something I look forward to in any event."

Anna smiled sympathetically, thinking it would be like throwing a lamb to the wolves. She hoped Tatiana knew what she was doing, especially when her husband returned from patrol duty and found Marya living here.

"She is also sending Keeah to be your maid," said Anna.

She frowned. "I don't want a maid."

"A Russian lady needs a maid to help her with her toilette and her hair, *Mademoiselle*."

Marya cast a mischievous grin as she kicked off her boots and yanked the comb out of her hair, letting it fall like raven wings past her shoulders. "Right now I don't feel much like a Russian lady."

Anna laughed and said, "Right now you don't look like one either, more like---"

"An Aleut, right?"

At Anna's nod, she said, "A *Creole* is actually two different people with two different names. To the Russians, I am Marya Nikolayevna. To my mother's people, I am Tooch, which means Little Duck. It is the same for Keeah, only she refuses to answer to a Christian name. The *Kolosh* are a proud stubborn people. Her name means the Dawn."

"I think both Tooch and Keeah are pretty names," said Anna. "Perhaps, if Keeah ever becomes a Christian, she will take another name."

"The *Kolosh* are not interested in what they call the white man's religion. They blame Christianity for turning my people, the Aleuts, from an independent nation to slaves of the Russians. My mother was once a princess, the daughter of an Aleut chief, who was my grandfather. Now there is no more royalty for the Aleuts. Nobles and commoners alike, we all live to serve the Russians. But the *Kolosh* are wrong. It wasn't Christianity that destroyed my people, it was the *promyshlenniki*'s greed for furs and the wealth they sought. They cared nothing for human life."

She looked at Anna. "Have you heard the saying, 'God is in heaven and the Czar is far away'?"

As Anna shook her head, Marya said, "It was the Russians' excuse for the massacre of my people. Mama told me many things of the early days of Russian America when the *promyshlenniki* invaded our islands after being told a man could be rich for life after one voyage. They were evil men who showed no concern for my people. They enslaved our men to hunt while they lived like kings in the villages with our women.

"Then came the taxes. It was decided that the Aleuts should pay tribute to the government and Russian Cossacks were sent to collect it. One collector, among other crimes, was known to cause the deaths of over twenty Aleut girls.

"Another time one Russian captain wanted to demonstrate how powerful their muskets were. He lined up twelve Aleut men in a single row, one behind the other, to see how many bodies one musket ball could penetrate. The answer was nine."

She ignored Anna's gasp of outrage and continued speaking in a bitter voice, "Finally, the natives of Unalaska and their neighbors revolted by killing the crews of five Russian ships. But the Russians took a horrible revenge by torturing and murdering hundreds of Aleut men, women, and children. They destroyed dozens of villages and my people have never recovered from these terrible reprisals. After forty years, the original population of twenty five thousand Aleuts was down to one third of that."

"My husband, Ethan, once told me how the Aleuts have suffered under the Russians, but I never imagined this," said Anna. "Why didn't the Czar interfere?"

"Mama told me that your former Czarina, Catherine the Great, tried to put a stop to the atrocities," admitted Marya. "When she heard of the mistreatment of my people, she sent priests and nuns to convert the Aleuts and to see to their humane treatment."

"Catherine the Great helped my people, too, *Mademoiselle*," said Anna softly. At Marya's expression of surprise, she said, "I am not a true Russian, but a Mennonite." Then she briefly explained the history of her own family's persecution and flight from Holland to Prussia and ultimately, to Russia.

"It seems that the Russians have saved your people then, Anna, and I wish I could say they did the same for mine instead of destroying them."

She sighed heavily. "I loved my father, but there are times I curse the Russian blood in my veins. After he died, I wished I could mourn him in the old ways. When a man as important as Papa died, the family would grieve for up to forty days, pulling out their hair and tearing their clothing to show their love and respect. It is not done now, of course, for the Russians have civilized us. But now my people are civilized to the point where they cannot function on their own any longer. Mama said many times that she feared our culture was becoming forgotten and would one day be gone forever."

"Do you feel like you are a Russian or an Aleut?" Anna asked curiously.

"In my heart I am an Aleut, but my people are of the past. They have lost their pride as a nation and will eventually be no more. The Russians are a powerful people and I believe some day they will rule the world."

She smiled sadly. "I am a product of two different worlds, and I don't belong in either one."

"Nonsense!" came Tatiana's brisk voice as she stepped into the room. "You are a Bolkonsky, Marya, and you mustn't ever forget that. In fact, now is a good time to declare it. Andrei Leonov is downstairs, requesting to speak with you."

"Andrei is here?" she repeated in a frightened tone. "How did he know so quickly?"

"Perhaps your uncle told him you moved out. I will come with you when you break off your betrothal. Anna, help her to fix her hair, and find a gown to make her more presentable. Then we shall face this Andrei Leonov together."

* * *

Andrei stumbled away from the Volodins' front door, his heart beating rapidly and his head pounding, not from exertion, but from a deep inner rage. There was something else, too, an unfamiliar ache, a feeling of loss, like he felt on the day his mother died.

Now he had lost his betrothed, his future wife. All his grand plans for a fine life as a respected member of the community were burnt to ashes. He should blame Marya, but on her own, little Marya would not have the nerve or the means to break off the betrothal. It was her arrogant sister who had just ruined his life and his happiness.

Tatiana Nikolayevna. How he hated her and her mean-spirited husband, Lieutenant Dmitri Volodin. The pair was the epitome of everything he despised about the Russian nobility, the superior manner in which they ruled everyone and everything. It was absurd to think that the Aleut girl known as Tooch would now be a part of the aristocracy.

"My sister will not be marrying you, *Monsieur* Leonov," Tatiana had said in haughty voice. "My father's last wish before he died was for me and Lieutenant Volodin to find her a Russian husband suitable to a member of the Bolkonsky family. You are not that man."

A cruel smile was on her beautiful face and he could not bear to look at her. He turned to Marya, his beloved. He had never seen her looking so lovely or so fashionable. Her often unruly black hair was neatly parted in the center and fastened into a plait held by an ivory comb while a few dark curls escaped around her ears. She wore a white muslin frock hemmed with puffs of muslin and a pleated flounce.

The effect was startling. With her complexion only a shade darker than a white woman, she truly looked like a young Russian lady. Her eyes rested on him, anxiously awaiting his reaction.

He had been stunned and speechless, not expecting anything more than hearing that Marya had been hired as a servant in the house. To discover that her half-sister had decided to acknowledge her as family was a shock. He recovered quickly.

"And you, Marya, my little Tooch," he said gently, "what do you say? Is it your wish to end our betrothal?"

Her gaze slid away, almost guiltily, as she clenched and unclenched her gloved fingers. He stared, realizing he'd never seen her wearing anything on her hands but fur lined mitts.

"Yes, Andrei," she whispered, "I do not wish to marry you."

There. It had been said. Nothing was left to say or do. With the words cutting him like a dagger in the heart, he left, finding his own way out.

Now he headed towards home, his dark cold empty house that would never know the beauty and grace of Marya Nikolayevna. The only thing waiting for him there was a bottle of vodka. He intended on drinking himself senseless tonight.

In his misery Andrei wasn't aware of the two men standing in the path until he crashed into them, knocking one into the bushes. They both yelled and swore at him in English, and he realized they were two of the Americans sailors.

How he wished the governor had not released all the crew into the town. They caused nothing but trouble. They resented the fact they were forced to work constructing buildings in the cold rain for the Russians, when all they wanted was to leave on their own ship. He really couldn't blame them, he supposed. But they were as surly in their own way as the Russians, and fights broke out constantly in the evenings when the men were in their cups.

These two were already drunk, smelling of rum and vodka. He tried to apologize for the accident, but neither man would hear of it. The fists came out of the gloom of the winter afternoon before he could dodge them. One smashed into his face, another to the side of his head. He threw up his arms to protect himself, but it was too late. He crumpled to the frozen earth where he felt the sharp heel of a boot grind into his ribs. Pain flashed throughout his whole body, from head to toe. There was another blow to his head. Then he felt nothing as he slipped into unconsciousness.

CHAPTER TWENTY ONE

"And this must be your half-sister," gushed Irina Trotskaya, her long nosed face forcing a smile as she extended a gloved hand towards Marya.

She smiled hesitantly and took the offered hand, shaking it slightly then dropping it as if stung by a bee. Marya dipped her head and curtsied. "I am most pleased to meet you, *Madame*."

Irina whinnied, displaying her mouth full of large square teeth. "Oh, my dear, you need not bow to me anymore. After all, you are no longer a servant here."

"That's right," said Vera sarcastically. "You are now one of us, a member of the nobility."

Marya blushed, her eyes full of unhappiness, as Tatiana bit her lip in sudden anger. She had brought Marya to her first social tea at the governor's residence this afternoon, to introduce her to the officers' wives as her sister, Marya Nikolayevna Bolkonskaya.

Before the Trotsky women had come, everything had gone smoothly. Catherine Kornilova welcomed Marya graciously, pretending she'd never once been Marya's supervisor here at the castle. Elizabeth Pushkina also had nodded to Marya and politely asked about her welfare. Several of the other ladies had followed suit, accepting Marya as one of them, while everyone sipped their tea and nibbled at tiny dainty cakes and sugary biscuits which *Madame* Kornilova had instructed the cook to bake that morning.

Anna helped to serve the tea and food, keeping her face fixed in a pleasant smile, knowing many of the women there considered her an oddity, a Russian Mennonite woman married to an imprisoned American, and pregnant with his child. After she finished serving them, she planned to slip out to see Governor Muraviev in his office. She'd heard he was there working today, and she wanted to persuade him to allow her to see Ethan.

If that didn't work, she decided she'd speak to Father Sokolov and appeal to the priest's sense of Christian mercy to help her. At church services with Tatiana, he had nodded to Anna several times, although they'd never spoken. He must have heard she was a Mennonite, for there were few secrets in New Archangel, and she had no idea if he approved or disapproved of her own faith. She hoped it would make no difference to him.

She had not told Tatiana about her intention to see the governor this afternoon. Anna didn't want to cause trouble for her with Dmitri when he returned. He would most likely become angry if he knew his wife's maid had gone over his head by seeing the governor to get permission to visit her husband.

The appearance of Irina, Vera, and Sophie gave Anna the opportunity to leave. Tatiana was so absorbed in defending Marya to them, that she didn't notice when Anna left the drawing room. She walked down a long hallway to the office door and paused, hearing the sound of men talking inside. One sounded like the pompous Lieutenant Ivanoff, another was the governor, and the other was Father Sokolov's deep commanding voice.

His presence surprised her, but perhaps it was an answer to prayer. Taking a deep breath to calm her trembling nerves, she knocked on the door.

The men continued talking as the door was opened by the governor's valet, a tall ascetic looking man with a hooked nose and thick black eyebrows. He peered down at her with surprised disapproval and said, "May I help you, *Madame*?"

"Yes, please, I must see Governor Muraviev. It is very important."

"Do you have an appointment with His Excellency?" he asked in a doubtful voice.

"No, I don't, but I must speak with him regardless. It could be a matter of life and death," she ended in a note of urgency. It was true. Lately, she had been experiencing a terrible feeling that Ethan was in danger, terrible danger, and not only him, but also the other officers.

"Could be a matter of life and death," the valet repeated, raising his bushy eyebrows in mock concern.

"Who is it, Mikhail?" Anna heard the governor ask in an irritated voice.

"Just a woman, Your Excellency, the maid of *Madame* Bolkonskaya. She says she wishes to see you, but she does not have an appointment. Shall I send her away?"

"What does she want?"

"She says it is a matter of life and death, but I'm sure she is only exaggerating."

"It will only take a moment of your time, Your Excellency," Anna called out from the doorway.

Muraviev sighed and looked at Lieutenant Ivanoff and Father Sokolov. The three men had been discussing the latest incident involving the Americans. A few nights before one of the Company's valued employees, a warehouse supervisor by the name of Andrei Leonov had been found almost beaten to death.

Leonov had survived, though he would be a long time recovering with broken ribs, a nasty head wound and concussion, and a shattered face. He claimed his assailants were two sailors from the Yankee clipper, but he could not identify them. Muraviev had sent out a warning to the

American crew that they all would be imprisoned immediately if there were anymore unprovoked attacks on the town's inhabitants.

"I am weary of the entire American problem," he had told the lieutenant and the priest a few moments ago. "The crew is causing nothing but problems in town. The little work they produce isn't worth the trouble they create." Muraviev took off his powdered wig and scratched his sweaty head, then put it back on and said, "As soon as the winter gales abate, I intend on sending all of them and their ship back to Boston."

Ivanoff had scowled. "That will not sit well with our own officers, especially Lieutenant Volodin."

"I realize that, Lieutenant Ivanoff, but I believe it is in the town's best interests if the Americans are gone as soon as possible. And if Lieutenant Volodin or the other officers object, I will deal with them personally." He'd turned to the priest. "What do you think about this, Father?"

Sokolov pulled on his long gray beard thoughtfully. With his flowing gray hair and somber dark eyes and expression, he appeared like an Old Testament St.. As always, his presence made Boris very uncomfortable. It seemed to him whenever the priest looked at him, his gaze was piercing through his soul, as if he was weighing all of his sins, and finding him unworthy.

"I cannot advise you on this, Your Excellency," said Father Sokolov, "but I will pray that you will make the correct decision."

The typical vapid response of a priest, Boris thought with a sneer then nodded politely at Sokolov as he felt his penetrating stare. *He knows I don't like him*, he thought uneasily. *But what else does he know? That I'm too fond of the native girls? Perhaps it is time I married and became more respectable around here. But marry who? Plain little Sophie Trotskaya?*

Then he smiled as he thought of the very young and beautiful Marya Nikolayevna. She could be no more than fifteen, a delectable age. Now that she had been accepted into New Archangel society, she would be perfect. He'd even heard that she had an excellent dowry. Her father, Nikolas Bolkonsky, had left her one thousand shares of Company stock, a small fortune indeed.

As soon as his good friend Dmitri returned from patrol duty, he would ask if he would give his permission to marry his new sister-in-law.

He glanced at Father Sokolov, who was still looking at him like he was a despicable snake. It was with relief that the woman at the door caused an interruption, making the priest focus his attention on someone else.

"Let her in, Mikhail," said Muraviev, "we have finished our discussion for now."

He stood up from behind his desk and smiled politely as Anna walked in the room.

In a glance she took in the masculine interior of the office, the stale smell of tobacco, the faint brandy fumes, and the shelves of leather-bound books, the massive desk and oil paintings of ships hung on the paneled walls. She suddenly felt like an intruder as the three men stared at her, the obese lieutenant with his squinty eyes, the stern countenance of Father Sokolov reminding her of Moses, and Governor Muraviev, looking exhausted with puffy bags under his eyes.

But his voice was patient as he said, "*Madame* Campbell, what can I do for you?"

She was glad she'd dressed in a nice silk gown and was wearing her pearl drop earrings from Ethan. She'd told Tatiana that she wanted to look her best for the ladies, but her real reason was to appear presentable for the governor.

"I need your permission, Your Excellency, to visit my husband in prison. I haven't seen him since we arrived three months ago, and he needs to know that I am well."

"The Yankee prisoners are not allowed visitors," said Ivanoff in a gruff voice.

"But--but I am with child," she said, blushing in embarrassment, "and by now Ethan must be so worried about me, as I am about him."

Boris leered at her then said in an unfeeling voice, "Write him a letter and tell him how you're doing. There's no need for you to see him."

"But I tried that once," she protested, turning to the governor. "The guard in charge refused to deliver it to my husband."

Father Sokolov studied Anna, remembering what he'd heard about her. She was a Mennonite, which he believed to be a heretical religious cult of farmers from the Ukraine. Although he'd seen her in church, she'd never come to him for confession. From what little he knew about Mennonites, they had no use for priests. This irritated him no end, but it didn't stop him from feeling sorry for her being in such a delicate condition and separated from her husband.

"It's almost Christmas," said Father Sokolov. "Surely, Your Excellency can have compassion on this woman during such a holy time of year. Remember how even our Lord had to be born in a stable, because the innkeeper had no compassion for the Virgin Mary when she was with child."

"But that's against the rules," sputtered Ivanoff, feeling a stab of fear. The last thing he and Dmitri wanted was for anyone to discover how ill the prisoners were. Weeks ago they had been informed by the sergeant in command of the prison that all four men were sick with lung congestion, but they'd decided not to pass on that information to the governor. Since he and Dmitri had been denied the pleasure of watching the American officers whipped with the *knout* and hung like common criminals, they intended to let them die a slow death in prison. But it was imperative that they have no visitors until it was too late to save them.

He looked at the priest with dismay. He certainly picked a fine time to voice his opinion instead of piously promoting prayer to the governor.

To Ivanoff's further chagrin, Governor Muraviev agreed with Father Sokolov. "That is a splendid idea, Father," he said, taking a quill and dipping it in ink. "I shall write a letter of permission for *Madame* Campbell to see her husband on Christmas Day for one hour."

A few minutes later a smiling Anna left the office, clutching the precious piece of paper to her heart. Christmas was only a week away! Soon she would be able to talk to Ethan and also, see Captain O'Connell and John and Jake. Her mind was busy planning the gifts of food and warm clothing and blankets that would she take to them.

When she reached the drawing room she found Tatiana standing in the doorway. "Where have you been?" she asked with irritation. "I'm coming down with one of my headaches. I'd like you to fetch our cloaks so we can leave."

"I--I went to see the governor."

Tatiana arched one eyebrow in surprise. "That was brave of you, Anna. Whatever for?"

"To ask his permission to visit Ethan." She held out the letter. "And he gave it! Look!"

Tatiana took the paper and scanned it. "Well, congratulations, Anna. It looks like Christmas will be very merry for you."

* * *

The *Buldakov* returned on Christmas Eve. They had encountered some bitter weather, and several foreign trading vessels, American and British. All the ships had fled south at the sight of the *Buldakov*, and Dmitri was pleased with the success of his venture. What did not please him was the news Boris brought. The ship had barely dropped her anchor when his friend had himself rowed out in a longboat to see him before Dmitri went ashore.

As Boris sipped a brandy inside Dmitri's cabin, he gave him the twofold news. His wife had welcomed her *Creole* half-sister into their family, and her maid had been given permission by the governor to visit the American prisoners the next day.

Dmitri's face darkened in anger, but before he could explode in rage, Boris hastily said, "I also have good news. I'm willing to marry Marya Nikolayevna and take her off your hands in spite of her native blood. Her father left her a rich dowry, and I heard he expressed his wish that she marry a naval officer of the nobility. So my good friend, if you give your permission, we can be betrothed on Christmas Day."

Dmitri took a deep breath, feeling his anger diminish slightly. "Of course you have my permission, Boris, although I'm not certain you are making a wise choice in a wife. The girl is half wild."

Boris rubbed his hands together and grinned lecherously. "I'm looking forward to taming the wench."

Dmitri laughed. "Then Marya Nikolayevna is all yours." He raised his glass in a toast. "To wedded bliss!" He drained the brandy in one gulp then frowned. "But what about the problem of the Yankee officers, Boris? What can we do to stop the maid from visiting them?"

Boris shrugged his massive shoulders. "There's nothing we can do about that. But we mustn't worry. The four men are so ill, I think it's too late for some of them to survive, even with the best of care. I believe it is safe to say we've almost had our revenge."

"Almost isn't good enough, but it will have to do for now."

* * *

Although it was mid afternoon, it was already dark by the time Dmitri entered the parlor of his house to be greeted by a cozy domestic scene. Tatiana and Marya were sitting at a table, playing a game of chess. Two kittens were curled up by the stove, an unwelcome surprise to him since he never could abide cats. He paused in the doorway, as both kittens jumped up in alarm at his unexpected appearance and raced under the nearest sofa.

"Ladies," he said, bowing slightly, his expression bland save for the tiny twitching of the muscle under his left eye. Tatiana knew his nervous tic meant that her husband was struggling internally to control his temper.

She rose from her chair and went to greet him with a warm kiss. "Dmitri, darling," she said, "so good to see you back safely."

His anger faded a bit at the sight of her loveliness in her pale lilac gown. Since her father had been dead for six months, she was now dressing in lavender and gray gowns, which was considered proper attire for partial mourning.

But it was her half-sister who surprised him. The *Creole* girl looked like any young Russian lady with her raven black hair styled into a perfect coiffure, wearing a pale yellow silk gown that set off her exotic looks. He had never realized how pretty she was. No wonder Boris wished to marry her.

"You remember Marya Nikolayevna, my sister. She has come to stay with us."

Tatiana said the words calmly, while studying Dmitri's reaction. She noted how tired he appeared, with shadows under his eyes and deeper lines at the corners. His skin looked roughened from the exposure to the weather, and his fair hair was longer than she'd ever seen it. If anything, he was more ruggedly handsome than she remembered.

He set his bag down on the floor and took off his heavy coat and threw it on a chair. Then he walked over to the warm stove and spread his hands out towards the heat. With his back to them he said, "Boris met me on the dock and told me about Marya. I must say it has come as quite a surprise, so you both will have to forgive me if I seem rude by not rushing over to greet her as part of the family."

Tatiana and Marya looked at each other with relief. They had expected Dmitri to fly into an immediate rage and here he was acting so nonchalant about the matter.

"You---you are not angry, Dmitri?"

"Of course I am, but it's too late to change anything. Boris explained about your father's letter and his request that we take care of her. Since the entire town knew about this before I did, I have no choice but to accept the situation." He turned and forced a smile at Marya, a smile that did not quite reach his cold gray eyes. "Yes, I can see that you are quite a beauty, dear sister. I can even see a family resemblance to my wife." He paused then added, "But some good has come out of this. My good friend Boris asked permission to wed you, Marya, and I gave it. We will announce your betrothal tomorrow on Christmas Day at the governor's dinner."

Marya looked stunned, her face draining of color as Tatiana gasped, "But, Dmitri, how could you agree to such a thing without discussing it with me first?" A sudden anger gripped her at the thought of her innocent young sister being married to the loathsome lieutenant.

"There's nothing to discuss, my dear. I am the head of this family and I make all the final decisions concerning our future." He jerked his head towards the door. "Now, Marya, be a good girl and run off. I need to spend some time alone with my beautiful wife."

She jumped up from her chair and fled the room without a word, giving Tatiana a backward glance of horrified panic. After she was gone, the coldness left Dmitri's eyes, replaced by a flame of rekindled anger.

"Please, Dmitri," she begged, "don't marry Marya to Lieutenant Ivanoff."

"Why not? Boris's family is of the nobility; he is a fine naval officer and my dearest friend. If anything, Marya should be on her knees thanking me for making such a brilliant match."

Tatiana thought quickly. She dared not criticize Boris without making Dmitri even more furious with her. She tried a different tack. "It's not because of him. You must understand that I've only just found my sister after a lifetime of being apart. We are finally getting acquainted, and the thought of her leaving here to marry anyone makes me unhappy."

Dmitri considered briefly then shrugged. "I can see your point, my dear. We can make the betrothal last six months or even a year if you wish. But she will marry Boris. He is mad for her."

Tatiana shuddered slightly at the vile thought. "Thank you, Dmitri. A year's betrothal is very generous of you."

"If Marya is distressed at marrying Boris, you only have yourself to blame, Tatiana. She wouldn't even be in this predicament if you hadn't disobeyed me by seeing her again, and then had the audacity to take her in as your sister."

"I---I--apologize for disobeying you, Dmitri," she stammered nervously. "I know you forbid me to have anything to do with Marya, but when I read Papa's letter, I--I--"

"You felt you had to obey his wishes over mine, isn't that correct, darling?"

"It was his deathbed wish, Dmitri. As a dutiful daughter, how could I disregard that?"

"Obedience to a husband takes precedence over a father," he snapped, then took a deep breath. "It's Christmas Eve and I do not wish to quarrel over this. All these weeks I have been gone, I've spent every minute missing you."

"As I have missed you, my darling," Tatiana lied with a smile.

"Come," he said, seizing her by one arm and propelling her up the stairs towards their bedchamber. "I want you to show me how much you love me, but first," he squeezed her arm tighter, "you must be punished for disobeying me."

* * *

Christmas was a festive day for all of New Archangel's inhabitants, especially the aristocracy. After early morning services at the church, Governor Muraviev hosted a huge dinner for the officers and their families, including gifts of sweets for all the children.

Waking up that morning was difficult for Anna. She was haunted by the memories of last Christmas on the *Sea Rose* with Ethan when they rounded Cape Horn, and then the memories of the many happy Christmas celebrations with her family. At least she would be able to see Ethan today! She planned on visiting him that afternoon while Tatiana and Dmitri were at the governor's residence for Christmas dinner.

After breakfast Keeah told her that Marya wished to speak with her. When Anna entered her bedchamber she was shocked to see her face, puffed up from weeping with reddened swollen eyes.

"Whatever is the matter, *Mademoiselle*?" Anna asked with great concern.

"Oh, Anna, it is the most terrible news! Lieutenant Volodin has betrothed me to that horrible Boris Ivanoff ! He's going to announce it today at Christmas dinner. I would rather have married Andrei!"

She began to weep anew while Anna put her arm around her. "And *Madame* has agreed to this?" She sounded incredulous.

"Tatiana didn't know anything about it until yesterday when he came home and announced it. Then he told me to leave the two of them alone." She buried her head on Anna's shoulder. "Later I thought I heard Tatiana crying. I'm afraid he might have hurt her."

Anna's set her mouth in a grim line. "If so, it wouldn't be the first time."

"Lieutenant Ivanoff is a bad man, too, Anna. All of the girls from my village keep out of his way, because he's been known to do dreadful things to a girl if he catches one alone. How can I be the wife of a monster like that?"

She wailed loudly and Anna tried to hush her. "Now, now, Marya, don't carry on so. A betrothal can last a long time before the actual wedding takes place. Otherwise, perhaps, you should tell Tatiana that you wish to return to your village, that you don't wish to live here anymore."

"I cannot go back there," she sobbed. "I have disgraced my uncle for breaking off the betrothal with Andrei. I have no place but here."

"My papa once betrothed me to a man I did not love, a violent man I too was afraid of."

Marya sniffled and looked at Anna in surprise. "What did you do?"

"After spending a few nights weeping into my pillow, I finally trusted God to help me and He provided a way of escape by sending me to work for the Bolkonsky family." Anna gave her a sad smile. "I also disgraced my papa, and most likely, cannot return to my village in Russia either."

"Oh, Anna, I'm so sorry," said Marya, forgetting her own dilemma for a moment. Then she sighed. "You were very brave. I will try to be also. Perhaps Father Sokolov can help me find a way to get out of this unwanted marriage."

Anna gave her a warm hug. "I will pray for you. Now dry your eyes and I'll send Keeah up with some water so you can wash your face. You have a busy day ahead. Merry Christmas, *Mademoiselle*."

"Merry Christmas to you too, Anna, and thank you!"

* * *

Shortly after noon Tatiana summoned Anna to help her dress for the banquet. She stunned Anna with a Christmas gift of a beautiful silver and jade necklace, crafted by a local *Kolosh* native. It made Anna's present to her, a hand stitched neatly embroidered silk scarf, seem poor by comparison. But Tatiana thanked her warmly and Anna began to feel better, until her mistress took off her chemise to bathe.

Anna was shocked to see several deep bruises and welts on her lower back and buttocks. She obviously had been whipped with a belt. It was a miracle none of her delicate skin was torn.

"*Madame* refused to speak of it," she said to Keeah later, "as if it was her fault the lieutenant had beaten her. I couldn't believe my eyes. He knew just where to hurt her, so when she was fully dressed, her bruises would be hidden, and no one would know."

Keeah shrugged, her expression devoid of sympathy. "All men hit their wives. Same with my people."

"My husband has never struck me," she said. "He loves me."

"You have a good man." Keeah patted Anna's belly with a smile. "And you have a baby now. Maybe a daughter to help you work or a son to take care of you someday."

"All I need is Ethan to be free to take care of us."

Keeah gave her a speculative look. "What if something bad happen to him? Would you marry again?"

She shook her head firmly. "There will never be another man as fine as my Ethan, unless the captain..." her voice faded as she suddenly thought of Captain O'Connell. She remembered the strange attraction she once felt for him, the unexplained emotions he evoked in her that she never understood. But it was all nonsense. The captain would never be interested in her. He'd had eyes only for Tatiana, and perhaps still did, in spite of his claim to dislike her.

Keeah watched her intently. "Captain? Russian captain?"

Anna laughed slightly. "I was thinking of an American---"

"The Yankees captain? He sick, your man, all of them, very sick." And that's when Keeah, who was a part of the servants grapevine, from the governor's residence to the married officer's building, told her she'd just heard that the Americans were suffering from the coughing sickness.

"Keeah," said Anna, "I need you to come with me today to the prison. We're going to need medicines, clean cloths, extra blankets, and tell Helena to prepare a large jug of warm meat broth."

* * *

Sean was dreaming that he was surrounded by burning hot flames with his da standing over him, grinning like the devil. "You'll be with me soon, lad, here in hell where ye belong, ye murderin' son of a ---"

"No!" he shouted then woke with a start as a cool hand slid over his brow. He opened his eyes to see Anna staring down at him, her lovely face full of anxiety. Her hand moved over his forehead again, and he felt the delicious trickle of water from a wet cloth.

Had he died and gone to heaven? He wondered. Then he heard Ethan moan on the cot next to him and Anna vanished. He struggled to move his head to look for her when a flash of pain tore through his skull. He winced and said, "Anna, Anna, 'tis you?"

"Yes, Captain," he heard her low throaty voice say as if from a distance. "We're here to help you. Keeah will bring you some broth."

Keeah? Who was that?

A slim Tlingit girl came into view holding a small bowl of something steaming. His eyes blurred as he tried to fix his gaze on her face. All he could make out was a pair of dark eyes and a brief glimpse of her scarred mouth before a spoon reached his own lips. He opened them automatically and swallowed a mouthful of warm broth. At first it was pure bliss as the savory liquid traveled down his sore parched throat and hit his stomach. Then he choked as his lungs rebelled and he began to cough, his chest feeling like someone was stabbing him with a sharp knife.

"We must tell the governor at once that all the men need to be moved out of here and under proper care," he heard Anna say. "If only Doctor-Surgeon Behrs was still here."

"There is a healing woman in the Aleut village," said the girl Keeah. "She is better than the white medicine man."

"Who is she?"

"*Mademoiselle* Marya's aunt."

And who is that? Sean wondered again, as he managed to stop coughing long enough for another gulp of broth.

* * *

The news about the ill Americans reached Muraviev that evening after the banquet was over. He was relaxing in his office having his usual nightcap of warm brandy, when Mikhail entered in a huff to announce that *Madame* Campbell wished an audience with him.

"You do not need to see her, Your Excellency," he said, scowling. "It's late and it's Christmas and--"

"Precisely, Mikhail," said Muraviev, waving a hand at him, "because it is Christmas, I shall see her, but only for a moment.

He straightened up in his chair as the small pretty woman marched into his office, her hazel eyes sparkling with outrage. "Your Excellency," she began, "I am sorry to disturb you on Christmas night so late, but you must know that my husband, and the captain and the other two officers are dangerously ill with lung congestion. When I went to visit them this afternoon I was dismayed by their condition."

Anna had also been horrified at the appearance of the four men, especially Ethan. They were hardly recognizable as the once tanned and healthy officers of the *Sea Rose*. After three months in prison, they were all skin and bones, their faces were pale and gaunt and they had filthy lice-ridden hair and matted beards. They were burning up with fever and suffered from fits of deep coughing.

"They are in dire need of proper care and a warm dry room or I fear they might all die." Her voice choked on the last word. Ethan seemed to be the sickest. His fever had been so high, he was delirious, and he hadn't recognized her when she talked to him. But what frightened her most was that he'd coughed up blood. Her heart was seized with dread at the fear that she might have discovered his illness too late. *Pray God that isn't so*, she breathed.

Muraviev frowned with concern. "I had no idea your husband and the other prisoners were so ill. I'd heard some time ago that they were suffering from nothing more than the usual colds and runny noses. I'll have to interrogate the sergeant in command and find out why he hasn't seen fit to inform me of their dire condition." He turned to Mikhail and said, "Tell the sergeant to have the prisoners moved out of their cell and into one of the small workmen's houses with a good working stove. Post guards at the front door, and I'll find someone competent to take care of them." He then dismissed his valet and said to Anna, "How I wish our hospital was finished and that we had a real physician to run it. I can only hope the Czar sends us a permanent doctor soon."

"Our *Kolosh* maid says there is a healing woman in the Aleut village."

"Ah, yes, I've heard of her. She'll be better than nothing. I'll send for her first thing in the morning."

"Thank you, Your Excellency. And can I ask one more thing? May I have your permission to help take care of the prisoners? I am so concerned about my husband."

Muraviev smiled at her. If only his own wife was so kind, gentle, and loving, he never would've left her behind in Saint Petersburg. "You have my permission, *Madame* Campbell, as long as your own mistress gives her permission as well."

* * *

"You were out so late last night seeing the governor, I had to ask Keeah to ready me for bed," Tatiana complained to Anna the next morning. "And don't look at me like that, Anna, I do care that Ethan is so ill and I understand how distressed you must be."

Tatiana was sitting at her dressing table, staring at Anna in the mirror as she stood behind her and brushed her hair. "The governor gave me permission to help take care of my husband and the other men. But he said I had to ask you first."

"Well," Tatiana considered, "perhaps it would be allowable each day, only after you have finished your duties to me."

"Of course, *Madame*."

Tatiana saw the stubborn set to Anna's jaw and sighed. "Except for Ethan, I don't understand why you care about the other Americans."

"They are my friends."

"Even Captain O'Connell?" Tatiana inquired, raising one eyebrow.

Anna felt herself flush. "He has always been most kind to me."

"I wish I could say the same for myself," Tatiana snapped in irritation, "but he treated me dreadfully on the *Sea Rose*."

It was on the tip of Anna's tongue to reply that she had only herself to blame, but stopped the words, as she remembered the bruises on her mistress's body. Instead she said with sympathy in her voice, "I would say it is your husband who treats you that way, *Madame*."

Now it was Tatiana's turn to flush, only for her, it was in anger. She snatched the hairbrush out of Anna's hands and said, "You are dismissed, Anna."

She stepped backwards as Tatiana rose from her chair, holding the brush threateningly. "You must never, ever say a word against Dmitri, do you understand, Anna?"

Anna bowed her head and said, "Yes, *Madame*, I am sorry."

"Now go!"

She fled the room, but not before seeing the flash of tears welling up in Tatiana's eyes. After Anna was gone, Tatiana tossed the hairbrush across the room and it smashed against the window, causing a small crack in the glass.

"I hate them!" she cried out, then ran over to the bed and threw herself on top the soft blankets. For a second, she'd actually felt the urge to strike Anna, her beloved Anna. And for what reason? None of the mess that was her life was her maid's fault.

With a deep sob, she closed her eyes and thought how much she hated Dmitri and Captain O'Connell. They both had humiliated and hurt her, and she wished she had never met either one. If by chance, the captain died from his illness, then good riddance. As for Dmitri, if he ever hurt her again, she was going to find a way to be rid of him, too.

* * *

Anna stumbled down the hall, her heart full of sorrow and pity for Tatiana. She knew her mistress was suffering in her marriage. She was an unhappy, tormented woman and Anna had no idea how to help her. All the marriages she had known were between two people who loved each other, her parents and both sets of grandparents. The type of marriage Dmitri and Tatiana shared, if it was typical of the Russian nobility, was a true abomination in the sight of God.

She tapped on Marya's door. The girl was a much earlier riser than Tatiana since she had not spent her whole life living in aristocratic luxury. It meant Keeah had an easier job being her maid than Anna had in serving Tatiana.

"Come in," Marya called out, and Anna opened the door and stepped inside her tiny sitting room. The house had only the two apartments upstairs, one for the master and the other for a guest, which was now Marya's. The first thing she had done when she moved in, was to retrieve all the icons and pictures of the Saints from her father's trunks, where Dmitri had ordered them to be placed after he took up residence. They were now displayed in the corner mantels both in this room and in her bedchamber. Over her bed she hung a silver crucifix which had once belonged to her mother.

Marya was already dressed in a high necked gown of warm velvet, burgundy in color with white lace at the collar and wrists. She sat at a small table, having her breakfast of tea and scones. The cat Otter was curled up at her feet. Her green eyes widened with alarm when Anna first entered the room, then slit shut halfway as she yawned with recognition. Her purring filled the room with a low rumbling sound.

Marya smiled in delight when she saw Anna. "Would you like to share some tea, Anna?"

"It would not be proper, *Mademoiselle*," she answered, returning her smile. It was good to see Marya looking so cheerful after her unhappiness of yesterday. Had she come to terms with marrying Lieutenant Ivanoff?

Marya rolled her eyes in exasperation. "Not even if I ordered you?"

Anna laughed. "That would be different."

"Then I order you, sit down and drink some tea with me, Anna."

As Marya watched Anna sit down at the table across from her, she thought how strange it was they had become friends, in spite of the differences of their religious beliefs.

Marya was a true Russian Orthodox, raised to believe that her church was the only official one, with its ordained priesthood, sacred liturgy and church books, and long traditional history of strict rituals. At first, she was appalled that Anna did not believe in the holy sacraments, or confession to a priest for sins, or in infant baptism, or in using the sign of the cross.

She remembered the day, not too long ago, when she told Anna that her Mennonite beliefs were considered a sect by her church. Anna had smiled and said, "I'm not surprised at that, *Mademoiselle*. The Russian Orthodox Church is not the only one to think the Mennonites are a dangerous sect, but also the Catholic, and some Protestant churches as well. My ancestors suffered great persecution in the past for their beliefs, but yet, we have only grown stronger. We are a people who base all their beliefs on the Bible, God's holy written words to mankind. In the Bible, Jesus teaches that we are redeemed through our faith in Him, not in works or religious rituals. For us Mennonites, church is a gathering place for believers, who join voluntarily through adult baptism upon confession of faith. We believe faith is a gift from God and is free, not earned by repeating endless sacraments or being baptized as an infant. For, how can a mere babe understand faith?"

"I--I'm not sure," Marya had said, "I never thought about it before."

After that conversation, Marya had asked Anna more about her beliefs, and for the first time in her life, found herself questioning some of the rigid forms of worship when she attended church services. As she repeated the same words over and over, she would glance around the church watching everyone mumble the same prayers, and wonder if they truly believed in their hearts what they were speaking.

Then she'd think of Anna, and how she not only spoke her beliefs, she lived them. She prayed directly to God, confessing her sins to Him, and then had the assurance she was forgiven.

She'd heard Irina and Vera Trotskaya and others criticize Anna's beliefs as unorthodox and strange, but that didn't stop Marya from liking her and admiring her courage to worship God as she wished.

Marya glanced at her and noticed for the first time, the strained look of worry in her eyes. Of course, she chastised herself, Anna was anxious about the health of her ailing husband.

"Anna, I'm so sorry about Ethan. Is there anything I can do to help?"

"Yes, you can pray for him and the other three men, and if I may, could I borrow Keeah in the afternoons to help me care for them? The governor has given his permission, and so has *Madame*." Unless Tatiana was so angry with her, she withdrew her permission, Anna worried.

"Yes, you can take Keeah along." Marya nibbled her lower lip in thought. "Perhaps I may be able to come with you. This afternoon I am invited to one of those interminable social teas with the officer's wives and daughters." She groaned slightly. "But I would much rather do something useful than spend my time with those haughty white women and hearing them congratulate me on my betrothal to that--that pig of a lieutenant. It was all I could do yesterday at Christmas dinner to be polite to him. Thank goodness he was seated far away from me at the table."

She shivered with revulsion as she remembered how Boris had taken one of her gloved hands and brought her fingers up to his fleshy moist lips and kissed them. Then he had the audacity to tell her how happy she had made him and how he was looking forward to their future together. Somehow she'd managed to answer him without vomiting up her meal, but later when she returned home, she'd thrown her contaminated glove in the hot stove embers.

Anna smiled at her sympathetically. "You acted with courage yesterday, *Mademoiselle*. I believe if you keep your faith, God will make a way of escape for you from the lieutenant. And if you can come with me today, I will appreciate your help. But first, your sister must agree."

"Speaking of Tatiana," Marya frowned, "in these past weeks since I have come to know her, I sense she's deeply unhappy, no matter how much she pretends otherwise. As her maid, do you know why?"

"Even though your sister was raised in a lavish palace in Saint Petersburg with every known luxury, I think she had a miserable childhood. She had no mother and an absent father. And now," she hesitated, "I suspect her marriage to Lieutenant Volodin is not all that she wished." That was a great understatement, Anna knew, but it wasn't up to her to tell Marya about Dmitri's cruel abuse.

"Poor Tatiana," Marya agreed. "Even though my parents were not married, Mama was there every day of my life, and except for two voyages to Russia when I was little, Papa was nearby if I needed him. When I look back at my life, I see little reason to complain."

Those words stayed with Anna the remainder of the morning as she went about her duties as quickly as possible, mainly that of keeping Tatiana's immense wardrobe organized. As she pressed the wrinkles out of Tatiana's lovely gowns, she thought of the plain dresses of the Mennonites, and knew she had been blessed as a girl with riches more valuable than silk, satin, and expensive jewelry. She too had no reason to complain about her childhood.

After Helena had cooked lunch and left for her own home, Marya found Anna in the kitchen, feeding the cats some dried fish before putting them outside. Dmitri had forbidden them to stay inside the house, especially since the time he'd woken up one morning and found the cats sleeping between him and Tatiana. He was so angry he would have gotten rid of them altogether, except for Tatiana's tearful pleading.

"Keeah and I both are coming with you this afternoon," Marya said excitedly.

"How did you arrange that?" Anna asked in amazement.

"At lunchtime we were talking about my betrothal to Lieutenant Ivanoff, and I began to cry. Tatiana felt badly for me and asked me if there was anything she could do to make me feel better. I told her the last thing I wished to do today was see any of the officer's wives. She said I could stay home and rest and she left a few minutes ago without me."

"But won't she be angry with you and me when she discovers you tricked her?"

Marya shrugged. "Why should she find out? We'll be back before she comes home."

Anna shook her head, thinking how alike the two sisters were. They both could be devious when it suited them.

CHAPTER TWENTY TWO

The Aleut woman Tugidaq made her way through the muddy paths of the town towards the house where the white men lay sick. She was followed by her two oldest daughters, Anaay, age eleven, and Gheli, age twelve. Both girls also had Christian names of Anna and Sofia, but Tugidaq refused to call them by anything but their Aleut names.

She was in a foul mood, having been summoned by the Russian governor to tend to the prisoners. She was full of resentment, but dared not refuse, even though she had no liking for what the natives called the Boston men. She had seen first hand the results of their violent behavior, for she had been tending Andrei Leonov the past weeks. His injuries had been life threatening, and only now were beginning to heal. But his face would never look the same. As the swelling went down, she could see that he had lost his fine looks. His nose, cheekbones, and jaw had been so shattered there was little she could do.

Her heart was full of pity for the young man; not only for his brutal attack, but because her niece had broken their betrothal without her uncle's permission. Sergei was furious with the girl. They had lost face in front of the entire village and Marya was not welcome in their home any longer.

Marya had tried once to explain to them that her prospects were better now. But neither she nor Sergei trusted the Russians, the nobility most of all. They believed their Tooch had made a terrible mistake in leaving her mother's people for life with her aristocratic half-sister.

The prisoners were a short distance from the Indian market, well within the stockade. Their house was typical, one main room with a stove, and a small storage room in the back. Two armed soldiers guarded the front door. They leered at the girls, but stood aside quickly when Tugidaq spat a curse at them.

Inside the prisoners lay in four narrow cots near the stove. The men were asleep, but woke up as soon as they entered. Tugidaq instructed Anaay to heat water on the stove, and although the men protested loudly, she and her daughters stripped off their filthy clothes. Gheli threw the clothing into a pot, scrubbing them, while her mother and sister washed the men.

One of the men was too ill to notice and hardly reacted to being bathed. He had hair the russet color of the fox and mumbled strange sounding words in his feverish delirium. Tugidaq didn't like the looks of him at all, especially the reddened swollen end of his leg stump. It was oozing pus and obviously had become infected from the filthy conditions in the prison cell.

She clucked in disgust as she reached in her bag and pulled out a salve made with dried goose grass softened with fat to soothe skin wounds. Tomorrow she decided she'd bring some *xos cogh*, or devil's club. The root of this tall prickly plant, when pounded and heated, was helpful in curing skin abrasions and infections.

The other three men were not as critically ill. Although weak, they were coherent enough to complain about the humiliation of having two blushing, giggling girls wash them all over. Tugidaq ignored the mutterings and curses, and finally when she brandished her skinning knife, they fell silent as she trimmed their long tangled hair and shaved off their matted beards.

After the men were reasonably clean, Tugidaq boiled infusions of willow bark tea to reduce fever, and lungwort (chiming bells) to relieve the congestion in their lungs. She also applied poultices of warm spruce pitch as a chest plaster to ease their aches and pains.

By this time, Sean and Jake and John realized the Aleut women were only trying to help, and they obediently drank the bitter tasting tea, and endured the sticky plasters, all the while rolling their eyes at each other in amused irritation.

Tugidaq and the two girls were just walking out of the house when Anna and Marya arrived with Keeah carrying a large basket. Under the watchful eyes of the two Russian guards, the women stared at each other for a moment in silence.

Tugidaq nodded briskly to Marya, then turned away, still feeling too irritated with her niece to speak to her.

"Wait, Aunt!" she called out in Aleut. "Please?"

Tugidaq halted, keeping her back to Marya, who said, "Tell me, how is Andrei?"

"Better," her aunt grunted. "Why do you ask?"

"He is a good man, and I wish him well. Can you tell him I have remembered him in my prayers?"

Tugidaq finally turned around. "He doesn't believe in your Russian God or your prayers. And he does not ever, ever speak your name."

Marya knew her aunt was one of those stubborn Aleuts who still clung to the old gods of their people. It was something Tugidaq and Andrei had in common. "I understand your anger with me, Aunt," she said, "but I must ask you a favor for my friend, Anna."

Tugidaq looked at Anna and scowled. Anna did not understand anything they were saying, but recognized her name. She smiled at Marya's aunt and the two girls, who smiled shyly in return.

Tugidaq began to mutter something then Marya said, "My friend is a maid who serves the Russians like many of our people. Her husband is one of the men inside and she will have his child in three months time. Will you come and help her then?"

The Aleut woman's hard expression softened slightly as her sharp black eyes dropped to Anna's belly hidden inside her warm cloak. She spoke rapidly to Marya in Aleut, her wizened face looking troubled. Then she and her two daughters left, heading back towards the village.

Marya sighed with relief. "My aunt is the best midwife in New Archangel, Anna, and she has promised to help you when your time comes."

"What else did she say? She seemed disturbed about something." Anna felt uneasy about having to trust the brusque-mannered Aleut woman with such a life and death matter as childbirth.

Marya frowned and glanced away, unable to meet Anna's inquiring gaze. "She's still angry with me because of Andrei."

But that hadn't been her words at all. Her aunt had said, "There are four very sick men in the house. One will die. I hope he isn't your friend's husband."

Anna raised her eyebrows, but didn't press the issue. They entered the small house, and walked into the main room, where the men lay on their four cots, alternately shivering and sweating under their covers. Anna saw at once that Marya's aunt and cousins had washed and shaved the men, and covered them with clean clothing and blankets. She could smell the pine scent of the spruce chest plasters and the sharp tang of willow bark tea. Obviously, Tugidaq knew what she was doing. Except for Ethan, who was sleeping as still as one dead, they appeared much better.

"Captain O'Connell, Mr. Hill and Mr. O'Riley," she said with a cheerful smile, "how glad I am to see you. I have brought my friend, Marya Nikolayevna, and her *Kolosh* maid, Keeah."

She spoke to all three, but she kept glancing at the captain. Unlike the day before, his black hair was clean and fell to his shoulders in a dark curly wave. It outlined his rugged lean face like the frame of an oil painting, his green eyes alight with surprise. There was a sudden warmth in them that made her heart flutter.

"Anna, I am glad to see ye." he said, struggling to sit upright. He coughed sharply and grimaced, then gave her a weak grin. "Ye just missed the local witch doctor and her minions."

"That was Marya's aunt, the best healing woman in New Archangel," she said dryly.

"Her aunt?" He echoed with confusion, noting the wealthy appearance of the beautiful Russian girl. She didn't look anything like any native he'd ever seen.

"I am a *Creole*, Captain," said Marya without embarrassment. "My mother was an Aleut and my father was Captain-Lieutenant Nikolas Ilyich Bolkonsky."

Anna saw his shock as he recognized the name of Tatiana's father. "*Madame* Volodina did not know she had a half-sister until she arrived here last year," she explained.

He smirked. "I bet your former mistress was not too pleased about that."

Anna hesitated then said, "She is still my mistress."

A flash of anger crossed his face. "Ethan an' I were afraid she'd force ye back to bein' her maid." He swore softly, then apologized. "I'm sorry, Anna."

She hastened to reassure him. "I'm fine, Captain, really I am. The work is easy and I'm treated well."

"Is everything all right?" he asked with concern. "With the babe, I mean?"

She glanced downwards. "Yes," she laughed lightly, "not to worry. Marya's aunt will deliver it in three months' time."

"The old crone?" he blurted, then apologized to Marya as another coughing spell seized him. He winced in pain and Anna gestured to Keeah.

"We've brought beet *borscht* and fresh bread. Whether you are hungry or not, all you men need to eat."

The captain gave Anna a lopsided grin, and Marya saw how his gaze fastened hungrily on her, as if it was her he wanted, and not the food. Was the captain in love with Anna?

Then, as Keeah ladled the soup into bowls, Marya noticed one of the men could not take his eyes off of her. He had blond hair that curled around his face, and dark blue eyes glittering with fever. She thought him a very handsome man, especially with that interesting looking scar near his mouth.

She brought him a bowl of soup and helped him sit up. He smiled at her. "I'm John Hill, the third officer of the *Sea Rose*. Pleased to make your acquaintance, Ma'am."

He coughed, looking embarrassed at the harsh hacking sound. She smiled at him with sympathy. "You must promise me that you will rest all you can and eat nutritional foods, *Monsieur* Hill."

"I promise," he said, his smile growing wider. "You may call me John, if you wish."

Marya felt her ears burning at his obvious admiration and she said, somewhat flustered, "Well then John, we will visit you every day until you are well."

"Perhaps I should stay sick as long as possible to prolong the attentions of such a lovely young lady as yourself."

She blushed at his compliment, and not knowing how to answer, went to fetch him some bread. She was aware of his eyes following her every movement as he ate his soup with trembling hands. Keeah noticed the

Yankee officer's interest in Marya, and smiled, then found the third man staring as intently at her.

He was the most fascinating man she had ever seen. He had wiry hair the color of the bright reddish orange mushrooms which grew in the rain forest, and his eyes were as blue as the jays who scolded her from the tree branches. His face was covered in faint brown dots, like the tattooed skin of her people.

She handed him his soup and bread, feeling uncomfortable under his steady gaze. Finally he grinned at her, and his whole face lit up like a ray of sunshine. "Me name's Jake," he said. "Jacob O'Riley, second mate."

She found herself smiling back, suddenly liking the strange looking white man. "Jake," she repeated, then tapped her cheek. "Keeah."

"Nice," he said, as he took a mouthful of bread. He noticed the scar on her lower lip, but somehow he didn't think it detracted from her native beauty. Too bad he was too sick to do much more than grin like a daft idiot at her.

While Keeah and Marya helped the three men eat, Anna moved to Ethan's cot, and bent over him. He needed nourishment even more desperately than the others.

She placed a hand on his forehead. It felt like touching a burning brand. "Ethan," she said softly, "Ethan, wake up. You must eat, or at least drink some tea." A half filled mug of willow bark tea sat on the floor beside his cot.

Anna looked at him with despair. His skin was flushed almost as red as his hair and his lips were crusted with fever blisters. She peered underneath the blanket and saw the irritated flesh of his leg stump. She saw that the Aleut woman had smeared an ointment all over it, and she felt thankful for her knowledge of the local herbs and medicines.

Ethan shifted restlessly and turned his head toward her. With painful slowness his eyes opened and at first they looked blank, then gradually awareness dawned upon his face. "Anna," he murmured. "Ach, Anna, are ye really here, or am I dreamin'?"

"Yes, Ethan, it's me, and I'll be here to see you everyday. Do you remember being brought out of the prison last night to this house?"

He glanced around the room at the other three men and then looked at her. "Aye, I remember a bit here and there. I couldna walk, so two big men carried me in a litter like a helpless bairn." He coughed, a deep wrenching sound that left him momentarily winded.

Anna saw a flicker of pain cross his face. "Does it hurt when you cough?"

"Aye, in my chest, something fierce. And I'm so hot an' thirsty, lass. Feels like we're caught in the doldrums with nary a breeze blowin'."

She picked up the mug of lukewarm tea. "Here, drink this down. It will ease the pain and fever."

She supported his head up with one hand so he could drink it all. After he finished he tried to smile. "'Tis hard to believe you're here, Anna. And how's our wee bairn?"

She took one of his hands and pressed it to her abdomen just as the child kicked inside of her. "Feel that, Ethan? He's as strong as an ox, and kicks just like one. Sometimes he keeps me awake half the night with his antics."

His eyes widened with wonder and he kept his hand there, even though it began to tremble in his weakened condition. "Could be a bonny lass, just like her ma."

"Is that what you want, a daughter?"

"Aye," he grinned, "but I'll take a lad, too."

She laughed lightly, thinking how much better he was looking when suddenly his eyes bulged and he coughed, again and again. She gave him a handkerchief to hold over his mouth and seized him by the shoulders, trying to give him support until the spasms halted. When he took the cloth away from his lips, she saw the blood in the phlegm. Exhaustion made the pallor of his face gray and he sank back onto his pillow, closing his eyes.

"Ethan, dearest, you rest and have sweet dreams. God will take care of you."

He didn't answer and she saw that he had fallen asleep. She stooped over and kissed him gently on his cheek, then took a cool wet cloth and placed it across his forehead. *He is a very sick man*, she thought, trying to swallow her dread and fear. *Please, Lord, don't let him die.*

"Anna," said the captain from the next cot, "I'm sorry I couldn't find a way to get Ethan out of the prison sooner. I tried every day to tell those cursed guards to get us help, but no one ever came."

"It's not your fault, captain. It's the fault of the Russians." She sighed heavily. "At least he will have better care now. I just pray it's not too late."

"He's strong. He'll make it through this, just like he did when he lost his leg. We all thought he was a goner then, but Ethan said God had other plans. And I guess he was right."

Anna smiled at him, surprised. "Thank you for those encouraging words."

He gave her an almost boyish grin then he flushed slightly. "Anna, I've a favor to ask. Can ye find someone to bring Samuel and Wang Li here to take care of us? 'Tis a bit embarrassin' for me and the lads to have those young lassies washing us."

* * *

"So, Lieutenant Ivanoff, what do you have to say for yourself?"

Governor Muraviev leaned backwards in his comfortable armchair sitting behind his desk and frowned sternly while he waited for Boris's answer. He had spent the past hour interrogating the sergeant in charge of the prison. The man had declared his innocence, saying he'd passed on the information about the ill prisoners to both Lieutenant Ivanoff and Lieutenant Volodin. Then after the *Buldakov* sailed in early November, he'd sent messages to Lieutenant Ivanoff each week, asking him to tell the governor that the prisoners were so sick, they were possibly in mortal danger.

Ivanoff mopped his perspiring forehead with his handkerchief. Why did His Excellency keep his office so hot during the winter? He could feel the sweat running down his neck and back and gathering under his armpits.

"The sergeant is lying, Your Excellency," he said. "I never received any messages about the prisoners. He should be whipped with the *knout*."

Muraviev looked at Dmitri. "And do you say the same, Lieutenant Volodin? Did you ever receive a message from Sergeant Dvorak?"

"*Nyet*, Your Excellency. I agree with Lieutenant Ivanoff. The man must be lying to save his own skin."

Muraviev closed his eyes for a moment and thought. Dvorak was a small weasel faced man with a pot belly and sharp crooked teeth. But his unattractive appearance was not the issue here. It was the man's character. And nothing about him had made Muraviev believe he was not telling the truth. Dvorak had acted frightened, to be sure, but who wouldn't be, accusing the two most powerful naval officers in New Archangel of hiding important information from the governor?

He was well aware of their hostility towards the American prisoners. He remembered the day *Madame* Campbell first came to his office, begging to visit her husband, and that Ivanoff had protested. Was it because he didn't want the woman to find out how ill the prisoners were?

But he had no proof. Dvorak had said he'd written the messages, but of course, if they existed, they would be destroyed by now. It was all one man's word against another, or in this case, two men's word against one. That meant he should believe his lieutenants rather than the sergeant. He hated punishing any man if there was a chance he was innocent. But someone had to be held accountable for this embarrassing lapse of communication in the ranks. And he couldn't very well whip Ivanoff and Volodin, the two sons of men on the Company Board of Directors, even though he suspected they were guilty.

He rubbed his eyes wearily, then opened them and looked at Boris and Dmitri. Both men appeared to be nervous, Ivanoff sweating like a hog and Dmitri with his twitching eye. If the charge wasn't so serious, he would've laughed to see the two pompous officers squirm. How he wished he could see them lashed with the *knout*, just long enough to humble them so that they might learn to show mercy to their fellow man instead of brutality.

But the Company would have his head if he dared to harm either one of them. That meant Dvorak would have to be the scapegoat; poor man.

"Tomorrow at dawn I will have Sergeant Dvorak given ten lashes with the *knout* for insubordination. Meanwhile, we have other matters to consider, such as how to feed our settlement for the rest of the winter and in the year to come."

Supplies of fresh vegetables, fruits, meats, flour, rice, molasses, and sugar were dwindling away, and the town's diet consisted mainly of *Herr*ing and dried salmon, with occasional venison. It wouldn't be until spring that the tastier fish such as cod, halibut, and salmon, which stayed away from the coast during winter, would return to add a bit of variety to the table.

The subject of food always interested Ivanoff, and he eagerly voiced his opinions on the matter. Later Dmitri and Boris left the meeting with expressions of relief on their faces.

"We must be more careful in the future, my friend," said Dmitri. "We are lucky it's not us feeling the bite of the *knout* tomorrow."

"I agree. But perhaps all is not lost. The Yankees are still very sick, I hear. And if they do survive their illness," chuckled Boris, "it will be an easy matter to arrange an unfortunate accident in New Archangel for them."Then his expression grew more serious. "Is it true that you have agreed to a one year betrothal between me and Marya?"

"Da, my wife says the girl is so young, that it is best to wait that long."

Boris growled deep in his throat. "*Nyet*, Dmitri, a girl is best wed young enough to train to be a good wife. The older they are, the harder that is. I beg of you, please reconsider."

Dmitri smiled. "Consider it done. When do you wish to marry her?"

"A spring wedding would be nice, don't you think?"

* * *

It was January, a bitter month when the clouds hung low like a gray mantle sinking over the town, intermittently spewing out sticky snowflakes. None of the surrounding mountains were visible in the short daylight hours; out at sea no horizon could be seen, only a merging of gray water and sky. The slate-colored ocean looked forbidding and cold and Marya shivered as she made her way carefully on the slippery path leading away from the church.

She had just finished confession with Father Sokolov and felt more depressed and troubled than ever. She had gone with such high spirits, hoping he would agree to talk to Dmitri about breaking off the betrothal with Lieutenant Ivanoff.

When she'd broached the subject, the priest had looked at her with surprise. "Not long ago I remember you asked me to speak to your uncle to break off your betrothal to Andrei Leonov, and I refused. Why do you think it would be any different now?"

"Because there is such a huge difference between the two men. Andrei Leonov is a decent man, but Boris Ivanoff is--is a dreadful man. Father, I cannot marry him!"

"If Andrei Leonov is such a good man, then why did you refuse to marry him?"

"Because I did not love him."

"And you do not love Lieutenant Ivanoff either?"

"No, Father, I despise him! And not only that, I am afraid of him. He is a violent man!"

He'd given her a sad smile and said, "Most of the men in New Archangel are violent men, child. It is a town full of sinners. I don't think you'll find a perfect man here."

Unbidden, the smiling face of John Hill entered her mind. She'd only met him once, but she remembered the sensitive manner about him, a gentleness she'd not seen in any Russian or Aleut or *Creole* man. And when he'd looked at her she had drowned in his eyes, the color of the deep blue ocean on a sunny day.

"I'm sorry I cannot go against Lieutenant Volodin's wishes. He is the head of your family now since you have left your uncle's household. You will have to accept Lieutenant Ivanoff as your husband."

Father Sokolov's words promptly brought her back to reality. For the first time in her life, she felt angry with him. In a moment of madness she gathered her courage and said, "There's something else that has been bothering me. Why do I need to go through you to confess my sins to God. Why can't I pray directly to Him and be forgiven?"

He was quiet for a moment, then frowned. "Have you been talking to that Mennonite woman?"

“Yes, but--but I've also been reading Papa’s Bible, and I'm confused.”

He furrowed his eyebrows together in a sign of sudden indignation. "I warn you, Marya Nikolayevna, do not listen to *Madame* Campbell's heretical interpretations of the Holy Scriptures. You will put your own soul in eternal danger!”

She stared at him in surprise. "But I don't understand."

"Marya, child, think. What did your own parents believe? Your devout mother, Sonya Grigorevna, clung to the holy Orthodox faith to the day of her death. And didn’t your own papa turn to our faith and welcome it into his heart before he died?” He paused. “If you wish to see them again someday in heaven, do not turn from the faith of your parents!”

Stunned, she could only bow her head meekly and stammer, “Y--yes, Father, forgive me for such unholy thoughts,” as the priest then sternly absolved her of her sins.

Now as she stumbled away from the church, her mind was in a whirling turmoil. The last thing she wanted to do was risk not seeing her beloved parents again in the afterlife. And she had to admit it was ludicrous to think that a young woman like Anna knew more about spiritual matters than the well known and respected Father Sokolov. She would have to stop talking to her about religion.

Tears blurred her vision and she paid little attention to where her footsteps led her. Not many people were about on this brutal day, just the usual packs of mangy starving dogs, which she avoided whenever she could. Without thinking she suddenly found herself standing in front of the small house where the American prisoners were. At this time of the afternoon she knew Anna was probably inside tending her sick husband.

The two guards by the door, each armed with a musket and a sword strapped to their waists, were stomping their boots in the cold. The taller one leered at her while his partner demanded gruffly, "Who are you and what do you want?"

"My name is Marya Nikolayevna Bolkonskaya. I'm here to visit the prisoners."

"By whose authority?" he barked, trying to appear important.

Marya thought quickly. "Lieutenant Dmitri Volodin, my brother-in-law."

The guards' faces, ruddy from the icy wind, paled. At once they stepped back from the door and let her through. As she hurried by them, the tall one gave a lusty guffaw and said, "Ivan, we should have searched her first for weapons."

Both men erupted in coarse laughter which she quickly halted by slamming the door behind her. The abrupt sound startled everyone inside the room, except Ethan who lay very still on his cot, except for the rising and falling of his chest as he struggled to breathe.

Anna jumped up from her chair. "Marya!" she exclaimed. "Does your sister know you're here?"

"No, she thinks I'm at confession with Father Sokolov."

"Oh, dear, did you trick her again?"

"No, I really was at the church. I just came from there."

Anna could see at a glance how distressed the girl was. She remembered that Marya intended to ask the priest to help her break off the betrothal to Lieutenant Ivanoff. Obviously, he had refused.

Marya's lovely amber brown eyes were moist with unshed tears. "Father Sokolov will not help me, Anna. In three months time I will be wed to Lieutenant Ivanoff !"

Her voice ended in a note of such despair that Sean, Jake, and John all looked at her with startled concern, especially John. The women had spoken rapidly in French, but he knew enough of that language to understand what had been said. And he didn't like it.

"What did the lass say?" Jake asked. He and the other two men were feeling well enough to be out of bed for a short time each day. They were all sitting at a crude wooden table drinking tea and eating soup served by a smiling Wang Li. Their appearance was greatly improved; the men were wearing clothing from their own chests brought off the *Sea Rose*.

"She is being forced to marry Lieutenant Ivanoff," said John in a grim voice.

Jake spat on the floor in disgust. "Ye mean that fat pig of a Russkie who tied us up like trussed chickens--"

"That's the man," interrupted Sean. "He and Volodin make quite a nasty pair of husbands I'd think. Poor lass."

Marya knew enough English to realize the men were discussing her. She flushed in humiliation and darted a quick glance at Mr. Hill. He was smiling at her, looking particularly charming this afternoon with a few unruly fair curls straying across his forehead while the rest of his long hair was neatly tied back with a string. He was dressed in a white shirt and gray trousers, which Samuel had washed and neatly pressed.

At the moment, the steward was standing near the stove holding a broom, eyeing the gray glob of Jake's spittle on the floor with a look of dismay. Leastwise dere's no blood in it, he sighed, thinking of Ethan Campbell. *What's poor Missy gonna do if he goes, I jus' dunno.*

Taking a deep breath, Marya gave all the men a dazzling smile, resembling Tatiana so closely, Anna was startled. "Good afternoon, gentlemen," Marya said in English, "It is good to see you looking well today."

Sean and Jake mumbled a greeting while John stood, shaking slightly on his still weak legs. "*Mademoiselle* Marya, come and sit by the stove. You must be chilled to the bone."

He pushed his chair towards the chipped brick stove built into the wall. She gave him a grateful look and took the offered chair.

"Thank you, *Monsieur* Hill. It is a dreadfully cold day."

"Remember, you're to call me John." He stared at her with admiration, then spied the glimmer of an unshed tear at the corner of one eye. "I'm sorry that you are suffering such misery. Is there anything we can do to help you?"

She wiped the tear away with one gloved finger then sighed. "Thank you for your concern, John, but there is nothing anyone can do now. I am to be wed to a man I despise."

Not if I can help it, John thought, as a strong feeling of protectiveness washed over him. Not only was she the prettiest girl he'd seen in a long while, she reminded him greatly of his young Nootka wife. Right then and there, he vowed to himself, that as soon as he regained his health and the governor set him free, he was going to find a way to stop that wedding, no matter how much trouble it caused him.

"Don't despair, Marya. The lads and I will smuggle you aboard the *Sea Rose* this spring when the governor allows us to leave. We can take you anywhere you want to go."

Marya uttered a high tinkling laugh while Sean snorted in derision. "Nay, John. The last thing we need is the wrath of a jilted Russian naval officer upon us. An' at the moment, there's no tellin' if we'll be getting our ship back or no, much less our own hides set free."

"I've heard talk that His Excellency wishes to send all of you and your ship away as soon as you are well and the weather improves."

Anna looked across the room at Marya. "Would that include Ethan?"

"I don't know, Anna," she replied in a sad voice. She glanced at the long bony form of the Scotsman bundled under blankets, hearing the deep rattle inside his chest whenever he drew breath. She could see the how paper thin and dry his skin appeared, stretched taught across his flushed face, his closed eyes sunken into hollows, reminding her of too much of her papa when he was nearing death. She was so afraid that before much longer, Anna would be a widow. Then it wouldn't matter if the governor set Ethan free or not.

Now it was Anna's turn to feel the sting of tears as she lovingly held Ethan's hand in her own. Yesterday she had thought him much improved. He had managed to sip some willow bark tea for his fever, and also a bit of broth, and then had talked to her briefly.

"Anna, lass, I love ye." His gaze drifted to her abdomen and he'd given her a weak smile. "I see the bairn is growin' well. Pray God that I live to see the day she's born."

With alarm she'd said, "Of course, you will, Ethan. You are getting better every day."

"Aye, lass," he'd said agreeably, "but if the Lord decides he wants me home soon, will ye give my Bible to Sean?"

"Of course, Ethan," she'd said, swallowing the lump of fear in her throat.

Today right before Marya came, he'd been taken with a coughing spell, one that was so harsh, his face and neck turned purple, his eyes bulged out, and his every muscle strained as he gasped to breathe. She had held her own breath for a moment, praying, *oh, God, please help him breathe, help him breathe.*

Then he suddenly relaxed and his face drained of color. For one terrible moment she thought he was gone, but then he started to breathe again. He'd been unconscious ever since, a torturous sleep where every breath was an agonized challenge.

It wouldn't be long now, she knew, even though she had pleaded, begged, and prayed to God every day and every night to heal him. Was this how her papa had felt when he watched her mama die? She remembered how they'd all prayed unceasingly, but Mama had slipped away regardless. Watching Ethan's every movement, every pulse and every breath, was seeing Mama die all over again. Her lungs had been so full of fluid, she slowly suffocated to death. Anna feared it was the same for Ethan. She could hear the ominous liquid in his throat with each breath.

It was like watching a man drown from the inside out.

She felt the eyes of everyone in the room looking at her. Their glances were full of worry and sympathy, not just for Ethan, but also for her. Somehow it irritated her, especially when the captain stared in her direction. She wished they would turn away and act normally, discuss the weather, drink their tea, argue about how unfair they'd been treated by the Russian governor.

Then she felt ashamed of herself. These were her friends and Ethan's friends, and the captain was like a younger brother to Ethan. They'd known each other since the captain was a lad, for some fourteen years in all.

Suddenly Ethan opened his eyes and began to choke again as he strained to catch a breath. He turned his head towards Anna and she quickly bent over and took his limp hand. “Ethan, Ethan, it’s me, Anna, can you hear me?”

His eyelids fluttered and he groaned as air rasped in his throat. Sean stood up and walked over to them and knelt on the other side of the cot. His face was shrouded in dread and fear.

“I’m right here with you,” she said, taking his hand and laying it gently against her cheek. “I’ll take care of you, Ethan, and you’ll be fine soon. Just rest now.”

He was staring at something over her shoulder. He let out a strangled gasp and said so softly she could hardly hear him, “I see Da an' Ma.”

Chills prickled down her neck and she glanced at Captain O’Connell. He had a strange look on his face. “They died years ago,” he said.

“Yes, I know, he told me about them. His dad was a minister and his mother was a fine lady. Ethan loved them both dearly.”

Wang Li shook his head. “Not good,” he muttered. “When ancestors come, soul can fly away with them.”

Anna’s face paled and she said, “Ethan, don’t leave me.”

Jake frowned at the little Chinaman. “Enough of that crazy talk, Wang Li. Yer upsettin’ the Missus.”

Wang Li bowed to Anna, a deep pity in his slanted black eyes. “Pardon, Missy, pardon.”

“Ethan?” Anna called out. “Ethan? Can you hear me?”

Slowly, his gaze seemed to refocus and he looked straight at her. She thought she could see the love shining in his warm brown eyes. In the next second it was like seeing a light being extinguished. His eyes glazed over and she knew he could not see her.

“Ethan,” she said with a sob as she felt a spasm of fear choke her throat.

With a grim expression on his face, Sean placed his left hand on Ethan's chest then pressed his right thumb against his neck. There was no pulse.

He sighed heavily. “He's gone, Anna. I'm so sorry.”

* * *

Ethan Campbell was buried in the Russian cemetery on a hill above the town. Instead of a church service, Father Sokolov read from the Holy Scriptures at the graveside. The weather was dreary, intermittent rain and sleet blown by a cold southwest wind. With silent tears and raindrops both running down her cheeks in wet streaks, Anna stood between Tatiana and Marya. The rest of the mourners consisted of a few curious onlookers and the entire crew of the *Sea Rose*. Robby slumped dejectedly against a sad-faced Gregory Jones while Sean, Jake, and John were flanked by several armed guards.

Anna didn't notice them. Staring down into the deep muddy grave at the rough pine coffin, she kept twisting her bright silver wedding band around her finger. One day last summer Ethan had traded for a small piece of silver from a Haida Indian, then had Gregory Jones melt the silver on his forge, and fashion it into a ring. She remembered when he presented the ring to her, his soft brown eyes sparkling with love, his voice speaking in the peculiar Scots lilt of his Gaelic ancestors, telling her of his plans for their future and how deeply he loved her.

How short-lived their happiness was, she thought with a burst of anger, as she envisioned his gaunt, disease ridden body and his painful battle to live. How could the God who loved her, the God she'd trusted all her life, allow such terrible sorrow to pierce her heart? And why did God take away such a fine man as Ethan?

These tormenting questions had no immediate answers. Anna wondered how her mama could have born the anguish of losing so many babies, or her papa losing her mama. Yet, they went on, and kept their faith, never doubting that God still loved them. She would have to do the same, she knew, but it was so very very hard.

Although Anna believed Ethan was in heaven and that she would see him again someday, she wanted him here with her now. She wanted to talk and laugh with him again and feel his strong protective arms around her at night. She wanted him to help her raise their child in this foreign violent world. She wanted to be able to stop weeping.

Tatiana kept one hand on Anna's arm and Marya held the other. Both girls felt Anna tremble and knew she needed their support. To Tatiana's surprise, she could feel her own eyes filling with tears whenever she looked at her. It was almost as if she could feel Anna's pain as her own. If that was the meaning of compassion, Tatiana realized she'd never felt it before.

She gazed down into the grave pit, suddenly wishing it was Dmitri they were going to bury there, and not a man as kind and loving as Ethan Campbell. It was monstrously unfair.

Sean stood some distance away watching Anna. His heart felt like it was going to break, seeing the grief and anguish on her face. Her eyes were enormous, full of tortured pain. It was all he could do to stop himself from rushing over to her, taking her in his arms, and assuring her that everything would be fine again someday. But how could he make that happen?

They were all still stranded in New Archangel without the means to leave. He glanced around at the Russians. The governor was conspicuous in his absence. In his stead were the two lieutenants, Volodin and Ivanoff, both with the proper somber expressions on their faces, except for the smirks of satisfaction they occasionally exchanged.

Some time ago Anna had told them that the sergeant in command of the prison had been brutally punished for not reporting the severity of their illness to the governor in spite of Dvorak's claims to have told Ivanoff and Volodin. If that was true, because of them, a God-fearing woman, a woman who had never hurt a living soul, was a widow. And her innocent child was going to be born fatherless. Where was the justice in that? Where were Ethan's and Anna's God or the God of his ma and his sister? What good did their faith do for any of them?

Bitterness choked him suddenly like a foul blister in his throat and he almost gagged as anger and hatred twisted inside his soul. Volodin and Ivanoff were going to pay for this, he vowed, somehow, someday.

CHAPTER TWENTY THREE

Anna drifted through the next weeks like a sad ghost, performing her duties with an ashen, hollowed-out expression on her face. She rarely smiled and never laughed. At first Tatiana had urged her to stay in bed as along as she pleased, resting and recovering from the shock of her husband's death. But Anna refused. Sleeping had become a nightmare of troubled dreams punctuated by crying spells. The least time she spent in bed and the more she stayed busy, the better she could cope with the grief that wouldn't leave her.

Her appetite suffered. Helena scolded and nagged her constantly to eat more. The *Creole* cook baked all sorts of delicious pastries and made nourishing soups to tantalize her, but Anna ate only enough to keep her and the child within her alive. As her belly grew, her arms and legs and face thinned, making her appear awkward and unbalanced.

The women of the household worried and fussed over her endlessly, mistresses and servants alike, irritating Dmitri no end. He had little sympathy for the maid, and treated her with the same cold contempt that he'd always had.

Now that the three American prisoners had recovered from their illness, he and Boris tried to persuade Governor Muraviev to return them to the prison. But the governor refused, saying he feared they could suffer a relapse. His Excellency had been distressed at Ethan Campbell's death, and didn't wish to risk the health of the captain or his two officers. Muraviev ordered the three Americans to remain under house arrest until their six month sentence was finished in mid-March.

With Ethan gone, Anna no longer visited the men, though twice a week she sent Keeah with a basket of food cooked by Helena. Each time Keeah left, Marya wished she could go with her. She hadn't seen John Hill in weeks, and had spoken to him only twice in her life, but for some reason she could not stop thinking about the man. During the day he invaded her thoughts at the oddest times and at night, she occasionally dreamt about him.

What did it mean, she often wondered. She'd never felt that way about Andrei Leonov, and certainly not about Boris Ivanoff. Was she falling in love with John Hill, like her papa had with her mama?

Her wedding was planned for the first of April. Tatiana had tried to convince both Dmitri and Boris that April was too soon, with all the wedding finery and trousseau to be sewn, the banquet to be planned with music and dancing and tons of food. But Dmitri refused, accusing her of just trying to postpone the marriage as long as possible.

One cold snowy morning in early February, Tatiana, Anna, and Marya were grouped inside Tatiana's sitting room upstairs. She was struggling with some embroidery while Anna and Marya were knitting baby clothes. The room was snug with the warmth of the stove and filled with the aroma of hot tea from the steaming samovar.

"The next time Keeah goes to visit Captain O'Connell and his officers," said Anna, "I'd like to accompany her."

Tatiana and Marya looked at her in surprise. This was the first time she'd shown any interest in venturing outdoors in weeks. However, Tatiana did not approve. "Anna, it is too dangerous for you in your condition to walk to their house. You might slip on the icy path."

Anna set her jaw in an obstinate look. "I could fall down the stairs, too, but I haven't. For heaven's sakes, the two of you have been telling me for days to get some fresh air."

"We meant you should take a brief walk around the house, not venture so far into town," said Marya. She gave Anna a curious smile. "Do you miss your American friends?"

"I have something for Captain O'Connell. One day when I was nursing Ethan," she paused to swallow a lump of pain that the mere mention of his name wrought, "and he told me that if anything happened to him, he wanted me to give the captain his Bible."

"I can't imagine what that godless man would do with such a thing," said Tatiana dryly.

"Perhaps if he read it, he would no longer be godless," Marya pointed out. "I think that's a wonderful gift for Ethan to leave to his best friend."

Tatiana frowned. "I still don't think you should attempt the long walk to that house."

"I'd be happy to deliver the Bible," Marya offered. "I can accompany Keeah next time she goes."

Anna gave her a relieved smile. "Thank you, Marya. I would appreciate it."

"You'll have to get Dmitri's permission first," said Tatiana doubtfully.

"My permission for what?" he said, suddenly appearing in the open doorway.

All three women froze with looks of surprised dismay on their faces. If he noticed their lack of welcome, he gave no sign. He marched into the room and said, "Tatiana, my dear, what are you ladies planning to do that needs my approval?"

Tatiana forced a smile. "Anna would like to bring Captain O'Connell a final gift from her husband, but she doesn't dare walk so far in her condition. Marya has graciously offered to deliver Ethan's Bible herself, as long as it is acceptable to you, of course."

"A Bible?" Dmitri laughed. "I believe it would take more than the Good Book to make a decent God fearing man out of that scoundrel!" He glanced at Marya. "Certainly, my dear, you can go, but since it isn't seemly for a betrothed girl to visit a houseful of single men alone, I'll ask Boris to accompany you."

He turned away from her, missing the flash of disappointment on her face. How glad he would be to have Marya married and out of the house, he thought. He was still furious that Tatiana had allowed the girl into their family. Although his fellow officers and their wives acted politely as ever towards him on social occasions, he saw the censure in their eyes whenever they looked at Marya.

Having a *Creole* sister-in-law was a constant source of humiliation to him. But when she became Boris's wife, she would no longer be his problem.

"Do you know if His Excellency plans to send the Americans away in their own ship this spring?" Tatiana asked.

Dmitri gave her a sullen frown. "If it wasn't for the Czar's *ukase*, I believe he would restore their ship to them, and let them all sail away." He grunted in anger. "He may do it regardless."

"Papa always liked the Yankee traders, as he called them," Marya blurted. "He and Alexander Baranov both believed that they were necessary to the survival of New Archangel."

Dmitri glared at her. “What was needed in the past is not any longer. You best keep those treasonous thoughts about foreign trade to yourself, my dear sister.”

Marya lowered her gaze, pretending to be chastised. *What fools the Russians are*, she thought rebelliously. *Anyone with two eyes can see how much this town needs the foreigners for trade and supplies.*

“Enough of this,” Dmitri said impatiently. “I must return to the governor's office where His Excellency and I are having a meeting. I only came back here to retrieve some documents.”

He crossed the room to his desk, opened a drawer, and snatched up a pile of papers. Nodding briskly to the three women, he exited the room, closing the door partly behind him.

He was about to step away, when he heard Marya say, “If you ever thought of marrying again, Anna, would you consider Captain O’Connell?"

“Sean O’Connell?” Tatiana repeated. “Why on earth would you mention him?”

“Keeah says he asks about you all the time, Anna, and I've seen the way he looks at you--"

“Oh, Marya, no,” protested Anna, “the captain only thinks of me as a friend.”

“In what way does he look at Anna?” Tatiana demanded.

"He stares at her all the time like a lovesick puppy. Keeah agrees with me."

Anna flushed with embarrassment. "That is so ridiculous! He may be in love with someone, but it's not me!"

"Nonsense," sniffed Marya. "Who else would he love, if not you?"

Anna shot Tatiana a questioning look. She suddenly glanced away, blushing furiously. Marya stared at both of them then laughed.

"You, Tatiana?" she exclaimed. "He's in love with you?"

Out in the hallway, Dmitri scowled and kept listening. As he waited for her answer, he clutched the papers so tightly he crushed them into a wad.

He heard his wife utter, "Hush, Marya! Why would either of you think there's anything between me and Captain O'Connell?"

"Marya is only guessing, *Madame*," Anna said with a serious expression, "but I remember one night on the *Sea Rose* when you returned to our cabin very late. You were with the captain, were you not?"

"How dare you imply such a thing, Anna!" she said sharply.

"Then tell me it isn't true."

There was a silence inside the room that seemed to last an eternity to Dmitri. At last he heard Tatiana say quietly, "It is true."

The blood roared inside Dmitri's brain as a deep rage possessed him. His wife, his beautiful Tatiana, was not the pure virgin bride he thought he'd married. She had betrayed him with a common Yankee sailor!

His first instincts were to rush into the room and confront her then slap her around until she begged for mercy. As a boy, he remembered his father beating his mother, hearing her cries for help. He had wanted to rescue her, but his fear of his father was greater. Now he wondered if his mother had deserved her beatings. Perhaps she too had betrayed his father.

He stood in the hallway and trembled with anger, the crumpled papers slipping to the floor unnoticed. As he took a step towards the door, he heard the boom of the harbor cannon fire a welcoming shot to an incoming vessel. The sound made him pause. What ship would be arriving in the middle of winter? Curiosity and a deep sense of duty temporarily overcame his rage. With a supreme effort, he forced himself to walk away. His Excellency would need him. He would deal with his wife later.

Back inside the sitting room, Anna and Marya ignored the crash of the cannon as they watched Tatiana wring her hands in agitation. "Nothing happened between me and Captain O'Connell," she said rapidly, "He was so drunk all he did was sleep. Because he couldn't remember anything the next day, it was easy for me to make him think we'd been intimate. It was the only way I could think of to get him to change his mind about leaving me in Rio de Janeiro. I swear he doesn't mean a thing to me!"

She glanced at Anna and Marya and frowned. “The two of you don’t have to look at me like that! I know what I did was wrong, but there was no real harm done.”

“What if Dmitri finds out?” asked Marya fearfully.

“It must be our little secret, between the three of us,” she said. “Do you both promise not to ever breathe a word of this to anyone?”

“We promise,” said Anna, “but you must be careful, Tatiana.”

“I will,” she said, remembering the fading bruises all over her body. Gossipy Natasha on the *Suvorov* long ago had been right. The Volodin men were a bad-tempered lot who thought nothing of hurting their wives and perhaps their own children. She suspected that Dmitri’s twin sister, Ella, had committed suicide for a good reason.

Now it was too late. She was part of their twisted family for the rest of her life. How she wished she could turn back the strands of time and be on the *Sea Rose* once again. If she hadn’t already been betrothed to Dmitri, with her head full of romantic visions of New Archangel and a new life, she might have fallen in love with Captain O’Connell herself. She deeply regretted throwing herself at the captain that one night. She remembered the next morning how he treated her coldly, with a distinct lack of respect.

How could she blame him? She had deceived him by pretending to be a loose woman even though she was not. And here all this time, Anna had known. A sudden wave of shame and nausea flooded through.

“My stomach has been unsettled all morning," she said. "I believe I should lie down for a spell.”

“Shall I help you, *Madame*?” Anna asked with concern.

“No, you and Marya run along. I just need some peace and quiet.” Tatiana headed for her bedchamber, holding one hand across her stomach.

After she was out of the room, Anna said to Marya, “I think she is with child. She has all the signs.”

“She must be very pleased.”

Anna looked doubtful. “Yesterday when I told her what I suspected, she became agitated, saying she was not ready to have children."

“When Dmitri finds out, perhaps he’ll treat her more kindly.”

“We can only pray that it is so,” said Anna worriedly.

The two girls stepped out into the hallway, almost bumping into Keeah. She was bending over, picking up a bunch of wrinkled papers from the floor. “You drop?” she asked.

“No,” said Anna. She and Marya exchanged looks of sudden horror.

“He was listening to our every word,” whispered Marya. “I hope he heard enough to know that nothing really bad happened between her and the American captain.”

"We must warn her as soon as she wakes from her nap." Anna then explained to the mystified Keeah what they were talking about.

The *Kolosh* girl looked at Anna and noticed how she appeared more energetic than she'd been in the weeks since her husband died. Maybe *Madame* Volodina's problem was a good thing, she thought. It had finally put the spark of life back in Anna.

* * *

Muraviev was in a fury, and at first he managed to hide it well. In a calm voice he instructed Catherine Kornilova to prepare a special banquet this evening. The *Alexandria*, a warship from Saint Petersburg, had arrived, and it was customary to welcome the weary officers to the finest foods New Archangel had to offer. Unfortunately, this time of year, it wasn't much.

He'd hoped the ship was carrying large supplies of badly needed provisions, but there was little left from their long voyage. The armed cruiser had been battered by storms as she sailed north and was deemed lucky to have survived at all. They should have been wiser, the governor fumed inwardly, and waited at Fort Ross in California for the calmer seas of April. But the young lieutenant in charge of the *Alexandria* had been impatient to reach New Archangel.

"It is his first command of a ship, but it could have been his last, the fool!" he finally spouted to Mikhail in the privacy of his apartment as his valet helped him dress for dinner. "I realize he was bringing important news for Lieutenant Volodin, but it could have waited a few more weeks. I expected more from someone with the name of Bolkonsky!"

"Perhaps it is due to his youth and inexperience that Lieutenant Bolkonsky was so reckless. And he might have been overanxious to tell his cousin and her husband about the sudden death of Baron Ivan Volodin, Your Excellency," he chided softly. "But I must say, Lieutenant Volodin took the news rather well."

"Yes, Volodin acted properly shocked and sorrowful," mused Muraviev, "but a part of him must be excited about becoming a wealthy baron. I know a greedy man when I see one. "

In fact, Dmitri was delirious with joy as he left the governor's office and hurried home. His mind was still trying to comprehend the good fortune that was now his, the title of baron and all the riches of the Volodin estate.

Mikael Bolkonsky had delivered the news to him in the governor's office. "I'm so sorry to have to tell you that last April your father, his Excellency Baron Ivan Volodin, suddenly collapsed and died from a stroke inside his brain. Please accept my sincerest sympathies to you and my dear cousin, whom I'm most anxious to see again."

His kind words belied the smug look of satisfaction lurking in his black eyes. Dmitri had never met the man before, but it seemed to him that his wife's cousin was as happy as he about his father's death. Then he recalled how Tatiana once told him about his father shooting young

Bolkonsky in a duel, because Mikael had insulted the entire Volodin family and his father had made him suffer for it.

All of this made Dmitri dislike Mikael Bolkonsky on the spot, but he stiffly shook his hand and accepted his condolences. There was something else about the younger man he didn't trust, the manner in which he spoke of Tatiana. He appeared too eager to see her again, as if they were very fond of each other, but Tatiana had never spoken of her cousin at all. He would have to keep a close on eye on Mikael Bolkonsky for the duration of his presence in New Archangel.

It was the problem of being married to such a beautiful woman, he thought, his mood darkening quickly as he opened the front door to his house and hurried upstairs. Tatiana belonged to him, but that didn't mean other men couldn't fall in love with her, such as the cursed Yankee captain.

He was going to take enormous pleasure in telling Tatiana she was now a baroness, then finding a way to make her suffer. She deserved to be beaten for deceiving him about her affair, but her punishment would have to wait until after the governor's banquet.

With a grim smile he entered his sitting room, and heard Tatiana speaking to her maid. Great, he thought, her nosy maid was always underfoot. Anna Campbell made him uneasy. She had a way of looking at him, as if she was staring all the way inside his soul and not approving of what she saw. He also resented Tatiana's close relationship with the girl, a common peasant as far as he was concerned. If only he could find fault with her work, he'd dismiss her services at once. He had no qualms in tossing a pregnant widow out of the house like he would an unwanted cat.

"Sir, *Madame* has just awakened from her nap," Anna said with surprise as he walked into the bedchamber.

"Leave us," he said curtly.

"Yes, sir." Anna pressed her lips together in disapproval, but left as he ordered without another word.

"I have good news and bad news, darling," he said with barely concealed excitement. "You heard about the ship arriving this afternoon?"

"Yes, what ship was that?" she asked automatically, not caring a whit. An hour ago she'd awakened and almost fainted from fright when Anna told her that she and Marya suspected Dmitri had overheard their earlier conversation about Sean O'Connell. Then Anna had urged her to tell Dmitri the truth about the captain, but Tatiana didn't know if she had the courage. If she told him anything, it would be about the child.

"The *Alexandria*, commanded by your cousin, Lieutenant Mikael Bolkonsky."

Mikael is here in New Archangel? Jolted by the shock, she gulped, swallowing down a burst of stomach acid, then said faintly, "Fancy that, Mikael's a lieutenant."

"He brought sad, but important news, my dearest, " Dmitri rushed on, "my father died last spring of a stroke, and do you realize what that makes us? A baron and a baroness! His Excellency is giving a banquet tonight to welcome your cousin and his officers, but I think we should use it to celebrate our new titles!"

To his surprise, instead of reacting with delight, she said, "I'm sorry about your father, Dmitri, even if you aren't. But I can't attend that dinner tonight."

Bewildered, he said, "But why not? I thought you'd be thrilled to see your cousin again."

Without thinking she blurted, "No, I'm not! I despise Mikael and when I left Saint Petersburg, I hoped I'd never see him again!"

Now it was Dmitri's turn to look shocked. "Whatever has he done for you to hate him so? I can assure you, the man doesn't hate you. On the contrary, he was looking forward to seeing you at the banquet tonight."

"When we were children, he and Olga were always mean to me. And one night, the night my grandmother died, Mikael killed my kitten that Papa gave me by throwing it out the window. I've never forgiven him!" she ended in a bitter voice.

"Ah, yes, you and your love for cats!" Dmitri gave her an amused look. "I suppose I better be careful around what are their names, Raven and Otter, or else you'll start hating me too?"

"How can you make light of a childhood experience that was such a nightmare for me?" Tatiana demanded. "Don't you love me at all?"

"Of course, I adore you, darling, but the greater question is, do you really love me?" He looked at his wife. Tatiana was still disheveled from her nap, wearing her violet silk dressing gown, her light golden hair tumbling past her shoulders to her waist. She had never looked lovelier. It filled Dmitri with lust and frustrated anger.

Tatiana saw his suppressed rage, saw how his muscle twitched under his left eye, and she felt a moment of panic. She knew she had better distract him from the subject of Captain O'Connell quickly before he lost control. Then she thought of the perfect defense, her child. Now that she was the Baroness Volodina with the heir to the family fortune growing inside her, Dmitri would never dare harm her. For the first time, she was glad she was with child. It was her protection from her violent husband.

"I'm not feeling well enough to play these games, Dmitri."

"You do look a bit peaked," he said with irritation, noting the dark circles under her eyes, even more pronounced against her pale face. "Are you ill?"

"Yes and no. I am to have your child. Anna says it will be born in September."

Dmitri broke into an astonished grin. He could hardly believe his ears. What a day! After a dreadful morning, when he discovered his wife was not the perfect woman he thought she was, then this afternoon, to hear the wonderful news of his father's demise, giving him the family title and wealth, and now, he was to become a father himself! His dream of founding his own Volodin dynasty was becoming a reality.

Excitement and a feeling of happiness coursed through him. He smiled at Tatiana. She was safe from his wrath for the moment. Not that he would ever forgive or forget that she betrayed him. But he would grant her a reprieve. As long as she never looked at another man again, he would treat her with the love and respect the mother of his heir deserved.

He strode across the room and crushed her into his arms. "I am so happy, my dear. So happy," he murmured next to her ear, breathing in the fragrance of roses from her perfume.

She closed her eyes and leaned against his chest, her knees feeling weak from relief. She was grateful to have escaped his fury, but it was still there between them, waiting for the slightest spark to ignite it. She would have to be extremely careful to never arouse his jealousy again.

As he caressed the silky strands of her hair, Dmitri thought of the American captain. Sean O'Connell had probably seduced his young innocent bride-to-be on board his ship. Instead of harming Tatiana, it was the captain who should be punished. He decided to consult Boris soon on the best way to plan his revenge.

* * *

Somehow *Madame* Kornilova had managed to arrange a feast. The long linen covered oak table in the banquet hall groaned under the weight of the platters of meats, smoked fish, and breads. All the officers and their wives were present, including Vera and Sophie Trotskaya, Lieutenants Ivanoff and Dohktorov, and Father Sokolov. The guest of honor, Lieutenant Mikael Bolkonsky, was seated near the new Baron and Baroness Volodin, and Marya Nikolayevna.

The men had already been entertained in the library by Muraviev and liberally plied with glasses of chilled vodka and appetizers of the traditional *zakuska.* Their faces were inflamed from the liquor and their voices loud as they attacked the meal with gusto. Mikael, who was ravenous, found his attention divided between eating and staring at the gorgeous women at the table.

His cousin, Tatiana, looked as delectable as the food. He could not take his eyes off her. She was dressed fashionably in a high-waisted amethyst silk gown with a low neck edged in a lace frill. The short puffy sleeves were caught up by bands of darker amethyst silk. Her golden hair was swept up under a silk turban trimmed with pearls and feathers, allowing a few side curls and ringlets to frame her beautiful face. Pearl and gold earrings dangled from her ears and she had draped a lace scarf shawl around her shoulders.

Her half-sister, Marya, was seated next to her. After the initial shock of hearing that his deceased Uncle Nikolas had an Aleut mistress for years and fathered a daughter by her, he had expected to meet a plain-faced native girl. But the fresh young beauty sitting across the table from him took his breath away. Dressed in a pale lemon dress of satin and white lace, the color contrasted dramatically with her shiny black hair and exotic amber brown eyes. If it wasn't for the slight bronze tone of her skin, she could pass for any girl of the Russian aristocracy.

She was also a cousin of his, a cousin he would've liked to get to know better, except that she was betrothed to the enormous Lieutenant Ivanoff. *Too bad.*

He turned from her and smiled at pretty Vera Alexisovna. It was unfortunate that she too was to be married to the dull Lieutenant Anton Dohktorov later in the summer. She returned his smile with a flirtatious grin. He nodded in recognition, recalling the days of their childhood when she and her family visited them in Saint Petersburg. Her younger sister, Sophie, he noticed with distaste, was still as mousy and plain as ever.

In a matter of one more minute he had included in his inventory of women, the faded beauty of Elizabeth Pushkina, the widowed housekeeper *Madame* Kornilova, and the horse-faced Irina Trotskaya, his mother's friend. His glances also strayed to the Aleut serving women, but dismissed them as too dark and savage looking for his taste.

He wondered about Tatiana's little maid, Anna. He'd heard she was widowed and expecting a child soon. *My, my*, he thought, *what a difference from the innocent young girl who spurned his attentions in the palace that night. She was probably fat and ugly by now.*

Tatiana saw him smiling at Marya and Vera with that all too familiar hungry look in his eyes, and she shuddered. Up to that moment, she'd hoped Mikael had changed along with his appearance. The rigors of sea life had thinned her cousin and hardened the soft flabby boy she remembered into a stocky muscular man. Only the prominent Bolkonsky nose and his thick red lips remained the same, and his deviant personality.

"We have much to celebrate tonight," announced Governor Muraviev. He lifted his glass of wine. "A toast to the safe arrival of the *Alexandria* and her commander and crew."

As everyone cheered and drank, Muraviev took a deep breath, preparing himself for his next announcement. It was a decision he had thought long and hard about. It was time he rid himself and New Archangel of the cancer that was Dmitri Volodin and Boris Ivanoff. And he had found the perfect solution without insulting the two men.

He stood up and straightened his shoulders. "All of you know the importance of Fort Ross to Russian America, and how for some time, there has been nothing but problems there due to the lack of proper leadership. I have chosen a new administrator, a man in whom I have the utmost faith, a man who will turn Fort Ross into the prosperous colony that was Alexander Baranov's original vision."

He paused then smiled, lifting his glass high. "Ladies and gentlemen, I give you the new commander of Fort Ross, Baron Dmitri Ivanich Volodin."

Once again, surprised delight rushed throughout Dmitri's entire being. It was another dream coming true. After turning Fort Ross into a success, the next logical step would be governor of Russian America. He stood and bowed to the noble assembly as everyone clapped with hearty approval. He motioned to his stunned wife to also stand up.

As Tatiana rose, she pasted a smile on her face, acknowledging the best wishes from all at the table. California, she thought with dismay. It was an outpost even more foreign and isolated than New Archangel. How was she going to bear it?

"And now," said Muraviev, "I have chosen a new commander for our fort at Kodiak Island." He gestured towards Boris with a satisfied smile. "Lieutenant Boris Ivanoff!"

Boris was startled, but quickly recovered. He grinned at Marya seated next to him and boomed out, "Then it is a good thing I'm marrying the daughter of a princess of Kodiak! The natives will welcome us both with open arms! Another round to honor the good fortune for myself and my good friend, Dmitri," he called out, gesturing to the nearest serving woman to refill his glass.

Spots of greasy meat and spilled wine stained his white and gold dress uniform, which bulged at the seams, and the brass buttons on his coat threatened to explode off his gut at any moment. Everyone burst into laughter and further applause as Marya struggled to mask her disgust of the obese lieutenant. *Kodiak Island*, she thought wearily, *where Papa first fell in love with Mama*. She'd dreamt of returning there someday with her own naval officer husband, but not someone as nauseating as Boris Ivanoff. She frowned unhappily, her eyes staring down at the food on her plate which had just become unappetizing.

Tatiana saw the distress on her sister's face and nudged Dmitri. "Say something," she whispered, "to change the subject."

"Certainly," he smiled. "I have a further announcement to make," he said loudly with his face beaming proudly. "Before dinner this evening, my lovely wife told me there will be a new addition to our family come September."

Now it was her turn to blush in humiliation. She felt queasy with the sudden attention and was conscious of all eyes upon her, especially cousin Mikael's. With an effort, she smiled at everyone, trying to maintain the image of the gracious baroness while longing to flee from the room and the sickening smell and sight of the rich foods.

She was afraid she was going to vomit. If she did, it would ruin Dmitri's hour of glory. He would never forgive her. Perspiration broke out underneath her clothes and her legs began to shake.

Sophie Alexisovna leaned across the table. "A child. How nice for you, Tatiana," she said softly, her face brightening, making her almost attractive.

Then Sophie's smile blurred and disappeared altogether as Tatiana swooned and toppled off her chair in a faint.

* * *

The following morning Anna was awakened by the child kicking her ribs with its tiny feet. She smiled ruefully to herself. He or she always seemed to be restless when she was trying to sleep, while during the day, when she was active, the child was quiet. She wondered if this was normal, wishing once again that her mother was with her to answer all her questions and fears about pregnancy and childbirth. There was so much she did not know.

The familiar pain over losing Ethan along with an added wave of homesickness engulfed her as she stepped awkwardly out of bed, and washed her face with the water in the chipped basin on the small table. A single tear slid out of her eye and mingled with the moisture on her cheeks. She longed to be home in Furstenau, surrounded by her beloved family. As a widow about to have a child, she would be well taken care of. And after the proper period of mourning was past, she would have her pick of any number of eager Mennonite bachelors or widowers to wed.

She shivered at the thought of remarriage. She couldn't imagine having another man as a husband. It was too soon to even consider it. Yet, what else was there for her?

As the birth grew closer, she felt more vulnerable and insecure about her future. Although she believed that God was watching over her, and that He would provide for her, she still worried how she was going to raise a child without a husband. What sort of life here would her child have as the offspring of a maid among the Russian nobility, a woman living in a society that scorned her as a member of a religious sect at odds with the established church?

Anna frowned at the wavy reflection of her face in the water inside the basin. She was weary of living in New Archangel with all its petty intrigues and conceited personages. She could only hope living in Fort Ross would be better. At least it would be a warmer climate in California. Yet, she dreaded the thought of moving to an unfamiliar place and starting all over again.

Wistfully, Anna recalled how content she'd been living on the *Sea Rose*. She missed the friendly camaraderie of the crew and the daily adventures of life at sea. Each morning she awoke to a new experience, whether seeing a strange bird, fish, or island, or using her mind to help navigate the ship, or educate an illiterate sailor. She knew she would have made Ethan a good captain's wife.

Ethan...a jolt of grief shot through her as she thought of how deeply she missed him! Not only the love and joy they shared, but how they used to pray together every night before they went to sleep, bringing them close in spirit with God and each other in a special intimacy she didn't believe she could ever find with another man.

There would never be a man like Ethan in her life again. Anna shook her hair out of its long braid and brushed it, then rebraided the strands into a plait and covered her head with a scarf. As she did so, she remembered yesterday when Marya had said she thought Captain O'Connell was attracted to her. How ridiculous! The man was only concerned about her welfare, because she was his best friend's widow. John and Jake also cared about her. Did that make them madly in love with her, too?

The thought once would've made her laugh if she had any laughter left in her soul. Now it only made her pity Marya. She was so young and fanciful, she saw romance even where it didn't exist. That's why it was so tragic she was being forced to marry Boris Ivanoff who was about as romantic as a walrus. Every day Anna prayed that the marriage would be stopped. She didn't want to see the spirited Marya become as bitter and unhappy as her older half-sister.

Poor Tatiana. Last night after her brief fainting spell at dinner, Dmitri had brought her home with what looked like a sincere expression of love and concern on his face. Anna had tucked her into bed, telling her not to worry, that in early pregnancy she'd also experienced dizziness, fainting, and nausea. But just to be on the safe side, she thought Tatiana should stay abed for several days. Dmitri had readily agreed.

"Good morning, Keeah," she said in Russian, as the Tlingit girl struggled upright in her bed, sleepily watching Anna fasten the tiny buttons on a loose-fitting gray wool frock and tie her apron around her bulging middle. "You were late coming back from the Americans' house last night. Was there a problem?"

Keeah smiled, the disfigurement of her lip almost hidden in a flash of white teeth. "No problem. I like to talk to Jake. He teach me English."

As long as the only thing they did was talk, Anna thought wryly. "Isn't there any young man from your own village that you would prefer seeing over him?"

"*Nyet*," she said, her smile vanishing. "My village is Wolf clan. It is forbidden to marry a man from my village."

"What is a clan?" Anna asked with curiosity.

"Is like a very big family," she said, explaining how the Tlingits were divided into clans. Each clan was composed of a group of brothers, their sisters' sons, sons of sisters of the second generation, and maternal cousins. A man's own sons belonged to the lineages of mothers according to rules of the matrilineal system. Every clan also had its own dwellings, berry grounds, fishing areas, and government by its own chiefs, who passed the right of succession from uncle to nephew.

"We have strict rules about choosing a wife or husband," she said. "A man from the Wolf clan has to take a wife from the Raven, Frog, or Eagle clan, and then their children become part of the mother's clan."

"Is there any man from one of those other clans who wishes to marry you?"

Keeah hung her head. "*Nyet*," she spoke softly, "My people think I am slave to Russians. I am now as dishonored as if I was living with a *promyshlennik*. Those Tlingit women who live with Russians cannot go back to the village, even if their husbands beat them, because it would disgrace their parents and they would be considered as lowly as a slave."

"How sad!" Anna exclaimed.

Keeah shrugged stoically. "My people think slaves are no better than dogs and treat them as poorly. Slaves have no rights and cannot marry or possess anything. They eat only the leftovers from someone else's meal. They have to obey their masters in all things, even if they are ordered to kill another. When I was a girl I remember once when the fate of a newly captured slave was decided at a party by the whim of our chief. He said he would listen to the loud cry of a wolf or frog. If the sound was joyful, the slave was to be freed. But as he was listening, a raven cried, and he ordered the slave to be sacrificed. After they killed him, instead of a proper burial, his body was thrown into the sea."

Anna decided she could never get used to hearing about the cruel manner in which humans treated other humans, whether Russians or Tlingits. Marya said Keeah's people were savages who spurned Christianity unlike her own people, the more peaceful civilized Aleuts.

In all these months of sharing the same room, Anna was well aware of Keeah's aversion to what she called, "*the white man's religion*." Each night before bed Anna would read her Bible, conscious of Keeah watching her with a scornful expression on her face.

To Anna's surprise, a few nights ago, Keeah finally became curious and asked Anna to read some of the words out loud. Anna began with the book of Genesis and the story of creation. When she finished, Keeah said her people also believed in a Creator of everything and in the immortality of the soul, but would speak no further about it.

The next night Anna read her the story of Noah, and Keeah became quite excited, saying her people had a similar story. "We believe there was a world wide flood long ago. One human family was saved by living on a big floating canoe. After the waters dropped, the canoe struck on a rock and broke into halves. My people are the one half, and the rest of the world the other half," she'd said in a proud voice.

Anna thought Keeah's story explained why the Tlingits were such a haughty people. She'd noticed many times how Keeah reacted to orders with a sullen insolent look in her eyes. Or perhaps the girl was as tired of serving the Russians as she was.

If only she had the money and the freedom to sail home to her own family. Anna sighed in exasperation. There was no time for daydreams. Both Tatiana and Marya would be awake soon, and needing their morning toilette. As she and Keeah hastened to each of their mistress's rooms to begin their duties, Anna asked God to give her the patience for another endless day of servitude.

CHAPTER TWENTY FOUR

With all the activity surrounding Tatiana's delicate condition, and with the arrival of the *Alexandria* and the news of his father's death, Dmitri forgot about asking Boris to accompany Marya to bring Ethan Campbell's Bible to Captain O'Connell.

Thus, one morning during a driving rainstorm Marya and Keeah went together, sloshing through the muddy paths, ignoring the jeers and stares of the *promyshlenniki*, the various sailors and soldiers, and the growls of the stray dogs that roamed the streets looking for food.

Marya clutched the black leather bound book under her hooded cloak to protect it from the rain. She was looking forward to seeing John Hill again. Even though she was a betrothed woman, she couldn't stop her growing attraction towards the American anymore than she could halt the rain and wind. She wondered if he felt the same towards her.

The house stank of drying wet wool, onions and cabbage soup, wood smoke and lye soap, with the underlying odor of male sweat. It was the typical smell of most of the Russian houses in New Archangel. Marya wrinkled her nose, thinking how spoiled she'd become since she moved into the Volodin's house where the scents of her own jasmine perfume and Tatiana's rose perfume mixed in with the warm yeasty aromas of Helena's freshly baked breads.

John Hill was seated at the table playing a game of cards with the captain and Jake. The black manservant, Samuel, was stoking the fire with more wood while the small Chinaman kept an eye on a bubbling pot. All five men turned to welcome the two girls with greetings and smiles.

Marya caught John's eye immediately. She nodded politely at him then turned to the captain and pulled out the Bible. "Anna bade me to bring this to you, Captain O'Connell. It was her husband's last wish for you to have his Bible."

Sean dropped the pair of aces he'd been holding in his hand. The cards fell unnoticed to the wooden floor. *Ethan's Bible*? What use would he have for that? A feeling of irritation pricked him, which immediately turned into shame as he realized it was his best friend trying one last time to reach out to him.

He accepted the book gingerly. "I dinna what to say, lass." He gave a few pages a cursory glance, then added, "Tell Anna I much appreciate it."

"She said for me to tell you to read the four gospels first, starting with the Book of Matthew."

Sean nodded, knowing that he would do no such thing. He would pack the book away in his chest along with his sister's rosary beads and the crucifix necklace that belonged to their ma. "And how is Anna these days?"

"She is well, but there is still sorrow in her heart. The child will be a great comfort to her."

She misses him still, as do I, he thought with deep sadness. Each night he was haunted by the thought of Anna crying into her pillow, and each morning, he imagined her drifting through the day burdened with the heavy weight of sorrow and her unborn child.

"Ye must tell me as soon as the bairn is born."

Marya saw the urgent plea in his eyes and once again, she sensed this man felt more for Anna than just a friend. "I will send someone with the news, I promise."

"Marya, can you stay for awhile?" John asked in an eager voice.

Keeah, who was handing out Helena's tasty dark rye bread to Wang Li, gave her a hopeful look. Marya saw Jake wink at her and suddenly realized Keeah had an admirer as well.

How interesting, she thought. She glanced at John and her heart caught in her throat as she felt herself drowning in the dark blue sea of his eyes. Her fingers ached to brush one of his blonde curls off his forehead.

"We can stay only a few minutes," she said. "We have another errand."

"In this nasty weather?" John raised his eyebrows in surprised disappointment.

"Keeah and I need to visit my aunt in the village to fetch some medicine for my sister who is suffering greatly from," she hesitated, her dusky cheeks heating into a flush, "from a stomach trouble caused by her delicate condition."

Sean and Jake exchanged smiles of amusement. "So, the beautiful baroness is also expecting a child?" Sean asked.

"Must give her Royal Highness 'r' congratulations," smirked Jake. "I expect the baron must be proud indeed."

Marya's lips tightened at the thought of Dmitri. "Yes, but he is especially glad to be the new commander of Fort Ross. They sail in the spring."

Sean inhaled sharply. "Does that include Anna and her child?"

"Yes, of course," said Marya, noticing the sudden distress in his facial expression. "And after my wedding on the first of April, I shall be sailing to Kodiak Island, where my--where Lieutenant Ivanoff is to take command."

The despair in her voice goaded John to say, "No maiden as fair as thee should be yoked to a man as despicable as he."

Marya choked with sudden laughter. John gave her a grin that did not reach his eyes and added more seriously, "There's still a few weeks for us to find a way to rescue you, Marya. Isn't that right, lads?"

"Aye," agreed Jake while Sean looked at him thoughtfully. Marya was not the only person needing escape from the Russians. There was Anna and himself and his crew. If only he could figure out how to steal his own ship away from under the noses of the Imperial Navy.

* * *

A short time later Marya and Keeah arrived at the Aleut village. The rain had finally stopped and a bone numbing wind was blowing the clouds east towards the mainland, allowing a thin watery sunlight to bathe the snow covered mountains and forests.

"No!" Tugidaq refused, her darkly creased face a wrinkled mask of resentment. "I will not help the Russian woman!"

"Please, Aunt," Marya begged. "My sister is suffering. The bouts of nausea have grown more frequent and vicious over time, instead of subsiding, and she stays abed most days. She cannot bear the sight or smell of any food, and I fear for the child. I do so wish to be an aunt someday, like you," she added softly.

Tugidaq's hard expression relaxed slightly. "I will come, but only for you, Tooch."

As she gathered up her pouches of medicinal herbs and placed them in a small woven basket, three men entered the *ulaq*, Uncle Sergei, her cousin Chignik, and Andrei Leonov.

Sergei was her mother's younger brother and they had similar features, but there the resemblance between the siblings ended. Whereas her mother's face was always full of love, her uncle had looked at her with a perpetual scowl of disapproval.

Now his dark round face was like a menacing thundercloud. He rattled off a string of questions to Tugidaq, who lowered her head respectfully as she explained about Tatiana. "I forbid you to go!" Sergei shouted, the sound of his angry voice silencing the children playing outside the house and reaching Keeah's ears as she waited for Marya.

Afraid to look at her uncle, Marya gazed at the smoothly packed dirt floor. When she finally glanced up, it was to see Andrei staring at her. The attack had drastically altered his face and she barely recognized him. Purple scars crossed his cheeks and puckered around his left eye, causing him to squint like an old man. His nose had been smashed to a pulp, and the cartilage inside his nostrils and sinus cavity was scarred, creating an obstruction. Now he had to breathe through his open mouth, a most unattractive sight, as most of his front teeth were missing.

She cringed at the sight of the man she once thought to marry, feeling both pity and revulsion.

Andrei saw her reaction and scowled, making him look even uglier. He sucked in a breath and wheezed, "So, Marya Nikolayevna, you spurn me as a husband and then agree to marry one of the most hated Russians in New Archangel."

"No, Andrei, it is not like that. My sister's husband betrothed me to Lieutenant Ivanoff against my wishes and that of my sister's."

Andrei appeared surprised. "You do not want this man as your husband?"

"No, he is a cruel and violent man just like Baron Volodin."

Her cousin Chignik spat at her boots. "You're getting just what you deserve for leaving our house and breaking your betrothal with Andrei! I feel no pity for you!"

Marya took a step backwards. Chignik was a short swarthy young man with a moody and unpredictable personality. As children they had quarreled constantly. When they had been ten years old, his father, Tugidaq's brother, had drowned in a storm at sea hunting otters for the Russians. His mother had died soon after from the coughing sickness. The young orphan was taken in by Uncle Sergei and was added to the family of four daughters. Overnight, Chignik changed from a child prone to laughter and mischievous pranks to a quiet and withdrawn boy who rarely smiled. He became animated only when he talked about the Russians, whom he blamed for his father's death.

And it was true. Chignik's father and ten other Aleut men had been ordered out to hunt one day when all the signs of an impending storm made even the *promyshlenniki* stay at home. Only one Aleut hunter had survived, and Governor Baranov had punished the Russian supervisor who had sent them out. But the damage had been done.

Chignik hated Russians, and he despised Marya for having Russian blood. After her mother died, and she also moved into the crowded *ulaq*, Chignik ordered her around mercilessly. She had no recourse but to obey him, as the Aleuts favored and fawned over boys. A son brought honor to a man. At a young age he learned to fish and hunt and contribute to the household, but a girl was just another mouth to feed. With five girls now in the family, Chignik was the favored son.

Marya remembered the hours she and Tugidaq spent sewing Chignik warm parkas and soft fur lined sealskin boots, her aunt carefully decorating them with exquisite beadwork and colorful feathers. He never showed a speck of gratitude, not once.

"Tooch," broke in her aunt, "you can take these herbs to your sister. Remember to seep the roots in hot water, but not boil them, to make her the tea that will soothe her stomach."

"Yes, Aunt, thank you," Marya replied and took the small basket. Without another glance at any of the men, she exited the *ulaq*, bending down to move through the small tunnel to the outside door.

She chatted briefly with Anaay and Gheli, and their two younger sisters, ages seven and nine, who stood shyly, not knowing how to reply to their cousin Tooch who was now a fashionable Russian lady. Others from her village, women and girls she had grown up with, also stared awkwardly at her, not returning her greetings. Marya sighed inwardly, feeling the gulf widen between her and all of them. She was no longer a part of this village, but yet, she knew she was not a part of the Russian nobility either.

As she and Keeah started to walk away, Andrei came out of the *ulaq* and hurried after them. He caught up to the girls before they reached the end of the village.

"Marya," he panted, "wait, please."

She turned in surprise. "Yes, Andrei, what is it?"

He took a moment to catch his breath then said, "I do not think like Chignik or your uncle. If you do not wish to marry Ivanoff then I will help you."

"How can you help me?"

He wheezed nervously. "If you will agree to still consider me for a husband, I promise I will stop this wedding."

Marya started in surprise. "But---but--" she began.

"She agrees," interrupted Keeah suddenly. "She has told me many times how deeply she regrets the day she broke off your betrothal."

"Keeah! That is not true!" Marya protested in shock.

"Do not listen to her," Keeah said quickly. "She will deny it. But it is true!"

A look of hope crossed Andrei's scarred face. "Then do not despair, my lovely Marya, I will save you from the wretched Ivanoff. And after I do, you will be my wife." He bent over and pressed his lips to her gloved hand, bowed briefly, then spun around back to the village, his footsteps light and eager.

Marya grabbed Keeah by her arm and hissed, "What do you think you are doing by telling him lies?"

Keeah gave her a slow smile. "My people have a saying, *'The enemy of my enemy is my friend.'* You need all the help you can get, *Mademoiselle*, even if it means using the scar faced man."

* * *

Putting aside personal differences, Dmitri soon found Mikael Bolkonsky to be a kindred spirit. The two men and Boris spent all their off duty time drinking, gambling, playing billiards, and discussing politics. One afternoon Mikael informed them of the latest revolutionary movement taking shape among the younger nobles of Saint Petersburg and Moscow. Some of these angry men were thought to be naval officers and even members of the Company staff. Their anger was focused on Czar Alexander I, who had turned from his earlier liberal views where he'd welcomed foreigners and their new ideas and reforms to a more conservative, repressive government, including giving the Russian secret police stronger power.

"It has become difficult for Russians to go abroad," complained Mikael, "and for visitors to enter the country. Not even the universities are immune to the reach of Aleksei Arakcheev, the new head of the secret police. He has dismissed most foreign teachers and even such subjects as Newtonian physics in case they corrupt the pious."

Mikael paused, gripping his billiard stick tightly. "I've heard a suggestion that His Excellency could be one of these men."

It was his own father, Count Vasily Bolkonsky, who had asked Mikael if he could quietly investigate the activities of Governor Muraviev, because there were rumors about his loyalty to the Czar. Mikael found the idea of being a spy both exciting and intriguing, but he knew he must not tell even his new friends in case they could not be trusted.

Dmitri and Boris looked at each other then Dmitri said very quietly, "It is true that His Excellency is unhappy with the Czar's latest *ukase*, that of restricting foreign trade here in Russian America, but--"

"Has he said anything about disobeying the decree?" Mikael questioned.

"Not in so many words," said Dmitri calmly, as he leaned over the corner of the billiard table with his stick to take aim at the group of painted wooden balls placed in the center. "But he has been so reluctant to properly punish the Yankee captain for trespassing in Russian American waters, trading arms to the natives, and assaulting my wife that Boris and I intend to take matters in our own hands soon."

Of the list of charges, Mikael heard only one. He gazed at Dmitri in shock. "Assaulting Tatiana?"

Dmitri made his shot, the balls clacking against each other, as one dropped into a corner basket. "Not only was she attacked and stabbed on board the *Sea Rose* by one of the officers, but I suspect that the captain himself might have ravished her."

Mikael was incensed. “Why hasn't the scoundrel been executed?”

“Unfortunately Captain O'Connell and his officers are under His Excellency's protection,” said Boris. He helped himself to a few appetizers from a platter containing pieces of smoked fish placed on suharji, a type of cracker made with poppy seeds. He smacked his full lips with satisfaction and mumbled, “I hear that His Excellency is thinking of releasing them this spring. He may even return their ship to them."

Mikael scowled then took a large gulp of vodka. “That is against the Czar's *ukase*!”

"They won't sail far without a captain," Dmitri said with an evil grin. "I plan to devise a way to have O'Connell whipped with the *knout*. Many a man has died after one of those punishments."

"Bah," grunted Boris, "you'll need his Excellency's approval, and he'll never give it."

"I have an idea," said Mikael. "As the governor's assistant, Dmitri, you must give him many papers to sign. Surely, with a few changes to one he's already signed and sealed, you can trick one of the illiterate sergeants into believing it's an imperial order."

Startled, Dmitri stared at Mikael. His mind began to churn through the possibilities. He suddenly remembered Muraviev's habit late at night to drink until he fell asleep. Often after he imbibed too many nightcaps, he was so disoriented and intoxicated he could barely walk straight, much less read an important document. The main problem with that would be getting around the governor's watchdog, Mikhail. But even that could be done.

"Thank you, Bolkonsky," he nodded appreciatively. "You may have solved our problem."

Mikael glowed with the young baron's approval. Now that he had finally met his cousin's husband, he found he admired him, something he was not prepared for. He had been jealous of Dmitri Volodin since the day he was betrothed to Tatiana. On the voyage over, he had indulged in fantasies where he killed his cousin's husband in a duel, thereby claiming her for himself and taking revenge on the Volodin family for his humiliation at the hands of Dmitri's father.

But he was finally realizing his love for her was hopeless. She still regarded him with haughty disdain. Therefore, if he could not have Tatiana, it was pure justice that she was married to Dmitri. He believed his arrogant cousin had met her match, and more. He suspected the baron ruled his wife with a strong fist, something she deserved after laughing at him long ago when he had declared his feelings for her.

Boris also looked at Mikael with admiration. "Your plan sounds like a piece of cake, lieutenant." He belched, exhaling fumes of alcohol and rancid bile. "Which reminds me, gentlemen, it must be close to dinnertime."

* * *

The pains had begun early that morning while everyone in the house still slept. Anna tossed and turned on her narrow bed, trying to ignore the dull aching in her lower back, which soon spread to her abdomen and developed into sharp stabs as her muscles contracted. She moaned with each one.

Outside she heard the rain lashing against the window. February was almost over. It had been a month of rainstorm after rainstorm, a month when the sun peeked out only three times in four weeks. Growing up in the dry climate of the Russian steppes, Anna had never seen so much water and mud in her life as she had the past winter. She longed for the first sign of real spring. But spring in New Archangel, she was told, only meant more rain.

As the weeks passed, she'd spent all her free time knitting tiny baby clothing and fretting. Her advanced state of pregnancy made walking in the town impossible and she was confined to the house. Perhaps it was just as well. She had never felt so bloated and uncomfortable and unattractive in her life.

But soon that was all to change, she thought as a burst of warm liquid gushed from between her legs. In a frightened voice, she called out to Keeah, “The baby. It’s coming.”

The Tlingit girl jumped out of bed and said nervously in crude Russian, “I go for help.”

Left alone, Anna wished with all her heart that Ethan was here, or her mother. Someone, anyone who loved and cared about her. She was afraid and worried that things might go wrong with the birth. Through all the past weeks of loneliness and sorrow, it was only the hope of the coming child which gave her comfort. But how could she bear it if she lost her child, too? With each new pain she clenched her teeth and prayed, Jesus help me and please, help my child to be born safe and strong.

The contractions squeezed a painful vise around her abdomen, then her tortured muscles relaxed, the agony flowing away like a river to nowhere, only to circle around and return. She was in the midst of a particularly vicious contraction when she heard a Voice whisper, “*Anna, do not be afraid. I am here*.”

She instantly felt a comforting Presence. Closing her eyes, she felt a renewed sense of strength and courage that carried her through the next pain and the next. Suddenly there was a burst of activity in the room. Cool reassuring hands were rubbing her forehead and a calm voice admonished her to relax and breathe deeply.

Anna looked up into Helena's kindly broad face and tried to smile her gratitude. “*Mademoiselle* is bringing her aunt, the midwife,” said the *Creole* woman. “You must not fret, Anna. All will be well.”

Tatiana, Keeah, and Maria hovered nearby, anxious looks on all of their faces. Helena ordered the two maids to bring lots of hot water and clean towels and extra blankets. Noting Tatiana’s extremely pale face, she added, “You will be of no help to Anna if you might faint, *Madame*.”

Tatiana swallowed and said, “I promise I'll be fine, Helena. I am feeling much stronger these days since Marya’s aunt sent me her herbal tea.”

Helena hesitated then nodded. “When the girls return with the water, you can take a cloth and wipe Anna’s face to keep her more comfortable.”

Tatiana drew a small stool next to the bed, and said to Anna, “Now it is my turn to take care of you.”

Anna smiled, resting briefly between pains. “You already did once before, in England, when I was so ill.”

"And then you nursed me when I was stabbed on the *Sea Rose*," she replied with a light laugh. She leaned over Anna and whispered, "We are more than mistress and maid, Anna, we are like sisters."

Anna was not certain she heard Tatiana correctly. "What did you say, *Madame*?"

Tatiana smiled. "I said we are like sisters, of the heart, not of the blood." She paused. "And I wish you would call me Tatiana from now on, unless my husband or some other illustrious person is nearby."

Anna started to smile then gasped as another pain tore through her. Tatiana winced in sympathy and gently sponged the perspiration off Anna's face with a wet cloth. She had meant every word about the sisterly bond between them. She could not imagine life without Anna, and Tatiana fervently hoped the babe would be born soon.

When Marya and her aunt came, Tugidaq took one look at Anna and clucked her tongue loudly. The girl was panting for breath in the stifling room, her sweaty hair plastered to her reddened face, her belly a huge mound hidden under a heavy pile of blankets. Anger sparked across Tugidaq's face as she spoke rapidly to Marya in Aleut.

"My aunt says she wishes Anna could get out of that bed and go to a proper birthing hut. Our women find it easier to give birth while standing than lying down like the whites do."

"How do they manage to give birth on their feet?" Tatiana asked, appalled at the notion.

"The woman in childbirth wraps a rope around herself that goes up through the mats of the roof and is tied to a strong branch of a tree above the hut. She hangs on to the rope, bracing herself through all the pains, until the baby falls from between her legs into the arms of the midwife."

"Tell her that is out of the question, so she will have to make do with Anna in bed," Tatiana snapped.

As Marya repeated her words, Tugidaq glared at Tatiana then she made a deliberate show of tossing the blankets off Anna, leaving her exposed in her thin chemise. Tugidaq pointed with her chin towards the one small window and spoke again.

"My aunt says if Anna has to remain here, the window must be opened to allow fresh air in to help her breathe easier."

Tatiana sighed in exasperation. It was the same old quarrel. Russians kept their homes heated snugly, and the natives complained that the rooms were too hot. But she did as the Aleut woman requested, and had Keeah pry open the window.

Cool air with the scent of rain, salt, and seaweed rushed into the room and swirled among the odors of sweat, blood, and birthing fluids. Anna took a deep gulp, then cried out as a wave of pain swelled slowly to a peak, then crashed over her before finally subsiding, only to begin again. She felt a terrible urge to push.

"*Nyet, Nyet*," muttered Tugidaq, as she slid a finger up the birth canal.

"She says not to push yet, Anna," said Marya. "The baby's head is not quite in the right position."

She had expected childbirth to be painful, but Anna had never imagined the horrible sensation of one's insides being ripped apart. She let out a small scream as the next pain attacked with a new viciousness.

"Go ahead, Anna," said Helena with sympathy, "scream all you want." She was the mother of several children and knew exactly how Anna felt.

Tatiana stared at Anna, appalled at how much she was suffering. It made her fearful of when her own time came, some months ahead. As she watched Anna writhe in pain, she found herself repeating inwardly, *please Anna's God, help her*. It was the first time she had prayed since she was a little girl.

Another spasm of pain gripped Anna, and soon all their faces blurred together into one gray mist. The hours went by, but she lost track of time as she existed in a world of never-ending torment. She no longer thought of Ethan, or her mother, or even the child. She just wanted it to stop.

The sun was setting when the impulse to push and bear down was so strong, there was nothing Anna could do to control it. In the distance, she heard the Aleut woman faintly say in Russian, push, push. Anna grunted and groaned and pushed, until a thin wailing sound jolted her to a new awareness.

"It's a girl," someone said.

Ethan, you were right, she thought wearily. We have a daughter. A feeling of joy shot through her exhaustion and she said a quick prayer of thankfulness. In a weak, but satisfied voice, Anna said, "Bring her to me."

A tiny squirming body was placed on her stomach and Anna saw her daughter for the first time. She was purple-faced, wrinkled, still covered with blood and liquids, her eyes scrunched closed as she howled her outrage. The thick blue umbilical cord jutted out from her belly, still pulsating from the bond of blood between them. She was the most beautiful perfect thing Anna had ever seen.

"She is small," said Tugidaq, with her gap-toothed smile, "but she is a fighter. She will live."

Marya repeated her aunt's words and all the women in the room let out a collective sigh of relief. Taking some string from her pouch of birthing utensils, Tugidaq tied off the cord first at the baby's navel and then several inches away. With one quick motion of her sharp *samiq*, she cut the cord, severing forever the physical tie between mother and child.

The afterbirth gushed out in a flood of red fluids, and she placed it in a bowl, telling Keeah to burn it later. They both understood, Tlingit and Aleut, of the necessity in protecting mother and child from any evil spirits who wished to harm them if the placenta was not totally destroyed.

Anna and Tatiana were oblivious to the superstitious undercurrents between Tugidaq and Keeah. But Marya, who was well acquainted with the ancient beliefs, frowned in disapproval. When she opened her mouth to question her aunt, Tugidaq glared fiercely at her.

"Tooch," she said in Aleut, "clean the child, wrap her in a blanket, and return her to her mother."

Marya pressed her lips together, but did as she was ordered, tenderly washing the protesting infant until her body glowed pink and clean. Tugidaq showed her how to swaddle the baby tightly in a soft blanket. Then after Keeah finished tidying up Anna, her new daughter was given to her to nurse.

The tiny head was covered with a fine down of silky reddish gold hair. She was truly Ethan's daughter, Anna thought with happiness, as the baby began to suck greedily.

"What are you going to name her?" she asked Anna.

"Ethan and I decided if we had a daughter, to name her after both of our mothers." A few tears misted her eyes as she added, "Her name is Katharina Maureen Campbell. I'd like to call her Katya."

Tatiana watched the touching maternal scene with interest. Both mother and child appeared quite healthy after their ordeal. Had her prayer actually been answered, or was it only a coincidence?

* * *

That same night, Governor Muraviev was sitting in his office, sipping his fourth brandy and enjoying the warmth of the stove and the peace and quiet of the late hour. It had been a particularly long and exhausting day. He'd spent most of it dealing with several complaints about the *Kolosh* living outside the stockade. Many of the natives were increasingly unhappy with the ban on trading with who they called, the Boston men. Lately, some of the younger *Kolosh* had been quarreling with some of the Aleut hunters and even a few *promyshlenniki* over food and furs. After trying to settle some of their disputes, he'd been given a report from one of the warehouse supervisor's about the shortage of grain and sugar and molasses. This was the time of year when Baranov had used British and American ships to trade for the food New Archangel needed. What he really wanted to do was send a ship to the Sandwich Islands for fresh provisions until Fort Ross could send more supplies. However, all his navy vessels were too occupied in patrolling the waters to make such a voyage.

If only I could send Captain O'Connell and his ship to the islands, he mused. *But that is impossible unless I ignore the Czar's ukase. Still, it is tempting. I will have to give it some thought. Meanwhile, I may as well have a toast to the safe delivery of Madame Campbell's new daughter. It's a sorry state of affairs that the child has no father because of me.*

He refilled his glass from the decanter on his desk. As he took a swig, someone knocked on his door. “Come in, Mikhail,“ said Muraviev automatically.

To his surprise, it was not his valet who entered, but another member of his staff, Ivan Putin. The man carried a pile of papers. "Your Excellency, I beg your pardon in disturbing you, but I was given these construction permits for you to sign."

Muraviev gave him a bleary-eyed look. "Give them to Mikhail and I'll sign them in the morning"

"Your valet is ill, Your Excellency, and has retired for the evening."

Muraviev frowned in puzzlement. "But he seemed fine earlier when he brought me my bottle of brandy."

"It seems he ate something at dinner which disagreed with him. He should be better by morning."

Muraviev sighed. His work was never done. "Leave the papers, then, Putin, and I'll sign them tomorrow."

Putin hesitated. At age twenty two, he was the youngest member of the governor's staff. As such, he rarely answered to the governor himself, but was directly under the authority of Baron Volodin, the governor's assistant. The baron had given him the papers just moments ago, with the strict order that it was imperative for all of them to be signed tonight. His fear of Volodin's bad temper was greater than his fear of the more mild tempered governor. He knew if he failed, his boss was not above ordering him to feel the lash of a whip, even the *knout*.

He crossed the room and placed the documents on the desk in front of the governor. "It will only take you a moment, Your Excellency. I was told these permits had been waiting so long, the supervisors in charge of these building projects are having difficulty in keeping the native workmen in line. Some of them are chafing at the delay and returning to their villages."

There were about twenty papers and Muraviev glanced down at the top one. It was a permit for the meteorological observatory on Yaponsky Island, one of his own projects. He looked at the next two papers and saw they were for bathhouses to be built at Mineral Springs, another one of his ideas. He quickly rifled through the papers, his eyes struggling to focus on each paragraph, but he was so tired the lines blurred across the pages in wavy black smudges.

"All right, Putin," he said wearily, "I'll sign them."

He reached for a quill, dipped the point in the ink pot, and wrote his name on the first paper, then pressed it with the Imperial seal. Since each permit needed his signature only at the bottom of every page, he didn't even glance at the rest of the documents. By the time he reached the last one, his head felt so heavy, he had trouble holding it up.

He shoved the pile towards Ivan. "Take them and goodnight, Putin."

Feeling relieved, Ivan clicked his heels and nodded respectfully. "Thank you, Your Excellency. Goodnight."

* * *

Winter did not want to lose its grip on New Archangel. The storms rolled in from the Pacific, dumping more snow in the mountains and blowing rain and sleet in town. Regardless of the inclement weather, all the navy ships were in and out on patrol duty, including the *Buldakov*. When Dmitri was gone, Tatiana was invited to dinners at the married officer's quarters. But she disliked the thought of eating with all the gossiping women and their quarrelsome children, especially with her still queasy stomach and instead, spent most evenings with Anna and her baby, Katya.

She was a good baby and slept well, but when she was hungry, she had a sharp cry that commanded attention. Tatiana had never been interested in babies. She had always thought of them as smelly little creatures, not much different from a wiggly ill-trained puppy.

But now that she was going to have one in the near future, Tatiana became quite fascinated with watching the new mother take care of her child. Anna was an expert in all facets of baby care, feeding, cleaning, burping, rocking and singing her to sleep. Not that Tatiana would be doing any of that. Women of her class had wet nurses and nannies to take care of their infants. Tatiana had no intention of ruining her figure with breast feeding.

For Anna, her figure was the last thing on her mind. She lived in a world where the storms roared unnoticed. Each moment of her life, whether sleeping or awake, was centered on the needs of tiny Katya. Every day she marveled at the wonder of her daughter. Katya looked so much like her father with her silky soft strawberry colored hair that Anna sometimes told him, "If only you could see how beautiful she is, Ethan. And then she imagined he answered in his soft Gaelic, *"The wee bairn is as bonny as her ma."*

Her body healed more quickly from the birth than her heart and soul did from her grief. Yet, whenever she held her daughter in her arms, she could feel the painful past slowly receding as her main concern became the present and the future.

It was one morning, about ten days after the birth, that Anna discovered how difficult it was going to be to raise Katya in their own Mennonite faith. She was in her small room, swaddling Katya after changing her soiled linens when Keeah announced that Father Sokolov was waiting in the parlor to talk with her.

“Will you look after Katya for me?” Anna asked. “She has been fed and cleaned and should be content for a time.”

Keeah’s nut brown face broke into a wide smile of delight. “*Da,*” she said as she welcomed the baby into her arms. Katya fussed slightly at the change, then settled down and stared solemnly at the *Kolosh* maid.

Anna smoothed the folds of her gray frock, tied her white apron around her more slender waist, and tucked a few stray wisps of her golden brown hair underneath her white scarf. She pinched her cheeks to give them a bit of color and hoped she looked presentable. Without a mirror in the room, it was hard to tell.

She made her way through the kitchen, past Helena who was stirring a large pot on the big brick stove. She grinned her gap-toothed smile at Anna through the savory steam wafting through the air. Anna recognized the aroma as beet *borscht*, made with beef broth, beets, carrots, onions, fried bacon bits, chopped cabbage, and topped with sour cream when served.

New Archangel *borscht* was made differently than the Mennonite way, but then, for all of the Russian dishes, there were as many ways of making *borscht* as there were Russian cooks. It was the mainstay of the masses, and although Tatiana ate it without complaint, Dmitri refused, saying it was "peasant soup." Helena made *borscht* only when he was away on patrol duty.

Anna returned her smile, and sniffed appreciatively. There was also the warm yeasty scent of fresh bread baking in the oven, making her mouth water in anticipation. It reminded her of *twaback*, and when she felt stronger, she decided to teach Helena how to make it. Perhaps the lieutenant would appreciate a hot *twaback* smothered in wild strawberry jam.

Nursing a baby made her hungry all the time, and tired as well. Fatigue was her constant companion since Katya was born. Otherwise, she had made a remarkable recovery, according to Tugidaq, Marya's aunt.

The Aleut woman had visited the day before and after examining Anna, muttered something that sounded like, "*ugheli*."

At Anna's questioning expression, Marya explained, "My aunt said it is good."

"I am thankful to God for giving me a safe birth and such a fine daughter," said Anna, "but also for your aunt's invaluable help." She smiled at her. "Thank you, Tugidaq."

The woman's wrinkled face creased into a grin and she nodded her acknowledgment. Then she stared at Anna quite intently for a moment. Her black eyes widened and she turned to Marya and spoke rapidly.

Obviously unsettled, Tugidaq hastily donned her *suk*, an exquisitely sewn parka made of the skins of many birds. It reached down past her knees and though hoodless, had a standing collar around her neck. In cold weather, she would wear it inside out with the feathers on the inside for warmth.

After she left, Anna said, "Tugidaq does not care much for me."

"It is true that she despises the Russians, but not you, Anna. She says you are to be treated with respect."

"How so?" Anna asked curiously.

"My aunt has what my people say, a gift of sight. She can look at someone and see into their soul and know what kind of person they are by the color that surrounds them. She says she sees a yellow light surrounding you, an aura of power."

Anna was startled. "What sort of power?"

"I do not know," said Marya thoughtfully. "Perhaps she sees God in you, and that makes her very nervous indeed, because she still clings to the old gods of my people. She and my uncle both disapproved of my mother's Christian faith and after she died, tried to stop me from attending church. Father Sokolov visited them one day and they had a bitter argument. After that, I was allowed to go to services, but they never forgave him for whatever it was he said to them."

The thought of the priest waiting to speak to her now made Anna's mouth dry. She could not imagine what he wanted with her after their last meeting. It had been one Sunday in January when she'd wished to partake of Communion. She had gone forward to receive the wafer and sip of wine, but he had refused to give it to her, saying she needed confession first.

Before she could stop herself, she had said, "My sins are between me and the Lord only."

His expression had turned thunderous and he ordered her to return to her seat. She had not attended church since.

Now Anna entered the parlor, seeing Father Sokolov standing by a window, wearing his usual black robe and cape with a gold crucifix around his thin neck. He was a tall man and had a curly gray beard and a thick mustache. The sun streamed through the glass behind him, making his gray hair shimmer like a slight halo around his head.

For one brief moment, Anna thought of Tugidaq and her gift of seeing people's auras. She did not believe in such a thing, but at the moment, looking at the golden sunshine around the priest, she fought a hysterical urge to laugh.

Instead she swallowed uneasily. Father Sokolov did have a powerful presence. He was not just any priest, but was revered all over Russian America. The last thing she needed was another confrontation with a man of such spiritual authority and power.

"You wished to see me, Father?" she asked nervously.

"Yes, *Madame* Campbell," he said in his deep voice. He looked at her with a penetrating gaze that seemed to bore right through her, reminiscent of Elder Klassen. "I came to discuss the baptism of your child."

"Katya?" Anna squeaked. "But she's only a babe, barely born."

He smiled benevolently at her. "It is your duty as a Christian mother to make certain of your child's eternal future if anything unforeseen should happen to her."

Anna blinked in surprise. "What do you mean, Father? Katya is perfectly healthy."

"Yes, praise God that is so, but in this interminably damp climate, infants have a high mortality rate. Certainly it would give you peace of mind to have her baptized soon, just in case, God forbid, she should become ill."

Anna knew the priest was only performing his duty. She tried not to let her irritation show as she said, "If my child should die, God would take her directly to heaven, whether she was baptized or not."

His smile faltered. "I am aware that your people, the Mennonites, preach against infant baptism, but here in New Archangel, you and your child are under my spiritual authority and guidance. Surely, you can set aside your personal beliefs, and allow your daughter to be baptized for the sake of her eternal soul."

Anna felt a stirring of anger amongst her fear of Father Sokolov. She felt like he was an Inquisitor accusing her of being a heretic. It reminded her of the persecution of her ancestors centuries ago in Holland.

Taking a deep breath she said, "My daughter will be baptized someday when she is old enough to understand what baptism means, as a public demonstration of her faith and commitment to Jesus Christ. Until then, her soul is safely in God's hands whether she lives or dies."

Father Sokolov's face darkened. "Then you refuse to have your child baptized?"

Her heart was beating rapidly and she could feel the perspiration running down her body as she faced him squarely. "Yes, Father."

The priest opened his mouth to speak again, but at that moment, Tatiana entered the room. "Oh, Father Sokolov, I didn't realize you were here. I was just looking for Anna."

He closed his eyes briefly then turned an artificial smile upon her. "Ah, Baroness Volodina, I have no further business with *Madame* Campbell. You are welcome to her."

With a respectful nod towards Tatiana, he walked stiffly out the door, ignoring Anna completely. She glanced at the departing back of the priest then at Anna.

"Have the two of you come to some sort of disagreement?"

"We have differences of religious beliefs."

Tatiana pursed her lips in surprise. "You are either very brave or very foolish to anger such a man, Anna."

Now that the intimidating presence of the priest was gone, Anna felt herself grow weak with relief. She sat down in the nearest chair. She didn't know whether she was courageous or an idiot, but she did know she had just made an enemy of Father Sokolov.

CHAPTER TWENTY FIVE

In the middle of March, Governor Muraviev announced his pardon of Captain O'Connell, his officers and crew, thereby freeing them from their house arrest and returning their ship, albeit empty of the original cargo of furs. He timed it on purpose to coincide with the absence of most of his naval officers, especially that of Baron Volodin and Lieutenant Ivanoff, who were both away on patrol duty on their ships, the *Buldakov* and the *Kamchatka*. The only remaining officer was Lieutenant Bolkonsky, who took note of his Excellency's orders in a secret missive to be dispatched with a letter to his father on the next ship returning to Saint Petersburg.

One night Governor Muraviev asked *Madame* Kornilova to arrange a small banquet in honor of the Americans as his way of apologizing for their ill treatment. He had suffered from frequent bouts of guilt over the death of Ethan Campbell and wished to demonstrate to the Yanks that the Russians were not all brutes. He invited all the officers' wives and at the last minute, included the widow, *Madame* Campbell, to attend as another token of his goodwill.

On the morning of the banquet, Tatiana opened her eyes, feeling the familiar waves of nausea churning inside her stomach. When would this interminable illness ever end? How she envied Anna having it all behind her, but she thought it was unfortunate Anna had birthed a girl. Tatiana hoped to give Dmitri a son, a male heir for the Volodin name, and pray that would be the end of her childbearing.

She glanced towards the window. The sunshine outside surprised her after last night's storm, when gale force winds had pounded the glass with slashing sheets of rain for hours.

The *Buldakov* was due to return any day now, in fact, was a bit overdue. What if the ship had been caught in the storm and sank? Dare she imagine what her life would be like without Dmitri?

Smiling, she envisioned returning to Saint Petersburg, a rich and powerful baroness, and living a life of luxury. She would remarry eventually, but only when she wished to, and only to the man of her own choosing. Her next husband would be a man who was kind and gentle, a man who would give her anything she asked, a man she could bend to her will.

Perhaps he would be a man like Anton Dohktorov. Did Vera Alexisova even realize how fortunate she was in being betrothed to the nice handsome lieutenant? She didn't believe so. Tatiana had heard the rumors how Vera was seen flirting with Mikael Bolkonsky whenever Anton was out at sea on the *Buldakov* as Dmitri's second in command.

It was also said that Irina, Vera's mother, was encouraging the flirtation. Tatiana could understand why. Although Anton's father was a wealthy shipping magnate, the Dohktorov's were of the lesser nobility and Mikael was the heir to the Bolkonsky title and fortune. Vera was her mother's pride and joy. If the betrothal was broken, it would be a dream coming true for Irina to have her oldest daughter marry the only son of her dearest friend, the Countess Irene Bolkonskaya and someday become the next countess.

Tatiana stretched her arms lazily over her head and chuckled at the thought of how miserable the mean-tempered Vera would make Mikael if they married. It would be just as he deserved. Then Anton could find himself a better wife, perhaps little Sophie Alexisova, who was always casting looks of unrequited love at him.

As for herself, she would rather have power over a man than have his love. Power was more important in life than love. I wish I had the power to sink the *Buldakov* so Dmitri would never come back.

Anna would tell her it was wicked to even think of such a thing, but Anna didn't know what it was like to have a husband who abused her. Even though their marriage was short-lived, Anna was lucky to have married a man like Ethan Campbell. For the thousandth time, Tatiana thought how unfair it was that Anna's husband was gone, but not Dmitri. To her it seemed, if there was a God or gods, they were laughing at the injustice of it all.

But if any of you do exist, she begged silently, *please destroy the Buldakov. And save everyone except Dmitri.*

A soft tap on her bedchamber door announced Maria with breakfast. The young Aleut girl was substituting for Anna while she was recovering her strength. Maria was short and plump with a moon shaped face and dull black eyes which came alive only when Tatiana yelled at her. How she loathed the natives.

The aroma of hot tea and the sight of the *pletjonaja boolka*, the thick slice of rich braided sweet roll, made the bile rise from her stomach. "Put the tray on my dressing table," she said sharply, as she pressed a hand against her throat. "And fetch me a basin at once!"

Maria did as she asked, but moved too slowly. By the time she reached the bed with the basin, Tatiana was already gagging, the bile burning up and out her mouth, splattering yellow liquid on the fine linen sheets. She struggled upright, choking and coughing.

"You idiot!" she gasped. "You are as sluggish as a snail in the forest!"

The girl muttered an apology in halting Russian. She set the basin on the bed by Tatiana and went to bring her a pitcher of water. As she began pouring the water, Tatiana slapped at her arm and snarled, "Never mind that, just bring me a towel! I need to wipe my mouth!"

Maria dropped the pitcher in dismay and water poured out all over the bed, soaking the sheet and blankets and Tatiana's nightgown. She shrieked in anger and smacked the girl in the right cheekbone with the palm of her hand.

"Aieee!" Maria screamed, jumping back in shock.

At that moment Marya entered the bedchamber. She took one look at the scene and with a sigh, dismissed the girl in a kind tone, telling her to put a cold compress on her swelling cheek, then helped Tatiana out of the bed and handed her a towel.

"I need Anna," Tatiana sputtered. "That stupid maid is just a clumsy oaf of a girl!"

Marya made no comment. After all the time she worked for the Russians as a servant, enduring their abuse herself, her sympathy went to the Aleut girl.

Tatiana yanked off her cold wet nightgown. "How much longer do I have to put up with that creature until Anna is better?"

"Anna said to tell you that she'll be returning to her maid duties in a couple of days." Suddenly her gaze narrowed. "What's that on your leg?"

Tatiana glanced down at the creamy pale skin of her inner thigh and saw a spot of red. "Just a bit of blood."

"Blood? But you shouldn't be bleeding now, should you?" Marya's voice was uncertain, as she knew very little about carrying a child.

"It's nothing to worry about." Tatiana shrugged carelessly, but as she did so, she felt a slight cramping deep inside her.

Marya shook her head. "We better make certain. I'll go find Anna and Helena."

"No! Don't tell anyone! They'll make me stay abed the rest of the day and I'll miss the banquet tonight. And if I can't go, you can't go either."

Marya didn't like that idea at all. Ever since the invitation came, she had been in a state of anticipation, looking forward to dining with John Hill. She hoped to make quite an impression on him by dressing in her finest gown and looking her most beautiful. And with her betrothed gone, it made it even more exciting.

"Promise me, Marya, you will not tell them!"

"Well," she hesitated, "do you have any pains?"

"Not even a twinge," Tatiana lied. "Now, do you promise?"

With reluctance, Marya said, "I promise."

But as she left the bedchamber, she felt a nagging sense of worry.

* * *

The longboat pitched up and down as the men rowed through the chop in the harbor toward the wharf. Another nasty storm during the night had produced a heavy swell from the open ocean. Sean turned his head to look at the *Sea Rose* behind them, straining against her anchor like a fish caught on a hook pulling to be free.

Soon, milady, he spoke silently to her, *we'll be gone from this wretched place.*

Since their release ten days before, he had hardly stopped working. From early dawn to late in the night, the *Sea Rose* was a frenzy of activity. He and the crew spent every waking hour repairing sails, rigging, ropes, and spars, repainting the woodwork, and provisioning the ship. Most of the men were grateful to finally have the chance to leave New Archangel. A few refused to rejoin, having spent the winter living with native women, and even signing on with the Russian American Fur Company.

Those men were deemed traitors to the rest of the crew. Many threats were muttered against them, and although Sean shared their sentiments, he cautioned his men to make no more trouble in New Archangel for any reason. He did not wish Governor Muraviev to change his mind about allowing them to soon sail away.

He could hardly wait to be gone. First they had to get through this banquet Governor Muraviev was giving them tonight. After that, storms or no, nothing was going to stop them from seeing the last of Russian America.

Or Anna, he mused. When we leave I might never see her again either. A feeling of depression gripped him at the thought then he shook it off. He was determined to try and see her later and beg her to leave with them. Since she was a servant, he did not expect her to be at the banquet. Afterwards, he would seek her out, if only on the pretext of seeing Ethan's child.

He remembered the day Anna's daughter was born. He'd paced around the small house, eating little, and consumed with fear and worry. Childbearing was dangerous and it had worn his own ma out, until having the last bairn killed her. His da had been too stingy to pay a good doctor for his ma to receive the medical attention she needed. Sean had felt even more anxious knowing there wasn't a doctor in all of New Archangel. Anna's child was being delivered by some toothless Aleut crone.

Finally, that evening, Robby had come to the house, allowed inside by the one of the guards with his message. "The missus had her babe, Cap'n, a girl!"

Sean had looked at the gangly fifteen-year-old youth and let out a deep breath. "And how's Anna?"

Robby's freckled face puffed up in importance as he said, "Both ma and child are' fit as fiddles, they say."

It was the best news Sean ever heard. He'd been so ecstatic, he even patted Robby's new puppy on the head. Named Jimmy after his brother, he was a frisky yellow dog with floppy ears and large intelligent brown eyes. "Good dog," he'd laughed when the puppy whined and jumped up to lick his face with his large pink tongue.

Now as his men tied up the longboat to the wooden dock under the watchful eyes of their Russian escorts, Sean glanced up the hill to

Baranov's Castle. The last time he'd been there was for another dinner some years ago, when he first met Irina Alexandrovna, Baranov's lovely young daughter. What an idiot he'd been then to think he was in love with her!

And here he was, at age twenty eight, in the same predicament. In love with a woman who cared not a whit for him.

His gaze caught the bulky lines of the warship, *Alexandria*, at anchor about three hundred yards from his own ship. Otherwise the island studded harbor was empty of vessels, with the rest of the Russian brigs out on patrol, searching for foreign traders to sink or seize. If the Russians found any, Sean hoped they would be lucky enough to escape.

Personally, he thought the Russians were stupid to restrict trade. He'd heard of all the food shortages in New Archangel, and how desperate they were for supply ships from Russia. But the rumors were that only more warships were coming to defend the borders of Russian America.

He wondered if Baron Volodin would have any success as the new manager at Fort Ross, their colony in California which supplied wheat and beef. Somehow he couldn't imagine the haughty baron knowing a fig about agriculture and ranching cattle. Certainly his wife did not. He thought it fitting that the arrogant deceitful baroness would be living in the isolation of such a wild place surrounded by the Pomo Indians and the hostile Spaniards. However, it was not for Anna and her child. Sean was determined to stop the Volodins from taking them along. How he was going to manage that, he had no idea.

The "castle" seemed to him a bit shabbier in appearance than when Baranov lived in it. A few shingles were missing from the cupola on top and he noted the sign of wood rot in the siding. The constant dripping of moisture on the wooden buildings grew fungus and mold, and the sea air rusted any type of exposed metal. He supposed it wasn't much different than living aboard ship.

Yet the background to New Archangel was a scene of unsurpassed beauty. As they climbed the stairs, he saw the snowcapped Mount Edgecumbe glistening in shades of mauve and rose in the dying rays of the setting sun. The Russians called the extinct volcano Saint Lazaria. To the north stood The Sisters peaks and Harbor Peak, their tops crowned with glacial ice and snow. And spreading southeast was an endless parade of misty green mountains.

Stunning scenery, but I will be missing none of it.

At the entrance, he and John and Jake were admitted by a uniformed guard and taken to the same library where Sean had first met Baranov's daughter. The gleaming mahogany pianoforte was still there, silent now, and he wondered if anyone was talented enough to play it.

Only three men were in the room, Governor Muraviev, Lieutenant Mikael Bolkonsky and Father Sokolov. Both the governor and the lieutenant were dressed in naval uniforms of the highest rank with flashing diamond and gold buttons and gold braid. In comparison, the gray bearded priest looked like a drab black crow in his dark robes. Only the large gold crucifix with gleaming red rubies around his neck declared his position of power.

Muraviev greeted the three Americans with a sincere smile while Father Sokolov gave them a brusque nod. Priests, Sean shuddered inwardly, how he disliked and distrusted them.

"Pleased to meet you, Captain O'Connell," said Lieutenant Bolkonsky politely. *So, this is the barbarian who harmed Tatiana*, he thought, remembering with pleasure the document Dmitri Volodin held in his possession. It was an order signed and sealed by his Excellency to have the Yankee captain whipped with thirty lashes of the *knout*, enough to kill any man. The punishment was to be carried out secretly one night this week, as soon as the *Buldakov* returned.

The lieutenant smiled, but Sean noticed Bolkonsky's black eyes narrow in unconcealed hostility. "Likewise, Lieutenant," Sean said with a forced grin. He knew the man was Tatiana's cousin and he looked like he was cut from the same despicable cloth.

Mikhail, the governor's valet, entered the library carrying a silver tray in each hand, one of crystal goblets with chilled vodka, and the other with the traditional *zakuska*. John and Jake eagerly reached for the vodka, but Sean politely refused.

Muraviev raised his eyebrows in surprise and said in accented English, "Captain, you do not wish the vodka?"

"Thank you, Your Excellency, but I am not fond of it," he said with a smile.

"But you must drink something, Captain O'Connell. Brandy, cognac, rum?"

Sean gestured towards the always present samovar, bubbling and hissing with steam, on the tiled stove. "I could fancy a cuppa tea."

Muraviev nodded brusquely to Mikhail, who quickly poured a stream of the amber colored liquid in a glass and carried it to Sean.

"A sea captain who does not drink anything but tea," commented Muraviev, glancing at the priest. "What do you make of that, Father?"

He gave Sean a surprising smile of approval. "I shall quote King Solomon from the Bible. He was the wisest man that ever lived. '*For the drunkard and the glutton shall come to poverty, and drowsiness shall clothe a man with rags.*'"

Then Father Sokolov took a large swallow of his own vodka and added, "But he also said that '*A merry heart maketh a cheerful countenance,*' and what makes a man more cheerful in his heart than a good glass of spirits?"

"The love of a comely lass," Jake blurted, "but as a priest, ye would nae ken such a thing."

There was an awkward silence in the room. Sean stifled a laugh as he saw Father Sokolov's face turn a mottled shade of purple. The priest's large hands twitched as if he'd like to strangle Jake right on the spot for the insult.

Muraviev decided to quickly change the subject. "How are the preparations for your voyage coming along, Captain O'Connell?"

"Very well, Your Excellency," said Sean, "thanks to your generous supplies."

"I wish there could be more, but as you know, we are short of many food staples here ourselves."

It's your own fault for restricting foreign trade, he thought. "We'll find more provisions at the Sandwich Islands, our first stop. 'Tis unfortunate we do not have our cargo of furs to trade, so I'll have to rely on Mr. Hill here to sign a credit voucher to pay for the goods."

"My uncle's credit should be almost as good as gold," said John. "Hill Shipping is well known all over the Pacific. Since I am the heir to the company, anyone granting me credit now will have a financial benefit in their future."

Muraviev looked at John with interest. "That is why I wish to make amends for all the difficulties you have experienced here. I hope someday Czar Alexander will rescind his *ukase* against foreigners, and your uncle's ships will be free to trade in Russian America again."

"So, Your Excellency," said Lieutenant Bolkonsky, "you do not approve of the Czar's *ukase* against foreign trade here in Russian America?" *This might be what I'm looking for*, he thought, hiding his eagerness behind a bland expression.

Muraviev hesitated. There was something about Bolkonsky that he distrusted. Ever since his arrival in New Archangel, he'd had the feeling the man was judging each word he said. He was well aware of the lieutenant's close connection to the Company Board of Directors and the Imperial family. Years ago his grandfather, Count Ilya Bolkonsky, helped put Czar Alexander on the throne. Muraviev knew he was treading in dangerous waters by speaking against the *ukase* and pardoning the Americans, but he wasn't about to allow this young puppy to intimidate him.

"You misunderstand me, Lieutenant. I am not questioning His Imperial Majesty's decree. However, I do question how well advised Czar Alexander is by others in Saint Petersburg, most specifically, a few men on the Russian American Fur Company Board of Directors. Some of them are so greedy for the riches of this land they do not care how they obtain it. For example, the sea otter has been over hunted in the Aleutians and is disappearing. Now I have reports of the same thing happening in the islands around here. So far, there is still an abundance of them south from Vancouver Island to the coast of California. But I wonder for how much longer?"

Mikael frowned in disappointment. The governor had neatly sidestepped around his question and took the offensive by challenging the integrity of some of the Board members. "Your Excellency, I trust you are not accusing my own father of being greedy and dishonest?"

"Of course not, Lieutenant," Muraviev denied in a curt voice while believing the opposite. He knew for a fact that Count Vasily Bolkonsky was one of the most rapacious board members when it came to glutting himself with furs and wealth. "I am only stating that it is time for the Company to realize there might be a limited supply of otters and other fur bearing animals. It is against our own best interests to hunt them to extinction."

Sean looked at Muraviev with new respect. He still blamed him for Ethan's death, but he had to admit the Russian governor was a man of uncommon foresight and wisdom. However, he was a rarity among the pompous naval officers such as Volodin.

Samuel, who had spent the winter mingling freely among the common Russian seamen, soldiers, fur hunters, *Creole*s, and the Aleut hunters, had told him that the opinion of all the inhabitants of the town was against the current influx of officers. Baranov's stable leadership was sorely missed as the young naval officers from the aristocracy became harder and harder to deal with. Many of them were sent out here fresh from the naval academy, inexperienced, arrogant, and having no regard for anyone or anything except their own interests.

Sean predicted difficult times lay ahead for Russian America if men like Volodin and Bolkonsky were the cream of the crop, their only hope for the future.

"Perhaps all of us, you Russians, we Americans and the British, should practice some sort of conservation of Alaska's resources," said Sean, "before all the otters, beavers, fox and mink cease to exist."

"That is an admirable thought," said Father Sokolov, "but hardly practical given the covetous nature of man."

"The natives are more respectful of their resources than the white man," said John. "After spending two years with the Nootkas, I saw firsthand how they consider the land, the sea, and all the creatures and plants that live in them, as gifts to be used and treasured, instead of exploited or destroyed."

Lieutenant Bolkonsky's face creased into a smirk. "Somehow I do not believe that is how an Aleut hunter feels when he is clubbing dozens of sea otters to death each day."

"That sort of hunting did not exist for them until you Russians came and forced them to it," said John, his blue eyes darkening with anger. "Now they are your slaves and have no choice but to kill everything in sight."

"We Russians have only enhanced the Aleuts' miserable lives by bringing them civilization and most importantly, Christianity," said

Father Sokolov stiffly. "For the first time in their heathenish history, they have a chance at heaven with the salvation of their souls."

"But at what cost?" countered John. "There are only a fraction of the Aleuts left as compared to the thousands who once lived in the Aleutians."

"No matter," said Bolkonsky with a sneer. "The savages breed like rabbits."

Governor Muraviev did not like where this conversation was leading. He cleared his throat loudly. "Mikhail, tell the ladies we will now be joining them for dinner." He turned to the men. "We can discuss our differences of opinions later over brandy and cigars. It is time to enjoy the company of the most beautiful women in New Archangel."

* * *

When he walked into the banquet room, the unexpected sight of Anna almost took Sean's breath away. Her dark honey hair framed her face in girlish ringlets as her lips curved into a sweet smile of welcome. She was wearing a silk gown of iridescent green shot through with gold thread that complimented the golden cast of her hazel eyes. The bodice was fashionably low-cut, but she modestly hid her *décolletage* under a green silk fichu. An exquisitely carved necklace of silver and emerald green jade encircled her slender neck. She had never looked lovelier.

Anna found herself staring back at him. He looked splendid, dressed in a stylish black frock coat with a white waistcoat and elaborately knotted black cravat. He had foregone the customary wig and instead had tied back his long unruly black hair with a black bow. There was a spark of energy about him, a firm set to his recently shaved jaw, and a gleam of new purpose glowing in his green eyes. It was the sight of a man freed at last to live life as he chose.

Sean was placed at the huge table between Anna and Tatiana. He bowed to both of them, giving a chilly smile to Tatiana, who was a vision of glamour with her shimmering blonde hair, glittering diamonds in her ears and around her neck, and dressed in a low-cut violet blue silk gown studded with diamonds and pearls. He eyed the swelling curves of her *décolletage*, and thought she had gained a considerable amount of weight since he last saw her. One glance around at the sumptuously laden table and he wondered if she had attended too many feasts, and then he remembered that she was with child.

Tatiana was startled at his handsome appearance. Was this well dressed gentleman the same brusque sea captain who had insulted her repeatedly? She was amazed at the transformation a fine suit of clothes could do to a man. Then she caught the cold contempt in his gaze and she felt her admiration for him harden into the old antagonism.

Father Sokolov sat across from her with Jake O'Riley to his left, and John Hill and Marya Nikolayevna to his right. Elizabeth Pushkina, the

Trotsky women, Irina, Vera and Sophie, and Mikael Bolkonsky were also seated at both sides of the table with Governor Muraviev at the head.

The food was served swiftly by the Aleut servant women. The main courses were the usual, fish, duck, and venison, accompanied with freshly baked breads and cooked vegetables, all washed down with liberal amounts of wine and hot tea.

Everything looked and smelled delicious, but Anna found she could hardly eat with the captain sitting so close to her. Out of the corner of her eye, she watched his every move, noticing the strength in his long fingers as he cut his meat, and almost jumped out of her chair once when his arm brushed hers, sending a shock wave of tingling all the way to her stomach.

Immediately she felt guilty. How could she react to another man in such a manner so soon after Ethan's death?

Ashamed of herself, she kept her eyes on her plate, conscious of Father Sokolov glowering at her frequently from across the table. Her appetite waned even more.

Tatiana also picked at her food. There was a slight pain in her abdomen that made her uncomfortable. She assumed it was from indigestion. If it didn't go away soon, she was going to have to excuse herself and find the nearest chamber pot.

She glanced across the table at her sister. Marya looked especially lovely tonight, dressed in a silk gown patterned in golden yellow flowers which complimented her dark amber eyes and skin. She was sitting between the priest and John Hill, and politely divided her conversation between them. But Tatiana noticed how her face glowed like a lit candle each time she spoke to Mr. Hill. And the young man responded in kind, his lean handsome face brightening with obvious pleasure whenever she looked at him. *Which is much too often*, she thought uneasily, sensing something amiss. The couple seemed to be dwelling in a private world of their own, smiling and talking softly to each other. Tatiana frowned. It was a good thing Boris Ivanoff was not here.

A quartet of musicians played quietly in a corner of the room. Anna listened intently, enjoying the harmonic blending of the three violins and one cello. She'd never heard such beautiful music and wondered how everyone could ignore it by drowning it out with their loud voices.

"Anna, is there a way I can see you alone after dinner tonight?" Sean asked quietly, just as she picked up her glass of tea.

Startled, Anna almost dropped it, but caught herself in time. "Won't you be in the governor's office for brandy and cigars."

"Aye, I should make my appearance, but since I care for neither, I should be out of there shortly."

She glanced up at him and her heart turned upside down. His face was only inches away from hers. Strange how she never noticed before how his brilliant green eyes were framed by such thick and dark eyelashes.

Her fingers twitched in an urge to touch the thin scar that angled down from his left eye across his cheekbone. It gave him such a dangerous look. How had he gotten it? A brawl with a sailor or from his father?

There was so much she didn't know about him. And so little time to find out. The *Sea Rose* was sailing next week.

"I would be glad of your escort home later," she whispered. "I am still easily exhausted by too much walking."

"Aye, I'll be happy to take ye back, Anna." They both smiled at each other then glanced up to see a frown of disapproval upon the priest's face.

"*Madame* Campbell," he said, "You might be interested to know that I baptized several *Creole* and Aleut infants last Sunday evening. One of the mothers inquired when you were going to bring your child to church for her baptism and christening. You should have seen the astonishment in her face when I said you've refused to have this done."

Anna squirmed uncomfortably in her chair as a silence fell around the table and all eyes fastened upon her. Sean set down his fork and looked at the stern forbidding expression on Father Sokolov's face. To his shock, all his hostility was aimed at Anna. A feeling of protective anger began to stir inside him.

"Anna is a Mennonite, Father Sokolov," he said politely, but firmly. "She has different beliefs than yours and they must be respected."

The priest stiffened and opened his mouth to retort when suddenly Jake said, "I was baptized as a wee bairn, but not much good it ever did me." He patted Father Sokolov on the arm and with a slightly drunken chuckle said, "Beggin' yer pardon, Father, but did ye ever hear the joke about the priest an' the tavern wench---"

"Excuse me, Your Excellency," said Father Sokolov, bolting upright from his chair as he brushed Jake's hand away like it was a bothersome flea. "It has been a splendid meal, but I must beg your permission to leave. I have several native acolytes waiting for me this evening to practice the chants for the service this Sunday."

Amusement glittered in Muraviev's eyes as he nodded towards Father Sokolov. It was a rare occurrence, he thought, when someone could make the normally intimidating priest uncomfortable enough to depart a banquet early. He glanced down the table and caught the carrot-haired O'Riley giving *Madame* Campbell a comical wink. Perhaps the Yank was not as inebriated as he appeared to be.

He hadn't wished to invite Father Sokolov this evening, but Mikhail had advised him not to insult the priest. He'd reminded him that Sokolov had the ear of the Bishop in Saint Petersburg. Muraviev believed that religion and politics should not mix, but in Russia, the Orthodox Church held tremendous wealth, power, and influence. Priests were not to be trifled with, even for the Imperial family themselves.

Immediately after the priest was gone, Vera said in a loud voice, "Father Sokolov is right. Everyone knows the baroness has a heretic for a maid."

She tittered as Mikael smiled at her in approval, thinking how Vera didn't like Anna Campbell any more than he did. He had been shocked and outraged earlier to see the pretty well dressed maid at the banquet table with the nobility. Obviously, it irritated Vera as well. He gave her an appraising stare. Her brassy blonde looks and sarcastic wit were a stark contrast to Tatiana's cold loveliness. He had a feeling that if he pursued her, Vera would not spurn his attentions as *Madame* Campbell had long ago in Saint Petersburg. She had humiliated him and it was time to get even.

With a spurt of anger, he pointed a finger at Anna. "*Madame* Campbell also has no respect for her betters," he said. "When she was a servant at my father's palace in Saint Petersburg, she once refused to obey me."

"Mikael, how dare you say such a lie about Anna!" Tatiana rose and threw her white linen napkin down the table at her cousin. The cloth landed right in the middle of his plate, splattering his immaculate uniform with foul brown droplets of gravy and meat grease. "The only time she ever refused your orders was when she rejected your unwanted advances!"

There was a collective gasp around the table. Vera's eyes widened in dismayed surprise while Mikael's face reddened in sudden embarrassment. "I don't know what you're talking about, Cousin," he said, grabbing his own napkin and trying in vain to wipe the stains off his coat. "But this isn't the time or place to discuss it."

As Sean saw Anna's face drain of all color, he was filled with instant rage. "Lieutenant Bolkonsky," he said in a dangerously quiet voice, "perhaps we could discuss this later after dinner."

Mikael lifted his eyes and found himself staring into the flat green eyes of a cobra. His mouth went dry. "What are you suggesting, Captain?" he blustered. "A duel over the lady's honor?"

Startled, Anna looked at the captain. Why did it matter to him what happened between Lieutenant Bolkonsky and herself years ago? Could it be that Marya was right? Did the captain have feelings for her that was more than friendship? Or was he only defending her because of Ethan? Either way, this entire situation was getting out of control.

"Captain," she said nervously, "there is nothing to argue about. The lieutenant and I once had a misunderstanding, but no harm was done." She turned to Mikael and gave him a steady look. "Isn't that true, Lieutenant?"

"Yes, *Madame* Campbell," Mikael said grudgingly, also wondering why O'Connell was so quick to come to the maid's defense. Perhaps he liked her. If so, nothing would come of it with only a few days remaining to him on earth before he faced the brutality of the *knout*.

At that moment, the battery cannons at the mouth of the bay boomed out in unison, rattling the dishes and silverware on the table. Feeling relieved at the interruption, Mikael shoved himself away from the table and said, "Your Excellency, it must be our ships returning from patrol duty."

"Bring me my looking glass, Mikhail," said Muraviev. He and Mikael hurried to the windows overlooking Sitka Sound. Although the sun had set, the Alaskan twilight already lingered late with the spring equinox next week. There was enough light outside to see the outlines of several ships sailing through the tiny islands towards the town.

Mikhail handed the governor his telescope, and Muraviev peered through it. "The first one looks like Pushkin's brig, the *Finlandia*, and there's a smaller one following...Ivanoff's sloop, the *Kamchatka*, and the last one is Trotsky's brig, the *Kuskov*." He was silent for a few moments then said, "I wonder where the *Buldakov* is. She should be with them."

All eyes were drawn to Tatiana, who reached for another glass of wine. "I'm not concerned," she said, shrugging her bare shoulders, "Dmitri always brags how he likes to sail farther out to sea than the others. The *Buldakov* will be here by tomorrow."

Muraviev acted like he hadn't heard her and said, "They all seem a bit banged up; must have encountered a few too many squalls. Lieutenant Bolkonsky, I want you to send some men to meet the ships and bring their commanders here to report to me as soon as possible."

He turned to Sean and said, "I am sorry, Captain O'Connell, but you and your officers must excuse me. As you can tell, I have important business to attend to. Please feel free to stay as long as you wish and finish your dinner. Afterwards, Mikhail will send you back to your ship with several bottles of my best brandy and a box of fine cigars. Thank you for your company this evening."

As Muraviev and Bolkonsky hastened out the door, Mikhail said, "I insist that you all stay until after the dessert course. *Madame* Kornilova has ordered a delicious dessert and someone must be here to enjoy it."

"We'll be delighted to stay, sir," said Sean, although his interest in food had disappeared along with the governor. This turn of events piqued his curiosity. Had something unfortunate befallen the *Buldakov*, or was she only delayed?

A murmur of appreciation went around the table as two serving women carried in a large tiered cake, frosted with blue and white icing, topped with a miniature sailing vessel carved of crystallized sugar. Instead of the notorious hot punch bowl from Alexander Baranov's time, plain tea or hot tea with rum was served with the cake. Conversation was subdued as the dessert was eaten, the thoughts of all the guests upon the ships in the harbor. Soon the banquet hall began to empty as the women left to find news of their husbands and fathers. Vera and Sophie were the last to leave.

"Aren't you coming with us, Tatiana?" Sophie asked with concern. "You must be worried sick about your husband."

"Dmitri is like a cat," she said flatly. "He always lands on his feet." She looked at Vera. "Sort of like your sister."

Taken aback, Vera shot her a venomous frown and stalked out of the room, pulling Sophie behind her. After they were gone, Anna, who had been toying with her cake, rose suddenly from her chair. "*Madame*, may I be excused? I need to tend to Katya."

Sean also stood up. "I'll escort you back, Anna." He looked at his officers. "Mr. Hill, O'Riley, no need to wait for me."

John gave Marya a quick look. "Would you like me to see you home, also, Miss Bolkonsky?"

"It wouldn't be proper," Marya said softly then gave Tatiana a hopeful smile.

She shrugged carelessly. "No, Marya, it's not proper, but since I need to stay here until I have news of the *Buldakov*, Mr. Hill may as well escort you home."

In a matter of minutes the banquet hall was deserted except for Tatiana. She sighed heavily. Dmitri once said she was the most beautiful woman in Russian America, but here she was, sitting by herself at an empty table. Even the musicians had departed. Several serving women peeked in the room, obviously wishing to begin clearing the dishes. Tatiana struggled to her feet, feeling awkward and uncomfortably bloated. Perhaps it was time for her to find that chamber pot.

As she swayed towards the doorway, feeling slightly ill, Mikhail appeared. "Baroness," he said, "His Excellency would like to see you."

He put a firm hand on her left elbow, guiding her out of the dining hall and down a few doors to the governor's office. As they walked in the room, she noted Muraviev and her cousin Mikael engrossed in conversation, serious expressions on their faces.

When they caught sight of Tatiana, Muraviev said, "We have news of the *Buldakov*. She was struck by lightening during a fierce storm this morning by the rocky headland near st. Lazaria. The ship was set on fire and sank with many lives lost. Luckily, the *Finlandia* was nearby and Captain-Lieutenant Pushkin was able to save the rest of the crew."

Tatiana's breathing stilled as she waited for the next words.

"Dmitri?" she said softly, not certain of what she wished to hear.

Muraviev gave her an assuring smile. "Thanks be to God that both he and Lieutenant Dohktorov are alive and well."

Not dead then, she thought, clenching her fists in disappointment and anger. At that moment a sudden stab of pain cut through her womb.

"I need to sit down," she said, feeling a gush of liquid trickling down her legs. Was it blood? She wondered in near panic. Was she losing her baby? How ironic it would be if her prayers to get rid of her husband resulted in the loss of her child instead.

A swirling dizziness danced around inside her head and she started to laugh, as she thought she heard the faint sound of all the gods laughing at her too.

CHAPTER TWENTY SIX

Sean felt Anna trembling slightly as they climbed down the stairs from the governor's house. He tightened his grip on her arm, feeling with his other hand for the pistol in his coat pocket and the knife at his belt. He never went unarmed, even to a banquet held in his honor.

They set off down the path towards the Volodins' house with Jake walking ahead and John and Marya following behind. Murky shadows shrouded their every step, cast by the warehouses and buildings nearby. As they walked along, they could hear the waves lapping along the rocky shore and the shouts and laughter of men carousing in the town.

Finally he could see the house up ahead, with a faint light glowing from an upstairs window. I hope she invites me inside so I can talk to her, he thought, then stiffened as four large *promyshlenniki* suddenly appeared in front of them. Jake halted abruptly and Sean and Anna almost bumped into him.

"Hey, dirtee Yankees!" one of the men taunted in crude English. He was a tall brute with pitted cheeks, a crooked nose, and no front teeth.

Even his grandmother would have a hard time saying something nice about his face, Sean thought wryly.

Under normal circumstances, they would be respected as ship's officers and left alone, no matter how much they hated Americans. But he could smell their reek of sweat and alcohol fumes and he suspected they were drunk.

His right hand slipped inside his coat pocket and fingered his pistol. He didn't wish to shoot anyone, but he doubted these men were going to leave without a bit of persuading. "Out of our way, men, at once," he snapped in Russian, in his authoritative captain's voice.

At first the fur hunters automatically stepped backwards, trained as they were to follow orders. But then the pock-faced man cursed, using a mix of Russian and English words, as he raised his huge fists threateningly.

Jake snarled under his breath, "Tis a fight they want, I be glad to oblige."

"Nay, man, think again," said Sean. "Not with the lasses here."

Anna stared at the crude-faced *promyshlenniki* as a memory stirred from long ago. Their black beards and the Mongol slant to their eyes reminded her of the Tartars who roamed the steppes, terrorizing both Russian and Mennonite villages alike. She remembered that night when the wounded Tartars broke into their house and held a knife to her papa's throat, and how her mama had calmed them.

"The Bible says, '*A soft answer turneth away wrath*,'" said Anna quietly to Sean.

"What?" Startled, he turned and looked at her.

"If you've read any of Ethan's Bible, you might remember what Jesus said about treating those who curse you," she whispered.

Sean paused. Although he had ignored the Bible at first, in the long days and nights of his convalescence, he had eventually begun to browse through the pages. To his surprise, he had found a note Anna wrote to him, saying he should start in the Book of Matthew and read through the New Testament. Taking her suggestion, he'd already read the first four books.

Most of it was new to him. As a boy, he'd heard the Holy Scriptures quoted from the mouths of priests, but it had made no impact. Now he found the Bible fascinating, from the story of Jesus' birth to his crucifixion and resurrection. There was so much to absorb and remember, but one thing stood out. Jesus called ordinary men to be his disciples; carpenters, fishermen and sailors like himself.

And yes, he did recall a verse where Jesus said to bless those who curse you. And to turn the other cheek if your enemy should strike you.

It went against every instinct he possessed, but he withdrew his hand from his pocket. "Anna, tell them that we are under His Excellency Governor Muraviev's protection, and if they harm us, they will be arrested."

Taking a deep breath, she repeated his words in Russian, then added louder for all to hear, "I am maid to the Baroness Tatiana Nikolayevna and this other woman is her sister. If anything happens to me or my friends, Baron Dmitri Ivanich Volodin will be greatly angered."

At the mention of the name, Volodin, all four men flinched. They looked at each other uneasily then one of them made the sign of the cross. The others followed suit as if to ward off evil. With one last look of hatred, they melted away into the dark fog.

"Whew," said Jake, wiping a hand across his face in relief. "Fer a bit there, I thought we was goners. Much thanks to ye, Mistress Campbell."

Anna smiled nervously. "I think we should give thanks to our Lord who is watching over us."

"Well," Jake shrugged, "Ye sure did put the fear of God in 'em with yer talk of Volodin."

"More likely the fear of the devil," said John with a short laugh, as he squeezed Marya's arm reassuringly.

"I best be getting back to Katya," Anna said, her legs shaking all over again.

* * *

The bairn looks like most babies, Sean thought, staring at the infant cradled in Anna's arms. She was snub-nosed with a tiny pink mouth that dribbled a gooey substance which looked like a mixture of saliva and milk. He tried not to think of where the milk came from.

Instead he noticed the child's hair, a soft fuzz of dark red gold which reminded him of a cross between Ethan's auburn locks and Anna's tawny hair.

"She has blue eyes like my younger sister, Tina," said Anna proudly.

"Aye," he said, smiling, "she's quite the little beauty, just like her mother."

Anna's cheeks turned pink at the compliment. "Would you care to hold her?"

"Err," said Sean, suddenly feeling awkward, "I have to admit I don't know how."

"Just keep one hand under her neck and head for support like this," she demonstrated, then slid the baby into his arms before he could pull them away. Katya was swaddled tightly in a soft fleece blanket, and Sean thought it was a bit like holding a doll. He could not believe how little she weighed.

They were seated on a sofa in the Volodin's parlor. To his initial irritation, Anna had invited all of them inside to meet her daughter. Jake, who was not fond of bairns, quickly declined, saying he would wait outside. Luckily, John had realized Sean wished to have some time alone with Anna, and had stayed only a few minutes to see the child and say goodnight to Marya.

After overhearing John tell her that he'd see her soon, Sean decided he'd better ask John later what he was planning concerning the *Creole* girl. If he was still thinking about rescuing Marya from her upcoming wedding, it would mean nothing but trouble.

He held the child stiffly and she stirred at the unfamiliar tension in his arms as if realizing she wasn't being coddled by a soft cooing woman. Suddenly she scrunched up her tiny features and let out a howl of protest.

Sean immediately looked horrorstruck. "What did I do?"

Anna laughed. "Nothing. She's probably tired. Try rocking her slowly back and forth, and singing to her."

"Singing?" he repeated. "I can't carry a tune, Anna."

But he began to hum softly while gently swinging his arms. The baby stopped in mid shriek to listen to the strange noise of deep rumbling, and finding the sound and the arm motion soothing, ceased whimpering altogether.

Anna watched silently, at the incongruous picture made by the broad muscular man holding the delicate infant. There was a tenderness in his proud chiseled features that she'd never seen before,

"See, nothing to it," she said, smiling. "She likes you. Look, she's going to sleep."

With surprise, Sean saw the child close her eyes, her dark eye lashes fanning out in two tiny semicircles. An unfamiliar feeling of protectiveness washed over him.

"Keeah brought her bed in here," said Anna, pointing to the small wooden cradle sitting near the stove. "Do you think you can lay her down without waking her?"

Carefully and quietly, he put the sleeping baby down and gingerly tucked the blanket around her. Katya made a few sucking sounds with her lips, but her eyes stayed shut, and she slumbered on.

"Ethan would be so proud," said Sean, staring down at Katya.

"He would call her his wee lassie," she said with a sad smile.

They were both quiet for a moment, as they each thought of Ethan. Then Sean looked at her. "Anna, I'll be gone in a week's time. I don't like the idea of leaving ye and the bairn here. Will ye consider coming with us to Boston?"

Anna hesitated. Ever since she'd heard the *Sea Rose* was to sail soon, she had dreaded the thought of never seeing Captain O'Connell again. It was a tempting thought to be able to leave her life of servitude to Tatiana. But there were two problems. She had little money, and she couldn't in good conscience, leave Tatiana in her delicate condition with an abusive husband.

"I have only a few rubles saved from my wages," she said nervously. "Not enough to pay my passage and Katya's."

"Come here," he said, taking her small hand in his large one and leading her over to the blue and gold brocade upholstered sofa. She started slightly at his touch, but did as he asked, and they both sat down. Without letting go, he grasped her other hand, and pulled her towards him, gazing deeply into her eyes.

"Anna, I'm not asking ye to come as a passenger. I'm asking ye to come as my wife."

"Your wife?" she repeated, not believing she was hearing correctly. "You wish to marry me?" She was utterly dumfounded at his proposal and could only stare at him speechless.

He took a deep breath. "Aye, but I think I'm doing this all wrong an' I need to start again before ye think I'm daft. Ethan was my best friend and--"

"Are you asking me out of a sense of duty to Ethan's wife and child, or because you love me?"

He tightened his grip and groaned, "Aye, I love ye Anna! I've loved ye for a long, long time. The day ye married my best friend I was heartbroken."

He bent his face over hers, and kissed her deeply. The warm touch of his lips on hers set her every nerve on fire and she began to melt into his arms. Then she jerked her head backwards and stared up into his ruggedly handsome face. “You were in love with me before I married Ethan?”

“Between the two of us, he was the better man. He deserved ye. I did not.”

“And why would you think that?”

“Because of his faith in God.”

“He always said that he was just as much of a sinner as any other man. If he was here now, he would say the only difference between the two of you, was that he was a saved sinner.”

Sean smiled wryly. "That sounds like Ethan! Once he told me a story in the Bible about a son who ran away from home, away from his father. Ethan said he'd been like that son, and one day he finally came to his senses and asked God to save him from his sinful life. But I think he also told me the story, because he wanted me to believe that God was my father, too. At the time and all the years since, I’ve dismissed it as impossible that God, if He exists, could actually love someone like me. I’ve not known a real da’s love, so 'twas something I’ve n’er imagined. But now, after holding Katya,” his voice trailed off as his eyes fastened upon Anna’s face. “I know I could learn to love a bairn, an' to be a da.

“So, Anna, I’ll ask ye again,” he paused and swallowed tensely, “will ye be my wife and let me be a proper da to Katya?”

She was silent as she remembered how she’d been taught that it was a commandment from God to forbid marriage between believers and unbelievers. Also, it was frowned upon among Mennonites to wed those who were not Mennonites. Although Ethan hadn't been a Mennonite, he had shared her faith, and one day, she'd hoped to bring him home to meet her family. But the captain? He was a proud immoral man who believed in no one but himself. Somehow, she could not imagine him ever meeting her papa’s approval.

Then there was that day he had confessed to killing his own father. She realized how little she knew about Sean O'Connell. And as much as she needed a father for her child, she was not desperate enough to marry a possible murderer.

He had been watching her, seeing the war of emotions play across her face. He knew he had lost when he saw the hard determination creep into her golden hazel eyes.

"I cannot marry you, Sean. It's too soon for me after Ethan's death to even think of caring for another man, much less marrying again."

"That's not what your kiss told me a few minutes ago," he said almost angrily. "So, then it must be because I'm not a saved man like Ethan was."

She blushed and pulled her hands away from his. "Yes, in a moment of weakness I let you kiss me, but you and I are from two different worlds. We can be friends, but not man and wife."

His face blanched as if she'd struck him a mortal blow. "Then when we sail away next week, I'll never see ye again. Is that what ye want, Anna?"

Before she could answer, the front door opened and John burst in. "Sorry to interrupt, but Jake just rushed over with a warning for us to get back to the ship because the Baroness Volodin is on her way home. She became hysterical at the news that his ship sunk in a storm yesterday, drowning twenty sailors. Then she collapsed and they are afraid she might lose her child."

Anna's face whitened and she said, "I must fetch Keeah and Marya at once."

Sean rose abruptly and strode towards the door. "Good-bye, Anna."

"Goodnight, Sean." When he was gone, Anna realized with a sinking heart, how final his farewell sounded.

* * *

After spending a tormented sleepless night, Sean was summoned to Governor Muraviev's office the next morning. There, he was faced with a hot crowded room full of agitated Russian naval officers, all talking loudly, with reddened faces and gulping tea and vodka. Muraviev stood behind his desk, his coat unbuttoned and his manner unnaturally disheveled as he mopped his forehead with a handkerchief. He looked up when Sean entered and gave him a brief smile.

"Ah, Captain O'Connell. So glad you could come."

Lieutenant Dohktorov also nodded politely, but it was obvious that they were the only two men in the room who welcomed his presence. The others, the corpulent Lieutenant Boris Ivanoff, along with Bolkonsky, Volodin, Trotsky, and Pushkin glared at him as if he was their worst enemy.

"My officers and I," said Muraviev with an expansive motion of his hands, "need your help and cooperation concerning the *Sea Rose*."

Sean felt a sense of foreboding as hostile eyes were cast in his direction. "I just heard about the unfortunate accident to befall the *Buldakov*," he said. "My condolences to the families of the lost sailors. But how can I be of help?"

"You are aware that Baron Volodin and the *Buldakov* were to sail to Fort Ross in several weeks." It was more of a statement than a question, and Sean nodded as Muraviev went on, "It is imperative that Fort Ross has a new manager as soon as possible. With the Czar's orders for extra patrols here, I cannot spare any other vessel for the voyage. Thus, I have a request to make."

All of a sudden, Sean knew where he was going. "A request, Your Excellency, or an order?"

Muraviev gazed at him with an unblinking stare. "We need the use of your ship, Captain, to transport Baron Volodin and his wife and servants to Fort Ross as soon as his wife recovers from her illness."

“This means we cannot sail next week as planned.”

“It will be a short delay, a month or less.”

Sean opened his mouth to protest further, then stopped as a thought struck him. Anna was coming with them. It would take several weeks to reach California, perhaps more, if they traded along the way. That gave him plenty of time to persuade her to stay on board after leaving the Russians at Fort Ross. Even though she'd refused to marry him, her response to him when he'd kissed her gave him hope that she might change her mind eventually.

“However, Captain O'Connell," said Volodin with a sly grin, "it will mean that for the first part of your voyage, I am in command of your ship, plus we will be sending enough armed sailors along to make sure my orders are obeyed by your crew."

"Impossible!" Sean retorted. "My crew would mutiny first!"

In fact, Sean wondered if even the Russian sailors would obey Volodin. The strange sinking of the *Buldakov* had started rumors around town that the Volodins were cursed. Sailors were a superstitious lot and it was a rare occurrence to have a ship struck by lightning in a storm and burn and sink. Usually, any fire started by lightning in a thunderstorm was put out by the accompanying deluge of rain, along with a few well aimed buckets of water.

But this storm had struck without warning and blown itself away before anything more than a few sprinkles had spattered down. A flashing bolt had struck the forward mast first, splitting it right down the center and setting it ablaze. When the two burning pieces of the mast and all the rigging collapsed onto the wooden deck, the gusting wind had spread the fire rapidly. All the men knew when it reached the barrels of gunpowder stored below for the ship’s cannon, the *Buldakov* would explode. It had been hopeless from the very beginning.

With tongues loosened by strong drink, the surviving crew spread the story that Baron Volodin had insisted his crew fight the fire, even when apparent to all but himself that it was a losing battle. When Volodin saw that some of the sailors were launching the longboat without his permission, he went berserk with rage, took out his pistol, and shot a man.

If this story was true, Sean thought that Volodin would have much to explain to Governor Muraviev. Even if it wasn’t, it was obvious to him as a ship’s captain that Volodin should have ordered his crew to abandon ship earlier. With the *Finlandia* standing by, most of his men could have been saved. Instead there were twenty families who had lost husbands, fathers, sons, and brothers.

"Your crew will not mutiny if they're well compensated," said Muraviev. "I will pay you for your trouble, Captain O’Connell. You may take forty percent of your original cargo of furs with you. It is worth many rubles, many American dollars. Perhaps enough to sail to Canton to trade, so you can return to Boston with some tea and spices and Chinese goods instead of an empty cargo hold."

Sean considered. The better the profit, the more the crew would be paid at the end of the voyage, and the more willing they'd be to put up with the Russians onboard. "Sixty percent, with the same percentage of all furs bought from the natives on our way south."

Muraviev hesitated while Bolkonsky uttered a short sneering laugh. "Don't push your luck, Yank."

The governor wiped his brow again and coughed sharply. "Fifty percent of everything."

Sean gave a brusque nod. "I accept."

* * *

During that same day Tatiana drifted in and out of consciousness. Her body had become a stranger to herself, a place of deep searing pain as her womb cramped and contracted, forcing out its small inhabitant long before its time. Finally, the pain disappeared, but before she could feel any relief, she sank into a coldness that wrapped its glacial fingers around her heart and soul, and sent tentacles of pure ice through every vein in her body.

Her teeth began to chatter like the pounding of tiny drums and she could not stop shivering. More blankets were piled on top of her, their weight crushing her.

"She has lost too much blood," she heard Marya say. "Should I send someone to fetch my aunt?"

No, she thought, *don't let that hideous old woman near me. She hates me*. Tatiana struggled to open her mouth to tell them, but found she was so weak, her jaw wouldn't open. She tried to open her eyes, but her eyelids felt too heavy. Then she lost consciousness once more.

Sometime later she heard Anna in a faraway voice ask, "Was it a boy or a girl?"

She strained her ears to hear the answer, but heard only some unintelligible Aleut words. Who were they talking about, she wondered, feeling detached and emotionless as she floated in her cold gray world.

"She lost a son," came the whisper and she fell back into the dreamless void where time did not exist.

When she woke again, it was to hear the sound of someone crying, a man. She thought it was Dmitri. Once again, she struggled to open her eyes, but found she couldn't. She drifted back into sleep, thinking, is he crying for me or for our son? And why is he still alive when our son is dead and gone?

* * *

At first Dmitri was inconsolable. When he burst into the bedchamber and Anna told him the child had been a boy, he crumpled against the bed where Tatiana lay unconscious, and sobbed. Both Anna and Marya were surprised to see him expressing such deep grief. They hadn't thought the baron was capable of any emotion except anger.

After telling him that Tatiana would recover, they left him alone with his wife. Minutes later he rushed out of the bedchamber, muttering, "How could this have happened? There must have been some sign." He glared at Anna, then at Marya.

It was evening and the girls were in the sitting room sewing. The wedding was ten days away and neither the bridal gown nor Marya's trousseau was ready. Anna was an excellent seamstress, but she didn't have the time with taking care of Katya and now Tatiana, to do more than some of the delicate embroidery. Luckily, there were several dressmakers in town, and they had been hired to sew the rest.

Now Anna looked up at Dmitri, seeing his rough unshaven face, the dark circles under his eyes, and felt a stab of pity. One tragedy after another. First, his ship and many of the crew were lost, then his child.

"I had no idea she was ill, Your Excellency," she said. "Yesterday before the banquet when I helped *Madame* dress she was in fine spirits and looking forward to the dinner. If she wasn't feeling well, she kept it to herself."

Dmitri grunted, and glanced at Marya. She kept her eyes on the handkerchief she was embroidering for Boris as a wedding gift, and said nothing, remembering the spot of blood on Tatiana's thigh. She dared not tell a soul, much less Dmitri. He would ask her why she hadn't made Tatiana stay in bed. But no one could make her sister do anything when she set her mind to something. And Tatiana had been determined to attend the banquet no matter what.

Marya tried to squelch a nagging feeling of guilt. It wasn't as if she hadn't tried to save the child. She had sent for Tugidaq, but when her aunt came, she'd shaken her head sadly, saying the child hadn't wanted to be born to two such mean selfish parents. At least she'd managed to stop the bleeding, or they would've lost Tatiana, too.

"I want one of you with my wife day and night," said Dmitri, as he strode through the room to the hallway. "I'll be staying at the governor's house until she's recovered." He paused and frowned. "This means we'll have to postpone the wedding. Boris will not be pleased, but he'll have to understand. Oh, and one other thing, *Madame* Campbell," Dmitri turned and gave Anna a smug smile. "Have you heard that His Excellency has commandeered the Yankee ship for our voyage to Fort Ross? And I'm to be the captain in charge, not O'Connell. We'll be sailing as soon as Tatiana is well enough."

With those startling words, he exited the room, leaving both Anna and Marya staring at each other in surprised dismay. "The captain must be livid," said Anna. Then she suddenly realized she also would be sailing on the *Sea Rose* and would be seeing Sean every day for several weeks. The thought both terrified and gladdened her.

"I wish I was going with you and Tatiana, too," said Marya sadly, "instead of marrying Boris and sailing to Kodiak. At least the wedding is put off for awhile."

With Boris gone on patrol duty, the past month had been a reprieve for her. Otherwise since their betrothal, he had stopped by the house several evenings a week to see her. Tatiana never left them alone in the parlor, but even with her presence the brief visits were interminable. Boris fawned all over her, his squinty piggish eyes studying her in a manner that made her flesh crawl. She never had anything to say to him. But since he was the type of man who loved to speak about himself, he didn't notice her silence. The thought of spending the rest of her life with him made for a bleak future.

Anna gave her a tremulous smile. "Let's not give up hope that God will make a way for you to escape this marriage."

Marya suddenly burst into tears. "I already had an offer of rescue! Last night John said he would sneak me onboard right before they sailed next week. But now it's impossible!"

Anna's mouth fell open. "Goodness, Marya! I thought the two of you were only engaging in a harmless flirtation. Now you are telling me Mr. Hill has serious feelings for you?"

"Yes," she sobbed, throwing Boris's handkerchief on the floor, "I think he's in love with me, just like I am with him!"

"Oh, my."

* * *

At that moment on board the *Alexandria* inside Lieutenant Bolkonsky's cabin, Vera was hastily donning her scattered clothing. "Mikael, must I leave already?" she pouted, her blue eyes narrowing as she struggled with the tiny buttons on her gown.

He pulled on his polished black boots, then glanced at her and chuckled. "Now, now, my sweet, don't be tiresome. You know I have duties to attend to."

She tossed her head, her brassy blonde hair tumbling around the shoulders of her low cut gown. "Duty," she scoffed, "that's all you men know."

A dark look passed over Mikael's proud Bolkonsky features, but she didn't notice. "Duty to the Czar and to Russia is the most supreme honor any man can perform in his life. But I don't expect you, a mere woman, to understand."

She gathered up her hair and twisted it behind her in a knot, shoving her jeweled combs into the thick coils. "Of course I understand duty, Mikael." She sidled up to him and gave him a sultry smile. "A woman always obeys her husband. If you should marry me, I will do anything you ask, anything."

Important aristocratic men like me toy with women like you, but we do not marry them. He bent over as if to kiss her, then took his hand and pinched her hard on the cheek.

She gasped, "You brute! Why did you do that?"

He laughed coldly. "Don't pretend you don't like me to play rough with you, Vera. Something I doubt your boring Anton will ever do."

"Perhaps I will not marry Anton after all."

"If that is true, then someone should tell the poor fellow soon. He believes the two of you will be wed this summer."

She shot him a calculating look. "What if I should ask Papa to break off our betrothal, would that please you, Mikael?"

He hesitated. This was the fourth time in as many weeks the two of them had secretly met onboard his ship, and he was already becoming weary of her incessant nagging.

"A dutiful daughter always obeys her father," he said stiffly as he grabbed his coat, hat, and gloves, making sure his pistol and knife were tucked inside his belt. "Now come, Vera, I want you safely in your room before he starts asking too many questions."

She stamped her dainty slipper. "I don't care what Papa thinks. Besides, my parents think I'm at the Volodin's house inquiring about the health of your poor cousin."

Mikael frowned. "Ah, yes, most unfortunate for Dmitri and Tatiana to lose their child."

"They can always have another," Vera shrugged heartlessly.

As he wrapped her cloak around her, he appraised her slim form appreciatively. "Thank goodness that's a problem you don't have, my dear."

Vera smiled at him, but inside she felt a twinge of worry. Since the first time she'd been with Mikael, her monthly flow was late, and she was never ever late.

* * *

Tatiana made her way slowly down the stairs. Since the miscarriage ten days ago she had finally regained enough strength to take short walks about the house. She went through the kitchen past the two sleeping cats, Otter and Raven. They were curled up together cozily near the stove, which Helena had banked for the night before she returned to her house. Since Dmitri was staying at the governor's house, the cats had been allowed back inside.

If only he'd stay there forever, she thought as she opened the door to Anna's and Keeah's small room. When she stepped inside, she saw Anna sitting on her narrow bed, quietly feeding her daughter. The sight of mother and child brought a sudden pang of grief and loss, but Tatiana tried to focus instead on the pungent baby odors of soiled linens and sour milk in the cramped stuffy room.

Babies really are messy smelly creatures. She wrinkled her nose in distaste. I should be grateful I won't have to put up with any of this after all.

Anna gave her a smile of surprised welcome and said, "Oh, *Madame*, is it time for me to help you undress for the night?"

Tatiana gave her an exasperated frown. "Really, Anna, you can call me Tatiana when we're alone. Maria has gone back to her village and Keeah is upstairs trying to help Marya get ready for bed. But would you believe, even after all this time, she's still not comfortable having a maid wait on her!"

Anna laughed slightly. "Perhaps her Aleut blood is thicker than her Russian blood."

Tatiana made a wry face. "We'd better not let Boris know that or he might change his mind about the wedding." She sighed. "Poor Marya. In two weeks on Easter Monday, she'll be married to that dreadful man. Then she'll be off to Kodiak and out of my life for who knows how long. Thank goodness I have you, Anna! Whatever would I do without you?"

"You'll have me with you for quite awhile yet since we'll be sailing together to Fort Ross."

"Yes, it will be like old times on the *Sea Rose* again," she said sarcastically.

"Except that your husband will be the captain and not Sean."

"Sean?" Tatiana said sharply. "When did you start thinking of Captain O'Connell as Sean?"

Anna flushed and dropped her gaze down to the child at her breast. "When he asked me to marry him on the night of the banquet, the night that you lost--"

Tatiana looked at her in shock. "I don't believe it! That despicable, insulting man actually asked you to marry him? I hope you turned him down!"

"Yes, I did, but not for those reasons. Sean O'Connell has always behaved honorably towards me." Anna gave her a sad frown. "It's too soon after Ethan to even consider marrying again, and also, he is not of my faith."

Tatiana let out her breath in relief. "I'm so glad to hear that, Anna. Captain O'Connell is all wrong for you. But he must have been very angry when you refused to marry him. Won't it be awkward sailing with him on his ship? We'll all be so cramped and crowded together, how will you be able to avoid him?"

"It will only be for a few weeks. And I'll be very busy taking care of Katya and you. I don't expect to see much of the captain."

She glanced down at her daughter. Katya was so full of milk it was trickling out of her mouth. Anna gently placed her against her shoulder and began patting her on her back. The child let out a loud burp, and

Anna laughed then kissed her button nose. The tiny face brightened into a toothless grin and she gurgled happily.

Tatiana winced as a jolt of jealousy and guilt shot through her. *I shouldn't have gone to that banquet. I should've listened to Marya and stayed in bed. And now at night I 'm haunted by terrible nightmares. An infant that never stops crying, and when I try to find him, all I see is Dmitri accusing me of murdering our son. I see the* Buldakov *on fire and men with hideous burns all over their bodies screaming in torment, then they are silenced forever as they drown in a wave of icy cold water.*

Hadn't she pleaded and begged and prayed that the *Buldakov* would sink? And hadn't someone or something heard her? Since the night of the double tragedy, the loss of the *Buldakov* and her own child, she did not think she was an atheist any longer. God or some gods had answered her selfish pleas for disaster then thoroughly punished her by taking away the innocent life inside her.

Where was her dead baby? Did the unborn have souls? If so, would he be in heaven? Or did he no longer exist?

These were questions she should be asking Father Sokolov, but she shrank from the thought of talking with him. She had not been to confession for ages and she knew he disapproved of her almost as much as he disliked Anna. What would his reaction be if she confessed to murder in her heart? She remembered her catechism lessons well enough to know that the church taught to wish a deed done was the same as doing it.

Anna and Marya would also be horrified if they knew what she had prayed for. They used prayer as a means to talk to God, to worship and praise him. But she had used it to ask for a terrible thing, death.

Anna gave her daughter a tender smile and glanced up at Tatiana, suddenly noticing the pain in her eyes as she watched Katya. Her heart softened. As horrible as it was to lose a husband, it was even more unthinkable to lose a child. "Tatiana, is there anything I can do to help?"

She hesitated then said, "I would like you to pray for me."

Anna looked at her with surprise. "But of course. And I shall pray for your husband as well. You both are going through terrible suffering."

"He---he blames me for what happened," Tatiana suddenly confessed. "He said it was my fault, because I wasn't careful enough, and that he will never forgive me for losing his son." Tears sprang into her eyes and she rubbed them away with irritation.

"Your husband is grieving and you mustn't believe everything he says, Tatiana. Give him some time to heal, and he will realize that these things just happen. My mama lost several of her babies, and she always said it was because God wanted them in heaven with Him to grow up with the angels."

Tatiana gave her a pathetic look of eagerness as she said, "So, you believe that my son went to heaven?"

"In the Bible Jesus said that little children were welcome into the kingdom of heaven. All infants, the unborn and the born belong to God whether or not they've been baptized." Anna smiled at her. "Yes, Tatiana, I believe your son is in heaven and he hopes someday to see his mama there."

But if God and heaven are real, she thought, *then so is hell. And I am such a sinner that when I die, I will go straight to hell.*

She gave Anna a sad smile. "Thank you for telling me that. It is of some comfort." She stepped towards the door and looked back. "Anna, promise me you will always be my friend, no matter what happens."

"Of course, I promise."

After she left, Anna felt a deep pity for Tatiana. She was the unhappiest person she had ever known. Then she thought of Sean O'Connell. He was another deeply unhappy person.

"Ah, well, my little Katya," she said to her daughter, who was falling asleep in her arms, "I can always pray for them both. God can work miracles even in the hardest of hearts."

CHAPTER TWENTY SEVEN

Sean tapped his fingers impatiently on top of his desk in his cabin. He was concerned about the foul mood of the crew and while it was not yet mutinous, they were full of resentment.

Ever since he'd announced he was temporarily handing over the command of the ship to Baron Volodin, along with the addition of his wife and servants, plus several armed Russian naval escorts and four Aleut fur hunters, there'd been nothing but a general spirit of unrest aboard.

About an hour ago at the beginning of the evening watch, he'd tried to appease his men by reminding them of the benefits of their extra passengers. Governor Muraviev was giving them extra provisions, food supplies, and restoring most of their original cargo of fur skins. Plus, he was adding trade goods in case they encountered any natives on their way south, albeit no extra guns or powder. His Excellency stood firmly against the further arming of the native tribes.

"Won't get any good skins from the Injuns fer some beads an' trinkets, Cap'n," Jeb Drake had yelled. He was a barrel-chested fellow with hair of an undetermined color tied back in a long greasy braid.

Several of his friends mumbled in agreement, until Jake shouted, "Shut yer traps, mates, or I'll shut 'em fer ye! The Cap'n ain't done speaking yet."

The mutters subsided somewhat as Sean further explained how he believed they had enough furs to sail to Canton and make a profit on the voyage. "All of you will be well paid," he promised. "In return, I need your promise ye will obey Baron Volodin's orders, and the will to work hard. The ship will be crowded, and till we reach Fort Ross, I expect you men to keep your mouths closed and your fists to yourselves whenever the Russians are around. The first man who starts a fight with one of them will find himself flogged and put in the brig. An' those are my orders. Understand?"

Many of the men nodded, but most still scowled, and some were heard grumbling about the Volodin curse. The ill fate of the *Buldakov* was as suspect to the American sailors as it was to the Russians, and having Baron Volodin sail with them on the *Sea Rose*, made his crew even more fearful and nervous.

Sean knew it was going to be a difficult challenge to keep order onboard. The first thing was to make certain the Russians and the Americans were quartered separately. With such limited space that would be difficult. They would have to double up on the hammocks below in the cargo hold for the Russians and Aleuts, while his crew stayed in their usual berths forward near the bow.

His important passengers also posed a similar problem. He would have to give up his spacious captain's cabin to Volodin and his wife until they reached California. It angered him, but since it was only temporary, he knew he would manage. Anna could have the cabin she once shared with Ethan for herself and her child. He would reassign John and Jake to other cabins. Everyone was going to have to sacrifice their privacy for a few weeks.

Sean picked up a gold ring sitting on top his desk. He had paid a Russian craftsman who was skilled in fine metal work to fashion the ring from a gold nugget he'd traded from the nearby Tlingits. The yellow rocks meant little to the natives, and he had obtained several for a small barrel of molasses. Sometimes he wondered how much gold there was in Alaska, and if the Russians realized that the land here held more wealth than only furs.

The shiny gold band had his and Anna's initials carved on them, S & A. He knew it was premature, but he intended on wedding her one way or another. He believed the day would come when Anna would remove her silver wedding ring from Ethan, and slip this gold ring on. Sean imagined how perfectly his ring would look on her delicate finger

He set the ring down and took hold of his mug, sipping the lukewarm tea. Today was Easter Sunday and tomorrow was the wedding of Boris Ivanoff and Marya Nikolayevna. On Tuesday all the Russians were coming aboard and on Wednesday they were sailing.

His thoughts went back to the problem at hand, his crew. He was not surprised that the men were uneasy about this voyage. Not only were they angered at having to obey Volodin's commands, they were mumbling about the two women bringing bad luck. They already resented the baroness, and even though Anna had earned their respect a year ago as the wife of Ethan Campbell, some of the superstitious crew blamed her presence on board for their capture by the Russians the previous fall.

Sean rubbed his eyes wearily. He was also concerned that the *Sea Rose* might be overloaded. More passengers meant more luggage. During the past two days they'd already stowed the Volodins' thirty large trunks plus some pieces of furniture. The rest of the hold was full of furs and provisions. The last thing he needed was for the ship to be so heavy she sat as deeply in the water as a fat woman in a tub.

It would be spring when they sailed, but that was no guarantee of fair weather in the Pacific. Unexpected gales, thick fog and rough seas were common in April.

Fortunately, he would be sailing the *Sea Rose* through the more protected inland waters, trading at several Indian villages until they reached Vancouver Island. Then it would be open ocean all the way south down the coast to California. If all went well, they should arrive at Fort Ross in June.

Another worry concerning him was the condition of the ship's cables, the long iron chains which fastened the ship to her anchors. Gregory Jones had brought it to his attention that after sitting in the harbor for months, many of the iron links were rusty and had deteriorated to the point where it was questionable if the cables could hold the ship's anchors safely in a big blow. Forging new links was the armorer's job, and Jones had been busily working at it, but there wasn't enough time to properly repair all the cables before they sailed.

A knock rapped on his door and he automatically said, "Come in."

Samuel poked his head in. "Two Russkies here to see yuh, Cap'n. They say yuh wanted at a meeting with the Gov'nor."

Sean frowned. "But I thought Muraviev was too sick to see anyone."

The governor had been fighting a lingering cough the past weeks. He'd heard just yesterday that he was quite ill with a fever and had taken to his bed. His valet Mikhail and the housekeeper *Madame* Kornilova were taking turns nursing him. Baron Volodin was in charge of the business of governing until he sailed, then Lieutenant Dohktorov was to take charge.

"Maybe yuh better take Mistah Jones. Nobody mess wi' yuh if he come along."

Sean sighed as he stood up and grabbed his coat and hat. "That won't be necessary, Samuel. Just tell Mr. Hill and Mr. O'Riley where I've gone, and that I expect to be back before midnight."

"Yessuh," said Samuel in a doubtful voice.

* * *

The night was pitch black with a cold wind blowing across the harbor, swirling salt spray from the choppy waves into Sean's face where he sat in the bow. At least it wasn't raining at the moment. As the boat pulled away from the hull of the *Sea Rose*, it didn't take Sean long to realize they were not heading for shore. The Russian sailors were rowing in the opposite direction towards the dimly lit *Alexandria*, anchored a half mile away.

The scars on his back prickled as he sensed something amiss. "Turn this boat around!" he demanded in crude Russian. "Take me back to my ship at once!"

The sailor sitting nearest to him said, "*Nyet*. We go to meet the governor."

"You're lying!" Sean shouted. "You're taking me to see Bolkonsky! That's his ship over there!"

"Quiet!" the man hissed as he pulled a pistol out of his coat pocket and aimed the muzzle directly at Sean. "You come willingly or not, it's up to you."

Sean snarled at him then looked back at the rapidly fading outline of his ship already a couple hundred yards away. A lantern flickered on top of each mast, but their light grew fainter by the second. He glanced down at the inky dark water and wondered if he could manage to swim back to the *Sea Rose* before the sailor shot him. If he stayed underwater as long as possible and with some luck, he might make it.

He tensed his muscles for the jump, but before he could move, something heavy crashed against his skull, blinding him with a stab of pain, and he slumped over into the two inches of brackish sea water sloshing back and forth on the bottom of the boat. He felt the shock of the cold water and the hardness of the wood floor before he blacked out into nothingness.

* * *

Shaking her head in sad empathy, Tatiana watched Marya stomp out of the parlor. Tomorrow was her wedding day and the poor girl had been weeping all evening. If she didn't stop crying soon, she was going to look like a wreck instead of a beautiful bride. Moments ago Anna had offered to bring her some chamomile tea to soothe and help her sleep and finally, Marya agreed. As Tatiana decided to go upstairs and see if Marya was better, a knock sounded on the front door.

"Keeah," she called out, "someone is here."

Instead of responding, Tatiana heard the *Kolosh* maid in the kitchen, singing one of her heathenish songs to Katya. The child had been fussing for hours, as if sensing Marya's distress. Little Maria and Helena had already left for their respective homes.

Who could it be this time of night, she thought, feeling irritated that she had to answer her own door like a common housewife who had no servants.

She flung open the door and found herself facing Lieutenant Dohktorov.

He appeared as surprised as she. "Please forgive me for bothering you so late, Baroness," he said. "But I must speak with your husband. Is he home?"

She was a tall woman and used to being the same height as many men, but she had to look up to see the lieutenant's face. He was even taller than Captain O'Connell. And though the captain's shoulders were broader and his arms and legs thicker with muscles, Anton exuded a wiry strength from head to toe, like a lean but powerful panther.

She had forgotten how handsome he was. He had the most extraordinary golden brown eyes, large and set apart, surrounded by thick dark eyelashes most women would die for. She also liked his face with his strong straight nose, square firm jaw, and his mouth that flashed white teeth when he smiled, with two dimples on each side.

He was smiling now, studying her as well, and Tatiana suddenly felt self-conscious of her appearance. The hectic evening had loosened her hair from tightly curled ringlets into a golden mass of half curls and half snarls tumbling around her face and shoulders. She thought she must look frightful.

"Dmitri is not here at present," she said, "but I expect him back soon. Would you care to come in and wait?"

Anton hesitated, glancing around the empty parlor then nodded. They both sat down in two comfortable armchairs near the stove, which had been banked for the night, but was still radiating some heat. Anton unbuttoned his coat and took off his cap, resting it on his knees. He glanced at Tatiana and thought how lovely she looked in her gown of lavender velvet and lace.

"It must have been terrifying for you on the *Buldakov*," she said, clenching her fingers together as a renewed sense of guilt assailed her. "I am so thankful you escaped without injury, Lieutenant."

He made a swift sign of the cross and said, "God was looking out for me that day, Baroness, as He was for your husband and many others."

A shadow crossed her face, like someone drawing a dark curtain over a brightly lit window. "Yes, Dmitri is a lucky man," she said in a blank tone.

"If it was luck, many of them were unlucky," he said as a haunting sadness crept into his eyes, "Yet, I cannot second guess the Almighty when it comes to life or death."

He is a religious man then, she thought. Once that would have disgusted her in a man, but not anymore. A man of faith was a man of depth and sensitivity, a man a woman could depend on to take care of her, a man like Ethan Campbell. Did Vera Alexisovna have any idea how fortunate she was?

"Vera must be overjoyed that you survived."

Hardness passed over his face. "Yes, she is delighted that I came back," he said flatly, thinking about the rumors he'd heard of her flirting with Mikael Bolkonsky while he was gone.

Tatiana raised one eyebrow then said, "I haven't seen much of her lately. I've been so busy with the wedding plans. Tomorrow after the ceremony in the church, if the weather is fine, we hope to have the reception outdoors."

It was the only thing Marya had insisted on. She wanted to have her wedding feast along the Indian River instead of celebrating with one of those interminable banquets. She said it was more traditional for her people, even though none of her family would be attending. Dmitri said he didn't care, so Tatiana went ahead and arranged a special picnic, complete with food, drink, and servants to carry it all. The only person who was not pleased was Boris. He detested any type of exercise, and the hike to the river was several versts away.

"I shall be escorting Vera, of course," said Anton. He passed a hand wearily over his face. "Do you have any idea where the baron went tonight?"

"He mentioned something about meeting Boris and my cousin Mikael on board the *Alexandria*. I imagine they're toasting Boris's last night as a free man, and Dmitri will come home roaring drunk." He had been drinking more heavily since the *Buldakov* sank and she lost their child. *Not that I blame him.*

"Then he may be back quite late," frowned Anton, wondering if more than just a bachelor celebration was taking place aboard the *Alexandria*.

That evening he'd been working in the governor's office and talking to young Ivan Putin. The aide had asked him if he knew any reason why the governor would wish to have the Yankee captain flogged. Anton was shocked at the very idea and was astounded when Putin said he'd once seen a signed document with an order to have Captain O'Connell flogged with the *knout*.

"The order was in a stack of papers which Baron Volodin had sent to the governor to sign, Sir," Putin said. "I saw His Excellency sign the paper himself without questioning it."

"Then what happened to it?"

"Baron Volodin took possession of all the papers, including the order for flogging."

Anton was well aware of the hostility Volodin felt towards the Americans, their captain in particular. He did not trust him or Ivanoff or Bolkonsky and suspected they were all involved in some plot to harm O'Connell. But was it with Governor Muraviev's permission?

Immediately, he'd left the office to see the governor upstairs in his bedchamber. But Mikhail had refused to admit Anton, saying His Excellency was asleep and must not be disturbed. After that, he decided to ask Volodin about the document and hope he received a straight answer.

"Is something wrong with the governor?" Tatiana asked, noting the worried expression on his face. "Has he taken a turn for the worst?"

"No, no, nothing like that," Anton hastened to assure her. "It's only a matter of a missing document and I thought your husband might know where it is."

"It must be an important piece of paper to bring you here so late on Easter Sunday."

He looked at her. She has the most beautiful eyes I've ever seen, a soft violet like pansies in the spring. "There might be some danger to Captain O'Connell," he blurted without thinking.

"What do you mean? He's in danger from my husband?" She shivered suddenly, remembering how Dmitri believed that the captain had once seduced her on board his ship. I should have told him the truth long ago, she thought guiltily. But then his anger would be against me.

Anton cursed himself when he saw her tremble. He reached over to her and took one of her slender hands in his. The smooth feel of her skin seared his fingers like heated silk. She jerked a bit at his sudden touch, but did not pull her hand away.

"Forgive me if I've alarmed you, but I'm sure there's nothing to worry about," he said in a soothing voice.

His strong fingers felt so warm and comforting wrapped around her hand she wished she could leave it there forever. "I sincerely hope not," she said, then gave him a shy smile. "You may call me Tatiana, Lieutenant."

He flashed her a handsome grin. "And I am Anton, your friend," he said.

They stared at each other for a few moments, and Tatiana felt herself blushing under his steady gaze. *What a nice, kind man,* she thought, *and what a terrible tragedy it would have been if he had died on the Buldakov. And it would have been all my fault.*

Anton saw her beautiful face flush and he quickly released her hand, believing she was embarrassed because of his bold and improper manner. He knew if Volodin ever saw him holding his wife's hand, he would be the next person on the baron's list of enemies.

After the disaster of the *Buldakov*, when he had witnessed firsthand Dmitri Volodin's cowardly and irrational behavior that led to all those unnecessary deaths, he believed the man to be selfish, cruel, and perhaps even evil. Since that day, he had tormented himself, trying to decide if he should be bold and take his accusations against Volodin to the governor, or stay silent like a coward. But it would be his word against Volodin's, as none of the surviving crew would dare speak against their commander. His Excellency would have no choice but to dismiss the matter, and then he, Anton, would have made a deadly enemy in Dmitri Volodin.

Tonight's situation was no different. He had no proof of any wrongdoing, only hearsay evidence that this document even existed. And now after spending these moments with Tatiana, and seeing how frail she appeared after her recent illness, he had no wish to accuse her husband of anything and cause more trouble in her life.

"It's late and I can talk with the baron another time," he said, rising from his chair. "I'll bid you goodnight, Tatiana."

"I will tell him you were here, Anton." She stood up and walked him to the door, her arm brushing his as he passed her.

She was only inches away from him and he tried not to notice the faint rose fragrance from her hair and throat, and how her necklace, made of gold with a large diamond and amethyst pendant, nestled inside the creamy whiteness of her *décolletage.* With difficulty he fought the urge to sweep her up into his arms and kiss her luscious mouth.

Shocked at himself, he wondered what was wrong with him. Here he was, almost a married man and he was tempted by another woman. Then he thought of Vera and Mikael. Perhaps my marriage to Vera is a mistake. Perhaps we should call off our betrothal. Meanwhile, I must be careful to never be alone with Tatiana again.

* * *

"He's coming around," Sean heard a familiar voice say in Russian, as he fought his way to consciousness some time later. His head felt like a hammer was hitting it. Wincing, he opened his eyes and found himself stripped to the waist, lying on his bare back with his wrists and ankles bound by ropes. The stench of the bilge, sewage and brine, filled his nostrils and he knew he was imprisoned deep in the hold of the *Alexandria.*

One oil lamp swung gently from the bulkhead above as the ship rolled at her anchors. It was enough light for Sean to see Boris Ivanoff and Mikael Bolkonsky standing next to Dmitri Volodin a few feet away.

"Hoist him up and tie him to the post there," ordered Volodin.

The same burly sailors that had fetched him from the *Sea Rose* both grabbed him under the armpits and dragged him upright as they jerked his arms above his head and fastened them tightly to the wooden post.

"Gentlemen," said Sean, glaring at all three officers, "what's the meaning of this outrage?"

"It's really quite simple, my dear Captain O'Connell," said Volodin in English, smirking slightly. "It's called revenge."

"For what?"

"Not for what, for whom. It's about my wife. When she was a helpless passenger on board your ship, not only did you fail to protect her from a cowardly attack by your own officer, but then you took advantage of her and raped her in your cabin one night!"

Sean was shocked speechless for a moment, then quickly recovered. "If that's what she told you, she lied!" he shouted.

"So, you deny that my wife ever spent a night in your cabin with you?"

Sean twisted his wrists and grimaced, feeling his muscles stretch painfully from his shoulders to his hands. "I'm only sayin' I never ravished the woman. One night I awoke to find her in my bunk with me. I don't know what happened after that, because I had too much to drink, and I passed out. She claimed I had my way with her, an' if I did, 'twas she fancied it, not me."

Volodin strode over to him and hit him in the face, splitting his bottom lip open. "You are the one who lies, not my wife!"

Sean spat a mouthful of blood at him, the red glob nearly striking his immaculate coat. "Your wife is the most deceitful woman I've ever met. You and she are a match made in hell!" Volodin's face whitened in anger and his left eye began to twitch. "And that's exactly where I aim to send you soon, Captain."

"I've already seen the tail end of a whip and survived, Volodin," said Sean with more bravado than he felt.

He glanced at the lines of puckered scars crisscrossing Sean's back. "Yes, I can tell you were once flogged quite soundly, for good reasons, I'm sure. But nothing you Yanks use for a whip can compare to our Russian *knout*. After fifty lashes, you'll be begging for death, if you aren't dead already."

Sean grunted, feeling a trickle of fear. The *knout* was a punishment peculiar to the Russian military. It was the most dreaded of all the whips. Made of a long thick rope, it had three thongs of hard tanned elk hide attached to the end. Each thong was the length of a finger and could cut the bare skin of a man like a knife. After only several lashes of the *knout*, a man's back looked like the flayed hide of an animal, a shredded mass of blood and tissue. At the end of the whipping, the victim was usually more dead than alive.

"Ye won't get away with this, any of ye," Sean threatened. "I'm under the Gov'nor's protection!"

Boris and Mikael looked at each other and laughed. They were enjoying watching Dmitri get his revenge on the Yankee captain. They had all waited weeks for this moment, but as the date for the Yankees departure came closer and closer, they'd worried there might be no time or opportunity to make use of the permit Muraviev had unknowingly signed, to authorize the corporal punishment of Captain O'Connell. But fate had intervened with His Excellency's unexpected illness. If luck stayed with them, they hoped the governor would never hear about the deed until after the *Sea Rose* sailed. To insure extra secrecy, Mikael had used the excuse of Easter Sunday to allow his crew to stay ashore to celebrate the holy holiday until the morrow, keeping only two sailors on board to administer the flogging. He had already bribed their silence with extra rations of vodka and a hundred rubles each.

Dmitri pulled a paper out of his coat pocket and brandished it under Sean's nose. "This is a signed and sealed document from His Excellency, ordering you to be lashed fifty times with the *knout*. He wants to make certain you are in no condition to override my command of your ship after we sail."

Sean glanced at the paper written in Russian and recognized only the press of the Imperial seal. "Since I canna understand a word of it, I'll have to trust ye, Baron," he said in a sarcastic voice, "but somehow I smell a rat here. I still dinna believe Muraviev has ordered this."

Dmitri shrugged and pocketed the document. "You can believe what you like, Captain O'Connell. But I do suggest that if you're a praying man, you better start praying."

He nodded to the largest sailor, a tall brute with a bulbous nose and thick lips and arms as meaty as hams. "Gorki, you may begin."

With the whip handle clutched tightly in his massive hand, Fedor Gorki gave a cruel-sounding chuckle, then snaked the *knout* back over his head before swinging the sharp thongs forward towards Sean's naked back.

* * *

As the longboat from the *Sea Rose* bumped against the hull of the *Alexandria*, the thirteen occupants heard a man bellow in sudden pain.

"'Tis comin' from the hold," said Jake, grabbing the slick rope ladder. "We've no time to waste, men!"

John climbed up quickly after him, followed by Gregory Jones and ten sailors, all armed with pistols, muskets, and knives. He glanced around the empty deck, feeling puzzled. "There's not one man on watch. How odd."

Earlier both he and Jake had tried to dissuade the captain from going ashore alone with the Russians to meet the governor. It had seemed strange that Muraviev wanted a meeting so late at night when he was ill. But Sean insisted he'd be safe enough with his knife tucked in his belt and a pistol in his coat pocket.

While the Russian boat carrying the captain disappeared into the murky darkness of the harbor, John and Jake stood at the rail, talking quietly about the wedding the following day. John felt depressed at the thought of the young and lovely Marya marrying the obscene lieutenant and how there was nothing he could do to stop it.

"I feel like I've failed her," he said to Jake when suddenly they heard the captain shout faintly in the distance. The sound carried across the water from the wrong direction, away from the shore, surprising them both.

"Where are they taking him?" asked John, peering through the misty gloom of the evening, but seeing nothing.

"Sounded ter me like he was yellin' from over there," said Jake. He pointed towards where they knew the *Alexandria* was anchored, although the ship was not visible except for the dull flicker of her mast lantern. The two men exchanged glances of alarm as the realization hit both of them---the captain had been kidnapped!

Now, less than an hour later, John, Jake, and Gregory plus the ten sailors crept cautiously towards the main hatch. The deck of the Russian brig looked eerie in the shadowy darkness with only a bare glimmer of light moving back and forth across the ship as she heaved slightly with each swell. Stars twinkled overhead, a tantalizing promise of a fair day on the morrow.

"I don't like this," mumbled Jake. "Where's the crew?"

"I hope they're not all waiting for us below," said John quietly as he clambered down the ladder with Gregory right behind him. The big man had a knife clutched in his teeth as he swung down another ladder to the bowels of the ship. He and the others followed the two officers aft toward the stern where they could see a light wavering ahead and hear the sounds of men laughing. Another sound, much more ominous, was the sharp crack of a whip snapping to and fro, striking its target like a lethal razor.

As the *knout* sliced across his back Sean jerked spasmodically against the post and uttered a low guttural moan of anguish. Every nerve, every muscle, every inch of skin felt like it was on fire, burning deeply into the fiber of his entire being. He had lost count of the lashes after the tenth one, and was now half-conscious. He existed in a state of hellish torment where each breath drawn was agony, each second alive was too long. Soon the only thought he had left was that he wished to die, even if his da was waiting for him. He longed for the moment when he could leave his pain-wracked body and fade into the sweet blissful oblivion of death. It was the only way to stop this unending torture.

He was unaware of the commotion around him; the shouts of his officers and crew; the surprised grunt issuing from Fedor Gorki as Gregory Jones threw his knife with dreadful accuracy stabbing him right between the shoulder blades; the yells of rage from Volodin, Ivanoff, and Bolkonsky as pistols already primed with shot were drawn and aimed directly at them. All Sean knew was the sudden absence of the slashing *knout* before darkness came rushing at him as he collapsed into the welcome nothingness of a deep faint.

* * *

After Anton was gone Tatiana went upstairs to her sitting room and poured herself a glass of Dmitri's fine brandy from the crystal decanter on the polished wood table. Then she sat down on the soft cushion of a curved armchair near the stove and drank it as fast as she could without gagging.

The April night was chilly and the radiating warmth felt soothing to her weary body. She hoped the brandy would bring some comfort to the ache deep inside her as well. Tears threatened to spill down her cheeks and the thought of crying made her angry. Even as a child, she'd despised tears as a sign of weakness, and scorned Olga who cried over every little thing.

But lately, she found to her dismay, tears frequently springing to her eyes, usually over nothing at all. At the moment, however, she believed she had good reasons to cry. Tomorrow her unfortunate sister was marrying the disgusting Boris Ivanoff, and then she would also be trapped in an unhappy marriage.

If only Dmitri was a man like her papa, she sighed, missing him suddenly with a fierceness she hadn't experienced in ages. She was certain he'd never struck her mama, but then her papa was different from most Russian aristocrats. He was a truly kind and loving man. If only they'd had more time together as father and daughter.

Sometimes she wished she'd stayed with her uncle and aunt in England. The Suttons had welcomed her into their family as if she'd always belonged. She could have watched her young cousins grow up, and eventually, found a nice husband among the English nobility. But she never would have seen her papa again or met Marya.

Perhaps she should have married outside of the Russian aristocracy to find herself the kind of husband she always dreamed of. But who, a poor Scotsman like Ethan Campbell, or Sean O'Connell, a common Irish-American, or an even poorer Mennonite from Anna's own village?

She snorted softly at the thought of herself wearing the dowdy clothing of a Mennonite woman and living in a plain house attached to a stable, kneading dough and scrubbing floors all day. No, that was not the life for her. She liked the feel of fine silk against her skin and having servants and wearing expensive gowns and jewelry.

Taking another sip of brandy, the image of Lieutenant Dohktorov flashed through her mind. "Anton," she whispered, liking the sound of his name.

She would swear on a stack of Bibles that he would make a strong, but loving husband. How could Vera risk losing him by her infatuation with Mikael? He was like Dmitri and would be a typical abusive husband of the Russian nobility. It was well known that Uncle Vasily had used physical force to control Aunt Irene in their earlier years. Vera must be dazzled by Mikael's family prestige, titles, and wealth. Didn't she have any idea what a cruel husband Mikael would make, and that she should do everything in her power to keep Anton?

He had called himself her friend. The thought brought a warm glow deep inside her, and she smiled.

Downstairs she heard the front door open and slam shut. Dmitri was home. She set her glass down and went out into the hallway. Down the corridor from Marya's room she could hear Anna speaking to Marya. It sounded like she was praying or reading the Bible. Tatiana stepped down the first few stairs then paused when she realized Dmitri was not alone.

"Bolkonsky's an idiot! He should've posted guards all over the ship! Instead those cursed Yanks snuck on board and almost killed Gorki, putting a halt to the flogging. Now O'Connell might survive!"

"Dmitri, my friend, calm down," came the low rumble of Boris's voice. "Gorki struck him with more than twenty lashes of the *knout*. I've seen less than that kill a man. O'Connell might be dead by this time tomorrow."

"I want him dead by the time we sail," snapped Dmitri.

"If not, he will be soon after. You saw the man's back, Dmitri. What was left of it can only fester into a massive infection."

"At least my wife is finally avenged."

Tatiana had heard enough. With mounting horror, she realized her husband and her cousin and Boris Ivanoff had somehow taken Captain

O'Connell to the *Alexandria* where he'd been whipped so badly he might die. And all because of her!

Her stomach heaved as the brandy inside threatened to erupt. She fled back into her sitting room and stood, taking deep breaths. So, that was why Anton had come. He was afraid Captain O'Connell had been arrested by Dmitri. What should she do? Find Anton and tell him? But the deed was done. It was too late to help. At least the American crew had rescued the captain. Perhaps he would survive after all.

How had Dmitri obtained the permission from the governor to do such a terrible thing? Or had the three men planned this on their own? If so, when the governor discovered what they'd done, would they be arrested?

She moaned, feeling even more ill as she thought of Anna. She mustn't be told, not yet, not until after the wedding tomorrow.

How dare Dmitri use revenge for her as an excuse for attempted murder! What a twisted way he had of showing his love! But wasn't she just as despicable? How could she fault him when her prayers were responsible for the destruction of his ship and the death of so many innocent men? And then there was their child...

Now she believed it was true what was said about the Volodin family. They were indeed cursed. Perhaps it was a blessing after all then, that her poor babe was no longer alive.

She buried her face in her hands and wept.

* * *

Later that night while most everyone in the household finally slept, Anna fed and cleaned two-month-old Katya. Then she rocked her for awhile, softly singing the special songs she and Jack used to sing at Easter service. Because Father Sokolov disapproved of her, she had not attended church that day and it saddened her.

Easter was the most joyful holiday of the Russian year. On the days before were the Holy Week services, which Marya told Anna were solemn affairs full of poetic and soul stirring hymns and scriptures. Then on Easter Eve, Marya and Tatiana colored boiled eggs and Helena prepared a roasted pig. At the church many decorations were placed in readiness for Easter worship, beginning with a short service at midnight on Holy Sunday, followed by a mass.

So now, even though Katya would not understand, Anna spoke of how Easter was such an important church and family day to the Mennonites.

"In the morning, Elder Klassen preaches his sermon directly from the Resurrection story in the Gospels. And after the service, Easter is a day of family reunions. Your Great-uncle Heindrich and *Tante* Sarah and my cousins all come from Silberfeld. We have such fun. There's good plain food like baked ham, *pluma moos*, dark bread and fresh churned butter, and hard-boiled eggs that my mama, your Grandmama, let us dye with different colors the day before. Then later in the afternoon, coffee and tea is served with *twaback*, raisin bread, and special sweets."

Anna sighed with frustration as she wondered if Katya would ever know her Mennonite family. She reminded her so much of little Tina. By now her stepmother Agatha had added at least one child to the Teichroew household. If she had any more children, Anna was afraid that Katarina might be forgotten among her papa's new family.

She glanced down at her sleeping daughter. She knew it was up to her to teach Katya the Mennonite traditions, but how could she do that as a serving maid in Russian America?

Tears welled up in her eyes, and she also wept.

* * *

Upstairs in her bedchamber, Marya tossed and turned on the soft mattress in her four posted bed, tormented by thoughts of becoming a wife to Boris. Earlier Anna had told her to keep trusting God because He would provide a way of escape."

But now she was almost out of time. Who was there to rescue her? Andrei Leonov or John Hill? It was too late for either one to help her.

She groaned like a mortally wounded animal trapped in a snare, then faced head down onto her white linen covered pillow and wept.

CHAPTER TWENTY EIGHT

Easter Monday dawned overcast with a steady drizzle, but by ten o'clock, the sun slanted rays of golden light through the clouds, promising a fine afternoon. At the Church of Saint Michael, the sunshine lit up the stained glass windows, which many viewed as God's blessing upon the wedding couple.

Most of the nobility of New Archangel attended the traditional Orthodox service. Marya wore a pale blue silk wedding gown, the color of a Russian bride. With her glossy raven black hair curled in fashionable ringlets framing the light dusky tones of her face, she was a striking beauty. No one seemed to notice the wretched misery pasted on her face as she spoke her vows in a soft halting voice. Her small slender form next to the beefy figure of Lieutenant Ivanoff made it seem as if Boris was wedding a mere child.

An extremely pale looking Tatiana was fashionable as always in a mauve gown of rich satin with ivory colored lace. Purple shadows under her eyes made them appear an even richer hue of violet than normal. Her fair skin was almost translucent and gave her beauty a wraithlike quality. While Tatiana struggled to smile at everyone, Dmitri fairly beamed with pride and delight at having his wife cling to his arm, depending on his superior strength to get her through her sister's wedding.

Anna waited in the rear of the church for the ceremony to be over. Marya had begged Tatiana to allow Anna to be there to give her added support. Afterwards Anna was also invited to the outdoor reception. Keeah promised to take care of Katya for the afternoon.

As Anna watched the ceremony, she remembered the day on the British naval ship when she married Ethan. At that time, she had believed she was in love with Ethan, but in reality it had been the other way around. Ethan was madly in love with her while she'd mistaken like and respect for real love. But because his love for her had been so strong, she eventually could not help but love him back.

She would always cherish her memories of Ethan, but his smile had never made her knees quiver like jelly, nor had his touch ever sent her blood singing through her veins like she was on fire. This is what happened to her whenever she was near Sean O'Connell. If she was honest with herself, she had been drawn to him from the very first weeks on the *Sea Rose*. How shocking it was to learn that he had felt the same.

Her attraction to him then had frightened her, and she had fought it by turning to Ethan, safe dependable Ethan.

He had promised her that someday they would return to Furstenau to see her family. Her papa might have accepted Ethan as a son-in-law, but she didn't believe he would ever accept an Irish-Catholic man like Sean into the family. Instead he'd rather she marry someone like Gerhard Yoder.

She closed her eyes, preferring to envision marrying the captain even though it would never happen. How surprised and envious her cousins and Susannah would be if they ever laid eyes on the devilishly handsome Captain O'Connell. And her brothers' reaction? She thought Jack, Jacob and Peter might find the captain fascinating, especially Peter, who loved ships.

As Father Sokolov bestowed the final marriage prayers and blessings on the couple, Anna sighed, her heart full of pity for Marya, and for Tatiana and her miserable marriage, and for herself and her fanciful daydreams of marrying a man who not only wasn't a Mennonite, but had a suspicious past. She decided that no matter how tempted she might be on the upcoming voyage to California, she must keep away from Sean O'Connell.

* * *

The favorite picnic spot of the town's residents on the Indian River was a wild and beautiful place. This time of year in late April, the river was a rushing torrent of water cascading down from the melting snows and glaciers of the mountains of Baranov Island.

With an escort of armed soldiers and a bevy of Aleut servants carrying enormous baskets of food, Marya and Boris, as the newlyweds led the way. They were followed by a small group of guests, Dmitri, Tatiana, and Anna, Mikael Bolkonsky, Elizabeth Pushkina and her three children, Anastasia and the twins Fedor and Nikolai, Captain-Lieutenant Alexis Trotsky and his wife Irina, with their daughters, Vera and Sophie, Lieutenant Anton Dohktorov, and Captain-Lieutenant Shekolov from the newly arrived warship, *Czarina*.

Basil Pushkin's *Finlandia* was out on patrol duty, and later in the week, Bolkonsky's *Alexandria* and Trotsky's *Kuskov* were to join Pushkin. Spring meant the fur trade among the Indian villages had just begun and if the Russians were to prevent the British and Americans ships from trading in their waters, they needed every ship the navy had to repel the invaders.

Father Sokolov was also leaving soon. He was sailing with the Ivanoffs in the *Kamchatka* to Kodiak Island and eventually to the other settlements. The governor was sending Father Sokolov as his emissary to inspect the outposts while he was overseeing their churches and meeting with several newly arrived monks to Russian America.

The route to Indian River lay around Crescent Beach and through the forest. As the party of wedding guests made their way along the pebbled beach, Boris huffed and puffed, complaining to Marya that it was too far. She still wore her wedding gown, but had exchanged her satin slippers for more practical boots, as had all the ladies. Instead of her veil, she wore a blue silk bonnet decorated with white flowers and ribbons. Unlike Boris, she tromped through the mud and rocks without complaint, her face set in a stoic expression.

Boris felt the perspiration rolling off every part of his body in the warm afternoon sun. A mosquito whined past his ear and he flinched in distaste. Whatever had possessed Dmitri to allow such a ridiculous wedding celebration? They should all be sitting comfortably inside the governor's banquet hall enjoying a sumptuous feast. Instead he had a long hike through the bug-infested, marsh-ridden forest before he could collapse into the large chair one of the Aleuts was carrying for him.

He glanced down at his new wife and some of his irritation vanished. She was a stunning vision in her beautiful gown and the warmth of her gloved hand in his as they continued their stroll was a promise of the night to come. The thought of that delightful pleasure made him sweat even more, but this time he didn't mind.

The trail through the forest passed under clumps of spruce, hemlock and yellow cedar trees, their branches so long and thick, the sun could not penetrate.The light was a diffused green, slanting in emerald rays to the forest floor. The pungent scent of pine and spruce needles and the moist odor of decaying logs and mushrooms filled the air. On both sides of the path, the vegetation was impregnable, a tangle of salmonberry and elderberry bushes with luxuriant ferns spreading out like giant green fans.

The forest made Anna feel claustrophobic, as used as she was to the wide open steppes of southern Russia. Looking at the verdant wall of greenery all around her, she imagined how easily it could hide a black tailed deer, or even more ominous, a ferocious bear or an unfriendly *Kolosh* native. It made her grateful for the armed escorts in front and behind them.

On the brighter side, the sounds of the forest were like music to her ears. Birds of many species abounded, thrushes, hummingbirds, orange-crowned warblers, and wrens, all twittered and chirped, flying and fluttering from tree to tree. Gray and brown squirrels added their chatter as they sat above on tree branches, scolding angrily down at the intruders crashing through their quiet forest home.

As they grew closer to the river the tumultuous roar of the rushing water crowded out all other sounds. The trail climbed gradually to an open area, the picnic spot, where a meadow with large flat rocks bordered the river, offering some places for comfortable sitting.

Patches of snow lay on the ground in shady places, a reminder that April showers sometimes brought snow. Looking east up the Indian River valley Anna could see a beautiful view of the Sisters Mountains, a cluster of white-capped peaks. Tatiana told her that if they continued on for a few more versts, the trail finally ended at a spectacular waterfall.

"Not today," she laughed, glancing down at the mud spattered on the hem of her gown. It was silk the color of golden amber trimmed with leafy green lace, another one of Tatiana's castoffs. She carried a silk fan to match and on her head wore an amber gold bonnet with green ribbons.

"I don't think we ladies are dressed for any further walking."

Her toes were already pinching uncomfortably in her tight laced boots, and she was thankful to sit down as one of the Aleut servants spread a thick quilt on a sunlit spot where the ground was soft and spongy with moss and fragrant with grass and pine needles.

Tatiana sat next to her, and Dmitri, Mikael Bolkonsky and Captain-Lieutenant Shekolov settled themselves nearby on another blanket. Boris and Marya were seated comfortably on two cushioned armchairs under a spruce tree while the other guests were all spread out in the clearing.

Fedor and Nikolai ran to the river, and immediately began to throw rocks into the water, squealing with delight at the resulting splashes.

"Come with us, Anastasia," called out Nikolai, who thought his older sister was the most boring person in the world.

Anastasia, a younger copy of her aristocratic mother Elizabeth, sniffed in disdain. She was dressed in a pale pink silk and lace dress, and wore a matching bonnet with pink silk ribbons tied under her small pointed chin. Her stockings were white and immaculate, and she wanted to keep them that way.

She had no intention of going near the dangerous looking river. The trek through the dirty forest had been dreadful enough. Each step had brought a risk of slipping on slimy mud or tripping over a thick gnarled tree root across the path.

Ignoring her little brothers, she stuck her nose up in the air and placed herself carefully on a blanket, arranging the folds of her dress just right so it wouldn't wrinkle. Elizabeth gave her a glance of approval, then frowned as she watched her sons as they headed up the river, skipping over the stones and laughing.

"Fedor! Nikolai!" she called out, "Don't go too far!"

"We won't, Mother," said Fedor without turning around.

The servants kept busy distributing the food and drink. There was smoked salmon and halibut, cold roasted chicken, pastries, cheese, jugs of tea, and champagne chilled with ice cut from Swan Lake. Somehow they'd even managed to transport the wedding cake, carried in a large box. This was placed in the shade, as the icing was already beginning to soften in the unusually warm afternoon.

The day was perfect except for the uninvited swarms of mosquitoes. They weren't as thick near the river where a nice breeze kept them at bay, but in the more stagnant air by the trees, the Aleut servants had to use the ladies' fans to sweep away the biting insects.

As Dmitri slapped at a mosquito trying to crawl inside the high collar of his cravat, he said, "Would you two gentlemen care to hear how our local natives once used these bloody insects to torture their captured enemies?"

"Certainly, Your Excellency," said Captain-Lieutenant Shekolov, a man about thirty years of age with a bushy black mustache, long sideburns, and a long aquiline nose.

"First the *Kolosh* stripped their captives, then they whipped them until their skin was flayed so raw all you could see were the muscles; then while they were in that bloody condition, they were tied to trees. It didn't take long until they were black with mosquitoes, and in a couple of days, they wasn't much left of them. The insects ate them all up."

Anna and Tatiana had overheard the story and they both gasped while Mikael burst into laughter. "Dmitri," he snorted, "that's what we should've done last night with--" he broke off as Dmitri gave him a hard nudge.

Shekolov frowned at Mikael then looked at Tatiana and Anna with apologetic eyes. "Pardon, ladies, I don't believe that was a story for your delicate ears."

"No, it was not," said Tatiana, giving both Dmitri and Mikael an angry stare. How could they make light of the horrid thing they had done to Captain O'Connell? Thank goodness poor Anna had no idea what they were talking about.

Some distance away, Anton, Vera, and Sophie were sitting on a blanket together. Sophie had been eating with her parents, but Anton graciously invited her to join him and Vera for cake and champagne. He always felt sorry for Sophie and the callous way her sister treated her. It was yet another character flaw in the woman he once wished to marry.

Pity he hadn't noticed sooner, he mused, but he had been blinded by her bold beauty, and hadn't seen the ugliness within until recently.

While finishing his dessert, Anton told Vera he wanted to speak with Baron Volodin about Fort Ross. She smiled agreeably, but privately noted how strange it was that he seemed to be so interested in the voyage to California, when he should be spending his time ingratiating himself with Governor Muraviev. Now that Baron Volodin was leaving New Archangel, the prestigious position of governor's assistant was open. Next to marrying her, nothing else was so important.

After Anton walked away, she tried to swallow some of the delicious tasting wedding cake, but found the crumbs sticking inside her throat. She managed to wash them down with a large gulp of champagne. Her sister, Sophie, had no such problem as she finished her piece of cake then greedily looked at Vera's plate.

"If you don't want your cake, I'll eat it," she said.

Vera handed her the plate. "You're welcome to it."

Sophie took a big bite then looked at her sister with a puzzled expression. "Why aren't you hungry?" She paused, thinking a moment then added, "In fact, you haven't been eating much at all lately. Is something the matter with you?"

Oh, not at all, Vera thought with a creeping sense of panic. *I just feel so ill each morning, I can't abide the sight and smell of food, and I have a terrible feeling that I'm going to have a child, a child that doesn't belong to my betrothed.*

"I'm fine, Sophie," she said irritably. "But I have many things on my mind these days. There is such a mountain of planning to do before my own wedding in three months. Of course, that's something you wouldn't understand."

Sophie flushed in sudden anger, as Vera's cruel meaning cut into her sensitive feelings. She knew she wasn't as attractive as her sister, but she considered herself a kinder, more intelligent person, and someday she vowed she would find a husband as handsome and wonderful as Anton Dohktorov. Vera didn't deserve such a fine man. Her sister was a shallow and self-centered young woman who didn't care about anything or anybody unless it directly concerned her.

Lately, Vera had grown extremely secretive, and Sophie suspected her sister was sneaking out to see Lieutenant Mikael Bolkonsky. She was keeping her suspicions to herself until the day she might need to use them. Now, looking at her sister, she noticed how puffy her face looked and the shadows under her eyes. It couldn't all be from planning the wedding, she wondered. There must be something else wrong. And she was certain it had to do with Mikael Bolkonsky.

At that moment she glanced up and saw the lieutenant himself standing in front of them. He was dressed in his gold-braided naval coat and wore his hat with the Imperial crest of the double eagle. He peered down his large nose at them and said, "*Mademoiselle*s, how delightful you both look."

Vera blushed with pleasure as Sophie glanced down at her plate, suddenly losing interest in her cake. Being near men like Lieutenant Bolkonsky and Baron Volodin made her feel gawky and uncomfortable. She felt his dark eyes settle on her only for an instant, then dismiss her as of no account. When his gaze centered on Vera, she sighed with relief and resumed eating.

"And how are you today, Lieutenant?" Vera asked with a bright smile on her face, showing every inch of her small sharp teeth.

"Marvelous," he said, also smiling broadly. "Would you two lovely *Mademoiselle*s like to take a short walk along the river with me? There are less of these pesky mosquitoes near the water."

Vera shot a quick glance at Sophie, who shook her head. "You go on, both of you."

Mikael stretched out his hand and helped Vera rose gracefully to her feet. "Be a dear, Sophie, and tell Anton I'll return shortly, will you?"

Sophie nodded, thinking that perhaps she might tell Anton more than that. "Certainly, Vera," she answered with a sweet smile, "I'll take care of Anton."

The two strolled away toward the river, walking as close to each other as they dared without touching. After some minutes, they disappeared down river around a bend. Many pairs of eyes watched them go, her mother Irina's with satisfaction, her father Alexis's with confusion, and one pair in deep anger, Lieutenant Dohktorov. But instead of rushing after them, he kept speaking to Dmitri for another twenty minutes.

Tatiana was one who had noticed the couple leaving together, and she felt a stab of pity toward Anton. For some reason when he had first stepped over to talk to Dmitri, flashing her a winsome smile of greeting, her heart had started to beat faster. As the two men stood side by side, deep in conversation, she could not help comparing them. She had always thought Dmitri was handsome with his perfect features, but his looks had such a cold haughty cast, whereas Anton's face held warmth and humor. No two men could be more different.

How can Vera Alexisovna humiliate him so blatantly in front of everyone? Tatiana thought. Yet, she dared not say anything to him with Dmitri there. Her husband became instantly jealous if she even glanced at another man, much less talked to him. And it wasn't only a man who inflamed his jealousy. A few nights ago when she sat in the sitting room reading a book he had become angry with her because the black cat, Raven, was sleeping on her lap.

"How can you let that filthy animal touch you?" he had yelled.

His angry voice immediately woke up Raven and he'd flown off her lap like any wild raven. As the cat shot by Dmitri, he kicked him with the sharp toe of his boot and Raven had let out a screech then disappeared into the kitchen.

"That was cruel thing to do, Dmitri," she'd protested.

He'd laughed at her. "I'm only showing it who is the master around here. A dog would know immediately and grovel at my feet, but a cat has no master, or so it thinks."

"Is that why you hate him, because you can't control him?"

His laughter ceased abruptly, and he frowned at her. "No, my dear wife, it's because you seem to shower these bloody cats with more affection than you do to me."

Tatiana opened her mouth to retort, then shut it with the realization he was right. She did love her cats more than her husband. Instead, she forced herself to say, "But you know that is not true, Dmitri. I love you more than anyone or anything in the world."

"Ah, Tatiana, my love, you have no idea how happy it makes me when you tell me such things." He crossed the room in one bound and pulled her upright, the book falling to the floor. Embracing her, he added huskily, "The sooner we start another child the better. Don't you agree, my lovely wife?"

She'd bowed her head in submission, hoping he wouldn't see the revulsion she felt at his closeness. "Yes, Dmitri."

Blocking out the remainder of that particular evening, Tatiana now sighed and knew she must not speak to Anton. She would play the dutiful wife and stay quiet. Underneath her thick eyelashes, she covertly watched as Anton left them and walked over to Sophie. She wished she could hear what they were talking about, for suddenly, Anton stiffened and marched off in the same direction Vera and Mikael had taken.

"Poor Sophie looks so lonesome," she said to Dmitri. "May Anna and I sit with her for awhile?"

He glanced over at the girl with little interest and said, "Certainly, my dear." then began to question Captain-Lieutenant Shekolov about his voyage from Saint Petersburg.

"Thank you, Dmitri." She motioned to Anna and the two made their escape before he changed his mind.

The plump brown-haired girl was so surprised to see them approach her that her mouth fell open. She had poor teeth, similar to Vera's, and Tatiana tried not to notice the food particles stuck between them.

They arranged themselves on the blanket next to her. Anna smiled and said, "How are you today, *Mademoiselle*?"

"Very well, Anna," she answered with a shy smile.

"Isn't it a lovely day for a wedding?" Tatiana asked politely.

"Oh, yes, Baroness, and your sister is such a beautiful bride," she added, looking towards the newlyweds sitting in their chairs, Marya picking at a plate of food while Boris smacked his full lips hungrily over every morsel.

Tatiana acknowledged that fact with a brief nod then said, "Your sister will be the next bride in New Archangel. I'm so sorry that my husband and I will not be here to attend the wedding." She paused then went on, "However, I could not help noticing that Lieutenant Dohktorov seemed a bit distressed just now. Did it have something to do with my cousin and your sister?"

Sophie's eyes slid away for a moment and her cheeks flushed pink. "He was not happy that they took a walk together."

"Ah," she said, nodding. "And so he has gone after them."

"Yes, and---and I'm afraid of what might happen when he finds them."

Tatiana studied the girl carefully, noticing the mixture of guilt and fear on her face. “And why is that, Sophie?”

“Be---because,” she stammered, “of what I told him.”

“And what was that?” Tatiana pressed.

Sophie’s brown eyes suddenly filled with unshed tears. “I told him that I thought Vera has been secretly meeting Lieutenant Bolkonsky behind his back, and now,” she said shakily, “I’m so afraid something terrible might happen between them.”

A shriek resounded over the roar of the river and all three young women jerked with surprise. They looked at each other in trepidation, until Tatiana realized the sound came from the opposite direction that Anton, Vera, and Mikael had taken.

Except for Boris, who continued to eat, everyone in the meadow scrambled to their feet, talking at once. Some of the soldiers grabbed their muskets in readiness and began to stride towards the river.

Several more shrieks were heard, this time much closer, as three figures came into view, Fedor, Nikolai, and a stocky man with black hair. As they came closer, Marya and Tatiana were surprised to recognize Andrei Leonov. The boys were sniveling and complaining as Andrei, a hand gripping each of their arms, pulled them roughly along. He was cursing as loudly as they were whining. All three were drenched to the skin, their hair plastered wetly on their heads, their nice clothes dripping with muddy water, looking like three drowned rats.

Choking back a cry, Elizabeth jumped up and lifted her skirts, moving quickly towards them. Anastasia followed, her eyes dancing with barely suppressed mirth.

“Fedor! Nikolai! What in heaven’s name happened to you boys?” She looked at Andrei and seeing the dreadful scars across his face, she paled. "What are you doing with this--this *Creole* man?"

Andrei scowled at her. “Andrei Leonov at your service, *Madame*,” he rasped through gritted teeth. “I just saved your two sons from drowning in the river.”

She was shocked into silence momentarily as Marya and Anna rushed over with blankets, and wrapped them around the white-faced, shivering boys, their teeth chattering behind their bloodless lips.

Marya handed another blanket to Andrei. Their eyes locked and his ugly face relaxed into a lopsided grin. "Good afternoon, *Madame* Ivanoffova."

"Andrei," she breathed, "what good fortune that you found them just in time!"

“Fedor and Nikolai Basilvich,” Elizabeth said sharply, “is it true this man came to your rescue?”

Both boys hung their heads guiltily and looked at the ground, then nodded. “Yes, Mama," said Fedor.

"It was his fault!" Nikolai shouted, pointing at Fedor. "He pushed me into the river!"

"No, I didn't!" Fedor yelled back. "You pushed me first!"

Nikolai's chubby face turned purple with rage. He kicked Fedor right on the shins. Fedor yelped in pain and jumped away, knocking over Anastasia, who was standing next to him. Fedor landed on top of her, the dirty blanket and his clothes smearing her lace pink dress and white stockings with streaks of wet black mud.

"Get off me, you oaf!" she shrieked in anger then gave a wail of dismay as she realized her dress was ruined. "Mama, Mama, look what he did..."

Elizabeth pursed her lips in disapproval and opened her mouth to scold both the boys when Fedor sprang to his feet and punched Nikolai squarely in the eye. The boy screamed in fresh outrage and pain then covered the eye with his hand, as tears spurted down his fat freckled cheeks.

"Enough of that lads!" Andrei snarled, stepping in between them. "Here you both could be food for the fish by now, and all you can think of is fighting again." He looked at them in disbelief.

"*Monsieur* Leonov is right," said Elizabeth. "You both should be ashamed of yourselves!" She gave him a polite smile, her eyes staring over his head rather than at his mutilated face. "Thank you so much for your help. I will make certain my husband rewards you well."

Andrei looked at Marya. "The only reward I need is *Madame* Ivanoffova's permission to join her wedding party for the remainder of the afternoon."

Elizabeth shrugged, then turned to her children and shooed them over to where the Aleut servants were standing, their faces full of curiosity. She quickly gave orders for two of them to help her escort her muddy bedraggled children back to town, along with one armed soldier.

"Of course you may stay, Andrei," said Marya generously. "And help yourself to any food and drink that you wish."

Andrei gave her a slight bow. "Thank you, *Madame*."

It was at that moment, Anton, Vera, and Mikael returned.

Vera was weeping, her arm held firmly by Anton as he propelled her into the meadow and towards her surprised looking parents. His face was grim and unsmiling and his eyes smoldered with suppressed anger. Mikael slowly followed them, nervously glancing around at the assembled guests, but not meeting anyone's eyes.

Standing next to Tatiana, Sophie gave a soft sigh of relief. But her relief was short-lived as Anton practically threw Vera down at her father's feet and said, "Tell them, Vera, or should I?"

She covered her face with her hands and knelt down on the blanket, weeping louder. Anton looked at her with disgust as Captain-Lieutenant

Trotsky glared at him. "What is the meaning of this, Lieutenant?" he demanded.

Irina bent over her daughter and patted her on the shoulder, murmuring consolably to her. Then she straightened up and said, "What have you done to our Vera?" Her long thin face was drawn into a look of unconcealed dislike, her large horse-like teeth bared in a grimace.

"It's not me who has done anything to her, *Madame*," Anton answered politely, "but it is your daughter who has done the unforgivable to me."

"Explain yourself, sir!" snapped Trotsky, his usually dignified face mottled with reddened spots of rage as his blood pressure mounted.

"Vera?" asked Anton once more then as her only answer was another choking sob, he squared his shoulders and looked both of her parents directly in the eyes. "I came upon your daughter and Lieutenant Bolkonsky arguing by the river. They did not see me as they were in the middle of a quarrel, but I was close enough to hear every word they said." He paused, lowering his voice, "Vera is going to have a child, and it will not be mine."

His words exploded like musket shot and all eyes were drawn to Vera, expecting her to protest them. But she only sobbed harder, keeping her face buried in her hands, as if she was afraid to look up at her parents.

Trotsky and his wife Irina both blanched as white as the icing on the wedding cake. He looked past Anton and his gaze fastened on Mikael, who stood a short distance away, appearing most uncomfortable.

"Bolkonsky!" Trotsky shouted. "I demand a word with you immediately!"

With reluctance Mikael sauntered over. "Come now, sir, isn't all this a bit premature? Vera might be mistaken about having a child---"

"Is it yours, Bolkonsky?" asked Trotsky bluntly.

He shrugged his shoulders with exaggerated nonchalance. "Perhaps." Then he looked at Anton and sneered, "or perhaps not."

Anton clenched his fists, but only said in a calm voice, "It is impossible for her child to be mine, as I have never touched her beyond a goodnight kiss on the cheek."

As if she had just sprouted two horns and a tail, Trotsky glanced down at his daughter with an expression of revulsion. "Is this true, Vera Alexisovna?" He reached out and shook her slightly on one shoulder. "Tell me at once!"

Vera choked back a sob and finally took her hands away from her face. Her blue eyes were swollen and reddened and her nose was dripping with snot. She rubbed it away in a most unladylike gesture and sniffed loudly.

"Yes, Papa, Anton speaks the truth. He has always been the perfect gentleman to me." She then glanced at him. "I--I'm so sorry, Anton."

He ignored Vera. Looking at both of her parents he said, "As of this moment, in front of all these witnesses, I am breaking our betrothal."

Then he glared at Mikael with an expression of pure hatred and strode away, heading back into the forest towards New Archangel.

Tatiana watched him go, wishing she could run after him and offer her sympathy. Perhaps she could find a way to express her condolences to him another time, when Dmitri wasn't standing two feet away.

Trotsky also looked at Mikael with hostility. "Bolkonsky, you have ruined my daughter's honor. As soon as I return to New Archangel, I intend to ask His Excellency's permission to challenge you in a duel."

At those words, Mikael's face turned ashen. The memory of his one and only duel with Dmitri's father came flooding back. And like the Baron Ivan Volodin, Alexis Trotsky was a crack shot and swordsman. "But they are illegal, sir!" he protested immediately.

"Not if His Excellency gives us permission," said Trotsky in a cold voise. "It is either that or you will marry my daughter as soon as possible."

In near panic, Dmitri looked at Boris, who had finally heaved his bulk off his chair and was glowering at everyone for interrupting his wedding feast. "Boris, what should I do? You know His Excellency better than I do. Do you think he will agree to a duel?"

Boris picked a piece of meat out of his teeth with a greasy fingernail as he pondered the situation. Muraviev was very old fashioned where women were concerned. He held a lady's reputation and honor above all else. He would be livid with Mikael for cuckolding Dohktorov.

"I'm afraid Captain-Lieutenant Trotsky is correct," said Boris. "His Excellency is likely to permit a duel."

Irina gasped and Mikael's face turned a peculiar shade of green as if he'd suddenly been punched in the stomach.

"No," he said quickly, "no duel." He glanced around at everyone, and saw not a speck of sympathy in anyone's eyes. He took a deep breath and said, "If Vera Alexisovna agrees, I promise to marry her."

Irina Trotsky's thin lips twitched in a triumphant smile. She glanced down at her daughter.

"Vera," she scolded, "get up at once and dry your tears. You have nothing to cry about. Your wedding will go on as planned, only sooner and with a different groom."

In an instant Vera ceased sobbing, and gave her hand to her father, who gently pulled her upright. Relief was written all over her watery blue eyes, and she cast a tentative smile at Mikael, who stood as still and stiff as a wooden statue.

Trotsky suddenly grinned at his future son-in-law, a smile that held no humor or affection, but rather the satisfied grin of a hunter who had just caught its prey.

"Welcome to the family, Mikael," he said.

Sophie hid a smile. Seeing her sister humiliated in front of the cream of New Archangel society was a rare treat never to be forgotten. And even better, now the way was clear for her to catch the interest of Lieutenant Dohktorov, who was suddenly an eligible bachelor.

Tatiana tried not to gloat. Two of her childhood enemies had caught themselves in a web of marital disaster of their own making. Vera and her mother obviously thought they had found the better man for her husband, but Tatiana knew that Vera was throwing away her life into a pit of unhappiness as deep as her own.

Anna could not believe the ridiculous melodrama she had just witnessed. She and Marya exchanged glances of disgust. With a wave of her hand, Anna motioned Marya away from the group and they walked to the river. The crisp mountain breeze felt refreshing as they stood and watched the green foaming water swirl around and over the rocks.

"*Monsieur* Leonov should be congratulated on saving Fedor and Nikolai," said Anna with a shudder. "That current looks swift enough to carry away the strongest swimmer, much less a child."

"I wonder what he was doing upriver when he saw the boys. Was he spying on our wedding party?"

"Why would he do that?" Anna asked, puzzled.

"He once told me he was going to save me from marrying Boris, but instead he saved Fedor and Nikolai."

Anna glanced behind them. "Here comes Boris now."

With difficulty, he lumbered around large boulders and across the many rocks protruding from the uneven ground. When he reached them, he mopped at his shiny forehead with a handkerchief. "Marya, my dearest wife," he grinned, "come, we must be going. It is time for us to finally be alone and get to know each other better."

Marya gave Anna one terrified look, reminding Anna of a deer cornered by a predator. "God go with you, Marya," she whispered, her words fading into the thunderous roar of the river.

Some distance away, Andrei Leonov watched the fat lieutenant as he placed a possessive paw on Marya's slender arm, guiding her firmly towards the forest trail. He ran a hand through his damp black hair and smiled to himself. *Chignik should be ready. Not much longer now.*

* * *

Supported by two thick pillows behind him, Muraviev was propped up in his huge bed. His valet Mikhail fussed around him, handing him a cup of tea. "Lieutenant Dohktorov is here to see you, Your Excellency."

The governor reached for the cup and grimaced as his hands trembled. He spilled a few drops down the front of his nightshirt, but the liquid tasted so refreshing and delicious on his parched tongue he didn't care. His fever had broken the previous night, leaving him as weak and thirsty as a babe.

"Tell him to come in, Mikhail," he said.

The valet frowned in disapproval but did as he requested. The tall lanky lieutenant entered the bedchamber and gave them a smile. "Thank you for seeing me, Your Excellency. I promise not to stay long."

This last statement was aimed more at Mikhail, the governor's watchdog. The valet nodded, looking pleased, and left the room to give them privacy.

"It feels wonderful to have visitors again," Muraviev said. "I need to be informed on what has been happening in New Archangel since I've been so ill."

Anton noticed how pale and shaky the governor appeared. Without his customary wig, he looked like a balding middle-aged man with large puffy bags under his eyes. "I've come to request a favor, Your Excellency. I would like to accompany Baron Volodin to Fort Ross."

Muraviev looked shocked. "But you are betrothed to Vera Alexisovna, and your wedding is scheduled in July."

"Not anymore, Your Excellency. This afternoon I discovered she was being unfaithful to me, and I have broken our betrothal."

This shocked Muraviev even further. "But with whom is she---?

"Lieutenant Bolkonsky. She is expecting his child."

Muraviev spit out a mouthful of tea. "He has admitted this?"

"Yes, and has agreed to marry Vera as soon as possible."

"Unbelievable! And you, lieutenant," Muraviev gave him a sharp look, "are you angered enough by this that you are tempted to challenge Bolkonsky to a duel? You must remember that duels are illegal here."

Anton shrugged carelessly. "Not to worry, Excellency. An unfaithful woman is not worth fighting over. All I wish is to leave New Archangel."

Muraviev sighed in relief. "Then I have your word on it, Dohktorov?"

"Yes, Your Excellency."

"Well, under the circumstances, your request is a reasonable one. I admit Volodin will be needing all the support he can get as Fort Ross's new manager. Although I had been considering you as his replacement as my assistant here in New Archangel, you may be of more value to me as Volodin's assistant in Fort Ross."

It was suddenly clear to Muraviev that no one would be better to help Volodin than the intelligent, dependable Lieutenant Dohktorov. But then who should he appoint as his assistant here, Lieutenant Bolkonsky? If he did, he knew he would be well rewarded by the Company Board of Directors, especially by Count Vasily Bolkonsky. Yet he felt uneasy giving the spoiled young aristocrat such power. He had hoped Bolkonsky would be as capable a commander as his uncle Nikolas had been. But now with this latest scandal, he doubted it very much.

Mikhail opened the bedchamber door and cleared his throat. "Your Excellency, I apologize for the interruption, but *Monsieur* Putin is here with two important messages."

As Muraviev nodded to his valet, he said, "Lieutenant Dohktorov, I grant your request. When the *Sea Rose* sails in two days, you will be on board as Volodin's assistant. I will inform him of your new position."

"Thank you, Your Excellency." He bowed briefly and turned to leave as Ivan Putin rushed inside the room.

The young aide glanced at him. "Wait, lieutenant, don't leave yet. You need to hear my news."

He clicked his heels and saluted the governor. "Your Excellency, I have just received two reports of tragic circumstances." He took a deep breath. "The first concerns the American captain. After the flogging with the *knout* on board the *Alexandria* last night, his officers report he is near death and they request the physician off the newly arrived *Czarina* to attend him."

"What bloody flogging?" Muraviev exploded, dropping his half empty teacup unheeded in his lap.

Putin gulped, his eyes bulging in fearful nervousness. "Why, the one you ordered a few weeks ago. I saw the permit myself, Your Excellency."

"I never signed such a thing!" Muraviev looked at Anton. "Do you know anything about this, Dohktorov?"

"I just heard of it last night when *Monsieur* Putin came to me and said the flogging permit was missing. He thought Baron Volodin might have taken it. So, I went to his house, but his wife said he was with Lieutenant Bolkonsky and Lieutenant Ivanoff on board the *Alexandria*. She thought they were having some sort of bachelor's party for Ivanoff."

"That must have been some party, all right!" Muraviev sputtered angrily. He looked at Putin. "By all means, send Doctor-Surgeon Prebelov to the *Sea Rose*. And then, tell Lieutenants Bolkonsky and Ivanoff and Baron Volodin that I wish to see them at once! I don't care if it is Ivanoff's wedding day! I intend to get to the bottom of this no matter how long it takes!"

Muraviev glared at Ivan. "Well, Putin, don't just stand there, go!"

But the young man didn't move, looking as if he was frozen in place. "I--I cannot tell Lieutenant Ivanoff, Your--Your Excellency," he stammered. "The--the second report I have for you, is that the lieutenant was shot--shot to death about an hour ago as he and his bride were walking back from the Indian River."

Both Anton and Muraviev gasped in unison as Putin went on, "They said Lieutenant Ivanoff was eager to return to town, so the couple went ahead of the rest of the guests. They were in a thick brushy part of the forest, and before anyone realized what was happening, a musket ball roared out of the bushes striking the lieutenant on the side of his head."

Putin lowered his voice. "Most of his head was blown off. His poor young wife was screaming, covered in his blood and brains, but she wasn't harmed."

"Did they catch the assassin?" Muraviev asked worriedly.

"Yes, Your Excellency. Several soldiers pursued him through the forest and shot and killed him before he could escape."

"Who was it?"

"An Aleut called Chignik. He's a cousin of *Madame* Ivanoffova."

Muraviev frowned in surprised dismay. "Her family must have greatly disapproved of her marriage to Lieutenant Ivanoff."

"It's unfortunate the Aleut was killed," said Anton in a troubled voice. "He might not have been acting alone. But now we'll never know for certain."

Muraviev coughed. "Mikhail, help me dress. It's time I take control of this town again. I've been lying in this accursed bed far too long!"

CHAPTER TWENTY NINE

As soon as they returned to the house Anna told Maria to heat up water for a bath for Marya in the tin tub inside the kitchen. The girl was filthy with dried blood on her face, hair, gloves, and wedding gown. She was also in a state of shock. She careened from moments when she became hysterical, then fell silent, looking numbed. She was acting like any young bride whose groom had been suddenly taken from her, but Anna knew it wasn't because Marya was full of sorrow. It was most likely the aftermath of the bloody violence.

"Andrei Leonov," she kept mumbling as Keeah helped her out of her clothing. "I know it was Andrei."

"But *Mademoiselle*," said Anna, holding a fussing Katya in her arms, "*Monsieur* Leonov was with us on the trail the entire time and they said the murderer was a young Aleut man."

Marya burst into tears again. "It was my cousin, Chignik," she sobbed. "He and Andrei must have planned it. Chignik never would've done this by himself. Now Uncle Sergei and Aunt Tugidaq will really hate me! They loved Chignik like a son! They'll blame me for his death!"

"Hush, Marya," said Anna, glancing fearfully back towards the door. "The baron is upstairs with *Madame*, and if he hears you, he will have Andrei arrested for questioning. And I think the poor man has suffered enough."

Her wails triggered Katya into a crying jag and Anna rocked her back and forth in an effort to calm her. Keeah shook her head, then took a bar of scented lavender soap and began to scrub Marya's hair. She closed her eyes tightly as the soap ran down her face, mingling with her tears.

Marya exhaled a mighty sigh and said quietly, "Yes, Anna, you're right. I must keep my thoughts about Andrei to myself. I don't wish to add to his troubles. Besides, now that Boris is--is dead, I must pretend to be a grieving widow, even though in my heart I am glad he's gone. May God forgive me!"

She made the sign of the cross as Keeah said, "I remember when the scar faced man said he would stop the wedding. And if he did, he will wish you for his wife."

Anna's mouth fell open. "What are you talking about, Keeah?"

"And if I remember correctly, Keeah, you led him to believe I was sorry about breaking off our betrothal and had a change of heart towards him!" Marya grimaced as the *Kolosh* maid rinsed the soap out of her long hair, the wet tendrils rippling down to her slender waist like glistening black snakes.

Keeah smiled slyly. "I had to pretend you would, *Mademoiselle*, so he would take action. And whether he did or did not, you are now safe from the man my people call the Evil Whale."

"But am I safe from Andrei Leonov?" Marya whispered, shuddering.

* * *

Upstairs in their sitting room, Dmitri handed Tatiana a glass of brandy. "I think we both could use this."

She accepted the crystal goblet half full of the golden liquid and immediately took a sip. The brandy burned all the way down to her stomach and she choked slightly. "My poor poor sister," she sighed, "to see such a terrible thing happen to her new husband."

Dmitri grunted. "All I care about is that the Aleut was caught and killed. We can't have these savages shooting Russians without facing the consequences!"

"But now what should we do with Marya? We can't just leave her here alone without family."

Dmitri gave her a hard look. "What do you mean without family? It was her own cousin who killed her husband! It seems to me she has plenty of family. As far as I'm concerned, she can go back to her village and marry some ugly savage and skin hides and raise brats the rest of her life!"

Tatiana set her glass down on the table and faced him. "No, Dmitri, she is my only sibling. I wish her to come with us to California. I promise she will be no trouble."

"She's been trouble enough already! It's because of her I've lost my best friend, Boris!" His voice broke slightly and he turned away before she could see the glimmer of tears in his eyes. Crying was for women and children, not a man such as he. Immediately he swallowed the painful lump in his throat, a strange ache that he felt whenever he thought of Boris. Twice before in his life he'd felt a similar emotion, once when his twin sister Ellie died and then when his mother died.

"Yes, I am sorry about Boris," said Tatiana quietly. "And you may not be the only one who blames Marya for his death. Now that her cousin is dead, her uncle and aunt might blame her as well. Please, Dmitri, I ask so little of you, but I will be heartbroken if Marya stays here."

He looked back at her and smirked. "If you spend the rest of the night comforting me for the loss of my friend as a good wife should, your sister may come with us."

Tatiana gave him a frigid smile. "Whatever you say, Dmitri."

A knock rapped on the door and little Maria called out, "Your Excellency Baron Volodin there's a soldier downstairs who says he has a message from His Excellency the governor."

"We will finish this later," said Dmitri. He gave her a quick kiss and quickly exited the sitting room, brushing past Maria as if she was invisible, and stomping down the stairs to the parlor. Curious, Tatiana followed after him part way, then decided to see how Marya fared. When she entered the kitchen, her sister was dressed in a clean gown and slippers and Keeah was drying her hair with a fluffy towel.

"How are you feeling now, Marya?" Tatiana asked with concern.

She smiled wearily. "Much better, but very tired. All I want to do is go to bed."

"Come back upstairs with me then. I'll sit by your bedside until you fall asleep."

After Tatiana and Marya left the kitchen, Keeah slid the large tin bathtub towards the back door to dump out the bath water. "Wait," said Anna, "I'd like to bathe Katya first. You go on ahead and help Marya settle for bed."

"Should I bring her food? Helena left a pot of *borscht* on the stove and biscuits in a pan in the oven warmer."

"I don't think Marya will be hungry, but the rest of us might be later."

Keeah nodded and walked out the door towards the stairs. Anna laid the wiggling child on the table and began to unwrap her from her blanket and tiny gown. As soon as Katya felt the freedom from the clothing she broke into a gummy grin and crowed with delight. Anna laughed and tickled her with a kiss on her soft little stomach.

"Anna," said Keeah suddenly from the doorway, "I hear something you need to know."

Anna gathered up her naked child and carried her over to the tub. "What is it?"

"Soldier said the baron must go see the governor. There is trouble about the Boston man, the captain. Last night he was hurt on Russian ship by *Madame*'s husband and cousin."

Startled, Anna stopped herself just in time from dropping Katya into the water. Instead she clutched the child to her chest and stared at Keeah. "What happened to the captain?"

Keeah gave her a pitying look. "Soldier say he was whipped and might die."

* * *

Governor Muraviev wiped a trembling hand across his eyes in disbelief as he read the permit on his desk, an order for Captain Sean O'Connell to be flogged fifty lashes with the *knout*, signed in his own hand, stamped with the Imperial seal and dated two months ago.

He looked up at Lieutenant Bolkonsky and Baron Volodin. "Gentleman, I have no memory of writing out this permit and then signing it. But I do recognize my own signature, so this must be legitimate."

Perspiration gathered under his armpits and behind his neck as he forced his still weakened body to sit upright in his chair with as much dignity and authority as he could muster. He glanced at Ivan Putin sitting next to Lieutenant Dohktorov.

"You say you saw me sign this very document?"

"Yes, Your Excellency. It was with a pile of construction permits." The young aide was also sweating, but from fear and not weakness. He was conscious of the baron and the way his left eye kept twitching as the lieutenant fastened his steely gaze upon him. Right before the meeting in the governor's office, Volodin had pulled him aside and said that if he valued his position and his own skin, he would not tell the governor that the permits had come from him.

I must be losing my mind, thought Muraviev as a wave of dizziness overwhelmed him. *I never would have knowingly authorized such a severe flogging for O'Connell when I had already promised him and his crew safe passage out of Russian America. But the signature doesn't look forged, so I must have signed it. Somehow I think Volodin and Bolkonsky are behind this, but I have no proof.*

"If I signed this permit two months ago, gentleman, then why did you wait so long to use it?"

Dmitri cleared his throat as he prepared his lie. "I didn't know of the permit's existence until a few days ago when I happened to see it sitting on my desk with other papers. I must confess I was surprised that Your Excellency wished to have the Yankee captain flogged, but it is not my place to question your decisions. I immediately brought the document to Lieutenant Bolkonsky and Lieutenant Ivanoff," he hesitated as he thought sadly of Boris, "and asked for their opinions."

Muraviev frowned. "Why did you not bring the document to me for my explanation, since I'm the person who supposedly authorized it?"

"You were too ill to see anyone, Your Excellency," said Mikael quickly. "Your valet had forbidden all visitors."

"That is true, Your Excellency," said Anton in a reluctant tone. "Last night I tried to see you concerning this very permit, but your valet said you were asleep and could not be disturbed."

But I was disturbed all night, Muraviev thought, remembering how every hour was a nightmare of strange dreams as he tossed and turned in his sweat-soaked sheets after the fever broke. Some time after dawn his valet Mikhail had brought him fresh linen and hot tea, but had not mentioned Lieutenant Dohktorov's request to see him. Obviously, his valet was overprotective, but Muraviev knew he owed his recovery to Mikhail's nursing and wasn't about to chastise him under the circumstances.

"There's one other thing," said Mikael Bolkonsky, shifting uneasily in his chair. "One of the Yankees, the armorer Gregory Jones, stabbed one of my men, Fedor Gorki, in the back and he may not survive. The American must be arrested at once, Your Excellency."

Muraviev knew why Jones had stabbed Gorki. He believed he was doing his duty to save his own captain from the man with the *knout*. But Gorki was also only following orders and if he died, then Bolkonsky was right, Jones had to be charged with his murder.

He nodded at Mikael. "I will have Jones taken into custody and if Gorki dies, he will be executed. If not, he's looking at a long prison sentence. Either way, he won't be sailing with his ship."

Muraviev paused as he surveyed the four men sitting in front of him and gave each one a hard stare. "Doctor-Surgeon Prebelov says Captain O'Connell may not survive. His back is flayed open almost to the spine and he's burning up with fever and infection. He gave instructions to the steward and the cook and left laudanum, ointments, willow bark, and fresh linen bandages, but said there was nothing else he could do." He paused, remembering the agony of his own fever the past week. "I will have to delay the sailing of the *Sea Rose* until the captain recovers enough for the voyage, or until he dies."

"But Your Excellency," Dmitri protested, "there have been enough delays already with my wife's illness. If Captain O'Connell is as critical as the doctor says, his men can take care of him at sea just as well as they can here. The ship is already loaded and ready to sail. I beg you to reconsider."

Another wave of weariness rushed through his body, making his arms and legs feel like dead weights. Doctor Prebelov had visited him just that morning and was pleased by the absence of his fever, but had cautioned him not to overdo or he'd have a relapse. He coughed, feeling the familiar soreness tighten across his chest. Suddenly, all he wanted was to return to his bedchamber and go to sleep. And as much as he hated to admit it, Volodin was probably right. O'Connell's life was now in God's hands, whether he was on land or at sea.

He yawned tiredly and his eyes watered as he tried to focus on Dohktorov and Bolkonsky. He noted how they were ignoring the existence of each other. Two men at odds over a slut of a woman. That reminded him. He had another announcement to make.

He looked at Volodin. "Father Sokolov is planning on conducting Lieutenant Ivanoff's funeral in two days. You may sail the following morning on Thursday. But you will be taking an extra passenger." He waved a shaky hand towards Anton. "I've appointed Lieutenant Dohktorov to be your administrative assistant at Fort Ross."

As Dmitri opened his mouth to complain, for he did not like Anton in the least, he spied the relieved expression on Mikael's face. Of course, he thought, because of the scandal with Vera, the governor has been wise to separate the two men.

He smiled at Anton. "I am pleased to welcome you aboard, Lieutenant."

Anton gave him a stiff nod. "Thank you. I look forward to serving under your command."

With an effort, Muraviev rose to his feet, hanging on to the edge of his desk for support. "Baron Volodin, before I adjourn this meeting, I must have your word that you will do everything possible to insure Captain O'Connell's recovery, because if he dies enroute on the *Sea Rose*, you might have a mutiny on your hands. And if that happens, may God help you all."

* * *

Somehow Anna managed to finish bathing, dressing, feeding, and singing Katya to sleep. Then she went upstairs to help Tatiana ready for bed. Her mistress was in her sitting room drinking brandy. Anna looked at the almost empty decanter with disapproval. But she knew better than to say anything about Tatiana's fondness for spirits. It would only provoke an argument and after this traumatic day, she had no wish for quarreling.

"Marya finally fell asleep," said Tatiana with a smile. "But before she did, she said what a relief it was to be spending the night alone in her own bed instead of with Boris on the *Kamchatka*." She made a face. "Between you and me, Anna, I think Marya is one very lucky girl."

Was it luck, or had God allowed an evil deed to save the girl from an evil husband, Anna wondered as she went about unfastening Tatiana's plait in order to brush her hair. She remembered all the prayers in hopes that God would stop the wedding. He hadn't stopped the wedding, but now the bridegroom was dead and Marya was free from Boris forever.

And was Sean the next person to die on this dreadful day? At the thought her hand jerked and the hairbrush caught in a snarl. Tatiana's head snapped backwards and the brush fell to the floor with a clatter.

"Ouch!" Tatiana complained. "What's got into you, Anna?"

She bent over swiftly to retrieve the brush as a tear crept from one eye. "I'm sorry. Did I hurt you?"

Tatiana rubbed her neck. "Yes, a little. There was a time when I'd have my maid whipped for such a thing."

When Anna made no comment, Tatiana whirled around and saw the moistness in her eyes. "Goodness, Anna, I was only joking." Her eyes narrowed. "Whatever is the matter?"

"A whipping is nothing to make light of. A short time ago Keeah heard the baron talking to the soldier about Sean--Captain O'Connell. Last night he was taken to one of the Russian ships, and--and whipped so badly, he might--"

"I know, Anna," she interrupted, taking the brush out of her limp hand and guiding her over to a chair. "Sit down for a minute. You look very pale."

"How did you know?"

"Late last night when Dmitri came home, I overheard him talking to Boris. They had taken the captain to the *Alexandria* and had him flogged with the *knout*. From what I could understand, they would have killed him, if it hadn't been for the American officers and some of their crew, who stormed the ship and rescued him."

"Why didn't you tell me first thing this morning?"

"With Marya and her wedding, it was impossible. I was planning on telling you later, but so much has happened since, it slipped my mind." Tatiana gave her a contrite look. "Please, forgive me, Anna."

"He might die, Tatiana, and I never told him I love him."

The words rushed out of her, startling both of them.

"You love him?" Tatiana finally squeaked.

Anna flushed. "I--I think I do, but this is the first time I've ever said it, or even admitted it to myself." Her eyes filled with tears of desperation. "Tatiana, can you help me get on the *Sea Rose* as soon as possible?"

She arched one eyebrow and pursed her lips in disapproval. Captain O'Connell was not the type of man Anna should be emotionally involved with. He was a blackguard and a rogue and would never make her happy. But he was dying, and it wouldn't do any harm to humor her.

"I'll tell Dmitri that I need you on board a day early to unpack my trunks and ready our cabin."

Anna gave her a grateful smile then she thought of Marya. "Will your sister be coming with us?"

"Yes, and I intend to bring Keeah along as her maid. Tomorrow I will have her trunk transferred from the *Kamchatka* to the *Sea Rose*."

"She will be very happy to hear the news," Anna said, remembering Andrei Leonov and his threat to wed Marya.

* * *

The funeral service for Lieutenant Boris Ivanoff seemed to last forever, Marya thought, as she listened to Father Sokolov's deep voice resounding throughout the Church of Saint Michael. Her husband's coffin sat on a platform, shrouded in black, with four uniformed sailors from the *Kamchatka* standing at each corner with drawn swords. Traditional in the Orthodox Church, the lid was open and Marya could see the top of Boris's rounded belly above the coffin's edge. It looked like a balloon ready to burst.

Nausea choked her as she tried to sing the hymns. Since it was right after Easter, Father Sokolov spoke of the resurrection of the dead and eternal life in heaven. Somehow, she could not imagine Boris in heaven with her Mama and Papa. However, she could easily imagine him in hell.

Feeling guilty, she crossed herself and then forgot Boris as she remembered yesterday's events. In the afternoon she and Keeah had gone to the Aleut village where she attempted to visit her family. Uncle Sergei refused to allow them inside the *ulaq*, barring the small entrance with his arms folded stiffly across his chest.

"Go away!" he'd shouted, his brown leathered face a dark mask of rage. "It is all your fault my son is dead! Never come back! You are nothing but bad luck!"

Tearfully, she took the basket of food they'd brought as a gift of sympathy and placed it on the ground at his feet. Then she stumbled away, her heart as heavy as lead. Behind her she could hear her young cousins crying her name as her aunt wailed in sorrow, "Our beloved Tooch is as dead as our beloved Chignik!"

Tears now sprang into her eyes at the memory. Except for Tatiana, those around her believed she was mourning the loss of her new husband and gave her smiles of sympathy.

She turned her face away from all the inquisitive eyes, remembering the first time her uncle told everyone she was bad luck. Still a child of nine, one day Uncle Sergei announced he was going to teach her how to paddle his *baidarka*. When they were only a short distance out from the beach, she became frightened to death of the cold gray water and the alarming manner in which the light craft bobbed up and down. She refused to take the paddle and began to cry. In disgust he took her back to shore and sent her home where she dreaded both her aunt's and her mother's reaction. But the two women merely clucked over her, telling her not to worry, that paddling a *baidarka* was a man's work, not a girl child's. Later when her uncle returned, Tugidaq had scolded Sergei. Angry and humiliated, he never allowed her near his *baidarka* again and told everyone in the village that she was bad luck on a sea hunt.

His anger towards her the day before had not been a surprise. Yet it still hurt deeply, and as she and Keeah walked out of the village, she had wept.

"Marya Nikolayevna, do you mourn your dead husband?"

The two girls were startled to find Andrei Leonov blocking their path. His mouth gaped open in a hideous smile as he breathed noisily.

Marya sniffled once, but recovered quickly, then drew herself up and faced him squarely. "No, Andrei, you know I do not."

"My condolences anyway," he said, "at least on the death of your cousin." His smile vanished. "Chignik was a fool! He should have run faster and he would've escaped the soldiers! We had it--" he stopped.

"We?" Marya echoed, her heart pounding so loud she was afraid he could hear it. But she had to ask him. "Was it your idea to ambush Boris in the forest? I find it hard to believe Chignik cared enough to rescue me from an unhappy marriage."

He shook his head in denial. "*Nyet*, I would never do such a thing! Chignik has always hated the Russians and blamed them for the death of his father years ago. And he couldn't stand the thought of his beautiful cousin being forced to marry the detestable Ivanoff against her will."

Leonov spread his arms outward from his sides in a gesture of innocence. "I had nothing to do with it."

"I don't believe you," she said, then turned to Keeah. "Come, we must go. We have more packing to do if we're to sail the day after tomorrow."

His face darkened. "You are going away?"

Marya gave him a sweet smile. "Yes, my maid and I are departing for California on the *Sea Rose* with my sister and her husband. So, I shall say goodbye, Andrei, and wish you a long and prosperous life."

Leonov stared at her in shock and then as they began to walk away from him, he shouted,

"This is not farewell, Marya! Just wait and see!"

"Scar Face does not give up," Keeah had said later back at the house.

Now the church bells pealed the end of the service, and Andrei's threats faded from Marya's memory. She watched as the coffin was sealed and the burly sailors struggled to lift it to their shoulders. They carried it out to a wagon where Boris would be taken to the cemetery. With a cross in his hand Father Sokolov led the procession. Marya, Tatiana, Dmitri, and Mikael followed the wagon, along with numerous naval officers, their wives, and the rest of the crew of Ivanoff's *Kamchatka*.

The weather was fine that afternoon. The sun was growing warmer and the ground was spongy with mud and new green grass. Crows cawed in a rowdy fashion from the building rooftops while sparrows chirped along the fences and white and gray seagulls swooped overhead. A few mangy dogs slunk away from the crowd of people.

At the burial site, the sailors began to carefully lower the unpainted wooden coffin into the gaping hole, which held two feet of water, a normal occurrence in spring from the high water table. The ropes wrapping around the coffin groaned as they strained to hold the immense weight. Suddenly one of them snapped and the coffin tilted at a steep angle. Everyone held their breath then several women cried out as the lid popped open slightly and one limp white hand and one bare foot dangled out.

The sweating sailors huffed as they tried in vain to keep control of the coffin. Then another rope broke and the coffin tumbled the rest of the way into the grave, making a splash when it hit the bottom, lying on its side. Father Sokolov peered down into the muddy, watery grave and shook his head. There was no room for anyone to jump down and try to straighten the coffin and push Boris's hand and foot back inside. He would have to be buried as is.

Marya caught Tatiana's gaze. Her sister's eyes were dancing in suppressed mirth. Marya held her hand over her mouth to stop the urge to giggle. Boris was as undignified in death as he was in life.

She thought of tomorrow and her spirits lifted. They were sailing at dawn and she would see John Hill again. As Father Sokolov murmured the final prayers over Boris, she gave her own private prayers of thanksgiving.

* * *

At the same time Anna, carrying Katya in her arms, was being helped aboard the *Sea Rose* by John and Jake. Both men were wreathed in welcoming smiles, but Anna could see the hollows of worry in their eyes.

The first words out of her mouth were, "How is the captain?"

"Not good," said John, shaking his head sadly. "But he still lives. Samuel and Wang Li are tending him while the rest of us pray the Almighty will spare his life."

Anna smiled at him. She had not heard John speak of God before, even though Ethan once said he'd been raised in a God-fearing home by his uncle and aunt. But isn't that human nature, she thought. God is always there watching over mankind, but sometimes it takes a crisis to make a man acknowledge Him.

"So, this is your wee bairn, is it?" Jake commented, his bright blue eyes fastened on Katya's sleeping face where one red-gold curl peeked out from underneath her lacy white cap. "Does the lassie have red hair like Ethan then?"

"Yes, she does," smiled Anna. "And she's as sweet and good-natured as her papa, too. I promise she won't be a speck of trouble on the voyage."

They both chuckled and John said, "Having a child on board will be good for all the crew, especially when they have to put up with the likes of Volodin and his men."

"It will only be for a short time," she said, "and then we'll be off your ship, and you can sail her across the Pacific to Canton."

"That's not what we were told yesterday," said John. "Volodin is planning on taking the whole summer and stopping at every Indian village between here and the Columbia River to trade for as many furs as he can get. And they won't be furs for us, but for him. He'll be offloading them at Fort Ross. Volodin is a greedy man."

"After living in his house for several months, I can also say he is a cruel and heartless man," said Anna.

"All the Russkies are a bunch of liars, even the Gov'nor," said Jake angrily. "He said we were free to go, then went an' had the Cap'n flogged by that cursed Volodin. Some of the men are fer hangin' him as soon as we're gone from these shores."

John frowned, his blond mustache curving down over his mouth. "But as I understand it, O'Riley, Volodin will be well guarded by armed men at all times. If any of our crew lay a hand on him, this ship will erupt in violence."

Nervously, Anna glanced down at her daughter. "I feel like I've just stepped into a nest of vipers."

"Don't ye worry none, Missus Campbell," Jake said quickly, "nay harm will come to ye or your bairn. But I can't vouch for the rest o' them. An' now that they took Jones---"

"The Russians arrested Gregory Jones?"

"Aye, missus" Jake scowled, "they came for him yesterday. 'Twas naught we could do."

"I'm sorry to hear that," Anna said quietly, thinking it was probably the last anyone would see of the gentle giant of an armorer.

John looked at her with a grim expression. "If the Russian dies, my good friend may be executed, even though he was only trying to stop the flogging to save Sean."

Jake's freckled face twisted in hate. "If Jones or the Cap'n dies, Volodin will pay."

At that moment a yellow haired dog dashed up to Anna. Robby ran after him, holding a rope in his hands. The floppy eared dog greeted her with a whine and began to sniff her cloak and boots with his wet black nose.

"Beg yer pardon, Missus Campbell," Robby puffed as he grabbed the dog and pulled him away from her. "Jimmy, come on now, you bad mutt, leave the lady alone!"

Anna laughed. "I don't mind, Robby. I once had two dogs of my own."

As he fastened the rope around Jimmy, he glanced up at her in surprise. "You did?"

"They were called Gerda and Alexi, and Gerda looked a lot like Jimmy. I hope he doesn't like to chase cats, though, because *Madame* Bolkonsky will be bringing one of hers along."

Robby rolled his eyes and groaned. "I dinna think this ship is gonna be big enough for the two o' them."

"You'll keep the dog below," said John, "and the Baroness can keep her cat in her cabin." He turned to Anna. "I'll take you to the cabin you're to share with Miss Bolkonsky and her Tlingit maid. Her trunk has already arrived from the *Kamchatka*." His handsome face brightened when he mentioned Marya, a fact not unnoticed by both Jake and Anna. "It must've been quite a shock to have her--her husband killed on her wedding day."

"Yes, it was, but she's doing quite well." Anna gave him a pointed stare. "You know she didn't want to marry Lieutenant Ivanoff."

"Aye, she told me that," he said as he took Katya from her, while she arranged her skirts to climb down the hatch ladder. The familiar ship odors assailed her nose, the stuffy air smelling of tar, pitch and damp sea water, the aroma of tea and cooking beans from the galley, and something else she could not quite place, a coppery smell, almost of blood. Immediately she thought of Sean.

"And where is the captain, in his cabin?" she asked as they entered the salon.

"I wish he were." John shook his head. "Volodin and his wife will be staying in the captain's cabin. We put Sean in the cook's cabin next to the galley. Wang Li and Samuel can tend him much better there."

Anna took Katya back in her arms, the child stirring restlessly, but still asleep. "I'd like to see him."

* * *

He was the dreaming the old nightmare again. The one in which his da was speaking to him from the depths of hell, begging him to forgive him. This time when he refused, his da laughed at him and said, "See ye soon, laddie."

Hot orange and yellow flames flared up between him and his da, searing his entire body with unbearable heat. He felt like he was burning up. He opened his mouth to scream out his torment, but nothing came out.

God save me. Jesus save me. Somebody save me. I don't want to die and go to hell.

Suddenly Ethan was standing by his bunk. "Sean," he said in a kind voice, "forgive your da for everything. Confess your hate and let it go. Then ye'll be forgiven."

Forgive Da for all the pain and suffering he'd inflicted on my family? Forgive Da for letting Ma die and for beating Rose over and over again?

"Aye, Sean," said Ethan. "Your ma and Rose have forgiven him."

And if I do forgive my da, who will forgive me for killing him?

"Jesus died to save you from all your sins."

Even the sin of murder?

"Aye, Sean, even the sin of murder."

But I don't deserve to be forgiven.

"No one does, Sean. We are all sinners. All ye have to do to receive eternal life is accept God's gift of grace through faith."

It sounds too simple.

"Aye, so simple that even a child can understand."

You have a daughter, Ethan.

"Aye, I know. A bonny lass. Take care of her and Anna. Hard times lie ahead for all of ye, but if ye trust God, He will see ye through it."

How can I take care of them when I'm dying?

But Ethan didn't answer, and when Sean looked again, his friend was gone. "Ethan?" he muttered, his face pressed against the pillow as he lay upon his stomach wrapped in bandages. He moved slightly and his back turned into a fiery mass of pain. He groaned.

"Sean, Sean," came a quiet feminine voice, breaking into his agony. "It's Anna. I'm here to help you."

He tried to speak, but couldn't. He tried to see her, but his eyes refused to focus. All he could to do was keep breathing as he fought the torturous never-ending pain. Then he felt her hand, cool and soft, brush his fevered forehead. It felt like the touch of an angel.

"Sean, stay strong. Don't give in," he heard her say. "I need you. Katya needs you. You must live for us. Please."

I'll try, Anna. I'll do my best. Ethan told me to take care of you both, because something bad might happen in the future. But what can be worse than what is happening to me right now?

The black pit of unconsciousness yawned before him again, and as he felt himself slipping down into it, he cried out silently, *Jesus, please forgive all my sins and accept me into your kingdom in case I never wake up again.*

PART THREE

1822-1823

To the Pacific Northwest Territories

CHAPTER THIRTY

The snow frosted cone of Mount Edgecumbe and the lush green forests of Baranov Island receded into the morning mists as the *Sea Rose* began her voyage south. Holding Katya in her arms, Anna stood at the stern rail between Marya and Keeah. The little round harbor islands covered with spruce trees faded in the distance along with the outlines of New Archangel and the Tlingit Indian village of the Raven.

All three women were staring back with solemn expressions on their faces, but Keeah looked the saddest. Anna gave her a smile of sympathy as she remembered how the Tlingit maid once said her people called the harbor Sitka Bay, which meant "In This Place." Her people also believed the rocky ground where New Archangel was built was sacred, and that the Russians would never be forgiven for claiming the land there as their own.

Marya was also feeling glum and a little queasy. She thought she would be relieved to see the last of New Archangel, but it was the only home she'd ever known. She had no idea what the future had in store for her. All she hoped was that it would somehow include John Hill.

Her melancholy lifted as she watched him relay Baron Volodin's commands to the crew to hoist more sail. She thought he cut a fine figure of a man. Under his officer's cap his long wavy hair was tied back in a queue, but the wind had loosened a few fair locks and they whipped around his face, giving him a youthful look. He turned in her direction and she saw his eyes gleam like two dark blue sapphires as his gaze fastened upon her. He gave her a boyish grin and she felt her cheeks burn with embarrassment as her stomach suddenly heaved.

"I think I'm going to be sick," said Marya in a panic.

The *Sea Rose* was heading into open ocean and the ship's bow rose up to meet each swell than nosed down into the trough of a wave before starting to climb again. The familiar movement was a welcome feeling to Anna, but she took one glance at the unnatural pallor of Marya's and Keeah's faces and felt guilty.

"The two of you need to go below and lie down on your bunks," she said. "After we round Cape Decision, the seas will be calmer, and you both will feel better."

The girls nodded and made their way gingerly toward the main hatch. In Anna's arms, Katya began to fuss and stir, her tiny white hands emerging from her blanket and waving around, signaling her displeasure with her new surroundings. Anna doubted she was feeling ill, too, but she knew it was near Katya's feeding time. She turned to follow Marya and Keeah then stopped.

Lieutenant Dohktorov and Baron Volodin were standing near the hatch with Tatiana between them. Two big coarse looking Russian sailors, each holding a pistol, flanked all three. As she approached the trio, Anton smiled down at Tatiana and murmured something so softly only Tatiana heard it. She laughed and for one second, Anna imagined she saw a flash of intimacy pass between them. Luckily, Dmitri was too absorbed in watching the workings of the ship's crew and officers to notice.

"Lieutenant Dohktorov," she said, diverting his dangerous attention away from Tatiana, "Could you please help me take Katya down below?"

It was a legitimate request. Climbing down a steep wooden ladder on a moving ship in full skirts while holding a wiggling infant was a feat Anna had not yet dared to try.

The lieutenant broke into a friendly grin. "It would be my honor, *Madame* O'Connell. I can see the difficulty in trying to balance your child in one arm and navigate the ladder with the other. Shall I carry you or the child first?"

Both she and Tatiana burst into laughter as Dmitri swung his gaze around to them, irritation showing in his cold gray eyes. Anna felt the chill of his disapproval on her, which was exactly what she was trying to accomplish.

She gave him her sweetest smile and said, "Good morning, sir, would you like to carry my daughter down the ladder, or should I allow Lieutenant Dohktorov the privilege?"

Dmitri appeared startled then he cleared his throat. "Err, I think it's best if the lieutenant took your daughter, *Madame* Campbell. As the commander of this ship, I need to stay topside to make certain my orders are obeyed by these lazy Yanks." He paused, smirking, "And how is O'Connell faring this morning?"

"Still the same, sir, mostly unconscious with a high fever. Whenever he comes to, he's in so much pain, we have to give him laudanum and willow bark tea if he can swallow it."

"Tell the steward to use the laudanum sparingly. No use wasting precious medicine on someone who will probably die."

His harsh words angered her. Anna raised her chin and said calmly, "That would not be wise, sir. If the captain is denied laudanum, he will be yelling with pain. The crew will hear his cries and much turmoil will result."

Volodin scowled, but he knew she was right. The crew was already surly and sullen and he sensed they followed his instructions only because they came from Hill and O'Riley. He'd been on board just a short time, and already he was thankful for the constant escort of the armed

sailors from his crew of the *Buldakov*. He'd brought eight of them to work twelve hour shifts, two to guard his cabin and Tatiana and two with him at all times.
He nodded at Anna and said stiffly. "We will do as you wish for now, *Madame* Campbell."
I do not trust that man, Anna decided as she followed Lieutenant Dohktorov down the ladder. The lieutenant held Katya tucked under one arm as if she was a precious loaf of bread. When they were all safely at the bottom, Katya let out a squawk of protest. Anna was surprised when instead of giving Katya back, the lieutenant bent his head over the baby and made a soft cooing sound.
Katya looked up at him with her round blue eyes and suddenly ceased her whining. He smiled and she responded with a small gurgle then grinned her gummy smile.
"She's beautiful," said Dohktorov, as he carefully handed her to Anna. "You are fortunate to have such a daughter. There's nothing more important in life than family."
Anna saw the hint of sadness in his eyes, and she felt a rush of pity for him as she remembered the callous manner in which Vera Alexisovna had treated him. The girl was a fool, she thought, and deserved to be married to such a despicable man as Lieutenant Bolkonsky. As for Anton Dohktorov, he could do much better someday. However, she hoped he wasn't falling in love with Tatiana. Only more misery would lie ahead for him if that was the case.
"Thank you, Lieutenant," she said. "I appreciate your help."
"Anytime, *Madame* Campbell. Although I am second in command on this ship, after watching how competent Mr. Hill and Mr. O'Riley are with the crew, there may not be much for me to do until we reach Fort Ross."
"But once the trading with the Indians begins, since Mr. Hill will be spending his time as supercargo, I expect you'll be handling more of the crew then."
"Mr. Hill is no longer the supercargo. Last night a *Creole* employed by the Russian American Fur Company approached Baron Volodin and asked to sign on. The baron wouldn't have considered him at all, except that he is very well traveled up and down the coast and is experienced in taking charge of the trading goods with the natives. He is skilled in communication and has an ear for Indian dialects, having mastered Tlingit and a smattering of Haida and Nootka. Andrei Leonov will make an excellent supercargo for us on the voyage."
Anna couldn't believe her ears. "Andrei Leonov?"
"Yes, you may have heard of him. He once sailed with Captain O'Connell on the *Eastern Wind*. Unfortunately, he has a rather badly scarred face. I hope he doesn't frighten you ladies when you see him. The man is quite harmless."

No, he is not, thought Anna worriedly. *I must warn Marya at once.*

* * *

The ship was near to bursting with humans and cargo, plus one dog and one cat. Dmitri had reluctantly given Tatiana permission to bring one of her cats from home as long as it wasn't Raven. The superstitious sailors did not need a black cat continually crossing their paths, so the gray and white Otter now made her home in the after cabin. With the dog confined below in the sailors' quarters, it was hoped Jimmy would never know the cat was on board.

Inside the main salon Samuel dusted off the blue damask sofas and mahogany tables, mumbling in his deep voice to Otter, who was crouched on the floor staring at him suspiciously as if he was a strange monster. He smiled when he saw Anna and Katya enter.

"Missus," he bowed respectfully, "is dere anything I can get you?"

"No, thank you, Samuel," she said, "but I may need you to bring me some of Wang Li's remedy for Miss Bolkonsky and her maid. They aren't feeling well."

"Ah," he exhaled with a look of understanding, "*mal de mir*."

He was delighted to see Anna and her child, but was deeply disturbed to have the Russian woman back on board with her husband acting as captain. He could not imagine a haughtier pair, nor did he appreciate how they both ordered him about as if he was their personal slave. He had already spent the entire morning making certain they and everyone else had their trunks placed in the correct cabins, and if he had made one mistake, he was sure he would hear about it.

Because of the shortage of space, the three women and child were squeezed in one cabin, the Russian lieutenant and new supercargo Leonov in another, and the officers Hill and O'Riley were sleeping in hammocks in the chart room.

It was all temporary until they reached Fort Ross, thought Samuel, and sooner the better.

He did not trust the Russians and both the Baron Volodin and the supercargo Leonov made his skin crawl. There was something evil about both of them and they bore watching.

The women's cabin was cramped and in such close quarters reeked of sour baby smells, stale perfume, and the chamber pot under the lower bunk. But it was quiet and private and Anna sighed with relief as she sat on the edge of her bunk, and fed Katya while Marya lay groaning above her. Keeah was curled up on a thin mattress on the wooden floor. Otter had raced in with her and had settled on the soft wool blanket next to the maid, purring loudly, her front paws flexing in happiness.

Drops of milk dribbled down from the corner of the baby's pink bow-shaped mouth, and Anna patted her gently on the back until she gave a resounding burp, then she placed her in the cradle. The wooden cradle was tied next to the bunk, but in a storm Katya would be nestled between her and the bulkhead for safety. The child put her tiny thumb in her mouth and fell asleep, soothed by the rocking motion of the ship.

Anna untied her head scarf, and ran a hand through her soft honey colored hair. "*Mademoiselle*, are you awake? I need to tell you something important."

"What is it, Anna?"

"Andrei Leonov is aboard ship as the Russian's supercargo. He's staying in the cabin with Lieutenant Dohktorov."

Marya sat up so quickly she bumped her head on the ceiling, her nausea forgotten. "He followed me? Oh, no, what if he asks Dmitri for permission to marry me when we reach Fort Ross?"

Keeah opened her eyes and petted the cat. "Scar Face Man will not marry you, mam'selle."

"How do you know that?" Marya demanded.

"I've seen the way the yellow-haired Boston man looks at you. I think he's the man who will be your next husband." Then Keeah looked at Anna. "And I think the captain will be your next husband, if he lives."

Anna blushed. "Keeah, you talk too much."

* * *

By nightfall the *Sea Rose* rounded Cape Decision, approximately fifty versts south of New Archangel, and the sea became as smooth and glassy as a lake. The ship glided through the grand scenery, the dark green forested mountains rising out of the water, sheer and mysterious, some topped by foaming waterfalls, others by icy blue glaciers.

Dinner was served by Samuel in the forward cabin at the big table to the Russian and American officers and the ship's passengers. It was traditional to celebrate the first night out and Wang Li cooked a splendid meal from food procured from the governor's kitchen. Platters of steaming roasted venison, salmon, halibut, and buttered potatoes, carrots, peas, and tender biscuits filled the room with delicious aromas. Mugs of hot tea, some laced with rum or vodka, were handed out to everyone.

At first the atmosphere was tense and awkward. There were four Americans at the table and all felt ill at ease with the two armed Russians, silent as statues, standing behind Volodin and his wife. The carpenter and cooper Ebenezer Cartwright, the new armorer Edmund Wilde, and officers John Hill and Jake O'Riley ate quickly, keeping their eyes on their plates. They were soon finished and except for John Hill, excused themselves to go topside.

Tatiana felt uncomfortable being the only woman at the table and also in the presence of Samuel the steward. This morning when they boarded he had greeted her civilly, yet, she knew underneath his polite veneer he despised her.

If every meal together was going to be like this, Tatiana thought wryly, it was going to be a long and miserable voyage. She missed Anna and Marya. Keeah had recovered quickly once the ship entered the inland waters, but Marya still complained of a delicate stomach. And Anna was spending the evening at Captain O'Connell's bedside.

"Is your sister still unwell, Baroness?" John asked Tatiana. He had looked forward to seeing Marya at dinner and was dismayed that she stayed in her cabin.

"Yes, Mr. Hill. Perhaps after a good night's sleep, she will feel better tomorrow."

Andrei Leonov cast a sharp glance at the American officer. Why was he so disappointed by Marya's absence? Did the man have feelings for his betrothed? A swift anger flared through him, but he quickly suppressed it. He would bide his time and observe and then take action, if need be.

"*Monsieur* Leonov," said Baron Volodin, sitting in the captain's chair at the head of the table, "before we begin trading with the natives, I wish to go over the cargo lists with you. I need you to meet me in my cabin tomorrow at noon."

"Certainly, Your Excellency. What is the first village you wish to see?"

"I will leave that decision to you. For all my experience as a naval commander, none of it has been with the natives."

Leonov appeared pleased at the honor and twisted his face into a semblance of a smile. "Then I suggest Henega on Prince of Wales Island in Sea Otter Sound. The *Kolosh* or the Tlingit there always have a goodly number of skins to trade. After that we might stop at Cocklane's Harbor (Petersburg) and Stikine (Wrangell), and then on to the Queen Charlottes."

John glanced at Leonov with irritation. Not only was it hard to sit at the same table with him, watching him noisily chew his food while breathing with his mouth open, but the man was too full of himself. "I've heard that Chief Shakes of Stikine is a very sneaky fellow and one to avoid. He is still out to revenge the death of one of his wives' elderly father who was killed years ago during a confrontation between the captain and crew of the Boston brig *Otter*. Two of the Americans and several natives were also killed. "

"Those bloodthirsty *Kolosh* have a long memory," said Dmitri, his proud features set in an expression of disapproval. "But then, who can blame them when the Yankee traders have deceived, cheated, and murdered so many of the natives along the coast. It is amazing that any of them still trust a white man at all."

"For once I agree with you, Baron," said John. "There have been atrocities committed by my countrymen and the British on the northwest coast, but yet, nothing we've done here can compare to the extermination and enslavement of the Aleuts by you Russians."

Volodin glared at him and a muscle twitched at the corner of one of his eyes. Tatiana knew his nervous tic was a sign he was about to explode. She frantically tried to think of something to distract him. Under the table she brushed her shoe against his boot and he tore his hostile gaze away from John and looked at her.

She was dressed simply for her, in a pearl gray muslin dress with a white cotton shawl draped around her shoulders. Her hair was modestly tucked away under a white silk cap, but a few pale gold tendrils had escaped and framed her delicate face. Her violet eyes were alluring with hidden meanings and his mouth suddenly went dry with anticipation of their first night together aboard the ship.

My beautiful Baroness, he thought, stroking her shoe with the tip of his polished black boot. *One day you will be the Queen of Russian America after we get rid of Governor Muraviev.*

Dmitri remembered that Mikael Bolkonsky suspected Muraviev of belonging to one of those secret groups who wished to depose Czar Alexander. Muraviev's leniency toward Captain O'Connell and his officers, plus his complaints about the lack of foreign trade in New Archangel, made Dmitri think it would be prudent for him to write a letter about Muraviev to certain people in Saint Petersburg. He would send it off after he reached Fort Ross.

When Muraviev was gone, he planned to be the next governor. Eventually he and Tatiana and their children would return to Russia with the prestige and power of a new Volodin dynasty.

He smiled at the thought, and then at his wife. Tatiana returned his smile with a bright one of her own, as she shuddered inwardly, dreading the evening ahead.

She looked at Anton Dohktorov then glanced away. It was going to be difficult to disguise her growing interest in the lieutenant without Dmitri suspecting. She was going to have to be very careful indeed.

* * *

A few yards away through the bulkhead walls in the cook's cabin, Anna heard the low mumble of men's voices at dinner. Wang Li had prepared some meat broth for Sean, and she now held the lukewarm bowl in her lap trying to wake him up to coax him to drink something. His fever still raged, his skin as dry as parchment, his lips cracked and bleeding.

Earlier Samuel and Wang Li had cleansed his wounds and placed fresh strips of linen bandages across his back. She had wished to help, but Samuel kindly and firmly refused, saying it was an unpleasant two man job. It caused the captain so much excruciating pain, that Samuel used all his brute strength to keep him still while Wang Li doused the raw gaping wounds with rum then gently applied a special ointment of his own making with herbs he bought from Tugidaq.

The cook had tossed aside the greasy ointments from the Russian doctor. "Healing woman knows more," he'd told Anna.

And Anna had to agree. After all, the Aleut woman had successfully helped Katya into the world. Even so, infection had set into Sean's injuries and she could smell the sweet sickly odor of pus mixed with the metallic tang of blood.

"Sean, please wake up and have some of this tasty broth."

He lay on his stomach, covered by a warm quilt with half his face pressed into a pillow, the other half turned towards her. His long black hair fell in dark waves around his muscular neck and coarse stubble surrounded his mouth and covered his chin. Normally a clean shaven man, he now looked scraggily and rough. His eyelids fluttered as if he was struggling to open them.

"Ethan," he mumbled.

She frowned sadly. "No, Sean, not Ethan. It's me, Anna. Can you hear me?"

He let out a deep sigh and said, "Anna. I love you."

Her breath caught in her throat. She leaned over him and whispered in his ear, "Sean, I love you too."

He jerked as if startled and his eyes opened a slit, their green color glittering with the fever. "You love me?" he gasped.

She repeated it. "Yes, I love you. But you must drink some broth."

He opened his mouth obediently. She tilted his head back and managed to dribble in two good spoonfuls that he swallowed before he closed his eyes and sank back into a delirium ridden sleep. She reluctantly placed the bowl on the floor, knowing he needed more liquids.

"Da," he muttered weakly, "da, don't hurt Rose."

His father, Anna thought, he is talking about his father.

"Leave ma alone!" he said more forcefully. "Don't--don't hit her!"

Anna stared at him. He seemed to be dreaming that his father was beating his mother and his sister. Or was it something that really happened a long time ago?

"Don't cry, Rose, don't cry...I'll save ye. He won't hurt ye anymore...I'll fix 'em good this time..." his voice trailed off.

With a heavy heart she watched him moan and groan, the torn muscles in his back knifing him in agony whenever he twitched. Suddenly he shivered and said in a pain wracked voice, "Forgive me, Da."

Had his father been a violent man like Baron Volodin? Had Sean killed his father to rescue his mother and sister from the abuse? And how old was he when this happened? Still a boy himself?

Anna felt ashamed of herself. She had been too quick to judge Sean. She doubted he was a cold blooded murderer. A strong longing to know all about him swept through her. But was it too late? Wang Li said the crisis would come in the next two days. Either Sean would conquer the relentless fever and infection poisoning him, or it would finally kill him.

She knew they were doing all they could do. All that was left now was prayer, constant prayer. She bowed her head.

* * *

"How are you feeling, Marya?" Tatiana asked her sister in an anxious voice.

A peaceful homelike scene greeted her inside the crowded cabin. The infant was asleep in her cradle, Keeah was wringing out her cloths, and the cat dozed on the bunk, twitching in her sleep as if chasing dream mice.

Marya was abed in the upper bunk, a recently emptied chamber pot nearby in case it was needed again. Her hair was plaited in two black braids and her face was ashen in color, making her look like a very young Russian girl. Her full lower lip trembled slightly as she struggled to smile.

"Not much better. I should have told you sooner about my problem, but I was afraid you'd leave me in New Archangel."

Surprised, she said, "What problem is this?"

The ship was tacking into the evening wind and she rolled a bit to port. The movement caused the timbers to creak and Marya's face went even whiter.

She pressed a hand to her throat and swallowed, then said hoarsely, "I've never told you that I have a fear of the water, a fear of drowning. And--and because I am so afraid and nervous, my stomach becomes upset and I cannot stand the thought of food or drink."

"It is called seasickness, Marya, and it is very common among passengers and even sailors on their first time out. It is nothing to be ashamed of." She smiled. "I missed you at dinner. It was hard being the only woman with all those men. You must get well and keep me company."

Tears glistened in her eyes, making them appear like two amber brown dewdrops. "Even after I'm well I dare not leave the cabin. I don't want him to see me."

Tatiana arched an eyebrow. "Who are you talking about?"

"My former betrothed, Andrei Leonov. He is aboard this ship and has threatened to take me back as his wife!"

Tatiana frowned, recalling *Monsieur* Leonov, the ugly-faced *Creole* who was now Dmitri's supercargo. She remembered seeing him at the wedding, but even then, she hadn't recognized him as the man she had met months ago when she'd broken his betrothal to Marya.

"He was at dinner tonight. I can't believe he's the same man. Whatever happened to his face?"

"He was attacked by two drunken American sailors last winter."

"It must have addled his wits, too, if he believes he can win you back now that you're a wealthy widow."

Before leaving New Archangel the governor had given to Marya, Boris's pension of one thousand rubles, which now were stowed away in a box inside her personal trunk.

"He cares nothing for my money."

Tatiana uttered an unladylike snort. "All men care for money, and so do women." She patted Marya sympathetically on her arm. "Don't fret, dear sister, for all his unfortunate looks, the man does not seem dangerous."

"Oh, but he is, Tatiana." Marya bit her lip and glanced at Keeah, who shrugged. "I believe Andrei used my cousin, Chignik, to kill Boris so he could marry me."

"What?" Tatiana stared at her in disbelief.

"A few weeks before the wedding I saw Andrei in my village. He said if he could find a way to stop the wedding, he expected me to become his wife."

"But *Monsieur* Leonov was not involved in the ambush. He was with the wedding party."

"That was his clever alibi. He and my cousin planned the whole thing, except that Chignik was supposed to get away safely without being seen."

"I still don't believe it," Tatiana repeated uncertainly.

Keeah folded an infant cloth and placed it inside an open trunk. "It is true, *Madame*. The Aleuts all say that the Scar Face Man killed the Evil Whale."

Tatiana paled. "If this is so, then I must tell Dmitri. He will leave *Monsieur* Leonov at the first Indian village we come to."

Marya shook her head. "No, Tatiana, we have no proof. Your husband trusts Andrei and needs him for trading. He would only laugh at you or become angry."

Tatiana fell silent. The thought of Dmitri's anger never failed to frighten her. "Does Anna know about this?"

"Yes, and she said we need to be careful around him."

"That is good advice, but Marya," Tatiana continued in a firmer voice, "you cannot allow that creature to keep you imprisoned inside this tiny cabin for weeks. There is nothing he can do to you aboard this ship. Tomorrow morning, I expect you to walk with me up on deck for some fresh air. And remember, we have armed guards to escort us."

Marya had forgotten the Russian soldiers. "Yes," she breathed in relief, "you are right, Tatiana. I--I'm feeling better already."

* * *

The morning dawned foggy and drizzly with the *Sea Rose* moving slowly through sullen gray water. Tatiana yawned and rolled over in the bunk, noticing with relief that Dmitri had already risen and left the cabin. He had not allowed her much sleep the night before, and she ached all over and felt very tired. It was a night she wanted to forget, much like the first one she'd spent in this very bed when she'd tried to seduce Captain O'Connell. What a foolish idiot she'd been, but desperation could drive a girl to do anything.

Although Dmitri never mentioned the incident, she knew thoughts of it had driven him to perform like a lustful animal. Was every night aboard ship to be like this, she wondered, shivering in repulsion. Or would he finally tire of punishing her for something that never happened?

She slipped out of the wide bunk and reached for her robe, glancing around the cabin. It had changed very little since the last time she'd slept here. There was still the same handsome desk and shelves of books, but now there was a slight feminine touch with her own hairbrush and comb and toiletries sitting on the table and her favorite lavender fragrances mingled with the more masculine scents of leather, tobacco, and musty books.

With a slight tap, the door opened and Anna peeked in. When she saw Tatiana up, she came in with a welcoming smile. "Good morning, Baroness, I have a tray of tea and breakfast scones for you."

"Baroness?"

Anna pointed with her chin towards the two guards outside the door. Tatiana rolled her eyes. "How is Marya this morning?"

"She is weak, but her stomach has settled and she already ate her breakfast and kept it down. She is anxiously awaiting your walk together on deck."

"Good." Tatiana sat down at the table and sipped her tea. "How is the captain?"

"He is alive, but barely."

"I'm so sorry, Anna." She hesitated then said, "Did you ever get your opportunity to tell him you love him?"

"Yes, I did, and I hope he understood me before he passed out again."

"Dmitri is disappointed that he still lives," Tatiana said in a flat voice.

"I have surrounded Sean with prayer. And I believe if it is God's will, he will survive."

Tatiana gave her a sad look. "Not many men can survive so many lashes of the *knout*."

"God is infinitely more powerful than the Russian *knout*."

"If the captain does live," she said thoughtfully, "I will know God answered your prayers."

* * *

The mountains were shrouded in cool mist as Marya and Tatiana, followed by a Russian sailor, walked along the rail to the stern where they were more protected from the stiff breeze. They were bundled snugly in their cloaks with head scarves to protect their hair and gloves to warm their hands. John was speaking to the helmsman, giving him orders, when he spied the two young women.

He noticed the pink color in Marya's cheeks and felt glad that she was over her illness. He bowed slightly and smiled at them. "We are fortunate to have two such lovely ladies to grace our humble ship with their beauty."

His words included both of them, but Tatiana saw how his eyes never left Marya's face. She remembered the night of the banquet, the same night of her miscarriage, when the two of them sat at the table engrossed with each other. Warning bells had gone off inside her then as they also did now.

"Officer Hill," she said stepping in front of Marya, "when will we reach a native village? I believe it will be interesting for us to watch the trading."

"In a few days, Baroness Volodin, but I'm afraid you ladies will have to stay in your cabins every time we anchor at an Indian village until the trading is over."

Tatiana pouted. "But that sounds quite tedious."

"Believe me, Baroness, when I say it is for your own good. Most of these coastal natives have never seen a white woman before. If any local chief saw you, he would either try to buy you or kidnap you for one of his wives. That would not please your husband."

She laughed at his warning. "Very little pleases Dmitri." She hesitated. "And how is my husband treating you and the crew?"

"This is only the second day, but so far so good. The baron looks right through the men as if they don't exist and they are careful to stay out of his way. As for myself and Mr. O'Riley, the baron gives us his orders only through Lieutenant Dohktorov, and we pass them on to the crew. When we begin trading, I believe it will be Andrei Leonov in charge."

"In regards to *Monsieur* Leonov," blurted Marya, "he was once my betrothed, and since my--my husband was killed, he now considers us betrothed again. But this is not true, and I do not wish to spend any time in his company."

John's face tightened. "Frankly, ladies the man is not fit company for a dog, much less you, Miss Bolkonsky. If you ever feel threatened by him, let me know."

Marya gave him a brilliant smile. "Thank you, Mr. Hill."

Tatiana nudged her arm. "Here he comes now along with Lieutenant Dohktorov."

Both the lieutenant and Andrei Leonov were smartly dressed in well fitting naval coats and caps with their trousers tucked inside shiny black boots. Only the absence of gold braid denoted Leonov's lower rank to the lieutenant. However, his position of supercargo ranked him well above that of the Russian sailor guarding Marya and Tatiana.

The sailor's name was Smirnoff and he had the brutish face of a *promyshlennik*. He wore a *kurtka*, which was a black jacket, and white cotton trousers, double soled boots that came up to his knees, and a *bezkozirka*, a black visorless cap, on his head.

Marya felt uncomfortable under Smirnoff's gaze each time his dark squinty eyes darted slyly back and forth from her to Tatiana. And whenever she glanced at him, she noticed him leering at her from underneath his bushy black mustache. Yet, she found his presence far preferable to that of Andrei.

"Baroness, *Mademoiselle* Bolkonsky," he greeted them with a nasally wheeze, "so nice to see you today. I trust you both are well and enjoying the voyage."

She gave him a stiff nod of acknowledgment, but did not speak. Tatiana saw the apprehension in her sister's face and said, "*Monsieur* Leonov, have you finished your meeting with my husband in our cabin?"

"*Da*, and we are anxious to reach Henya for trading, perhaps as soon as tomorrow."

Lieutenant Dohktorov looked at John. "Mr. Hill, Baron Volodin has ordered more sail hoisted to increase our speed."

"Aye, Lieutenant," John answered politely then strode away to instruct the crew. He gave Marya one backward glance, noting with great irritation how Leonov was eyeing her with the eagerness of an ugly mastiff.

"Come, Marya, we should return below," said Tatiana, hoping to get her sister away from Leonov's attention.

Lieutenant Dohktorov smiled charmingly at her. "Do you ladies have to leave so soon?"

Tatiana flushed slightly. "Perhaps not," she said, changing her mind. After all with the guard looming protectively behind them, what mischief could Leonov do?

"Oh, look," Marya suddenly exclaimed, leaning over the rail and pointing down into the water, "there are two black sharks swimming next to the ship!"

Leonov immediately stepped to her side and looked over. "They are dolphins, *Mademoiselle.*Quite harmless, I assure you."

"They are so graceful and swift! And look, one just jumped ahead of the bow!" She glanced at him in concern. "But what if the ship hits it?"

Leonov tried to laugh, his damaged nose emitting a strangled sounding snort. "That never happens, *Mademoiselle.* The creatures are much too quick." He reached for her arm in a proprietary gesture. "Come, would you like me to show you more of them on the port side?"

Marya snatched her arm away from him. "No, Andrei, I do not."

A look of hurt and brief anger flashed across his ruined face. "Another time then," he said coldly and left.

The lieutenant raised his eyebrows questioningly at Tatiana. She pulled him aside, away from the guard and her sister and said quietly in French, "He once was betrothed to Marya and is still in love with her, but she cannot abide him."

"It is a shame about his face."

"Not because of his looks, but because she suspects he had something to do with Lieutenant Ivanoff's death."

He gave a start of surprise. "How can that be? It was her own cousin who killed him and besides, *Monsieur* Leonov was walking with us in the forest at the time."

"Marya believes *Monsieur* Leonov used her cousin as the assassin while he had the alibi of being with the wedding party. But she has no proof, and when she confronted him, he denied it."

"Perhaps your sister is still in a state of shock over her husband's death and isn't thinking clearly."

"Marya never wished to marry Boris in the first place. Dmitri forced her into it."

This bit of information also stunned him. "Your husband has a way of making others do his will whether they want to or not."

"Yes, and that also applies to me," she said tersely.

He saw the shadows under her lovely violet eyes and felt a deep anger stir at the Baron. "Does--does he hurt even you?"

Before she could answer, she heard Marya whisper, "Dmitri comes."

Immediately she released Lieutenant Dohktorov's arm and whirled around, plastering her face with a false smile. Anton moved quickly away, his arm tingling with pleasure where her gloved fingers had pressed. He hoped the Baron did not notice how close he'd been to his wife.

Dmitri wore a thunderous expression, and both Anton and Tatiana prepared themselves for the worse. But to their surprised relief, he was tense about something entirely different.

"I've just received news from the steward," he said. "It seems Captain O'Connell's fever has lowered and he is asking for food and water. I don't understand how he could be improving. By now he should be dead."

Tatiana smiled. "God must be answering Anna's prayers."

CHAPTER THIRTY ONE

September 1822

Anna took out a batch of golden brown *twaback* from the oven, brushed back a strand of hair that had loosened from under her white lace cap, and smiled at the little Chinaman. "You are a great cook, Wang Li!"

He grinned with happiness at the praise and bowed his shiny shaved head to her, his long braided queue swishing sideways behind him. Then he tugged one corner of his long drooping mustache thoughtfully as he surveyed the pans of the cooling buns. "We make too much, Missy?"

"My mama used to say you can never have too many *twaback*," she answered. "After we've eaten our fill of them at dinner tonight, we can give the rest to the crew."

Samuel, who had been in and out of the galley all morning watching the preparation and baking of the *twaback*, poked his head in the doorway and said, "The Cap'n sure do need fattenin' up."

"Yes, he lost too much weight when he was ill," Anna agreed, then she looked up to see Robby. He was also peering inside the small hot room, drawn by the aroma of the delicious yeasty fragrance, making his mouth water in anticipation.

"Canna have one, Missus Campbell?" He towered above her, having shot up several inches since the summer before. He was all knees and elbows, a gangly youth with a thin frame begging to be filled out. Anna felt a rush of affection as she handed him a warm *twaback* and watched him stuff both of the buns at once inside his mouth. He reminded her of her brother Jack.

"Mmph," he nodded with approval, both of his cheeks bulging like a well fed chipmunk.

"You go," said Wang Li, making shooing motions with his hands, "or I cook dog for dinner." He barked a short cackle.

Anna stifled a laugh as Robby's freckled face paled into a look of horror. "He's only joking," she said. "He'd never put your Jimmy in a stew pot.

"Maybe and maybe not," Robby said uncertainly, spewing out some crumbs, "but I don't aim to stay here an' find out." He knew that the Chinese as well as many coastal natives ate dog meat, considering it a delicious delicacy. He shot Wang Li a distrustful frown then hastily exited the galley.

The ship rose on a swell and two of the pans slid off the table. Wang Li caught them deftly before they spilled the *twaback* onto the wooden planked floor. They were sailing in the open ocean near the northern tip of Vancouver Island and after two days of inclement weather, the seas were running six to eight feet.

Recently the ship had crossed the new southern boundary of Russian America into neutral waters. It bothered Sean and all the American crew that in September of 1821, exactly one year before, the Russians had extended their southern border from 54 degrees, 40 minutes latitude, a line north of the Queen Charlotte Islands, to latitude 51, just north of Vancouver Island.

Of course, that wasn't the only thing that irritated Sean, Anna thought. He had spent the entire summer snapping with impatience at most everyone as he struggled to become the strong man he used to be.

She recalled her visit to him the day after his fever broke and he was finally coherent and conscious. Her heart had raced in nervous expectation. Would he remember she told him she loved him or were her words lost somewhere in his feverish dreams?

He was sound asleep on his stomach and she could see the toll the fever had taken on him. His face was tinged an unhealthy gray and his eyes were shadowed and sunken with deep exhaustion.

After a few minutes he woke and she asked, "How do you feel, Sean?"

"I'm alive thanks to your prayers, Anna, but whenever I move, my back is on fire," he moaned, looking at her sideways from his pillow. "If not for the laudanum, I'd be screamin' my guts out."

"At least you aren't raving in a fever any longer."

He winced. "I'm a feared to hear what strange things I mighta said."

"You talked mostly about your parents and your sister."

"And my da? What did I say about him?"

Anna hesitated, remembering his cries of anger at his father. Perhaps it was not wise to remind him, but her deep curiosity about his past overcame her caution. "You were begging him not to hurt your mother and sister."

At the look of dismay which crossed his face, she reached out her finger and tentatively traced the scar on his left cheek. "I've always sensed you are a man of many scars, Sean, not only here and on your back, but inside you as well."

He grabbed her hand and pulled it away from his cheek, flinching in pain. "I told ye once that I kilt my da. Ye've never asked me about it, Anna, but I can see in your face all the questions."

"I would like to know," she said quietly, "if you dare tell me."

He sighed and released her hand. "I've not told a soul about the night my da died. I was a lad of fifteen and my sister Rose was fourteen." He paused. "My da used to beat my ma, and after she died giving birth to a bairn who did not live, he beat poor Rose. He used to hit me too, 'till I grew big enough to hit him back."

During the next hour Sean told Anna all about his miserable childhood in the Irish slums of Boston. When he came to the night his father died, he closed his eyes in shame, unable to look at her. But he told her all of it, including every detail of how he choked the life out of Paddy O'Connell. When he was through, a silence fell into the small cabin, punctuated only by the usual shipboard sounds of water hissing by the hull, the creaking of the timbers, the clatter of pots and pans in the galley, and the muted thumps of feet overhead.

"So, Anna," he said finally, staring her full in the face, "do ye find me some sort of monster, then? A man who murdered his own da?"

Her eyes swam with unshed tears. "You had no choice, Sean," she whispered. "You were protecting your little sister. He was a beast, not a father."

He stared at her in surprise. "You forgive me, then?"

"It's not my place to forgive you, Sean. Only God can do that."

"Aye," he said sadly, "that's what Ethan told me in my dreams when I was sick."

She wiped at a tear and gave a soft laugh. "That sounds like Ethan. What else did he tell you?"

A strange expression came over his face. "Not much."

"Do you have any memory of anything I said to you when you were so feverish?"

He moved slightly on his stomach and he groaned with the pain. "I remember you calling my name. Nothing else."

Taking a deep breath, she said, "I told you I loved you, Sean."

He appeared stunned, his eyes wide and blank. Then a slow smile crossed his face. "Now I do remember ye sayin' that, Anna, but I thought 'twas only a dream."

"It wasn't a dream. I love you, Sean."

She knelt by the side of the bunk and kissed his damp forehead. He smelled sourly of sickness and male sweat, but she didn't care. He tried to laugh with pleasure, but the sound came out more like a strangled chuckle.

"Anna, do ye have any notion of how long I've been waiting for this? An' now instead of kissin' ye back all I can do is lay here like a trussed chicken," he grumbled.

She smiled and kissed him again. "You'll be better soon. Wang Li has some nourishing soup for you to eat and after that you need to sleep."

"Before ye go, Anna, I need to tell you something else. When Ethan came to me in my dream, he said I needed to ask God to forgive me for all the terrible things I've done."

Anna caught her breath. "And did you?"

"Aye, I thought I was dyin' ye see, an' I didn't want to go to hell, so I cried out to Jesus to save me. And now, here I am, more like a helpless bairn than a man, but I'm a forgiven man."

With a deep joy in her heart, she said, "Oh, Sean, this is what I've been praying for you for a long time."

"Does that mean ye'll marry me now, Anna?"

She choked. "I—I don't know. The most important thing is getting you well and back on your feet."

"But ye won't tell me nay?"

"I'm saying I might marry you, Sean, but I have to think about it."

"Ye'll have to decide before we reach Fort Ross." He shut his eyes and groaned, "Tell Samuel I need to use the chamber pot."

* * *

The days passed by quickly with busy shipboard routines. On occasion Anna visited Sean, sometimes bringing Katya while they discussed the weather, the trading, and the constant tensions among the American crew and the Russians.

On a lighter note, they joked about all the hidden flirtations between Tatiana and Anton Dohktorov, John and Marya, and Jake and Keeah. She also filled him in about Andrei Leonov and Marya's suspicions that he had something to do with Lieutenant Ivanoff's murder.

If Anna had extra time she read to him from the Bible. Sean was full of questions about all the knowledge she had taken for granted growing up as a Mennonite.

His recovery was slow and painful. The raging fever and infection and loss of blood from the flogging left him weak and crippled. Sleep was elusive and the nights were a torment. It was two months before he could lay on his back without being in agony.

As each muscle in his back healed, he began to exercise, but his back was so stiff at first he could not stand upright or walk normally. Instead he would hobble across the floor, bent over like an old man. It was an excruciating process that left him bathed in sweat, exhausted and trembling.

Eventually, he progressed enough to limp around the ship and Dmitri soon put him to use in the chart room plotting their navigational course. When he was stronger, Sean became the officer in charge of the night watch, a position lower than even John's or Jake's. Anna knew it was Dmitri's way of using his power to further humiliate the proud captain. It also kept the two men separated most of the time.

As the summer passed Sean's recovery made Dmitri even more irritable than usual. His foul temper spilled over into the women's realm of the ship. He endlessly criticized Samuel and Robby as they polished the salon furniture, cleaned the carpets, scrubbed the skylight and windows.

Whenever one of them helped Anna string up Katya's newly washed cloths to dry in the salon, the sight brought a string of oaths from Dmitri.

"Is this a ship or a bloody nursery?" he would demand as he stalked out of the salon, heading above decks, while muttering something about it being the "only place on this cursed tub where a man could think without some chattering woman or screaming brat interrupting."

It was true that the four women, the infant and the cat had taken over the main salon. They used the room like a parlor in a house, for conversation, reading books, playing chess, sewing and embroidery, and visiting with the other officers. If Anna hadn't been so wary of Baron Volodin, she would have found his reaction to their domestic clutter amusing.

This morning she was also a bit hesitant to invade Wang Li's personal domain of the galley, but he readily accepted her offer to show him how to make the special buns of the Mennonites. He said it would be a good change from the daily hard biscuits. She was pleased to see the ingredients for *twaback* were already in the pantry: flour, salt, lard, cakes of yeast, and tins of powdered milk from London.

Wang Li was a quick learner, and soon was helping Anna mix and knead the dough like any expert *hausFrau* from Furstenau.

Today, September twenty-nine, was Sean's twenty-ninth birthday. For days she had been knitting a scarf for him as a gift. Then the idea came to her to have *twaback* served at dinner as a special treat to surprise him. Afterwards, she hoped to give him the scarf before he started his duty on night watch.

After Robby left the galley and she and Wang Li were alone again, he startled her by blurting, "Missy, I want to know about your Jesus God."

It was the last thing she expected to hear from an opium smoking Chinaman and she wasn't certain how to explain. Perhaps if she started with something he might understand. She remembered Ethan once telling her about the Chinese expression, *to lose face*.

"In China what does it mean to'lose face'?"

"If son disobey father in front of family or village, father lose face and so angry with son, son has to go away, maybe forever."

Anna nodded and began to explain about the first man and first woman, Adam and Eve, in the Garden of Eden, and how they wished to be like God, knowing good and evil. "It was their disobedience in eating the fruit of the forbidden tree that caused mankind to be separated from God."

Wang Li listened intently. He thought the story of the son of God who died to save humankind from their sins and eternal damnation was fascinating.

As a Buddhist, he had been brought up to believe that God existed only as one with the universe, distant and detached from the petty problems of men. The idea of a personal God who loved people so much He would sacrifice His only son was startling, as foreign a concept as the Christian teachings of sin.

"Buddha taught not much different between good and evil," he told Anna, "Everything that exists and happens is part of sameness of universe. We not worship God or Buddha. We believe in Four Noble Truths to give us better life."

"What are they?" Anna asked curiously.

"You have your Holy Book, Missy. We Chinese have sacred teachings, too. We believe in Four Noble Truths," he said, holding up four fingers. "One, all life is disappointment and suffering. Two, most suffering is because we desire pleasure and power. Three, only way we not have suffering and pain, we must stop bad desires. Four, only way we stop bad desires is, follow Noble Eightfold Path."

Anna was fascinated. "And what are those?"

He chuckled. "I think I forget them, because I still like pleasures, good food and opium." His expression darkened briefly. "Too bad opium almost gone. I buy more in Guangzhou."

"Guang---what?" she repeated in confusion.

"We say Guangzhou, you say Can-ton."

"Oh," she said with understanding. "You mean, when you sail to Canton, you intend to buy opium."

She frowned slightly. "Shouldn't you think about giving up such a bad habit? Smoking opium is addictive and not good for you."

He shrugged his narrow shoulders. "It give me peace of mind, great tranquility."

Anna opened her mouth to argue then thought better of it. His opium addiction was none of her business. Instead she asked him, "Will you get in trouble with the Chinese authorities when we reach Canton?"

"I hide below where men of Empress do not find me."

"And if they did find you?"

"They bring me back to Empress. Execute me," he added, using one finger in a slicing motion across his throat.

"Then it is very dangerous for you to return there," Anna said thoughtfully. "But you do not seem worried about it."

"If I die, I die," he stated matter-of-factly.

"So, do you believe in life after death?" she asked.

He shrugged again. "Some teachers say we born again here after we die, and if we good in this life, we get better life next time. Or some say if we follow Four Noble Truths, we reach nirvana."

"Nirvana?" she questioned, as she peeked at another batch in the oven that was browning nicely.

"State of nothingness, like what happens when you blow out candle," he answered with his brown toothed grin. All his front teeth were stained a mahogany color after years of opium smoking.

Anna looked surprised. "What does that mean, you no longer exist?"

He frowned, appearing slightly troubled. "I worry that too. But some teachers say, in nothingness of nirvana we find fulfillment we don't have here."

"I think I'm confused," she said, shaking her head.

Wang Li patted a flour covered hand on her shoulder, dusting her dress and apron with white powder. "I think you be more happy with your Jesus, Missy, than with Buddha."

Anna smiled at him. "And what about you, Wang Li, are you happy with your beliefs?"

He tugged at his mustache again, a habit when deep in thought. "No, Missy," he finally said with a sigh, "Buddha confuse me too. No help to me when Lily Flower die. Only opium," his voice trailed away as a haunting expression of grief appeared in his slanted dark eyes.

Anna remembered Ethan telling her the story of Wang Li's young Chinese wife, and how she had helped him escape China to save his life from the wrath of the Empress, but probably lost her own life in the process.

"Promise me you'll think about one fact," she said. "Buddha died a long time ago, but Jesus Christ rose from the dead and He lives in heaven."

His eyes widened briefly in astonishment. "You may be right, Missy," he mumbled, "you may be right."

After that, he wouldn't talk about anything except the *twaback*, but Anna saw him fingering his mustache thoughtfully as they finished up the baking.

* * *

That evening Sean glanced around the table at his usual dinner companions, John Hill on his right, Lieutenant Anton Dohktorov on his left, and around the table, Ebenezer Cartwright, Edmund Wilde, Andrei Leonov, Volodin and his wife, her sister Marya, and Anna.

As he chewed a bite of fried fish, his eyes focused on Anna dressed nicely in a pearl gray gown and rose colored shawl. She caught his gaze and smiled at him. His heart twisted and he almost lost his appetite as his fear of losing her choked him.

She hadn't agreed to marry him as yet. Time was running out. He knew she loved him, so it wasn't her feelings for him that were in doubt. Was it her love and loyalty to Tatiana? Was she still mourning the loss of Ethan too much? Or was it because she had married one cripple and didn't want to be stuck with another?

Sometimes when he shuffled around like he was seventy years old, he could see the pity in her eyes. It made him realize that she deserved a man so much better than him, a man well in body, mind, and soul.

But even if his body never completely healed, he was thankful for the cleansing of his soul. He no longer had the nightmares about his da and whenever he thought about him, the old rage and hatred were gone. It felt like a dark heavy weight had lifted up out of him and was cast away. Little by little as time passed, he began to take enjoyment in the simple things of life again, the taste of food, the colors of a sunset, the haunting cry of a seabird, the sight of a powerful whale, and especially, the sight of Anna laughing with her child.

All the assembly were eating and drinking heartily, except for Marya who still had little appetite. He felt a twinge of pity for her. Too bad she wasn't more like Anna, who became ill only in the strongest of storms, none of which they had encountered so far. A fine captain's wife she would make, he thought wistfully.

"What are these odd looking biscuits?" Mr. Cartwright asked, his long thin face wearing a puzzled expression as he stared at the basket of *twaback* Samuel was placing on the table.

"Birthday treat for the Cap'n," he mumbled softly, knowing that the Baron did not like to hear Captain O'Connell referred to with his American title.

As expected, Dmitri shot the steward a dark frown of disapproval. Ignoring him, Anna turned her glowing hazel eyes upon Sean. "Captain O'Connell, this morning Wang Li and I made these special buns in honor of your birthday today. They are a tradition in my family."

Most of the men around the table lifted their mugs in Sean's direction and chorused "Happy Birthday!" as he flushed in embarrassed pleasure. He couldn't remember anyone celebrating his birthday since his ma had died when he was a lad.

"I thank ye, Mistress Campbell," he said and gave her one of his old handsome smiles that took her breath away and set her pulse throbbing.

Marya helped herself to a *twaback* and told Anna how good they were. "You will have to teach me how to bake them."

Tatiana shook her head at her sister. "Now Marya, you forget that a lady of the nobility does not cook. It is something Anna can teach Keeah, however."

Marya frowned in disappointment. John glanced at her from across the table and gave her a wink of sympathy which Leonov happened to see. The *Creole* glowered at John with a jealous expression so malignant; it made his face a mask even more vile than normal.

Anna looked away from him and caught a quick glance exchanged between Tatiana and Anton Dohktorov. She sighed inwardly. All summer long she had been watching a situation unfold aboard ship which she would call two love triangles, two very dangerous love triangles.

"Some of the crew is still complainin' about leaving those slaves," said Edmund Wilde the armorer.

Sean gave him a hard look. Mr. Wilde was not a competent blacksmith and Gregory Jones was sorely missed, not only for his skills with the forge, but as a friend who had tried to save his life. It had made him furious to hear that the Russians had arrested Jones.

"Who are the latest troublemakers?" he asked.

"Jeb Drake an' Nate Tyler. They keep telling all the men how those lads would a brought us more otter skins, more money."

A few days before they had traded at Cumshewa, a Haida village dotted with tall totem poles, located along the eastern shore of one of the Queen Charlotte Islands. The chief there, Tooschcondolth, had offered many otter skins if the *Sea Rose* would transport two slaves to the Nootkas. He said they were a special gift to Chief Maquina as a part of a dowry for Tooschcondolth's daughter who was to become the Nootka chief's fourth wife.

The two slaves were young boys, about ten years old. They came from the Salish tribe in Puget Sound, and were captured as infants with their mothers.

It was common for American ships to carry Northwest Coast Indian slaves from one place to another. Slavery was universal up and down the coast, with most of the slaves coming from the more peaceful tribes on Puget Sound and the Columbia River.

The Haida chief's request had triggered an argument. Volodin and Leonov wanted to transport the boys, sensing a huge profit, but John, Jake, and Sean had protested.

"We dare not stop at Nootka Sound," said John. "If Chief Maquina recognizes Captain O'Connell and Mr. O'Riley from the *Eastern Wind* years ago when they rescued me and Mr. Jones, Maquina will seek further revenge for the death of his brother. We could all be slaughtered and the women captured as slaves. Are a few otter skins worth that risk, Your Excellency?"

Dmitri was angry and disappointed, but he wasn't stupid enough to endanger his life and especially that of his wife. So, he had Leonov politely tell Tooschcondolth that there was no room on board for extra passengers.

Sean knew the Haida chief found that excuse unlikely since the ship looked huge to him, but there was nothing he could do to change the white men's minds.

"Tyler and Drake do have a point," said Leonov grudgingly, at the same time wondering if the two Yankee sailors were the ones who had attacked him and left him for dead last winter.

He'd spent all these past months on board and still hadn't discovered who the culprits were, but he was most suspicious of Tyler and Drake. Unfortunately, there was no way to wring the information out of them.

But at the moment Leonov had a more pressing matter to attend. For weeks he had observed the smooth talking Mr. Hill showering his attentions upon his Marya Nikolayevna. It was obvious the officer was smitten with her and he was afraid she was beginning to feel the same towards the detested Yankee.

However, tonight he was making certain Mr. Hill never saw the light of day again. It was the same type of plan that had eliminated Lieutenant Ivanoff from Marya's life. And once again he had another idiot like Chignik to do his dirty work. All he needed this time were a few rubles and a couple bottles of vodka to pay his newest assassin, the greedy imbecile, Vladimir Smirnoff.

With a sly expression Leonov glanced around the table. "If we'd agreed to transport the slaves we could've doubled our money by taking the otter skins from the Haidas, and then instead of giving the slaves as gifts to the Nootkas, we could've sold them for even more skins."

"That would have been dishonest," said Sean.

Dmitri shot Leonov a smile of admiration, and said, "Oh, I forget, O'Connell, you are a man of principles."

Immediately Sean bristled at the sarcasm and would have retorted when Lieutenant Dohktorov said to Dmitri, "If there were more honorable Yankees like Captain O'Connell, a man who lacks greed and deceit, our Czar never would've had to issue his *ukase* against foreign trading in Russian America."

Dmitri scowled. "You over simplify the matter, Lieutenant."

"I think not, Your Excellency," he answered as the two men glared at each other, both as stiff and unyielding as two totem poles.

The trading that summer had not gone well. The natives were eager to barter their beaver, fox, and weasel furs, but not the more profitable otter skins. The Indians claimed there was a scarcity of otters, and Sean thought they were telling the truth. The days were gone when the American and British traders could purchase eighteen thousand otter skins in one season, like they had in 1801.

But the Indians also were turning their noses up at the Russian goods they had brought. Sean knew they were inferior to the higher quality English goods he had originally bought last year in London, such as: hoes, axes, hatchets, adzes, knives, rat traps, snuff bottles, fish hooks, beads, jewelry, brass pans, pewter porringers, skillets, tin kettles, razors, mirrors, combs, saws, wire, tobacco, and especially plain iron bars called chisels.

There was a great demand for chisels, because the Indians could hammer them into weapons and tools. The only trade goods the Indians wanted more than chisels were copper, clothing, and muskets, ammunition and powder, which were forbidden by the Russians.

One year ago he had traded away all of his English cargo for furs before the *Sea Rose* was captured. Now he would give anything to have even a fraction of those goods.

"Dmitri, Lieutenant Dohktorov," said Tatiana lightly, "don't be angry with each other. We have enough enemies without us Russians being at odds with each other." She gave a slight shudder. "I'm so frightened each time we anchor near a village and are surrounded by savages."

When the ship was anchored near the shore at Cumshewa she and the other three women had hidden in their cabin as usual. Tatiana had peeked out the window and was awestruck by a huge totem pole standing guard at the entrance to the largest house in the village. It was carved out of a massive cedar tree and had images of animal faces with fierce teeth and wild eyes, topped by a giant bird beak. The faces were painted in black and bright red and yellow colors.

Keeah refused to look at it, saying the totem was bad luck. Her people, the Tlingit, carved the poles as well, every one with a meaning all its own to each clan and family. But the Haida totems were the biggest and most terrifying she'd ever seen, making her feel nervous and agitated until the ship sailed away from Cumshewa.

Out of the corner of her eye, Tatiana saw Anton staring at her with concern, but it was Dmitri who answered in a soothing voice, "Don't be worried, darling. There are plenty of men and guns on board to protect you and the other women if need be. Isn't that correct, Dohktorov?"

"Yes, Your Excellency, and we have eight mounted cannon on board, four on each side of the ship that could blast their canoes right out of the water if the natives attacked us."

Tatiana fluttered her long thick eyelashes at him. "That does make me feel so much safer, Lieutenant."

Dmitri gave her and the lieutenant a penetrating look. It had crossed his mind lately that his second in command was a bit too friendly with his wife. More than once this summer he had found them playing chess together in the salon; never alone, of course. Either Marya or Anna or both would be sitting nearby reading a book or sewing. At least with these rougher seas there would be no more chess games.

Still, he would watch Anton and Tatiana more closely.

"The natives are more clever than you think," said John. "If they intended to attack us, they would resort to trickery and stay far away from the cannons."

As a look of dismay crossed Tatiana's lovely face, Anton said quickly, "But not to worry, Baroness, we are finished with the natives and our hold is full with bales of furs."

"Almost too full," Sean muttered to no one in particular.

The ocean swells were running near eight feet, a height the *Sea Rose* once glided through as gracefully as a swift dolphin. But tonight the overloaded ship was lumbering slowly through the water, feeling sluggish and awkward at the helm.

Heaven help them if some larger waves arose from a storm.

"We can never have too many furs, O'Connell!" Dmitri snarled at him. Then he looked at John and steadied his voice, "Mr. Hill, I understand why we cannot stop at Nootka Sound, but I still think we should consider trading at some other villages on Vancouver Island."

"I disagree, Your Excellency," said John quietly. "The other villages can cause us trouble as well as the Nootkas. When I was a captive with them, Maquina often visited the villages of Clayoquot Sound and Barkley Sound at the southern end of the island. He would have told those natives about us by now.

"And then, there are the other visiting chiefs, such as the fierce Makahs of Classet, which is near Cape Flattery on the tip of the Olympic Peninsula. The Makahs' hatred of white men is well known. We are better off avoiding any contact with them."

"Is it true that the Nootkas and the Makahs are related?" Anton asked curiously.

John nodded. "Aye, when I was living with the Nootkas, whenever there was a big *potlatch*, many of the powerful Makah came, as the Nootkas called them cousins."

"What is a *potlatch*?" Anna asked.

"Tis a great feast given by the chief or any other rich and important man in the tribe. Each guest brings gifts, and the smart ones know how to accept gifts with the least amount of obligation. The host shows how rich he is by giving away, or even destroying much of his property, valuables like furs, blankets, baskets, copper, iron, tools, tobacco, or food.

"Once at a *potlatch*, I saw Maquina burn one hundred otter skins and throw fifty bundles of tobacco in a river, so everyone would know how rich and important he was. Of course, after that, he was inundated by gifts from the other guests and ended up with more property than before."

"A *potlatch*," said Marya, "is like a war without blood. The tribes can battle for supremacy without killing anyone. It is something white men should emulate."

"No white man in his right mind would destroy a hundred otter skins. It's like burning rubles," said Dmitri in disgust.

"The society and tribal rituals on the Northwest Coast are quite complex, perhaps even more so than in Boston and Saint Petersburg," John pointed out. "I spent two years with the Nootkas, and I never understood them."

"Bloody savages, all of them," sputtered Dmitri, who had drunk more than his share of rum.

* * *

After dinner Sean went up on deck to relieve Jake O'Riley on the night watch. Anna followed carrying a parcel wrapped in paper. By then the strong northwest wind had died down to a light breeze and she only needed her shawl and scarf instead of her heavy cloak. The forested rocky coast of Vancouver Island slid by on the port side as the ship sailed south. A huge orange sun was beginning to slip into the sea on the horizon and the rays were coloring a pathway of burnished gold across the turquoise blue swells.

Anna watched the sky and clouds change from gold to dusky rose and as the sun sank out of view, a sudden explosion of emerald fire blazed on the horizon. It was gone in a split second.

"A green flash!" she exclaimed with pleasure. "I just saw it for the first time!"

Sean smiled down at her, his mouth tipping up slightly at the corners. "I remember in the tropics how ye used to wait many evenings at sunset for a glimpse of the green flash. Now ye finally see it in these usually foggy northern waters. Isn't life strange, Anna?"

The breeze ruffled his black curly hair that had escaped his cap and his green eyes, a shade darker than the emerald flash, studied her lovingly. "Yes, it is always full of surprises," she said, handing him the parcel.

"What's this then?"

"Your birthday gift from me. Open it."

He laughed like an eager boy and tore off the paper, which the wind caught and flung over the rail. He unfolded the long neck scarf, made of soft green wool. "You can tuck it under the collar of your great coat to keep you extra warm on these cold nights on deck," she explained.

"I thank ye, Anna," he breathed. "I've never had a scarf so fine."

"I have another gift for you as well," she added, her eyes dancing with a mischievous light. "I accept your proposal of marriage, Sean."

With a small cry she swayed as a large swell tipped her off balance. Instinctively his long arms enfolded her before she could fall. For a few moments she melted into him, closing her eyes and savoring his protective embrace.

"My dearest Anna," he murmured into her ear, "ye have no idea what a happy man I am today."

Suddenly a ball of golden fur hurtled into their legs, shoving both of them backwards into the rail. Startled, they jumped apart as the dog Jimmy bounced around them with his bushy tail whipping back and forth like a furry flag.

"Sorry, Cap'n, sorry Missus Campbell," Robby yelled out, running after the dog with a rope. "Poor Jimmy's been cooped up below all day and needs a bit of exercise." He glanced at them with a knowing grin on his face.

Sean turned red. Soon it would be all over the ship that Captain O'Connell was seen holding Mistress Campbell in his arms.

"I think our secret is out," she said, laughing.

CHAPTER THIRTY TWO

Captain Matthew Hunter, of the British trader, *Elizabeth Ann*, ordered the longboat lowered to investigate what appeared to be a man floating on a crude wooden raft. Using his telescope, he saw how the man had lashed himself to the raft with a frayed rope. *Amazing that it had held through such a storm*, he thought, *and even more amazing, that the man was alive.*

The late autumn hurricane had come roaring out of the Atlantic days ago. If Captain Hunter hadn't recognized the signs, the falling of the glass barometer in his cabin, the sultry yellowish cast to the sky, the ominous looking clouds of mares' tails hugging the horizon, and the oily sheen to the swells building in height from the east, the *Elizabeth Ann* might have foundered along with many other unlucky ships.

But they managed to slip into a sheltered bay on the southern coast of Cuba, and the storm brushed by them, heading north to the Gulf. As it was, a glancing blow from a hurricane was bad enough, liken to a full gale otherwise. The ship had sustained some damage, even in the bay, dragging her anchor and almost beaching herself several times. It had taken all his expertise as a captain to keep her afloat and safe.

Now they were on their way to round the Horn and head for Alaska to trade for furs come spring. He'd heard the Russians were on the prowl against both British and Americans, however, and he knew this voyage was to be a tricky business.

His sailors were returning with the rescued man, who looked barely alive. His tattered shirt and pants had been no protection against the relentless sun, which had toasted his skin to the color of a rare beef roast. As they brought him closer to the ship, Hunter leaned over the rail, thinking what a fortunate soul he was, the only survivor of his ship.

"Do you know the name of his ship?" Hunter called out.

"Aye, Cap'n," said his second mate. "She was the *Jupiter* out of Boston."

Hunter frowned in dismay. Everyone in the Caribbean and the East Coast of the United States had heard of the *Jupiter*, a notorious privateer smuggling slaves and rum and other contraband. It seemed the captain and her crew had finally met their just reward at the bottom of the sea, unless this man was the captain.

Hunter watched as the poor wretch was helped up the rope ladder onto the deck. He collapsed into a pile of shivering rags. His lips and tongue were swollen from dehydration and his pockmarked face was as red as a boiled lobster.

“Get him below,” said Hunter, “and give him some food and water, but not too much.”

As his men hurried to do his bidding, Hunter asked his second mate, “Mister Adams, did you get the man’s name and rank?”

“Aye, Cap’n, he’s the first mate, goes by the name of Horn, Arthur Horn.”

* * *

Marya sat on the edge of her bunk with a damp cloth clutched in her hand. The small amount of food she'd eaten at dinner churned inside her with every roll of the ship.

"How are you feeling?" Anna asked her, keeping one eye on Marya, another on Katya. At the moment her daughter slept peacefully in her cradle, rocking back and forth with the ship's movement.

Marya grimaced. "I feel like such a burden to you and Keeah being ill all the time. You'd think by now I would be used to the sea."

Anna remembered Natasha Chernyshova, the sickly wife of Igor, the commander of the *Suvorov*. "Some people have a harder time than others on a ship, *Mademoiselle*. It is nothing to be ashamed of. When we reach the calmer waters off California, you'll likely be better."

"I hope so," she muttered, wiping the cloth across her perspiring face. "Anna, did you notice *Monsieur* Leonov behaving strangely tonight at dinner?"

"It seems to me he is always strange."

"But tonight he was odder than usual. He was staring at John with such hatred in his eyes. It worries me. I'm afraid Andrei might do him some harm."

"Yes, I have noticed his jealousy of John, but what can he do here aboard the ship with so many people about?"

Marya sighed. "I don't know, but I think I'm going to find John before he retires for the night and tell him my concerns." She stood up and patted her hair into place, then slid a shawl around her shoulders.

She opened the cabin door and stepped into the salon where Tatiana was stooped over, looking under the tables and sofas. "Have you seen Otter anywhere, Marya? The cook gave me some leftover fish from dinner for her. She should be hungry by now, but I can't find her."

"Perhaps one of the crew accidentally let her out of the salon."

"I hope not," Tatiana said worriedly. "Could you go find out from the steward if he's seen her? If I ask him, he won't give me a straight answer. He always behaves as if he doesn't understand me, even if I talk English very slowly."

"I don't think Samuel likes you, Tatiana."

She shrugged. "Or else he's as stupid as he looks."

Marya rolled her eyes and left the salon, walking along the narrow passageway to the forward cabin where Samuel and Wang Li shared their quarters with Captain O'Connell. Along the way, she stopped at the chart room and knocked on the door, hoping to speak to John.

She heard a muffled giggle coming from inside the room and a soft oath, then Jake called out, "Who is it?"

"It's Marya, Mr. O'Riley. Is Mr. Hill with you? I'd like to see him for a moment."

"He's not here, Miss," Jake answered, opening the door a crack and peering at her. "He went down to the hold. The supercargo, Leonov, came by some time ago to say there was a problem with some of the cargo shiftin' around below an' Lieutenant Dohktorov wanted John to meet him down there."

"If it's not too late when he returns, could you tell Mr. Hill that I'd like to speak with him?"

"Aye, Miss, I'll tell him," said Jake, shutting the door swiftly, but not quite swiftly enough. Marya was positive the bright yellow scarf she saw on the floor belonged to Keeah.

Shaking her head and frowning, she continued towards the forward cabin to talk to Samuel and found him in the galley helping Wang Li tidy up for the night. When she asked if either one had seen the cat, they both said no. After thanking them, she returned to the salon, then halted before going in.

Andrei! He was plotting something, she was sure of it! The thought of John in the dark cargo hold at this time of night alone with all those Russians made her very uneasy. Then she remembered that Lieutenant Dohktorov was meeting him and she let out a breath of relief.

But her relief was short-lived. When the armed Russian standing next to the salon door slowly opened it for her, she saw the lieutenant sitting on a sofa talking to Tatiana.

"Do you still love Vera Alexisovna," she heard Tatiana say softly, "or are you finally over her?"

In the entrance Marya paused, listening as Anton answered in a tender voice, “I now realize that I never loved Vera at all, because I am in love with someone else.”

Tatiana blushed and said very quietly, ‘Who, Anton?’

"You know," he whispered, leaning towards her in an intimate manner.

At that moment Marya cleared her throat and they both were so shocked to see her, they quickly moved apart and Anton jumped to his feet.

Tatiana appeared flustered, but her voice was steady as she asked, "Did the steward know where Otter is?"

"I'm sorry, Tatiana, neither he nor the cook has seen her." Marya gave Anton a puzzled look. "Lieutenant, aren't you supposed to be meeting Mr. Hill below in the cargo hold?"

Now it was his turn to look confused. "What are you talking about, *Mademoiselle*?"

"I just spoke to Mr. O'Riley and he said that *Monsieur* Leonov sent Mr. Hill a message from you to meet him below; something about a problem with the cargo."

"I know nothing about it," said Anton. "And there certainly isn't anything wrong with the cargo, at least, not to my knowledge."

Marya felt a feeling of panic bubble up inside her. "Please, you must do something, lieutenant! I'm afraid Mr. Hill might be in danger!"

"Marya!" Tatiana exclaimed, "whatever are you talking about?"

Anton appeared startled. "I can see that there has been some misunderstanding, *Mademoiselle*, as I never sent *Monsieur* Leonov with a message for Mr. Hill, but why do you believe he is in danger?"

Marya swallowed nervously. "I've known *Monsieur* Leonov for a long while. He used to be my betrothed and for some reason, still thinks we will be married someday. I'm afraid he is jealous of Mr. Hill's attentions to me, and I believe he might have planned to do him some harm tonight."

Anton looked at Tatiana, who smiled slightly. "She also believes *Monsieur* Leonov was the mastermind behind the Aleut assassin who ambushed and killed Lieutenant Ivanoff."

"My cousin never would have done such an evil thing on his own."

"Then why haven't you mentioned this before, dear sister? Boris was my closest friend!"

Dmitri stood in the doorway of his cabin with a belligerent expression on his face and swaying with too much drink. He glared at Marya. "Well, speak up!"

"I--I--" she began in fright, "I never had any proof against *Monsieur* Leonov, sir."

Anton faced Dmitri with a stern look. "Your Excellency, if *Mademoiselle*'s suspicions are true, then there's no time to waste talking. Give me your permission to take some armed men and investigate the cargo hold at once!"

Dmitri gave him a wave of dismissal. "Go Lieutenant, and then bring Leonov to me. I wish to interrogate him in my sister-in-law's presence."

Anton noted the look of apprehension on Marya's face, but at the moment he was more interested in what might be happening below.

* * *

As in most ships, the cargo hold of the *Sea Rose* was chilly and damp with the rank stench of the bilge, and crowded with countless trunks, boxes, barrels, and bales of furs, all roped together and carefully stacked to keep the ship's ballast steady and to prevent shifting during heavy seas. John threaded his way aft towards the stern through the maze of goods. Ahead he could see two oil lanterns burning, a continual shifting light that cast moving shadows everywhere. Between some of the boxes were strung the rope hammocks for the eight Russian sailors.

Some of them stood in a group speaking the guttural sounds of their language punctuated with a burst of coarse laughter. There were other noises, too, water rushing alongside the hull and the scuttling sound and occasional squeak of a rat.

Need to get the baroness's cat down here, was his idle thought as he approached the Russians. The first thing he noticed was that Anton was nowhere to be seen. "Where is Lieutenant Dohktorov?" he called out.

The Russians fell silent at the sound of his voice and suddenly Andrei Leonov, who had been sitting on a trunk, stood up and said in English, "Glad you could meet me here, Mr. Hill."

John stopped abruptly. "So, what is the problem with the cargo then, Leonov? Everything looks fine to me down here."

Leonov uttered a harsh laugh, his ravaged face appearing more ghastly in the flickering light. "The problem is your unwanted attentions towards Marya Nikolayevna! You can't have her, Hill! She's mine and always has been!"

In that instant a tremendous weight bludgeoned down upon his head and everything went black. His last thought before the darkness descended was, if my enemy is in front of me, then who just hit me from behind?

* * *

Robby had lost control of Jimmy. As soon as they entered the cargo hold, the dog raced off and disappeared into the mess of trunks, boxes, and barrels. He was sniffing madly, obviously chasing something. *Probably a rat*, he decided. That was to be expected, but what he didn't expect was the commotion among the Russians aft in the stern section where they were quartered far from the American crew in the bow. He was some distance away when he saw a man strike Mr. Hill on the head with a wooden club, then Mr. Hill collapsed.

Swift anger seized him and Robby ran as fast as his long lanky legs could carry him, until he smashed into the man who had hit Mr. Hill.

"Oomph!" the man cried out as they both sprawled onto the floor. The Russians began to jabber excitedly at the sight. Robby jumped on the man's back, pinning him down face first.

"*Nyet*, *Nyet*," the Russian yelled, then twisted and heaved as he tried to throw Robby off.

"You bloody Russkie!" Robby shouted furiously and grabbed the sailor's head and began to slam his face over and over again into the hard oak planks of the floor. Blood spurted from the Russian's nose and mouth and he choked, sputtering with rage and pain.

"Halt, boy, I say, halt!" ordered Andrei Leonov in English.

Strong hands grabbed Robby's shoulders and tried to pull him off the Russian, but he refused to release his grip on the sailor's head. Suddenly

Leonov kicked Robby on his right ear with the sharp toe of his boot. The unexpected blow caused Robby to fly off the Russian's back, and deposited him on the floor next to Mr. Hill.

Agonizing pain blasted into his ear and Robby almost fainted as dizziness swept over him. Somehow he heard a deep throated growl and Jimmy flew by him, coming to his master's rescue. The dog took a mighty bound and pounced on Andrei Leonov, knocking him off his feet. Leonov fell backwards with the snarling dog trying to bite his throat.

"Get it off me! Get it off me!" he shrieked, his hands grabbing at the dog's head in a vain attempt to stop the attack.

The Russian sailors seemed frozen as they watched the scene before them with fascination. It wasn't every day they got to see the arrogant *Creole* fighting a mere puppy with his bare hands. Some of them snickered and finally Vladimir Smirnoff, his face dripping with blood, pulled a knife out of his boot.

Robby saw the knife flash and cried, "No!" as he forced himself upright, frantic with fear for his dog.

Smirnoff hesitated and at that moment Lieutenant Dohktorov arrived, not believing what he was seeing, especially the sight of John Hill lying unconscious on the floor.

"Call your dog, Robby," he ordered then said in Russian, "Smirnoff, put the knife away!"

Robby whistled, the sound sending another wave of pain through his right ear. "Come here, Jimmy! Good boy, come here!"

The dog suddenly let go of Leonov's coat collar. Luckily for Leonov, Jimmy's teeth did not come in contact with his throat. But all the men there knew when the dog was full grown and no longer a pup he had the makings of a fierce fighter. With a whine, he slunk over to Robby, panting heavily as saliva drooled from his mouth. Robby hugged the dog around the neck and held on to him, uttering soothing words of praise into one of his floppy ears.

"What is going on here?" Anton demanded angrily. He held a pistol and behind him stood Jake, Mr. Cartwright, Mr. Wilde, and Samuel along with two American sailors armed with muskets.

The steward immediately knelt at John's side. "Who done this?" he growled in his deep booming voice.

"He did," said Robby, pointing at Vladimir Smirnoff. "I seen him hit Mr. Hill right on the head wi' that piece of wood thar." He gestured toward a blunt three foot long stick lying near John's boots.

"Mr. Cartwright," said Anton sharply, "take Smirnoff to the brig and put him in irons."

"Not so fast, lieutenant," he protested in Russian. "It wasn't my idea to kill the Yankee officer. It was the *Creole*, Leonov here. He gave me some coins and vodka."

By this time Leonov was on his feet, trying to wipe the sticky dog saliva off his face and coat. "Nonsense," he said, "Smirnoff is lying to save his own skin. Why would I want to harm Mr. Hill?"

"Why, indeed?" Anton commented dryly. "Mr. Wilde, tie up *Monsieur* Leonov and bring him to Baron Volodin for questioning."

"How dare you!" Leonov sputtered as the big armorer grabbed him and fastened his wrists together with a piece of sturdy rope.

Anton glanced down at the boy and his dog. "Robby, help Samuel carry Mr. Hill to the salon. And have your head looked to," he added, noticing a thin red line glistening down from the boy's right ear.

Robby whistled for his dog to follow as he and the steward struggled to lift John and take him away. Anton turned to Jake. "Mr. O'Riley, please thank your men for their assistance and tell them to return to their quarters." He could feel the tension from the two American sailors, who muttered in outrage that the Russians dared attack one of their own officers.

"Come on mates," Jake ordered, "we'll let the lieutenant sort this mess out. I'm sure Mr. Hill will recover soon."

The two men grumbled under their breath and gave the Russians hostile glances, then reluctantly did as Jake commanded. Anton looked at his countrymen, shuffling their feet restlessly with sober expressions on their rough bearded faces.

"I'll be questioning the lot of you tomorrow," he said as he left to follow Jake and the others.

Halfway to the ladder he heard a soft meow from above. He glanced upward and saw Tatiana's cat sitting on top a stack of boxes, her huge slanted eyes reflecting a luminescent golden green from the distant glow of the lanterns. She stared down at him with an inscrutable expression.

"Come, kitty kitty," he called out softly, impulsively reaching up towards the cat. He liked animals, especially cats, and had spent much of the summer attempting to befriend this one. Tatiana would be pleased if he returned her pet. He imagined her gorgeous violet eyes fastened upon him in gratitude and his heart quickened in anticipation.

Otter recognized him as one of the humans she trusted, but she hesitated, trying to decide if she should go to him or ignore him as if he didn't exist. Finally, practicality won over feline pride. She was ready to exit the cargo hold. Over the course of the evening she had stalked, killed, and eaten two plump rats. Then came the smelly slavering dog who tried to turn herself, the huntress, into his own prey. Frightened, she'd hid herself in a remote corner of the hold. To her relief, when the humans began yelling the dog had given up trying to find her. Now that the dog had left, she wished to leave also. With another meow, she leaped into the man's arms.

* * *

"So, Leonov, I find you to be a very intriguing man," Dmitri said in a deceptively bland tone as his left eye twitched. "According to my sister-in-law, Marya Nikolayevna, not only were you once betrothed to her, but still hope to marry her, correct?"

Marya trembled on the sofa as Andrei Leonov, bound at the wrists and wearing a dirty torn coat, gave her a dark look from across the salon where a guard kept hold of him.

"*Mademoiselle* is full of imaginative fancy, Your Excellency," he rasped. "Don't believe any of her wild claims about me!"

Dmitri grunted with irritation. "But it does seem to be a strange coincidence that two men who were fond of her, have both come to harm recently, her newly wedded husband ambushed and killed in a forest, and now Mr. Hill. Vladimir Smirnoff claims you paid him rubles and vodka to attack Mr. Hill. What did you pay the Aleut assassin to murder my best friend, Boris?"

Leonov's swarthy face drained of color. "I am innocent of both crimes, Your Excellency! Smirnoff is lying! It's his word against mine!"

"I'll have Smirnoff's belongings searched and see what we can find. Meanwhile, Leonov, you will join your accomplice in the brig. Guard, take him away! The very sight of him disgusts me!"

After a protesting Leonov was forced out of the salon Anton said, "The Americans will be demanding you hang the two men for attempted murder of their officer, Your Excellency."

"Bah!" Dmitri growled, "I can't waste the life of two Russians because of a bloody Yankee! We'll be needing both Smirnoff and Leonov in Fort Ross. However, if I ever find proof that the ugly *Creole* was involved in Boris's murder, I'll have him lashed with the *knout*, then executed by hanging him very slowly."

As he uttered those words, a cruel smile crossed his thin lips, a smile which Dmitri aimed at Anton and Tatiana. "Earlier when I came into the salon and heard Marya speaking about Leonov, I thought the two of you looked quite cozy together. If I didn't know better, I'd think something was going on between the two of you."

"What a ridiculous thought!" Anton exclaimed as Tatiana pealed off a false sounding laugh of derision.

Marya said nothing, remembering how Anton almost told Tatiana that he was in love with her. If she hadn't interrupted them, Dmitri might have overheard from his cabin, and then there would be three men in the brig. What dangerous kind of game was Tatiana playing?

* * *

During the next few days the favorable northwest winds died. When the *Sea Rose* reached the southern end of Vancouver Island, thick fog shrouded the coast, hiding the entrance to the Strait of Juan de Fuca, the channel of water leading east into Puget Sound, another inland sea of green islands and remote mountains.

They were becalmed for several days, drifting with the tides and sea currents. Dmitri gave orders for the *Sea Rose* to shorten her sails and tack off the entrance to the Strait, which had disappeared into an impenetrable gray haze. It reminded Anna of the Doldrums, the Horse Latitudes of the tropical Atlantic, except for one major difference, the near presence of the treacherous rocky coast.

The tranquil weather was the only peaceful thing about life aboard ship since the attack on John. The crew was in a state of turmoil and thirsty to avenge the attack on their officer. It was all Sean and Jake could do to keep them in hand by reminding them that the Russians would soon be gone, and that Mr. Hill would survive. He had suffered a concussion and Wang Li said he was lucky his skull was not fractured. Besides a gigantic lump on his head, whenever John tried to sit or stand up, he suffered a blinding headache and his stomach rolled with nausea. To his chagrin, he was forced to stay in bed until his equilibrium stabilized.

Marya soon became a frequent visitor to the chart room. With the calmer seas her energy returned and she spent many an hour coaxing him back to health with hot drinks, soups, and her vivacious company. In spite of his worries about Leonov brooding below in the brig, John found his heart lifted from her lovely smiles and laughter.

"Twould take more an one bump to crack yer thick noggin," Jake teased John, while secretly he was furious at both Smirnoff and Leonov and like the crew, wished to hang both men from the yardarms until dead.

Robby was another who hated the two Russians, but especially Leonov. The blow from the supercargo's boot to his right ear had perforated his eardrum and had affected his hearing. Wang Li gave him willow bark tea to lessen the pain and said the rupture should heal itself in a few weeks.

A handful of rubles and an empty bottle of vodka were found in Smirnoff's possessions. None of it incriminated Leonov, but when John told Dmitri and Anton what Leonov had said before he was attacked, they decided the supercargo was as guilty of attempted murder as Smirnoff. Both were given a sound flogging, but not with the *knout*, and kept chained in the brig. Even so, the mood of the sullen crew was dangerous. Dmitri and Anton kept their pistols handy and were always escorted by armed guards when they were on duty.

After making certain John would completely recover, Sean's immediate concern was rounding Cape Flattery safely. The tip of the cape jutted way out to sea, with a series of towering rock pillars, called sea stacks, rising up from the water like deadly stone castles. Near the cape there was the jagged rocks of Tatoosh Island to avoid.

Dmitri was not familiar with this coast, but prided himself on his skill in navigation. When the breezes returned he told Sean to set a southerly route. The two men argued over the charts. Sean told Dmitri he plotted their course too close to shore, and Dmitri accused Sean of wasting time by wishing to sail the *Sea Rose* too far west. Because Dmitri was in command Sean had no choice but to obey his orders and instruct the helmsman to keep closer to shore. To his immense relief, they eventually passed Cape Flattery and Tatoosh Island without any mishap.

One evening in mid October the women were eating dinner together in the salon. Dmitri had ordered the Russian *kapoosta* as a change from Wang Li's tiresome American fare of beans and biscuits, but none of them had much appetite for the lukewarm stewed cabbage and fish in their bowls.

Tatiana picked at her food then rubbed a hand across her forehead. "Where is that Keeah? If she doesn't return soon with the willow bark tea my head is going to explode!"

Marya hid a smile. "Are you certain Keeah didn't go visit Mr. O'Riley again?" She had told both Anna and Tatiana about the time she suspected Keeah was in the chart room with the officer.

Tatiana's eyes snapped with disapproval. "I sincerely hope not! Keeah has no sense when it comes to him. I suppose she believes he will make an honest woman out of her someday."

Marya uttered a mocking laugh. "Believe me, men like him do not marry a native girl. I've tried to tell her, but she won't listen. The Tlingit are a stubborn people."

"Sort of like the Irish," Anna smiled, thinking of Sean and his persistent pursuit of her. Then her smile vanished. This afternoon the wind had dropped and now the ship was at a dead calm. The canvas hung limply from the rigging and in the distance everyone heard the low rumble of surf crashing onto rocks. Dmitri ordered all anchors dropped to hold the ship fast, but Anna knew that Sean was uneasy about their situation.

An hour ago he had told her the ship's position, Latitude seventeen degrees, fifty-six minutes North. That meant they were near Destruction Island, a small island with high cliffs of jagged rocks, located off the mainland just far enough to be a hazard to ships. Its name explained the fate of many an unlucky or careless ship carried onto its sharp rocky teeth. The summer before they had sailed north past the island on a sunny day, and Anna remembered how Sean had steered the *Sea Rose* well to the west to avoid it.

Unfortunately, Dmitri is not as wise of a captain as Sean, Anna thought, as the salon door opened and Keeah walked in with a steaming pot of tea.

"Oh, you're back," Anna said. "Can you keep watch over Katya while I go up on deck to for a breath of air? She's asleep in our cabin." She wondered how close they really were to Destruction Island and wanted to find out before night fell.

The maid nodded, then caught Anna's arm. "I feel something bad happen soon. I feel it in the wind. Both captains must be careful."

"Keeah, what are you talking about? There is no wind."

The Tlingit maid dropped her hand from Anna's arm and gave her a sorrowful look, then began to mutter in her native tongue.

Superstitious Indians! Anna thought with exasperation as she climbed up the main hatch to the deck. She breathed deeply of the salty brine scent of the sea and noted the air was still calm while the ocean heaved slightly under an opaque greenish gray surface. The sun had set minutes before and the sky was fading from rose pink and apricot orange to a hazy gray twilight. On the southern horizon Anna noticed a dark line. Probably a fog bank, she mused, then forgot it as she saw all the activity on deck.

Dmitri strutted from bow to stern, barking out commands right and left. Looking a bit unsteady on his feet, John was helping some of the crew in taking soundings of the water depth with long poles, while Jake O'Riley and Lieutenant Dohktorov were making crude sketches of the shoreline and landmarks. In the fading light she could barely see Destruction Island to the north, an ominous looking black island jutting abruptly out of the sea. It seemed a safe distance away.

Bundled in her cloak, Anna sought out Sean, who was standing at the helm, glancing at the sky and sea. "Why are they making those drawings?" she asked him.

"The currents here are very strong an' the shore's riddled with rocks hidden under the water."Tis low tide now and many of them are exposed so we can mark where they are. Later at high tide the rocks are covered again and become a danger."

"But it's so calm right now," she pointed out. "We can't be in any danger without wind to push the ship towards the rocks, can we?"

"The lack of wind can be almost as dangerous as the wrong wind. There're swift currents on this coast that can shove us too close to the rocks. Without the wind we can't control the ship. We're at the mercy of the tides."

"But won't the anchors keep us safe?"

"Aye, they should," he said in a concerned voice, "but many of the cables are still in poor condition. In Sitka Gregory Jones was repairing the rusty links in the chains, an' if we'd had him along, he'd have finished the job by now. We'll have to hope the cables hold if a gale blows in, always likely this time of year in these waters."

"*Madame* Campbell," said Dmitri, striding over, "is my wife still feeling poorly?"

"She will feel better after she sleeps off her headache, Your Excellency." She paused. "And the rest of us will be more relaxed after we're further away from Destruction Island."

He gave her a pompous smile. “It's nothing you and the other ladies should worry your pretty heads over. As you can see, everything is under control. As soon as the north wind returns, we’ll be sailing south again.”

"I don't like the looks of that dark bank of clouds in the south," said Sean.

Dmitri jerked his gaze in that direction. "All I see is the usual evening fog approaching, O'Connell. Why don't you make yourself useful and help Mr. Hill with the soundings? He looks slightly woozy tonight as if he's imbibed too much rum." He uttered a mocking laugh. "Save your weather forecasts for when you're in command again." still chuckling, he strolled away.

Sean frowned and looked at Anna. "Don't stay too long. 'Tis almost dark."

He left her at the rail and walked stiffly over to John. Anna watched him go with a deep pang of sympathy. How hard it must be for him, forced into a subservient role on his own ship, under the command of a man he despised. She knew he was often humiliated and frustrated, yet, she admired the humble manner in which he behaved. The Sean O'Connell she'd first met wouldn't have reacted to this situation with such grace. *He is truly a changed man*, she thought.

A splash in the water caught her attention and she leaned over the stern rail where she spied two seals, a mother and her pup. She smiled down at the glossy silver and black spotted creatures, one large and one small, with their huge dark eyes and white whiskers. For a second they both stared up at her then with a graceful flip, they submerged into the gray swells. They were as adorable as sea otters. How she hated the cruel slaughter of the fur trade even though it was the livelihood of the man she loved.

Feeling disloyal at the thought, she glanced around at the ocean and realized something was different. A small breeze was disturbing the surface, rippling the water where seconds before all had been as smooth as glass.

“Yer Excellency!” came a voice from the lookout perched up high in the crow’s nest. “There's a squall comin' from the south!”

Everyone stopped what they were doing and looked at the southern horizon where a mass of thick clouds, purple and black, boiled against the darkening sky. In the next instant, a gust of cold wind blew across the deck, making Anna's cloak billow. She shivered as a spatter of icy raindrops pelted across her face.

All the officers and crew on deck looked at Dmitri expectantly, waiting for his commands. "Hoist the anchors," he yelled, "Spread the sheets!"

"There's no time to pull the anchors and set sail!" Sean shouted, rushing over to him. "We're too close to shore! We need to hold the ship fast and hope the wind doesn't blow us onto the rocks!"

Dmitri flushed with anger. "Are you countering my orders, O'Connell?"

"He's right, Your Excellency," said Anton, coming up to them. "It's too dangerous to hoist the anchors with the wind coming from the south."

"She'll end up on the rocks for sure!" Jake bawled out.

"If the cables hold, we'll be safe where we are," John said in a firm voice.

Dmitri stared at the four men, all seasoned officers, and knew with a sinking heart that they spoke the truth. And also he had to admit that O'Connell had been right all along. He should have sailed the ship further from the coast. Because of his stubborn pride, he had made a costly blunder. Now he was afraid they were all going to suffer for it.

He squared his shoulders and said, "Men, inform the crew to stow away any loose gear and secure items below. We'll be staying put until the worst blows over."

Sean walked over to Anna. "Tell the women we're in for a gale. Make sure everything is tied down in the cabins. And Anna," he added, "it wouldn't hurt to say a few prayers."

Feeling frightened, Anna hurried below. When she reached the salon Samuel was already busy securing everything. "Dere's a storm a comin', Missy," he said with a face full of misgiving.

"Yes, Samuel, and we are too close to the rocky shore for comfort. We may be in for a long night."

Samuel grunted. "If de Cap'n was still in charge, we'd not be anywhere near de rocks! Dat Volodin don't know nothin' 'bout sailin' on dis coast!"

Marya stood by the stern windows and glanced outside fearfully. "Is that true, Anna? Are we in danger?"

Anna hesitated, then said, "I'm sure the Baron will have everything under control, but why don't you keep your sister company tonight until things calm down? I'll be staying in our cabin with Katya and as soon as I can, I'll send Keeah to you."

Marya's face was pale, but she nodded and disappeared into Tatiana's cabin just when a blast of wind hit the ship and the *Sea Rose* creaked and groaned as she pulled against her cables.

Samuel's eyes narrowed. "I don't like de sound of dat wind."

"If you are a praying man, Samuel, perhaps now is a good time to pray."

Inside their cabin Keeah was waiting for her, trying to calm a fretful Katya. Anna told her to store all their toiletries, books, shoes, and any other loose objects in the trunks and lash them securely. She obeyed quickly, her black eyes darting nervously around the room.

When she was finished, Anna said, "Go and take care of *Madame* Tatiana and *Mademoiselle* Marya. They will be needing your help if the seas get rough tonight."

Keeah left reluctantly, saying, “I had dream, Anna. I--”

“No, don’t tell me,” Anna interrupted. “I don’t wish to hear.”

After Keeah was gone, Katya began to cry hungrily. Anna bent down and picked her up and fed her the usual bedtime meal. As the baby nursed, Anna stroked her soft red-gold curls, thinking how innocent, how beautiful, how utterly helpless her child was. If anything bad happened to the ship, Anna hoped she would be able to protect her daughter.

When Katya was full, she smacked her tiny rosebud lips in contentment. Anna burped her and changed her dirty cloth, then placed the child beside her on the bunk. Her little face was turned towards Anna and she stared drowsily into Anna’s eyes, giving her a smile of trust before falling asleep. Feeling nervous, Anna kept one arm around her and prayed they would see the night through safely.

She began to doze. As sleep stole softly over her she thought she heard the familiar slap of canvas in the wind and felt the ship lift her bow to the waves. They must have found a way to bring the ship about and we are sailing safely away from the shore. In her dream she chastised herself for all her worry.

But it was the snapping sound of a cable breaking that she heard and not the sails filling with wind in the rigging. And the ship’s sudden movement meant that the *Sea Rose* was freeing herself of the anchors, one by one.

CHAPTER THIRTY THREE

"Anna, wake up! Wake up!"

The sound of Keeah's voice, sharp and full of fear, invaded Anna's dreamless sleep. Instantly she was wide awake. Katya still lay in her arms, peaceful in her own infant slumber, but not for long. The ship gave a sudden lurch and Anna and Katya both rolled across the bunk to the bulkhead as Keeah fell over on top of Anna's legs. With an effort the two girls slowly untangled themselves.

The oil lantern overhead was swinging wildly, and finally flickered out, plunging the cabin into darkness. Anna could not see Keeah or Katya. Outside the wind was screeching like a thousand outraged seagulls and Anna could hear the heavy footsteps of the crew running around on deck overhead. The ship was bucking and turning unusually hard. The worst gales she had ever experienced were around Cape Horn, but the *Sea Rose* had never twisted and shook in such a sickening manner. The ship felt as if she was fighting for her life.

Anna remembered how worried Sean had been about the overloading of the cargo, and how the ship lay so much deeper into the water than normal. Could that be a problem now, making her wallow and act sluggish, instead of her normal buoyancy?

"Where are Tatiana and Marya?" she asked. "If the ship hits the rocks, we could be trapped here. We must go up on deck."

"They wait for you in the salon," said the Tlingit maid. Moaning with fear, she helped Anna find the thickest blankets to wrap around Katya. Anna stumbled around the dark cabin, feeling for her boots and cloak and quickly putting them on. Katya was crying softly and Anna knew she wanted to be fed and comforted, but there wasn't time. A few minutes later, with her daughter clutched tightly, Anna met a frightened Marya and Tatiana in the darkened salon. All the oil lanterns had extinguished there too. Grabbing each other for support, they made their way out of the salon to the ladder to the main hatch. Anna wondered where the Russian guards had gone and didn't know how she could manage climbing up with a babe in her arms in such a storm.

As she was pondering this situation a torrent of sea water spilled down the ladder from the open hatch. The women jumped aside, but some of the cold water splashed Anna and Katya. She stirred restlessly in the blankets and began to whimper.

Sean clambered down the ladder and the four women, still holding on to each other, struggled to keep their balance on the tilting floor. He felt rather than saw them and said, “Ladies, ye must return to the salon. 'Tis not safe on deck. We're caught in a southeasterly gale. All three cables broke from the strain and our anchors are gone. We've set some sail to try an' maneuver the ship against the wind, but we've been pushed north all night."

He put one arm around Anna's shoulder and helped her make her way back into the salon with Marya, Keeah, and Tatiana following slowly and carefully. Once inside they sat down in a huddle on the floor.

Sean knelt beside them and said, “Don’t go into your cabins. stay away from the windows and the skylight."

"But how close are the rocks?" Anna asked frantically, grabbing at the sleeve of his wet oilskins, jostling Katya as she did so.

The child gave a cry of protest and Sean sounded tense as he answered, “We won't know exactly till the mornin'."

“O'Connell,” interrupted the steady voice of Lieutenant Dohktorov, “you're needed topside. All hell's breaking loose up there. None of the crew will listen to me or Volodin. They blame him for everything and are demanding you take command at once!"

"That's mutiny," Tatiana whispered.

"I'll take care of it," said Sean impatiently. "Lieutenant, stay with the women. If we hit the rocks, bring them up on deck.”

“What about my men in the brig, Leonov and Smirnoff?”

Sean hesitated then said, “If we're in danger of sinking, I’ll send Jake and some men down to release them.”

He touched his wet hand to Anna’s cheek in a loving gesture, then he was gone. Anna felt a sudden rush of hot tears, and a sense of being abandoned. She knew it was foolish and selfish of her, because his first duty was to the ship and crew, and not to her.

Tatiana whimpered in fear and clutched one of Anton's arms in his slippery wet oilskins. She had never felt so glad for a man's comforting presence. Her uncle, her husband, even her papa did not mean as much to her as Anton. It was a realization she had come to on the night he had returned her missing cat. She’d taken one look at the handsome lieutenant cradling her beloved Otter tenderly in his arms and had known instantly that she loved him.

A sharp cracking sound came from above and the ship veered sharply to starboard, gave a shudder then began to pitch and yaw in no definite rhythm like a drunken dancer.

"God help us, what was that?" Anton muttered as he kept hold of Tatiana.

They heard men shouting above the roar of the wind and seas and a few minutes later, Robby burst into the room. "Lieutenant, the foreyard cracked an' broke an' the foresail tore! We're headed fer shore and ‘tis naught we can do---”

Somehow Anton stopped himself from uttering a curse. "Calm down, Robby. I'm going to need your help taking care of the ladies here, especially if we hit the rocks."

A terrible fear seized Anna at those words and Marya and Keeah let out a high-pitched wail simultaneously. Their voices were drowned out by the heavy crashing of the seas against the hull and as each wave subsided Anna could hear the ominous roar of distant surf. Katya was startled by the women's shrieks and began adding her own to the melee. Grasping her tightly, Anna could do nothing to comfort her child. She clenched her teeth and began to pray.

It seemed like hours, but was only a short time later when the *Sea Rose* lurched violently to a stop. There was a tremendous crashing sound of splintering wood somewhere deep inside the bowels of the ship and the floor heaved wildly. Robby lost his balance and fell down as the rest tumbled forward into a heap. Katya slid out of Anna's arms and out of her blankets, and began to roll across the slanting floor. As she gave a piercing cry Anton reached out his hand and grabbed the child by her tiny muslin nightdress.

"Katya!" Anna screamed and struggled up onto her knees, wishing she could see in the dark salon.

"We've hit a rock!" Anton shouted. "Robby, help them get up to the deck! Anna, I'll bring your child! Now hurry!"

When he left her side Tatiana felt a moment of panic, then Marya grabbed her and forced her to her feet. Robby helped Anna and Keeah stand up, then the group inched their way towards the salon doorway, hanging on to each other for support. They stumbled out of the salon to the ladder. Anna gasped as icy water poured down from the open hatch and drenched her, soaking into every layer of clothing down to her skin. Her hair under her wet scarf was plastered to her face and her fingers could barely hold onto the rungs as she climbed with Keeah shoving her from behind.

When the women emerged onto the deck, they stepped into another nightmare. Men were running in different directions like a scattered herd of sheep, yelling and cursing. Dark dirty waves smacked against the port side of the ship, sending cold frothing water through the railings and across the deck. Rain pelted down from a leaden sky. It was dawning and the sickly gray light revealed their predicament in all its true horror. The ship was impaled near the bow on a tall craggy rock called a sea stack. Many more of the jagged stacks dotted the water north and south, each one encircled by a white ring of breaking surf.

Anna glanced around, expecting to see the cliffs of Destruction Island looming nearby, but the island was nowhere in sight.

So, we did clear Destruction Island after all, she thought, suppressing an urge to burst into hysterical laughter.

She looked towards shore and with surprise noticed a sandy beach a short distance away. The roar of the surf was frightening to hear and she shuddered to think that their only chance to save themselves was to try and make it through those monstrous breakers to the shore. But the thought of staying aboard the *Sea Rose* was even more terrifying. The ship shook and trembled from the force of each wave bashing against the hull. It seemed any moment the ship could break apart.

Robby made certain the women were safe together near the aft mast, which was still intact, then he went below to see to his dog. Wild-eyed sailors ran everywhere ignoring the shouts from Dmitri. He stood with three of his guards near the ruined foremast. Above them the slender wooden spar called the foreyard was shattered and the foresail hung in shreds. The deck was a tangled mass of ropes and wreckage and swirling green sea water.

Anna's boots were soon awash and the penetrating cold set her teeth to chattering. Then Sean was at her side, his face peering out from underneath the hood of his oilskins. His mouth was drawn with exhaustion, but his voice was steady as he said, “Ye must take courage, Anna. All is not lost. As soon as the seas have abated we’ll head for shore. The holds are full of water, but I don’t believe we’re in immediate danger of sinking.” He glanced at Tatiana, Marya, and Keeah with a puzzled frown. “Where’s Katya?”

“She fell out of my arms, but Lieutenant Dohktorov caught her. He said he will bring her up soon.”

A worried look passed over him. “When we abandon ship I'll tie Katya securely to me.”

The words “abandon ship” struck new terror to Anna’s heart and to the other women. Sean must have noticed for he tried to smile reassuringly. “Ye ladies need not fear. The wind's dying and at low tide we can easily reach the shore. Ye must trust God to help us.”

“Yes, Sean, I will try.” Her words sounded hollow to her ears, but he seemed satisfied and left her to see to the ship. He had said the holds were full of water. That meant the cargo of furs were ruined and all of the Volodins' possessions. She glanced at Tatiana and wondered if she realized she had lost everything to start her new life in California.

But material things could be replaced. It was their lives which were most important, and especially that of her own daughter. Anna anxiously scanned the deck, looking for the lieutenant and Katya. What was taking him so long?

Then she almost collapsed with relief when she finally saw Anton walking slowly towards them. When he reached Anna he slowly unfastened the front of his coat. “I think the child bruised her head when she rolled across the floor.”

Katya was in a makeshift cloth sling held against him by several strands of rope tied around his chest. She was crying, her tiny fists clenched as her mouth opened with wails of fright and pain. There was a small reddish lump on her forehead.

He also carried four black sealskin capes and as he handed them out he said, “Your cloaks are useless in this weather. These *kamleikas* will keep you ladies dry.” Then he carefully untied the sling and gave her child to Anna.

She smiled in gratitude. "Thank you, Lieutenant."

Tatiana threw her soggy cloak on the deck, its fine velvet material crushed and ruined. She wrinkled her nose at the sight of the strange Aleut garment, but when she fastened it over her gown she was pleasantly surprised at its smooth soft feel and the efficient manner in which the gutskin shed the rain. The bulky *kamleikas* were way too large for her and the other women, and she had to smile at the comical sight they made, like a flock of fat black crows. She glanced at Anton with undisguised admiration. *What a gallant, brave, kind man*, she thought, *to care for a child who is not his and also to care about our comfort at a time like this.*

Then her smile died as she remembered her cat. “Oh, Anton,” she said, “what about Otter? We can’t leave her to drown on the ship.”

Anton frowned, obviously perplexed. “I’m sorry, Tatiana, I forgot her, but I promise I’ll fetch the cat as soon as I see you ladies safely ashore.”

At that moment Samuel and Wang Li joined the group, the steward hoisting a bag over his shoulder and the cook carrying a covered wooden box. “We put Cat in box, Missy,” said Wang Li to Tatiana with a short bow.

“Oh!” she exclaimed in surprise, “I’m so grateful to you both. Thank you!”

Samuel said nothing, only glowered down at her, but she was too relieved to care. She was used to the big black man’s disapproval and took no notice. Then she turned and saw Dmitri walking in their direction. His normally immaculate lieutenant’s coat and pants were sodden and wrinkled. His mustache drooped with moisture and there was dark blonde stubble on his chin. Except for when he was ill, she had never seen him look so disheveled. Uncertain, she took a step forward, giving him a tentative smile.

Dmitri saw her lukewarm response and how close she stood to Anton. With a short harsh laugh he called out, “Ah, my dearest wife, so glad to see you safe! Who do I have to thank for taking such good care of you, the Lieutenant here?"

Anton flinched slightly, but answered in a cool voice, “Yes, Your Excellency. I have made certain your wife and her sister and the maids came to no harm below when the ship hit the rock."

Tatiana froze, her heart pounding so hard she was afraid everyone would hear it. Now Dmitri would go into a jealous rage and accuse her of infidelity. To her surprise he did neither. He gave an exaggerated sigh and said, “Then I thank you, Lieutenant, for being such a good, loyal friend to me and my wife.”

Anton nodded and smiled politely, not fooled for a second at Dmitri’s bland tone. He and Tatiana both could see the distrust glinting from Dmitri's steel gray eyes and knew he suspected something between them. Instinctively, she edged away from Anton and moved closer to her sister and Keeah.

Marya had never been so terrified in her life. The only good thing about the ship hitting the rock was that its crazy motion was now stopped and her queasy stomach was settling. But the sight of the pounding waves between the ship and beach and the frightful thought of having to somehow get through that monstrous surf to safety was making her dizzy.

Swaying, she closed her eyes and made the sign of the cross. Then she felt a man take hold of her arm. Her eyelids fluttered opened in surprise.

“John,” she breathed and leaned against him gratefully. "I'm so frightened."

“Be brave, Marya, I'm here to help you,” he said into her ear. “And look, the rain is lessening and the sky is brightening. Soon the sun will come out.”

“I hope so,” she tried to smile then choked as she noticed two men staring at them with scowls on their faces. Several yards away Vladimir Smirnoff and Andrei Leonov stood, their hands tied behind them and iron chains still wrapped around their ankles.

Jake waved a pistol at them. "Move it, lads, move it," he yelled, herding the two Russians away from the women. Some of the crew spat at the prisoners while others grouped nearby looking worried or frightened, each man holding his bag of belongings.

As the morning wore on, the seas began to calm and the southeast wind, which had driven them into this disaster, turned into a brisk westerly breeze. The clouds overhead were breaking up and a few rays of sun streaked down from the sky.

Dmitri and Sean were everywhere, shouting commands to the crew to gather the critical gear and provisions they would need ashore, food, weapons, tents, blankets, clothing, and any personal possessions they could not part with.

Shortly before noon, when the tide was at its ebb, Dmitri told Sean to order everyone to make for the beach. Most of the ocean bottom was exposed now, dotted with rocks, large and small, some pointed, some flat, and all covered with slippery greenish brown seaweed and sharp white barnacles. Due to the outgoing tide the heaviest surf had receded away from the ship. The walk to the shore would be through shallow water and tidal pools. Everyone would be wet, but there was no danger of drowning.

Robby hooted with laughter as Jimmy jumped into the water eagerly, swimming for shore without hesitation. The dog was the first one there, and he stood on the sand, shaking the drops of water off his fur. Robby was a close second, and he quickly tied a rope around the dog's neck, not wanting him to disappear into the nearby forest where he could be lost forever.

Katya was strapped tightly under Sean's oilskins as he and Anna made their way to shore, accompanied by John, Marya, Keeah, Dmitri, and Tatiana. Trying to ignore the cold sea water freezing her legs and feet, Tatiana clung to Dmitri's arm, conscious of Anton a short distance away, his eyes always following her.

"Do you know where we are?" Anna asked Sean.

"The gale blew us way north of our position last night. Luckily, we missed Destruction Island. Now I think we're somewhere south of the mouth of the Quillayute River. 'Tis an unlucky place to go ashore."

"Why is that?" Looking at the beach ahead, she thought it looked quite hospitable with pale fine grained sand and plenty of large logs and driftwood with which to make a fire. But then she glanced at the thick green forest standing behind the beach like an impenetrable dark wall, and a tremor ran through her.

He tightened his grip on her arm as a small wave broke and swirled around their legs, then sucked back out to sea. "This part of the coast is called the Quileute Needles, because of yonder sharp rocks like the one we hit. Some years back an East India Company ship named the *Imperial Eagle*, also ran aground near here. Her entire crew was killed by natives. We must be very careful as we head south to Gray's Harbor, about seventy miles from here."

Anna had not thought about the Indians of these shores. Last year on their voyage north, Sean had told her about the Makahs and Quileutes and how those tribes were the most feared of the coastal Indians for they hated white men. And they had never seen a white woman. Anna shivered suddenly and it had nothing to do with icy water in her boots.

She took a deep breath. "Why are we going to Gray's Harbor?"

"'Tis a common meetin' place for ships in fall along the coast here. If we're lucky, we'll be rescued by a British or American trader." Sean looked at Dmitri, who was listening intently to their conversation. "Don't ye agree, Your Excellency?"

It irked Dmitri that the Yankee captain had already thought of a rescue plan. Dmitri was determined to stay in command of all the men even if it meant taking O'Connell's knowledge and making it his own.

With reluctance, he nodded. "*Da,* I have heard of Gray's Harbor. I agree it's the best place to try and find a ship, but it seems too far for the ladies to walk."

Sean smiled grimly. "The ladies will have no choice but to walk, Your Excellency. We can follow the coastline, covering five to ten miles a day, and be there in two or three weeks."

Looking down at his wife on his arm, Dmitri snorted with disbelief, trying to imagine his beautiful, but fragile baroness hiking over a hundred versts through rough wilderness terrain.

When they reached the beach Anna was amazed at the huge piles of wiggling sea foam deposited on the sand by the stormy waves. At first glance the foam appeared a dirty brown, but then as a burst of sunshine flooded through the overcast, she saw a rainbow of colors, blue, green, purple, and rose, glistening in the bubbles.

She sat down on a large driftwood log well away from the water's edge. It once must have been a gigantic tree, for the log had an immense root system, bleached white by the sun and salt. As she took off her boots and dumped out the water, she was conscious of the lush green forest behind her, so dense she could imagine a group of Indian warriors hiding in it and watching her every movement undetected. With an effort she shook the thought away as Marya, Tatiana, and Keeah walked up to her, the hem of their gutskin capes and wet gowns coated with sand, but smiling their relief at being on stable land once again.

The first tent to be erected was for the women. Made of canvas sail and tied down with ropes, Sean ordered it situated well above the highest tidal mark. As Keeah spread some blankets on the sandy floor for them to sit on, they felt grateful to have a sheltered place to rest. Anna unstrapped Katya from her sling and the sudden movement woke the child. The lump on her forehead was still red and swollen, and her skin felt slightly hot to the touch. She fussed and whined, her mouth dripping with drool.

Sean poked his head through the tent's entrance flap and said, "Ladies, the baron has requested that ye stay inside this tent. We're posting two armed men outside to stand guard while we set up camp."

He stepped aside as Wang Li brought in the wooden box holding Otter. The cat yowled with unhappiness, but stopped when Tatiana started talking to her through the holes in the top. As Sean walked away, he wondered how in the world they were going to manage to tote a cat through the rugged wilderness all the way to Gray's Harbor. There was Jimmy the dog, too, but perhaps the puppy might help them in hunting animals later on when they needed fresh meat.

Anna settled down on a blanket and cradled Katya in her arms. At age seven months she was a plump little thing with vivid blue eyes and the most charming smile. But the child was not smiling now. Her face was flushed and wore a cranky expression.

"Keeah, does Katya seem too warm to you?"

The Tlingit girl edged over and gently pressed her hand against the baby's forehead and frowned slightly. Then she ran a finger inside

Katya's mouth, feeling the gums. "New tooth is coming. Sometimes that brings fever."

"I wish there was a doctor among us," Anna said, sighing worriedly.

"In my village the *shaman* can drive the sickness out of the baby's body," said Keeah.

"What is a *shaman*?" Anna asked.

Keeah and Marya exchanged knowing glances, and Keeah answered, "*Shamans* are powerful medicine men or sometimes a woman is one. They can heal the sick, but if they get angry, they can send curses. *Shamans* are respected and feared by everyone."

"Enough, Keeah," said Tatiana in a sharp voice. "Anna does not wish to hear of the *Kolosh* witch doctors."

Keeah frowned slightly and a stubborn look crept into her black eyes. "Then spirits will watch over Katya," she said and shrugged.

"You mean God will take care of her," Anna corrected automatically. "And we can pray to Him for Katya's healing. Do you understand, Keeah?"

She nodded agreeably, but her eyes narrowed with a crafty look and Anna knew she remained unconvinced. No matter how many years she'd spent among the Russians in New Archangel, Keeah still retained all the superstitions of her native childhood and her Tlingit tribe.

Despite her flirtations with Jake, Anna suspected if a young Tlingit warrior had ever offered her marriage she would have left Tatiana's employ for life among her people again. She did not want to be a Russian servant all her life, and Anna could not blame her. Whenever that deep sadness stole across Keeah's face, Anna felt sorry for her. Perhaps when they reached Fort Ross, Tatiana could find her a husband among the Aleuts who lived there...if they ever reached Fort Ross.

The day dragged on endlessly. Vladimir Smirnoff and Andrei Leonov were kept in their irons, complaining loudly as they were chained together inside a small tent. With Anton in charge, the rest of the Russian sailors were put to work, helping the ship's crew unload supplies from the ship and setting up more makeshift tents. More of the women's personal belongings were brought, including combs and toiletries, Tatiana's jewels, Katya's cloths and Anna's Bible.

When dusk fell Dmitri ordered fires started to dry their wet clothing and boots, but Sean and John pointed out to him that the smoke would attract any natives nearby. With irritation Dmitri reluctantly agreed.

Dinner consisted of soggy bread and cold *kapoosta* or cabbage stew. Wang Li apologized for the poor meal, but no one complained, knowing the food was important to keep up everyone's strength for the long trek ahead.

All the clouds were gone by sunset, and when the women looked out of the tent, they were amazed to see a rosy pink glow in the western sky and beyond the white frothing surf the sea was turning a beautiful turquoise blue. It was hard to believe such a fierce storm had happened, but the sight of the doomed *Sea Rose* thrust upon the rocks was a grim reality. Anna thought Sean's heart must break each time he looked at his beloved ship, knowing she would never sail again.

There was much grumbling among the crew that their bad luck might have been caused by the women on board. Nate Tyler and Jeb Drake were the most vocal. Sean noticed how they shot many an angry look at the women's tent and he felt uneasy. He had the officers' tent pitched next to the women to keep a closer watch over them and advised Dmitri to post extra guards around the entire camp.

During the night Anna kept Katya at her side. She dozed off and on, waking frequently as the baby was restless and fussy. Sometime in the wee hours of the morning Katya began to wail and when Anna touched her, she realized the child was clammy with perspiration. Her skin felt cooler, and Anna knew the fever had broken.

Tatiana, Marya, and Keeah also woke up and started talking excitedly. A few feet away through the thin canvas walls of the adjoining tent, Sean heard the women murmuring and the child's sharp cry. Immediately he jumped up, grabbed an oil lantern, and raced into the women's tent.

"Anna," Sean called out, groping around in the darkness as he lit the lantern, "how is the bairn?"

"She's much better, Sean," said Anna in a relieved voice.

The flame of the lantern flickered, shining on the sleepy, but smiling faces of all four women and glinting off the reddish gold curls of Anna's daughter, who was gurgling happily. "Thank God!" Sean said, noticing the lump on her forehead had shrunk to a slight redness.

"Our miracle babe," Anna announced, as Keeah shook her head in amazement.

"If the white man's God is so powerful He can heal Katya, "said the Tlingit girl, "then why didn't He stop the storm?"

Sean had been wondering the same thing. Although he had remained calm and in command since the ship ran aground, inside he was struggling to deal with this horrific disaster and what it meant for him personally. He had lost the ship and cargo of furs, worth a small fortune to his employer, Thomas Hill. Now it was his responsibility to see that his crew and the Russian passengers were rescued and taken to their destinations, whether Fort Ross or Boston.

The loss of his ship was a terrible blow. He loved the *Sea Rose*, knew her more intimately than anyone or anything. Watching her death throes on the rocks and the thought of never sailing her again made him sick to his stomach.

He knew the reasons for some of this disaster, the shoddy condition of the anchor cables and Volodin's errors in navigation on these dangerous shores. Still, none of these things actually caused their doom, it was the storm itself. Why did God allow that to happen?

"Sometimes there is no immediate answer to those questions," said Anna. "But I believe when bad things happen to us, like the storm, God can turn them into something positive. Right now we don't know what that could be, because our ship is gone and the future is uncertain. But we have to keep our faith and trust in God who loves us."

Unconvinced, Keeah gave Anna a sullen look and said, "I wait and see what happens."

"It's hard to have strong faith when trouble like this comes," Sean sighed and set the lantern on the sandy floor. "Here, Anna, ye can keep this lit for a few more minutes, than blow it out, aye?"

She could hear the anxiety in his voice and could tell he was worried about the lighted tent being seen by the natives. Even though Dmitri was supposedly in command, Anna knew Sean felt responsible for the safety and rescue of all of them. They had a long, difficult, and dangerous journey ahead, and she could see how it weighed on his shoulders like a heavy burden. Lines of worry and fatigue creased his face, but there was a feverish joy in his eyes as he looked at her and the babe.

"Sean, take care of yourself, too."

He smiled wistfully. "Aye, sleep well, Anna," he said and departed, feeling a sense of foreboding for the future, not only for himself, but for Anna and her child and the other women.

Tatiana and Marya shared the same blanket and after he was gone, Tatiana whispered to her sister, "Captain O'Connell doesn't seem like the same man I met on the *Sea Rose*. Has falling in love with Anna changed him that much?"

"I think it is something even deeper. Anna told me the captain has become a Christian."

"I don't believe it," Tatiana murmured. "Leopards don't change their spots. He's pretending to be religious so Anna will marry him."

Snuggled inside her blanket with Katya, Anna heard Tatiana's comments and winced. Could she be right? Could Sean have tricked her into believing he shared her faith?

No, she decided, it was just Tatiana speaking out of spite, trying to cast doubts upon Sean's love for her so she would change her mind about marrying him.

Tatiana had made it clear to Anna all summer that she was unhappy about her marrying Sean and leaving her employ as maid. There was such hostility between the two of them, all stemming from that night on the *Sea Rose* when Tatiana had deceived Sean into thinking they had made love when all he did was sleep off a drunken stupor.

Anna remembered his reaction a few weeks ago when she told him Tatiana had confessed the truth to her.

"That lying witch!" he had exploded. "Volodin had me flogged with the *knout* because of her! He believed I took advantage of her so-called innocence when she was the one who used me! The sooner we leave her and Volodin at Fort Ross, the better!" Then he had noticed the sad expression on her face. "Even after all she's done, ye still dinna want to leave her, do ye, Anna?"

"She's not as hard a person as you believe, Sean. She suffers greatly in her marriage to Dmitri and I often fear for her."

"How can that be? Everyone knows how Volodin adores his wife."

"There's a dark side to his affections for her. Sometimes he hurts her. I've seen the bruises and welts on her skin."

"If that's true," he had said grimly, "than Volodin is more of a beast than I thought. As much I distrust the baroness, I dinna condone a man beating his wife. I saw too much of that with me own da and ma. But even so, Anna, there's naught ye can do to help her. She's his wife and he can do what he likes with her."

Giving him an uneasy frown, she'd asked, "Is that how it will be between us, too, Sean?"

They'd been standing together at the rail with many of the crew around. Ignoring the whistles and rude comments, he'd smiled tenderly and held her close.

"Nay, Anna, I believe a man and his wife should be equal partners. On the day ye become my bride, I vow to always put your welfare and happiness afore mine."

Now as Anna listened to the muffled roar of the surf outside the tent, she wondered when and if that day would ever come.

* * *

The next morning dawned cloudy and cool with a light rain. Dmitri gave the instructions for the crew to organize the packs of gear and supplies to be carried on the trip to Gray's Harbor starting on the morrow at first light.

For Anna and the other women, that meant spending another long day confined in the tent with a temperamental cat and a fidgety child. For Andrei Leonov and Vladimir Smirnoff, the thought of a long trek down the coast with irons wrapped around their ankles made them both apprehensive and angry. After eating their breakfast of stale biscuits and cold beans, Leonov demanded to speak with Baron Volodin and Captain O'Connell.

Around noon after receiving the message from one of the guards, Sean met Dmitri inside the prisoners' tent. Both Smirnoff and Leonov crouched on the sandy floor, their hands and feet still bound. Glaring at Sean and Dmitri with an insolent expression, Smirnoff looked like a filthy peasant with his dark unkempt beard and greasy hair, but he said nothing and let Leonov plead their case.

The *Creole* appeared shabby and dirty and he had a wild glint in his black eyes. "Your Excellency, we implore you to release us from our chains. We promise that if you do, we will---"

"What I should do, is have both of ye flogged one hundred lashes, then left here for the natives to find while we set off tomorrow," Sean growled at them.

Fear sprang into both men's faces as Dmitri gave Sean a sardonic look. "O'Connell, even though I've agreed to your suggestions about not starting any fires, so far we've not seen a sign of one native. I've since come to doubt there are any hostile Indians in this vicinity."

"Have ye never heard of the John Meares report? Some years past Mr. Meares told of the location of a stockaded Quileute Indian village very near to here. 'Tis named Queenhithe and 'tis perched on a high perpendicular rock inside the great forest. By now 'tis certain they know of our presence on this beach."

Dmitri looked skeptical as Leonov said, "Captain O'Connell, if that is true, then you should free us from our irons, because you'll be needing every able-bodied man on this expedition to Gray's Harbor. If we are attacked by natives, we need to join together and face the enemy we both have in common on this shore, and believe me, Captain, it isn't Vladimir or me. We both have learned our lesson, and we'll not cause any more trouble."

Sean considered his words thoughtfully, then said, "Well spoken, Leonov, but if you men are released from your chains and given weapons, what's to stop ye from stabbin' Mr. Hill in the back some dark night?"

"Your Yankee crew, Captain. They hate me and Vladimir and will be watching us like hawks. We're more a feared of them than any natives out there."

"I don't trust either of ye," said Sean, "but there are more practical matters to consider right now. Once we leave on the morrow we need to move fast. Having men in leg irons will only slow us up."

Dmitri nodded. "We'll remove your irons on the morrow before our departure."

"But," said Sean, staring intently at each man, "neither one of ye will be issued a weapon, not even a knife. And if either of ye cause one bit of trouble, I'm giving orders to shoot on sight. No questions asked."

With those hard words he stepped outside the tent, Dmitri following behind him. "You don't have the authority to have those men shot, O'Connell."

Sean stopped and turned around. "You have only ten men under your command, Your Excellency, and two of those are prisoners. I have a crew of twenty plus two officers, all of whom will obey any order I give."

Dmitri scowled at him and opened his mouth to argue, but suddenly he sensed something amiss. The camp, which a moment ago, had been bustling with activity, was strangely still except for Jimmy the dog who began to growl and whine, pulling hard on the rope that tethered him to a large log. All the men had stopped what they were doing and were staring at the forest. Dmitri looked in the same direction and his gut tightened in sickly surprise.

A group of ten half-naked barefooted Indians were cautiously stalking toward the camp, each armed with a long sharply pointed spear.

At the same time Tatiana and Anna with Katya in her arms were standing outside their tent breathing in the tangy salt breezes wafting off the ocean. At the sight of the natives they both froze in disbelief.

"Marya, Keeah," Tatiana hissed, "Indians!"

The two women immediately peeked out the entrance and both sucked in their breaths. Keeah said something to Marya who called out softly, "Tatiana, Anna, you both must come inside. Keeah says it is dangerous for the natives to see you. They will be attracted by your light colored hair."

"My scarf is covering most of my hair," she said irritably. "And I'm tired of being in that musty smelly old tent."

Anna gave her a worried glance as she and Katya ducked inside the tent. "Please, *Madame*, it is folly to tempt the Indians. Perhaps we outnumber them at the moment, but this is their land and they are everywhere in the forest."

"I'll be right there, Anna," Tatiana said, but found she couldn't move. She was fascinated by the drama unfolding before her. Nate Tyler and Jeb Drake wanted to shoot the Indians and Captain O'Connell and his officers were ordering them to hold their fire. She saw Anton standing with them, gesturing to the Russian sailors to stay quiet as well. She felt a rush of admiration for him then she saw Dmitri standing by the prisoner's tent. He saw her, too, and motioned to her to hide herself.

Tatiana lifted her chin defiantly and turned her gaze from him and looked at the Indians. Except for the sharp spears they carried, they didn't appear hostile. When they came closer to the camp, she could see their eyes darting around as they examined everything and everyone.

"They are Quileutes," she heard the captain say to John. "Can you understand their language enough to speak with the chief?"

"The Quileutes speak Salishan which is a different language than what I learned from the Nootkas. However, there are some similarities between the two and I'll try to communicate with them."

The captain smiled in relief, as the chief stepped forward. He was of medium height, his hair and eyes were inky black, his nose was straight and he had a broad forehead. He appeared to be near thirty years old, and Tatiana would have thought him a noble-looking savage, except for the wide purple-red scar that ran from his right eye across his cheek to the corner of his mouth. It gave him a sinister and cruel look.

John held his hand up in greeting and the chief did the same. "Hoheeshata," said the Indian in a deep voice.

It was his name, and after John spoke his own name they began to converse. Hoheeshata uttered a series of explosive sounds that he pronounced with a forceful click. At first John had trouble following his words, but soon he came to an understanding. Using hand signs and gestures, he explained that Dmitri and Sean were the two men in command.

Watching nervously, Dmitri, Anton, Sean, and Jake stood in a group next to John. He finally turned to them and said, “The chief, Hoheeshata, welcomes us to his shores. He insists that his men are friendly and are only curious about us. He would like the permission of our yellow haired chief and our green eyed chief for them to visit the camp.”

All four men exchanged glances of dismay, then Dmitri said, “And if we refuse?”

Keeping his voice calm and his expression polite, John said, “I would advise allowing them to satisfy their curiosity. It may give us more time in which to prepare for our journey without worrying about the Indians.”

"Perhaps we should agree," said Sean to Dmitri.

As Dmitri reluctantly nodded his head, Hoheeshata spoke again. John listened intently, then frowned and glanced at Tatiana standing several yards away. “The chief also states that he would like to get a closer look at the goddess from the sea with her white skin, eyes the color of the hyacinth and hair of the moon and sun.”

Dmitri flushed with annoyance. "Tell him that she is my wife and not for him to see."

“Tatiana,” Marya whispered from the tent’s entrance, “will you come inside now?”

Tatiana suddenly felt the gaze of every man on her, especially the chief who was staring at her boldly with what seemed to her a malignant gleam in his black eyes. She quickly backed into the tent, her pulse racing with a mixture of fear and excitement and sat down on a blanket. “You were right, Marya,” she said in a voice full of dread. “I shouldn’t have let them see me.”

Keeah peered outside, her face full of interest as she studied Hoheeshata. He was a chief and he exuded an aurora of power that she found irresistible.

“Keeah, close the tent!” Tatiana ordered.

She ignored her mistress and instead, said excitedly, “Look! Quileute chief gives sign and many more come now.”

This time all four women looked out. It was true. The dark interior of the heavily wooded forest was coming alive. From behind every tree an Indian stepped out. Their camp was being invaded.

The women were appalled to see the Indians suddenly swarming everywhere, pawing over the goods, breaking open boxes, looking for food, trinkets, blankets, and tools, anything they could find that looked interesting. The crew became agitated as some of the Indians began to dump onto the sand the few precious goods they had saved from the *Sea Rose*.

Muttering angrily, the Americans and Russians alike were showing signs of losing their patience, if not their tempers. Dmitri, Sean, Jake, and Anton watched the chaos with their muskets loaded, primed, and ready to fire.

John stood next to Hoheeshata and kept trying to communicate with him. The chief appeared to listen, his proud face impassive to the circus around him. Then he spied Samuel and interest flickered in his eyes. Samuel stared back at him, his black face registering almost the same haughty expression as the Quileute chief's. The two men gazed at each other until Hoheeshata said something to John.

John looked at Samuel. "The chief said he would like to touch your skin, to see if the darkness comes off."

Before Samuel could reply, a fight broke out. The Indians had started to drag some of the boxes and barrels off into the woods. Cursing angrily, Mr. Wilde, the burly armorer, punched the Indian nearest to him. Seconds later another man did likewise, and the camp quickly turned into mayhem. Spears and rocks began flying overhead.

Hoheeshata knocked John to the ground and ran off toward the forest. Then a sharp stone smacked into Dmitri's cheek, slicing it open. Enraged, he immediately shouted an oath and fired off his musket.

Inside the tent the women huddled together, Marya and Keeah sniffling with fear. Tatiana had an angry gleam in her eyes as she listened to the shouts and cries of the men. Her fear was more for Anton than anyone else. Anna clutched Katya protectively and her mouth moved silently in prayer for God's deliverance from the Quileutes.

More guns began to fire, invoking dreadful shrieks from the Indians as the bullets found their marks. Then as soon as it had started, it was over. Except for Jimmy's frantic barking, the camp was quiet; all the Indians had fled to the forest.

The women emerged from the tent to find three dead Indians in a bloody heap on the sand, and a number of slightly injured men with mainly bumps and bruises and cuts.

Dmitri immediately stumbled over to Tatiana, his cheek bleeding. "Tatiana," he called out, "you should not have allowed that savage to see you!"

"I'm sorry, Dmitri, it was a mistake," she said then exclaimed, "your cheek is cut!" She made a show of wifely concern by taking the corner of her scarf and trying to wipe the blood off his cheek.

He accepted her ministrations with pleasure, fighting the urge to sweep her off her feet and carry her to one of the tents. How dare that savage covet my beautiful wife! He fumed angrily.

"Good job, men," Jake O'Riley suddenly shouted, rubbing the top of his head where a rock had glanced off, giving him a lump. "We've won our first battle with the Injuns!"

"Ye can save the victory speech, O'Riley," said John Hill loudly. "The Quileutes will never forgive us for killing three of them. They'll be back any time to take revenge. They've declared war on us and they'll not rest 'till every one of us is dead or captured."

His ominous words hung gloomily over the camp. Jake frowned, his mood of jubilation clearly deflated. He and the other officers soon began to bark out orders for the men to tidy and reorganize the camp, attend to the injured, and make ready for the coming night.

Anna walked over to Sean who was telling Wang Li to start a fire to cook their dinner. Now that the natives knew they were here, there was no reason not to have the warmth of a big driftwood bonfire.

"Oh, Sean," she said, "I am so thankful you were not harmed."

"I'm thankful ye had enough sense to stay in the tent, Anna. Whatever possessed *Madame* Volodin to flaunt herself so?"

"As a baroness, she's used to giving orders, not taking them. She didn't realize the danger at first, but now she knows better."

Sean tensed. "She's not safe yet. John told me Hoheeshata's last words to him before he fled was that he was coming back for her."

CHAPTER THIRTY FOUR

Anna spent her second night on the beach, tossing restlessly, unable to get Sean's words out of her head. Under normal circumstances, she would have enjoyed the novelty of sleeping in a tent just yards away from the ocean's edge, the constant thunder of the surf soothing her into a peaceful slumber. Before going to bed, she had glanced up at the stars, twinkling across the night sky in their brilliant diamond studded constellations. There was no moon, but the waves glittered with a strange florescent light as they broke onto the dark sand. While Anna was awestruck by the eerily beautiful scene, she was also afraid of its raw untamed nature. It reminded her too much of the wild Indians lurking nearby.

If she slept at all it was to dream of Katya being taken away from her by the Indians. Towards dawn, she awoke to find Katya sleeping soundly, her sweet little face just inches from her nose, sucking on her thumb. Relief mingled with a nagging worry about the day ahead and the days after. Then she remembered the men with their guns, and that the natives didn't have anything but the crude weapons of spears and rocks.

They would be safe, she thought and almost laughed at herself. What would her papa and brothers say if they knew she was glad to be surrounded by men with guns? They would think her a Mennonite of poor faith, if a Mennonite at all. The thought gave her pause. Was she a Mennonite anymore? Without being a part of the church and the community, had she lost her roots, her family heritage?

She had no answer to that, and as she listened to the stirrings of the camp around her, she could only be thankful they made it through the night without another Indian attack.

There was much to do before they could begin their journey to Gray's Harbor. All the heavy equipment from the *Sea Rose*, such as the cannons, had to be thrown into the sea. They had to destroy everything from the ship that the Indians could use as a weapon against them.

As for the mortally wounded ship herself, the sea was taking her apart slowly, the large ocean breakers splintering her in two sections, then demolishing the wooden beams and hull piece by piece. Soon the *Sea Rose* would no longer be a ship, but a wreck. For Sean and Anna and the crew who loved her, it was a gut wrenching sight.

Except for Andrei Leonov and Vladimir Smirnoff, Sean issued each man two muskets and a pistol. Slings were made to carry kegs of gunpowder, bags of shot, axes and other tools, provisions, trade goods, and their most valuable personal possessions. Dmitri ordered the two prisoners to carry extra heavy loads. Besides a large sling full of provision Leonov had to carry the box with Tatiana's cat inside, a chore he found extremely distasteful, and he and Smirnoff were assigned to walk with Anton who promised to keep a watchful eye on them.

And so they set out that afternoon. Leading the group was Jake O'Riley with ten armed crewmen, and Robby and the dog, which was wildly sniffing everything in sight. John, Sean and Anna, with Katya nestled warmly underneath her parka in a sling, followed them. Next were Anton, Dmitri, Tatiana, Marya, and Keeah. The Russian seamen with Wang Li, Samuel, and the rest of the armed crewmen were in the rear. All in all they were a company of thirty-nine souls, plus one dog and one cat.

The wind was blowing a chilly fog from the north and it was damp and penetrating to the bone. They were dressed in their warmest clothing, and some wore *kamleikas* and sealskin *mukluks*, the favored footwear of the Aleuts, which were more practical than boots for hiking along the coast. Anna took one last glance at the beach, now gray and bleak-looking with its stacks of sharp rocks standing offshore, and the forlorn wreck of the once lovely *Sea Rose*. Then the fractured outlines of the ship disappeared into the mist.

The tide was ebbing and the wet sand was hard and firm under their boots. The beach was littered with broken seashells, but some were whole, flat and round and white with a pattern of a starfish etched on top which Sean called sand dollars. There were large and small clam shells of different varieties, and an occasional carcass of a crab, picked clean by the ever present seagulls.

At first the mood was light and there was quite a bit of cheerful talking and singing among the men. It was not long until the wide expanse of flat sandy beach ended abruptly against a steep rocky headland that jutted out into the sea. Luckily, the tide was low enough so they could walk around the point, but the going was treacherous on the slick rocks covered with seaweed and sharp barnacles. More than one person slipped, sometimes spilling precious supplies out of their sling.

Dmitri had refused the *mukluks* and insisted on wearing his fancy Hessian boots, impractical as they were. Eventually he caught a boot heel between two rocks and twisted his ankle. He stumbled against Leonov who dropped the box with Otter inside. The box landed on a rock and slid sideways down to another flatter rock. The cat let out a terrible yowl, seconded by Tatiana's screech of horror.

"Dmitri, you must be more careful!"

Anton, who was several yards ahead of them, stopped and turned around. "Would you rather I carried Otter, Baroness? *Monsieur* Leonov might have weak arms and legs after being in irons for a week."

Dmitri cursed softly then picked up the box with the hissing cat. "I'll carry your cat, darling," he said to Tatiana.

He gave Anton a dirty look, wondering why the lieutenant seemed to be as concerned as his wife over the wretched cat. He resented the protective manner in which Dohktorov appeared to behave towards Tatiana. Warning bells went off in Dmitri's head. Perhaps it was time he stopped being jealous of Captain O'Connell and his past relationship with his wife, but focused on a new and more dangerous threat, that of Lieutenant Dohktorov.

Ahead of them, Anna made her way carefully over the rocks. She was amazed at the purple and orange starfish and the brilliant green sea anemones living in the tidal pools. Here and there she also spied a pretty stone among the dull ones, a translucent agate shining like a gem, or a piece of golden amber. These she placed in her pocket.

Truly, she thought, *this coast is as wondrously beautiful as it is deadly.*

When they rounded the headland, they reached a pebble and sand beach which continued for several miles, then ended at another rocky promontory, also too steep to climb. Dmitri and Sean called a halt to consider the problem.

"I'm afraid the entire coastline is a series of beaches and headlands," Sean said, remembering all the voyages he'd made in the past.

Dmitri cast a searching glance at the forest of towering cedars and firs. "I wonder if an easier path might lie in there."

"It's too easy for the Indians to ambush us in the dense growth of the forest," said John. "I would advise against it."

"Normally, I'd agree with you, but we need to round that point," said Sean, pointing at the steep headland surrounded by crashing waves from the incoming tide.

"Now the tide won't be low enough 'til after midnight, and by then, 'tis too dark to see safely. We're losing precious time having to wait on the tides. I say, come the mornin,' we head for the forest."

John tightened his mouth with disapproval, but said nothing more, as they made camp for the night on the beach. They set up several tents away from the high tide mark, but it meant they were closer to the forest. As a precaution, hoping the Indians were not aware of their presence on this beach, Sean forbade any fires and he posted guards to watch in shifts during the night.

Inside the women's tent, Tatiana let Otter out from her cramped quarters. The cat was happy to have some room to stretch and run around, and also was delighted to use the sandy floor to relieve herself. She seemed none the worse for her spill earlier.

"Make sure no one opens the tent when Otter is out of her box," Tatiana warned. "If she gets outside, I'll lose her for sure."

"I don't think your husband would mind if that happened," said Marya with a laugh as she brushed sand out of her black hair. The wind blew sand into everything, hair, eyes, nose, mouth, and clothing. Thankfully, the wind had dropped by nightfall, and it was warm inside the tent with the four women.

"He would be overjoyed if she disappeared," Tatiana said, rubbing her aching feet. She was not used to hours of walking and her back and neck were sore from toting a small bag over her shoulders with her most valuable items, her prettiest combs and precious jewelry. Keeah carried her clothing, extra petticoats and chemises, stockings and scarves, two gowns, one of muslin and one of silk, and a pair of slippers. She wanted to look her best when they were rescued, as a Russian baroness should.

Dmitri was livid about the loss of their furniture, luggage, furs, and especially, several thousand rubles in gold coins he'd stashed in a metal box in their cabin. When he'd returned to fetch it before the ship broke apart, there were gaping holes in the bulkhead and water was sloshing back and forth throughout the cabin. The box was nowhere to be seen. Only a few of Captain O'Connell's books were floating around, their leather bindings and pages ruined forever. At least he'd managed to stuff some of her jewelry in his pockets, so they weren't totally destitute.

"This entire debacle is the fault of O'Connell," Dmitri had muttered to her earlier that day as they walked together. "He allowed the condition of the ship's cables to deteriorate to such an extent they couldn't hold the ship in the storm. If only we still had the *Buldakov*, we never would have run aground. He is the most incompetent man I've ever seen as a ship's captain!"

"The storm came out of nowhere," Anton had replied. "That was hardly the man's fault."

"A good ship's captain is prepared for anything," Dmitri had snapped, "especially storms. All I can say, he better know what he's doing, or none of us are going to make it to Gray's Harbor alive, much less rescued by any ship!"

Tatiana gasped, causing Anton to give Dmitri a stern frown. "Perhaps you should keep your opinions to yourself, Your Excellency. You are frightening your wife."

Dmitri glared back at Anton, then said to her, "My apologies, Tatiana, I'm certain we will all be rescued in due time."

But she hadn't believed him then, and she didn't believe it now. The thought of walking for two weeks or more on this rough terrain made her wince. She was so exhausted after only one day. How was she going to endure it? And then there were the savages...

Marya was thinking along the same lines as Tatiana, but she had more experience than her half-sister in physical hardship, and it wasn't the difficult hiking that bothered her, but the hostility of the natives. John kept trying to assure her that their spears and rocks were no match for their guns, but she remained unconvinced. As an Aleut, Marya understood how the mind of a native worked, and she was afraid the

Quileutes were plotting some trickery against the white men as an act of vengeance.

And now the captain said they were heading into the forest in the morning. She and John both knew it was risky and dangerous. Her stomach clenched whenever she thought of the dark woods with its deceptive beauty. Marya imagined a Quileute lurking behind each tree and she much preferred the open spaces of the beaches, no matter how hard the way.

Only Keeah appeared unperturbed about their situation. Her face was set in her usual stoic expression as she busily saw to the women's needs, bringing them their cold supper of salted cod and hard biscuits from Wang Li, and helping Anna with the babe.

"I have no way to wash her soiled cloths," Anna complained after cleaning Katya's bottom. "I'm afraid she's going to get a bad rash."

"My people use moss," said Keeah. "It is soft and clean and we throw it away when dirty." She gestured with her chin to the east. "The forest is full of moss."

"And most likely, Quileutes," said Anna, dismissing the idea at first. Then she noticed the irritated redness on Katya's delicate skin and sighed. "Tomorrow when we go through the woods, can you gather some moss on the way, Keeah?"

She nodded and smiled as she tossed Otter some tidbits of fish. The cat ate the pieces then daintily washed her face, purring contentedly.

"Quileutes never see a cat so small, only cougars and mountain lions. Otter worth much as gift or trade."

Tatiana looked appalled. "I'd never part with Otter for any reason, nor allow the savages here to have her."

"I suppose there are wolves and bears, too," said Anna, thinking that the natives weren't the only wild creatures in the forest.

Suddenly the women fell quiet as a man's voice right outside the tent declared belligerently, "I say we give them Injuns the Russkie woman! She's the one they want an' if they have her, they'll let us be!"

"Aye, she's bad luck, that's fer sure," agreed another man. "Why else did that storm hit us in the midst of a calm? She's brung us bad luck!"

"Enough of that daft talk, Drake, Tyler!" Jake O'Riley roared. "An' git yer arses outta here afore the Cap'n or the Baron sees ye hangin' around the ladies tent!"

The men left in a huff, grumbling loudly, as Jake stuck his head inside the tent. "Beggin' yer pardon, Baroness, 'bout those dumb lads shootin' their big mouths off."

"Is that how most of the crew feel about me?" Tatiana asked, her large violet eyes full of apprehension.

Jake looked uncomfortable then saw the cat edging towards the entrance. He avoided her question and warned, "Ye better fetch yer cat afore it gets away."

Keeah snatched the cat around the stomach and put her back into the box on top a woolen blanket. She shot Jake a slight smile.

"Keeah," he said, his freckled face flushing, "Would ye fancy a walk later?"

She looked at Tatiana with a questioning expression. "No, Keeah, it's not safe out there," said Tatiana, staring at Jake with distaste.

"I'll look after the lass, Baroness, don't ye worry," Jake grinned, "an' have her back here afore ye know it."

"Not tonight, Mr. O'Riley," she said, refusing him the second time.

His grin faded and he pretended not to care by shrugging his shoulders and saying in a careless tone, "G'night to ye ladies then."

After he returned to his guard duty Tatiana said, "So, he's still sweet on you, is he, Keeah? You two haven't done anything er, intimate by now, have you?"

Keeah hung her head and refused to meet her eyes. "No man of my people want me for wife, only Jake."

"Mr. O'Riley isn't the marrying sort either," said Tatiana bluntly. "Besides, the way those men were talking about us women being bad luck, it isn't safe out there for any of us."

Especially not for Tatiana, Anna thought later as she bedded down on a blanket with Katya. The crewmen said she had brought them bad luck, and the Quileutes thought she was a goddess. But that was Tatiana, people either loved her or they hated her.

As she drifted off to sleep, Anna felt thankful that she was just an ordinary woman.

* * *

Soon after sunrise Sean announced he had found a very narrow path leading from the beach into the forest. "'Tis most likely an animal path, but we can walk single file," he said.

More fog and drizzle had rolled in overnight and the forest was shrouded in a mist so thick Anna could not see the treetops. Each branch dripped with the heavy moisture and the mossy ground squished underneath her *mukluks* as she and the other women walked in the middle of the line, protected front and rear by armed men. The roar of the ocean was quickly muffled behind them and soon she could hear it no more.

The silent forest awed all of them. She had thought the forests of New Archangel had big trees, but nothing prepared her for the ancient sentinels of the Olympic rain forest, the gigantic red cedars, hemlocks, and spruce trees. Some fallen trees, now logs lying on the ground, were as tall as houses. Huge brown mushrooms and orange fungus sprouted everywhere and the pungent odor of moist decay and soil filled her nose with each breath. Shallow creeks crossed their paths frequently, the cold running water refreshing to drink when anyone was thirsty.

Keeah was delighted, feeling at home as she never could onboard ship or in the confines of the white man's buildings. The forest was her native habitat and she recognized many familiar plants. As she strolled along under her heavy pack, she collected moss which grew green and thick on every log and hung down from every branch. Looking up, instead of blue sky, she saw only a never-ending canopy of moss.

The rest of the group was nervous and nobody spoke, unless in whispers. Dmitri sent several men up ahead as scouts, including John. The animal path soon ended and they were forced to hack their way through the dense undergrowth. It was slow and difficult going as the bushes and prickly berry vines scratched their hands and faces and they tripped constantly over tree roots half hidden in the ground. After a couple hours the men in front suddenly halted, calling back that their way was blocked by several Quileutes.

This what they'd all feared, and Sean, Jake, Dmitri and Anton hurried forward where John was engaged in a conversation with three Indians. The natives were smiling and gesturing to the south.

"They want to show us a path through the forest," said John.

"Do you trust them?" Sean asked, a doubtful look on his face.

"No."

The Quileutes kept smiling and motioning with their hands, then began to walk in the direction they had indicated.

Dmitri hesitated only for a few seconds. "They appear friendly enough. I say we follow their lead. By now we're all weary of this hard struggle through the thick forest."

Sean nodded his agreement, but John looked uneasy. "They could be leading us into an ambush."

Thinking quickly, Sean scratched the rough dark stubble on his chin. "Aye, they could, an' then again, not. We'll chance it for now." He turned and said in a loud voice, "Carry on then, men. Keep a tight hold of your muskets, but fire them only as a last resort. We need to save our ammunition."

Marya reached out and squeezed Anna's hand nervously and said, "I don't like this. I wish we could return to the beach."

"I believe we'd be safer there, too, but there's naught I can do about it," she sighed, noticing how most of the men appeared worried and some were grumbling under their breath.

"We should turn around," Leonov said behind her, "before those savages attack us."

"*Da*! *Da*!" agreed all the Russians.

Keeah, who was walking with Tatiana, glanced at all of them with scorn in her eyes, then without saying a word, lifted her head bravely and marched forward. It shamed the big burly Russian sailors, and they soon followed, along with Leonov, who had no choice.

Soon they came to a well marked path and their Quileutes guides melted away into the lush undergrowth of the towering trees. Anna had to admit that following this wide trail was much easier than shoving their way through the forest, but she could not shake off a feeling of anxiety.

After continuing this way for what seemed like several miles the mist began to dissipate. Sunshine entered the top of the forest, yet the trees were so immensely tall, the sunbeams could not penetrate to the emerald world below. Once they came to a small clearing where the sun slanted golden sheets of light to the ground, and it was so bright, it dazzled her eyes. But mostly, she had to crane her neck backwards and look straight up through the heavy green branches of the trees to see any sunshine at all.

Their group was making so much noise crashing through the forest, that all the animals, from the predators such as bears, coyotes, and cougars to the deer, rabbits, squirrels, were aware of their presence, and fled or hid themselves. If they were a hunting party, they never would've found one animal to kill. The clumsy white men did not have the ability to move silently with the stealth of the natives.

Thus, the only wild creatures Anna saw were the ones on the ground, a variety of insects or a slow moving slug, which was a fat snail without a shell. The slugs were ugly and glistened with slime. Once Tatiana slipped on one and almost fell. After that all the women tried to avoid stepping on them, but the slugs were not easy to see, their colors of brown, black, or spotted greenish yellow, blended with the leaves and soil of the forest floor.

It was while she was watching carefully where to place her feet on the trail, she heard a rock whistle by her head and thud against a nearby tree trunk. Startled, she stopped abruptly and Marya bumped into her back. Tatiana gave a short cry as a spear flew out of the ferns and crashed down a short distance away, narrowly missing Dmitri.

Sean and the men up ahead began to shout as more stones and spears were thrown. At the rear of the column, Jimmy started to bark frantically and lunged at the bushes. Robby had to keep a tight hold of the dog's rope to keep him under control. Dmitri took one frightened glance around and dived to the ground, somehow keeping hold of the box with Otter. He yelled at Tatiana and the other women to duck for cover.

All the men readied their muskets, including Samuel and Wang Li, but the Indians were too well hidden to form any targets for them to aim at and shoot. When no one was hit by the missiles being tossed, it soon became apparent that the Indians were missing their marks on purpose. They could hear the natives convulsing with occasional bouts of laughter as they amused themselves with taunting the white men.

Sean, followed by Jake, John and the scouts, sprinted back down the trail. "Retreat, men!" he called out. "Back to the shore!"

He grabbed Anna's arm and said, "Come, we must hurry! At any moment the Quileutes might get tired of playin' games with us and start aiming their weapons for real. John was right. We should've stayed on the beach no matter how slow or rough the way."

As soon as they all turned around, the shower of rocks and spears halted. During the next couple hours they rushed back through the forest the same way they had come. It was with great relief and utter exhaustion when they finally exited the woods and saw the ocean again. That evening they made camp on the same beach as the night before with extra guards posted all around.

Everyone knew they had not seen the last of the natives.

* * *

"The Hoh River," said Sean, staring at the rushing torrent of water with dismay, "which to the Quileutes means, 'fast moving water.' How right they are."

One week had passed since the shipwreck. During that time they'd stayed well away from the forest and kept marching along the shore, always in constant fear of attack. Anna, Tatiana, and Marya grew wearier with the brief snatches of sleep at night and the demanding physical activity they were not used to. Their nerves were stretched almost to the breaking point and at times, Anna wished she could find a rock to crawl under and sleep undisturbed for twenty-four hours.

Only Katya and Keeah seemed to thrive. The infant was lulled contentedly by the constant roar of the sea and the warm closeness of her mother, and the comfort of the soft, absorbent moss on her skin. Keeah was like a pack mule, her wide shouldered body and sturdy legs carrying herself and her large bundle effortlessly across either rocks or sand.

The weather was different from morning to afternoon to evening, changing from fog to sun, to drizzle, to rain, sometimes very windy, sometimes calm.

Sean tried to joke, saying, "If ye don't like the weather here, wait fifteen minutes, and it'll change."

But he was not laughing now. His black bearded face held a grim expression and his eyes looked bleak as he considered how they were going to cross the mouth of the Hoh River, which was swollen with the fall rains almost to flood stage.

"We need some of those canoes from the natives over there," Dmitri pointed out.

On the opposite bank of the river was a village of large huts with many cedar dugout canoes secured on the shore, some of them quite long. There were also about two hundred Indians standing about, staring across the river back at them.

Sean looked at the Indians then glanced at Anna. She could see a deep uneasiness in his eyes that bordered on fear. She knew he was afraid of losing her. Frequently the past week she had found his attention fixed on her instead of his men. Whatever she seemed to be doing, hiking along the beach, sitting around a campfire eating, washing her hands in a cold clear stream, or resting exhaustedly on a driftwood log, she would lift her eyes and see him staring at her with a hungry burning desire in his green eyes, the color of the rain forests. Such a look from him set her heart racing and weakened her already tired knees to pudding.

On the other hand, Tatiana was relieved she couldn't spend any time alone with her husband. Dmitri had always prided himself on his immaculate uniform complete with shining buttons and braids, boots polished to a glossy ebony sheen, and a tall cap with the gleaming Imperial Eagle on his head. Now his uniform was torn and filthy with missing or rusted buttons, his cap discarded, and his boots caked brown with mud. Without the benefits of regular bathing, his close cropped blonde hair had darkened in color with excess oil, the skin across his increasingly hollow cheeks was blotchy and his mustache was matted. With his newly roughened beard, he looked more like an unkempt peasant than a lieutenant in the Imperial Russian Navy.

Gone was the swaggering arrogance of the aristocratic baron. Increasingly, Dmitri radiated a frantic insecurity as if taking him out of the precise naval environment which he was used to left him floundering confusedly on these alien shores. The Russian sailors had long since turned to Anton as their true leader.

Lieutenant Dohktorov seemed to be the type of man who flourished under rough conditions. There was a new strength and maturity in his freshly bearded face, giving him a rugged handsomeness that his dirty rumpled clothing could not take away. Tatiana found herself covertly watching him, admiring the calm assurance in his gold flecked brown eyes.

As if sensing her gaze upon him, Anton glanced at her. She had grown thinner, as had all the women and her delicate skin was stretched taut over her high cheekbones, giving her a haunting loveliness that brought an ache to his throat. How he loved her, but she was as forbidden and unreachable to him as if she was a Grand Duchess, a daughter of his Imperial Majesty, the Czar himself.

He forced himself to look away from her, turning his attention to the crisis at hand. This time he had to admit Dmitri was right about the canoes. "There is no other way to cross the river, Captain," he told Sean, who reluctantly agreed.

Using gestures and a few shouted words from John, they eventually communicated their need for the canoes to the Quileutes. The Indians appeared to be discussing it among themselves, and after a time, they finally brought two canoes across the river. Both were painted red and were highly decorated with elongated bows ending in a sharp point a few feet above the water line which served to break the surf in landing on a beach, or to slice through a wave on a rough sea.

The largest canoe was paddled by two Indians and was big enough to carry ten people, and the smaller one could take five passengers plus the lone Indian paddler. It would take several trips to get everyone and all their provisions and baggage across, but Sean thought that was just as well. He didn't want them all to be on the river at the same time.

Anton and Jake went with the first boatload, encouraging the reluctant men that they would all be safe enough in a few minutes.

As they watched the canoes being expertly guided through the roaring river by the strong muscular arms of the natives, John said, "I have a bad feeling about this. If any of these Indians are from the band that we attacked a few days ago, they will be plotting for revenge."

"Dmitri," said Tatiana worriedly, "I don't like the idea of stepping into one of those canoes at the mercy of the Indians."

Dmitri sighed with exasperation. "My love, you will not be at the mercy of the natives. Our muskets are fully loaded and if the savages try anything we can shoot them."

"But they outnumber us," she pointed out.

Sean glanced down at his musket, thinking that wasn't the only problem. It had been raining all day, and he was afraid the firing mechanism of his gun and all the others might be too wet to spark shots if they needed to fire them.

Dmitri ran his fingers lightly across her cheek. "Don't worry, Tatiana, we will protect you."

The Indians slid the canoes stern first onto the riverbank and indicated they wanted only men in the big canoe and the four women in the smaller one. Dmitri and Sean protested that idea immediately.

"We don't want the women to be separated from us," he said to John. "Ask them why they want to split us up. I think they have a trick up their sleeve."

John tried to convey to the Indians their displeasure at the seating arrangements, but the natives shook their heads stubbornly and one of them spoke a few terse words then pointed at the river.

Frowning, John said, "They refuse to carry us across unless we do what they say. He insists it's for the ladies own safety, because the smaller canoe is easier to maneuver than the big one when the river is high like this. He also says one of our men can go with the women, but not me or any of our chiefs."

"That's preposterous!" Dmitri exploded. "I refuse to hand my wife over to these treacherous savages!"

"As much as I agree with ye, Your Excellency," said Sean, "I'm afraid we have no choice but to do as they say. Otherwise, we'll be left stranded here with no way across the river." He gave Dmitri a grim look.

"If it makes you feel better, why don't you send one of your men along with the lasses."

Dmitri nodded abruptly and gestured to Vladimir Smirnoff. Of all the Russians, he was the strongest and most brutal looking.

"Give Leonov and Smirnoff each a gun," Sean snapped to Jake.

With reluctance he handed a musket to both men. "Now Mr. Leonov, I dinna care to see ye shootin' anyone but the Injuns," he said, scowling.

Andrei Leonov's ravaged face was wild with worry. The thought of his fragile Marya being carried away defenseless in the canoe by the Quileute maddened him. Somehow he managed to keep his voice steady as he said, "Not to worry, Mr. O'Riley, you can depend on me to protect all the women."

But when the cold steel of the gun hit his hands it was all he could do to stop himself from aiming it at John Hill. He took a deep breath. *Patience. I'll have the chance another time to make sure the Yankee has an unfortunate accident.*

The three Indians were bare-chested and wore only a strip of cedar bark cloth around their waists. Although soaking wet, they seemed oblivious to the cold rain. At first they looked askance at the huge burly white man towering over them with a face as hairy as a black bear, but then they shrugged in agreement.

None of the women made a move towards the canoe. Finally Anna glanced around at the three women and said, "We must do as the Indians say. I am certain we will not be harmed."

With a brave expression she took a step forward, but Sean stopped her and gave her a quick embrace, whispering in her ear, "I love ye Anna. Keep a tight hold of Katya, and I'll see ye both in a few minutes."

"God be with you, Sean," she said, her voice quavering with fear. Then she looked at the rest of the men, "And may He be with all of you, too."

Dmitri pulled Tatiana into his arms. "If the savages ever touch one hair on your head, I swear I will kill them all."

She endured his husbandly kiss and murmured with barely subdued irritation, "I'll be fine, Dmitri."

"Wait, Baroness, you forgot your cat." Startled, she glanced at Anton, who gave her the box with Otter and flashed a smile so warm she felt herself blush as she thanked him.

John and Marya held hands briefly, staring with love into each other's eyes then with a tremulous smile, Marya walked bravely to the canoe and sat down. Tatiana and Keeah stepped in after her, both trying not to show their nervousness.

Anna held her head high to disguise the trembling of her legs, and settled into the center of the canoe with the other women, as Smirnoff and the Indian paddler pushed it off the bank. The big Russian positioned himself in the bow, his hands on his musket, facing their Indian paddler who propelled the canoe expertly into the river with a few bold strokes.

Immediately Sean picked out six of his crew while Dmitri ordered Andrei Leonov and three Russian sailors into the bigger canoe, along with their muskets and boxes of ammunition. He told the men to follow the women's canoe and be ready to give protection to them when they reached the opposite shore. As officers, Dmitri and Anton, Sean, Jake, and John would be the last men to cross.

The smaller canoe tipped sharply to starboard as it met the swift current then righted itself. Marya moaned in fear and she and Keeah clutched the sides, their eyes wide with fright.

"Be of good courage, ladies," said Anna calmly, all the while looking back to make certain the large canoe was following. Even with two Indians to paddle it, the big canoe was too heavily loaded to catch up with the smaller one. As the distance between the two canoes widened, Anna and the other women became more and more anxious.

They were past midstream when Tatiana suddenly pointed back to the big canoe. "Look!" she shouted, trying to make herself heard above the roar of the water. "Their Indian paddlers have jumped overboard!"

Smirnoff swore loudly. "The renegades have pulled the plugs from the bottom of the canoe and took their paddles with them!"

The big canoe was beginning to sink even as the men were trying frantically to cover the holes in the bottom with their feet and turn the canoe around by paddling with their muskets. At that moment dozens of Indians lined up on the bank and shot a volley of spears and arrows at the men stranded in the sinking canoe. They tried to shoot back, but their muskets would not fire. Some of the spears fell short into the water, but most of the arrows found their targets. Screams of pain were heard echoing over the water.

"We've been tricked!" yelled Smirnoff. He jumped up, rocking the canoe wildly, and aimed his musket at their Indian paddler.

But the Quileute anticipated his movement and he quickly swung his paddle at Smirnoff. The paddle was no ordinary oar, but was five feet long, made of hard ash wood with a broad blade, in the shape of an inverted crescent with a cross at the top, like the handle of a crutch. The crescent shape of the blade allowed the paddle to be drawn through the water without making any noise, so when hunting, the Indians could sneak up on sleeping sea otters, or when raiding, attack an unsuspecting village.

The paddle also made a fearful weapon and it knocked the musket out of Smirnoff's hands and into the water. The Indian swung it again, with extra force, and the blade smacked Vladimir on the right side of his head, splitting it open. Instantly he lost his balance and toppled over the side of the canoe, falling into the river with a mighty splash. The current tore him downstream and Anna did not know if he was dead or alive.

It had all happened so fast, the women could only cling to each other, paralyzed with stunned horror. Speechless, they watched as the men from the half-sunk canoe leaped overboard and struggled to the bank where Dmitri and Sean and the rest of the crew were hastily drying their muskets in order to shoot back. But it was too late to provide cover for the helpless men and when they reached the shore, every one of them was wounded.

By then the women's canoe was slicing through the current faster and faster, and instead of heading for the opposite shore, they soon disappeared around a bend up the river.

CHAPTER THIRTY FIVE

Dmitri would not stop ranting and raving like a madman. He cursed and swore and shook his fists and screamed, "Tatiana! Tatiana Nikolayevna! Come back! Come back!"

As Anna vanished from sight, a deep inner rage filled Sean, a murderous anger he'd not felt since the night his da died. A tiny voice inside kept telling him not to lose faith, to keep trusting God, but he refused to listen. All he wanted to do was kill every Indian in sight.

With a supreme effort, he struggled to maintain his composure. He could see that the Indians had noticed they were having trouble shooting their muskets, and were now moving upstream to cross over to their side of the river. The Quileutes obviously assumed this was their chance to exterminate all the white men.

"Let's get these guns dry, lads," he ordered, "and prepare for an attack. The savages aren't through with us yet!"

"Nor are we finished with them!" John snarled, suddenly possessed by a raging hatred against the Quileutes. His fear for Marya was so great he could barely see straight, but he knew now was not the time for him to lose control like Volodin.

Dmitri stood next to him, his gaze centered on Anton, who was staring upstream, his face white and hard like a slab of cold marble. Dmitri's left eye twitched in a nervous tic and for a second, he was tempted to fire his own gun at Dohktorov. Earlier when the lieutenant had handed Tatiana her cat, he'd noticed Anton smiling at her in a manner so intimate, a flush crossed his wife's beautiful face.

When this business with the savages was completed, and Tatiana returned safely to him, Dmitri vowed that Dohktorov would then discover his deadly mistake in trifling with his wife these past weeks. He couldn't believe how his life had turned into one disaster after another. First, his plan to kill O'Connell with the *knout* had failed. Then the ship ran aground due to O'Connell's incompetence and his entire fortune was lost. Even worse they were now stranded in the wilderness, had been attacked by savages and his beautiful Tatiana, his aristocratic Baroness, the mother of the future Volodin dynasty, was gone.

A picture of her being brutalized by dirty natives flashed through his mind. It was imperative they find her before that happened. He was not sure he could bear to ever touch her again if she was ravished by savages.

He groaned in helpless rage as he checked over his gun, making sure it was ready for firing. He couldn't wait to put a bullet right between the eyes of one of those smug Indians.

"Cap'n, Suh, we got lots of hurt men here," called out Samuel. He and Wang Li and Robby had been trying to attend to the injured men. Three had leg wounds from arrows so severe they could not walk, and six had various puncture wounds in the arms, hands, shoulders, and back. The most critical was Andrei Leonov, who was suffering from an arrowhead buried deep inside his belly that had severed his large intestine. It was a mortal wound.

"Lay the injured on blankets behind those big boulders over there," said Sean, motioning to more of the crew nearby to help. He didn't like their position on this exposed riverbank. Except for those few large rocks, there was little shelter they could use for cover. As soon as they could move everyone safely, he wanted to set out for higher ground.

"Here they come!" Dmitri suddenly roared. He fired his musket at a group of yelling Indians who were shooting off arrows as they ran towards them on their side of the river. He was so anxious his one shot went wild, missing all of them.

The rest of the men were better shots, their muskets exploding almost simultaneously. Many of the Indians fell and the rest halted their charge, surprised that the white men's guns worked after all. They didn't retreat, however, but ducked behind trees, rocks, bushes, anything they could find, and continued to rain arrows towards them.

For an hour Sean kept the men reloading and firing, reloading and firing, until they realized no more arrows were being launched in their direction. The Indians had gone, taking their wounded and dead with them.

Immediately he checked to see how many more injured men they had besides the ones wounded earlier, but miraculously, no one else had been struck by an arrow. Even Jimmy was unharmed, tied up behind a tree, whining and trembling with fright.

During the next half hour Sean held a meeting with Dmitri and their officers and they decided they would be safer inland this time of year when all the Indians were living in their permanent villages along the coast. By now it was likely most of the natives on the Olympic Peninsula were aware of their presence and they needed to find a place in the mountains where they could set up a fortified camp.

With haste Sean told the men to quickly organize their provisions for the long trek. The more seriously wounded men would be carried. Unfortunately they had to abandon much of their heavy equipment, such as the portable forge and blacksmith tools used to repair guns. But time was of the essence and they needed to move fast and hard without the extra weight to slow them down.

They set off upriver, each man nervously clutching a musket and keeping a sharp eye out for any native hiding behind a tree or bush. After hiking only a short way Leonov began to shriek in such anguish, the two men carrying him had to place him down on the ground.

“I can’t stand the pain. Somebody please shoot me," he begged in a piteous voice. His face was slick with perspiration and his eyes bulged in fierce agony as he clutched his bleeding abdomen. He knew he was dying and he welcomed it. Anything was preferable to this hideous torment. There was nothing left for him in this life without Marya anyway. And she was gone from him forever. He might as well be dead. His only consolation was that John Hill wouldn't ever see her again either. He started to laugh, but managed only a strangled cough that tore his insides up even more in the most excruciating torture imaginable.

The stench of his perforated bowels was sickening. Sean stared down at Leonov and knew there was nothing they could do for him. He would die, the sooner the better. Sighing with pity, he pointed to a nearby clearing secluded by salal bushes and thick blackberry vines. “Cover him with a blanket and leave him in there. Give him a jug of water and a knife. Then we best be going.”

“Captain," said Anton with a pale shaken face, "perhaps you should say a prayer for him."

Sean hesitated, feeling inadequate. He'd never prayed out loud in front of anyone before. Then he remembered what Anna called the Lord's Prayer from the Bible. "*Our Father who art in heaven*," he began, but before he could go any further, Leonov rolled his eyes and passed out.

Sean figured he wouldn't last another hour. “May God have mercy on your soul, Leonov,” he muttered as some of the men made the sign of the cross.

After they left the *Creole*, Sean felt something hard twist inside him. "Anna," he cried out silently, "how can God make any of this work for our good now?"

It was a question with no answer. He had lost his ship and he had lost Anna, and now he was torn with doubts about his newfound faith in God. At the very least, he was ridden with fears for the future.

With a bitter expression he drove the men relentlessly through the great forest, and in the days ahead, a deep inner rage consumed his every waking moment.

* * *

“They’re going to make us slaves,” whispered Marya. Her long black hair lay tangled and snarled in a dark mass around her shoulders. Her eyes were shining with tears and her full mouth quivered in alarm.

It was dawn of the following morning. Since their capture the day before, the women had been taken through the forest to a large Quileute village and put inside a small dank hut with a dirty damp earthen floor. They had no fire, nor had they been given any food or water. Their sealskin parkas and *mukluks* had been instantly confiscated by the chief's first wife, who marveled at the unusual garments made by the Aleuts of Alaska, a people none of them had ever seen.

Imagine her further delight, Tatiana thought glumly, when the woman discovered her pearl necklace, diamond earrings and necklace, her sapphire and diamond engagement ring and gold wedding ring in her coat pockets.

The women huddled together in misery, their dresses too thin for warmth and their feet sore and cold in their torn stockings. Shivering, their teeth chattering, they tried in vain to comfort each other and the fretful Katya who sensed all was not well along with the irritated and hungry cat in her box.

The Indians had not taken Otter. When one of the native women opened the box, the cat hissed and extended a sharp claw, scratching the woman's hand and drawing blood. Surprised and alarmed, the woman had shoved the box back at Tatiana. After that, she and the others quickly left the hut, casting suspicious and fearful glances at the box.

"You'll not be a slave, *Mademoiselle*," said Keeah. "But I will. My people raid on this coast and the Quileutes will know I am Tlingit and take their revenge on me."

"Then what will happen to us?" Tatiana asked quietly.

Keeah considered. "You might be held for ransom. You have a husband who will trade many guns to get you back."

"What if John and the others were killed yesterday?" Marya cried out.

Keeah patted her hand to reassure her. "They still live. They not easy to kill. They will come to free you."

"John told me once that when he was living with the Nootkas, he had actually taken part in several successful raids on other Indian villages. He knows how it is done," Marya said hopefully.

"I imagine my husband has had a nervous breakdown by now," Tatiana commented with sarcasm. "So, if anyone can rescue us, it will be up to your John and Captain O'Connell."

Anna looked up from nursing her daughter. She was dehydrated from lack of water and feeling weak from hunger and little sleep. She was fearful of her milk drying up, and then she didn't know how Katya was going to survive. Rescue couldn't come soon enough for her. She had been praying almost continually for them to be freed and returned to their men.

"God will help us," said Anna.

"Yes, He will," Marya agreed, making the sign of the cross.

Just as she did so, two Indians entered the hut. Early morning light streamed in behind them and the women recognized one as Hoheeshata, the leader of the band that had attacked their camp on the beach after the shipwreck. They could never forget his face with its jagged scar down the right cheek or the cruel gleam in his eyes.

He was smiling now. Hoheeshata had taken his revenge on the whites and had their women in his power, especially the woman with the hair of moon and sun. Or were there two of them? He peered at Anna in surprise, not remembering this one, who had hair the color of honey and eyes the golden green of hazelnuts. She had an infant, too, with the most astonishing curls of burnt amber. He recalled seeing a white man with a head of hair like a flaming sunset, and wondered if he was the child's father. Truly, the white's were a strange type of human!

The other two women were black haired like the women of his village, but one had the lighter skin of a half breed. He didn't know from what tribe she originated, but she was very lovely to look at. The other girl was a Tlingit, their old enemies, which made her a prize indeed.

Chief Xawishata, Hoheeshata's older brother, was quite intrigued with their captives, although there was some talk about a small hissing animal with sharp claws and a face like a wildcat which belonged to the sun and moon woman. Perhaps it was her animal spirit helper. They would have to ask the *shaman* what to do about it. They'd never had a captive with a spirit helper before. He eyed the box on the floor with faint trepidation.

The women instinctively shrank back from the two Indians. Anna held Katya protectively against her, thinking the men looked like brothers, having similar facial features and the same broad foreheads which sloped backwards. The other man was two inches taller than Hoheeshata and was more wide shouldered with an older, more authoritative air about him. For a few minutes he intently studied all four women, then with a curt motion, indicated they were to stand up.

Giving Keeah a cursory glance, he walked over to Tatiana. The two were of nearly the same height, and smiling slightly, he put out his hand and touched her hair, running his fingers through the long golden locks that had come undone from her braided plaits. Tatiana tried to hold herself still, but she could not help shuddering with fright when he lightly stroked her cheek and let his gaze travel down the length of her damp clinging gown.

Then he turned his attention to Anna and saw how she clutched the infant to her breast. His eyes widened briefly at the sight of Katya's red-gold hair. Anna lifted her chin and met his stare head-on, determined not to let him know the fear inside her. His black eyes burrowed into hers, and he grunted, acknowledging her courage.

He saw Marya next and halted, giving her a smile of pure admiration. *Surely Many Baskets once was as beautiful as this one*, he thought. *She looks like a captured doe with those frightened eyes so huge and soft a man could melt in them.*

Hoheeshata made a lewd comment about the women and Xawishata's smile vanished. He pointed his chin at Hoheeshata and spoke a few words. Hoheeshata suddenly scowled and burst into a rapid speech that Xawishata silenced with a sharp gesture and an arrogant look.

A few seconds later they were gone. All the women sat down, feeling weak and shaken.

"Hoheeshata is brother to big chief," stated Keeah. "His name is Xawishata." She glanced at Tatiana. "He might want you or *Mademoiselle* for wife."

Both women exchanged fearful looks and Anna said, "I pray you are wrong, Keeah. Perhaps he was just looking us over to see how much we are worth to him for a ransom."

The door flap was flung aside and three women entered. Anna and Tatiana were scandalized to see that two of them were half naked, wearing only fringed skirts made of woven cedar bark. They jabbered excitedly among themselves, staring at all the captives with much interest, taking in every detail of their clothes and hair and exclaiming over their unusual appearance.

The one woman who was fully clothed in a cedar bark jacket and skirt issued an order to the other two, who apparently were slave girls. A fur headband encircled her head and her long black hair was parted in the center, flowing loosely to her shoulders. Around her neck was a necklace made of curved brown bear claws. Her ears were pierced several times each with one large shell earring in her lobe and other small copper earrings around the rim of her ear.

She was a short, plump woman of obvious importance and she chattered incessantly to the slave girls. They carried food and bowls of water, which they placed on the floor. The woman with the necklace motioned to them to eat, still speaking rapidly. There was a wooden platter of dried fish and smoked clams, a basket of dried berries made into small cakes, and a bowl of greasy fish oil.

Marya and Keeah helped themselves immediately, but Tatiana looked at the food with dismay, having little appetite for it. Anna had no hesitation. She knew she needed the food for Katya. First she took several gulps of the cool water then ate several bites of a berry cake, enjoying the tart fruity taste. The fish was smoked salmon, dried to a tough chewy texture. When she took a bite she almost choked on the strong salty fish flavor.

Keeah looked at Anna, her mouth stuffed with food, and pointed to the bowl of fish oil. "We dip food in oil."

"To the natives, fish oil is their cream, butter, and salad dressing," explained Marya. "At home my aunt always served dried berry cakes with whale oil." She smiled at the repugnance on Tatiana's face and added, "It tastes better after you get used to it."

Anna nodded, but could not bear to coat her food with the rancid smelling substance. Tatiana eventually followed suit, struggling to keep a polite expression on her face as the Indian women watched their every move.

Suddenly Katya, who had been wiggling on her lap, let out a howl. Anna tried to shush her, but she wouldn't stop crying.

"Poor Katya has a rash," said Anna in frustration. "They took all our belongings away yesterday, including the moss for her changing."

She unwrapped Katya from her blanket and drew back her tiny dress and petticoats to show all the women in the hut the infant's angry red bottom.

Immediately the older woman clucked in sympathy and spoke to the slave girls, who both rushed out of the hut. She held out her arms towards Katya and smiled a smile which transformed her homely face to one of near beauty, revealing a set of perfect sparkling white teeth.

Anna froze, understanding that this native woman wanted to hold her child, but she did not want to let her go. What if she took Katya away from her? She'd heard the stories of white children being adopted into Indian families and raised as their own.

Tatiana and Marya and Keeah watched, knowing this was something Anna had to decide on her own. The plump Indian woman waited patiently, talking all the while in a soothing voice, her arms outstretched. After a few more moments of deliberation, Anna walked over to her and slid the fussing Katya into her arms. Somehow Anna knew she had to keep demonstrating courage to her captors, or they would not respect her. And she would have to trust God to take care of the rest.

The Quileute woman's black eyes softened with delight and wonder as she gently rocked Katya, who continued to cry. She gave Anna a kind smile, as if she understood how difficult it was for the white woman to hand over her child and began to hum a strange tune to Katya.

The two slave girls entered the hut, one carrying a bundle of shredded cedar bark and a basket of herbs, and the other a wooden cradle board. Anna bit her lip and stepped back as the girls took off Katya's soiled clothing and cleaned her, then mixed the herbs with some of the fish oil from the bowl, and carefully rubbed it all over the infant's buttocks and groin. In an instant, Katya ceased her wailing and a big grin broke across her face. She gurgled happily, and for the first time since their capture, Anna felt herself relax.

One of the slave girls took the cradle board, which had been carved from a section of a slender tree trunk and hollowed out like a tiny canoe or wooden serving dish, and filled it with shredded cedar bark. Then she showed Anna how to place Katya comfortably inside, putting a soft pad under her neck and knees, leaving her feet higher than her head. The shredded cedar bark had a twofold purpose, to be used as a soft mattress and as an absorbent material like moss to be thrown away when dirty.

While Katya squirmed around and waved her fat little hands, accustoming herself to the cradle board, Keeah told Anna if Katya had been a child of noble birth among the Quileutes, they would also place a pad across her forehead. The pad would be left for the first few months while the bones were soft to flatten the forehead. Without hurting the child, this produced an altered profile of a broad forehead and cone shaped head that was considered a mark of beauty and high rank.

Anna glanced at the woman with the bear necklace and noticed she had such a forehead that sloped gently back, as did the chief, Xawishata, and his brother, Hoheeshata.

She thought it was a strange custom, similar to the Tlingits inserting lip plugs in their young women to make them more beautiful. Privately, she thought it all quite barbaric and ugly. "They won't make me do this to Katya, will they?" Anna asked Keeah.

She shook her head. "They only do it when child is born, but not to children of slaves or people of low rank. They not allowed to flatten heads."

Anna felt relieved as the native girl, ignoring their conversation, demonstrated how she could strap the board to her back, so Anna could walk and work with her hands free, and still have her infant with her. Anna nodded with interest, thinking how sore her neck was from the makeshift sling she had carried Katya in during the past week. She had to admit the idea of the cradle board was much more practical.

Now that Anna realized the women were only trying to help her with her daughter, and not take her away, she smiled her gratitude at them. She was amazed at how quickly Katya appeared to adjust to the cradle board, falling asleep soon after she was tucked snugly into the shredded cedar bark.

Just when the problem with the baby was solved, the cat decided she'd had enough of the confines of the box. She also smelled the dried salmon and began to meow for the food. When Tatiana went to remove the lid from the box, all three native women scampered towards the door.

"Keeah, can you tell them not to be afraid?" Tatiana asked. "Tell them that the cat is only hungry."

Keeah tried to convey this to the Quileutes, but they stayed by the entrance, staring with alarm as Tatiana lifted the gray and white spotted cat out of her box and fed her fish tidbits from her hand. Otter ignored the native women and ate her meal with relish, purring loudly.

The strange rumbling sound from the small animal caused the girls to exclaim in wonder. The woman with the bear claw necklace turned to Keeah, and tried to ask her some questions in a few halting words of the Tlingits.

When Keeah answered her, the woman blanched and frowned nervously, then spoke to the girls. Their eyes grew huge and they shrank away even further from Tatiana and her cat.

Noticing this, she asked Keeah, "What are you telling them?"

"She want to know if the little cougar is your spirit helper and I said yes."

Tatiana could see at once that Keeah's words had frightened the Quileute women even more. She had no idea what a spirit helper was, but it was obviously the wrong thing to say.

"Why did you tell them that, Keeah? Now they are more scared of Otter than before. What if they tell their men my cat is dangerous and they decide to kill her?"

"They never dare harm someone's spirit helper. If they do, that animal always haunt them. I tell them this so they leave Otter alone." Keeah smiled proudly at her own cleverness.

It seemed to work, for the women waited patiently until the cat was finished eating, had washed her whiskers clean, had relieved herself on the dirt floor, and been placed back inside the box. Then the woman with the bear claw necklace motioned for all of them to go outside.

They gladly left the dark hut and walked out into a gray overcast morning. Tatiana told Keeah to carry Otter's box. As they followed the women, Anna strapped the cradle board to her back and glanced around at the village. It was situated well back from the Hoh River bank and had two rows of large wooden houses and a number of smaller huts. She recognized it as the same village they saw yesterday when they tried to cross the river in the canoe. Hope rose in her and the feeling that Sean and the men were somewhere close by.

The damp cold air was filled with wood smoke and smelled pungent with drying salmon and other fish. Women and children were busily preserving food for the coming winter by smoking the fish in strips on wooden racks. The smallest children used sticks to guard the food from the village dogs. No men were in sight.

A group of black haired, dark eyed children broke away from their work and surrounded the captives, giggling and gawking at their pale skin, odd colored hair, and strange clothing. Their mothers were about to order them away when their own curiosity got the better of them and they came to see the odd white women.

Anna thought they must look a miserable sight, as the hems of their gowns and petticoats all hung in tatters around their muddy ankles. She and Tatiana tried not to flinch as a myriad of brown fingers and hands touched their hair and the fine muslin of their colorful gowns. Marya's gown was inspected as well, but Keeah was left alone. Besides the fact she was a hated Tlingit, she was holding the box with the cat inside. By now all of the Indians had heard about the small fierce wildcat which belonged to the woman with the hair of the sun.

Finally the bear claw woman issued a sharp command and everyone reluctantly returned to their chores. She continued to lead the captives away from the village and to a secluded area of ferns and bushes upriver where the water pooled by a small sandy beach. They were ordered to remove all their clothing and then bathe in the river.

Anna and Tatiana and Marya had been feeling dirty for days, but they still felt reluctant to undress in front of all these natives. Keeah placed Otter's box on top of a large rock, then stripped off her filthy maid's gown and tossed it carelessly onto the riverbank. She splashed into the water and called out to the others to come.

One of the slave girls held the cradle board with Katya while Anna took off her clothes. Since the shipwreck she had carried her small Bible in her apron pocket. Now she slipped it out and slid it under Otter's box. She had a feeling she wouldn't be seeing her apron again, and she couldn't imagine captivity without her Bible.

Then she and Tatiana stepped into the pool, feeling shy and embarrassed about their nudity exposed to the scrutiny of strangers who had no sense of modesty themselves. The water was icy cold and she and Tatiana gasped with the shock of it. Marya and Keeah were more stoic, having bathed in rivers and streams most of their lives. They splashed water all over themselves, and soaked their long hair well. They were given a sort of soap made from the bruised leaves of a plant called mock orange, and this gave their hair a pleasant smell.

Anna had to admit it felt wonderful being clean again, the first time since leaving New Archangel. There hadn't been the luxury of washing in a tub of warm water on board the ship.

That was why the natives complained the white men stank, Keeah told them, for the coastal Indians bathed every morning, no matter what the weather.

After their baths, the slave girls dried the women with blankets, exclaiming over the paleness of both Anna's and Tatiana's bodies. While they'd been in the river, their own clothing had been taken away, probably to be torn up and distributed among the village women.

Tatiana was appalled when she realized she would have to wear native garments. She and Anna shivered in the chilly wind, looking apprehensively at the flimsy fringed cedar bark jackets, and the skirts that the slave girls strung around their waists on a cord and fastened with several rows of twining. The skirts weighed scarcely a thing and ended at their knees, a length so short Tatiana imagined what a scandal it would be if any of the ladies of New Archangel saw them.

Anna had a similar thought, knowing her papa and Agatha and the women of Furstenau would be horrified to see her now. She could not help a small hysterical giggle at the idea.

Tatiana heard the slight noise and looked at her. "Oh, Anna," she said, uttering a slight laugh, "how indecent we look! What would Anton say?"

"He would be shocked, and so would Sean," she answered, noticing how Tatiana didn't even mention her own husband's possible reaction to their new clothing.

"At least they don't expect us to be half naked like their slaves," said Marya with a relieved expression.

"Are we expected to go without footwear?" Tatiana asked, staring down at her feet with concern. She had the tender white feet of an aristocrat, and had never gone barefoot in her life.

"When I was girl in Furstenau," said Anna, "I went barefoot all summer except at church on Sunday. It was fun," she added.

"Fun?" Tatiana's eyebrows arched in disbelief. Then she remembered the hot summer days on the country estate when she and Olga would watch the peasant children run barefoot across the grass to swim in the river. She'd always envied their laughter while they enjoyed playing in the cool water. Olga had mocked them and said they were simple-minded and barbaric.

Her cousin would never recognize her now, Tatiana realized wryly; nor would her Uncle Vasily and cousin Mikael. She wondered if she would ever see any of them again. And Anton, she thought, as despair suddenly washed over her.

She looked at Keeah. "What will happen to us now?"

"We might go separate ways," the Tlingit girl answered in a sober voice.

That was the last thing Anna, Tatiana, and Marya wanted to hear. They looked at each other fearfully as the woman with the bear claw necklace pointed at them with her chin, then gestured impatiently for them to follow her.

"Who is she anyway?" Anna asked as they hurried back towards the village.

"I think she first or second wife of big chief, Xawishata," Keeah answered. "Soon we find out if any of us will be third wife or only slaves."

CHAPTER THIRTY SIX

"No!" Robby shouted, his arms encircling his dog's neck so tightly, the animal whimpered. "Yer not gonna eat my dog!"

"The mutt's not good fer nothin' anyhow," replied Jeb Drake. "An' the Chink can make 'im into mighty fine stew." His mouth started to drool at the thought as his starving stomach clenched in anticipation. "Come on, now, lad, let us 'ave im."

Robby tightened his grip even further until Jimmy's tongue hung out of his mouth. As if sensing danger, the dog intently watched Drake and Wang Li.

Two weeks had passed since the women disappeared, a long fortnight of plunging haphazardly east through the great forest, always staying north of the Hoh River. Four more men died from their wounds. Out of the original company of thirty-nine that had set out after the shipwreck, they were now down to twenty-eight. They'd lost four of the crew, two Russians, and the four women and infant.

Still, there were too many mouths to feed. It didn't take long to run out of all their provisions and they had yet to find a decent campsite which offered an adequate food supply. Sean organized hunting parties, but they found no deer or elk and the incessant rains made it impossible to keep the ammunition dry. They tried using axes or makeshift spears to hit a bird or rabbit, but the men were too clumsy and unskilled to actually kill one. John was the only one patient enough to occasionally spear a fish or two, but it was never enough to feed the group. Instead they subsisted on late fall berries, if they were lucky to find any, mushrooms, roots, leaves, tree fungi, and some of the men even gnawed on shoe leather and their gutskin *kamleikas*. As a result many of the men showed the early symptoms of scurvy, the bleeding in the gums and loosening of teeth, and most suffered from chronic diarrhea.

On this raw morning everyone was famished and desperate for meat. They were camped in a clearing near a rushing stream which flowed among the towering cedars, firs, and spruce trees. Samuel had built a crackling fire in hopes that Wang Li would have something substantial to cook in the iron pot hanging over the flames. So far, the only food in the pot was roots and wild onions and mushrooms and the shredded flesh and bones of one unlucky squirrel Sean had hit in the head with a rock.

"We need Jimmy. He catches rabbits an' possums," Robby said with desperation.

"He ain't no huntin' dog," laughed Drake unpleasantly, his teeth stained yellow from years of tobacco chewing. "I seen him eat what he catches 'afore we can get it from him."

"Did any of ye ever hear of the Lewis an' Clark Expedition of 1806?" asked Nate Tyler. "They ended up spendin' the winter hereabouts on this coast down south near the Columbia. I heard they an' their men got a hankerin' fer dog meat an' said they downright preferred it over venison or elk."

"Cap'n, please," Robby begged, "don't let 'em take Jimmy. Please---"

The sight of the scrawny freckle-faced youth hugging his floppy-eared dog almost brought tears to Sean's eyes. The last thing he wanted to do was give the order to slit the throat of the faithful Jimmy to provide meat for the cooking pot. But yet, the dog could provide nourishment for all of them for one more day. Maybe tomorrow they'd find a herd of elk or even a deer.

With sadness he reluctantly opened his mouth to tell Robby he had to give up his dog, when he heard someone shouting from the woods.

"Captain O'Connell!" yelled John as he and Anton emerged from the trees, their thin faces alight with enthusiasm. Sean looked at them with hope. Had their scouting expedition turned into a successful hunt?

"Have you found meat?" he asked as all the men waited expectantly.

Anton shook his head, causing groans from around the campfire. Then he said, "But we have found an Indian village not far away."

"It looks to be deserted," John added with excitement. "Everyone's gone hunting and there might be dried fish we can take. If we make haste, we can be there and back before the natives return!"

All the men swung their gaze towards Sean, especially Robby, who had a flare of hope in his eyes. The lad was lucky, he thought. He and his dog just got a reprieve.

"I'll take ten of the strongest and fastest to carry the fish," he said, motioning to Jake, Samuel, the carpenter Ebenezer Cartwright, the armorer Edmund Wilde, Robby, and five other men, two of whom were the biggest Russians.

"May I come, Captain?"

The cultured voice of Baron Volodin surprised Sean. He had not heard him speak more than a few grunts in the past weeks. The man had withdrawn inside himself, talking to no one, not even to Dohktorov or his own countrymen. Sean knew Volodin was grieving the loss of his wife and was in such a sorry state that it was impossible to look at him without some compassion. The man acted as if he had no reason left for living.

Because Volodin usually turned up his aristocratic nose at the meager fare the forest had to offer, he was more emaciated than any of them. He still wore his Russian Imperial uniform with its tattered and filthy gold shoulder epaulets and a few tarnished buttons. His once shiny black

Hessian boots had long since been discarded. He now wore the *mukluks* of one of the dead seamen. All the men were heavily bearded and had long, shaggy hair, but Volodin's hair, once fair and thick, had gone white with a bald patch on top of his head. Sean didn't think that Tatiana would recognize him except for the perpetual nervous tic in his left eye.

"Ye aren't strong enough, Your Excellency," he said bluntly. "We'll be travelin' hard and fast and carryin' back heavy loads of food."

"Then I suggest you leave me in command of the men while you're gone."

Sean looked him over uneasily, but decided he could do little harm. "Aye, Volodin, I'll give ye permission to take charge of the camp till we return. "

"Cap'n, Sir," Robby called out anxiously, "can we take Jimmy?"

"Nay, lad, not this time." Sean shook his head. "Ye can tie him to a tree. He'll do fine."

Robby reluctantly did so then buried his face into the dog's golden fur, and murmuring his farewell. Jimmy licked his face and whined and commenced barking in protest when his young master ran off with the other men and disappeared into the trees.

They followed Anton and John through the timber and after hiking several miles south, they could hear the rushing roar of the Hoh River. With great caution, they crept through the thick underbrush and peered through the bushes at a small village of wooden houses situated on a bank above the river on one side and a small stream running out of the forest on the other.

Although they could see wisps of smoke from several small smoldering fires, the village appeared to be empty of people. Anton and John were right. All the men must be gone hunting and the women and children out gathering the last of the roots and berries.

There were no totem poles in the village, but each house had a decorated house post on which an ancestor spirit guardian was carved. As quickly as possible, they entered the vacant dwellings through the doors, small oval openings raised several feet from the ground made for protection against sudden enemies, such as themselves. Over each door hung an elk hide curtain. There were no windows in the buildings and the interiors were dark and reeked of stale sweat, smoke, and bear grease.

Ignoring the rank odors, Sean couldn't help noticing how well-constructed the houses were built with long flat planks of cedar for the walls and flat roofs. Cracks in the walls were chinked with moss to keep out drafts. There was furniture made in the shape of built-in platforms which went around three sides of each house and were used for beds and seating. Bedding was made up of soft warm furs and animal skins, and some houses were carpeted with cattail mats. The chief's house had wooden planked flooring.

It was the cooking areas the men were most interested in. These were complete with fire pits, cooking stones, tongs, expertly woven baskets and carved cedar boxes, all arranged neatly as if in a kitchen. They rifled through the baskets and boxes, emptying their contents of roots, dried berries and herbs onto the dirt floors. With eagerness the hungry men confiscated all the baskets of dried salmon, halibut, and cod that they could carry.

Some of the men also wanted to steal blankets, furs, fishhooks, and any weapon they could find. In the chief's house Nate Tyler found a three pointed sealing harpoon, but Sean told him to put it back. He was insistent they were not to take anything but food. Tyler grumbled loudly, but did as he was ordered.

On the return trip, Sean thought about the Indian village and how their houses were a whole lot cozier and drier than the evergreen branch shelters they'd made at their own camp. It gave him a small comfort to imagine Anna and Katya living in such a place, safeguarded from the wilderness and inclement coastal weather.

Samuel was the last man out and it wasn't until they were halfway back that Sean realized his steward was wearing one of the Quileute rain hats made of spruce root and decorated with red and yellow geometric patterns. It made the tall black man with the grizzled beard look like a wild African tribesman.

Tyler protested immediately. He spat on the ground and said, "That good fer nuthin' darkie disobeyed yer orders, Cap'n!"

"I's sorry, Cap'n," Samuel said, "but mah daddy in Africa has a hat like dis. I's just a boy when the slavers came, but I does 'member him wearing a red and yellow hat when we has special occasions. Mah momma and big sister made hats and baskets, jus' like dose I seen back dere."

Sean saw the sadness in his face and told him to keep the hat. He knew it would cause jealousy among Tyler and Drake and some of the other men, but Samuel was the hardest worker they had and Sean thought he deserved more than a measly hat.

He often wondered if the private investigator he'd hired in Boston before they sailed had ever located Samuel's older sister. The two siblings were separated at the slave auction block when they first arrived in Virginia, and hadn't seen each other again. But then, Sean realized, if they never were rescued from this miserable place and never returned to Boston, it hardly mattered.

Just thinking of slavery made him wince. Were Anna and the other women slaves of the Quileutes by now? The tormenting question dodged his every step as they dashed through the forest with their stolen plunder. And even more tormenting, were they wives of some cruel savage like Hoheeshata?

An hour later as they approached their camp, Sean and the men suddenly smelled a delicious aroma wafting through the air.

" 'Tis meat cookin'!" one of the men cried out.

John smiled at Anton and Sean and said, "Maybe Volodin actually organized a successful hunting party while we were gone."

"Maybe so," said Sean, but he kept his face grim as he realized the camp was too quiet. He could hear the sounds of men talking, but there was one thing lacking, Jimmy's barking to announce their arrival.

Robby must have had the same thought, because he rushed ahead and ran into the camp, dropping his basket of fish on the ground. "Where's Jimmy?" he shouted, his blue eyes wide as he frantically looked around at the men seated on logs, shoveling stew into their mouths.

Wang Li stood at the cook pot, stirring the contents with a long metal spoon, keeping his face carefully averted from the boy.

With a cry, Robby lunged at the short slight man. "You murderin' Chink!" he screamed. "You kilt my dog!"

Wang Li jumped aside and smacked Robby on the head with the spoon. "Get away, Boy. I not hurt dog. I only cook dead dog." He pointed with the spoon at Dmitri. "That man kill dog."

Robby swung away from Wang Li and lowered his head like an enraged bull, then charged straight at Dmitri. The baron was spooning the last bites of his stew when he saw Robby coming. He set his bowl down on the log beside him and calmly withdrew a knife from under his coat.

Sean and Anton saw the glint of the knife at the same time, and Anton rushed towards Dmitri, yelling, "No, Volodin! Put it away!"

Sean already had his pistol in hand, loaded and ready to fire, and he aimed at the ground near Dmitri's feet and squeezed the trigger. The sudden roar of the gun froze everyone in their places as dirt exploded around Dmitri's *mukluks*. He swore loudly and jumped in fright, noticing as he did so, that he was not hurt. The bullet had plowed harmlessly into the ground. He dropped his knife and leveled a deadly stare at Sean.

Jake quickly grabbed Robby by the arm and pulled him back, saying in a soothing voice, "Nay, lad, there's nothin' more to be done now. Yer Jimmy 'tis gone an' that's the end of it."

Robby was trembling and he glared at Dmitri with a look so dark and full of hate that even Dmitri gave pause. "The dirty Russkie kilt my dog!" he shouted, "an' I'll never forget it! Never!" With those words, a deep sob wrenched from his throat and he spun around and fled into the woods. Jake made a move to follow him, but Sean said, "Let him go. He'll be back by dark."

Then he looked at Dmitri and shook his head. "Well, Volodin, I leave ye in charge for what, an afternoon? And all hell breaks loose! Why in heavens name did ye kill the poor dog when ye knew we were coming back with food?"

"The men were starving and we didn't know for sure if you'd be returning with anything," Dmitri said defensively. "Before you left you almost had the dog killed yourself. I didn't think it would matter."

"It matters to the lad," said Jake, scowling angrily.

Dmitri shrugged. "He's just a boy. He'll get over it."

"You better hope he does," said Anton quietly. "Because otherwise you've made yourself an enemy."

The mood around the camp stayed somber the rest of the day, even though there was real food to eat for the first time in weeks. Sean told Wang Li to portion out the rest of the dog stew to whoever wished to eat it, then scour out the pot and make another stew from the dried fish they brought. As for himself, he had suddenly lost his appetite.

Robby returned late that night, shaking with weakness from hunger and drained from hours of weeping. His bloodshot eyes had the dull sunken look of grief, and Sean knew he had been mourning more than the loss of his dog. Jimmy had been named after his twin brother and now both of them were gone. Sean made certain Robby had a bowl of fish stew then sent him to sleep it off. He hoped things were calmer the next morning.

That night he spent another restless sleep, haunted by dreams of Dmitri Volodin standing over him brandishing a *knout* while Jimmy the dog howled mournfully. He woke up sometime in the middle of the night and rubbed his eyes, thinking angrily about Volodin. He'd had no right to kill Jimmy. His heart was full of pity for Robby over the loss of his dog. He also felt guilt. Sean knew it was only a matter of time before the dog would've been sacrificed for the cook pot. The dried fish they'd taken yesterday would not last more than a week.

His thoughts turned to Anna as an image of her sweet face appeared in his mind. "Please God," he prayed, "watch over Anna and Katya and all of them, and bring us safely together again soon." After repeating the prayer numerous times, he finally fell into a dreamless sleep until morning.

But at the crack of dawn there was more trouble. Now with their bellies full, some of the men wanted to cross the Hoh River upstream where it was less wide, and make their way south towards the coast and Gray's Harbor. It was early November and the summer trading season was over, but perhaps it wasn't too late to hope for rescue by a passing ship.

"What we hangin' 'round here fer?" Jeb Drake demanded and was instantly seconded by Nate Tyler, Ebenezer Cartwright and several others. "We ain't never gettin' those women back from the Injuns. 'Tain't no use waitin' for somethin' that's not gonna happen."

Sean stood in front of the disgruntled men, about ten in all, and admitted that their fears were real. The longer they stayed in the forest, the slimmer their chances of finding a ship this fall. "But as ye all know, I'm planning on weddin' Missus Campbell and I willna leave without her and her child," he told them. "And I speak the same for Baron Volodin and his wife. As long as the women are alive, we must find and rescue them."

He knew having women on board the ship had never been popular with the crew, and looking at their surly faces, knew it was even less now.

"What if we don't want to wait for yer women?" Cartwright, the carpenter, asked. "Don't we have the right to try and save ourselves?"

Sean hesitated then nodded brusquely. "Aye, men, ye do. If any of ye wish to leave, I won't be stoppin' ye. However," he added, "bear in mind that ye go with only one weapon each an' ye'll have to fend for yerselves in the matter of finding food."

A few of the men shuffled their feet and sniffed the air, remembering the gnawing emptiness of their stomachs the past weeks. Wang Li already had breakfast started, a simmering pot of savory fish stew spiced with wild onions and mushrooms.

Cartwright opened his mouth to argue further when an arrow whizzed past him and thumped into a nearby tree trunk. Another arrow just missed Sean's head and clattered against the iron cooking pot, causing Wang Li to jump in fright and start jabbering in Chinese.

Pandemonium erupted across the camp as everyone ran to find their muskets and powder and prime their guns for firing. Some of the blackberry bushes rustled near the stream and O'Riley, who was the quickest, fired in that direction. The bushes shattered in a shower of yellow gold leaves, leaving a gaping hole in their midst with nothing else to be seen.

In the distance they could hear a few whoops of laughter and then silence. No more arrows shot overhead and Sean decided their attackers were gone, for the moment at least. To be on the safe side, he gave the order for some of the men to guard the perimeter of the camp.

"Jimmy woulda smelled them Injuns," Robby declared. "He woulda started barkin' long afore they coulda loosed them arrows at us."

"True, lad," agreed Sean. "He was a good dog and we miss him."

The boy had more color in his cheeks, most likely due to the Indian attack, but his appetite was still poor and Sean noticed he'd a hard time accepting any food from Wang Li that morning. As for Baron Volodin, he and Robby avoided each other entirely.

"Sean, I need to talk to you," said John, walking over to him with the Indians' arrows in his hands. His curly blond hair was tied neatly back by a leather string but his scruffy beard and drooping mustache gave him a rough appearance. "I'm certain these arrows are from the village that we raided yesterday and I think they'll keep harassing us if we stay here. We need to go inland, into the mountains where the Indians rarely hunt. If we follow the Hoh River east we'll end up near Mount Olympus. The Quileutes believe that mountain is holy and haunted by spirits. They'll never follow us there."

"But that will take us further away from the lasses."

John looked at him with dull eyes that no longer twinkled when he smiled. Sean saw the furrows of sorrow lining his forehead and knew John hated the thought of putting even more miles between them and the missing women as much as he did.

"We have no choice at the moment," John said quietly.

Sean nodded, knowing he was right. With great reluctance, he called a meeting and announced their new plan, waiting for Jeb Drake, Nate Tyler and the other men to object. This time there was no comment. The morning's attack had refreshed everyone's memory as to the worst danger of the forest, not wild animals, not starvation, but the savages themselves. If they split up into two smaller groups, they were more vulnerable to future attacks.

It was a unanimous decision that they pack up immediately and head east into the mountains.

* * *

"*Hokwat! Basi!*"

Chief Xawishata's First Wife, named Many Baskets for her exquisite basketry, spat the insulting words at Tatiana and Anna. *Basi* meant bad, and *hokwat* meant drifting house people, the term for whites because they came on ships. The two were inside their small gloomy slave hut, which had become their prison for the past weeks. Their meager furnishings consisted of one cattail mat on the dirt floor, a thin fur robe each for warmth and bedding, Otter's box, and Katya in her cradle board.

Many Baskets had once been beautiful. Her eyes were almond shaped and soft brown in color. Tiny dark eyebrows arched over each one. Her face had delicate features and her mouth was blessed with full red lips. But it was her ravaged skin that erased any thought of beauty.

Ten years ago when she was fifteen, Many Baskets' village north on the Quillayute River had been decimated by smallpox, brought by a Chinook slave who claimed to have caught the illness from the white traders at Fort Astoria on the Columbia River. She and her family had contracted the disease and only her father, the village chief, and she had survived. Her mother, two younger brothers and infant sister had died.

Her father was given wise advice by the *shaman* to quarantine the village until the disease had run its course. No one was allowed in or out. Then he ordered the village burned and the rest of the surviving people scattered up and down the coast. At the time Many Baskets had already been betrothed to Xawishata. Her father brought her to the Hoh River village, then took his canoe and paddled out to sea, never to be seen again.

Xawishata was a man of honor and he married her in spite of her scars. She had fallen in love with him immediately, but he'd never felt anything but pity for her, for her scars were more than skin deep. She was a brooding, reclusive girl who never smiled.

He soon married again and favored his second wife, Talks A Lot, a plump cheerful woman who bore him many daughters. As the years passed and Many Baskets remained barren, perhaps due to the smallpox, she became bitter and full of hatred for the whites whom she blamed for all the misfortunes of her life. Now her frustrations were aimed at the two white captives who were at her mercy.

Xawishata had commanded they were not to be harmed, because he was holding them for ransom. But Many Baskets could not help frightening the women whenever she had the chance. She enjoyed the quick looks of terror in their strange colored eyes, especially if she pretended to threaten the infant in the cradle board. Not that she would ever harm such a beautiful girl. Her arms ached to hold the little one with the hair of the sunset to her heart. But she dared not try. The young hokwat mother was as fiercely protective as any mother bear around her cub.

Anna snatched Katya to her breast before Many Baskets could get any closer. She did not trust the way the woman's eyes slid towards her daughter.

"Leave us alone or I'll let my cat out!" Tatiana said sharply, moving towards Otter's box. The cat was meowing restlessly and wanted to stretch her legs. When Tatiana opened the lid, she leaped out with an extra loud yowl. The cat had become scrawny and ill-tempered with her constant confinement and she had no affection for anyone except Tatiana and Anna, who fed her whenever they could.

Many Baskets thought the cat was possessed by an evil spirit, and she hastily backed away. At that moment the door flap swung aside and Talks A Lot entered the hut, followed by Marya and Keeah.

Otter froze, arching her back at all the sudden commotion and spit, looking like a demented animal. That was all Many Baskets needed to see and she disappeared out the doorway. Tatiana and Anna breathed a sigh of mutual relief.

"I detest that woman," said Tatiana then smiled a greeting to Marya and Talks A Lot, who always wore her bear claw necklace. The Quileutes hunted very little, as they were a seafaring people, but Xawishata had once killed a grizzly, a feat so great, it had brought him immense honor. When they married, he gave Talks A Lot a necklace made of the giant claws. She treasured it, especially since Many Baskets had nothing so fine.

Grinning broadly, Keeah and the other girl set down baskets of freshly roasted fish, steamed clams, and dried blackberry cakes, a veritable feast. Keeah looked healthy and well cared for. She was a slave in the chief's household and in a few days was to be given to his new Third Wife, Marya, as a wedding gift. At that time she hoped Marya would choose a new name for her besides the ignoble one of Tlingit Girl, which the Quileutes now called her.

"I have wonderful news for the two of you," said Marya, forcing a smile on her face.

She was dressed in native jewelry, wearing a necklace of slender white shells around her throat, which the natives called money beads and the white men called dentalium. They looked like small ivory tusks, an inch or two long and were considered as gold to the Indians. Dentalium was found only in the deep water off Vancouver Island where the little creatures inside them clung upright to the rocks. The Nootkas fished them up and traded them along the coast. Keeah had thought it quite impressive that the chief had given a necklace of money beads to Marya.

Tiny shell earrings dangled from her ears and shiny copper and brass bracelets encircled her arms. A headband of fur was wrapped around her head and her long ebony hair flowed to her waist. Gone was the sophisticated Marya Nikolayevna wearing gems and expensive gowns. In her place was a beautiful native girl with the saddest eyes Anna ever saw.

She felt a rush of pity for Marya, who was in a terrible position. If she went through with the marriage, and she had little choice, her chances of ever reuniting with John were slim. Anna was so thankful Chief Xawishata had decided against marrying her or Tatiana, nor had they been given to any of the warriors.

It had almost happened, however. Keeah, the source of all their information, told them Hoheeshata had demanded one of them be given him for a wife. Both of his previous wives had died in childbirth, and he was looking for another. In order to save them from the cruel Hoheeshata, Keeah had urged Marya to tell Chief Xawishata that both Tatiana and Anna were wives of the white chiefs. Even though Anna was only the captain's betrothed, Marya agreed. When the chief heard this, he refused his brother's request, saying he wished to save the white chiefs' women for ransom. He expected many guns in trade. Angry, Hoheeshata soon left with a small band of men to raid other villages in the south, vowing to steal a wife if he had to.

Since then, she and Tatiana and Katya lived a strange existence in the village. Neither wife nor slave, they were prisoners, allowed out of their dank hut each morning to bathe in the river then returned to long hours of boredom. At first they were not permitted a fire, even when the winds howled and thundered over the hut and the rain drummed constantly on the roof. Not until it turned bitterly cold was a fire finally allowed.

One morning the ground was frozen solid and a thick frost coated all the tree branches and ferns like a dust of sparkling white diamonds. Anna could hardly stand the icy shock of the river water and was worried the cold baths might make them ill. Yet, she and Tatiana stayed healthy with only an occasional runny nose.

Often in the dim light of their fire, Anna read her Bible out loud to Tatiana, who for the first time in her life, admitted the holy book contained some very interesting stories. They saw Marya and Keeah occasionally. As a slave, Keeah's days were spent fetching wood and water, cleaning fish and skins, and helping with the perpetual cooking. She lived in the chief's big plank house, but her bed was the coldest in the house, the furthest away from the fire, and she could eat only after the family had eaten.

She was never mistreated, as the Quileutes did not believe in whipping, starving, or punishing their slaves. A badly treated slave could not work. Sometimes Many Baskets lost her temper if she was too slow to obey, and gave her an occasional blow. Keeah's greatest sorrow was that she could not rise in position. A slave to the Quileutes was a slave for life.

Marya also lived in the chief's huge house. The building was divided up into four family compartments belonging to Hoheeshata, Many Baskets, Talks A Lot and her children, and Marya, who was given one of her own. Since Many Baskets retained the honor of First Wife, Xawishata kept all his possessions in her compartment, but he rarely slept there.

As Marya waited for her wedding day, Talks A Lot taught her the duties and responsibilities of becoming a chief's wife. Besides learning the Quileute rules, traditions and rituals, the work was not much different than the sewing, weaving, and cooking she did as a young Aleut girl. Talks A Lot was a kindly person and a good mother to her four daughters, ages six months to seven years.

At first the three oldest girls were shy around Marya, never having seen a half-Aleut, half-white person. But they reminded her so much of her young cousins in New Archangel, that she showered them with smiles and warmth. They soon welcomed her into the family by treating her like a favored aunt and trying to teach her their language. That was no small task, for the Quileutes spoke without any nasal sounds and used a series of explosive sounds that were pronounced with a forceful "click," which was difficult to learn. It was helpful to Marya that the chief and some of the Quileutes also spoke "Chinook jargon," a type of pidgin language mix of English and native words which developed between the coastal Indians and the white traders.

The only two people in the village Marya feared was Hoheeshata and Many Baskets. Since Hoheeshata was away, it was Many Baskets who made no secret of her jealousy and tried to make Marya's life miserable. As soon as Marya moved into the chief's house, Many Baskets began to screech insults at her. She had gone into Marya's compartment and was about to strike her with her fist, when Xawishata stepped inside and strode between them.

He was like water thrown on a fire. Her hand dropped to her side and she smiled up at him, a smile that would have been lovely even with her pitted skin if it had reached the coldness in her eyes. He spoke sternly to her and ordered her out of his sight, then turned to Marya, his black eyes alight with desire.

She had been fearful he would take her to his compartment then, but he only touched her cheek and hair gently and left her alone. Later Talks A Lot explained that though polygamy and divorce were common among the Quileutes, premarital relations were frowned upon.

Marya was relieved the chief wouldn't expect her to share his nights until they married. She dreaded that day so deeply, there were times she wondered if she was better off taking her own life. Then she remembered Boris and how she'd been saved from becoming his true wife in the nick of time.

Now she prayed continually that God would help her. She knew after being an Indian wife, no decent white man like John would ever want her again. Inside her heart, she felt broken in many pieces.

It wasn't that Chief Xawishata was a cruel man like his brother. As time passed, she watched him closely and decided there was much about him that reminded her of her Russian father, Nikolas Bolkonsky. Like her papa, he was strong yet gentle, and of noble lineage. The village respected him as their leader and a fearless hunter of whales, which had made him very rich. At age thirty five, he was in the prime of his life, and though Marya did not find him traditionally handsome, because of his sloping forehead, he had an attractive smile and his eyes were etched in laughter lines.

Even more important, he also had a generous nature that earned him the adoration of his whole family. His daughters worshipped the ground he walked on. Since their betrothal, he had showered her with gifts of ornaments, furs, and promised she could keep her friend, Tlingit Girl, as a slave instead of selling her off. Perhaps if she had never known John, she could have learned to love Xawishata in time.

This evening he'd told her startling news. Accompanied by Talks A Lot, she'd come at once to tell Tatiana and Anna, even though her heart was shattering. "The chief has made contact with the white men," she said stiffly, trying to keep the envy from her voice. "He has made arrangements for you both to be taken to a meeting place and be traded back to them."

Joy suddenly coursed through Anna's veins and she and Tatiana laughed excitedly at the same time. Then Tatiana stopped laughing and looked at Marya with worry. "And what about you, Marya?"

"I am not Marya," she said, her eyes misting with tears. "Chief Xawishata has named me Whispering Doe. In two days I will be his third wife." Her lips trembled and she fought to control them, conscious of Talks A Lot's puzzled expression. As far as the Quileutes were concerned, her past life no longer existed and they expected her to forget it no matter how she felt. When she became their chief's third wife, she became a Quileute forever.

"I'm sorry," said Anna softly, hearing the unbearable anguish in Marya's voice as she struggled to hide it from Talks A Lot.

"You are to leave tomorrow morning," she said, keeping a smile pasted on her face.

"Did the chief say anything more about our men?" Tatiana asked. "Do you know how they are faring in the forest?"

"He said they have been watched ever since our capture. Several of the most badly wounded have died, but," she hastened to add at the looks of alarm on their faces, "not the captain or Dmitri or--or John." She took a deep breath. "They say the rest of them are in good health, though not well fed. They are poor hunters. Some weeks past they retreated up the Hoh River near the holy mountain, Mount Olympus, where they've built a fortified camp at a lake near the river's headwaters. I understand negotiations for your release has been going on for some time."

"But we can't leave you behind! You are my sister. Doesn't the chief understand that?"

Marya's mouth twisted bitterly. "It is too late for me. I'll be married soon and I will never see John again. Even if I do, he will never forgive me." She glanced at Anna's Bible sitting next to her on the floor. "Soon I will become the wife of a heathen and my children will be born pagans. I will never have a priest to confess my sins to. The best thing the two of you can do is go and forget all about me. I am a lost soul."

A sob tore out of her and Talks A Lot frowned in dismay. She put an arm protectively around Marya and murmured to her.

Tatiana felt furious. She and Marya had gone through so much. First, they had hated each other on sight, then their father died, and finally, they'd learned to love and respect one another as true sisters.

"I refuse to be ransomed unless you are too," she said stubbornly.

Marya shrugged off Talks A Lot's arm and stepped over to her. "No, Tatiana Nikolayevna, you must not do anything to jeopardize your situation. You are truly a white woman. I am a half breed, a *Creole*. I remember well the ways of my mother's people. It will not be too difficult for me to learn how to be a Quileute. I will have many children. I will be an honored wife the rest of my days. John will forget me like his Nootka Princess and marry a proper white woman. You must tell him I am dead."

Anna stood up, handing Katya to Talks A Lot, who took her eagerly. "Listen to me, Marya Nikolayevna, you are not a lost soul. You are a Christian woman caught in a situation not of your own doing."

"I should refuse to marry him," she said, "but I'm too much of a coward. I'm afraid of being a slave or sold away. I wish I had Father Sokolov to talk to."

"I'll leave you my Bible," Anna said, handing it to Marya. "Here, read it whenever you can. It will help you in any situation you find yourself, especially when you feel alone and you need God's strength."

Hope flared in Marya's heart, replacing the utter desolation she'd felt moments before. "I miss my Papa's Bible," she said. "It was lost the day we were captured. Won't you need yours, Anna?"

"I will miss it, too," she admitted frankly, "but I learned so much Scripture as a child, that I now carry God's words in my heart." Anna gave her a smile. "You know, Marya, as Whispering Doe, God can use you here in this village to bring Christianity to these Indians."

"I never thought of that before," she said, her eyes suddenly brightening then fading as quickly. "But--but there is the *shaman.* He would oppose any new religion."

"God is more powerful than he is," said Anna, remembering the night two weeks before when White Panther the village *shaman* came into the hut, demanding to see the spirit animal.

He was an elderly man of about seventy years, toothless and shrunken with wisps of long gray hair hanging down his back and fierce black eyes set deeply into his wizened face. He carried a wooden staff almost as tall as he was and a conical hat of colorful designs sat on his head. A white panther's skin was thrown over one bony shoulder like a Roman toga.

Keeah accompanied him, trembling visibly, as she translated his requests. First, he wanted to see the cat.

Tatiana removed Otter from her box, trying to stroke her into submission, but failed utterly, as the cat turned her glowing green eyes upon the *shaman* and hissed. He flinched slightly, but held his ground, then spoke to Keeah.

"He wishes to know how you came to have this animal, *Madame*," she said in a quivering voice. *Shamans* and their powers terrified her.

"Tell him when I was a child I had a cat as pure white as his mantle. One day it flew out my window, and then reappeared many years later as this cat."

Anna coughed into her hand as she tried to stifle her laughter. She knew the story of Snowball and how Tatiana's cousin Mikael had thrown the poor thing out the window. Now Tatiana was twisting it to serve her own purposes.

White Panther appeared skeptical also and then his eyes alighted on Anna's Bible which was sitting on the floor near Katya's cradle board. He pointed to it with his staff.

"He wants to know what that is."

"Tell him it is God's holy book," said Anna, picking it up.

Since there was no word for book in their language, she told him it was a holy object that spoke the words of the white man's God, a very powerful Spirit. The *shaman*'s eyes narrowed with interest and he set his staff aside as he indicated he wanted to see it.

With reluctance Anna gave him the Bible. He flipped through the pages and saw the odd black markings which made no sense to him.

As he ran his fingers over the thin paper, he muttered, "Feels like butterfly wings."

Suddenly his hands began to shake and he dropped the Bible as if it had scorched him. He hissed a sound so similar to Otter's that the cat stared at him in surprise and growled.

White Panther appeared even more rattled and said a few terse words to Keeah, then snatched up his staff and vanished out the doorway.

"What was that all about?" Tatiana asked as she struggled to put Otter back into her box.

Keeah fidgeted in agitation. "He say holy thing turned hot and burned his fingers and must be evil. He say cat is evil, too." She twisted her hands nervously together and added, "*Shaman* very powerful man. You must guard Otter from him. Hide Bible."

The rest of the night Anna could hardly sleep, pondering the mystery of the Bible turning hot in the *shaman*'s hands. Was it the old man's imagination or had something supernatural taken place? Had the power of the Holy Spirit in the Bible marked the *shaman* himself as evil?

When Tatiana had asked her to explain it, Anna said she could not. Tatiana became very thoughtful, very subdued, and listened even more closely the next day when Anna read from the Bible about a young man named Daniel and how God saved him from a lions' den. The story of Daniel living as a captive in Persia far from his home in Jerusalem brought much comfort to Anna. Though he had every reason to forget God, Daniel's faith never wavered, and God protected him and his friends from wild animals, fiery deaths, and evil men.

White Panther had not returned since and Anna hoped they'd seen the last of him. Yet she knew it was unlikely he would forget the incident anymore than she could.

Talks A Lot now looked uneasily at the Bible in Marya's hands. The news of the strange black object had spread throughout the village.

Tatiana noticed the suspicion on her face and said, "Will you be allowed to keep it?"

Marya smiled wryly. "At the moment the chief is besotted with me and he denies me nothing. If I beg him to let me keep the Bible, he will override the *shaman*'s wishes. When he tires of me," she shrugged, "then I don't know."

"He won't have the chance to tire of you," smiled Tatiana, giving her a quick embrace. "I intend to ask our men to offer a ransom for you as well as us. Do not give up hope, Marya Nikolayevna."

A sob caught in her throat. "I will try to keep faith, dearest sister."

Then Anna hugged her warmly. "I will pray for you every day, my dear Marya, and God will watch over you. If He wills, we will see each other again."

"Not to worry," said Keeah, "I will take care of *Mademoiselle*." Her eyes lingered mournfully on the sweet face of the sleeping Katya, whom she had taken care of as tenderly as if her own, then all three slipped out the door.

Tatiana and Anna sighed sadly at first then Tatiana burst into a grin, her eyes sparkling with happiness. “We will be with our men tomorrow, Anna!”

She reached for the food, eating hungrily. Nodding in agreement, Anna helped herself to the salmon, privately suspecting that Tatiana was not speaking of her husband, Dmitri, but of Anton Dohktorov.

CHAPTER THIRTY SEVEN

For weeks the weather had been wet and windy, but now a rare arctic cold snap blew in from the north. The day of Anna's and Tatiana's release dawned clear and brisk with a brilliant blue sky overhead. A bright sun streaked through the trees, but the rays could not reach the forest floor and the ground remained hard and frozen with frost.

The voyage up the Hoh River in the canoe was a bitter cold, yet exhilarating experience for both young women after their weeks of confinement in a dank smoky smelly hut.

Pale and thin, they knew they didn't look their best. Their hair was unevenly braided and they were dressed in poorly sewn robes of muskrat fur. Since they were still captives, the chief didn't want to give the women a valuable fur robe, such as sea otter, bear, marmot, or martin, so they wore the coarse skins of the common and lowly muskrat thrown over their flimsy cedar bark clothing.

The girls had to admit the material was excellent in shedding the rain and keeping them dry, but they could never stop shivering in the thin garments. They had been told the Indian women wore them all winter, usually without anything else and never became cold.

It made Anna and Tatiana feel inferior, but soon they expected to be back with their men, and it wouldn't matter what the Quileutes thought of them.

Katya was strapped in her cradle board on Anna's back, her bright blue eyes soberly watching the Indian behind her as he steered the canoe skillfully against the current. Tatiana sat in front of them with her feet resting on top of Otter's box. Chief Xawishata and a small band of his warriors followed them in another canoe.

Many creeks flowed into the Hoh, adding to the river's volume, and at this time of year, the current was swift and strong, making dangerous rapids whenever the water met a jagged rock. There were numerous gravel bars, too, but the Quileutes avoided these obstacles with ease as they paddled their canoes tirelessly up the river.

Walls of towering moss draped trees lined the banks. Behind them the lush forests loomed dark and forbidding. Once they saw several deer munching on some leaves. When they saw the canoes, their dark eyes widened with alarm and they flicked their white tails then bounded away into the trees.

The warriors laughed and several aimed their bow and arrows at the animals, wishing they were on a hunt.

The surrounding scenery was breathtaking. As the canoes rounded the bends in the river, there were brief glimpses of majestic Mount Olympus to the east, covered with snow and frozen glaciers.

Keeah had told Anna and Tatiana that the Quileutes believed the Blue Glacier was the lair of their Great Spirit, Thunderbird, who sent thunder and lightening and certain rains. It was also the place where the white men had wisely settled, safe from all native attacks.

The meeting place was a quarter of the way up the Hoh River Valley, which stretched over fifty miles from the Pacific Ocean to the foothills of Mount Olympus. The river narrowed here as the terrain steepened and became more treacherous with white water and rapids. The Quileutes landed their canoes on a gravel beach on the south side of the river. Across the rushing water on the opposite bank the group of white men was already gathered.

At first Anna and Tatiana could not recognize anyone. The men's clothing was in rags and each had a thick beard and mustache and long dirty hair. Then four men stepped forward.

Tatiana stifled a gasp of distress as she saw her husband. He had aged considerably; his hair and matted beard was near white, his face haggard and gaunt, his eyes sunken into darkened hollows, and his arms and legs appeared painfully thin. He looked more like a prisoner of war than a lieutenant of the Imperial Navy.

Anton stood besides him, tall and almost as bony, dressed in the same shabby clothing, but his face with its trimmed brown beard and mustache was wreathed in a welcoming smile, giving him an air of health and strength. Tatiana sighed in relief at the sight.

From this short distance across the water, Anna spied Sean immediately. Like the others, he had lost much weight. His *kamleika* hung loosely from his broad shoulders and the skin was pulled taut across his cheekbones. He looked like a pirate with his thick black beard and long black hair. She could feel the magnetic pull of his green eyes glittering towards her as he waved and grinned, displaying a flash of white teeth in his face darkened from his life outdoors.

"Anna!" he shouted over the roar of the water.

"Can we talk to our-- our husbands?" Anna asked Xawishata, hoping he would understand her. To her surprise, he seemed to gather her meaning and pointed to the water's edge, nodding his assent. She and Tatiana stood on the edge of the rough beach, gingerly balancing their tender feet on the rocks and pebbles.

"How are you?" Sean and Dmitri both shouted in unison, their voices full of anxiety.

"We are fine," Anna called out.

"Have the savages harmed you, Tatiana?" Dmitri demanded.

"No, Dmitri, we have been well-treated," she answered. "And how are all of you? Are you well?"

"We're surviving!" Sean said. "We've built a small fort in the mountains. 'Tis room for all of us." His gaze focused on the cradle board strapped to Anna's back. "And Katya, how is she?"

"Growing like a weed," said Anna, her voice trembling with emotion. She wanted to say so much more, but then John shoved forwards, anger written all over his bearded face. She felt a moment of panic. What were they going to tell him about Marya?

He cupped his hands around his mouth and yelled, "What has happened to Marya?"

"She's my sister," said Tatiana quietly. "I'll tell him." She took a deep breath and answered firmly, "John, Marya has not been harmed. But the chief would not allow her to leave with us."

"Why not? Did they make her a slave?"

"No, but she needs to be ransomed quickly! Chief Xawishata intends to make her his third wife very soon!"

John's dirty face went pale with shock and he swore loudly. Sean and Anton also appeared disturbed while Dmitri did not change his expression one whit. Instead he said something to John that caused his body to stiffen.

"What do you mean that I'm better off without her?" John demanded, his face contorted with rage. "Is that how you'd feel if it was your wife being married to the chief?"

"My wife is a pure blooded white woman, the daughter of one of Russia's most noble families. It would be an abomination for her to marry a savage. But my sister-in-law is a half breed," he sneered. "She's finally going back to her own kind."

"Why, you--" John began as he grabbed Dmitri around his scrawny neck with his hands and squeezed. "Marya is a Bolkonsky just as much as Tatiana! How dare you!"

"Stop it at once, men!" Sean ordered. He seized John by the waist and tried to pull him off Dmitri. "John, this won't help matters any. The Indians are laughing at us."

Dmitri's eyes were bulging and his face was turning purple when John finally released his grip, dropping his hands at his side. Robby stood nearby, watching eagerly, and frowned in disappointment when John let him go.

John saw his scowl and muttered, "Another time, lad, another time." He stalked away without any apology, distancing himself from the group. Sean caught the bleak expression on his face and decided not to pursue the matter.

"Ye need to watch your mouth, Volodin," he said, as the baron coughed and sputtered, rubbing his reddened neck. "One of these days, I won't be around to save ye."

Chief Xawishata and his warriors were smiling and tittering at the sight of the white men at each other's throats. Anna and Tatiana felt dismayed and Tatiana was particularly embarrassed, knowing her husband had provoked the confrontation by insulting her own sister.

The Quileutes suddenly ceased laughing as Xawishata decided he'd heard enough of the shouting in the alien English and Russian languages of the white men. He strode forward and faced them, gesturing to John to come closer as he began to speak. John listened carefully then translated the chief's speech to Sean and the rest of the men.

"Chief Xawishata demands eight guns, four for each woman."

This started all the men arguing among themselves and brought a worried look on Sean's face. "We don't have eight guns we can spare," he said.

"We have no choice!" Dmitri exploded. "We have to give them what they want. They can even have my gold epaulets," he added, as he began ripping them off the shoulders of his uniformed coat.

John ignored Dmitri's tantrum and hailed the chief, telling him he would personally give him his finest musket in trade for the woman he planned to take as third wife.

"She is not for trade," said Xawishata, folding his arms across his bare chest. "She will bear me many sons."

John's face blanched at that and he yelled, "But she is the woman I want for my wife! You have no right to her! Give her back!"

The chief refused to answer and only repeated his demands for Anna and Tatiana. John turned to Sean and said, "He won't budge. He wants eight guns for the women, but not for Marya. I wash my hands of this whole affair." With a tormented groan he walked off into the forest, a look of utter desolation upon his face.

"What are we to do?" Sean said to Anton, "We've twenty eight men and only have twenty five usable guns left, and some of those are bound to break eventually."

"If only we still had the forge and all the tools for repairing guns," said Anton in frustration. "Then it wouldn't matter so much if we gave away a third of our guns."

"We can't give them Injuns eight of our best muskets," complained Nate Tyler. "Why they'd just turn around an' use them guns against us. I say we let 'em have the women."

Dmitri growled in anger. "You wouldn't say that if one of them was your wife, you black-hearted bag of scum!" He turned to all the men and pleaded, "Don't listen to him, men. Listen to your consciences and do the right thing and give up your guns to rescue our women. How can you live with yourselves if you don't?"

"Captain," he then said to Sean, "why don't you order them to hand over their guns? One of those women is your betrothed!"

"Tyler's right. If we gave eight guns to the Quileutes for Anna and Tatiana, half of us be dead in a week. They'd pick us off one by one like sitting ducks."

"They can have this gun," said Jeb Drake with a smirk, holding up an obviously damaged musket.

Chief Xawishata saw the gun and shook his head, grunting in dissatisfaction. He stared at the white men with a thunderous expression, then turned heel and marched back to his canoe.

While Anna and Tatiana listened to all of this, their hopes had quietly ebbed away. As much as they longed to be rescued they knew it was foolish for the men to surrender any of their guns to the Indians. The white men's sole power lay in the fact that the Indians feared their weapons and had left them alone for that very reason.

Across the water, Sean and Anna exchanged glances stricken with despair. Anna longed for him to order the men to trade their guns, but she knew he would not do it. Not even for her and Katya. He stood still, a look of helplessness and anger upon his face. His eyes reached into hers, begging for forgiveness.

Anna bowed her head, wondering if she could do it. This time when they separated, it might be forever. There would be no further hope for negotiations and ransom. But if this was the final time they might see each other, she couldn't leave without letting him know she understood and still loved him.

She lifted her head and smiled at him through her tears. "I'll always love you," she said. "Don't lose faith. God will bring us together again."

Her bravery brought Sean close to tears as well. "I love you, too, my Anna. I promise I will come for you. Never forget that!"

Dmitri was shrieking insults at the Indians then began to lament loudly, "My beautiful Tatiana Nikolayevna, my love, do not despair! I will rescue you!"

Tatiana said nothing, her shoulders slumping in defeat, as her eyes sought Anton's face one last time. He nodded at her and smiled sadly, but neither one dared speak. She looked at Dmitri with an expression of disgust, refusing to say farewell to him, as one of the Indians seized her and dragged her back toward the canoe.

Another took hold of Anna and she and Tatiana began to sob with bitter disappointment as their hopes of freedom disappeared. Katya, who had remained silent throughout, heard her mother crying, and let out a sympathetic wail.

All the men stood on the riverbank and listened sadly to the pathetic sounds of weeping women fading into the roar of the river as the two canoes vanished from sight. Even Nate Tyler and Jeb Drake appeared abashed when they saw their captain lower his head in obvious pain, his broad shoulders heaving with silent sobs.

Dmitri finally quieted and collapsed on the ground, looking at the river with a wide unblinking stare. He hunched over and wept, and when he stood up again, he had the shrunken face of an old man.

In grim silence, everyone gathered their gear and guns and prepared for the long march upriver to their mountain fort where the only thing awaiting them was the icy rains and heavy snow of the long winter ahead.

* * *

After returning from the trip up the Hoh River valley Anna and Tatiana were taken back to the hut and given neither food nor water. The chief was obviously angry that his valuable captives had proven to be worthless. But the lack of sustenance didn't matter to them since neither one had any appetite. If it wasn't for Otter's and Katya's demands for nourishment, they wouldn't care if they saw another morsel of food.

The next day brought a flurry of activity to the village. Anna and Tatiana awoke to the sounds of chattering women, laughing children, and barking dogs. They were sounds of anticipation and excitement, exactly the opposite emotions of the two severely depressed women. They'd lain on their furs all night, curled up in fetal positions, having cried so long, they now felt drained of any feelings except despair and hopelessness.

"It sounds like today is Marya's wedding," said Anna, struggling to sit up and feed Katya, who had also spent a fretful night.

At age eight months she was well aware of her surroundings and had a sensitive ear towards her mama's moods. When Anna was unhappy, Katya became crabby and irritable, knowing something was not right in her tiny little world. She also had begun to crawl whenever she was out of her cradleboard, usually aiming for the attractive flickering and crackling of the fire which kept Anna and Tatiana busy keeping her away from the danger.

"It makes me wonder who is the more cursed, she or us," said Tatiana dully. "At least she knows what her fate is." She looked at Anna. "What do you think your God has in store for us now?"

"I don't know. I was so certain we were going to be ransomed. Now I don't know what to think."

The door flap swung aside and Marya entered. She was beautifully dressed in a luxurious robe of velvety sea otter skins. Flashing amber earrings dangled from her ears, necklaces of blue abalone shell beads hung around her neck and silver bracelets encircled her arms. Her hair had been freshly washed and oiled and flowed down her back in a gleaming black waterfall. She looked every inch a bride.

"You must pull yourself together, my sisters," she said in a firm voice. "Today is the first day of my wedding feast, a celebration of great importance that the Quileutes call a *potlatch*. Many chiefs and nobles from other villages have been invited and Chief Xawishata wishes to present you to them."

"Don't you want to know what happened yesterday, Marya?" Tatiana asked, arching one eyebrow at her with surprise at her sister's appearance and calm demeanor.

She stiffened. “I already heard from Chief Xawishata that he was insulted and dishonored by the white men’s refusal to trade for you.”

“And John,” said Tatiana with emphasis, “don’t you wish to know how he is?”

Marya’s expression faltered then, and her eyes misted. “How---how was he?” she whispered.

“He tried his best to trade for you, but the chief refused. John was beset with grief as were Dmitri and Captain O'Connell .”

Marya hung her head. “I knew it would be hopeless. I came to a decision after you left, that I would try to forget my past life and live each day here as a Quileute. This is what I still must do. I do not know any other way to survive and find life worth living again.” She stared at both of them. “Forgive me if I become Whispering Doe.”

Marya would not meet her sister's angry gaze and kept her head bowed like a guilty parishioner before a priest. She was afraid both Anna and Tatiana would never understand her acceptance to become a Quileute. Her only other choice was to become a slave, or end her life. And she did not have the courage for either.

“My mama used to tell me a favorite Mennonite saying whenever I couldn’t let go of my guilt over a confessed sin,” Anna suddenly blurted. "She’d say, ‘Yesterday is gone, so I’ll just forget about it. Tomorrow is something I can’t do anything about since I can’t reach it. That leaves today, which is a gift from God, and that is why we call it the present.’”

Marya appeared startled then she smiled gratefully. “Thank you, Anna.”

Tatiana huffed, but before she could say anything, two slave girls stooped through the doorway carrying baskets and bowls. They brought salmonberry juice, dried fish, fish oil, and slices of camas bread for dipping. Camas was a type of starchy tuber that looked like an onion and grew in open fields. It was pounded into flour and mixed with water and then baked into loaves. These would keep for months and slices from them were eaten with fish or seal oil. Both girls thought camas bread tasted like wet wood chips.

“Eat,” said Marya, “then you will be taken to the river for washing.” She slipped out the door, saying, “Be brave, my sisters, and don’t despair.”

“Easy for her to say,” muttered Tatiana resentfully. “She knows exactly what her future holds. We do not.”

The slaves had brought more shredded cedar bark for the cradle board and as Anna replaced the fouled material with the fresh, she said, “I can survive anything as long as I still have my Katya with me.”

* * *

Otter was missing. After Anna and Tatiana returned to the hut from bathing in the cold river, the first thing they noticed was that the cat and her box was gone.

"Where is my cat?" Tatiana demanded. "Who has taken her?"

The two slave girls who accompanied them had no answer. They were both about seventeen years old and had been traded from the Chehalis tribe to the south. Shy and timid, they shrank back from the fierce expression on Tatiana's face. Before they could stop her, she brushed past them and ran outside.

Their hut had never been guarded and both she and Anna could have walked out anytime. But there was nowhere to go and no way of escaping the Quileutes on their own, so they had never tried to leave.

Now Tatiana was so maddened she had no intention of staying placidly inside.

"Tatiana, wait," Anna called out, following her with Katya strapped on her back.

One of the slaves grabbed Tatiana's arm to try and pull her back into the hut, but Tatiana shook off her hand like a troublesome flea. She glanced around at the surrounding houses, wondering which one belonged to White Panther, the *shaman*. She was positive he had stolen Otter. No one else would have dared.

There was a commotion some distance away past the last house at the end of the village, near the forest's edge. Dogs barked and whined, women and children shouted, and they could hear the deeper gruff voices of men.

"What's happening?" Anna asked, looking in the same direction.

Tatiana tensed her jaw. "I'm not certain, but I'm going to find out."

Anna hesitated only for a moment. "I'm coming with you."

They set off towards the hubbub of people and dogs with the slave girls right on their heels, chattering in great agitation. Tatiana and Anna ignored them, and soon saw a crowd of men, women, and children standing beneath a towering cedar tree.

A pack of snarling dogs circled the massive trunk, sniffing and looking up into the branches.

As the girls came closer, they both knew what they would find. Peering upwards, they spotted the white and gray cat perched more than fifty feet up on a branch. She was staring down, her slanted eyes glowing green with fright. Except for her precarious perch, she appeared in one piece. Obviously the dogs had chased her up the tree.

The Indians fell back from Tatiana as she approached, muttering at her with wide eyes as if they expected her to perform some magic in fetching her cat down. But she knew Otter would never come down until all the people and dogs left. And how was she to make that happen?

The people retreated even further when White Panther limped through the crowd, leaning on his staff. Tatiana whirled on him and spat in French, "You! You're responsible for this! You stole my cat and let her go and she could've been killed by the dogs!"

The villagers were shocked beyond belief that the white captive dared shout at their powerful medicine man. However, the *shaman* was even more shocked than they were. No one had spoken to him like that since he was a boy scolded by his mother.

He recovered his composure quickly. He pointed a long bony finger at Tatiana and said in Quileute, "If this animal is indeed from the spirit world and is truly your spirit guardian, the dogs cannot hurt it and it will find its own way out of the tree."

The crowd murmured their agreement at his wise words. It was apparent to them that their *shaman* had decided to test the white women's animal to see if it was mortal or spirit. If mortal, it could be killed without worry. If spirit, then he could perform some magic spells to make the creature leave the village without any harm to them.

Tatiana was incensed beyond reason. For weeks she had lived in submission to the Quileutes. They had taken her freedom, her clothing, her jewels, threatened her, starved her, kept her from her husband and the man she loved, and now they'd stolen her only possession, her pet cat. Who did they think they were, she fumed, her temper near to the explosion point.

Unnoticed by her, a group of visiting Makah warriors who had just arrived for the *potlatch*, stood nearby watching. One man in particular stared at Tatiana with fascinated admiration. He was close enough to see how her eyes changed color the way the sky after sunset darkened from topaz to sapphire blue to violet and then darkest indigo. With the wind rustling through her freshly washed golden hair as it tumbled past her slender waist, he decided he was seeing the vision of the sun goddess. He also noticed the other white woman, small and slight, with hair of darkly burnished honey. She stood quiet and meek in sharp contrast to the taller woman, who was possessed of a magnificent spirit

I need another wife, he thought. *At the* potlatch *tonight, I will offer so many gifts to Chief Xawishata; he will give her to me. I shall name her Daughter of the Sun.*

Tatiana continued to rant and rave at White Panther, who suddenly lost his patience. He marched stiffly over to her and as he raised his staff to smack her on the head the Makah warrior grabbed the end. He and the *shaman* glared at each other, challenge written all over their faces.

"I'll remove this troublesome woman from your village forever," said the Makah in Quileute. "But do not strike her."

Slowly, the *shaman* lowered his staff, his arm trembling. At his advanced age, he wasn't used to sudden physical exertion any longer. He spat at Tatiana's feet. "If Xawishata agrees, she's yours. Both of them," he added, giving Anna a hostile glance.

With all the dignity he could muster, he hobbled away, whacking a few of the dogs with his staff as he passed by them. They yelped and ran off, and the rest of the dogs followed. He disappeared into the forest where he had his medicine hut and soon the villagers dispersed as well.

The Chehalis slave girls tugged at Anna's arm, indicating that she and Tatiana were to return to their hut. The group of Makah warriors turned to leave, except for one, the man who'd saved Tatiana from the *shaman*'s wrath.

He stood smiling at Tatiana, and she looked at him, her anger dissolving into curiosity. The Makah warrior was taller than any of the Quileutes, even taller than she. He was as broad shouldered as Captain O'Connell and when he moved, muscles rippled across the light copper colored skin of his bare chest. He wore a blanket fastened around his loins with a girdle and reaching halfway down his thighs.

Tatiana glanced up at his face. He seemed to be in his mid thirties and his features were bold and arresting. Although he had the typical broad forehead of a noble Indian, he had a straight nose and his lips were sculpted full and sensual. She could not see his hair, for he wore it tied back like an Englishman. He had a straight thin mustache and a small goatee on his chin. A colorful hat rested upon his head, painted with whaling scenes and topped with a pear shaped bulb.

His eyes were dark and hooded like a hawk. They gazed into Tatiana's eyes with a smoldering look of such intensity that she felt her blood course through her body, hot and quick. Instinctively she knew this man was a danger to her, but not in the same manner as a savage like Hoheeshata.

Confused, she stumbled away after Anna and the slave girls, conscious of his burning stare following her. In her haste she forgot poor Otter stuck in the tree.

"Who was that strange Indian that stopped the *shaman* from hitting you?" Anna asked her a few minutes later when they reached their hut.

"I don't know, and I don't care if I never see him again."

* * *

Earlier that morning the Makah from Cape Flattery were the first of the *potlatch* guests to arrive. The rest of the day saw dozens more of the huge ocean going canoes from up and down the coast lining up at the mouth of the Hoh River, waiting for the invitation to land. There were some Nootka from Vancouver Island, neighboring tribes of Quileutes from nearby villages, and Quinaults from the south. Those who traveled the farthest were welcomed first, and when all the tribes were ashore, there was a great feast of roast elk, salmon, and razor clams.

In the following days the entire village resounded with laughter, singing, and feasting as everyone celebrated the wedding of Chief Xawishata. At night huge bonfires were lit outside for storytelling and dancing to drums. In the daytime dozens of shouting young men played games of prowess and skill, including wrestling contests, tug-of-war, and canoe racing on the smooth water of the river at high tide.

Anna and Tatiana were forbidden to attend. On the first day Marya sent Keeah with food and instructions to take care of them for the duration of the *potlatch.* The girls and Katya were to stay hidden until the final night. It was a long three days and nights, but Keeah's company and explanations of what was happening helped them pass the time.

The many ceremonies of the *potlatch* were held in Chief Xawishata's big house. Keeah described how all the partitions inside were removed so the guests could gather together. Gifts of food, beads, baskets, knives, weapons, furs, blankets, and slaves were given away. The more a man gave, the more he impressed everyone how rich he was. Other ceremonies included the recitation of Chief Xawishata's mythological heritage. The chief was a member of a secret society called the whaler society, which involved intense spirit preparation, ritual cleaning, and physical training.

The Quileutes had several other societies; the warrior or wolf dance society, also called the Black Face, the fisherman society, the elk hunter society, and the *shaman* society for those trained to interact with the spirits.

Keeah spoke in awe of the chief and Anna assumed the Tlingits had similar societies in the village where she'd been raised. She wondered how Marya would fare with her Christian beliefs in such a foreign culture. At least she had a Bible, and that gave Anna some consolation.

"I'm so relieved Otter managed to get down from that tree, but I'm worried about her getting lost in the forest," Tatiana said on the final evening of the *potlatch.* Keeah had heard some of the children claimed to have seen the animal running through the bushes near the village. Another said he saw the cat seize a large rat in its jaws and scamper away.

"She'll find a way to survive," said Anna. "She's probably glad to be out of that box."

"At least Otter is free, unlike us," Tatiana said, frowning nervously.

Anna felt her tension as she finished weaving her hair into one long braid. They were both waiting to be presented to Chief Xawishata's guests. What that exactly meant, they were not certain, but they were afraid of being sold or given to some strange tribe, further away from any hope of rescue.

"I don't want to leave this village," said Tatiana. "Our men know we're here and now that my sister is wife to the chief, perhaps we might be treated with more respect."

"What if they make us slaves, or force us to marry one of their warriors?"

Tatiana gave a harsh laugh. "Any husband might be an improvement over Dmitri."

"Many Baskets say you must come now," said Keeah, suddenly appearing at the hut's entrance. "She outside waiting."

They stood up and Anna picked up Katya, who was babbling happily in her cradle board. Keeah shook her head. "Many Baskets say Katya stay here with me."

Anna did not like the thought of being separated from her daughter, not even for a short time. But if it had to be, there was no one she trusted more than Keeah to take good care of her.

She brushed her lips across the soft fluffy curls on top of Katya's head, breathing in the sweet milky scent of her daughter. "I'll be right back, sweetheart," she murmured.

They walked behind Many Baskets through the village to the Chief's long house, and found themselves inside for the first time. Over two hundred people were crowded together, wearing their finest garments and jewelry and talking, laughing, and singing. It was hot and suffocating with the press of many bodies and all the fires in the cooking pits. The air was thick with wood smoke and rank with sweat, bear grease, fish oil, and the aroma of dried bearberry leaves called kinnickinnick, which the Indians were fond of smoking in their pipes, long hollow cones or tubes of stone fitted with a stem of some hollow plant stalk.

The women could barely breathe nor could they see clearly through the dim smoky atmosphere. Many Baskets urged them forward to the center where Chief Xawishata and his brother, Hoheeshata, sat cross legged on the floor, entertaining a large group of chiefs. Tatiana immediately recognized one of them as the strange Indian she'd seen a few days before.

She tensed as he glanced at her, his gaze lingering briefly then drifting away. His black hair gleamed with oil in the firelight and his copper skin glowed like shiny coins in the flickering firelight. Next to him sat an older man with a long gray braid. She was surprised to see him wearing brown European trousers and a faded yellow shirt. He would have looked quite ordinary if it wasn't for the bit of abalone shell dangling from a hole through the septum of his bold nose, and the tiny piece of ivory inside a hole in his lower lip. According to Keeah these ornaments were worn only by the very rich nobles.

Hoheeshata had painted his face in black and red lines, and he stared boldly at both Anna and Tatiana, his facial scar a black jagged line running down his cheek, giving him a nightmarish appearance. To Tatiana's consternation, she recognized her diamond earrings hanging from his earlobes. They looked ludicrous on him, and if she wasn't so afraid of him, she would've burst into laughter.

Keeah said he'd returned from his raiding party with two young women for wives, sisters from a tribe of Chehalis near Gray's Harbor. They were the only daughters of the chief, and Hoheeshata bragged how he had stolen them right off the beach when they were clam digging with a group of women.

The two girls, aged fourteen and sixteen, were being instructed by Talks A Lot and Marya to help serve food to their husbands and guests. Their soft young faces were pictures of misery and Anna felt great pity for them. She understood how anguished they must feel, to be torn from their homes and loved ones and forced to live with strangers.

Yet according to Keeah, the girls were fortunate Hoheeshata had not captured them for slaves. Among the coastal tribes, if a girl was taken as a slave it was the ruin of her whole life. The shame lasted forever. Only a chief would try to find a kidnapped daughter and would have to pay a large price to buy her back or fight to rescue her. If they were successful in getting the girl back, the family would try to wipe out the disgrace with a feast and gift giving. But as time passed, there still could be rumors following the girl and her children and grandchildren. People would whisper, "That family wasn't much. She was once a slave,"

Chief Xawishata was speaking and laughing with the Indian dressed in white man's clothing. He looked near sixty years old and had a heavily lined face. A few gray whiskers sprouted from his chin. When he smiled and chuckled, gaps showed in his teeth and his eyes crinkled at the corners. Except for the shells in his nose and lips, in an odd way, he reminded Anna of her Grandpapa Teichroew, her papa's father.

He and the warrior sitting next to him studied her and Tatiana with great interest. Fear and dread began to sweep through them both as it was becoming increasingly apparent that they might be traded to these men. They exchanged glances of sheer panic, feeling as helpless and trapped as an insect caught in a spider's web.

Tatiana tried to catch Marya's attention, but her sister kept her face averted, speaking only to Talks A Lot and Hoheeshata's two young wives. With a sinking heart, Tatiana knew it was Marya's way of telling her she could do nothing. Indian women were not allowed to speak in front of male guests and dared not interfere in the business of trade or gift giving.

Moments later Many Baskets motioned them to follow her again. With relief they left the chief's long house and the hundreds of inquisitive eyes. Outside it was raining and a salty breeze was blowing in off the ocean, a refreshing change from the stuffy claustrophobic atmosphere inside. Anna never thought the privacy of their dirty hut would be so welcome. She was anxious to see Katya again.

"I'm afraid we're going to be sent away," said Tatiana with despair. "Oh, Anna, what are we going to do?"

"I wish we could steal a canoe and escape upriver and find Sean and the men."

"We're not strong enough to paddle a canoe against the current, and even if we were, the Indians would catch up to us before we found them."

Many Baskets whirled around and spoke tersely to them, her hand raised in warning. She made it clear she didn't like them speaking in their own language, so they walked the rest of the way in sullen silence.

When they reached their hut Many Baskets halted as two warriors stood in front of the entrance. They both carried spears and in the faint light of the fire burning within, the expressions on their faces were not friendly. Many Baskets spoke to them and they stepped aside, allowing the three women to enter the hut.

"It looks like we have guards," said Tatiana nervously.

Inside the hut Anna saw at once that Keeah and Katya were gone. Her stomach gave a sickening lurch and she cried out, "Where is my daughter? What have you done with her?"

Many Baskets gave her a sly smile and shrugged as if she didn't understand. Anna almost lunged at the woman, but stopped herself in time. Becoming violent was not a solution.

"Perhaps Keeah took Katya for a walk because she was fussy," said Tatiana, only half believing her own words.

Hysteria rose in Anna's throat and she struggled to force down a scream. Then the door flap swished aside and Keeah entered, but without Katya. Many Baskets spoke to her, then she flashed Anna a triumphant smile and quickly exited the hut. Anna immediately ran over to Keeah and grabbed her, shaking her slightly.

"Tell me where Katya is!" Anna said with gritted teeth.

Keeah trembled and could barely meet her gaze. "Katya good, Anna. Not to worry. She with Talks A Lot's daughters. She sleeping."

Bewildered, Anna released her grip. "But why didn't you bring her back with you?"

Keeah took a deep breath then spoke quickly, "Chief Xawishata is trading you to Makah Chief Utramaka and *Madame* to his son, Black Hawk. He happy he didn't trade you to your husbands. The Makahs give him many skins, halibut, money beads, whale blubber, and two slaves for you. In the morning you leave here." Her voice dropped with sorrow. "Utramaka not want Katya. He say infant is useless. He want you for slaves or wives."

"And---and Katya? What will happen to her?" Anna asked in horror.

"She stay here. Chief Xawishata give Katya to Many Baskets for daughter."

CHAPTER THIRTY EIGHT

The voyage north up the coast around Cape Flattery to Classet, the Makah village, took two days. Anna and Tatiana sailed in two huge ocean going canoes, capable of holding twenty to thirty men each. The black canoes were almost forty feet long and six feet wide, pointed at both ends and hollowed out of giant cedar logs. The interiors were painted red and the edges all around the sides were attractively decorated with little shells. The Makahs were reported to be the best canoe men of North America and their canoes rarely shipped water, keeping dry even in the wildest weather with someone bailing.

As handsome and sleek as the Makahs' canoes were, they could not compare to the solid sturdiness of the *Sea Rose*. Both girls were ill with seasickness the first day. They had no stomach for riding in an open canoe with snarling foam crested waves only inches from their heads. The same size waves that they hardly noticed on board the *Sea Rose*, were terrifying monsters of mountainous proportions when viewed upwards from the bottom of a canoe.

Yet the Makahs took little notice of the weather or the seas. With the confidence and expertise born of generations of experience, they paddled in long firm strokes as each canoe rose gracefully to the crest of a wave then glided down into the trough without so much as the slightest shudder.

They each rode in a different canoe, Anna with Chief Utramaka and Tatiana with his son, Black Hawk. Being separated only added to their misery, for they could not communicate with or console one another. After awhile Anna was too sick and depressed to care. Time passed and became meaningless as she spent each minute either retching into the sea or slumped against the side of the canoe in an exhausted stupor. The old chief took no notice of her discomfort. She was ignored as he and the other warriors continued in high spirits, singing and laughing as they paddled and talked to one another in their own peculiar language.

All the Makahs had smeared a greasy red paint over their faces and bodies, giving them a frightening and hideous appearance. At first Tatiana thought it was war paint, but then recalled Keeah telling her how her people, the Tlingits, painted themselves when sailing on the ocean. The oily substance helped keep their skin from becoming chapped by the cold salty wind and gave added warmth.

When they first set out to sea, the man called Black Hawk had offered her some, but she refused, finding the idea repugnant. Instead she wrapped herself warmly inside her muskrat robe, sheltering her face as best as she could from the constant wind and bursts of cold rain showers, sometimes mixed with sleet. He turned his broad back to her after that and left her alone.

The day was endless, but as miserable as she felt, Tatiana felt worse for Anna. She knew the poor girl was heart broken and in a state of shock with the loss of her child. It was unbelievably cruel that Katya had been given to Many Baskets to be raised as her own daughter.

When they'd left that morning, she'd managed to speak with Marya briefly as they said their farewells.

"Tell Anna that Keeah and I will make sure Katya is well treated and loved, " Marya said. "And tell her it is possible she will see her child again someday."

"How could that be? I've heard that the Makahs and the Quileutes are more enemies than friends."

"That is true, but they raid each other only when there is a debt to be settled. Otherwise, they often trade. I believe we all will see each other again, Older Sister."

Marya had subconsciously slipped into calling her by an Indian term. Tatiana felt she was losing her sixteen-year-old sister in more ways than one. She was still so young that as the years passed, her childhood in New Archangel and her brief marriage to John Hill might dim in memory. She truly would become Whispering Doe.

"Are you happy with your husband?" Tatiana had asked.

Marya's large expressive eyes filled with tears. "He's kind to me, but he is not John," she whispered. "He expects me to give him many sons."

"Don't they all?" Tatiana answered with sarcasm, thinking of Dmitri and his obsession with continuing the Volodin line.

Marya also embraced Anna, who stood stiffly, unable to respond. Her face wore an expression of terrible grief, but she did not weep. As she was taken to the canoe, her eyes looked longingly towards the chief's house where her daughter was sleeping. Most women would have become hysterical, but somehow Anna kept her composure until they were out to sea. Then she let the tears of pain flow silently down her cheeks.

The skies finally cleared as the day wore on and the sun broke out, bathing the ocean in a sparkling blue color. Tatiana's nausea lessened gradually and the urge to vomit finally ceased. As they kept paddling north, she recognized the same beaches and headlands where they had spent all those days marching south. She kept a lookout for the wreck of the *Sea Rose*, but they passed the mouth of the Quillayute River without any sign of it.

Late in the afternoon the warriors turned the canoes towards a long sandy beach near a large headland. Tatiana held her breath as the canoes shot through the wild curling breakers, tipping crazily to the right and to the left, surrounded by thundering green walls of foam-flecked water. Frightened, both Anna and Tatiana clung to the sides with all their strength, believing any second they could be hurled into the dangerous surf.

By some miracle they all made it safely to the beach. On shaky legs the girls stepped out of the canoes and stumbled over to the nearest driftwood log where they huddled together, weak from lack of food, water, and seasickness.

The days were short this time of year and darkness was approaching rapidly. A cold wind blew from the north. Both girls shivered, wondering how a fire could be made with all this damp driftwood. But the Makahs were prepared for anything. One man was opening matching clamshells which contained glowing coals from that morning's fire, while another was arranging cedar bark tinder and kindling in a box full of beach sand. Soon they had a blazing fire going.

Tatiana looked at the warmth of the fire with longing. Suddenly it occurred to her that it would soon be Christmas and then January, 1823. A new year and a new life awaited her, a life that any civilized person would consider worse than death.

The tide was low and some of the men were busily digging in the sand with sharp sticks for razor clams. Tatiana watched as the clams were cleaned and rinsed with sea water, speared with sticks, then cooked over the fire. She remembered their tasty flesh as sweet and tender and her mouth watered.

When the clams were roasted the chief, his sons, and their men sat around the fire eating them and also some smoked fish they had brought along. Tatiana knew she and Anna would not be offered any food until the men were finished. She had learned from her short stay with the Quileutes that the men always ate first, then the women and children, and the slaves last. When they passed around the bowls of drinking water she knew the men were done since it was considered bad manners to drink during a meal.

Her eyes fastened on Black Hawk as he drank heartily, then set the bowl aside. He was sitting a short distance away and he lifted his head as if sensing her gaze. The light from the fire flickered across his painted face as he looked at her. She was transfixed. It was like staring into the dark hooded eyes of a hawk mesmerizing its prey.

Expressionless, he motioned Tatiana to his side. She glanced at Anna. Her friend seemed oblivious of anything. She sat on the log with a dazed expression on her pale face, staring out to sea as if she had no idea of where she was.

"I'll be right back, Anna," she whispered.

Anna gave no inkling that she heard. Tatiana patted her on the arm, then rose and walked over to Black Hawk. She sank down onto the soft sand a few feet away from him. His gaze still held hers in a snare. It reminded her of the staring contests she used to have with Mikael and Olga when they were children. Whoever blinked or looked away first, however briefly, lost. Mikael usually won.

The man who stared at her now was no child. He frightened her with his intensity as if he could see into her very soul, yet she could not tear her eyes away. How long this would've lasted she did not know, for her stomach suddenly gave a loud growl.

Black Hawk glanced down at her belly, then threw his head back and laughed a rich happy sound. Chief Utramaka began to chuckle, too, and the other men soon joined in. With a wide smile Black Hawk handed Tatiana a large chunk of dried halibut.

She took it and started to eat. The white fish had a mild smoky flavor and was slightly tough and chewy. She had never tasted anything so delicious and could not help giving him a small smile of gratitude.

Her smile pleased him greatly and he handed her a roasted clam, then spoke in a deep voice and nodded. She wished she knew what he'd said. She missed Marya and Keeah desperately and their quick ability to understand the Indian dialects. Now it was up to her and Anna to learn their language.

He watched while she ate and when she had swallowed the last morsel he offered her a bowl of water. She drank thirstily. When she was through she said, "Thank you," in English instead of the usual French which she conversed in with Marya and Anna.

To her great surprise he answered, "I speak words of Boston man. My father speak it too. We learn from Nootkas, our cousins. They trade with Boston man."

Tatiana was speechless with amazement. American and British traders were known to the coastal Indian tribes as "Boston" men and their language would be English. She couldn't wait to tell Anna.

A squawking sound above Tatiana caused her to look up at the dark sky. Through a break in the clouds, the moonlight outlined a sharp formation of geese flying south.

"I didn't know geese flew at night," she said.

Black Hawk glanced upwards and laughed, "Geese? We name them They Who Talk While Flying."

She giggled. "I like that name better than geese."

He reached out with one of his strong brown hands and gently touched her right cheek, then slipped two fingers across her mouth. The warmth of his fingers burned into her lips and she jerked her head away instinctively. His eyelids blinked in displeasure at her reaction and he frowned slightly.

What was this man's intentions towards her, Tatiana wondered. Was he to be her master or her husband? Either way she was filled with apprehension, but she hated the idea of slavery the most. She dreaded the thought of all that hard menial work no different from the life of a

Russian serf. If she could choose, she would rather marry a chief's son and live a life of respect and authority like Many Baskets. It would be a far cry from the life of a Russian Baroness, but she knew she could survive it.

Deep inside she still retained hope of rescue one day. There was one thing she knew about Captain O'Connell. As long as there was breath in his body, he would move heaven and earth to find Anna again. And she believed Anton loved her enough to do the same. As for Dmitri, she didn't expect him to even survive the winter in the mountains, much less have the strength and ability to rescue her. From now on, she would think of herself as widowed and free to marry again.

She gave Black Hawk another tentative smile. He was a fearful looking savage, but so far, he had treated her honorably and with kindness, something Dmitri rarely had. She would prefer her next husband to be Anton, but if it couldn't be him, it might as well be this man.

Then there was Anna. Tatiana sensed forces at work surrounding her friend that she didn't understand. The incident with the Quileute *shaman* claiming her Bible burnt his fingers was mystifying. And now the God Anna believed and trusted in, had allowed her to be robbed of all she held dear, first Ethan, then the captain, and now her own daughter. Tatiana was puzzled by all of this. She didn't expect God to care what happened to her, a worthless sinner, but she did expect Him to take care of Anna.

While she was pondering these things, the object of her thoughts softly slipped off the log and fainted face first into the sand. Black Hawk and Tatiana both jumped up and hastened to her side as Chief Utramaka, with a concerned look on his face, spoke urgently to three of his braves. The trio then ran off into the trees.

Black Hawk gently rolled Anna over and wiped the sand off her face. "She hasn't eaten all day," said Tatiana worriedly, "and the sea made her sick."

"We take her to Ozette. Women there help her."

Tatiana looked askance at the dark forest. "Is it far?"

"No." He nodded to a couple men, who carefully picked Anna up and headed towards the woods. "Come, Daughter of the Sun," said Black Hawk, taking her by the hand.

Tatiana's eyes widened at the name he had given her, but she said nothing. His large hand enclosed her smaller one and he guided her through the darkness to a trail. His father, the chief, followed along with several warriors. Another group stayed with the canoes.

It was a surreal experience walking through the blackness of the rain forest, hand in hand with an Indian. At least he knew exactly where they were going, Tatiana thought. As it was, she stumbled more than once over hidden tree roots and rocks in the path. Each time she tripped his grip tightened, not allowing her to fall, and after a couple miles, they emerged on the north side of the headland to another beach.

The Makah town of Ozette was about twice as big as the Quileute Hoh village. There were several rows of big cedar plank houses, some over a hundred feet long. Each house was cleverly constructed with its own elaborate drain system of cedar plank and whalebone gutters to divert the ground runoff from rainfall away from the house floor surfaces.

Barking dogs heralded their arrival, although the three Makah warriors sent by Chief Utramaka had already announced the coming visitors. The chief and his sons and warriors were given a warm welcome by the Ozette chief and his family. They took all their guests into the largest house and placed Anna on one of the platform beds. A group of women clustered around her, chattering and shaking their heads, and staring with curious eyes at Tatiana. They had heard rumors about the white women and were excited and pleased to have them in their village.

Three of the women were wives of the Ozette chief, and the two younger ones were his daughters. The oldest woman, obviously the first wife, ordered the others to serve the men a meal while she prepared an herbal tea to strengthen Anna when she revived. Tatiana sat by Anna's side, whispering to her to wake up.

Black Hawk and his father and their men sat in the center of the house, eating heartily of the feast that was set in front of them, platters of freshly roasted salmon and halibut, camas bread, smoked clams, and ripe berries. As the evening wore on, they talked, laughed, smoked pipes, and shared stories.

The smell of the smoke and the sound of the unfamiliar voices finally penetrated Anna's consciousness. Gradually she stirred, coming out of her dreamless faint, and opened her eyes. The first person she saw was Tatiana.

"Where am I?" Anna asked weakly.

"At the Makah village of Ozette," said Tatiana, smiling with relief. "You fainted on the beach, so they carried you here. Do you remember?"

Anna's eyelids fluttered in disappointment. "Yes, but I was hoping we were back with the Quileutes."

"Perhaps we will visit there someday, Anna, but now you must take care of yourself. I have some tea for you to drink. And after that, you must eat some food."

"Why does it matter?" Anna asked in a dull sounding voice.

Tatiana snorted in exasperation. "Because if you don't, you'll make yourself ill, then you'll be no use to anyone, least of all to me. I need you, Anna. I can't endure all this without you. And think of Katya and Sean. Someday that captain of yours will come looking for you and you better be ready. He's going to need you to be strong and healthy to help him get your daughter back again. You'll help no one, least of all yourself, by feeling sorry for yourself and refusing to eat and live again."

Her sharp words sliced into Anna's feelings of self pity and she realized Tatiana was right. No matter how tempting it was just to give up and die, she knew it was wrong.

With a supreme effort she struggled to sit up and take a sip of the steaming liquid Tatiana held in a bowl. The hot tea ran down her throat and instantly warmed her, and at the same time, caused her swollen breasts to leak.

Anna winced in painful embarrassment as she opened her robe and wiped her wet skin. "It's been twenty four hours since I last fed Katya and now I'm so full, it hurts terribly." Her voice trailed off and she wondered with a heavy heart who was nursing her daughter now. It certainly couldn't be that mean-spirited Many Baskets.

The Ozette chief's first wife, a short round woman with a kind lopsided smile, peered at Anna then clicked her tongue in sympathy. She sent one of her daughters to fetch a strip of cloth which she wrapped tightly around Anna's breasts. The added support would relieve the aching pressure until her milk dried up.

A terrible sadness fell upon her at the thought of never holding and feeding her daughter again. She felt the urge to weep, but somehow fought against it, remembering Tatiana's words of courage and hope.

And then there was God. Although she felt like He had abandoned her, deep down she knew He was still there watching over them all.

Mennonite women had lost their babies all through the generations. Her mama had buried several and so had both of her grandmothers and great-grandmothers. Even Tatiana had lost her unborn child. Somehow, all these women had tucked their grief away in their hearts, and found the strength to go on with their lives. Could she do no less?

It wasn't as if her child was dead. Katya was still alive and well. And Tatiana was right. One day Sean was going to find both of them and they would all be rescued.

With renewed purpose, she accepted a basket of food and began to eat.

* * *

They reached the Makah village of Classet by nightfall of the following day. It was situated inside a cove, located between Cape Flattery and Neah Bay near the entrance of the Strait of Juan de Fuca. As they rounded the cape they passed the Fuca Pillar, a strange but remarkable looking rock almost in the form of an obelisk. Anna and Tatiana remembered seeing it months earlier on the *Sea Rose*.

Riding up and down the blue green swells in the canoes made them both nauseated again, but not as badly as the day before. It was another chilly, but sunny day, a blessing that kept them relatively warm and dry.

When they neared the village the girls saw a great crowd of people on the beach. Barking dogs ran excitedly to and fro, and it looked as if every man, woman, and child was on hand to greet their chief and his men.

When they landed the canoes were pulled out of the water by the eager throng and Chief Utramaka disembarked, hailing his people in his gruff voice.

There was a hush as Anna and Tatiana rose and gingerly placed their feet onto the sand. A sea of amazed faces stared at them. Tatiana was the tallest woman they had ever seen, almost at a level height with their chief's son, Black Hawk, deemed the tallest man in the tribe. Like the Quileutes they were awestruck by the sight of her golden hair and pale skin. Surprised eyes fastened on Anna as well, and she realized that they were the first white women to ever step foot on these shores.

Quivering with fear, both Anna and Tatiana were grateful that their full length fur robes covered their trembling legs. They sensed the moment to be critical. If the Indians suspected their fear, they would lose all respect.

Tatiana was thankful for her training as an aristocrat, raised to hide her true feelings. She gazed back at all the Indians with a calmness she did not possess. While they studied her she studied them, noting that some had faces with wide sloping foreheads similar to the Quileutes, revealing their high rank. They were a short sturdily built people with light copper skins. Some of the men were clean shaven and others had small mustaches and short goatees. The men wore only some cloth around their waist, and many of the women were bare-chested. She and Anna could never get used to seeing so much naked flesh.

Out of the group of Indians two women and a boy stood slightly apart. One of the women was the first wife of Chief Utramaka. Gray Cloud was excited and relieved to see her husband back safely, but she hid her emotions by keeping a dignified frown on her deeply lined face. It wouldn't do for the chief's wife to act as silly as some of the women were behaving when greeting their husbands, although deep down she wished she could run down the hill and throw her arms around Utramaka.

She had not wanted him to go to the Quileutes *potlatch*. The voyage to the Hoh River was always fraught with dangers from the unpredictable weather and from the sea itself. The night before he left, she had dreamed he was swallowed up by a whale. The dream had frightened her greatly, but she had told no one, not her husband, nor Utilla, the *shaman*. He was Utramaka's older cousin and would have counseled her husband not to go if he'd known. Utramaka would've become angry with her then, and would've refused to speak with her for a long time. That was something she could not bear. After all the many seasons of their marriage, he was like the other half of her whole being. She lived only to please him as his dutiful wife. It was never her place to question him or disobey him in any way. Thus, their relationship had always been harmonious. She had given him two fine sons, Black Hawk and Strong Elk, both of whom had families here in the village, and two beautiful daughters, one married to a Makah chief in Biheda, the other married to a Nootka chief on Vancouver Island.

Gray Cloud tilted her head proudly towards the two strange white women standing together by the canoes. She thought they were quite ugly with their pale skin and odd colored hair. But she saw the manner in which Black Hawk and the other men looked at them, and she knew at once that they were trouble.

She glanced at the young woman standing nearby, her daughter-in-law Soft Fern. Had she noticed the way Black Hawk eyed the white women? Soft Fern was the perfect wife for him in every way but one. She had been able to give Black Hawk only one child. Thank the spirits it was a son.

Gray Cloud smiled fondly at her grandson, Red Hawk. Almost thirteen years old, the boy had the skinny build of an adolescent, but he held himself tall and straight, smiling slightly with a hint of arrogant pride on his face so like that of his father.

The boy had eyes only for Black Hawk. He yearned to run to him, but forced himself to wait politely until his father and grandfather had finished greeting the older members of the village, including his uncle Strong Elk, his father's younger brother, who had taken over the chief's duties in their absence.

When Black Hawk's attention was finally turned towards his family, the boy broke into a great smile of joy. Soft Fern's round face mirrored his happiness as Black Hawk strode over to them, his handsome face creased in a big grin. Out of respect he greeted his mother first, then his wife and son. He put one arm around each of their shoulders and they walked together towards the village.

Gray Cloud waited patiently for Utramaka to reach her side. The old chief acknowledged her with a grunt then patted her fondly on the buttocks. She knew that was the only sign of affection he would give her until later that night in their sleeping furs. Content, she followed her husband and her son and his family to their house. For the moment the white women were forgotten.

Not so for Utilla the *shaman*. Shivering in the raw wind off the Strait, he clutched the edges of his warm bearskin robe and wrapped it more tightly around the aching bones of his thin hunched frame. His matted and unkempt gray hair blew around his shoulders, a few strands fluttering across his sunken cheeks. His sharp eyes settled on the two captives with a great sense of unease. Like Gray Cloud he felt that they were the harbingers of something bad to the village. As yet, he did not know what it was. But he could see a power around them, an unfamiliar power that made his soul restless and if he was honest with himself, almost frightened.

It wasn't the tall golden woman he was concerned with. Yes, she was striking enough to attract any warrior but except for her outward beauty she held little power. It was the small slender woman he was concerned about. There was something about her that boded ill for him, and perhaps all of them. He would have to keep a close watch on her.

Anna and Tatiana started to walk after Chief Utramaka and his family. All around them were cries of joy as each man was welcomed by his family. The reunions could be thought of as touching, thought Tatiana, similar to the happiness she'd felt whenever her papa returned to visit her in Saint Petersburg. Why did everyone in the world have a place they belonged to except her? Even Marya seemed to have adjusted to her role as wife to a Quileute chief and Keeah had resigned herself quite cheerfully to that of a slave. She had never felt she belonged anywhere---not in the Bolkonsky's palace, not with the Suttons in England, not with Dmitri in New Archangel, and most certainly, not here in this Makah Indian village.

Tears of self-pity welled up in her eyes and came dangerously close to spilling out. She blinked them back furiously and continued walking after the chief and his family. If she had a place in this village, she assumed it was with them.

No one stood in their way. The men nervously glanced at them, then averted their faces as they passed by, but the women stared openly, some with suspicion, some with hostility, and some with friendly curiosity.

Unlike the Quileute village which sat in the open, a high stockade of posts surrounded Classet, similar to the wooden stockade in New Archangel, but without the blockhouses. There were no totem poles to be seen. Instead Anna and Tatiana were startled by the shocking sight of a grisly collection of shrunken heads on poles stuck in the ground near the entrance to the stockade. The heads were blackened and shriveled with a few wisps of hair still attached.

The girls exchanged looks of horror. All the stories of the fierce warlike Makahs were true. Not only were they were the most savage and dangerous of all the coastal tribes, they obviously chopped off their enemy's heads. And now they were at their mercy.

For the first time since leaving the Hoh River village, Anna realized that God might have had His reasons in keeping Katya with the Quileutes.

To the rear of the village stood the forest, out of which flowed a large stream of water that emptied into the cove. Inside the stockade there were three rows of large flat-roofed wooden houses, a number of sheds, a sweat house, and multiple drying racks for curing fish and meat.

The largest of the buildings was the chief's house. As Anna and Tatiana headed towards it, three young boys carrying sticks approached. With sly grins on their dark-eyed faces they stepped around Tatiana and blocked Anna's way, waving the long pointed sticks in front of her face. Like most children, it hadn't taken them long to figure out which of the two white women was the most vulnerable.

Their sticks narrowly missed Anna's nose. Feeling increasingly irritated with their little game, she shielded her face with one arm and said sharply in English, "Leave me be!"

The boys laughed at her strange words and drew closer. The biggest boy, a fellow with a large round head and plump cheeks, aimed for Anna's head. His stick struck her outstretched hand, slicing through the skin of her palm.

The sight of blood on Anna's hand roused Tatiana's fury. With one quick motion she grabbed the end of his stick and wrestled it out of his surprised grasp. She swung it upwards and was about to smash him in the face with it when a tiny white-haired woman ran into their midst, screeching angrily at the boys. Tatiana dropped the stick on the ground as the boys, still shocked at her unexpected aggressiveness, scattered in all directions.

Anna clutched her bleeding hand and gave the frail old woman a smile of gratitude. She grinned back, practically toothless, her face creased by many wrinkles. Her age was difficult to guess. She was under five feet tall with a stooped back that gave her the appearance of an ancient witch, yet her eyes twinkled merrily like two shiny black beads. She shook one small gnarled fist at the rapidly disappearing boys then broke out in a cackle of glee, releasing an odor of sour breath and rotting gums. With surprising strength she tugged on Anna's arm, peered at her hand and muttered.

Laughing Gull was Chief Utramaka's mother and the oldest woman in the village. She was held in high esteem by all the people. Even the *shaman*, Utilla, respected her knowledge of herbs and medicines. She was also known for her screeching laughter and for being a mischief maker. The arrival of the two white women delighted her with many future opportunities to stir up trouble. But she had a strong sense of empathy for the weak and did not like the manner in which the small white woman with the sad eyes was being harassed by the boys, especially since one of them was the incorrigible Muddy Feet, one of her great-grandsons.

The entire incident had been watched by Black Hawk and his wife and son, who now paused at the house entrance to allow Chief Utramaka and Gray Cloud to enter first. Laughing Gull motioned to Anna and Tatiana to follow her. As they approached the chief's house, Tatiana saw Black Hawk smirking at her. How dare he find amusement at her and Anna's humiliation by those dreadful boys, she fumed inwardly. She flashed him a smoldering look.

Soft Fern caught her angry glare and she glanced at her husband to see his reaction to his slave's open defiance. She felt surprised, then dismayed, when he smiled at the tall woman instead of frowning. She was even more discomforted when Black Hawk took the woman's hand and drew her to a spot right in front of them.

"Soft Fern, this woman will be your new sister, my new wife," he said to her in his deep voice. "I call her Daughter of the Sun." Then he turned to Tatiana and said in broken English, "Soft Fern, mother of my son, Red Hawk."

Tatiana looked at Soft Fern with dread. If she was to become Black Hawk's second wife, then she expected his first wife to dislike her on the spot. What woman enjoyed sharing her husband with another woman, especially one of a different race and culture? Marya and Keeah had explained to her that polygamous marriages among the natives were a sign of prestige, power, and wealth. But she couldn't imagine how any of the wives could be truly happy and content.

Tatiana smiled at Soft Fern and Red Hawk. The young woman nodded politely, but the boy scowled and shuffled his feet as if he wished himself elsewhere. Tatiana decided that so far she wasn't impressed by the manners of any of the Indian boys.

Then she dismissed him as unimportant and instead gave his mother a quick appraisal. Tatiana judged her to be near thirty years of age. Soft Fern was not a beautiful woman, but she had retained her youthful figure and her face glowed with health and a certain dignity. She was petite with a smooth round face and skin the color of dark copper. Tiny lines radiated from both of her eyes and her shoulder length black hair was parted in the middle and lightly streaked with gray. She wore a twined cedar bark cape edged with sea otter fur and had decorated herself with many ornaments. From her ears hung exceptionally long dentalium earrings with small beads at the end of each tusk. Around her neck she had a choker necklace made of many beads and underneath that, another necklace made of small ivory dentalium tusks. Her arms were covered in silver and copper bracelets. Black Hawk obviously lavished expensive gifts on her.

Tatiana was conscious of her scrutiny as well. The woman's dark eyes swept over her from head to toe. She stiffened as she prepared to meet her hostility face on.

To her amazement Soft Fern's face broke into a wide smile. Two tiny dimples played on either side of her mouth, giving her a sudden impish look, and she laughed with a slight tinkling sound. She grasped Tatiana firmly by her hand and led her to the entrance of the house.

Anna followed them, noticing that the house was huge, bigger by far than Chief Xawishata's house, possibly measuring eighty feet long and forty feet wide and twelve feet high. The small oval door opening was raised several feet from the ground and covered with an elk hide curtain.

Soft Fern brushed aside the door flap to allow Black Hawk and their son to enter first. As Red Hawk climbed through the opening after his father he shot Tatiana and Anna a quick glance. Tatiana drew back hastily, startled by the venomous hatred gleaming in his black eyes. His mother must have noticed it also, for she frowned and shook her head at him. He ignored her and stalked off into the house.

She patted Tatiana's hand almost apologetically and Tatiana sensed that this woman was making a supreme effort to be hospitable to her at whatever cost to her own personal feelings. She had to admire her for such a noble gesture and she responded with another smile. Soft Fern appeared relieved that she was not offended by her son's rudeness. Tatiana wished she could tell her that she did not blame him for resenting her presence here. He probably knew that his father intended to make her his second wife, and as a result, she was a threat to his mother's happiness.

The old woman clambered through the door opening after Anna and grinned at her in a friendly manner. Anna assumed she must be an honored grandmother or aunt since the Indian boys had obeyed her so readily. Now that Tatiana had been accepted by Black Hawk's wife, it seemed everyone had a place in this family, but her. So far, Chief Utramaka had seemed to have forgotten her existence. Perhaps it was just as well. Anna thought his gray haired wife looked like a formidable woman, reminding her of Gerhard's mother, *Frau* Yoder.

Laughing Gull gestured Anna to follow her and proceeded to give her what she thought of as the grand tour. Through the middle of the building from one end to the other, ran a wide passage. Each side was divided into many compartments, the first for the chief and his wife, and the others for their sons and their families. Every compartment had its own fireplace, a shallow pit dug into the floor and walled with stones to keep the fire from spreading. Above each pit was a rack for drying fish. Smoke escaped by moving certain boards apart in the roof.

The floor was covered with wooden planks, a sign of great wealth. Anna couldn't help recalling the earthen floor of many poor Mennonite homes in Furstenau. She supposed that if her papa and her siblings saw this fine house they would think the Makah Indians were a civilized people, that is, until they saw the shrunken heads displayed outside.

The furniture in the house was similar to that of Chief Xawishata's home. Built-in platforms went around three sides of each family's compartment, a couple feet from the ground and two planks wide so that two people could sleep side by side on their bedding of furs. Anna was finally taken to Gray Cloud's compartment where she noticed a second tier of bunks above the first, packed tightly with baskets and boxes. Laughing Gull managed to pull a small cedar basket down and produced a foul smelling paste of some type of herb which she smeared on Anna's cut palm. The substance immediately reduced the stinging pain and Anna smiled her thanks.

Gray Cloud appeared to be an excellent housekeeper. She had a place for everything. Cooking stones, tongs, boxes of dried fish and other foods were neatly arranged and stored under the bed platforms as in a kitchen cupboard. Cattail mats were everywhere, on the floor as carpets, spread on the bunks as mattresses, and hung over shelves. Cattail mats could not be washed, but a woman kept rolls of new ones ready. If the Indians judged a woman's wealth and industry by her supply of mats, Gray Cloud had much of which to be proud.

By this time slave women were removing some of the partitions in the house so the entire family could come together for a welcome home feast being prepared by Gray Cloud, Soft Fern, and the wives of Strong Elk, the chief's youngest son. His two wives were sisters, Brown Bird the eldest and his first wife, and Swift Deer, the younger second wife, who was obviously with child.

One piece of furniture overshadowed all else. Chief Utramaka reclined in a seat which reminded Anna of a king's throne. It was elevated about two feet above the others and had a hide canopy ornamented with the sharp teeth of some type of animal. Black Hawk crouched at his side, Strong Elk at the other, and Red Hawk at his feet. All three men were talking excitedly as their wives supervised the meal, although Black Hawk's gaze never seemed to leave Tatiana.

A girl of about twelve years old was showing Tatiana how to boil water. She was Small Fawn, Brown Bird's daughter. They also had a ten year old son, He-Who-Has-Muddy- Feet, but he was nowhere to be seen.

Tatiana had shed her robe in the stuffy warmth and was wearing the same type of cedar bark garments the other women wore. Her fair complexion had darkened over the past weeks, and except for her golden braids and violet eyes, she looked like a native woman, bending over a box in which water was heating with hot stones. When near boiling, Small Fawn handed her pieces of fish to drop into the box, and the stew soon sent out a delicious aroma.

The domestic scene made Anna feel like an intruder. She lingered forlornly on the outskirts of the gathering as sharp pangs of homesickness assailed her. She missed Sean and Katya and her *Tante* Sarah and her cousins, her papa and her brothers and Katarina and her friend Susannah. At the moment, she would've even welcomed the sight of her stepmother, Agatha. Why had God watched over her in all the many miles traveled from Furstenau, just to bring her to this savage pagan place?

Then she heard a soft whimper coming from the platform to her right. No one paid the slightest attention to the sound. Anna looked and saw something moving underneath the bedding of furs. A small fist suddenly emerged and waved wildly in the air. Without hesitation she hastened over and yanked the furs back.

A naked infant girl stared up at her with the soft melting dark brown eyes of a baby calf. She appeared about a year old and was strapped in a large cradle board filled with shredded cedar bark. Her skin was light for an Indian baby but her hair was black and thick and mussed in a sweaty tangle around her face. She studied Anna intently for a few seconds then her cute little face crumpled as she realized Anna was a total stranger. She let out a wail, sounding exactly like Katya when scared or hungry.

Anna stepped back as Gray Cloud hurried over with an irritated frown on her face. She pinched the child's nostrils shut and covered her mouth as if she was trying to suffocate her. Anna was shocked, but then remembered Keeah saying that Indian babies were taught not to cry at a very early age. Would Many Baskets be treating Katya as cruelly?

Seconds later Gray Cloud took her hand away from the child's face and the infant gasped and sputtered. Gray Cloud unstrapped her and picked her up, motioning Anna to come closer. Without another word, the woman shoved the child into Anna's arms and walked back toward the fire pit. This time the little girl did not cry at the sight of her, but kept sniffling as Anna instinctively murmured soft words and soothingly rubbed her back.

Who was this child's mother? None of the women seemed to care as Anna carried the infant to the nearest platform and sat down. The child acted hungry and kept grabbing at Anna's chest, causing her milk engorged breasts to swell even more.

Then Chief Utramaka stood up and stared in her direction. In halting English he said to Anna, "My daughter. Her mother, my second wife, die when she born." He paused and his black eyes bored into Anna. "Now you are Second Wife. Take daughter." He sat down again and began speaking to Black Hawk in their own language, seemingly unconcerned that he had just exploded a cannon ball in the middle of his house.

Tatiana's mouth fell open as Anna froze in shock. Gray Cloud, Soft Fern, and the other women also reacted with confused consternation. They began jabbering among themselves, casting a variety of looks at Anna. Because of her vivid beauty, they'd expected Tatiana to be Black Hawk's second wife, but for some reason, thought Anna was to be Gray Cloud's slave. For her to be elevated to the position of Chief Utramaka's second wife was a shocking surprise. The chief hadn't even spoken to or acknowledged her since they arrived. They were astounded that he desired the small white woman at all. But then, their chief was an unusual man.

Unlike the other Makah chiefs, Utramaka was fascinated by the white men. He was curious to know everything about them, how their huge canoes flew through the sea and where they came from. He traded heavily for their goods, iron, copper, knives, blankets, and longed to have one of their thunder sticks called guns. He loved to wear their clothing and was interested in learning their language. And now, he wished one of their women for wife.

Utramaka watched the women's reaction with amusement. He noted the dismay on Gray Cloud's face, and he knew he would have to explain it to her later. He would tell her that he had no intention of sleeping with the little white woman, at least not yet. He actually did not find her that attractive.

His original intention in buying her was to be a slave, one that he could question to his heart's content about the whites. He hadn't wanted her to bring her child, thinking another infant in his compartment would be a nuisance. He was getting too old to keep fathering children when he already had grandchildren.

But ever since his second wife, who he had been slightly fond of, died giving birth to his daughter, the child had never had a proper mother. Gray Cloud complained she was too old to bother with the infant, and so a series of slave women had fed and taken care of her, producing a fitful unhappy child that they nicknamed She-Who-Never-Sleeps.

The Quileutes had claimed the little white woman to be a tenacious mother. On the trip back when he'd heard her weeping in the canoe for her lost child, he'd thought her tears were a good thing. It showed that the little white woman had a great heart.

And so, he had made his decision. The only way for his daughter whom he loved to have a real mother, was for him to make the little white woman his wife.

Anna was panic-stricken at Chief Utramaka's announcement, but she had no time for hysterics as the child was demanding her total attention by fussing loudly. Gray Cloud shot her a stern glance and Anna realized if she didn't do something, the infant would start to cry again, and then be subjected to another brutal punishment.

She turned her back to the men and unfastened her chest bindings. As she placed the child at her breast, it came to Anna that here in her arms was a motherless child. And here she was a mother without her child.

CHAPTER THIRTY NINE

Tatiana spent the morning on the beach digging clams. It was one of two chores for which she had some talent. During the past two months all her tries at basket making and cattail mat weaving had met with disaster as much as her sewing and embroidery efforts as a young girl had failed. But she was quick with her sharp digging stick and her clam basket filled faster than anyone else's.

The other chore she was good at was smoking fish. Whenever the weather calmed the men were out fishing day and night and the women stayed on shore, cleaning fish with sharp mussel shell knives and hanging the flesh to dry over what amounted to miles of drying racks. The fires of alder wood were built in rows along the beach. Over each one was a rack made like an arbor with open work tops. If the fish was very large, it was first sliced into narrow strips. Otherwise, the fish was cut open and spread apart with sticks, then hung down on the rack.

The Makah, the Quileutes, and the Quinaults were the only tribes who had the expensive equipment, ability, and bravery to attempt catching the huge halibut and cod that lay feeding on the ocean bottom, a hundred feet down on the bank, fifteen to twenty miles off shore. The Makah took more halibut than salmon and made a good trade in the dried fish.

Besides being a whaler, Black Hawk was an excellent fisherman. He told Tatiana how he caught the fish by setting out long lines with special hooks, then he watched all day in his canoe, waiting to see the skin buoy bob, indicating a feeding halibut. The lines were made of kelp, long stemmed seaweed so tough it was almost unbreakable and long enough to reach the ocean floor, its end weighted with a stone. The hook was made of wood, as large as a horseshoe and had a sharp piece of bone slanting from it in the shape of a halibut's head. The fish got its entire head inside and when it tried to pull back the bone barb caught its jaw. The fish was then pulled up and clubbed.

Usually the fish were left smoking for a week. It was a never-ending job for Tatiana and the other women. Every day they softened the fish by rubbing and squeezing them between their hands. This broke down the fibers so the air could get all the way through to the inside, so the fish would not spoil. There was always some fish to be moved further from the fire and other, fresher fish to be placed near.

Whenever it looked like rain, which was often, Tatiana had to hastily cover the racks because the moisture would rot the fish. She also had to keep a close eye on the village dogs, who would steal the fish, and the younger children, who loved to sneak up and play with the fish. After the fish was thoroughly smoked she folded them up like sheets of brown paper and Gray Cloud and Brown Bird stored them away in the woven baskets which formed their pantry.

During this time there was much trading done up and down the coast. Tlingits from southeastern Alaska and Nootkas from Vancouver Island often came to the village. They traded shell money or dentalium, slaves, dogfish oil, carved dishes, even splendid ocean going canoes, for the Makahs' highly prized supply of whale oil and dried halibut.

Two weeks earlier Black Hawk and several others had taken some of the new goods down the coast to the Quinault for sea otter skins and to the Chinook for dried shellfish and Columbia River salmon. It had surprised Tatiana that she missed him when he was gone.

The wind blew cold off the water and goose bumps traveled up and down her bare legs and feet. She would never get used to wearing skimpy garments, especially this time of year in early February, or what the Makah named *kluk-lo-chis-to-put'hl*, or the Moon of Better Weather, when the days were longer and the seas were safer. Thank goodness Black Hawk had given her a warm cape of soft marten to wear around her shoulders.

She was glad the worst of winter was now over. It had been a monotonous time to her. The people stayed inside their houses and spent the time on tedious tasks, the women and girls sewing and weaving and the men and boys working on their fishing and hunting equipment, and carving wood with their stone tools into ceremonial masks, dishes, and boxes. At other times some of the men sharpened their spears, put on their skin armor and set out on a raiding party. Every evening all the children were told the ancestral stories of the Makah.

As in New Archangel there was little snow. But the Makah had a different explanation than the Russians for the absence of snow from the coast. Their legends spoke of a time long ago when the coastal people fought the five Snow brothers and killed all of them but the youngest. This eliminated most of the icy snows of winter, but not the continual moisture which day after day drifted down through the towering firs and cedars in a monotonous drizzle or swirled a cold misty fog through the trees.

Tatiana and Anna had spent much of the winter learning the language. With a lot of effort, they'd eventually grasped the meaning of many of the Indians' words and gestures. Tatiana realized this now made her fluent in four languages, French, Russian, English, and Makah.

A small chuckle escaped her at the thought then she glanced down at herself, muddy up to her knees, mud plastered hands and smears of dirt and sand on her face where she absentmindedly rubbed herself. She laughed again and wondered why she felt so lighthearted these days when she should be feeling trapped and as miserable as Anna. Poor

Anna. Even though she had a husband who was kind to her and another baby daughter who adored her, she was continually tormented by the loss of her child

Anna still hoped they would be rescued by Captain O'Connell and the other men. As the weeks passed Tatiana thought it less and less likely, and though she missed Anton, she did not miss Dmitri, and was glad he was out of her life, hopefully forever. It was ironic that this savage barbarian she was now married to treated her with more gentleness and respect than her civilized Russian husband ever had.

Tatiana smiled as she thought of Black Hawk. She'd amazed and pleased him by learning to speak his language so quickly. They'd spent much of the long winter nights in their bed of furs teaching each other their respective languages. With Black Hawk's keen intelligence, he could now converse in English as easily as she could in his dialect. What would he say when she told him she suspected she carried his child? It was a secret she'd kept even from Anna, who she knew would be scandalized.

She carried her basket of clams over to the cooking fire, thinking how she and her husband had another method of communication between them that was even better than speaking. The mere thought of it brought the blood rushing to her cheeks and she quickly bent over the fire, hoping that Swift Deer, Strong Elk's second wife, would think the heat from the pit was searing her face and not notice her blushing.

She was helping Tatiana smoke the clams. Since clams rotted quickly, they had to be cooked the same day they were dug. The two women had first dug a hole in the ground and floored it with stones, then built a fire on them. Now they were letting the fire burn out, so they could place the clams, still in their shells, on the hot rocks. After that, they would cover them with seaweed and let them steam in their own juices for about an hour. The heat would pop open the shells and the clams would be ready for the family to eat at the evening meal. What was not eaten would be dried.

The Indians wasted nothing. Everything had a use. Tatiana had come to admire their self-sufficient way of life and the logical manner in which their society was structured. In one way it was much like Russian society with many czars instead of one. There were several villages in the Makah tribe, but no head chief for all. Each village had its own chief, usually the richest man. Once a chief's family had the ruling position, it tended to keep it. When Chief Utramaka died, Black Hawk would be his successor as the eldest son, no different than a Russian czar passing on his title to his firstborn son.

The next in line for leadership were the nobles, such as Strong Elk, Black Hawk's brother. These wealthy relatives were considered the aristocrats similar to the Bolkonskys of Saint Petersburg. The commoners and poorer Indians were like the Russian peasants and lived well enough by helping the more prominent members of the tribe. The poor reminded Tatiana of the serfs on Uncle Vasily's estate. They were forbidden to learn the skills of hunting and whaling, and had no skins for clothing, wearing only cedar bark garments and living in huts instead of plank houses. But unlike the serfs of Russia, the Indian poor had hopes to rise above their lowly position. If a poor boy had courage and a powerful spirit vision behind him, he could better himself, even above a stupid rich boy. Only a slave could never rise above his status.

The titles of the nobility of Europe and Russia gave them prestige even without riches, but wealth was everything to the Indians. The Makah reminded Tatiana of the rich men of America who had no titles but rose to power only because of their money. If the wealth of an Indian family disappeared, then that family was soon forgotten.

Black Hawk was a successful whaler and brave warrior. His father was the most powerful and wealthy chief of all the Makah chiefs and was spoken of with awe among them. When the two men had taken Tatiana and Anna as wives, they had given a *potlatch* celebration for all the chiefs and nobles from the other Makah villages. The event lasted five days, and this time she and Anna attended, mainly as observers.

Tatiana remembered how they were still in a state of nervousness and fear and only watched the festivities, the singing, dancing, game playing, story telling, and had little appetite at the constant feasting. On the final day of the *potlatch* the gifts were given out. This was the grandest moment for the feast giver, Chief Utramaka, who expected each gift, whether food, blankets, skins, slaves, or strands of money beads, to be repaid someday and with interest that might amount to one hundred percent per year. If not, the recipient of the gifts would lose face and fall in status. Names of all who were given gifts were called out in proper order that night by the Speaker, one of the elders. He also thanked each person who had helped with the *potlatch.* In a final display of generosity, Chief Utramaka threw the rest of the gifts out into the crowd where the children and poor people scrambled to catch them. It was feasts such as this one which made a man sure of his position among the wealthy.

The fire had died down and she carefully laid each clam on the hot stones, the salty moisture on the shells sizzling in the heat. As she covered the clams with long strands of seaweed, Tatiana thought about last night. She had made the mistake of asking Black Hawk if he would ever trade her away.

"Some of the people say you have put a spell on me, wife," he'd said with a husky laugh, "and they would like to see you go. Since you came I have gone whaling only once and the whale I harpooned got away. My brother says I should trade you back to the Quileutes or to the Nootkas so I will act like myself again. I know he is right, but I cannot help myself. I have never felt like this about a woman before."

After that, he had fallen asleep. Tatiana was awake for a long time wondering if he had answered her question. A strong feeling of insecurity gnawed at her as she thought of Strong Elk's resentment towards her because he thought she had bewitched his brother. She knew he wasn't the only one in the village. Most of the women didn't like her either. She didn't think she could survive another trade to a different tribe, so it was imperative that she keep Black Hawk infatuated with her, even though her heart belonged to Anton.

She sighed, thinking of poor Anton suffering out in the wilderness somewhere. It also made her feel guilty as she was well cared for, had plenty of food to eat, and always had warm shelter out of the storms.

"Daughter of the Sun," said Swift Deer, "you look as tired as I am. Why don't I find a slave to watch the clams for us and we can go back to the house and rest."

Tatiana smiled at her, noticing how heavy her belly had become. Her child would come soon. Swift Deer did not share her husband Strong Elk's dislike of Tatiana and was her only friend except for Laughing Gull, who enjoyed Tatiana's disruptive presence in the village. Soft Fern still treated her with the utmost respect, but Black Hawk's obsession with Tatiana had taken the laughter out of her eyes and the First Wife kept to herself most of the time, weaving mats and making exquisite little covered baskets out of shredded beach grass to hold all her jewelry.

"Your hair turns more like the sun every day," Swift Deer said with admiration, touching a hand to Tatiana's hair.

She'd recently had her hair trimmed to just past shoulder length, finding that her waist length hair to be too much of a problem without a maid to arrange it properly each morning. She now wore it parted in the center in the loose flowing style of the Makah women, although unlike their straight hair, hers curled and waved in an unruly manner. She kept the strands out of her face with a decorative headband edged in fur. With her fair complexion tanned to a light brown, Tatiana knew she resembled a civilized woman less and less these days. But at least she didn't wear facial ornaments like Swift Deer and the other young wives of rich men. The girl had a nose piece ornament, a small circular pendant with a serrated edge made out of a piece of shimmering blue-green abalone shell.

Her husband Strong Elk also wore nose and lip ornaments, but to Tatiana's relief, Black Hawk only had earrings. Both of his ears were pierced and he wore several earrings made of different types of shells in each lobe. He also had tattoos on various parts of his body, something she had discovered the first night they had spent together. These were permanent markings which were made by pricking holes in his skin, then rubbing charcoal into them.

On special occasions, such as a feast or ceremony, he painted his face and body a dark red with a paint made of colored powder mixed with whale oil. At those times Tatiana kept a careful distance from him, since his frightful appearance and the greasy fish odor of his skin transformed him into a wild looking savage.

Tatiana was thankful it was Soft Fern's duty, as his first wife, to sit next to him at the feasts. She also had a lovely singing voice and was often called upon to sing. Recently the Indians had overheard Anna singing lullabies in her low throaty voice to Chief Utramaka's daughter, and now she often joined Soft Fern in singing at feasts, their voices blending together in a delightful manner.

Soft Fern accepted Anna and often sought her company. In fact, most of the village women admired Anna for becoming such a good mother to She-Who-Never-Sleeps. Even Gray Cloud said nothing bad about her, and had shown no jealousy over having her for a second wife. Tatiana suspected that was because the old chief came to Anna's bed only to talk. Anna said his sole interest in her was learning about the ways of the white man.

"The first time he came to my bed, I was terrified he would expect me to act like a real wife to him," she'd told Tatiana. "But all he did was stroke my hair a few times like I was his pet dog, then proceeded to question me about my entire life. Since then, that's all he does when we're together. He wants to hear about the farms of my people, the Russian palaces in Saint Petersburg, and also about the Russians in New Archangel. He also wants to know details about ships and how the white man can sail across the oceans without getting lost. He asks me so many questions, I get very little sleep. And when Laughing Gull teases me about being exhausted the next morning, I let her think what she wants. She's so hard of hearing lately she can't hear us talking all night, but Gray Cloud does, and I think it makes her glad talking is all we do."

Anna had given a hollow laugh. "I know it's a relief to me, too, because I could not keep doing what you do with Black Hawk night after night."

Tatiana was hurt that even Anna disapproved of her relationship with Black Hawk when she of all people should know that she had no choice but to pretend to love him. Since that talk, Tatiana felt a strain between her and Anna and she supposed it was just as well the two of them had little time to spend together. Indian wives worked almost as hard as slaves, from sunrise to sunset, and now Tatiana understood why polygamy was so popular among the Indians. One wife could not possibly do all the work, unless she had many slaves.

At that moment Anna and Small Fawn walked up to her and Swift Deer. Anna carried She-Who-Never-Sleeps who was now out of her cradle board most of the day and learning to walk. The child was tugging on one of Anna's dark blonde braids and gurgling happily. Anna refused to wear her hair loose and in the Russian style, still braided it each morning after washing. At first the women laughed at her, but since she was a chief's wife, they eventually learned to accept how she looked. Some of the younger women even asked to have her braid their hair, much to the consternation of their husbands.

Tatiana was a bit jealous of how popular Anna was in the village. However, she had noticed one man who did not like her, Utilla, the *shaman*. As Chief Utramaka's cousin, he occasionally visited their house. All the women were nervous around him and made certain he had the best foods, but he refused any dishes that Anna touched. No one understood why.

As a part of the chief's family, Utilla could have lived with them. But the *shaman* preferred his own hut near the forest, where he could practice his magic spells and chants without the villagers' interference. He was training an apprentice, a young man named Lightning Eagle. Both men often disappeared for days at a time, returning with special wood that they used to carve frightful looking ceremonial masks and rattles.

Most of the Makah were in awe of the forest, a dark mysterious wall rising behind the village. They would prefer to face a storm at sea than be lost in the tangles of undergrowth, where they believed cannibal spirits would chase them and drive them insane by the frightful voice of the creature called, "The One Who Shouts in the Woods."

Their fear of the forest led the Makahs to be whalers, not hunters. Strong Elk was one of the rare men who had the courage to become a hunter. When he was a boy he went on a vision quest and received the spirit guardian of an elk, who he claimed protected him whenever he hunted. By killing many elk, deer, and even bears, he soon rose to such prestige he became one of the wealthiest and respected Makahs of all the tribes.

Tatiana realized that if he truly hated her then she had to be careful. It seemed she and Anna both had inadvertently made enemies of two of the more powerful men of the village.

"You are a good mother, Knows Much," Swift Deer said to Anna. She rubbed her round belly and added, "Some day you'll look like this. Make Chief Utramaka another son."

Knows Much was the name that the chief had given Anna after she impressed him with all her knowledge of so many things. Tatiana had laughed when she first heard it, but then she realized that Anna was the most intelligent woman she'd ever met, and the name was fitting.

Anna blushed at Swift Deer's words and tried not to show her dismay. She had no intention of ever having an Indian baby, but she wouldn't be surprised if Tatiana ended up having one someday soon. In fact, she wondered if Tatiana could already be with child. She had seen her in the special women's hut only once since their arrival.

The Makah believed a woman in her moon time possessed a harmful power. She must stay apart from her family, especially the men, for her very glance could injure a hunter or whaler and even cause the deer to run away or the whale to escape. At first they had been appalled at having to be quarantined for a few days as if they were lepers. Soon they both realized it was a time to relax and get extra sleep, have others prepare food and serve it to them, listen to village gossip, and mainly just take a welcome break from the grinding routines of never-ending daily chores. From then on, Anna looked forward to her time in the women's hut.

Anna hugged She-Who-Never-Sleeps tightly, enjoying the feel of her chubby body. She was such a constant delight, watching her take her first halting steps, forming her first words of speech, and finally, seeing the glad welcome in her impish grin every time she spied Anna.

The child already thought of her as her mother. A bond of trust and love had developed between them. Because of it the ache in Anna's heart over the loss of Katya had eased enough so that she no longer flinched with pain whenever she thought of her daughter being cared for by Many Baskets. The sorrow was still there and the anger, too, but Anna had come to terms with both emotions, and she trusted God to someday bring them back together. Until then, she had this adorable little girl to take care of.

Anna buried her face into the silky softness of the child's dark hair. She squealed with laughter and Swift Deer and Small Fawn tittered at the sound. Life in the early years for a Makah child was all affection. The Indians felt a child was not ready to understand much until he was five or six. At that time they learned a few strict rules. Children were taught not to cry for food and to eat what was given them, as the best food was for the old people. They were told not to make a noise in the house nor interrupt adults when they were talking. When a child disobeyed, he might be switched, but usually he was scared with stories about the Cannibal Woman who lived in the woods and carried off bad children to eat.

No wonder the Makahs were afraid of the forest, thought Anna, as she set She-Who-Never-Sleeps down on the ground a safe distance away form the pit of steaming clams.

Immediately the child grabbed a fistful of sand and dirt and shoved it into her mouth. Deciding that the dirt was not to her taste, she began to sputter and spit. Laughing, Anna knelt down and tried to wipe as much of the dirt out of her tiny mouth as possible.

Small Fawn giggled and said, "We should change her name to She-Who-Eats-Dirt."

Tatiana thought the girl was twelve or thirteen years old. She had pretty smile and a round face with thin crescent shaped eyebrows over her dark brown eyes. The Makahs plucked a girl's eyebrows before puberty and also pulled out some of the hair on her forehead to make a clean arching line. Due to her continual dieting Small Fawn was slender, and her skin was quite light because she used sunburn lotion made from sea lettuce which she shared with both Tatiana and Anna.

Swift Deer nodded in agreement. "She-Who-Never-Sleeps isn't a good name for her anymore since Knows Much has become her mother. Now she sleeps all night without a fuss. Gray Cloud says you have brought peace and quiet to our house."

"Why are infants only called by nicknames and not given a permanent name?" Tatiana asked curiously.

"We like to wait until a child is older to see what sort of person he turns out to be. Small Fawn used to be called She-Who-Always-Giggles until one day she found an orphaned fawn and tried to mother it. The fawn followed her around like a dog until a cougar killed the poor thing. And I am called Swift Deer because I used to run faster than anyone else in the village, even the boys, before my belly got so big," she laughed.

Small Fawn giggled. "My brother Muddy Feet is really called He-Who-Has-Muddy-Feet, because he loves to play in the mud and always has dirty feet. He hates it now, though, because he says it's too childish. He wants to have a naming ceremony for his permanent name, but my mother and father say he has to act more grown up first."

Privately, Anna thought that day would be long in coming. Muddy Feet was the boy who slashed her hand the day she arrived at the village. He still was a problem in the house, tracking in mud, talking when he shouldn't, taking food that belonged to Laughing Gull when she wasn't looking. As far as Anna was concerned, he was a boy who should be switched, or in the Mennonite way, taken behind the barn for a good spanking.

Black Hawk's son, Red Hawk, was another troublemaker, especially for Tatiana, whom he openly disliked, but he was soon to become a man and could not be punished like a child any longer.

"How did my husband get his name?" Anna asked.

"Utramaka is a traditional family name, belonging to an old ancestor," said Swift Deer.

"How come I have never heard the name of his second wife, the first mother of my daughter?" asked Anna. "All I know about her is that she was Soft Fern's younger sister."

Swift Deer gave her a serious look. "We never speak the name of a person who has just died, in case their spirit hears and comes back to haunt us."

"I've heard Muddy Feet say her name when he swears," said Small Fawn.

"That boy should be called He-Who-Causes-Trouble," Swift Deer muttered in disapproval.

"Red Hawk too," said Small Fawn. "When no one sees he pulls my hair until it hurts."

"He's as sly as a fox," said Swift Deer. "He should be called Red Hawk."

She-Who-Never-Sleeps was busily inspecting a white scalloped clam shell and suddenly she threw it down and began to cry, ending the women's conversation. Anna scooped her up, noticing the baby's skin felt extra warm, even though the sun was setting and the wind was growing colder. Swift Deer announced that the clams were ready to eat. She and Tatiana used a pair of tongs to place the hot clams in baskets to carry to the house for their husbands to eat.

When the women arrived at the house they noticed that all the men were gone. Brown Bird, Strong Elk's first wife, explained that there was trouble with some Clallams again. A canoe from their village had been fishing for seals in the Strait and encountered a canoe of Clallam men. A fight had broken out and two Makah men had been injured.

The Clallams were from a village on the eastern Strait that had stolen a whale from the Makahs last spring. At that time a whale which Black Hawk had harpooned out at sea, broke loose from his canoe and drifted into the Strait to the Clallam village's beach. Even though a dozen Makah harpoons were still sticking out of the whale, the Clallam took the whale for their own use. They ignored the Makahs' demands for payment and the return of their harpoons. Since then, a series of fight and murders had broken out between the two villages.

"Our men in the village have grown tired of the situation," Brown Bird continued, "and asked Chief Utramaka weeks ago to put an end to the troubles once and for all by attacking the Clallam village. He said it was for Black Hawk as our war chief to make this decision. Everyone knows," she paused, giving Tatiana a frown of resentment, "he has been too preoccupied with his new wife to go to war."

"Daughter of the Sun," said Laughing Gull, her leathery face breaking into a sly grin, "you will not have your husband to warm your bed this night. Even as we speak, your husband is in his sweat house preparing for war. When the sun rises he will attack the Clallam." She put her white-haired head back and her ancient voice cracked with laughter.

At first Tatiana did not believe she was serious. The old woman loved to play jokes on people and was always getting herself into mischief, like her great-grandsons. Older women in the tribe, past the age of forty five, had more freedom than any woman of Russia. They could spend their days as they chose, helping with the young children, going where they pleased, talking with anyone they wanted to without worrying about all the taboos placed on young girls and women.

Tatiana often thought Laughing Gull had too much time on her gnarly hands, and she could be a constant source of annoyance. But sometimes she reminded her of her own grandmother, Nana, and Tatiana felt a genuine fondness for her. Then she noticed with a prick of discomfort, the smile of gloating about Soft Fern's face as she instructed the slave women to finish preparing the evening meal for anyone who wanted to eat.

She looked at Soft Fern. "Does our grandmother speak the truth? I have not seen any war ceremonies in the village."

"It is true. This raid is a secret and must be carried out quietly and quickly. Our husband and all the men of our village will leave before the sun rises."

She and Anna exchanged worried glances, but Tatiana felt the most fear. If there was a battle in which Black Hawk lost his life, Tatiana knew she would be traded away as soon as possible. She also felt hurt. Why hadn't he warned her about this? Surely he must have known the night before that he was to leave on a raid soon.

Anna's position in the village was much more secure if anything should happen to Chief Utramaka. No one would dare trade away the mother of his daughter. But at the moment, it was the last thing from Anna's mind. She-Who-Never-Sleeps would not stop fussing and whining and refused to eat. Anna didn't like the flushed look on her little face, nor the hot feel of her delicate skin. She was afraid the child had a fever.

Soft Fern had noticed something wrong, too. With a concerned expression she took the restless child in her arms and rubbed her forehead and arms. At once she knew the infant was ill. It made her fearful as she remembered two of her own babies, a boy and a girl, both who died from fevers when they were only a few moons old. Since then she had been unable to give Black Hawk another child. She supposed that was why he was so anxious to have Daughter of the Sun as wife. He hoped she would give him more sons. It wasn't good for a man to have only one.

"I will make a tea for your daughter," she told Anna, "and you can wash her body with cool water to see if that will make her feel better."

Laughing Gull frowned. "Someone has made She-Who-Never-Sleeps unhappy." She gave Brown Bird and Soft Fern a hard look. "Someone has been quarreling or having unkind thoughts in this house. Maybe because of Daughter of the Sun."

"Not me, Grandmother," protested Soft Fern. "I am glad my husband has her for wife."

The old woman gummed her shriveled lips and said, "Mmph!"

Anna looked confused. "What are you talking about?"

"I can explain," said Gray Cloud, bending over her cooking pit where she was broiling freshly caught fish. She had taken the meat of the fish, speared it on the pointed ends of green sticks and propped them before the embers to roast.

"The souls of infants have a land of their own where they live and play without any adults. When a child is born on earth he is still talking the language of this baby land. In time he forgets. If he likes life on earth he grows to manhood. His soul also grows and when he dies, it goes to the regular land of the dead. If he does not like life on earth, his soul returns to baby land, where it plays until it feels like coming back, usually in a child of the opposite sex."

"So, that is why it is most important to keep a child happy," said Laughing Gull, "and to learn his likes and dislikes. Quarreling and bad thoughts in a household can make an infant sick. Then a sick child might tell his friends in baby language that he is not happy here and wants all of them to go back to baby land."

"Many times when one infant is sick in the village, others are sick, too, and many die," added Gray Cloud with a sad expression.

"Are there any other sick infants in the village now?" Anna asked worriedly, thinking of smallpox or measles or diphtheria or whooping cough. She'd had measles and the whooping cough as a child, and a slight case of the smallpox when the disease struck their village, causing many to die, including her papa's parents, her Grandpa and Grandma Teichroew.

"None that we know of," sniffed Brown Bird. She was a skinny woman with a large pointed nose like a bird beak and yellowed chipped teeth, worn from years of using her teeth to stretch skins tight when she sewed. Perhaps she had once been attractive when Strong Elk married her, but the passing of time had not been kind to her.

She had given her husband two fine children, Muddy Feet and Small Fawn, but now he favored his younger wife, Swift Deer. Strong Elk was hoping for another son and he showered her with gifts and attention. Although they were sisters, Brown Bird felt hurt and jealous and her shrewish nature became more bitter each day.

Her sister-in-law Soft Fern was suffering the same sort of indifference from Black Hawk, and the two first wives often commiserated their mutual unhappiness together. Only Gray Cloud seemed content with her husband's second wife, Knows Much, and this was because Chief Utramaka treated the white girl more like a daughter than a wife.

She-Who-Never-Sleeps would not stop her tiresome whimpering and Tatiana decided to spend the rest of the evening in her compartment she shared with Black Hawk. She had no appetite for food and with the men gone there was no need for her to help with the meal. She had contributed her part by digging and cooking the clams.

With a sigh, she sank down onto the luxurious furs covering her bunk. Her husband had given her many gifts in the past weeks, jewelry, robes, heavy woven blankets of mountain goat wool traded from the Tlingits, and several square lidded boxes artfully decorated with pearl shells in which she kept all her bracelets, necklaces, and personal belongings. As a wedding gift he had given her a beautiful cloak of sea otter skins. To the Makah it was worth a slave in trade, but to the white men it would be as valuable as a priceless gem.

The night ahead yawned empty and endless with only worry and anxiety as her companions. She closed her eyes and thought about Black Hawk in the sweat house. It was located behind the big house and crudely similar to the wooden bathhouses of the Russians.

During the long winters of Russia, both rich men and the poor were so weary of being cooped up indoors, that they became addicted to the bathhouses. Each house contained a stove, some tubs full of water, and stones. Cold water was thrown on red hot stones, producing hot steam. After two hours of sweating and rubbing their skins with soap and twigs, they ran outside and rolled around in the snow, a change in temperature of forty or more degrees.

In like manner, Black Hawk had told Tatiana that the Makah warrior stayed inside the sweat house until all the evil had perspired out of his body. Then he ran and jumped into the nearby stream, cleansing himself thoroughly with its frigid waters. Afterwards, he painted himself. She shuddered to think how her handsome husband was soon to become a savage warrior.

The hours passed and Tatiana found she could not sleep. She could faintly hear the crying of She-Who-Never-Sleeps and some time after midnight, she thought she heard the men gathering down at the beach. Slipping on her sea otter cloak and a pair of moccasins, she crept out of the house, unaware of the two boys following her. She quickly ran to the stockade entrance and halted, her eyes searching through the shadows for Black Hawk.

There were twelve canoes lined up on the beach, about twenty men in each. They were all well armed with bows and arrows tipped with barbed bone and large spears pointed with sharp mussel shells. Each warrior had a long, thin club made of wood and a knife made of sharpened stone or whalebone.

The night was clear but cold and there was a crescent moon in the sky to the west. Red Hawk and Muddy Feet stayed hidden in the shadows, watching as Tatiana crept almost to the water's edge, and slid behind a large driftwood log.

Her movement had not gone undetected. A man pointed in her direction and though she froze herself into total stillness, she was found and jerked to her feet. The fierce looking man who loomed over her was her husband, yet not her husband.

His face was painted black and in the sliver of moonlight his skin glittered with powdered mica. He wore battle armor, a long sleeveless shirt of elk skin, made in one piece with a hole for the head and sewed up the sides. In one hand was a club raised in a threatening manner over her head.

She flinched and tried to move, but his grasp on her wrist was as hard as iron. "Woman," he hissed, "you do not belong here. Go!"

Tatiana turned to him, pleading, "I did not wish to anger you, husband, only to see you once more before you leave."

His manner softened slightly and he lowered his club and released his grip. "Now is not the time for a warrior to think of a woman in such a way it will rob him of his power."

They gazed at each other for a moment. Only his eyes looked familiar, but there was a savageness in them she had never seen before. His expression settled into a grim mask and he said angrily, "Go, woman! Go before I beat you with this club for your disobedience!"

Tatiana gave a wounded cry and whirled around and fled back to the house. It was as if he'd turned into Dmitri only worse, a wild Indian Dmitri. Sobs tore at her throat as she realized she would never understand all the multitude of superstitions and taboos of the Makah. She didn't know her presence was not welcome when Black Hawk left for war. At home in Saint Petersburg, when her grandfather and uncle had left to fight Napoleon, all the women had seen them off.

Tatiana threw one backward glance at the Strait. There was a bank of fog developing over the water. The twelve canoes were dark shapes disappearing into the black mist as they paddled eastward in single file. She saw how they moved in zigzags like lightning bolts in their belief that the mighty spirit Thunderbird guided them on their way to war. Black Hawk once said that fog was good to conceal a warrior from the enemy. If so, then their god was taking good care of them.

As she stumbled back inside the house to her compartment, she wondered if she would ever find a real home or a husband who truly loved her. And now she was afraid he was so angry with her he might trade her away to some heartless savage like Hoheeshata.

The hours dragged by and she finally fell into a restless sleep. For Anna, the night held no sleep at all. She-Who-Never-Sleeps had finally stopped crying, but only because her fever grew so high, she had become limp and unconscious. Soft Fern and Gray Cloud did all they could to help, but when the morning light dawned, they told her it was time to ask the *shaman* to come.

It was the last thing Anna wished to do. She had spent the hours praying hard for the little girl, asking God to heal her, to save her life. If the *shaman* came, she was afraid his presence would be disruptive to her prayers. She was well aware of Utilla's dislike of her, although she had never even spoken to him. He reminded her of the old *shaman* in the Quileute village and she remembered the mysterious incident with her Bible. How she wished she still had it with her.

Her mama used to say that God's words were a living breathing force that printed paper could not contain. "You must hide His words inside your heart, Anna," she'd said, "in case there comes a day when you need them and you don't have a Bible to read."

This was that time. And as Anna prayed all night, many Bible verses came to her mind, among them the accounts of Jesus healing the desperately ill, the lepers, the crippled, the blind, casting out demons, and bringing the dead back to life. Truly, there was no greater power on earth or in all the heavens than that of the Holy Spirit. Her fervent prayer was for Him to touch She-Who-Never-Sleeps with His hands of healing and spare her tiny life.

A few feet away in the next compartment, Tatiana awoke, unaware of the anguish and spiritual battles her friend was facing. She assumed the child was better because she didn't hear her wailing any longer. She left the house without seeing anyone and walked to a secluded part of the stream where the women bathed each morning.

The Makah kept themselves very clean. Not only did both men and women bathe at daybreak, but several times during the day they washed their hands and faces with soap made of the bruised leaves of mock orange or boiled down thimbleberry bark. If someone was very dirty, they scoured themselves with cedar branches.

Usually after bathing in the cold rushing stream, Tatiana felt refreshed, but this morning it had no affect on her. Fatigued by little sleep and slightly nauseated, she felt burdened with worry and a fear for Black Hawk's life. She drew the warmth of her sea otter cloak around her and hurried back to the house, meeting Soft Fern and Brown Bird.

Tatiana stopped and said to Soft Fern, "When will our husband return?"

"Soon."

Abruptly she walked away, her small body swaying gracefully. Brown Bird lingered behind and cast Tatiana a knowing glance. "Perhaps Black Hawk does not return to you, but to Soft Fern."

Tatiana looked at her closely, seeing the hostility gleaming in her flat black eyes. "Why do you say such a thing, Brown Bird?"

She lifted her bony chin and preened herself importantly. "We know you angered him last night. He is not a man who forgets such a thing. Soon he will tire of you and trade you away."

She laughed, displaying her jagged stained teeth then swept herself down the path after Soft Fern without waiting to see Tatiana's reaction. There was none. Brown Bird had not spoken anything that was not already on her mind.

When Tatiana reached the house she saw the *shaman* Utilla and his apprentice, Lightning Eagle, being greeted by Gray Cloud at the entrance. They each carried a rattle and a wooden mask and she realized they weren't there for a friendly visit. Her first thought was for She-Who-Never-Sleeps. The child must be very ill. She hurried inside to Chief Utramaka's compartment and halted.

Laughing Gull and Anna crouched in a corner, both with a sad worried look on their faces. The child, her eyes closed as if asleep, was lying on a small bed of furs near the cooking pit. The *shaman* took some powder from a pouch around his waist and sprinkled it onto the hot stones. Smoke immediately puffed up and billowed around the child with a sweet cloying scent.

Tatiana stifled a cough and slipped in the room to sit with Anna. Gray Cloud stood next to her with a nervous expression on her usually calm face.

Utilla and Lightning Eagle put on their wooden masks and began to hum and move slowly around She-Who-Never-Sleeps as they shook their rattles. The masks had hairy eyebrows and huge indented eye holes, a large nose and a scowling mouth, and a short hairy beard made of smooth wood. It transformed the elderly man and his young apprentice into frightful looking creatures.

"If she wakes up and sees them," Tatiana whispered to Anna, "I think it would scare her half to death."

Gray Cloud glared at her then said sternly, "They're not trying to frighten her, but only the evil spirit inside her which is making her sick, so it will leave her body. Utilla says there is nothing else we can do."

"I believe in an all powerful all loving Creator God," said Anna firmly. "I have been praying all night to Him that He will heal her."

Utilla immediately ceased his tuneless humming and pointed at Anna with his rattle. "If what you say is true, then why is she still sick? Soon you will see how my power is greater than your Spirit God's."

He threw back his head and yelled a blood curdling shriek that sent shivers of fear down all the women's spines. Anna clenched her teeth and bowed her head and closed her eyes, and began to pray out loud, her words barely audible over Utilla's chants, which grew louder and louder.

He and Lightning Eagle whirled around the infant, shaking their rattles over her head, their masked faces giving them a demonic appearance. As Anna prayed, she sensed the presence of a growing evil in the room and from somewhere deep inside her, instead of fear came a feeling of peace and strength.

Suddenly she heard a quiet voice speaking, "Anna, go to the child and touch her."

She rose to her feet and walked over to She-Who-Never-Sleeps. Ignoring Utilla who almost hit her on the head with his rattle, she bent over the child and laid both her hands on her burning forehead.

Speaking in Makah as best as she could, she said forcefully, "In the name of Jesus, I pray that you will heal this child by the power of the Holy Spirit and deliver us from the evil one."

The strange words confused Laughing Gull and Gray Cloud. Utilla and Lightning Eagle heard them as well. They stopped singing. Utilla wrenched off his mask and dropped his rattle to the floor. His face was turning a mottled purple color and his eyes bulged with rage. He opened his mouth to speak, but nothing came out except a strangled choking sound. Gray spittle flew from his thin lips as his tongue tried to work.

He shot Anna a malignant look of pure hatred then stumbled out of the compartment to the door where he collapsed. Gray Cloud let out a moan of horror at the sight of the *shaman* stricken in her own house. She and Lightning Eagle hastened to his side to help him.

For once in her long life Laughing Gull was speechless. She never would've thought it possible for a mere slip of girl to stand up to the most powerful medicine man in all the villages. If she hadn't seen it happen with her own ancient eyes, she wouldn't have believed it.

Then an even more astonishing thing happened. As Knows Much kept her hands firmly on She-Who-Never-Sleeps' forehead, the child stirred restlessly and opened her eyes and began to cry. Laughing Gull forced herself to her feet, her arthritic joints protesting in pain, and staggered over to see the child.

Knows Much was smiling down at her, saying, "Thank you Jesus. Thank you."

Laughing Gull placed a wrinkled hand upon the child's forehead and felt the coolness of her soft baby skin. Somehow it didn't surprise her.

* * *

Later that morning a cry went up from the flat rooftops of the houses where the women and children had gathered to wait for the warriors return. Tatiana kept herself apart from them, standing by herself at the forest's edge. She had spent most of the morning here, escaping from the turmoil inside the chief's house where Utilla lay on a bunk, one side of his body paralyzed, unable to speak. He was being attended to by Lightning Eagle.

The child, however, had fully recovered from her illness. She was eating, babbling happily, and crawling around the floor as if nothing had happened. She was oblivious to all the arguments going back and forth between Gray Cloud, Soft Fern, Brown Bird, Swift Deer, and Laughing Gull. None of them could agree exactly on who had actually healed her, Utilla or Knows Much. The only thing they knew for sure was that the child was fine and the *shaman* deathly ill.

The entire incident gave Tatiana the shivers. She'd doubted most of her life that God even existed, but today she had seen a miracle. It happened right in front of her. She was convinced there had been supernatural powers at work in that room, good and evil, and because of Anna's faith and prayers, good had won out. But she was worried. What was going to happen to Anna now? Would the Indians blame her for the *shaman*'s illness? She remembered how Keeah once said a *shaman* could be a woman, and now she was concerned the Makah might think Anna was a *shaman*.

If so, would that make Lightning Eagle angry? There were several men and women in the village who sometimes helped Utilla with singing and dancing the evil spirits away from ill people. None of them had been specially trained like Lightning Eagle. If Utilla died, he was next in line to become the new *shaman*.

She wondered how old he really was. The Makah had a confusing way of measuring time. They didn't have a twelve month year. Their "year" consisted of six months or moons, with the first beginning in December when the days were lengthening and continued until June. From then as the days shortened was the second period or year. No one could explain to her anyone's actual age, but she supposed Lightning Eagle could be around sixteen. He still had the look of an adolescent boy about him, similar to young Robby.

A heavy overcast sky melded the horizon and water into a solid gray mass, but as Tatiana strained her eyes, she began to see first one canoe, then another and another. Soon she counted twelve. She let out a breath of relief. The raid must have been successful if all were returning.

As the canoes paddled in closer to shore she could hear the sound of the men singing. The words floated across the water to her ears.

"*The Makah have no equals in numbers or strength. It is nothing for us to have forty whales on the beach in a day. There is my head that I took. Do not think for a moment that you can defeat us. For we own slaves from all other tribes.*"

The women and children rushed down to the beach to welcome their triumphant husbands and fathers and sons. Some of the canoes held captured Clallam young women and boys, despair written all over their faces as they faced a future of slavery. Tatiana felt pity for them, for she could understand their hopelessness.

She stayed well out of the way, watching warily. Black Hawk stepped out of his canoe, tall and proud, his glittering black face making him look like a menacing stranger. Then her eyes fastened in shock on the terrible looking object in his hand. He and Strong Elk and eight others carried the heads of ten Clallam warriors. Blood still dripped from the freshly severed necks, spattering the sand with crimson drops. The gory sight made Tatiana feel ill and she doubled over and vomited bitter tasting bile onto the ground

She closed her eyes, seeing Black Hawk's blood stained hands, the same hands that he used to stroke her lovingly at night. How could she stand for him to ever touch her again?

When she straightened up she saw Soft Fern greeting their husband proudly, her face breaking into her dimpled smile. He grinned down at her and put his arm around her slim waist. She didn't even seem to notice the butchered head in his other hand. Red Hawk whooped and hollered, jumping around his father with great joy and pride.

Strong Elk was welcomed by his family in the same manner. Brown Bird, Swift Deer, Small Fawn, and Muddy Feet encircled him, talking and smiling, oblivious to the ghastly thing he held. With Gray Cloud at his side, Chief Utramaka raised a bloody spear towards all the people, and announced that the raid was victorious. Everyone cheered and applauded.

Feeling repulsed and still sick to her stomach, she hurried away into the woods where Black Hawk couldn't see her. The forest welcomed her with silence and peace, a relief after the grisly return of the raiding party. The trees soared above her and the air was still and fragrant with the odors of fungus, pine needles, cedar, and rich damp earth. Moss grew everywhere, on the sides of the trees, over stumps and fallen logs, and carpeted the ground with a soft emerald coating.

She walked blindly, almost stepping on a yellowish green slug, moving slowly across her path, leaving a trail of slime in its wake. Harmless, but ugly, the Makah children liked to squish them with rocks until the yellow insides squirted out, a rather repulsive sight. Once she had seen Red Hawk and Muddy Feet chase a squealing Small Fawn, as they threatened to throw slug guts at her. Yet, the sight of a severed head bothered them not at all.

Eventually the forest thinned as she reached a bluff near Cape Flattery, overlooking the ocean and Tatoosh Island in the distance. The clouds had lifted slightly and the wind had a cold salty bite. Blowing from the northwest, it rippled the waves into frothy whitecaps and she wrapped her sea otter cloak tightly around her. To the north lay Vancouver Island and the Nootkas, and to the west lay freedom, if only one could fly or had a ship.

Her eyes scanned the ocean once more then froze. A faint smudge had appeared on the horizon. A ship! Squinting hard, she watched as the spot grew larger until she could make out the sails. The ship was sailing north and would soon pass right by Cape Flattery.

A sudden hope flared inside her. What if it turned into the Strait and came this way? Tatiana glanced around the bluff looking for something for which to start a fire. If the crew saw the smoke, they might investigate, and if they came close enough, they could see she was a white woman. Quickly she began to gather dry twigs and pieces of wood into a pile. Then reality set in. She did not have a source of flame, nor did she have the time to run back to the village and sneak away a few hot coals from a fire.

She soon saw that the lack of a fire did not matter. The ship was sailing steadily away and shortly was out of view. In despair she sat down on a nearby stump and thought of Anton and Dmitri and the rest of the men. Were they still surviving in their fortress in the mountains above the Hoh River? Or had they been captured by the Quileutes and forced into slavery? Either way, she did not believe she would see any of them again.

"Wife," said a deep voice behind me. "Why did you leave the village?"

Tatiana whirled around and fell off the stump, twisting her ankle. "Ouch!" she yelped and clutched it as a sharp pain radiated through her foot.

In an instant Black Hawk was at her side, helping her up. She flinched at the touch of his hands. At least he had washed away all traces of paint and blood from his body, face and hands, so now she could look at him without wanting to retch.

"I--I didn't think you needed me," she answered nervously. "You had Soft Fern to greet you."

"You are my wife, too."

"I was told you were so angry with me that you no longer wished me to be your wife."

"Who told you this?" His expression darkened in swift anger.

Tatiana tried to step back, but he was still holding her. "Brown Bird," she said softly.

His anger turned to disgust. "She is no one to listen to."

"You threatened to beat me with that club," she reminded him.

To her surprise he gave a throaty chuckle and took a strand of her hair, winding it around one finger, something he did as a sign of his affection. "All the men were watching. I had to make them think my woman knew her place. My anger against you vanished as soon as it came. I would never harm you, wife. I would kill anyone who does."

She trembled, envisioning anew the bloody evidence of his murderous instincts.

"Next time I return from war you will meet me."

It was a command and not a question. She gazed at him directly and somehow found the courage to say, "No, I cannot."

He was silent for a moment and she braced herself for his anger. Instead he said quietly, "I saw you watching me. Your eyes were full of fear and hatred."

"No," she protested, "not hatred. But I have never seen heads cut off," she swallowed, "and I felt sickened by all the blood and--"

"You think we Makah are cruel, but you do not understand. We take their heads, because it is necessary to frighten our enemies enough so they will never trouble us again. We do not fight as the whites' do, to conquer a people or a land. We left the Clallam a free people. They will not bother us for a long time."

In a crude barbaric way, she had to admit he made a certain sense. Taking a deep breath, she said, "Then tell me about the raid. I wish to understand."

Pleased by her request, he smiled and said, "We reached their village before the sun rose. It was at low tide and their canoes were far up the beach away from the water. We crept up to their houses behind the stockade and threw blazing torches on the roofs and waited for the people to rush out. It was a short fight. We killed ten of their men and took a few women and children for slaves. The rest of the Clallam escaped by running out of the side doors of their houses and into the forest. After the fires burned down we took what we wanted from the ruined houses. It was a successful raid."

She forced a small smile. "I am glad you returned safely, husband."

He gave a relieved laugh. "And I thought you might wish I'd never return."

"No," she said and realized she meant it. "I can never wish any harm to you."

Her words gave him a sudden joy and he pulled her tightly against him. Then he stiffened and said, "But while we were gone I heard some strange things happened between Knows Much and Utilla. Is it true she asked a Great Spirit to heal She-Who-Never-Sleeps? A spirit more powerful than our *shaman*?"

"Yes," she nodded, "a Spirit we call God. He is the Creator of the earth and all the plants, animals and people."

He grunted in disbelief. "Not of the Makah or the Quileute. Our ancient stories tell how the earth at first was flat, without mountains or trees. It was full of cannibal monsters with powers unknown to man. Some could swim under water, some could fly, and some had claws. They could do all the things fish and animals do now. Then came the Changer. The Quileute say this was the clever and crafty Mink, but we say the Raven. He created the earth and the animals and birds to what it is now. Then he created humans."

"Maybe your Changer is the white man's God."

Shaking his head, he grunted again. Then he shrugged and took her hand. "Come, wife, we must return to the village. There will be a celebration feast."

With a powerful stride he began to walk across the rocky bluff to the forest. Wincing in pain, Tatiana stumbled along next to him, her sore ankle barely holding up her weight. He glanced down at her foot and without a word, swung her easily up into his arms. His shoulders and arms bulged with muscles from all the time he spent picking up boulders to strengthen them. As a whale harpooner, he needed to be one of the strongest men in the village.

"Wife, you are more trouble than you are worth," he said, but his eyes danced with merriment as he added, "It's a good thing you are so good at warming my bed at night."

Black Hawk laughed at the blush on her face. As he carried her through the forest towards the village, Tatiana felt more confused than ever. How could a man be a murderous savage and a gentle considerate husband all in one day?

CHAPTER FORTY

The Hoh River ran swiftly downstream as Sean and Anton steered the crude wooden boat with long makeshift paddles. A second boat was behind them, propelled by the strokes of Jake and John. Fifteen men sat in each boat, along with what was left of their meager supplies after spending three months at their fort in the mountains.

It had been a disastrous time with the Russians and the Americans quarreling incessantly. Dmitri bordered on insanity and had so many enemies, it was a miracle he hadn't had his throat slit by now.

Finally one day John came up with the idea of building two boats to carry them down the river and out to sea. He thought they should be able to make it to Destruction Island, where passing ships could be signaled, or else they could try to navigate to the Columbia River, which was often visited by Americans. They could decide when they reached the ocean.

The construction of the boats had brought Dmitri out of his stupor and given all the men a renewed purpose. They dismantled the fort they'd built, fashioning planks out of the logs and reusing the few precious nails, then smearing the sticky pitch of tree sap to chink the gaps. So far, the boats were handling the river well, leaking only a small amount of water that was easily bailed.

The weather had been cold and wet, raining every day. At night they pulled the boats up on the riverbank and struggled to start a fire. They were all soaked, starving, exhausted, and miserable, yet they had a glimmer of hope that they could reach civilization soon.

This afternoon they were nearing the mouth of the Hoh and the Quileute village where they believed the white women were still held. Dmitri was already having second thoughts. He was urging Sean and John to make an effort to ~~found~~ find out what had happened to his wife and the other women.

This made the rest of the men angry. They all knew they didn't have enough guns or ammunition left to risk battle with the natives.

Secretly Sean sided with Dmitri. The thought of leaving Anna and Katya behind was tearing him up inside. But as the commander he was trying put aside his personal feelings and do what was best for all the men. John struggled with the same emotions, especially as he did not know how he could bear losing Marya in the same manner as he'd lost his first wife, by leaving her with the Indians.

Darkness was descending when Sean hailed the other boat and said they were heading into shore to make camp for the night. Tomorrow they should be able to reach the sea and freedom. As far as they knew, none of the Quileutes were aware of their presence near their village and they hoped to keep it that way for at least another day.

Sean ordered no fires made, which meant it would be a cold wet night of sheer misery ahead for all of them. For food, Wang Li rationed out dried fish they'd traded from some Indians upriver, and the men had to content themselves with that.

Dmitri vowed he was never going to eat fish again after he reached civilization. He was sick and tired of the taste, smell, and looks of it, but it was better than starving to death.

After he finished his small portion he walked away from the men, who he found to be a great source of irritation. The Americans were always staring at him and making unpleasant remarks while his own Russian sailors ignored him completely. They looked to Anton as their leader, not him. Well, that would change as soon as they were rescued and returned to New Archangel or Fort Ross.

He headed into the forest, did his business behind a tree, and suddenly heard rustling noises coming from the bushes a short distance away. He pretended not to notice and idly refastened his breeches, then sauntered a bit closer, wondering if it could be some edible animal he could catch, like a duck. His mouth watered at the thought of a roast duck dripping with fat.

The bushes kept moving and he tensed himself then lunged quickly, tearing apart the branches. To his shock he almost fell face first onto two young Indian girls. They both squealed and without thinking, he grabbed their arms and dragged them out.

He shouted in Russian for someone to come help as they twisted and turned, trying to bite his hands. Sean, Anton and John came running with Samuel right behind them. The girls saw the huge black man and they froze with their dark eyes wide in terror.

"They were spying on me," said Dmitri. "If we let them go, they'll run back to the village and tell the chief where we are."

"Right you are, Volodin," said Sean with a grim face. "Samuel, take these women back to camp and find some rope and tie them up."

The girls shrieked as Samuel picked one up under each of his massive arms and headed back. "If they don't shut up, gag their mouths," Sean called out after him, "before they alert every native around."

"Good work, Your Excellency," smiled Anton. "You just found us some hostages."

"Are you men thinking what I'm thinking?" John asked, his bearded face also breaking into a grin. "I can tell just by looking at those girls with all of their jewelry that they are not slaves. They could be daughters or wives of some important villager."

"We can hold them for ransom," said Dmitri eagerly, "until they release our women!"

Excitement gleamed in his gray eyes, igniting the same feeling of hope among Sean and John. "What luck," said Anton. "We can free the women and take them with us."

Dmitri shot him a penetrating glance then said, "Of course Tatiana will ride with me in the captain's boat, not with you."

"Whatever you decide,Your Excellency," he answered with a bland expression.

"I wonder why they brought these," said John. He'd been rummaging around in the bushes and now held up two deerskin bundles, obviously belongings of the women.

"Looks like they were prepared for more than a day's outing," said Sean, puzzled. "John, I need you to talk to them and find out who they are and where they were going."

They made their way back to the riverbank where Samuel and a grinning O'Riley were busily tying up the young women. John walked over to them, dropping a deerskin bundle beside each girl. They had their hands tied behind them and their backs up against a large boulder near the water's edge. Both girls moaned in fear and trembled like captured fawns as the men grouped around them. Some were making ribald remarks and all were looking at them like they were the daintiest morsels of food they'd ever seen.

Sean sensed trouble immediately and he fingered his pistol, hoping he wouldn't have to use it.

"All right, men," he shouted, "you've seen the lasses. They're our hostages and I want everyone to leave them alone."

"What we gonna do with them, Cap'n?" Robby asked, his gaunt freckled face sprouting a few scraggily chin whiskers.

"I know what I wanna do with them," said Nate Tyler in a loud voice, producing laughter all around.

"We're holding them for ransom," said Sean. "We aim to trade them back to the Quileutes for our own women."

"What about Keeah?" O'Riley questioned.

"We'll see about her, too," said Sean, watching as John crouched in front of the girls and began to speak to them, first trying a few words of Quileute, then some words in Chinook Jargon.

Sean thought the language of the tribes north of the Columbia River sounded like a combination of the grunting of a pig and the clucking of a hen. How in the world John could understand any of it was beyond him. But he wasn't the only one. Even the Indians had trouble communicating. He'd been told that the Chinooks, Chehalis, and Quinault tribes, all of whom lived only miles from each other, could not understand the language of the other. Usually only roving traders could communicate with the various coastal tribes. When the white men entered the area, the Chinook Jargon had been born, a confusing mixture of Chinook, French, and English.

At first he wondered if either girl understood John, but then he noticed some of the fright in their faces faded slightly. Neither one looked a day over fifteen.

Finally one of them spoke to John, her full lips quivering as her eyes filled with tears. He talked back to her in a soothing voice, nodding and smiling. That seemed to give the other girl the courage to speak, and she also began to converse, gesturing to her legs, which many of the men noticed for the first time were covered in purple bruises and reddened welts.

After a few minutes, John turned around and said, "These girls are the two young wives of Hoheeshata. He captured them from a tribe of Chehalis to the south last fall and they wish to return to their family. They said their husband beats them and they were trying to run away when we found them."

He and Sean exchanged sad looks, knowing there was nothing they could do to save the poor girls from Hoheeshata. "John, tell them we are sorry about their cruel husband, but we have to trade them back."

When John explained, both of the girls burst into weeping. Many of the men appeared ashamed of their lustful thoughts and began to mutter among themselves what savages the Indians were to treat their wives so brutally. Dmitri pretended not to hear, suddenly feeling guilty about all the times he'd hurt Tatiana. He swore to himself that after she was returned to him, he would never lay a hand on her again except in love.

"We better take the girls to a safe place while we find the Quileutes and begin negotiations," John said. "We should cross the river now before it gets dark and make a camp up on top that bluff over there. At least it puts the river between us and the village while we wait."

Sean saw where he pointed and nodded his agreement. "Sounds like a good plan. Men," he ordered, "back into the boats. We're crossing the river."

* * *

Hoheeshata was away on a whale and seal hunting trip up the coast and that's why no one noticed the disappearance of his two wives, Hummingbird and Buttercup, until the next morning. Many Baskets thought they were in Talks A Lot's compartment helping her with her four daughters, all who seemed to have caught the sniffles. Talks A Lot thought they were with Whispering Doe, who had befriended them, and Whispering Doe thought they were with Many Baskets and her daughter, Katya, who was now called, She-With-Hair-Of-The-Sunrise, or Little Dawn. Chief Xawishata didn't even notice their absence as he was spending the night with Whispering Doe.

Tlingit Girl and the other slave women were the only ones who knew they were gone and why. But they kept that information to themselves, hoping the girls could make their escape somehow. The slaves also had endured many a harsh beating from the chief's brother whenever they displeased him and their sympathies lay with Hummingbird and Buttercup. Even Tlingit Girl who belonged to Whispering Doe had suffered a blackened eye once from Hoheeshata's swift fist.

It was Many Baskets who discovered them missing when she stepped into Hoheeshata's compartment to ask one of them to watch Little Dawn while she bathed in the river. To her surprise the coals of their cooking fire were only a heap of cold ashes. It was that which alarmed Many Baskets, not the fact that the room was empty. After all, they could be bathing in the river themselves, but never absolutely never did a proper wife allow the fire in her cooking pit to go out. At once she knew something was very wrong.

Crying out, she dashed around the big house, peering into all the rooms to see if they were inside. Chief Xawishata was up in an instant with Whispering Doe at his side to see what all the commotion was about.

"Hummingbird and Buttercup are missing!" Many Baskets exclaimed.

"When did you last see them?" he demanded, his face full of irritation at being forced out of his warm bed furs with his favorite wife.

Talks A Lot appeared, rubbing her eyes sleepily. "Yesterday afternoon they said they we're going upriver to pick some pussy willow branches."

Many Baskets scowled. "Those foolish girls! They should know better than to wander off that far by themselves. Anything could've happened to them!"

"Maybe they were attacked by a bear," said Whispering Doe.

"Most of the bears are still asleep for the winter," said Many Baskets scornfully. "It's more likely they were clumsy and fell into the river and were swept away by the river spirits."

"Maybe a hungry cougar found them," said Talks A Lot. "Or that spirit cat of the white woman's. No one knows where it is."

The women were all speaking at once and their chattering was giving the chief a headache. "Will you all be quiet!" he said sharply. "I'll send out some warriors and we'll find them before my brother returns."

"Or he'll be very angry," added Talks A Lot.

At that moment a group of men were heard at the house entrance, calling for the chief to come. Xawishata sighed and ran a hand through his long black hair, then went outside. All his wives followed, including Tlingit Girl, who held Little Dawn. The child had just finished being fed by one of the slaves, a young Chehalis woman who'd been captured along with Hummingbird and Buttercup. At that time she had been married and recently given birth, but Hoheeshata had thrown her baby into the sea and now she was a wet nurse to Little Dawn.

Two men who had been fishing in the river early that morning had astounding news. "We were hailed by the yellow-haired white man who can speak our language. He and all the other white men were standing on the hill across the river. He said they had captured two of our women yesterday."

"Hummingbird and Buttercup," muttered Talks A Lot to no one in particular.

"The white men refuse to let our women go unless we bring them both of the yellow-haired women in ransom. They even dare to demand Whispering Doe and her slave girl."

"No!" Chief Xawishata shouted. "They cannot have my wife!" He grimaced in anger then took a deep breath. "But I will send a messenger to the Makah and ask them to return the yellow-haired women." He gestured to several of his strongest warriors. "Go and tell the white chief that it will take a few days time. It is all I can do."

Most of the village had arrived by this time, and a great murmuring surrounded them. Whispering Doe and Tlingit Girl stared at each other in shock. Neither one had ever expected such a turn of events. Little Dawn began to fuss at the noisy crowd of people and Tlingit Girl whispered in her ear, "Katya, you might see your real mother again soon."

* * *

Lightning Eagle thought he might be in love with Knows Much. He knew it was a forbidden emotion to him, not only as a *shaman*'s apprentice, but because she was the chief's second wife. Yet, he could not control the turmoil of feelings inside him whenever he saw her.

Since his master, Utilla, had been struck with the paralysis, he had taken over all the duties of a *shaman*. He had one middle aged slave woman to help with Utilla's care inside their small hut. Chief Utramaka had offered the use of his house for his cousin Utilla, but Lightning Eagle instinctively knew the *shaman* would be more comfortable in his own home, surrounded by his masks, amulets, charms, herbs, and sacred objects.

If only Utilla could speak. It was bad enough that he could not move his left side, but when he tried to talk, his tongue would not obey. Only an incoherent babble came from his mouth.

The *shaman*'s eyes followed him around whenever he was awake. Lightning Eagle still felt the force, the power of Utilla shining inside them. His spirit was trapped inside the worthless shell of his body, clamoring to get out. It was the most awful, terrible thing he ever imagined happening to a man.

Whenever he could, he escaped the depressing atmosphere of the hut. Most of the time he found himself wandering by the chief's house, hoping for a glimpse of Knows Much. Now there was someone who had power, more than he'd ever dreamed. Some of the villagers were terrified of her, but he believed she was a good woman. And he was curious, so very curious, as to the source of her power. Who was this Great Spirit she claimed healed the child? More than anything, he wished to talk with her, to ask her many questions. But he dared not. He was almost a *shaman* now himself. He was expected to answer all the questions, not ask them.

It was a path of life he had not chosen for himself. As a boy, he'd hoped to become a famous whale hunter. He was called He-Who-Loved-the-Sea. Paddling through the waves in a canoe was the most exhilarating experience he could imagine. When he reached puberty he went for his vision quest to seek his spirit guardian. His father left him in the forest in a small clearing at the base of an ancient cedar tree so huge its trunk was as large as a hut was round. He remembered little of the first three days except being frightened by every noise in the woods, imagining one of the Cannibal Monsters coming to eat him. He neither ate nor drank, and by the fourth day, had fallen into a fitful sleep.

He dreamed a great storm roared through the forest, and a lightning bolt struck down from the clouds, hitting the old tree. But the tree did not burn. Instead a strange white light glowed all around him and he heard a voice saying, "From now on, your name is Lightning Eagle. One day you will meet a Great Spirit and if you obey it, you will become a man of power among the people, but you must never ride on the sea again, or you will die. I, Eagle, have spoken."

When he awoke, it was morning, and he saw a smoking blackened hole in the side of the tree. An eagle perched on a branch above it, studying him intently with two black beady eyes. When Lightning Eagle staggered to his feet, swaying with dizziness the giant bird flew off, flapping his powerful wings as it circled above him three times then disappeared over the treetops. Three black and white feathers floated down and he picked them up, touching them with reverence.

Later that morning his father came to fetch him and was overjoyed to hear about Lightning Eagle's vision and new name. He said it meant his son would become a famous warrior, for lightning was the power that came from the spirit Thunderbird, a weapon more dangerous than any made by man.

But when Utilla the *shaman* heard of the boy's vision, he summoned him, questioning him in great detail. Then he announced that Lightning Eagle was meant to become a medicine man and if he ever stepped foot in a canoe again, he would bring bad luck and cause all those in the canoe, whether hunting or on a raid, to die. Utilla told Lightning Eagle's father that he would take the boy and train him as his apprentice. In return, the *shaman* gave his parents many gifts, for they no longer had a son.

His mother had been loathe to let him go. He still remembered her tears as she said her farewells to him. He never saw her again. That same winter she died from the coughing sickness. It was from her that he had inherited his strange looks, his height, his unusual facial features, and the red in his hair. Once upon a time white men had lived for a short time at

Deeah (Neah Bay.) Soon after they left in their big canoe, his mother was born to a slave girl. She would've become a slave, too, except for her rare beauty. His father, a wealthy whaler, had taken her for wife while she was still very young. Nine moons later she almost died giving birth to him. She never had another child.

To this day Lightning Eagle still had the three eagle feathers, which he wore around his neck in an amulet. He never took the pouch off, not even to bathe. Washing was the closest he ever came to water. The joy of the sea he'd had as a boy was now a source of dread and fear. From a distance he'd watch the whale and seal hunters return with their catches to the adulation of the village. From a distance he'd watch warriors paddle off to war and come back in victory.

But he dared not go near the canoes. He was considered as much a danger to them as a woman in her moon time.

The Eagle had told him he would someday meet a Great Spirit. It was a term he did not understand, nor could Utilla ever give him a satisfactory answer. Talking about it actually made the *shaman* nervous. Sometimes Lightning Eagle believed the only reason Utilla had chosen him was because he was afraid of this Great Spirit and was determined to banish it from the village whenever it decided to show itself to Lightning Eagle. One thing he knew about the *shaman* after all these years of living with him, he was a man greedy for power.

Lightning Eagle remembered well the contests Utilla entered with medicine men of other villages. To show which *shaman* held the most power, they would handle fire, dance on burning stones, then pick them up and carry them. Somehow Utilla never burned his feet or his hands. Next they would grapple with invisible objects or make objects disappear, using their magic chants and spells. Utilla always won.

Lastly, the most painful, was the drinking of an entire bucket of water or even worse, fish oil. Utilla was the only one who could drink the oil without vomiting. However, Lightning Eagle recalled how the *shaman* spent the next three days squatting in the forest over a latrine hole.

It wasn't until the day that She-Who-Never-Sleeps was sick did he hear the term, Great Spirit, again. Knows Much said the child was healed by the power of the Great Spirit she worshipped. He longed to find out everything about this spirit that was more powerful than Thunderbird, or Raven, or the trickster Blue Jay.

But since that day, Chief Utramaka guarded his little wife well and she was rarely seen without him or Black Hawk nearby. He knew many of the villagers thought her Great Spirit was an evil spirit and they blamed her for the *shaman*'s illness. Though more feared than liked, Utilla was still revered as their medicine man, and had healed many a sick child and injured warrior himself.

On this particular rainy afternoon, a canoe of Quileute warriors had landed in the cove, claiming an important message from Chief

Xawishata. This caused a great curiosity in the village and Lightning Eagle decided to find out what they wanted. After instructing the slave woman, Frog, to watch over the *shaman*, he made his way to the chief's house.

He slid inside through the back door which faced the forest, and immediately bumped into Knows Much standing in the center passageway. His heart practically jumped out of his chest before settling back into its usual rhythm.

She seemed as startled as he, but when she recognized him, she gave him a bright smile and said, "Welcome, Lightning Eagle. How is Utilla today?"

He marveled at her kindness in caring for a man who hated her. "The--the same," he stuttered, drinking in the sweetness of her face, the burnished gold of her hair, and her eyes the color of hazelnuts.

"I'm sorry to hear that. I was hoping he would be better soon."

Anna looked up at the young man, towering almost foot above her. They said Black Hawk was the tallest man in the village, but she thought it was Lightning Eagle. To her he looked more like a Spaniard than a Makah. Instead of being round-faced, short and stocky he was very thin, almost to the point of being gaunt. He had a long aquiline nose, high cheekbones, and a narrow face with deep set brown eyes.

Once Sean had told her about the very first white men to visit these shores. In 1792, over thirty years ago, the Spanish built a small fort near Neah Bay. They wished to trade for the sea otter, but within four months abandoned the idea. Too much conflict had developed between them and the natives, who the Spaniards claimed were warlike, treacherous, and full of thievery.

Anna believed it was possible Lightning Eagle was descended from a Spanish sailor. Sometimes in the sun, his long brown hair glinted reddish. And when he smiled, which was not often, his perfect white teeth made him appear quite handsome. Too bad he was covered in so many tattoos, she thought. The intricate black designs all over his forehead, cheeks, arms, back, chest, and legs would make him an object of envy if any American sailor saw him.

He was grinning at her now and seemed at a loss for words. She felt a prick of impatience. The Quileute guests were almost finished with their meal, and then they were going to give their message from Chief Xawishata, Marya's husband. What if they had news of Katya? Anna felt excited and anxious all at the same time.

"Would you like to sit with the men?" she offered graciously. "There is still much food."

"Thank you, Knows Much, I would like that." He hesitated then added haltingly, "Would you--would you ever consider telling me about--about your Great Spirit?"

She had started to move past him to fetch some more baskets of dried fish that Gray Cloud wanted from her pantry. At his words she stopped and stared at him in surprise. It was the last thing she expected to hear from Utilla's apprentice.

"You wish to hear about Jesus?"

"Yes, this Je--sus, who is He?"

"The son of God, the Great Spirit, who came to earth as a babe long ago---"

"There you are!" Tatiana exclaimed, coming up behind her. "Oh, Lightning Eagle, I didn't notice you. How are you?"

It was a question she didn't expect answered, for she went on rapidly, "You won't believe what the Quileutes want, Anna, I mean Knows Much. Our white men have captured Hoheeshata's two wives as hostages and are holding them for ransom. And the ransom they are demanding is us, the two of us!"

Anna's mouth fell open in shock. "What? You can't be serious!"

Tatiana laughed, feeling amazed and delighted at the audacity of the captain and Dmitri for their daring plan of playing the Indians own game of kidnap and ransom.

Suddenly conscious of Lightning Eagle's brooding presence, she calmed down and said, "Come, our husbands wish to speak with us. We may be going on a journey back to the Hoh River, as early as tomorrow morning."

She grabbed Anna's hand and the two of them sped down the long hallway towards the chief's compartment where the sound of many men arguing and talking was heard. Neither girl noticed the terrible look of anger and frustration on Lightning Eagle's face.

He smacked one of his fists into the other. *No*, he cried out silently, *not now. Not when I just came so close to hearing about the Great Spirit, this Je--sus.*

For the first time in his life as a *shaman*, he understood what drove people to pay medicine men to perform black magic against their enemies. If Utilla was well, he'd ask him to place a curse on Chief Xawishata and all the white men, so Knows Much would stay in the village forever.

He turned around and stumbled back outside. Perhaps he could do it without Utilla's help. After all, he was a *shaman* now, and he had observed how evil spells were cast.

* * *

The Quileutes demand for the return of Knows Much and Daughter of the Sun provoked a bitter debate that lasted most of the night. Black Hawk was vehemently opposed, saying it was no concern of theirs what happened to Hoheeshata's wives.

Chief Utramaka partially agreed with his son. Not only was Knows Much the mother of his daughter, but she was an integral part of his household and family, and if he was honest with himself, he had come to care for her. He also was in awe of her. He believed she could commune with a powerful spirit who obviously looked with favor upon his family, or his daughter would have died from her illness. He was angry that Chief Xawishata dared ask he return his own wife.

But he was the chief of the Makah and his principal duty was the prevention of war. His responsibilities to his family came second. The Quileutes had made it clear that if the Makah refused to return with the white women, Hoheeshata had sworn revenge on them. Normally, this would bother Utramaka little, but the Quileute war chief had an extremely bloodthirsty reputation up and down the coast. If he was on the warpath against the Makah, it meant that no group of women clam digging on a beach or gathering food in the forest, or even a small hunting party of boys were safe. With his fierce band of warriors, Hoheeshata was known to attack without warning, killing the very young, the old, the infirm, and capturing the rest for slaves.

Utramaka realized he had no choice but to give in to the Quileutes demands. He spent most of the night trying to explain this to Black Hawk.

Finally, Strong Elk came to his father's aid. He said, "My brother, are you so besotted with your wife, that you would put your own people's lives in future danger in order to keep her?"

This made Black Hawk flush with anger and shame. He bowed his head and said, "You are right, Strong Elk. I have been selfish. I will bring my wife back to the Hoh River. But," he added, raising his head and staring at both his father and brother, "if she refuses to return to the white men, I will not force her to go."

"You think her feelings for you are so strong she would rather stay with you than with her white husband?" Strong Elk asked with a trace of scorn. He was eager to see the last of both white women. They were nothing but trouble for his family, which Knows Much had already proved by cursing his father's cousin with an illness.

Black Hawk gave him a level glance. "I have seen the scars on my wife's back from the many beatings her white husband gave her. I have only touched her in gentle pleasure. If you were a woman, which man would you choose?"

Strong Elk was silent and his father gave a great sigh. "It is decided then. We leave in the morning."

* * *

The two day voyage south to the Quileute village was miserable. They took two of the biggest ocean going canoes with thirty of their best warriors. Rain, wind, rough waves, and penetrating cold soon took all the excitement out of the trip for Anna and Tatiana.

She-Who-Never-Sleeps stayed behind. Swift Deer had given birth several days before to Strong Elk's second son, and she had plenty of milk to spare. Anna knew the child would be well taken care of, but she would miss her. She loved her like a second daughter.

Both women were seasick again, and more than once, they were afraid their canoe was going to swamp with the frothing waves only inches away. It was with great relief to spend the first night at the village of Ozette in a warm house. As they settled into their bedding furs, Black Hawk asked Tatiana, "If I let you go, do you want to return to your white husband?"

She knew he had no intention of letting her go, that it was only a theoretical question, but her answer would be the same regardless. She never wanted to spend another minute of her life with Dmitri Ivanovich Volodin, even if it meant a return to civilization.

"No," she said.

Her answer pleased him so well he fell into a deep undisturbed sleep. She lay next to him, feeling guilty; because it wasn't Dmitri she wanted to see again, it was Anton. Then her hands slipped over her abdomen and she sighed. Anton would not want her back along with an Indian child. And Black Hawk would never let her leave him if he knew she was carrying his child.

A wry smile flickered over her face. That was one thing he and Dmitri had in common, their desire for sons.

A few feet away Chief Utramaka pondered his relationship with Knows Much. When he first bought her, he knew she grieved for her white daughter, but since then, he hoped she had mostly forgotten her. He had given her another daughter and in time, when she was ready, he was eager to show her that he could be a proper husband as well. A woman like her who was such a good mother needed more children.

Before falling asleep, he turned to her and said, "Wife, if you can talk any of the white men into giving themselves up to the Makah, I promise they will be well treated. You can even tell them if one of their white man's canoes pass by the village, I will allow them to leave." The thought of having white men in his village where he could talk with them and learn more about their ways was an intriguing proposition.

Anna said she would try to persuade them, thinking with excitement about the possibility of all of them being rescued. Then her heart sank in despair. It wouldn't include Katya, and how could she bear leaving her daughter a second time?

The next day dawned cloudy with a brisk wind, but cleared later and the sunshine sparkled golden on the dark blue ocean. When they reached the mouth of the Hoh River, Anna looked south and saw the steep rocky outline of Destruction Island. She remembered how close the *Sea Rose* had come to its treacherous cliffs on that fateful night when the ship encountered the sudden gale that eventually foundered her. It seemed a long time ago rather than just a few months.

With swift sure strokes, the warriors paddled the canoes through the curling foam capped breakers of the dangerous river bar, an experience that frightened both her and Tatiana. When they neared the Quileute village, Chief Xawishata, Hoheeshata, and many Quileute warriors joined them in their canoes. All in all there were more than one hundred Indians. Nervously Anna scanned the village, looking for Many Baskets, Katya, Marya, or Keeah, but no women and children were to be seen. Fearing possible trouble, they had been told to stay inside their houses.

The large group of natives headed upstream about a mile past the village to the appointed place where they were to meet with the white men. They landed their canoes on a sand and pebble beach and waited.

Both Anna and Tatiana were dressed in their finest clothes. Tatiana wore her beautiful cloak of sea otter skins, and Anna wore a cloak made of plush brown mink. They were covered in jewelry, silver and copper bracelets and choker necklaces made of blue and green glass beads. A month before they had consented to having their ears pierced, a practice considered as barbaric among white society, and now long ivory colored dentalium earrings hung from their ear lobes. Their hair was freshly washed and shining and on their feet were beaded moccasins made of soft leather.

Their Makah husbands were also dressed well, Black Hawk in a thick black bearskin robe and Chief Utramaka in his favorite European trousers and shirt with a fur hat, clothes he found once from a shipwreck off Cape Flattery. Anna thought it bizarre that he was an Indian dressed like a white man and she was a white woman dressed like an Indian.

Black Hawk and his father both looked grim as they waited for the white men to appear. They soon arrived, paddling down the river in a crude wooden boat. It was smaller than their canoes and looked unseaworthy, but they managed to handle it well enough, steering it near the riverbank. A handful of white men sat inside, each holding a musket. The Quileute hostages were nowhere to be seen, most likely left behind in the well guarded hilltop camp.

One man climbed out of the boat, unarmed, and strode along the river's edge toward the Makahs. He was very tall and thin and wore a fur hat over his long wavy black hair. Anna recognized Sean instantly. She was at once excited and dismayed. His bearded unkempt appearance was even more shocking than the last time she'd seen him months ago. His filthy coat, threadbare and patched, hung loosely from his broad shoulders and his boots were worn and full of holes.

When he reached the spot where she and Tatiana stood Anna's nose twitched uncomfortably as his odor hit her. His unwashed body reeked of dirt and strong sweat, as did all the white men. Yet, when his brilliant green eyes raked over her with the look of a hungry desperate man, her heart pounded so hard she thought it would leap out. She had forgotten how much she loved him.

Not so Tatiana. She took a few steps backward, repulsed. Was this the same man who once was the handsome captain of the *Sea Rose*? With dread, she craned her neck to see where Anton and Dmitri were, and if she would even recognize them.

Sean stared at Anna as if she was the most beautiful sight in the world. He took in her clean, healthy appearance and knew at once that she had been well cared for all this time. He breathed a sigh of great relief. One quick glance at Tatiana told him it was the same for her.

Suddenly he was aware of the two Makah men standing next to the women, a middle aged man in white men's clothes and a scowling younger man in a bearskin robe. He had a sinking feeling that Anna and Tatiana belonged to them, and not as slaves.

Chief Utramaka placed a possessive hand on Anna's arm and said in English, "Do not look so upon my wife, if you wish to keep living."

Sean jerked as if slapped and a horrified look of shocked disbelief crept into his eyes. Immediately a mask, hard and cold, slipped over his face. He tore his gaze from Anna and said, "I meant no offense, Chief."

Utramaka grunted. "Are you the chief of the white men?"

"Aye, I am in command."

Anna finally found her voice. "How is everyone, Sean?"

Without looking directly at her he said, "We're all hungry and exhausted and have kept our sanity only by working on this plan to free you and Tatiana and make our escape to freedom. After we release the Indian women we'll take ye both and all our men in two boats across the river bar to Destruction Island where we can signal a passing ship and be rescued. If we can't find a safe place to land there, we'll paddle south to the Columbia and find a ship."

Black Hawk had listened intently, understanding some of the words. He stepped forward and gave Sean a dark glare. "My wife and my father's wife wish to stay with the Makah."

Sean looked at Anna and Tatiana with growing anger. "Is this true, Anna?"

Before Anna could reply, Tatiana blurted, "We would be fools to cast our fates with you and Dmitri and your wild plan to reach Destruction Island. The Hoh River bar is treacherous enough for these big canoes, but it is insane to try and cross it in your flimsy boat. Both Anna and I lead a comfortable life with the Makah and I must tell you that I have no wish to suffer the hardships that all of you men are enduring."

His nostrils flared with fury and he turned to Anna. "Is this how ye feel, too?"

She could not meet his gaze. His eyes blazed like two emerald fires and a terrible feeling of guilt and sadness filled her. But she said in a clear voice, "Yes, Sean. And not only that, Chief Utramaka, my--my husband, says that if all of you give yourselves up to the Makah, he promises you will be treated kindly. You will be given food, shelter, and clothing--"

"Have ye lost your mind?" Sean interrupted.

"No, you are the ones who have lost yours!" Anna snapped to the surprise of everyone standing there, used to her mild manner. "Can't you see the wisdom of my words? Or will you remain foolishly stubborn! Occasionally ships pass by Cape Flattery and by our village in the Strait. The chief told me he is willing to ransom all of you eventually."

Sean fell silent, pondering this possibility which none of them had considered. John came up behind him, also having heard Anna's words. "She's right you know," he said. "Her plan makes better sense than ours. If we go with the Makahs, we have a better chance of survival. All we need to do is convince them how indispensable we are. Didn't you say you once learned how to use a forge like a blacksmith when you were on the *Eastern Wind*?"

"Old Bill Carter, the armorer, taught me during the War with the British in 1812 when we were laid up in the Sandwich Islands."

John smiled at the chief. "I know how to work with wood, make canoes and paddles, even toys for your children. Our chief can work with iron. He can repair spears and knives and make tools for you."

"I like to learn the way of the white man," said Chief Utramaka, giving them both a friendly grin. "You teach me many things. I take good care of you."

Somehow Sean sensed the Makah in the bearskin robe didn't feel the same, as he was still glaring at him. Tatiana spoke to him softly in his language and he turned and smiled at her in such an intimate manner that Sean thought it was a good thing Dmitri was still in the boat.

He looked at Anna. "How is Katya? Is she well?"

To his surprise, her lips began to tremble like she was about to burst into tears. "I don't know," she whispered.

"What do ye mean ye don't know? Where is she?"

"She's still here with the Quileutes. Chief Xawishata's first wife, Many Baskets, adopted her as her daughter when we were traded away to the Makahs. I--I haven't seen her since."

Sean winced inside at the obvious pain in Anna's eyes. *How she must be suffering*, he thought, *and I can't even help her.* Feeling powerless and frustrated, he gave the Makah chief a curt nod. "I'll tell my men of your plan and we'll talk about it."

During this exchange all the Quileutes were still seated in their canoes, watchful and silent. Hoheeshata stared at the white men with hatred and loathing while Chief Xawishata listened to Chief Utramaka explain of the new turn of events.

Sean and John went back to the boat with the news of the women's refusal to leave the Makah and Utramaka's proposal of refuge. Tatiana took a few steps after them, curious to see if Anton had come. He had not, but Dmitri had. She saw him standing up in the center of the boat as

Captain O'Connell spoke to him. Dmitri began to argue. He glanced in her direction, his words halting abruptly at the sight of her.

"Tatiana!" he screamed. "Tatiana Nikolayevna!"

She held up one hand in greeting, but said nothing, conscious of Black Hawk coming up beside her. She could not help feeling a rush of pity for the disintegration of a man who had once been such a proud naval officer, a Russian baron of the aristocracy. From this short distance she could recognize the symptoms of insanity, the wild twitching of his left eyelid, his saliva-flecked beard, the trembling of his hands, and the shrill desperate pitch of his voice.

"How can you refuse to come with me?" he shrieked. "How dare you prefer living with filthy heathens over returning to me, your lawful husband?"

Suddenly he whirled around and grabbed the musket from the man sitting in the boat behind him. Aiming it directly at Tatiana's heart, he shouted, "Tatiana Nikolayevna, if you do not come here at once, I will be forced to shoot you!"

Tatiana stiffened in suspended disbelief. A few paces away she was conscious of Black Hawk uttering a deep throated growl, an expression of pure rage on his face. Sean looked at her, then at Dmitri's hand shaking violently against the shooting mechanism. She knew he wished to grab the musket away, but dared not.

Swallowing her fear, she stepped closer to the boat and stared directly at her husband. "Dmitri," she said in a steady clear voice, "your threats have no hold on me anymore. You may shoot me if you wish, but I cannot go with you. Not now, not ever."

He was stunned. She had never stood up to him in public before. The temptation to kill her was very strong. But she was so beautiful with her pale gold hair shining in the sunlight. And that sea otter cloak she was wearing, it would be worth a small fortune in Canton. His Tatiana, his lovely lovely Tatiana. No, he couldn't harm her. He had sworn he would never hurt her again. Besides it wasn't her fault she was a captive.

He swung the barrel of the musket towards Black Hawk. This was the man he should kill, the savage who had defiled her. But then a glimmer of sanity returned. If he shot the Indian, they would all be massacred. With a cry, he dropped the musket and fell to his knees onto the bottom of the boat and sobbed, covering his face with his hands. Sean immediately snatched up the musket and gave an order to the men. They slid their paddles into the water and turned the boat into the current.

He looked back at the Indians and shouted, "I'll return tomorrow with the women!"

CHAPTER FORTY ONE

"I say both of the women have turned into Injun squaws," Jeb Drake declared, "an' we shouldn't trust 'em."

It was evening and the men were in the middle of a heated discussion as they ate their dinner. They stood around a roaring fire located in the center of a crude breastwork of logs and brush on top the hill above the river. Hummingbird and Buttercup had given Wang Li all the food in their deerskin bags, a goodly amount of dried fish, berries, and camas root bread. Together they had cooked a tasty fish stew that managed to feed everyone.

Having hot food in their bellies renewed most of the men's eagerness to be on their way in the boats. When Sean and John returned with the news of the Makahs' offer, almost all of the men decided against it, including Dmitri. He'd collapsed earlier, crying about his wife's betrayal, fueling the idea to the others that neither Anna nor Tatiana could be believed about their promises of safe treatment among the Makahs.

"Beggin' yer pardon, Cap'n, " said Jake, "but we men don't understand why decent white women would rather stay with savages than their own men."

"I can answer that, O'Riley," John said sharply. "Miss Bolkonsky, Missus Campbell, and the baroness are surviving among the Indians in the same manner that I survived captivity among the Nootkas," he paused, glaring at each one, "by becoming one of them."

A murmuring went around the group at that statement, some of the men looking shamefaced, but most shrugging it off.

"Well, I for one, ain't goin' to be a slave to them Injuns," said Nate Tyler, "'cuz that's what we'll all end up if we surrender to 'em."

"Hear hear!" Jake said loudly. "I say we vote democratic like. Who wants to go with the Cap'n and who wants to go in the boats?"

"To the boats!" yelled all the men from the *Sea Rose* except Samuel, Wang Li, and John.

Robby opened his mouth to agree with the crew, then remembered how well fed and healthy both Missus Campbell and Missus Volodin looked. He was still a growing adolescent and he'd never experienced such constant gnawing hunger as he'd felt the past months. He knew if he cast his lot with the men, he'd only be facing more starvation.

He looked at Sean. "Cap'n, did the Missus say they'd feed us?"

"Aye, lad, she said we'll be given food, shelter, and clothing."

"Then I'm with you," he said, his skinny freckled face cracking into a grin.

Sean looked at Samuel and Wang Li. "Ye two are free to leave."

Samuel gave a mighty sigh and shook his head, then showed a flash of white teeth through his kinky gray beard. "No, suh, Cap'n, suh, I don't aim to get myself drowned by goin' out to sea in dose little boats. I'm a comin' with you."

"I come too," said Wang Li with a sparkle in his eyes. "I help Makah wives cook."

Sean raised his eyebrows and smiled slightly. "I'm sure they'll appreciate that, Wang Li." He turned to Anton. "What about you and your countrymen?"

"I'll come with you," he said, then spoke to the seven Russian sailors. He assumed all of them would follow him rather than Dmitri, but to his surprise, only two of the sailors agreed. The rest voted to go with Baron Volodin and the Americans in the boats.

Sean motioned for everyone to be silent, then he said, "Men, it looks like we're splitting up into two parties, eight of us are going with the Makahs, including myself, and the rest of ye will be taking the boats. I wish us all to separate as friends and I pray to God for the safety of each one of us."

* * *

The Makahs made camp that night in the same spot by the river. It was bitterly cold with a wind blowing in from the sea. They huddled around a blazing fire, wrapped in their furs, but Anna could not sleep at all. She kept seeing the agony in Sean's eyes when he learned that she was the chief's wife. And she kept thinking about Katya. It was sheer torture to be so close to her without being able to see her.

Early the next morning she asked Tatiana what she should do. "I can't leave without seeing her. I have to know she's being taken good care of and loved."

Tatiana thought a moment then said, "I'll ask Black Hawk if he can get us permission to visit Marya. Since she's my sister he'll understand why we wish to see her. That should get us inside Chief Xawishata's house."

When she asked Black Hawk, he was more than willing to allow her some time with her sister, but Chief Utramaka refused. "I want to leave this morning while the weather is still fair," he said sternly. "There's no time for visits." Another reason, one he kept hidden, was that he did not want Knows Much to see her white daughter and start grieving for her all over again. The child was best forgotten.

Anna felt frustrated, but she kept silent. Utramaka would never understand her. Because he had given her She-Who-Never-Sleeps, he thought she should be content. He had no understanding of the depth of a mother's love. She would love Katya and miss her until the day she died, and no other child could ever take her place.

Chief Xawishata and Hoheeshata and a number of Quileute warriors soon returned to wait patiently for the white men to keep their promises. About mid morning eight men and the two Quileute women emerged from the forest.

Tatiana recognized Hummingbird and Buttercup. The girls looked in good health and to her surprise, seemed reluctant to leave the white men. John spoke kindly to them, urging them on, and they finally flitted across the camp to Hoheeshata. He didn't greet them like a loving husband, but instead, seized them by their arms and marched them down to his canoe where he deposited them both while giving them a few harsh words. The two young girls hung their heads, looking forlorn and ashamed. Then he jumped in and ordered a couple warriors to paddle the canoe back to the village.

For a second they reminded Tatiana of herself and Dmitri, and she felt compassion for them. Like Anna, she too had spent a sleepless night. Over and over she replayed the scene where Dmitri aimed the musket at her, a wild crazy look in his eyes. If he hadn't ~~have~~ come to his senses, either she or Black Hawk would be dead. The frightening experience left her feeling vulnerable and she instinctively moved closer to Black Hawk, the only security she felt she had any longer.

Her movement towards the Indian caught the attention of Anton. He stared at Black Hawk with a feeling of pure disgust. Even though John had explained why she was now an Indian wife, he still found it revolting. For once he understood Dmitri's ravings about his wife.

Tatiana saw the speculative look of disappointment on his bearded face and felt a twist of annoyance. How dare he judge her! Then she noted his bedraggled appearance and her anger dissolved. He had always been thin and wiry, but now his skin was stretched so taut across his tall frame that he seemed almost skeletal. His large brown eyes, which used to remind her of a puppy's, were dark rimmed and sunk into hollows. His uniform was unrecognizable as such and looked like the rags of a beggar. Tears pricked the corners of her eyes. How could a once splendid looking man be reduced to such a wretched condition? She felt so sorry for him.

"These men and I are the only ones who will come with you," Sean said to Chief Utramaka. "The others would rather starve than give up their freedom."

"They are fools following an even greater fool," said Anton in a bitter voice. "Dmitri actually believes those clumsy boats can safely cross the river bar to Destruction Island. If they do not drown, they will be captured."

"We tried to reason with him last night," said John, looking at Tatiana apologetically, "but he was beyond reason."

She nodded in understanding. "Dmitri was always a proud stubborn fool."

Chief Utramaka was delighted with his eight captives, one of which was a great black man and another was a small short man with strange slanting eyes and a long black braid sprouting off a bald head. *Very interesting*. He couldn't wait to get them all back to the village and start questioning them.

At that moment to his dismay, a group of Quileute women and children arrived, including Chief Xawishata's entire family. The chief walked up to him and said, "I cannot let you leave until my wife greets your son's wife, her sister. She has been bothering me about it all night. And then she insisted I bring the rest of my family." He shrugged helplessly and Utramaka sighed and gestured for Tatiana and Anna to come.

Talks A Lot, smiling and plump, and her four daughters chattering like blue jays, surrounded Tatiana and Anna while Marya embraced both of them with excitement. Then she became conscious of John standing by the riverbank, his face turned toward her.

Earlier she had told herself if he was there, she mustn't look at him. But his presence so close by drew her like an irresistible magnet and she glanced at him. Their eyes met. She had forgotten what a vivid blue his eyes were and how handsome he was, even though he was too skinny and his face was half covered in a rough blonde beard. There was an intense pain in his expression, the same deep pain she felt over their forced separation. She tore her gaze away.

"I'm going to have a child," she told Tatiana softly. "But don't let John know."

Tatiana blinked in surprise. "Oh, Marya, congrat--" she started to say then stopped, feeling flustered. Should she share her own suspicions that she too was expecting a child? It certainly wasn't something she wanted Dmitri or Anton to know.

"My husband hopes it will be a son." Marya smiled sadly. She knew this child would bind her even closer to the Quileutes.

Although Anna was standing there listening to their conversation, all of her attention was focused on Many Baskets, who was carrying Katya in her cradle board on her back. The woman's scarred face was set in a forced smile, but her eyes were flat and hard.

"Marya, I mean Whispering Doe," said Anna, "how has Many Baskets been treating my daughter?"

"She dotes on her and refuses to be separated from her. But you mustn't call her your daughter or Katya." Marya gave her a nervous smile. "Her name is She-With-The-Hair-of-the-Sunrise, or Little Dawn. Having a child has made Many Baskets a happier woman. Even our husband has remarked on this. We are all grateful to you for the sacrifice you have made."

As if I had a choice in the matter, Anna thought with a flash of irritation. She steeled herself to stay calm as Marya called Many Baskets to come over.

The Indian woman unstrapped the board from her back, and without a word, sullenly handed Katya over to Anna. She was naked and wiggling under a small fur and Anna immediately saw that her daughter was in perfect health. The second thing she noticed was how she'd grown, bigger, heavier, her red-gold curls longer, but the same deep blue eyes, Tina's eyes.

Anna gave her a huge smile and said in the Mennonite Dutch-German language, "Hello my darling Katya. It's me, your real mama, are you still my little girl?"

Katya studied her solemnly for an entire minute while Anna continued to talk to her. Then she wrinkled up her nose and opened her tiny mouth and screeched and howled. At once Anna saw she had grown several more teeth before Many Baskets grabbed her back, giving Anna a cold look of triumph. Speaking soothingly in Quileute, she had Katya quieting down in a few moments.

A crushing pain struck Anna in her heart. Katya no longer recognized her! Her own daughter was afraid of her! Tears coursed down her face and she whirled away, tripping over rocks towards the canoes. There was nothing more for her here.

Sean intercepted her by blocking her path. He reached out his hand to hold her, then remembered Chief Utramaka and simply said, "Anna, Anna, don't despair. I'll find a way to get her back and we'll be rescued by a ship soon. Don't give up hope."

"It's already too late," she choked. "She doesn't know me anymore. Many Baskets is truly her mother."

She slipped around him and hurried to Chief Utramaka's canoe, where she stepped inside, sat down, and buried her head in her arms, sobbing quietly. That was all the chief needed to see, and in an irritated voice, he ordered everyone to load up the canoes.

Out of the corner of his eye he watched Knows Much, his heart heavy. It was the one thing he feared, that she would see her white daughter and start mourning again. If he'd realized a white woman had the same strong maternal instincts as a Makah mother, he would've traded for her infant from the Quileutes. At the time he didn't think it mattered. Now it was too late. He could see that the child was already a Quileute.

Nervously he wondered if the Great Spirit which favored Knows Much would be angered by her grief. The Quileutes obviously hadn't heard of the incident with her and Utilla, or Chief Xawishata might have second thoughts about keeping the child of a woman who could strike a powerful *shaman* with the paralyzing sickness. Perhaps someday he should kidnap her daughter and bring her back for Knows Much. She could be a sister to She-Who-Never-Sleeps. He would have to consider this.

The eight captives were divided up among the three canoes. Sean, John, and Anton were in the chief's canoe; Samuel, Wang Li, and Robby were put in Black Hawk's canoe and the two Russians in the last one.

John hesitated before boarding, looking back at Marya with sad longing, drinking in her beauty for the last time. He didn't expect to ever see her again.

"Marya," he called out and waved to her. "I love you. Don't forget me."

She looked back and smiled, feeling tears prick her eyelids. She longed to tell him she still loved him too, but she saw Xawishata watching her. Instead she waved then with an unconscious movement she touched her abdomen.

John immediately understood what the gesture meant. His beloved Marya was with child by her Quileute husband. For all his brave words to the men the night before when he defended the women and their new lives with the Indians, he suddenly felt like retching. He turned his face away, so she could not see the tears glistening in his eyes, and stumbled into the canoe.

A stiff wind was blowing when they reached the mouth of the river and the bar looked very rough with twelve to fifteen foot breakers. The current was running at maximum ebb, the most dangerous time to attempt a crossing. Chief Utramaka wisely decided to wait until conditions eased. They headed for the north side of the river's mouth and pulled the canoes onto a sandy spit where they all disembarked.

Anna finally dried her tears and she and Tatiana sat on a log, talking. All the Indians left them alone, seeing that Daughter of the Sun was doing her best to comfort Knows Much. Sean ached to go over and take Anna in his arms, but he knew Chief Utramaka would kill him if he did.

Instead he prayed silently for her, asking God to watch over Katya and all of them, and for Anna to feel His comfort. He patted the small oilskin pouch around his waist and the square shape of Ethan's Bible inside. He wondered if Anna still had her Bible. If not, he'd find a way to give this one to her when they reached the Makah village.

"I don't like the looks of them there seas, Cap'n," commented Robby. "Are you sure them Injuns know what they're doin'?"

"They brought their canoes safely here just yesterday, Robby, so I imagine they can bring us back up the coast no problem."

"First we got to git across that bar," said Robby looking worried. Then he let out a yell and at the same time, pointed at the river.

Everyone looked in surprise to see the two makeshift wooden boats paddling by. Ten men were in one and eleven in the other, all their faces pale with fear as they aimed their boats toward the breakers covering the river bar. Dmitri was giving orders in the lead boat and Jake was supervising the other one.

The men on shore let out a cheer and Sean called out across the water, "We wish you God's help!" He knew they would need nothing short of a miracle to clear those breakers.

Then John gave a shout and gestured behind them. Several canoes full of Quileute warriors were in hot pursuit of the white men. Sean recognized Hoheeshata in the first canoe. His face was painted black and he had outlined the jagged scar on his cheek in bright red so that it looked like a fresh bleeding wound.

The Makahs stirred nervously, knowing the Quileute chief's brother was making a statement of war against the white men, and hoped he wasn't on the warpath against them, too. Chief Utramaka and Black Hawk ordered both Anna and Tatiana to get behind them in case of trouble.

Anna could see at once that both of the boats rode dangerously low in the water, overloaded with too many men and heavy guns and ammunition. Their bows were not high enough to shed the heavy seas of the river bar. With bated breath she watched as the first wooden boat was picked up by a large blue-green wave. For a moment, the boat teetered precariously on top of the white crest, then disappeared into a frothing maelstrom of sea water for a few moments before emerging half sunk. A second wave curled over the other boat, drenching the occupants with tons of cold foaming water. The two boats swirled out of control as the waves carried them back towards the opposite shore. Minutes later they both struck rocks and capsized. In horror Anna saw all the men and supplies thrown into the water.

"They're going to drown!" Tatiana cried out.

Black Hawk shook his head. "No. The Quileutes will save them."

Their forty foot long canoes, pointed at both ends, rode the turbulent water easily, as each floundering man was plucked from the water. The ones who made it to shore were immediately captured. Tatiana was astounded that Hoheeshata had not let them perish. He was not known for being a compassionate man.

"What will the Quileutes do with them now?" she asked, thinking of Dmitri.

"They will be sold to other tribes as valuable slaves," answered Black Hawk, smiling. He thought it fitting that the yellow-haired husband of Daughter of the Sun would now be a slave. He would never forget or forgive the man for threatening both him and his wife yesterday with the gun. If he ever had the chance, he intended to kill him.

Tatiana shuddered slightly. There was no way that Dmitri, with his already feeble grip on sanity, would be able to survive captivity among the Indians for long. She remembered all the times she'd wished him dead. Now her wishes might be coming true, but she found she couldn't rejoice at his misfortune. In his own twisted way the man had loved her.

She could see Dmitri sitting inside Hoheeshata's canoe, drenched to the skin, staring blankly straight ahead, the pallor of his face ashen. The Quileute paddled his canoe close to the north shore and scanned the Makahs. When he saw Tatiana looking his way, he let out a triumphant cry, so high-pitched, chills shivered down her spine. Then he began to shout in a loud voice, staring at Black Hawk.

She couldn't understand any of the words. "What is he saying?"

Black Hawk's bold features were set in a deadly expression of cold anger. Without taking his eyes off Hoheeshata's arrogant figure, he growled, "He say, 'Next I come for your woman.'"

At her gasp of fright his gaze hardened further. "Let him come. When he does he will die."

* * *

Lightning Eagle kept Utilla informed of all the happenings in the village. When he'd told him that Knows Much and Daughter of the Sun had been taken back to the Hoh River as a possible ransom for the Quileute women, Utilla's eyes brightened and he struggled to speak. With a great effort so painful to watch, he forced his tongue to pronunciate what sounded like, "I'm glad."

It was a good thing the *shaman* didn't know what he was doing in the forest each night. When he was certain Utilla was asleep, Lightning Eagle returned to the site of his spirit quest, the ancient cedar tree. This was a holy place where he could be alone, where no villager ever came with their fears of the forest. Here he built a small fire, mixed special herbs and powders, and sang a chant to bring Knows Much back to the village.

He found he couldn't bring himself to cast a curse or an evil spell on the white men. He had seen too much suffering when Utilla used his black arts to cause sickness or even death. People believed the *shaman* held a power so strong it could kill as well as cure. They didn't believe in chance or fate. No misfortune seemed natural to them except death from old age or wounds from war. Everything else meant the work of evil spirits.

Many times he had seen an important person of the village pay Utilla to keep him out of trouble or to scheme against a rival. Once Chief Utramaka had felt threatened by another prominent rich man who challenged his authority to rule the village. The chief came to Utilla secretly one night. Two days later the man mysteriously fell ill and eventually died after suffering painfully for a week. No one had dared defy Utramaka since.

Ten days after the canoes left they returned and Lightning Eagle was overjoyed to see Knows Much with them. When he went to tell Utilla he was careful to hide his happiness behind a blank expression.

To his surprise Utilla was not fooled. He immediately became agitated and tried to speak, making a gargling noise in his throat, but instead of words only flecks of saliva flew out of his mouth. Taking his right hand, the side that was not paralyzed, he pointed a long bony finger at Lightning Eagle and shook it in a scolding motion while he scowled his lopsided frown.

"He is telling you to beware of Knows Much," said the Chinook slave woman, Frog. When she was a young girl she had been captured from a rich family on the Columbia River and she had the high sloping forehead of a noble woman. Considered a mark of breeding and beauty, it looked out of place on her. She was the ugliest woman Lightning Eagle had ever seen.

Her name was Frog for a good reason. Her eyes bulged out and her round mouth had thick protruding lips with few teeth. Utilla had knocked most of them out over the years. He'd also broken her nose many times and it had never set properly. Now it was flat and crooked, and she snored with each breath she took, awake or asleep.

Utilla hated women in general and had abused her in every way he could. But she never complained, never spoke against him, always obeyed him without question. It was as if he had broken her spirit along with her body. Even now, in his helpless state, Frog waited on him hand and foot, attending to his every need. Lightning Eagle thought she was much too good for the mean old *shaman*.

"My father," said Lightning Eagle in the respectful way he always addressed Utilla, "there is no need for you to worry about me. I have no intention of going near the chief's second wife."

It was a lie and Utilla knew it. He tried to speak again, but only a strangled sound came out of his mouth. His angry dark eyes bored holes into Lightning Eagle's eyes and he could feel the man's immense power trying to reach him. He stepped back and looked away. He refused to allow Utilla to manipulate him ever again.

"Frog," he said, "take care of him while I go into the village. Father, I hear that Chief Utramaka is giving a great feast tonight to celebrate his new captives. I promise to come back afterwards and tell you all about it."

Without another glance at Utilla, Lightning Eagle fled the hut. As his feet carried him quickly towards the village, he kept looking back over his shoulder. Was someone or something following him? He could see nothing, but by the time he reached the chief's house he thought he felt a flutter of wings brush by him as if the *shaman* was sending his evil spirit along.

* * *

All the partitions inside the big house were removed and the most important villagers and their families were squeezed together in a crowd of exuberant celebrants. The atmosphere was thick with smoke and ripe with the stench of human bodies and rancid fish oil. Sean squatted on the floor next to the other captives, watching Anna and the other women serve all the men roasted fish and venison. Although he was very hungry, the food stuck in his throat and was difficult to swallow. To his amusement he noticed Robby consumed every morsel placed in front of him.

All the people were astir with excitement at the sight of the newcomers. Samuel astonished everyone, especially among the women. They kept touching and rubbing his skin to see if the black color was ingrained dirt. He sat patiently while they satisfied their curiosity, grinning widely whenever a particularly comely young woman ran her fingers over his arms and face. After questioning him several times about his first home in a far away land called Africa, Chief Utramaka announced his name was Black Crow. He was to be given as a slave to Black Hawk and his friend the whaler Brave Spear, to help them take care of their whaling equipment, and perhaps learn to paddle a canoe. After proper feeding, he thought Black Crow looked to be very strong.

An ancient wrinkled woman was intrigued with Wang Li. Sean was told she was the chief's old mother and was named Laughing Gull. When John mentioned to her that Wang Li was their cook, she gave a surprised chortle then she asked her son if the strange little man could be the women's slave in the chief's house to help with the meals. He agreed, and she motioned Wang Li to the cooking hearth at once. He grinned and bowed to her which made her cackle.

Minutes later he was busily demonstrating to her and Gray Cloud his knowledge of which herbs and roots complimented certain types of fish and meat. When he showed them how to rub the fish with wild onion and parsley before broiling to give it added flavor, he immediately attracted a group of interested women.

When the men were finished with the meal, Chief Utramaka passed around a pipe of kinnikinnick and dried salal. To his pleasant surprise Wang Li was eager to smoke with him, and in halting English told the chief that he had come across the sea from a land called China. After describing the Chinese Emperor and his palaces and gardens of exotic birds called peacocks, Chief Utramaka named him Small Man With Big Stories.

Soon the chief turned his attention to Sean and John, who he called Green Eyes and Yellow Hair. He told the people that the chief of the white men and the yellow haired man who once was a captive of the Nootkas, would be given a hut of their own to live in. Because of their special skills, they were to be treated more as honored guests rather than slaves. From across the crowded room, Anna sent Sean a tiny smile at this good news.

When he returned her smile, Chief Utramaka leaned over and gave him a steely eyed stare. "I know you like my second wife, Green Eyes," he said calmly. "But she is not for you. She is the mother of my daughter, She-Who-Never-Sleeps."

This news brought a hot flush of anger to Sean's face as he thought of Katya and how cold-hearted the Indians were to think they could replace a woman's child with another without a care for her feelings. He was about to make a retort when John nudged his elbow sharply into his side, warning him to stay silent.

"You may speak to my wife only in my presence," said Utramaka, "but if you ever touch her, I will kill you. Or maybe I will sell you," he added with a contemplative frown. "Killing you is a waste of a most valuable captive."

Well, that is clear enough, Sean thought with frustration as the chief looked at Robby. "You," he said, "the boy with the spotted skin. I give you to my son Strong Elk."

Brown Bird heard those words and glanced at her husband, who shrugged. She sniffed in disdain and said, "That boy is too weak and scrawny to be much use for anything."

With her newborn son in a cradleboard on her back, Swift Deer gave Robby a friendly smile and said, "He is a growing boy who is starving. If we give him a few days of sleep and all the food he can eat, I think he will be strong soon. Then we can set him to work hauling water and firewood to the house every day."

Brown Bird gave a caustic chuckle. "The way he keeps eating makes me think he should be named Hollow Stomach."

All the women tittered at that joke and Robby turned bright red, making his freckles pop out of his skin in a rash of brown dots. He didn't know what the women were saying, but he did know they were laughing at him. His large ears burned with embarrassment and he stared at the planked floor, wishing he could hide under it.

Then he heard a light feminine voice speaking to him. He looked up and saw a girl with long glossy black hair falling to her hips. She was smiling at him. His eyes widened with astonishment as he realized she was half naked, wearing nothing more than a cedarbark skirt. He'd noticed earlier, as all the captives had, that many of the Indian women were bare breasted in the heat of the house. Most of them were old and ugly like Laughing Gull, so he'd paid little notice.

But this girl was young and lovely, her upper torso draped with jewelry, necklaces of ivory dentalium, strands of blue and red glass beads, her ears dangling with copper earrings and her arms encircled with bracelets of silver. He found himself blushing even more furiously as he tried to look everywhere except at the light copper sheen of her delicate skin.

With one graceful movement she sat down next to him. "My name is Small Fawn and I'm glad you will live with my family and be our slave," she said. "I think you are strange looking, but handsome."

He had no idea what she was saying, until John translated for him. Robby broke into a big grin and blurted, "Tell her I'm happy to meet her an' I'll be the hardest workin' slave she's ever seen."

Just then an Indian boy carrying a bowl of fish oil tripped over Robby's big feet sprawled in front of him and spilled the smelly greasy substance all over his filthy worn trousers. The chubby faced boy smirked with laughter then sped away, bumping rudely into the crowd.

Some of the oil splashed onto Small Fawn's skirt and legs. "My little brother Muddy Feet," she said, throwing a dark look of annoyance after him. Still keeping her dignity, she rose to her bare feet and motioned Robby to follow her. "Come, Hollow Stomach. I will find you other clothes. You need to bathe anyway. All you white men stink."

With amusement John explained her last words, and as Robby stumbled off after her, Sean called out, "Be careful, lad, she's the chief's granddaughter."

At those words Robby hesitated, but then quickened his steps as Small Fawn led him to the rear of the house and out the door. At the same time Anna was coming back inside holding a squirming black-haired child. The chief's daughter, Sean thought, observing how Anna held her firmly but with the affection of any Indian mother.

Then he noticed another man staring at Anna. He reminded Sean of a Spaniard with his aquiline nose and proud bearing. Taller and thinner than any of the Makahs, he was dressed only in a loincloth, but his body was covered in tattoos. He wore shiny silver earrings, bracelets, and a silver nose piece as if he was very wealthy. He appeared young, yet his face had the wary intense look of an older man. Sean saw that most of the people there spoke little to him, but when they did, it was with a great respect.

Who was he, Sean wondered, another son of Chief Utramaka?

In the next minute he forgot about the tattooed man when he heard the chief say he intended to trade the two Russians to the chief of Neah Bay and Anton to the chief at Ozette, his son-in-law.

"I don't like the idea of us being separated," he said to Anton.

The Russian lieutenant was staring at Tatiana. He thought he had never seen her so beautiful. Her skin was tanned a light bronze in contrast to her sun bleached hair, now almost as light as dentalium. She was dressed in a cedar bark jacket with a skirt that came to her knees. He had never before seen her legs bare and he found he could not take his eyes off her slender calves. Then he saw Black Hawk pull her towards him and whisper in her ear, causing her to flush and giggle slightly.

"Perhaps it's for the best, Captain," he answered, his mouth tightening into a grim line.

Sean's gaze fastened upon the pair and he nodded with understanding. If Anton was living in another village, at least he would be spared the constant torment Sean faced, living each day seeing the woman he loved but not being allowed to go near her.

The level of noise inside the house was extremely loud, but in the middle of the babbling and raucous laughter, the sound of a high pitched crying penetrated, suddenly hushing the people. A woman pressed through the crowd, howling out for Chief Utramaka. She was the homeliest woman Sean had ever seen with bulbous eyes and a crooked nose and thick jutting lips.

She threw herself down on the floor in front of Utramaka and sobbed, "My lord chief, your cousin, the great *shaman*, is dead!"

Utramaka leapt to his feet, pulling her upright with him. "Frog," he said shaking her, "tell me this isn't so."

"It--it happened only a few minutes ago," she choked. "I was tending the fire when all of a sudden he gave a great sigh and his spirit flew away." She looked at Lightning Eagle. "Behold, our new *shaman*, the great Lightning Eagle."

Utramaka released her and turned to Lightning Eagle. Stunned, the young man stood, feeling self conscious as every eye in the house turned upon him. Suddenly the realization dawned that he was now one of the most powerful personages in the village and there was no one to hold him back from becoming a friend to Knows Much and learning all her secrets.

Nervous sweat trickled out of his pores. Already he could hear the mutterings against her as the villagers began to blame her for their *shaman*'s death. He knew he had to put a stop to this at once or her life would be in danger.

"Lightning Eagle," said Chief Utramaka, "as our new *shaman*, I would like to give you a gift. Ask and it shall be yours."

He inclined his head politely towards the chief and considered, then said, "The only gift I seek is for you to allow me to spend time with your wife, Knows Much."

Chief Utramaka appeared startled then he scowled suspiciously. "And why is that, Lightning Eagle?"

He leaned towards the chief, lowering his voice, "Now that your cousin is dead, many will think your wife killed him. She could be in danger. I can guard her from any ill will. When all of our people see their new *shaman* in her company, unafraid, they will believe she is harmless."

But she wasn't harmless, Utramaka thought. If he was honest with himself, a part of him was afraid of his own wife. Another part held her in great affection because she was a good mother to his daughter. But if she could curse a powerful *shaman* like his cousin and even kill him, what was to stop her from cursing him too, if he displeased her?

Last night at the town of Ozette he'd slept in his robe by the hearth. He had intended to share her bed furs in their guest compartment, but changed his mind when he heard her crying and talking. It hadn't been her tears for her lost child that disturbed him, but he'd seen her bowing her head, with closed eyes, talking to her spirit God.

What sort of spirit listened to a woman's voice? What sort of woman could talk to a spirit? Only a holy woman, or a witch, as he'd heard Strong Elk tell Brown Bird one day when they didn't know he was listening. Now the thought of ever sleeping next to her again unnerved him. He was getting too old for this. If Lightning Eagle wished to endanger himself by being with Knows Much, he was welcome to her.

The chief clapped a hand on the young man's shoulder. "You have my blessing, Lightning Eagle. You may visit with my wife whenever you wish."

While John was explaining to the captives about the old *shaman*'s death and the new younger *shaman* called Lightning Eagle, Sean recognized him as the young man with the tattoos who was staring at Anna earlier.

He felt confused. There was something more here he didn't understand. And it involved Anna. She stood behind Utramaka with the Indian child in her arms, having an odd expression of fear and dread on her face. Then the chief spoke to her and motioned to Lightning Eagle, who put a hand out and took her arm possessively. She flinched at his touch, but kept her attention upon him as he talked intently to her.

Sean wished he knew what Lightning Eagle was saying. Anna listened carefully, nodding, then smiled at him in something akin to relief. The *shaman* released her arm, a bit too reluctantly Sean thought, and headed for the front entrance, winding his way among the respectful throng.

As he passed Sean, he glanced at him and their eyes met. The *shaman*'s dark gaze gleamed with a strange look of victory, giving Sean an uneasy feeling. He didn't know why, but he felt an instant dislike to the man.

CHAPTER FORTY TWO

During the month of March, which the Makah called *o-o-lukh-put'hl*, or the Moon of the Finback Whale, winter settled in harsh and wet over Cape Flattery. The storms off the Pacific rolled in one after the other, bringing endless rain and howling gales that kept the people inside their houses. Once again it was a time for the women to stitch robes of furs and weave baskets and mats, a time for the men to repair old weapons and fishing equipment and make new harpoons, spears, bows and arrows, a time for the children to hear their elders tell the stories about the earth and the people's beginnings, and it was a time of ceremonies, especially of the secret societies.

Chief Utramaka and his two sons belonged to the black spirit society, an exclusive group comprised of only the wealthiest. If a boy wished to join, his father had to make a high payment and give a huge feast. Red Hawk had now reached puberty and was anxious to acquire the prestige of belonging to his father's secret society. He had seen how the people were in awe of its members and never gave offense to them, for they were noted for their ability to endure pain without feeling it.

One damp gray afternoon the women of the house noticed Red Hawk was missing. They were all in Gray Cloud's compartment sitting around a blazing cedar fire in the cooking hearth, working on various projects except for Laughing Gull, who was snoring in a corner.

Soft Fern was making small covered trinket baskets, no more than two inches across, using materials she'd gathered during the summer months when each twig, root, and strand of grass was at its best. Gathering was a tedious process and Soft Fern always said when she began to weave a basket, her work was already half done. Her favorite design was a white background with a black boat or whale, and Anna never tired of watching her nimble fingers intertwine a fine lattice work out of shredded white beach grass and shreds of a black sea plant.

Small Fawn and her mother, Brown Bird, were making cattail and cedar bark mats while Swift Deer worked on a cedar bark rain cape for Strong Elk. Her infant son slept nearby in his cradleboard. His cousin, She-Who-Never-Sleeps, was busily crawling around the floor and looking for objects to put in her tiny mouth. Gray Cloud was instructing Anna and Tatiana how to make fishing nets out of nettle strings, an intricate job of tying knots and loops that Anna mastered easily, while Tatiana was all thumbs.

"Where is my cousin?" Small Fawn asked with concern. "I haven't seen him in two days."

I hope he's lost in the forest, thought Tatiana with barely concealed dislike. The boy was bolder than ever in his antagonism towards her. Unless his father was present, Red Hawk made no secret of his hostile feelings.

Lately Black Hawk had been spending more and more time with Soft Fern and less time with her. Just last week she had seen him coming out of his first wife's compartment with a small smile of contentment on his mouth. She was on her way outside to the stream to bathe when they almost collided. Tatiana wished him a good morning, but he had brushed her aside brusquely without replying as if she was a troublesome fly.

Red Hawk had witnessed the incident. After his father was gone, he'd slyly commented to her that his father was getting tired of her ugly white skin.

Tatiana hadn't seen Black Hawk since, and at first she worried that he was indeed losing interest in her. Then Soft Fern said not to expect to see their husband for a few days because he was closeted with the other members of the society preparing for the ritual to initiate Red Hawk. It was considered a time as sacred as preparing for war, when relations with women were forbidden. Tatiana had not forgotten the night when he'd left to raid the Clallam village and her error in approaching him to say farewell.

"Red Hawk has gone to join the secret society of his father and grandfather," Gray Cloud now told them. "It is his first step towards manhood."

"Where did they take him?" Small Fawn asked with great curiosity.

Laughing Gull had been dozing by the hearth, but she suddenly opened her eyes and chuckled. "He has been eaten alive by the black spirit, the cannibal monster of old from those the Changer never destroyed."

The young girl gasped, along with Swift Deer and some of the slaves. "Is Red Hawk going to die?" she asked fearfully.

"The black spirit will vomit him out soon," spoke up Gray Cloud, bending over a basket to hide a gleam in her eyes. "And when this happens, he will be filled with a supernatural power."

Anna and Tatiana exchanged glances of suppressed mirth, both of them thinking how ridiculous the Indians' superstitions often were. Anna had an inkling that Red Hawk was safely inside Lightning Eagle's hut. The young *shaman* had told her last week he wouldn't be able to see her for a few days because he was going to have an important guest.

She had developed a strange relationship with him. After her previous two experiences with *shamans*, she had panicked when the chief told her that Lightning Eagle wished to visit her to discuss spirit matters. The first time he came, the other women were extremely curious, but the chief told them to leave the pair alone, so Gray Cloud showed him to Anna's compartment and kept her distance.

"I want to know all about the powerful spirit you talk to," he said with eager sincerity written all over his tattooed face.

And so she told him, starting from how God, the Great Spirit, created everything perfect in the world until sin entered the world. Sin was a word that the Makah didn't have in their language, so it was a challenge to Anna to translate the meaning. She used the Ten Commandments to describe what God considered sins, lying, cheating, stealing, murder, dishonoring one's parents, envy, and worshipping other spirits than the true God.

Lightning Eagle shook his head, feeling slightly angry. "Then, according to the Great Spirit, all the Makah have broken His laws."

"Everyone on earth has broken them, myself included. But Jesus, God's son, came to earth to save us from our sins and make us acceptable to God, the Father. When we are sorry for what we have done, we are forgiven and we receive His Holy Spirit to give us the power we need to obey God."

At the mention of the Holy Spirit, a glimmer of understanding dawned in his dark eyes. "The old *shaman* was right. You do have a spirit inside you, a powerful spirit."

"You can have the same spirit inside you, Lightning Eagle, if you believe in Jesus."

"I do not need your spirit power, Knows Much. I have my own. Yet, perhaps I will try it someday. I cannot help respecting a spirit power stronger than the old *shaman*."

"The Holy Spirit did not kill your *shaman*. God only helps us do good things, so after we die, we go to heaven where we live forever with God and Jesus and the good spirits called angels. It is a place where there is no sickness or tears or hunger or thirst. It is such a beautiful place no one ever thinks about coming back to earth."

She hesitated then added, "And for those who reject Jesus, when they die, they go to a place of never-ending fire and torment where all the evil spirits live."

"This is very interesting, Knows Much, but I find it hard to believe that such a terrible place exists in the land of the dead, or that we Makah need to change our way of life so we don't go there."

Anna sighed with frustration, then realized how foreign all this must sound to him. "Whenever the Makah take captives, that is stealing," she commented.

"No," he said, "we need captives for slaves and for trade like the white man has what you call money."

"But you're taking people away from their homes and families against their will. That's what happened to me and Daughter of the Sun."

She'd hoped to make him feel guilty, but instead he gave her a tender smile. "You two should be thanking us for rescuing you from the Quileutes and the white men. When you came here, you were sad, dirty, and too thin. Now look at you, you are healthy and very beautiful!"

She'd blushed slightly at the personal comment and awkwardness fell between them, which he hastily covered up by asking more questions. When he left that day, she realized Lightning Eagle liked her far too much for his own good. If the chief suspected his interest in her was more than just spiritual, she didn't know what would happen. *Perhaps nothing.* Ever since they'd returned from the Hoh River, he'd ignored her. He hadn't visited her at night, not even once. Not that she minded. She couldn't imagine having the old chief in her bed while Sean was sleeping in a nearby hut.

She rarely saw him. He was gone all day with the men, either fishing or working at the crude forge he'd made, melting iron to fashion sharper harpoons, spears, knives, and axes. John was busy building a new canoe for the chief, out of a huge cedar log he'd help to cut down in the forest. If by chance Anna and Sean ever met, they'd glance at each other briefly and nod, or perhaps smile. Only once were they able to see each other alone.

It was early one morning when she had gone to the stream to bathe. He was returning, half naked and still dripping wet. His appearance had greatly improved in the past weeks and he was no longer the gaunt shoddy looking man she had seen at the Hoh River. Plenty of nutritious food, proper rest and exercise had done wonders.

For a few seconds they'd halted in the path, staring at each other. She stood transfixed, her hands suddenly aching to brush back the damp tendrils of his dark curly hair from his forehead then trace one finger down that handsome profile of his across the scar on his left cheek.

"How are ye, Anna?" he asked in a low voice.

"I'm well. And you?"

"Never better, except I miss ye something' fierce."

"I miss you, too, Sean."

"How is the chief treating you? Is he-- does he--"

"If you're asking if he sleeps with me, the answer is no. He's never touched me like that. He bought me only as a mother for his daughter."

Relief shone bright in his green eyes and he burst into a grin. But before they could say anything more, they heard a group of women walking down the path.

"I must go," she said with reluctance and moved quickly toward the stream as he nodded and went in the opposite direction.

If only they could've talked longer, Anna thought now, as she pulled She-Who-Never-Sleeps away from the heat of the hearth flames. The child giggled and crawled over to Swift Deer's son and put out a tentative finger to touch him. "Da-da," she said and smirked at Anna mischievously. Then she added, "Mam-mam."

Anna held her breath in delight as Swift Deer laughed. "She calls you mother," she said.

It was a bittersweet moment for Anna, for it reminded her of Katya. By now she was one year old and was probably calling Many Baskets her mother.

* * *

When the sun went down that afternoon all the villagers were told to gather behind the stockade near the *shaman*'s hut. A cold east wind was blowing down the Strait of Juan de Fuca, and most of the people were wrapped warmly in capes and robes. A huge bonfire was lit and the bright orange flames roared skyward, casting out sparks and smoke everywhere.

The chief was nowhere to be seen nor were Black Hawk or Strong Elk. Anna and Tatiana stood with the other women, who were nervously talking to each other. Nearby was a group of slaves, including Robby and Wang Li along with Sean and John. Samuel was the only one missing, then Anna saw him arrive with a young woman at his side. She was an attractive widow called Starlight, the daughter of Black Hawk's boyhood friend, the whaler Brave Spear. Anna had heard she was smitten with Samuel and wanted her father to buy him from Black Hawk. As a husband or a slave, Anna wasn't certain. But she could tell by the broad grin on Samuel's face that he was happy to be with her.

Drums began to pound and her attention was caught by a frightening bunch of men leaping out of the forest. They wore ugly wooden masks of huge indented eyes with small holes, thick eyebrows made of human hair, and large noses and scowling mouths. All the children let out shrieks of fear while many of the adults gasped.

The masks were supposed to hide the identity of each society member, although everyone knew who they were. Anna recognized the chief and his sons and some other men, including Lightning Eagle. As they danced around the bonfire, singing and chanting, the members began to take arrows and pointed bones and slash and cut holes into their arms, legs, and even their ears, nose, and lips. Blood streamed from each man, yet none missed a beat of the drum. They were demonstrating the fact that they felt no pain.

Anna and Tatiana thought the scene appeared like a gruesome nightmare and they could barely watch. Some of the children, including Small Fawn and Muddy Feet, clapped their hands in rhythm, giggling and smiling. Tatiana glanced at Soft Fern. Her face was set in a proud expression as she stared at her husband and son.

A chill of repulsion shook her at the sight of the man who was her Indian husband. At the moment he looked like a half-crazed devil monster, dripping with blood and screaming high pitched cries that curdled her insides. Her hand subconsciously slid across her still flat stomach. And to think that she was almost three months gone with his child! How she hoped it would be a girl. She could not stand the thought of giving Black Hawk a son who would end up going through such a barbaric ceremony. Soon she had to tell him. Most of the women in the house had already guessed except Anna. Tatiana dreaded her reaction to the news.

She thought of Anton and sighed. How she missed him! She hoped he was being treated well by the chief of Ozette and that if he ever heard about the child he would forgive her.

Anna was also thinking how difficult it was going to be, to look at Chief Utramaka or Lightning Eagle again without feeling disgusted. She spied Sean and saw that he was calmly observing the ceremony with an expression of interest. He must have felt her gaze upon him, for he gave her a quick smile then shrugged, as if to say, what do you expect from a group of wild savages? She wondered what he thought of all the shrunken heads on posts by the stockade entrance. It was something she'd never become accustomed.

A great cry from all the villagers shook her back to the ceremony. Red Hawk was being brought out of the *shaman*'s hut, half-conscious, as limp as a string of seaweed. His legs and arms had been slashed and were reddened with his blood. The members sang over him, then raised him up four times, finally placing him on the ground.

Suddenly he came to, his black eyes darting crazily about. He gave a screech that did not sound human and jumped up, then ran wildly down to the beach. All the members rushed after him and caught him easily. Red Hawk collapsed and fainted. While he was passed out they dressed him in a costume with cedar bark fringes on the head, knees, and ankles. Then they blackened his face before placing a fierce-looking mask over his head.

For the next couple of hours Red Hawk lay unconscious while the members of the society danced around him and all through the village. Anna and Tatiana longed to retire, but there would be no sleep for anyone that night. As in the case of *potlatch*es, the rituals of the Makahs lasted for days. A great dance was held in the chief's house. Red Hawk was brought back to his senses and he and the other society members danced continuously, proudly displaying their wounds, while men pounded on boards with clubs and on the house rafters with long poles. Three long nights later Red Hawk and the members finally calmed down.

Luckily for Anna, she spent those days in the women's hut in the outside corner of the village. Otherwise, she would've had little sleep, if any. On the fourth day the entire village feasted and gifts were given by Black Hawk to the society and to the drummers, who were past the point of exhaustion.

For Anna and Tatiana, it was a relief when the whole affair was over and life returned to normal routines. For Lightning Eagle, the ritual of the black spirit society was his first test as head *shaman* and he knew it had been a success. But in another respect it had been a failure. On the first night of the ceremony he'd seen the expression of revulsion on the face of Knows Much, and he worried she might never want to speak to him again.

The day after she left the women's hut, he decided it was time she learned about the Makahs' religion. She had told him much about her own religion. Much of it he didn't understand, especially the story of Jesus, the son of the Spirit God who was killed by being nailed to a tree. That was a barbaric way to die, he thought, worse than anything the Makah did to their enemies. It seemed to him this Jesus was a weak and powerless spirit, and it puzzled him why he didn't strike down his tormentors. And how could any father allow such a death for his own son? Then it became even more confusing when Knows Much said the Jesus Spirit came back from the dead and went to live in the sky with his Father.

For the Makah, there was always the fear of the dead returning to take a soul back with them. Perhaps that is what this Jesus did, he pondered, as he walked stiffly towards the chief's house, feeling his scabbed skin pull tightly from all the puncture wounds on his legs. Perhaps the connection between the dead and the living had not been broken. Perhaps too many people kept calling out the Jesus name and he came back. One should never think or speak the name of a dead person in case he heard his name and thought he was being summoned.

Everyone knew that those who died were lonely in the land of the dead, even though it was a comfortable place with plenty to eat, similar to what Knows Much called heaven. What she called hell, a place of eternal burning and torment, was not something he'd ever heard of and he doubted it existed. At least he hoped not.

Everything about the funeral and burial for the Makah was planned to break the connection between the dead and the living. When the old *shaman* died, no one of his family would touch his body, and they hired outsiders to prepare him for burial by wrapping him in his favorite robe, putting his body inside a small canoe and placing it high on posts deep into the forest.

Knows Much said that the body of Jesus was placed in a cave covered by a huge stone. She said spirits called angels rolled the stone away, and Jesus walked out and was seen by his friends. It was a mystery to him why Jesus didn't take them all away with him when he went back to his father in the sky.

Lightning Eagle tucked these thoughts away and entered the chief's house, feeling nervous. What if Knows Much refused to see him?

He bumped into Red Hawk who was on his way out, carrying a bow and a quiver of arrows. The boy sprouted two red hawk feathers in his headband, and was full of self importance since his initiation into the black spirit society. His curt greeting to Lightning Eagle bordered on rudeness.

He decided to overlook the lack of respect, noting how gingerly the boy moved because of his still raw wounds. "Where is Knows Much?" he asked.

Red Hawk was irritated at the delay. His uncle, Strong Elk, had promised to give him a lesson in target practice before he left on a hunt, but he wouldn't wait long. Red Hawk gave the young *shaman* an impatient scowl. "How should I know? I'm not her keeper."

The boy saw a spark of anger kindle inside Lightning Eagle's eyes and he remembered just in time that his grandfather had once told him to never anger a *shaman*. He hastily covered up his blunder by saying in a friendlier voice, "I saw her down at the beach. She went with my father's second wife and my uncle's second wife."

So, she was with Daughter of the Sun and Swift Deer, thought Lightning Eagle. That is good. She cannot rebuff me if she is with the others.

He thanked Red Hawk for the information and made his way through the village. He met the young man with the spotted skin called Hollow Stomach carrying two heavy loads of firewood for Brown Bird's cooking pit. The white slave had finally lost that haunted look of starvation in his face, and had gained weight and muscle due to his tremendous appetite and daily chores. Small Fawn walked beside him, chattering away to him as if he could understand her words.

As usual, a pack of scrawny village dogs followed the two. Hollow Stomach attracted dogs the way a bear was drawn to a honeycomb. He shared his food with them, gave them names, and affectionately patted their heads. It was something none of the villagers understood. The Makah tolerated dogs, and some were used in hunting, but rarely did anyone treat them kindly. If Hollow Stomach wasn't careful, his name might be changed to Dog Man.

Lightning Eagle smiled at the pair then continued on, passing the hut where Green Eyes and Yellow Hair lived. A young Clallam slave boy was helping Green Eyes by keeping the fire going in his forge, which was placed outside. There was no sign of the white man, and Lightning Eagle felt relieved. He knew the man was fond of Knows Much and he couldn't stand the sight of him. It gave him much pleasure to have the chief's permission to be with her whenever he wished while Green Eyes risked great punishment if he so much as spoke to her.

When he reached the beach he saw Daughter of the Sun and Swift Deer, with her infant on her back, carrying baskets of mussels and clams. He didn't see Knows Much anywhere. He thought of asking them, but he suddenly felt awkward and shy in front of the two beautiful wives of the village's most powerful men.

Instead he headed back towards his hut. By now Frog would have his meal cooking. She was an excellent cook and housekeeper, but since the old *shaman* died, he had become uneasy with her around. He had no evidence, but he believed she had killed the old *shaman*. He remembered returning to the hut that night and finding him dead, a look of sheer terror upon his face. His one good hand and arm was mottled with fresh bruises as if he'd tried to fend off an attacker. Suspicions crowded his mind at once, noting the dried blood and purple bruising around the *shaman*'s nose. How easy it would've been for Frog to suffocate him by pinching his nose shut and covering his mouth.

He knew he should tell Chief Utramaka and each time he was determined to do so, he found he could not. If she was guilty, she would be killed and her body thrown into the sea, doomed to forever wander the path of the dead. After all the suffering Frog had endured in her life, Lightning Eagle decided he couldn't add to it. He hoped the old *shaman* was removed far enough away so he wouldn't come back to haunt either of them.

"You have too soft of a heart, Lightning Eagle," he'd told him long ago. "You must harden yourself to the emotions and pain of others or you will never achieve the effectiveness and power of a true *shaman*."

Perhaps he was right, Lightning Eagle thought. Because of his obsession with Knows Much, he wasn't focused enough to be the powerful medicine man the village needed. But at the moment he didn't know how to stop the trembling in his knees whenever he saw her, or the fluttering in his stomach whenever he heard her voice.

Like now.

Thick bushes and trees grew densely behind his hut, and as he approached he heard her low throaty voice coming from inside the foliage. He also heard an even deeper voice, a man's.

Softly, he padded past his hut and into the forest. He hid behind a big spruce tree with evergreen branches spreading to the ground like out swept arms. He peered through the pine scented needles and saw Knows Much talking to Green Eyes. They were speaking in one of the white man's tongues and he understood nothing that was said, but he did recognize the deep longing that was evident between them.

"And that's why most of the villagers blame me for Utilla's illness and death," Anna finished, after explaining to Sean the story of She-Who-Never-Sleeps' miraculous healing.

Sean was astounded. "God healed the bairn just like Jesus healed people in the Bible," he breathed. Then his eyes narrowed and he said, "But that means ye could be in danger here."

"Not as long as I'm the chief's wife," she said. "And now that the new *shaman*, Lightning Eagle, has befriended me, and he has come to no harm, the people will realize there is nothing to fear from me."

"Why has Lightning Eagle become such a good friend to ye?" Sean asked suspiciously.

"He is very curious about Christianity. We spend all our time talking about religion. I've been praying that one of these days he might believe in our faith. And as the spiritual leader of these villagers, he would have a great influence on them." Anna's eyes glowed as she imagined the people turning away from their false spirits, the cannibal monsters that frightened them so, and having the peace and love of God in their hearts and lives.

Somehow Sean doubted the only reason the young *shaman* spent so much time with her was his interest in religion. "Say, Anna, do ye still have your Bible?"

"Nay, I gave it to Marya months ago."

He fumbled at his pouch and drew out Ethan's Bible. "Here, ye can keep this one."

She smiled with delight as he handed her the small black book. "Have you or John seen a sign of any ships?"

"Nay, but soon the whales will start passing Cape Flattery on their way north and the trading ships will be sailin' right behind them. The main problem is how to find a way to signal them. 'Tis something me and John haven't figured out yet."

"You'll think of something. The two of you are so inventive. All the women in the house love the wooden dishes John makes and the children enjoy playing with the little wooden figures of whales, birds, and other animals he carves for them."

"John said as long as we keep our captors happy, we'll be treated well. But he warned me that the Makah are fickle in their affections. If they get tired of any of us, they'll start passing us around to other villages."

"I couldn't bear it if we were separated again, Sean."

"I won't let that happen," he vowed.

A gust of wind blew through the trees, rattling branches and swirling around them. Drops of rain pattered against their heads and Anna shivered. "I think we better go back, but not at the same time. You go first, and I'll circle around and come out of the woods by a different path."

"I love ye, Anna," he said and in one quick movement, took her into his arms and kissed her deeply. With reluctance he released her and then exited the forest, sauntering slowly back to his hut.

Anna watched him go with a smile on her face. She knew they shouldn't have met like this so close to the village, but minutes ago when she saw Sean disappear into the forest, she couldn't help following him. Tatiana and Swift Deer were busy digging shellfish, and she'd told them she needed to relieve herself in the bushes. By now they were probably wondering what was keeping her. She hid the Bible under her robe and began to walk in a different direction than Sean had. She was so engrossed in her thoughts she didn't see Lightning Eagle until he popped out of the bushes.

He seized her by a wrist and glared angrily at her. "You little fool," he lashed out in Makah, "do you realize what a dangerous game you are playing with Green Eyes?"

Anna was suddenly filled with dread as she realized he'd seen her and Sean not only talking together, but kissing. Was he going to tell the chief?

To her surprise he yanked her back into the bushes, pulling her away from the village.

"Where--where are you taking me?" she asked, as she stumbled along beside him with trembling legs.

His face was a scowling mask and he didn't answer. Instead his grip on her wrist grew tighter and pain shot up her arm. She gasped, but he ignored her as he propelled her along a narrow trail. It was slippery with the recent rains and her moccasins slid in the mud.

She pressed the Bible against her with her one free hand, wishing Sean hadn't left her so quickly. There was a look of menace about Lightning Eagle which she'd never seen before and he frightened her.

The wind blew stronger, whipping branches into her face. Raindrops pelted down and the weak afternoon light grew darker the deeper they went. After a mile or two they burst into a clearing where a mammoth cedar tree stood. Lightning Eagle released her wrist and Anna stopped, panting heavily as she clutched the Bible.

He looked down at her, a bit calmer now, but still angry. "Do you know what would've happened to you if anyone else but me saw you with Green Eyes?"

She shook her head timidly, staring at him with her eyes wide and full of fear.

"They would tell your husband at once and Chief Utramaka would have the right not only to divorce you, but to cut off the tips of your nose and ears, so you would never look beautiful to anyone again. As for Green Eyes, he most likely would be killed."

She cried out in horror and he softened his tone, "So you are fortunate it was I who saw the two of you." He glanced at the Bible in her hands. "What is that?"

There was no word for book in the Makah language so she said, "It is a holy object that speaks the words of God the spirit and his son, Jesus."

He frowned in disbelief. "How could that be?"

She opened the Bible at random and showed him the inside pages. "See, these black marks are words that I can tell you."

Anna glanced down at the Book of Mark in the New Testament, reading silently a few of the verses. Then she attempted to translate them into his language, "Here it says that Jesus was baptized, er," she knew there was no word for *baptism* in the Makah language, so she said, "washed in the river. And when he came up out of the water, He saw the clouds and sky open, and the Spirit like a dove came down upon Him. And then there came a voice from the sky, saying, 'You are My Son in whom I am well pleased.' And right after that the Spirit took him into a wild place where he stayed many days and nights."

Lightning Eagle appeared intrigued. "This Jesus received a dove for his Spirit Helper. They are small but powerful birds. When a pair of doves makes a nest, all the ravens and crows stay far away from them." He looked at her thoughtfully. "Then he went on a vision quest in a wild place for how long?"

The Makah had trouble counting past ten, so she said, "Four tens of fingers."

"That's impossible! He would have died from no food or water in that many days."

Anna translated from the Bible again. "It says he was taken care of by the wild animals and the," she paused, thinking of a word to substitute for angels, "good spirits."

Lightning Eagle nodded. "Yes, I can understand that. Tell me more."

She flipped back through the pages and it opened to Psalm 96. She read, "*Let the heavens rejoice, and let the earth be glad; let the sea roar, ... Let the field be joyful and all that is therein; then shall all the trees of the wood rejoice...*"

"What does that mean?" He interrupted her, his eyes startled.

"It means that all of nature, the earth, the sea, the grassy meadows and trees, will sing for joy to God who created it all."

"So, the white man's religion is like ours. Everything has a spirit."

Now it was her turn to be flustered. "Well, no, I don't believe that's---" her voice trailed away, feeling at a loss to explain.

He pointed with his chin towards the huge cedar tree. "This great tree is our holy tree. Sometimes when I come here I hear the tree spirits talking." He listened for a moment. "They are silent now."

Anna glanced furtively around the clearing. Had he lost his mind?

"Have you ever heard of a holy tree?"

She was about to say no, when she remembered once when she was a little girl her family had taken a trip to the town of Chortitza. There in the center of the village was a gigantic oak tree which the peasants called, "The Thousand-Year-Old Oak." It was regarded as sacred by them and the Cossacks who used to live there. Her parents told her the tree had provided shelter for the earliest Mennonite settlers before they had built their houses.

She recalled the massive branches of the oak that spread outward from the thick trunk like the many arms of an octopus, a frightening sea creature she'd never known existed until one of the Indians caught one while diving for oysters. Now looking upwards, the ancient cedar tree had such branches, but it was so much taller than the oak. She couldn't see the top.

"I once saw a sacred tree near my village," she said.

He smiled at her then and looked more like the old Lightning Eagle who was her friend. He took her hand gently this time and said, "Come, it is time you learned about my religion."

He drew her to the base of the tree and began to sing a chant without words in a strong tenor voice, a beautiful liquid voice such as she'd never heard. The sound of it flowed over and around her like molten gold. She closed her eyes as she listened, thinking how much she'd missed the sound of music. Instinctively she began to hum in melodic harmony with him, the way she used to with her brother Jack in their duets.

At the same time the wind whistled and whispered around the tree, the branches rustling as if they were alive. While she hummed she thought she heard moaning voices, or was it her own imagination? If there were spirits here as Lightning Eagle believed, she doubted they would be pleased to have a Christian in their presence. Feeling uneasy, she opened her eyes and saw he was kneeling in front of the cedar, his head bowed and his arms stretched against the trunk. She abruptly stopped singing. Was he worshipping the tree? She wondered with dismay.

Lightning Eagle had slipped into a trance and when he heard her voice, the low throaty sound blending so perfectly with his, tears of joy flooded his eyes. *She is my his soul mate*, he thought. *If only she wasn't married to the chief.*

He turned to look at Knows Much. His heart pounded violently as he observed her loveliness, the innocent eyes, the sweetness of her lips, and the curves of her body beneath her fur robe. He had never seen her unclothed like many of the women of his tribe, and it only made her the more desirable and mysterious.

When Green Eyes kissed her, he felt he would go mad with jealously and wanted to kill him at once. Now the thought came, if the white man dared kiss her, why not himself? The more he pondered it, the more reasonable it became. Without hesitation he jumped up and whirled around and rushed towards her, catching her around the waist and pressing her against him. The black holy thing fell on the ground as she protested. But he silenced her by crushing his mouth over hers. He'd never felt anything so wonderfully soft and moist.

She struggled to break free, but his strength overpowered her. His nostrils filled with her scent, the flowery fragrance of her hair and skin. He crushed her harder, his hunger for her almost out of control. How he longed to do more than kiss her!

It was then he felt an unseen presence searing his back. He tried to ignore it, but the prickling of danger penetrated to every pore of his body, sending out an alarm of warning inside him. He let her go and twisted around.

There were two red hawk feathers sprouting over the bushes at the edge of the clearing, the same kind of feathers Red Hawk wore in his headband. They waved wildly in the wind. Then suddenly they were gone.

He caught a glimpse of someone crashing away through the thick undergrowth. Red Hawk had seen them! A sense of panic enveloped him and all his desire for Knows Much fled.

Stunned and angry, Anna wiped her bruised lips with her hand, trying to get the revolting taste of him out of her mouth. She turned her face upwards and let the raindrops wash over her. What she'd suspected for some time was true. Lightning Eagle had been using the pretext of being interested in her religion only to get her alone. She was thankful that something had stopped him before he had tried anything worse than kissing.

She looked at him. He was staring off into the bushes with an expression of fear on his face. Keeping a wary eye on him, she picked up the wet and muddy Bible. As she wiped it clean with the hem of her robe she said, "I think there is evil in this place. Not holiness. And the evil entered in you, Lightning Eagle."

Her words jolted him. Could they be true? Had something possessed him to do such an insane thing? He turned towards her with a dazed expression. "Forgive me, please forgive me. I don't know what came over me. Did I hurt you?"

"A little," she said, rubbing her mouth again.

"I'm so sorry," he mumbled, looked ashamed. Then he added, "We were being watched."

"Yes, I know," she replied, staring firmly into his eyes. "God was watching."

"No, that's not what I meant." But the thought of her spirit seeing what he'd done made him even more fearful. Would he now be struck with the paralyzing sickness? He took a deep breath to calm himself.

"Red Hawk was spying on us." He pointed with his chin towards the bushes. "He was over there. I saw him run away. Unless I can stop him from telling his father or grandfather, we are in big trouble."

"We? What do you mean, we?" she demanded. "It was you! I have done nothing."

He hung his head in shame. "You are right, Knows Much. You are innocent. But it all depends on how Red Hawk describes what he saw. He may say you were willing."

She choked in outrage as he said, "Promise me, Knows Much, you will never tell a soul what I did. Not Green Eyes, not Daughter of the Sun, not anyone. Promise me!" His voice ended on a frantic note.

"I promise, Lightning Eagle, but only if you promise to stay away from me after this."

Sorrow rushed through him at the bleak thought, but he had only himself to blame by breaking her trust in him. He uttered a heavy sigh, saying, "I promise."

They stood looking at each other in silence for a few moments then Lightning Eagle motioned her to follow him. "Come," he said. "We must get back to the village at once. We will go together. I won't hide the fact that I took you to see the holy tree. I can explain that much to your husband."

She frowned, her brow creased with worry. "What will happen to us if Red Hawk tells him you kissed me?"

"He won't," Lightning Eagle said darkly, "not after I'm through with him."

He refused to explain further, and as Anna hastened after him through the windy wet forest, a strong feeling of fear and dread dogged her every step.

CHAPTER FORTY THREE

Red Hawk spent a sleepless night. He was in a quandary. He knew he held the power of life and death in his hands over his grandfather's second wife, the village *shaman*, and the white slave, Green Eyes. He spent the first part of the night, chuckling to himself at how smart he was to have followed Lightning Eagle into the forest. The rest of the night he tossed and turned on his platform bunk, worried that if he told his father or grandfather what he'd seen, Lightning Eagle would put a curse on him.

Yesterday after telling the *shaman* where the white woman had gone, he'd found his uncle feeling too ill from a belly ache to instruct him in target practice. His uncle complained that the new slave, Little Man With Big Stories, was not a proper cook and was poisoning them all with his penchant for cooking different foods together in a strange stew. Everyone knew that fish and meat should be prepared separately. Strong Elk had already asked if the yellow man could be traded away. It was being considered.

Since Red Hawk suddenly had a few hours of free time, he'd sauntered out of the village looking for his friends and spotted the *shaman* heading into the forest. There was something furtive about his movements and the way he kept looking around to see if anyone noticed what he was doing. It pricked Red Hawk's curiosity.

One thing he had learned well from his uncle was how to walk through a forest without a sound or being seen. It was easy for him to follow the *shaman* without betraying his presence. How surprised he'd been to see Knows Much not only kissing Green Eyes, but later, kissing Lightning Eagle as well.

The knowledge that his grandfather's wife loved two other men astounded him, because Knows Much always acted so meek and submissive and was such a good mother to She-Who-Never-Sleeps. She never flaunted her beauty like his father's second wife, Daughter of the Sun. Now she was the woman he'd imagined would be seducing all the men. Most of the boys he knew lusted after her, including himself. There were times he had to admit he wished she was only a slave and not his father's wife. Strange how he had misjudged both of the white women.

Knows Much was a loose woman and deserved punishment. His grandfather was being fooled by her innocent ways and if he didn't tell him, he would soon be the laughing stock of the village instead of their respected chief.

But it wasn't as simple as that. Lightning Eagle had seen him spying on them. Even now as he was trying to sleep, the *shaman* could be preparing a magic spell or curse to sicken him or even kill him. And then there was Knows Much. Some said she had greater power than any *shaman* they'd ever seen. The old *shaman* had hated her and now he was dead.

Sweat broke out all over his body as he tried to decide what to do. When the first light of morning crept over the house, he still remained confused.

* * *

During the next few days Anna waited for disaster to fall. But nothing happened. Life went on in the same routine, rising at dawn, washing in the stream, each member of the household busying themselves for the day's activities. If the weather wasn't stormy, the chief and his sons went out to fish or hunt and the younger women to forage whatever edible substances they could find in late winter. Gray Cloud and Laughing Gull stayed inside to watch over the two little ones while they swept the sand around their cooking pits with a cedar branch, then broke up cedar bark firewood and placed pieces on the fire, which had been left smoldering since the night before. Next they put cooking stones in the pit to heat and had the slaves fetch water from the stream in a wooden box. When the fire was hot enough, they would begin cooking so the men would have food whenever they finished their work.

No one seemed concerned about her jaunt in the forest with Lightning Eagle. When he explained to the chief about taking Knows Much to see the ancient sacred tree, he'd nodded in understanding and said, "It is good to teach my wife about such things."

Then he lost interest in the subject and asked Lightning Eagle if he could concoct a potion to help Gray Cloud sleep better at night. Lately she'd been plagued by the same dream where he fell out of his canoe and drowned. She was irritating him with her fear, begging him not to go to sea anymore. Ridiculous, he'd told her. He was the chief. Of course he would still go out in his canoe. And when his time came to die, it would not be in such an embarrassing way. He intended to die honorably, either fighting a whale or fighting in war.

Anna steered clear of Red Hawk whenever he was inside the house. But one night when she was clearing the dishes away after the men had eaten, he looked straight at her, his young handsome face so like his father's, holding an expression of knowing contempt.

"Will the *shaman* be coming to visit you tomorrow, Grandmother?" he asked in an innocent voice.

She flushed and her heart beat rapidly as she said, "I--I don't know. He's a busy man."

"Yes, he is," agreed the boy, smirking, then said, "Green Eyes is also a busy man."

Her face turned even redder and she could not meet his gaze. "I wish you well in your hunt tomorrow with your uncle, Red Hawk," she said, ignoring his reference to the white slave.

"Thank you, my grandmother," he said. "Perhaps when I return it is time for me to have a nice long talk with you and my grandfather."

A look of fear passed over her face and Red Hawk felt a surge of satisfaction. It was always easy and fun to scare women. They needed to know a man was their master.

Unknown to both of them, Laughing Gull had heard the entire exchange. She'd been dozing off as usual while the men ate, but had awaken just in time to witness the odd conversation between her great-grandson and her daughter-in-law. There was something here she was missing, something of importance.

She recognized that look of smug knowledge on Red Hawk's face. It was the same expression he had whenever he was hiding something. And that strange look of fright on her daughter-in-law's face, now that was even more mystifying. As yet, the girl had never acted afraid of anything, like a true Makah. But now, something was bothering her.

Laughing Gull stretched, feeling the familiar pain knife her wrists and elbows, shoulders, knees, and ankle joints. Old age was tiresome, she thought. It was funny how her memories of a little girl playing in the village were so clear when she couldn't even remember what she ate for breakfast that day, if she ate at all.

She struggled to her bony feet and decided to keep an eye on Red Hawk and Knows Much. She sensed trouble brewing between them. She might be old, but she wasn't stupid.

* * *

The next morning Red Hawk left with his uncle, Strong Elk, to hunt deer in the forest and was gone for several days. Venison was needed for an important feast Strong Elk and Brown Bird were to give soon to celebrate their daughter's passage into womanhood.

Small Fawn had reached the age of puberty, a time when the Indians believed that a dangerous power came to a girl. She had to be kept away from the others and their activities. A cubbyhole had been built in one corner of the house, high up above the bunks. For five days she had to stay there with her back against the wall, in the darkness, for she was not allowed to look at the sun or at a fire.

A slave attended to Small Fawn's needs, which were few. She ate only dried food once a day, from special dishes which were thrown away. She drank water through a tube. Every morning before the rest of the family woke up, she went bathing in the stream alone. She was not allowed to talk to anyone.

By the time her ordeal was over, she would be very slim, as an aristocratic lady should be. For the girl of a good Makah family, getting a rich husband was the main aim in her life. From now on, Small Fawn could not run around outside playing with the other children. If she went out, she had to be chaperoned. She could not speak to or look at a young man outside the family, and when she walked by a man, she had to keep her eyes cast down. She could not laugh when men were about, for that would show her as light minded and bold. During the day while food gathering or running around the house without her cedar bark clothing, she could talk and laugh. But when the men came in she had to retire to a corner and gather her blankets around her, speaking only rarely. When she ate after the men, she had to sip delicately from the tip of the wooden spoon, never showing her teeth.

Tonight Small Fawn's confinement was over, and Strong Elk and Brown Bird were giving a feast to announce her becoming a young woman. Makah parents saved for this feast from the day of a daughter's birth. It was to be a solemn affair in which gifts were given, but not to Small Fawn. In the moons ahead, she would have to prove what a good wife she would make by being modest and industrious.

"Unmarried girls here have as many rules as I had as a young lady of the Russian nobility," Tatiana observed to Anna that evening. They had spent hours helping Brown Bird with the preparation of the many food dishes. Wang Li was put in charge of making the vegetable stew, a mixture of camas, dried wild clover, and dried elderberries which were steaming in a pit all day.

When he complained that it was not tasty enough, Swift Deer reminded him that her husband, Strong Elk, preferred the food served plain. Wang Li grumbled to himself that all the Indian food lacked flavor, because they had no source of salt, except sea water or seaweed. Today he was tempted to slip some seaweed in the stew. Certainly that wouldn't harm Strong Elk's delicate stomach. Later he found his chance to collect seaweed when he went outside to fetch water and pieces of firewood that Robby was splitting out of dry seasoned logs.

Anna and Tatiana were keeping an eye on the roasting venison which Strong Elk and Red Hawk had carved from a slain deer. The roasts were skewered onto green sticks and placed over the smoldering heat of the cooking pit. The juices sizzled and dripped into the fire, adding to the already smoky environment.

"Of course, we young wives also have many rules to obey," commented Tatiana in a disgruntled voice. "We mustn't talk to strange men, or eat or touch something ceremonially forbidden. An Indian husband is as much as a despot over his women as a Russian husband is over his wife."

"Has Black Hawk ever struck you?" Anna asked.

"No, not yet," she answered, "but lately he has been ignoring me and I worry that he's thinking of trading me away."

"I think he's just been preoccupied with his son," said Anna, wishing she and Tatiana had some time alone so she could tell her about Red Hawk and Lightning Eagle.

Tatiana made a face. "Well, he may be having another one next summer."

Anna stared at her blankly then her mouth dropped open. "You are with child?" she whispered.

"Unfortunately yes," Tatiana hissed. "Maybe you've noticed I haven't been in the women's hut for more than two months."

"Now that I think about it, you're right. But you look so well, I never would've guessed."

Tatiana patted her belly. "I haven't felt ill hardly at all with this one. I only feel extra tired at night and have trouble getting up in the morning."

Anna eyed her friend, thinking how different her life was now. Instead of the pampered cloistered wife of an aristocrat, Tatiana spent all her time outdoors, getting plenty of exercise and eating natural foods. As a result, she and Anna both had lost much of their body fat and were more lean and muscular like the Indian women.

"Does Black Hawk know?"

Tatiana gave a secretive smile. "I'm waiting for just the right time to tell him."

Anna thought about Anton and Dmitri and decided it was a good thing neither man lived in this village. Once again, she marveled at how well Tatiana had adapted to life as a Makah wife. Sometimes she suspected that her former mistress was in love with Black Hawk, because in all the time she'd known Tatiana, she'd never seen her so contented and mild mannered. It was hard to believe she was the same imperious young Russian beauty she'd once served as a new frightened maid.

The feast that night was an endless affair, for it followed the form of all elaborate meals. First the men sat down, rinsing their mouths out with water, then they passed around shredded cedar bark which served as towels. After each man wiped the grime from his hands, a drink from the special drinking basket was taken. It was not proper to drink during meals.

Anna and Tatiana helped serve the first course of plain dried fish with oil by laying out the fish on a mat with a small bowl of whale oil for all the guests. The cooked food came next, consisting of roasted venison, smoked salmon and halibut, steamed clams and crab, whale blubber, and the vegetable stew. These foods were served in two foot long wooden platters shaped like a canoe and flat on the bottom. In the corner of each platter was an oil dish, for it was unthinkable to take a bite of fish without dipping it in oil first.

Chief Utramaka and his sons were served first, then the *shaman*, Lightning Eagle, the tribe elders and their sons. As Sean and John were still favored by the chief, they were included. Anna tried not to look at

Sean, but she couldn't help it, remembering their shared kiss in the forest.

Both he and John appeared more Indian than white. As in the days when the *Sea Rose* sailed through the tropics, their skin had deepened to a dark gold, a startling contrast to their green and blue eyes. They wore their long shoulder-length hair down to their shoulders with headbands to keep it out of their faces. They both were bare-chested and barefoot, wearing only a simple blanket tied around their waists. She thought Sean had never looked so handsome and she ached to be near him.

The men ate with ladles of wood and clam shells. Anna was always amazed at the correct manners of these so-called savages. Well bred Indians ate slowly, never took too much food, nor opened their mouths wide enough to show their teeth while chewing. Recalling the crude manners of most of the American sailors, she thought many a white man could take a lesson from them.

After the cooked food course, the wooden finger bowls and cedar bark napkins were offered again; then came a dessert of dried berries in oil. After the final hand washing, the drinking basket was passed around. No matter how salty the food, the well behaved person waited to drink.

Lightning Eagle was conscious of Knows Much as she gracefully served the food. His heart was heavy at the thought of their broken relationship. So far, the chief hadn't noticed he had stopped visiting his wife, but soon he would have to give an explanation. He saw how Red Hawk watched her with a smug expression, and he knew the boy would not keep quiet much longer.

He fingered the small pouch at his waist. It was filled with a powder of dried foxglove, a lethal herb which in small amounts could help a person with a weak heart, but in larger quantities could kill a man by stopping his heart. Utilla had used it only on his greatest enemies. Lightning Eagle planned to mix it in with Red Hawk's food, but he hadn't found the chance as yet. He knew it must be soon, though.

Earlier in the day he had seen the slave, Little Man With Big Stories, overseeing the pit of slowly steaming vegetables. When he left to fetch more wood, Lightning Eagle slipped a goodly amount of the ground bark of the cascara bush into the mixture, insuring that everyone would have a stomach ache and possible intestinal problems this evening, including himself. He was hoping it would cause enough chaos that he could poison Red Hawk. When the boy began to complain about his pains, no one would pay much attention until it was too late.

Lightning Eagle hated to ruin Small Fawn's feast, but Red Hawk had to be silenced. And the slave would be blamed for it all. Already his guts were rumbling even though he'd eaten sparingly of the vegetable dish.

Tonight the men wanted to smoke after the meal. While they puffed on their pipes, the women and children ate. Red Hawk felt starved and he helped himself to an extra large portion of everything, especially the venison, which he had provided by shooting his first buck with his uncle the day before. He had never felt so proud of himself and excited about the future.

Both finback and gray whales had been spotted recently on their way north. His father had promised to take him whale hunting soon for the first time. He had dreams of becoming the best hunter and whaler of all the Makahs. Most men were either one or the other, but he was determined to do both. Then he would become the most wealthy and powerful chief ever, raiding up and down the coast, striking fear and terror into the hearts of all the other tribes, and especially the white men. He did not share his grandfather's fascination with them, and thought they were a danger to their way of life. In the future he planned to kill or enslave every white man and woman he encountered.

He would start tonight. After the feast was over, he intended to tell his father about Knows Much and Green Eyes. He would leave out the part about Lightning Eagle. All his grandfather needed to know was that his wife desired the white man and she would be mutilated or traded away. The white man would be killed. Then he could start thinking of a plan to rid his family of Daughter of the Sun. His mother would never be happy again until she was gone.

As for the *shaman*, he would pretend he never saw him with the white woman. He was afraid of Lightning Eagle, and had been conscious of his menacing brown eyes staring at him all evening.

Suddenly he noticed everyone groaning and clutching their stomachs, and getting up to leave. His father was the first one outside, with his uncle and grandfather following right behind him. He stood up and left his platter of food briefly to ask Brave Spear, his father's friend, what was wrong.

The muscular man rubbed his belly and grimaced. "There's something wrong with the food. Excuse me, Red Hawk."

After he bolted for the entrance, the house erupted into a turmoil of people moaning and running around with most of the guests quickly disappearing. Small Fawn looked like she was going to burst into tears and her mother, Brown Bird, appeared horrified at the disastrous end of her daughter's special feast.

Red Hawk shrugged then sniggered at Small Fawn. The ignoble memories of this night would follow her for a long time. There would be laughter and whispering behind her back. What man would want her now? She'd be lucky to have a lowly commoner for a husband.

His shoulders shook with suppressed mirth as he turned back to his platter of food. To his dismay, Lightning Eagle stood next to it. Unlike the others, the *shaman* did not appear to be sick.

"Red Hawk," he greeted, "it looks like the new slave must have put a wrong herb into the steamed vegetables. But I'm certain everything else is safe to eat."

"That's good, because I'm still very hungry," he said, helping himself to a hearty bite of fish dipped in oil. He'd never liked vegetables anyway and now he had a good excuse not to eat them without his mother nagging him.

"I have the same problem as everyone else," said Lightning Eagle, sighing painfully. His eyes lingered briefly on the corner of the platter where the fish oil was. "Have a good night, Red Hawk," he said and swiftly moved away.

Laughing Gull watched the young *shaman* leave the house. She'd been napping in the corner as usual during the feast. Everything made her extra weary these days, especially crowds of people. She had little appetite, too. Tonight the only food which appealed to her was the whale blubber, but it hadn't been prepared properly. She only liked it when boiled in salt water with young nettles and other tender greens, none of which could be found this time of year.

So, she hadn't eaten anything yet, and now with most of the people ill, she wasn't about to. She fastened her eyes upon Red Hawk who was eating a bit slower now. Maybe he was finally getting full, she thought.

A small cackle of glee escaped her lips. The sight of all the nobles and their families fleeing the house as they grabbed their bellies was the funniest thing she'd seen in her whole life. And she knew exactly what happened.

The best thing about being so old was that everyone tended to ignore her. When Lightning Eagle had sprinkled the powder in the pit of cooking vegetables that morning, she had been in her usual corner snoring away. Only she really hadn't been asleep. Her left eye was cracked open and she'd seen what he'd done. At the time she hadn't questioned it. He was the *shaman*, and if he thought something important should be added to a dish for the feast, who was she to think otherwise?

After he'd left, before Little Man With The Big stories came back, she'd shuffled over to the pit, and dipped in a big round clam shell and tasted a tiny bit. She immediately recognized the flavor of cascara bark. It was a laxative that she'd given many a time to a person whose bowels refused to move.

She was mystified as to why Lightning Eagle would deliberately try to sabotage the feast. It was the type of thing a *shaman* would do if someone paid him to dishonor a rival by ruining such an important occasion for his daughter. But who disliked Strong Elk enough to want to cause him to lose face in front of the village?

Could it be Daughter of the Sun? She wondered. She was well aware of her youngest grandson's strong opposition to his brother's obsession with his second wife. But why would the white woman stoop to such a trick when she now had the power in her belly to be even a more favored wife?

She grinned to herself. Once again, by being old and practically invisible in this household, she'd gained priceless information. Earlier she overheard Daughter of the Sun telling Knows Much that she was carrying Black Hawk's child, a son, she'd hoped. Her grandson was going to be overjoyed when he knew, but Soft Fern was not. Recently she had rekindled her husband's passion and now that would be endangered.

Laughing Gull sighed with happiness. There was so much intrigue going on, she was never bored at all. Soon she was dozing off again.

Minutes later she and everyone still inside the house were shocked when Red Hawk suddenly keeled over with a sharp cry, regurgitating all his food as his face darkened into a deep purple color and his eyes bulged out like a boiled fish. His mother Soft Fern was the first one to reach his side. He gasped, his mouth contorted in silent pain, but he could not utter a word. As she reached out to hold him in her arms, his eyes rolled back in their sockets and he died.

The primeval shriek of pain and despair which filled the house echoed back and forth under the rafters and beams, sending chills down the spine of every person who heard the heart wrenching sound of a mother lamenting the loss of her only child.

* * *

Wang Li was frightened, even more frightened than he'd been in China years ago when the Empress had sent her guards after him. All day he'd been tied with his arms behind him to a post in front of the stockade entrance. At first, he'd only been blamed for making everyone ill at the feast by using the wrong herbs in the vegetable stew. He'd tried to tell the chief that he'd added only some seaweed, but no one believed him. Then came the second and worse accusation, that he'd poisoned Red Hawk.

Even though a cold wind blew off the Strait and rain was slanting down, sweat poured off his body at the sight of the shrunken heads grimacing toothlessly down at him from their perches on top their posts a short distance away. He closed his eyes and wept at the thought that his own head might be joining them at any time.

He was so dehydrated his thickened tongue stuck to the roof of his mouth. He'd had no food or water since the night before when the boy had died. He didn't care about eating, but he certainly wished he could have a sip of water. He kept hoping someone like Samuel or Robby or the captain would come and help him.

But he'd been left alone with only the crying seagulls and the cawing ravens for company. When the wind grew stronger, even they deserted him. Once a village cur came snarling and nipping at his bare feet. Wang Li cursed him, telling him he was fit only for the stew pot. Perhaps the dog understood, for he turned tail and ran off.

Wang Li knew he was doomed to die. The entire village was in mourning, the women wailing in a long musical chant. The endless keening had not stopped since the boy collapsed and died. All the women of the chief's family had cut their hair, even Missy and the Russian woman. Black Hawk and Soft Fern had slashed their arms and legs countless times and let the blood flow to show their deep grief.

It was a sad thing, but it wasn't his fault. Someone else had poisoned the boy. If only Wang Li could figure out who it was, then maybe he would be pardoned, or maybe not. Maybe the real murderer was too clever to be caught. Then he would die in his place.

That reminded him of the stories the little Missy used to tell him about her Jesus, the perfect son of God dying to save all mankind from their sins. He remembered how she said that if he accepted this gift from God she called salvation, he would have eternal life. He thought of Buddha and his own religion. At the moment there was nothing there that comforted him.

In desperation he lifted his head towards the sky, as the icy raindrops pelted his face, and cried out in Chinese, "Jesus, save me from my sins and save me from this death. If not, then take me to your heaven when I die here."

A strange feeling of calm entered his soul and he thought he heard the wind whisper in his ear, *"Peace, my child, I will be with you always."*

* * *

Hours later after the evening meal, Anna and Tatiana sat together by Gray Cloud's cooking pit, talking about Wang Li. At first they spoke in French, then when the chief's wife gave them looks of disapproval, they switched to Makah. Anna kept thinking about the little Chinese man and all the time they'd spent in the *Sea Rose*'s galley, cooking and talking.

She hoped and prayed that he had heard and understood all her talks about Christianity. She had done what her mama called, *planting a seed.* Then she said *it was up to God to water it and make it grow*. Her mama said someday when they got to heaven they'd find out how many plants grew from the seeds they'd planted. Anna fervently hoped Wang Li would be one of them.

Soon Gray Cloud said she was joining her husband for bed. The death of Red Hawk had hit the chief extremely hard and after almost twenty four hours of mourning, he was now sound asleep. The rest of the women were in their compartments and Black Hawk and Strong Elk were in Brave Spear's house.

Next to Anna was She-Who-Never-Sleeps, sound asleep in her cradleboard, her tiny black eyelashes curving over her fat dimpled cheeks. Hunched over by the fire, Laughing Gull was wrapped up in her blanket like a moth in a cocoon. Anna assumed she was asleep.

"Why do you suppose Wang Li would've killed Red Hawk and made us all sick?" Tatiana asked her. She fingered the ragged ends of her newly slashed hair and frowned. Neither she nor Anna had wanted to cut their hair, but it had been expected of them as a demonstration of their grief and they'd dared not refuse. Although Tatiana felt badly for Soft Fern and her heart ached for Black Hawk, another part of her was not sorry to see the last of Red Hawk. This made her feel guilty. But at least no one suspected her of poisoning the boy's food.

"He didn't," said Anna in a dull voice. "It was Lightning Eagle."

"The *shaman*?" Surprise sharpened her voice.

"Hush," said Anna as the old woman stirred slightly. Anna waited to see if Laughing Gull was awake and then she heard her snore.

She leaned closer to Tatiana and said, "You must promise to never tell a soul..."

* * *

In a cold corner of the chief's house, Robby tossed and turned on a thin blanket in a vain attempt to stay warm enough so he could sleep. But the cold and the thought of Wang Li tied up like a trussed pig outside in the wind and rain made it impossible. He was positive the little Chinese was innocent. If only he was brave enough, he would steal a knife, sneak outside, and cut him loose.

He squirmed around, thinking hard. If he was caught, the Indians would kill him. If he did nothing, Wang Li would die for sure. It was true he had never quite forgiven him for cooking Jimmy in a stew. But he was still one of their own, one of the crew of the *Sea Rose*.

He half rose from his blanket, then froze as he made out a bent figure shuffling towards the door. It looked like Laughing Gull was going outside for one of her frequent nightly visits.

His heart hammering, he sank back onto his blanket. He would have to try it later, if he tried it at all. His thoughts went to Soft Fern, the sweetest girl he'd ever met. If they were never rescued, which he believed likely, he had hopes of someday rising above being a slave. He'd heard of young men who proved their worth among the Indians and had eventually married into a rich family. That was his goal, if he was destined to stay with the Makah the rest of his life.

In Brave Spear's lodge, Samuel was banking the fire for the night after Black Hawk and Strong Elk had left. Brave Spear had retired to his compartment with his wife.

Samuel was full of grief and anger at the thought of Wang Li being falsely accused of the boy's murder. It was all he could do to stop himself from grabbing the nearest knife and running amok among the chief and his sons, and then freeing Wang Li. He knew his little friend was doomed if someone didn't do something soon. He'd heard Black Hawk say that tomorrow morning the slave was going to die.

"Black Crow," said Starlight, suddenly appearing in the soft glow of the coals, "I know you are sad. Is there anything I can do to make you smile again?"

He glanced at her, seeing her anxious expression. All her concern was for him, he realized with surprise. She actually cared how he felt. It had been many years since anyone had spoken to him with such gentle womanly kindness. The last time was when his poor mother told him she loved him before she died, gaunt and disease ridden, on board the slave ship in the middle of the Atlantic. Then his older sister tried to take care of him, a frightened little five-year-old boy, for the rest of that terrible voyage. Would he ever know what became of her?

He thought how strange it was that life here in this Makah village was bringing back other old memories from his life in his boyhood village in Africa. There was much about both villages that were the same; the laughing mostly naked children running about, the chatter of the women as they prepared food over their cooking fires, the men with their spears and great prowess in hunting and fishing, and the slaves. He did remember captive slaves from enemy tribes and his mother and grandmother warning him that slavery was the worst thing that could happen to anyone, even worse than death.

Starlight tugged at his arm and smiled up at him in a pretty display of white teeth. He glanced down at the young woman and felt his heart melt. She'd had her share of grief already. She couldn't be more than twenty and she'd already buried two husbands, both dying from different accidents. One was mauled by a bear in the forest, the other fell from a cliff over the sea, looking for bird eggs. She'd had no children by either man.

Now many in the village said she was barren and brought bad luck to her husbands. Even though her father was a great whaler and a rich man, no man had come forth to be her third.

Recently Brave Spear had said that as soon as Samuel helped him kill a whale, he would consider him worthy of finding a wife. Samuel knew he was talking about his daughter Starlight. If he married her Brave Spear would adopt him into his family and he would no longer be a slave, but a free man with a chance to have a family and life of his own. He would become the respected whaler, Black Crow.

It sounded so much better to him than being the ex-slave, Samuel. He didn't like the thought of returning to the white man's world. It was true he had his freedom papers, but most whites still treated him like he was a slave. In a moment of honesty, he hoped they were never rescued.

"Starlight," he said, flashing a grin. "Just being with you make me smile."

At the same time inside their hut, Sean and John were trying to figure out a way to save Wang Li from his awful fate. Now that Red Hawk rested in a canoe placed high in the trees in his beloved forest, his father intended to exact payment for his death.

The Makah had a system of fines, a law enforced by the chief to decide what a fine would be to give an injured person some material satisfaction when wronged. Fines were paid for insults, personal injury, using the names of the dead, and murder. Usually the dead victim's family bartered the worth of the dead man with his murderer. A man could be worth the cost of the same bride price paid for as his mother, or only a few blankets, and a slave or woman even less. A chief or rich man was so important that no payment was enough and his family must take the murderer's life, even for an accidental killing.

If the murderer had no payment, such as a slave, he would be killed.

"Wang Li did not kill Red Hawk," said John in frustration. "Nor did he poison the food that made everyone sick."

"Sometimes he's gotten carried away with too much garlic or onions, but never to the point of anyone feeling ill," agreed Sean. "And he had no reason to kill the lad."

"Well, someone hated Red Hawk enough to want the boy dead."

"He was an irritating young rascal," said Sean, "but most lads are at thirteen. What could he have done to anger someone so much they killed him?" He frowned in puzzlement then said, "We should free Wang Li and tell him to run."

John shook his head. "They'd only track him down and the punishment for a runaway slave is a gruesome death. I've seen what the Nootkas do and I'm sure the Makah are no different."

* * *

Later, much later, Tatiana lay in her bed, snuggled into the warm soft furs. She was wide awake, thinking about all that Anna had told her. It made sense. Lightning Eagle was the killer, and Wang Li would die for nothing. But she could tell no one, especially Black Hawk. He would tell his father, and then Anna and Sean would be the next ones to die some heinous death.

She stirred restlessly as he heard his footsteps come by her compartment. Surely, he wouldn't come to her tonight, she thought. He would go to Soft Fern and comfort her over the mutual loss of their son. But the footsteps paused outside her door, and to her great dismay, he came in.

He was wet and cold, and smelled of his bloody wounds and the *kinnikinnick* he'd been smoking. The mixture of odors offended her and caused her stomach to churn. For the second time since she was with child, she felt like vomiting. The first time was when he returned from the raid carrying the bloodied heads of the Clallam warriors.

"Wife," he said in his deep voice, "I need to be with you tonight."

"But-- but what about Soft Fern? She needs you."

"She's asleep." He sat down on the bunk beside her and sighed heavily. "There's something I must tell you."

She rose to an upright position, leaving the fur robe wrapped around her unclothed body. "What is it?"

"Two days ago I heard that a white man had died at Ozette."

Anton! She thought, gasping out loud. At her sharp intake of breath Black Hawk frowned in the dark and grabbed her arm roughly.

"You still care for your white husband," he accused her angrily.

"No," she protested in bewilderment, "I do not care about him!"

"You care that he is dead. I heard you!" He squeezed her arm tighter.

So, it wasn't Anton who was dead. It was Dmitri. Feeling immense relief she gritted her teeth against his painful grip and said, "I was only surprised, my husband. How did he die?"

"The Quileutes traded him to the Makahs at Ozette. He had no wish to be a slave and he ran away. The Makah warriors caught him easily. Four men held him down on the ground and forced open his mouth. They rammed stones down his throat until he choked to death. That is what we do to runaway slaves."

She shuddered at the horrible image of Dmitri's brutal death, then closed her eyes and tried to picture him when she first met him as the splendid young Russian lieutenant who had married her, loved her, then abused her. Next she saw him as a broken shell of a man, sobbing on his knees in the bottom of a boat....

Black Hawk waited in silence for her to recover from the shock of his words. Then he released her arm and touched her cheek gently. "You do not cry for this man?"

He sounded surprised, almost relieved. When Tatiana finally found her voice, she said, "I cannot weep for someone I feared and hated."

"Do you feel that way about me?"

Yes and no, she thought, *your barbaric savageness frightens me, yet you have never harmed me. And now that Dmitri is dead, you truly are my husband.*

"This is how I feel about the father of my child," she said, taking his hand and raising it to her lips.

Now it was his turn to gasp in surprise. "You--you are certain of this?"

"Our child will be born next summer. Our son," she added hopefully.

"Wife," he said, his voice breaking with emotion, "you have just presented me the greatest gift a woman can give a man. You have restored my lost child and given this family hope for the future."

He gathered her up into arms, apologizing for his soaked appearance. "From now on, you are my first wife, the special joy of my heart," he said, kissing her. "Whatever you wish, I will give it to you. Ask for anything and it is yours."

She bit her lip and gathered her courage. "Can you pardon Little Man With Big Stories?"

"No," he said harshly, disappointed in her request, "anything but that. The slave dies in the morning."

As Black Hawk slid under the furs with her, she thought about poor Wang Li. In her own way she had tried to save him. There was nothing left she could do, unless she told her husband the truth. And that was out of the question.

* * *

Early the next morning a terrible cry rang throughout the village. "He's gone! The slave has escaped!"

Black Hawk and Strong Elk bolted out the door, hastily followed by Chief Utramaka and the rest of the family, except for Swift Deer who was nursing her infant son. With her adopted daughter on her hip, Knows Much bumped into Hollow Stomach on her way to find Daughter of the Sun. The two shared a look of relief at the surprising news.

"God go with him," she murmured in English.

Robby grinned and nodded before rushing out after everyone. A sleepy looking Tatiana emerged from her bunk, her eyes brightening when Anna explained what had happened.

"But how did he get away?" she asked, wondering if Black Hawk had changed his mind.

"Someone cut his bonds during the night," said Anna, "and if they find out who it was, he will be severely punished."

From her platform bunk in her compartment, Laughing Gull heard all the commotion in the house and the village. She gummed her toothless smile in the dim morning light as she fingered the sharp knife under her robes. She hoped the slave was far away by now. She had done her best to free an innocent man. Now the slave's fate was in the hands of the spirits.

Her next dilemma was to decide how to bring the real murderer to justice, the young *shaman* Lightning Eagle. But he was a very dangerous and powerful man and perhaps there was nothing she could do about him without putting her own life in jeopardy.

Yet, the murder of her great-grandson had to be avenged somehow. She could feel his spirit walking restlessly about. He would never be happy in the land of the dead until justice was done.

She had to find a weakness in Lightning Eagle and use it to expose him. As she closed her wrinkled eyelids and fell asleep, she dreamed of Knows Much.

CHAPTER FORTY FOUR

The days passed one by one and the slave, Little Man With Big Stories, was never found. Some said he must have been eaten by the Cannibal Monster in the forest, or killed by a hungry cougar, or a pack of starving coyotes. Some said he might have been captured by the Clallam or the Quileute. Some said he could have found a white man's canoe and flew back to his land across the sea.

Then it was April, the Moon of Sprouts and Buds, or *ko-kose-kar-dis-put'hl,* and the slave was forgotten. Many whales were passing Cape Flattery on their spring migration north to the Bering Sea. The Makahs readied for their first whale hunt of the season. Early one morning when the rays of the sun streaked rose pink across the pearl gray sky, Chief Utramaka, Black Hawk, and Brave Spear set out in three canoes, each with a crew of seven men.

It had taken Black Hawk weeks to prepare. To hunt the whale was more than just a hunt, it was a spiritual journey. He fasted, bathed alone in icy streams and in the ocean, rubbed his skin raw with sharp barnacles, and talked to his spirit guardian, the black tailed hawk. This was how he projected his spirit into the spirit of the whale, telling it to swim closer to the canoe. He believed if a man had to do something beyond human power, he must have more than human strength for the task.

The hunt reminded him again of the loss of his son. The boy was to have been a part of Black Hawk's crew for the first time as a test of his coming manhood. Now it would never be.

As the harpooner, the man who did the killing, he had to put aside such thoughts. It was he who must have the magic on which the success or failure of the hunt depended. He could not dwell on past grief, but had to focus all his mental and spiritual energies on the job at hand. The winter had been long and one whale kill could provide the village with blubber and oil for a year as well as bone for tools and weapons.

Standing in the bow, Black Hawk clutched his harpoon as a whale was sighted, its telltale geyser of water gushing up toward the sky. His twelve foot long harpoon was made out of heavy yew wood with a sharp cutting blade of mussel shell. The blade was lashed between elk bone barbs, which prevented the harpoon from pulling out of the whale after it struck.

The gray whale was fifty feet long and covered with barnacles. It floated a short distance off the bow of the canoe.

Black Hawk aimed carefully and threw, as did his father and Brave Spear. All three harpoons smacked into the whale with such force, blood sprayed out over the sea in a shower of crimson drops. The whale reacted with a mighty splash of its tail then dove under the sea, creating a swell that rocked all the canoes from side to side.

Sealskin floats were attached to the harpoons by a rope of twisted cedar twigs. These were tossed overboard as the harpooned whale dived, marking the whale's position and keeping it from diving too deeply. Now the hunt would go on for a day or two, following the wounded whale. Whenever the whale would come up for air, the men would spear it again and again until finally it was killed.

For Samuel, or Black Crow, as part of Brave Spear's crew, it was the most exhilarating experience of his entire life. His arms, rippling with muscles under his black skin, flexed in rhythm with the others as they paddled over the ocean swells. Never had he felt so alive, so at one with his surroundings, as harsh and beautiful as they were. He didn't mind the blowing wind, the horizontal rain, or the moments of blinding sunshine. Joy filled his heart and he chanted and hummed in harmony with his fellow crew members. He had never felt so free.

Back in the village Gray Cloud was troubled. The night before the whalers left, she went to visit Lightning Eagle to ask him for special prayers to the spirits to guide and protect the chief. She was still haunted by dreams of her husband drowning. To her surprise Laughing Gull asked to accompany her. Using a wooden staff for support, the old woman hobbled painfully to the *shaman*'s hut. They were both greeted respectfully by the slave Frog, who made certain their honored guests were served tea and food.

Lightning Eagle was also surprised at the presence of the chief's ancient mother. She rarely ventured far from her house, as crippled as she was from her constant joint pains.

He supposed both women wished him to ease their fears about the whale hunt. If only they knew he was even more depressed in spirit than they were. Ever since the night of Red Hawk's death, there was a crushing weight upon his soul. He thought he would feel a great relief with the boy gone. Instead each morning when he awoke, he was consumed with a black despair.

He wished he could speak with Knows Much. But she had made it clear that she wanted nothing to do with him. Whenever he came near her, she found a way to disappear. He was miserable, knowing that she must despise him for what he'd done. He often wondered why he felt so much guilt.

The old *shaman* had never acted ashamed of any evil thing he did. If he was still alive he would tell Lightning Eagle he should rejoice at the loss of an enemy, that feeling guilt was a sign of weakness in his soul, and the only way to become a powerful *shaman* was to conquer such weaknesses.

Knows Much would say he felt guilty because he committed a terrible sin and had angered the spirit God. He remembered her talk of confessing such things to the Jesus spirit who sacrificed himself to save men from their sins. For the first time, he began to understand what she was talking about. But would murder ever be forgiven?

He remembered his vision quest when his spirit guardian, the Eagle, had told him that if he obeyed the Great Spirit, he would become the most powerful man in the village. By killing Red Hawk he was afraid he had disobeyed and now he was uncertain of the consequences.

"We haven't seen you visiting our house in many a moon," said Laughing Gull, her sharp black eyes studying him intently.

"That's right," said Gray Cloud. "You used to come almost every day to talk to Knows Much. Have you two quarreled?"

Lightning Eagle flushed slightly. "She is a busy mother and I am a *shaman*. We have nothing more to talk about."

"How can that be?" Laughing Gull questioned. "Each day brings new problems to the village. You and my son's second wife both have power. It would be good if the two of you brought your spirits together to fight off the evil around us."

"Is that why you are here?" Lightning Eagle asked. "You are suffering from bad dreams like Gray Cloud?"

The old woman was silent for a moment. Then she stared straight into his eyes and said, "My great grandson haunts me. He keeps asking why his murderer has not been caught and punished."

Lightning Eagle sucked in his breath. Did Laughing Gull suspect him? He gave her a patronizing smile and said, "Our warriors did the best they could to find Little Man With Big Stories. But he has vanished without a trace. Surely your great grandson can understand that."

"He has told me that the slave was not the person who poisoned him."

Now it was Gray Cloud's turn to be surprised. "Old Mother, why have you not told my husband of this?"

"If it wasn't the slave," said Lightning Eagle slowly, "then has---has your great grandson told you who the real killer is?"

Laughing Gull hesitated, conscious of the barely concealed hostility and fear in the young *shaman*'s eyes. "No," she lied, "but he said you might be able to help find him or her," she added quickly. "I think you should visit Knows Much again," she went on. "She is a woman of many secrets and powers. She can help you reveal the evil one in our village before he or she kills again."

"She?" Gray Cloud echoed nervously then realization dawned across her face. "Oldest mother, what are you saying?"

The old woman shrugged her shoulders. "I refuse to say anything more." She rose unsteadily to her feet and leaned on her staff. "Come, my daughter, we should be going now."

After they were gone, Frog turned her bulging eyeballs on him. "The old woman thinks Knows Much killed her great grandson," she said.

"It wasn't her," he said quickly, too quickly.

"Maybe not," the slave woman said with a knowing smile, "but Gray Cloud is a big gossip, and she's going to spread the idea around the village. Just you wait."

Sweat gathered under Lightning Eagle's armpits. What would he do if Knows Much was accused of Red Hawk's murder?

* * *

During the next two days everyone anxiously waited for the return of the whalers, but it was the most difficult for their wives. While their husbands were gone, they were required to lay still on their beds, and could not eat, sleep, or talk until the men returned. They believed this made the whale stay docile. The wives were not allowed to even comb their hair in case a broken strand might cause the lines to snap.

Thus, Anna and Tatiana spent two days lying motionless, feeling hungry, bored, and irritated at another Indian superstition they were forced to respect. Gray Cloud did her part without complaint, while Brown Bird, Swift Deer, Small Fern, and Laughing Gull ran the household and took care of She-Who-Never-Sleeps.

Early on the morning of the third day, shouts rang out that the whalers were back. It was not too soon for Anna and Tatiana, who felt weak, stiff, and starved after their own ordeal. They quickly stuffed themselves with some dried fish and smoked clams, then went down to the beach to greet their husbands.

The whole village sang songs of welcome when the canoes appeared, towing their twenty ton whale behind them. This was a difficult chore since the whale's enormous mouth kept filling with water, making the carcass heavier. When that happened, a designated swimmer had to jump overboard and tie the whale's mouth together. As the weary hunters paddled to shore, they sang songs honoring the dead whale. They believed if the whale liked their songs, other whales would return to their shores every year.

At high tide, the whale was pulled onto the sand and left for butchering. First more special songs were sung then everyone turned out to help cut the blubber off the whale. The men climbed on top of the carcass and began cutting it with their bone knives. The women stayed below, throwing cedar bark ropes up to them and pulling at them, slicing into the blubber and making long strips. The choicest pieces from the whale's back went to the chief and his family as the main harpooners. Then the rest of the whale was shared among the villagers.

Tatiana was surprised to see Soft Fern working right next to her. Since Red Hawk's death she had become a recluse. The day after her son's burial she had burned the boy's clothing and belongings like he'd never existed, then she had confined herself to her compartment, weeping inconsolably.

Many times Tatiana tried to show Soft Fern compassion. But whenever she approached the woman with a soft word, Soft Fern turned away. She obviously resented all the extra attention showered on Tatiana because she was carrying Black Hawk's child.

The women of the house fussed over her night and day. Laughing Gull gave her special herbs and food to make the baby grow well and strong. Brown Bird thawed in her attitude towards her and made sure she wasn't overworked. Swift Deer was overjoyed and gave her advice on caring for an infant, demonstrating with her own son. She showed Tatiana how to rub a child's limbs to make them straight, to pinch his nose high and thin, to see his ears lay flat, and most important, how to shape his head to the broad sloping forehead they preferred. Small Fawn was excited about having another baby in the house and helped Tatiana with all her chores.

Soon the beach was filled with the overpowering stench of the raw flesh as the huge mammal was hacked into pieces. Both white women found the experience tiring, grisly, and nauseating. They were covered with blood and guts and longed to wash in the stream.

Being four months with child, Tatiana was especially fatigued. As she tore into the thick rubbery skin of the whale with her mussel-tipped bone knife, she groaned with frustration. She knew that more work lay ahead the next day and the next as the women of the family cooked the blubber into oil to be stored in skin bags and wooden boxes for later use.

Her fatigue turned into astonishment when Soft Fern, her face spattered with blood, flashed Tatiana her old dimpled smile. That was the only thing left of her former beauty. She had aged greatly, her hair was heavily streaked with gray and her face seemed prematurely wrinkled. The life force appeared to have drained out of her as she went about her duties automatically with a dull expression of perpetual suffering.

"Daughter of the Sun," she said, "I have misjudged you. It is not your fault that I am no longer the honored mother of my husband's son, nor can I ever be of another. I can never give him the joy I see on his face now when he looks at you. You have restored to him his honor as a man and given him hope for the future." She sighed and added, "I am glad you are one of us. Your child is the same as mine. If you ever need help, I will be here for you."

Tatiana knew it had taken Soft Fern a long time to gather the courage to say such a speech to her. With tears in her eyes she hugged her. Soft Fern's slight form stiffened at first, then relaxed as she returned her embrace. When they drew apart, tears also glistened in her dark brown eyes. It was a highly emotional moment and Tatiana hoped it was the beginning of a special bond of affection and trust formed between them.

By dusk all the flesh had been ripped from the whale, leaving its bony carcass for the crows, ravens, and gulls to pick clean. In the next few days after the winged scavengers had finished, the bones would be carved into useful tools and weapons.

Anna and Tatiana were two of the last women to make their way to the stream to bathe. They took their time scrubbing away the foul blood and slime off their skin with sand, then they washed their hair in a solution of snow berries and vetch roots. Tatiana had a comb, made of finely polished wood about a hands breath wide with teeth about two to three inches long. They combed the snarls out of each other's hair, which had grown out to just past shoulder length. They wanted to look their best for the celebration feast that evening in the chief's house.

As they walked back towards the village, Anna said, "Laughing Gull and Gray Cloud have been acting oddly towards me the past couple days. I keep wondering if I've done something to offend them."

The two women were making her uneasy. As she went about her duties, she often caught the old woman gazing at her with the unblinking stare of a lizard. And Gray Cloud, who had always been so friendly to her, now avoided Anna as much as possible.

"I haven't noticed anything," said Tatiana, then she gasped as two men jumped out from behind a large cedar tree.

"What---?" Anna began to say when one of them grabbed her and twisted her arm viciously behind her back.

She screamed once, then a dirty hand clamped over her mouth. The other man did the same to Tatiana. She rolled her eyes to the left, seeing her attacker as a strange Indian, his body painted red and his face a hideous black. At the sharp nod of his head, dozens of Indians appeared out of the forest with spears, clubs, and bows in hand.

One turned towards Tatiana and in the gloom of the deepening twilight she barely made out the jagged outline of the painted red scar on his black cheek.

It was Hoheeshata. His band of warriors had come to raid the village.

With alarm Tatiana remembered the unsuspecting villagers gathering for the whale feast and she found the strength to struggle. In a flash she turned and brought up her knee and jammed it into the man's groin. Grunting in pain, he released her and she immediately fled towards the village, hoping Anna would be brave enough to attack the man holding her.

Tatiana had covered only a short distance when a rock smacked against the side of her head, and in a sudden wave of dizziness and pain, she fell to the ground, rapidly losing consciousness. The last thing she remembered before everything turned dark was the face of Hoheeshata, staring down at her with an evil smile.

* * *

Inside the chief's house, the atmosphere was one of festivity. Chief Utramaka strutted about wearing a headdress of flowing cedar bark, looking very proud and impressive. He was singing, "I am telling what the other tribes are talking about. I hear everything they say and they are all talking about me."

Black Hawk and Brave Spear joined him in the same refrain, bragging about the hunt to reaffirm their prestige among the people. When they finished singing, Brave Spear told Samuel to stand up.

"I welcome Black Crow into my family," he announced in a loud voice, "as a fearless hunter of whales and as my daughter Starlight's new husband."

Along with everyone else, Sean and John applauded enthusiastically, noticing the expression of pride and happiness on Samuel's face and Starlight's coy smile.

"I wanna get married, too," blurted Robby at Sean's elbow.

Sean raised his eyebrows. "And who's the lucky lass?"

In a low voice, he said, "Small Fawn."

"Ah," breathed Sean. "The chief's granddaughter. Ye will have to earn her hand, my lad."

"I know, Cap'n. Muddy Feet's been teachin' me how to shoot a bow an' arrow like his da. They might be takin' me huntin' soon, an' I aim to shoot me a bear or a wolf."

John nodded in approval. "If you impress Strong Elk enough he might consider you as a possible husband for his daughter."

"I wonder where Anna could be," said Sean, glancing around worriedly. "I don't see her or Tatiana helping the other women with the food. 'Tis past dark. They both should be back by now."

No one else seemed to notice the two women were missing. Swift Deer was watching both her infant son and She-Who-Never-Sleeps, as they slept side by side in their cradle boards, oblivious to all the commotion. Sean spotted Lightning Eagle talking to the chief and let out a sigh of relief. The young *shaman* had an uncanny way of lurking in the background whenever Anna was about, and Sean distrusted his motives. But he obviously wasn't with her now.

"I'm going outside to see if I can find them," he told John.

"I'll come with you."

"Me, too," said Robby.

* * *

It was dark by the time Tatiana drifted back to consciousness. She was lying on her back in the bottom of a canoe with her arms bound behind her and her feet tied together. Her head throbbed painfully, especially on the right side where the stone had struck. She could feel a lump growing there. She moaned then shivered in her scanty cedar bark clothing.

Anna was next to her, also tied up, and she said anxiously, "Tatiana, are you awake? Are you all right? You've been in a faint for a long time."

Tatiana took a deep breath of the crispy night air. She struggled to clear her mind of the fuzzy muddle it had become and said, "My head hurts and I'm cold, but otherwise, I think I'm all right." She thought of the babe inside her, and felt it move, giving her an overwhelming feeling of relief. Nothing must endanger her child, she thought fiercely.

The canoe belonged to the Quileutes, most likely to Hoheeshata. It sat halfway on the beach, the stern end on the sand and the bow in the water, ready for a quick getaway. Tatiana strained her ears for any sound other than the water hissing around the bow. She heard nothing. With a groan she forced herself upright. Wave after wave of pain and dizziness rolled over her and she hastily tucked her head down over her knees until everything steadied.

The silvery glow of a half moon bathed the beach in an eerie contrast of light and shadows. She could see the outline of a dozen more canoes, but not one person was guarding them. That meant Hoheeshata and his men were already stalking the village, waiting for the right moment to strike, most likely after everyone had gone to bed. A feeling of panic assailed her at the thought of the coming bloodshed.

"What are we going to do?" she whispered to Anna in a desperate voice.

"I've been praying," she answered, "and trying to think of how to escape these ropes. We have to warn the village before it's too late."

"I know, but how?" Tatiana glanced frantically around the canoe, looking for any sharp object to cut the ropes of twisted cedar twigs which were bound tightly around her wrists and ankles. Except for a few food supplies there was nothing. All the weapons had been taken.

Her stomach rumbled with hunger and she realized they had missed the evening meal. "By now Black Hawk will wonder where I am."

"Sean is probably out looking for me already," Anna said, remembering how he always seemed to keep a close eye on her.

"If he is, you better pray he doesn't run into an ambush. The woods are full of Quileutes."

It was at that moment Tatiana spied the two matching clamshells. After all the voyages she'd taken with Black Hawk, she immediately knew what they signified. When traveling long distances by canoe, burning coals were taken from the last fire and placed inside a matched set of clamshells. This was how the Indians started a fire when camping on a beach at night.

Hope spun in her heart as she stared at the shells sitting near the bow of the canoe. "Anna," she said, "I have an idea." Slowly, she scooted her bottom over to them and gently pried the shells apart with her swollen fingers, grown puffy with the poor circulation from the ropes wrapped too tightly around her wrists.

She sighed with relief at the sight of the glowing orange coals. "I'm going to burn off my ropes."

"Be careful," said Anna, struggling into a sitting position, "or you may be burning yourself as well."

Tatiana hesitated, trying to gather the courage she needed. Then a vision of Black Hawk appeared in her mind, his arms and legs bleeding with the self-inflicted wounds to demonstrate his ability to withstand injuries without feeling pain. She closed her eyes and gritted her teeth and with a small gasp, thrust the sides of her two wrists onto the hot coals. The pain was so excruciating and the sizzle of burnt cedar and flesh so nauseatingly strong, she could feel another faint coming on.

She fought it off by biting her lower lip, and with tears of agony streaming down her cheeks, she forced herself to endure the stinging torture one moment longer.

Suddenly the ropes fell apart. With a sob she tore at the bindings around her ankles, then flung her arms over the side of the canoe and plunged her inflamed wrists into the cold water. The relief was instantaneous, but short-lived. The pain returned as soon as her hands were out of the water. Clumsily, she unloosened Anna's ropes and set her free.

"You need one of Laughing Gull's poultices for burns," said Anna.

"There's no time to think of such things. Come, we must move quickly and quietly."

In the distance they could hear faint cries and Tatiana was fearful it was already too late to warn the people. The quickest route to the village was to follow the beach back, but they would be exposed in the moonlight to any possible Quileutes. The forest wasn't much safer, but she thought they could conceal themselves better behind trees and in the bushes, if they could find their way.

Feeling shaky and disoriented from the bump on her head and the constant misery of her blistered wrists, Tatiana clutched Anna's hand, and the two headed for the woods. Anna felt the thumping of her heart in rhythm with each step she took. They pressed on, keeping in the shadows of the trees, occasionally stumbling over roots and bumping into logs. An owl hooted overhead and they paused, listening.

When they neared the village there was the terrifying sounds of people screaming and yelling and they could see an orange glow in the sky. The stockade and the some of the flat roofs of the houses had been set on fire. The village was a scene of sheer pandemonium. Tatiana thought of Black Hawk's description of his raid on the Clallam village, and she was afraid it had become the Makahs' turn for a night of sorrow.

Shaking and trembling now, more from fear than the night chill, they hid in a thick clump of bushes and ferns on the edge of the forest, not far from Lightning Eagle's hut. It had not been torched as yet.

"It's too dangerous for us to go into the village," Anna whispered.

"I know. By now all the fortunate villagers have escaped into the forest and are hiding like we are. Look, there are some who have been captured."

A group of crying women and children were already being forced down the beach by the Quileutes to their canoes. What Hoheeshata would do when he returned and found them gone, they shuddered to think.

Anna's eyes were riveted on the blazing village with fascinated horror. "Oh, God," she prayed, "please help them and protect us."

Tatiana strained to see Black Hawk as she saw many of the Makah warriors struggling with the Quileutes, swinging war clubs and throwing knives. But she could not recognize any individuals in the leaping shadows made by the fires. She thought it appeared as a scene out of hell, the roar and crackling of the flames, the bloodcurdling war cries, and the shrill screams of the wounded and the dying.

A patter of rain hit Anna's head as a gust of wind tore in from the Strait. Another spring storm was approaching. She closed her eyes and prayed anew for a downpour heavy enough to put out the fires. It was sheer torture to watch all the homes being destroyed as she agonized over the fate of the inhabitants. Had Brown Bird, Soft Fern, Swift Deer, and Small Fawn been captured? And Gray Cloud and Laughing Gull and the babies, were they safe or had the Quileutes killed them, as they were too old or too young to use as slaves. Tears rushed down her cheeks at the thought of never seeing sweet little She-Who-Never-Sleeps again.

And what about Sean, and John and Robby? Were they in the middle of the fighting or had they escaped? Anna knew Sean would be as frantic by now to find her as she was to find him.

It was then that they saw Black Hawk near one of the burning houses, locked in mortal combat with a Quileute warrior. Both men held Indian knives, sticks made of hard wood, tipped with sharpened stone or bone. They circled each other like two wolves waiting for the kill. The Quileute spit a stream of saliva at Black Hawk and laughed, the menacing sound sending chills down both Tatiana's and Anna's spines.

Hoheeshata.

Watching, they held their breath, their attention so fixed on the two men that they neglected to notice the Quileute warrior sneaking up behind them until the cold sharp tip of his spear pressed first into Tatiana's back, then into Anna's. Shocked speechless, they both stared at each other in fright while he grunted something in his language as he prodded them forward. Tatiana tripped clumsily and the warrior snorted in impatience, then jerked his spear harder into her back, slicing through her skin.

She cried out at the sudden flash of pain and the high sound of her scream caught Black Hawk's attention. He glanced in her direction, seeing her held prisoner by the Quileute. It was the moment Hoheeshata had been waiting for.

He lunged at Black Hawk and Tatiana screamed a second time, "Watch out!"

Black Hawk saw him coming at the last second and sidestepped swiftly, moving just enough so that Hoheeshata's knife missed his heart and cut deeply into his left shoulder. The knife stuck into the bone and blood spurted out in a red gush. Before Hoheeshata could twist his weapon out, Black Hawk charged him, knocking him flat on the ground. He jumped on top the Quileute and slit a line across his throat, drawing blood instantly.

Hoheeshata's eyes were wide open with fear. Death stared him in the face and he knew it. As Black Hawk was about to strike the final blow, the Quileute warrior brutally shoved Tatiana forward until they stood in front of the two men.

"If you kill him, she dies," said the Quileute in the Makah dialect.

The hand that held the knife froze. Black Hawk glanced up at them, blood lust shining clearly in his eyes. Then he saw the spear nudging gently at the base of Tatiana's white throat, already pricking a few drops of blood. Indecision crossed his face and for one long dreadful moment Tatiana knew he was unable to let Hoheeshata go, even to spare her.

Then his gaze wavered and he looked directly at her slightly rounded abdomen and his unborn child. With a snarl of frustrated rage, he released Hoheeshata and waved his knife at the warrior who had Tatiana pinned against him.

"Give her to me," he ordered.

Hoheeshata sprang to his feet and laughed triumphantly, shaking his head. "No, Black Hawk. Dark Cloud never said you could have her back. Only that if you spare me, she will not die. Your woman now belongs to me." He pointed at her belly with his chin. "And so does your child. After it is born, I will kill it and then plant one of my own inside her."

Black Hawk stared at Tatiana, a look of helpless fury darkening his eyes as he longed to plunge his knife into Hoheeshata. She stared back at him, seeing Hoheeshata's knife still sticking out of his shoulder with blood running red rivulets all over his naked upper body. It filled her with a terrible rage.

She looked at Hoheeshata and shouted, "You will regret this night, you murdering monster! If you take me with you, someday I will finish the job my husband started!"

Her words startled Hoheeshata momentarily then he laughed, a venomous sneer on his face. The distraction was all that Sean needed.

He and John had been circling in the forest the past hour, avoiding the Quileute warriors. Earlier when they'd left the chief's house in search of

Anna and Tatiana, they had split up, Robby down to the beach, John and Sean into the forest. They headed for the stream, thinking the women might have gone there to bathe. On the way they noticed the woods were strangely silent, devoid of the usual chattering squirrels and twittering birds. Sean assumed that was because it was getting dark and such creatures bedded down for the night, but John thought something more ominous was afoot.

He told Sean they needed to move slower with greater stealth through the underbrush. "There might be hungry bears about. Many have just awakened from their long winter hibernation and they will eat anything, including us," he explained.

It was as they neared a clearing in the trees, they heard the low rumble of human voices. They crouched underneath a clump of tangled berry vines and bushes and saw a group of painted warriors carrying various weapons. The Indians were talking together, obviously planning a raid. The sight filled them with dread as they realized they needed to warn the village immediately, but they dared not stir and reveal their hidden position to the Quileutes.

And where was Anna? Sean thought as he struggled to control his feelings of panic at the thought of her being captured. He recognized Hoheeshata at once and an even greater sense of doom and despair descended upon him.

After an interminable period of time when it was totally dark, the Quileutes left the clearing, melting into the forest towards the village. He and John stood up and decided to go after them, but they both knew it was too late to warn the Makah of the coming attack.

Meanwhile on the beach, Robby had been sidetracked by the presence of Small Fern. She had seen the white men leave the house and had slipped outside after them. Unknown to her, her younger brother, Muddy Feet, had seen her leave, and decided to follow.

She hailed Robby as soon as they were alone. "Hollow Stomach," she called out, "what are you doing out here?"

He started at the sound of her voice. Then he turned, his face flushing with pleasure. "I look for Knows Much and Daughter of the Sun," he answered in halting Makah.

She smiled, her pretty face glowing in the fading light of evening. Dark clouds were building to the west and Robby knew it was going to rain later. "They went to wash before the feast," she said.

"They should be back by now."

She shrugged her delicate shoulders. "They will be here soon."

Robby was so delighted to have her all to himself he immediately forgot about finding Anna and Tatiana. Small Fawn was more than a foot shorter than he, and when she was near him, he felt like the biggest and strongest man alive. She was also the kindest girl he'd ever known. She never ordered him about like a slave, but would politely ask his help when she needed it.

During the next hour as it grew dark, the two walked by the beach talking together. Muddy Feet kept an eye on them. He liked Hollow Stomach and knew that the slave was sweet on his sister. But nothing must ever come of it. His father wished to marry Small Fawn to the son of a wealthy whaler in Neah Bay.

"I hear that some think Knows Much might have something to do with my cousin's death," Small Fawn said.

"That is crazy," he said.

"Yes, I think so, too, but Gray Cloud is talking about it."

"Why would she think of such a thing?"

"My great grandmother said that my cousin has talked to her in dreams. He says that the slave, Little Man With Big Stories, did not poison him."

Robby snorted. "I know he didn't. He is a good man, not a killer."

"You might be right," she said agreeably. "But he is a bad cook."

"He likes to spice up the food in the Chinese way. But that wouldn't kill anyone." Robby looked down at her and frowned slightly. "Knows Much wouldn't kill anyone, either."

"Most of the people believe she killed our old *shaman* and some have been afraid of her ever since. Some say even my grandfather is afraid of her, his own wife, and that's why he won't sleep with her."

Robby flushed, feeling relieved Small Fawn couldn't see his face in the dark. A decent white girl would never make a ribald comment like that, but the Indians were much freer with such things.

"I don't know anything about that," he said with a worried expression.

He wondered if the Captain knew what was being said about the Missus Campbell. If people were suspecting her of Red Hawk's murder, she could be in danger. Robby decided he'd best tell him as soon as he and Mister Hill returned with the women. That reminded him, what was taking them so long?

Feeling uneasy, he glanced toward the woods and to his initial relief noticed movement along the edge of the forest. Perhaps it was them. Then he squinted harder. The moon was shining and the area suddenly seemed alive in silver and black human forms creeping out of the brush towards the stockade entrance.

Muddy Feet, who'd been sitting in the dark shadow of the whale carcass, saw them, too. Immediately, he knew what they were. Enemy warriors! With a loud cry of warning, he ran towards the entrance, shrieking the alarm.

Robby took a step to follow him, but Small Fern grabbed his arm. "No!" she exclaimed. "Stay here!"

The words were barely out of her mouth when a Quileute warrior rushed towards her brother and swung his war club, hitting the boy on the back between his shoulders. He crumpled like a shot goose.

Small Fern choked out a soft cry. Robby glanced around frantically for a place to hide before they were seen. The only thing he could see was the whale carcass, a short distance away.

"Come," he hissed, pulling on her arm. He yanked Small Fern after him and she only halfheartedly protested when he shoved her inside the bloody hulk then flattened her to the ground, putting his body over hers.

"Shush," he whispered, as the rotting stench hit their nostrils. She struggled underneath him then quieted as she heard the sound of warriors whooping their war cries and the people screaming with shock and fear.

* * *

As Sean and John made their way back to the village, they knew they needed to find weapons. Sean thought of Lightning Eagle's hut, situated near the forest away from the burning village. The two men crept inside and saw the slave woman, Frog, crouched in terror by the back wall.

"Does your master have any spears or knives we can use?" asked John.

Frog looked at them with her unblinking stare, then shuffled over to a shelf and brought out a large bow and a quiver of arrows and a spear. Without speaking, she handed them over.

Sean nodded their thanks and they slipped out. They hadn't gone very far when they saw Anna and Tatiana being threatened by a Quileute warrior with a spear. Next to them were a wounded Black Hawk and a malevolent looking Hoheeshata. As Sean and John snuck closer they heard Tatiana shriek her insults at the Quileute war chief.

Sean took the bow and an arrow and aimed to shoot. By the time he and John were noticed, the arrow was already lodged deep inside Dark Cloud's skull, killing him instantly.

As the dead man toppled over backwards, he released his grip on Tatiana and his spear. It began to fall and without a moment's hesitation, she seized the weapon and rammed it as hard as she could into Hoheeshata's face. The tip pierced him right above the eyes.

For one long terrifying second, he wavered. He took one step toward her, his surprised expression fixed upon her at the instant of death. Then his body crashed to the ground and the spear slid away, leaving a gaping hole in the middle of his forehead.

CHAPTER FORTY FIVE

Using gentle strokes, Tatiana sponged off Black Hawk's feverish body with cool water, soothing his cries of delirium with the sound of her voice. It had been three days since the raid and the knife wound in his shoulder was a mass of festering pus. He slept in short spurts, and when he awoke he watched her every move with dark glittering eyes, as if needing assurance that she was still with him.

He did not know it, but she was the only wife he had left. The Quileutes had killed Soft Fern.

During the feast she had told Gray Cloud she was going to look for Daughter of the Sun. She had just stepped outside when she spied the Quileute warriors slinking through the stockade entrance.

"Enemies!" came her sharp cry as she began to ululate in a high pitched warning.

Everyone inside the house froze with disbelief for a moment then erupted into frantic activity, the men grabbing their weapons, and the women snatching infants and small children, and fleeing out the rear door to the forest.

In order to give them more time to escape, Soft Fern ran towards the approaching warriors, screeching at the top of her lungs. Her shrieks signaled the danger to all the villagers until the instant when the Quileute war club caved in her skull, silencing her forever.

But her sacrifice had roused the whole village, thereby saving many lives and making her death a brave and honorable one. All in all, thirteen Makah warriors were dead, twice as many wounded, and ten young women and girls had been kidnapped. But the Quileutes had suffered their share of casualties. Besides Hoheeshata and Dark Cloud, eight others were killed, their heads already severed and placed on posts outside the scorched walls of the stockade.

The heavy rains that night extinguished the fires and the damage to the village was not as extensive as first feared. Two houses were burned to the ground and also one section of the chief's house, Soft Fern's compartment. This was accepted as fitting.

Chief Utramaka killed two warriors himself before taking a slight wound in his right arm. Strong Elk, Brave Spear, and Black Crow each killed one, and Black Hawk killed two before Hoheeshata attacked him.

But all the village could talk about was the bravery of Green Eyes in shooting Dark Cloud and saving Daughter of the Sun, and then, the awesome courage of the white woman in slaying Hoheeshata. It was unheard of for a mere woman to kill in battle, and many said Black Hawk's young wife must have been guided by the spirit of Thunderbird, their god of war.

Tatiana knew better. As she wiped the burning face of her Indian husband, she looked at her blistered hands. The blood of death was upon them now. Even though she had killed a dangerous enemy, and had saved the life of Black Hawk and her unborn child, she felt a deep sense of guilt. It brought back the horror she felt after the *Buldakov* sank, taking all those men with her.

She was full of grief for the loss of Soft Fern and blamed herself for all the destruction and sorrow the raid brought. She remembered when Hoheeshata had threatened to steal her someday and how Black Hawk had scoffed at her fear. But he had come, and even though he was dead, the repercussions continued.

There had been another casualty in Chief Utramaka's household, that of Laughing Gull. As the women ran through the forest she'd tripped over a thick tree root and broke her neck. The chief had let out a deep cry of anguish at the sight of his dead mother and had spent the past few days in deep mourning.

After the raid Muddy Feet was found crumpled on the ground and at first, his parents thought he was dead. But the boy was only unconscious with a cracked shoulder blade. With proper care and bed rest, he was expected to recover in a matter of weeks.

Brown Bird and Strong Elk had also been frantic with worry over the whereabouts of Small Fawn. She had not been with the women in the forest and her mother assumed the worst had happened to her daughter, that she had been one of those captured.

Early the next morning, when everyone had returned to the village, they were astonished to see the slave, Hollow Stomach, and Small Fawn emerge unharmed from inside the whale carcass. They both reeked of the decaying odor and were filthy from the slimy skeleton. Small Fawn claimed that Hollow Stomach had saved her life by hiding her from the Quileutes. Strong Elk was so grateful he gave the boy his freedom, and said he would like to adopt him into his family as another son.

It was a bittersweet moment for Robby. He knew this meant he could never marry Small Fawn, who would become his sister. But on the other hand, he would no longer be a slave, so he accepted the honor.

Tatiana stepped aside as a group of people crowded into her compartment headed by Lightning Eagle. They were all mostly naked, the men only wearing a blanket around their loins and the women covered in necklaces of beads. All of them had red painted faces with black or blue stripes and wore elaborate bark headdresses. They were the *shaman*'s helpers come to sing and dance as he performed his duties as medicine man. This was the fourth day they'd visited Black Hawk, trying to frighten the evil spirits away from his body. So far, none of it had done any good.

She left Lightning Eagle and his novitiates to their chanting and went to look for Anna. She found her with the other women preparing food for the parade of endless visitors. Each day many Makahs arrived from Ozette and Deeah and the other villages to help with the burials and the rebuilding of the stockade and damaged houses.

"How is your husband?" Anna asked, a concerned look on her face as she heated cooking stones to boil water to soften dried strips of halibut.

"The same. I wish Laughing Gull was here to help us find the right medicines for him. I think she could help more than Lightning Eagle and his superstitious gibberish."

"He's doing what he believes will help."

"Yes, but it is not enough. Anna, if I thought God would hear me, I'd beg Him to heal Black Hawk."

"I have been praying constantly for him."

"Thank you, but I'm afraid God might not listen, even to you. Why would He care about a heathen savage like Black Hawk?"

"He loves these people. Remember how God healed She-Who-Never-Sleeps? And when I prayed for Him to send rain the night of raid, He heard and sent the storm to put out the fires to save the village. Jesus died for all mankind, not only white people like us."

That means He died for me, thought Tatiana. But how can He ever forgive me for killing Hoheeshata and wishing the *Buldakov* to sink, so Dmitri would die? And now he was dead. Her evil prayers had come true and in the civilized world she was a widow. If they were ever rescued, she would be one of the wealthiest baronesses of Russia, free to marry whoever she chose.

Anton? She wondered how he was faring in the village of Ozette. She had heard that many of the captives were being passed around from village to village, being given as gifts in *potlatch*es and traded for gambling debts. For all she knew, he wasn't in Ozette anymore.

"If Black Hawk dies, I don't know what will happen to me and my child."

"You are carrying the chief's grandchild. You will always have a place here."

"Anna, I need your prayers, too. I feel as if I've committed a terrible sin in killing Hoheeshata. Your own people, the Mennonites, would agree."

Anna sighed. "Yes, they probably would, even though you did it in self defense and saved us all from a wicked man." She bent over the box of boiling water and dropped pieces of fish into it to cook. "God will forgive you any type of sin, if you confess it."

"Even murder?"

Anna thought about Sean, and how he'd killed his own father. "Yes, even murder. In the Bible, in the Book of Acts, there is the story of Saul who persecuted and killed Christians. On the road to Damascus he had a vision of Jesus speaking to him, and he realized what a terrible sinner he was. He was forgiven and became the Apostle Paul."

Tears sprang into Tatiana's eyes. "Then God will forgive me," she whispered, hope dawning inside her heart.

Anna smiled and took her hand. "He loves you, Tatiana, more than anyone on earth ever has or ever will."

"Even more than my papa?"

"Yes, even more than our earthly parents. God is your Heavenly Father. He will never leave you nor forsake you. This is His promise through His son, Jesus."

Tatiana bowed her head and wept, praying for forgiveness. As she did so, an extraordinary feeling of relief and happiness bubbled up inside her. She remembered her lifelong fear of being abandoned and left alone, the fear that had been with her since the day she'd been born. Unlike her Russian papa who had always left her, her new Father in heaven would be with her always.

As Tatiana sobbed, Brown Bird and Gray Cloud and Swift Deer watched with sympathy, thinking that Knows Much was comforting Daughter of the Sun over the illness of her husband.

If only they knew, thought Anna joyfully, that Tatiana Nikolayevna, a Russian Baroness, the wife of a Makah whaler and warrior, had just been given God's priceless gift of eternal life.

* * *

In the morning Black Hawk was better. His fever broke and the wound was less swollen, showing signs of healing. He struggled to sit up and demanded food in his usual arrogant voice. Tatiana was delighted and thanking God, she brought her husband a bowl of venison broth with chunks of meat.

He ate it quickly then turned a questioning gaze on her. "Where are my grandmother and my other wife?"

Taking a deep breath she said, "They are with us no more, my husband. Your grandmother had an accident in the forest running away from the village and your--your wife was killed by the Quileutes when she warned the villagers of their approach."

Black Hawk appeared stunned. "Then they are with my son."

She was silent, her face full of compassion. He reached out and took her hand. "You are my only wife now."

"Yes," she nodded, "and you are my only husband."

"You killed Hoheeshata," he said with a smile of admiration. "You are the bravest woman I've ever met. You have the courage of a lioness. You will make a good mother for our child."

Then a terrible look of pain crossed his bold features. "Leave me now, wife."

He let out a wail of such deep sorrow that Tatiana could not bear to look at him. She left him to his mourning, knowing he would not be comforted until he decided it was time.

The evening was clear with a cool breeze and the village was crowded with visitors. Many of them stared at Tatiana as she walked to the beach, seeking a breath of fresh air. Dozens of colorfully painted canoes rested on the sand above the high tide mark. Slaves were busily unloading supplies and gifts from them to be given to the bereaved. One tall wiry man in particular caught her eye. He had long brown hair streaked with blonde, flowing over his shoulders and caught in a headband. There was something achingly familiar about him.

"Anton," she called out softly.

His back was to her and he stiffened then turned around slowly. His lean handsome face was bronzed by the sun and his warm brown eyes widened in pleased surprise when he saw her. Then his gaze traveled to her slightly swollen belly and he flinched.

They stood staring at each other for another minute before Anton said in French, the language of the Russian nobility, "You look well, Tatiana, very well."

She blushed. "And so do you, Anton."

"My name is not Anton any longer. My master, the chief of the Ozette, calls me Canoe Man, for my skills in navigating a canoe. He never leaves the village without me."

"I heard about Dmitri. He must not have been able to adjust to captivity like you."

Anton grimaced. "He was belligerent at the start, and refused to obey his new master, the chief's brother. This angered his wives, who beat him with sticks and gave him only rotten food to eat. Dmitri ran away the first chance he got." Anton glanced away briefly. "I won't describe what happened to him. It was the worst thing I've ever seen done to a man. The only good thing about it was, he didn't take long to die. I'm sorry, Tatiana."

"To be honest, I am relieved he is no longer my husband. He was cruel to me."

"You deserve a husband who worships the ground you walk on," he mumbled, then flushed. "Are you well treated by your Makah husband? "

"I have no complaints," she said.

"Neither do I, except I wish we could find a ship soon and be rescued."

Tatiana glanced down at herself. "I could not return to New Archangel looking like this."

The corner of Anton's lips twitched in suppressed amusement. "No, I suppose you would cause quite a scandal."

She laughed her first real laugh in a long long time. "Whatever happened to Mr. O'Riley?"

"He's a slave in my village and as feisty as ever. He's real popular among the ladies. They call him Man-With-Hair-of Orange-starfish."

She burst into laughter again. Some of the other slaves glanced at her curiously and Anton gave her a quick smile before he returned to his work.

Tatiana knew it was not proper for her to continue their conversation, so she stepped away, hoping she would have a chance to speak with him again. She had forgotten how much she enjoyed his company and that there was a time, not so long ago, when she thought she was in love with him.

But now it was Black Hawk she loved, wasn't it?

* * *

With all the visiting Makahs, came the talk and plots of vengeance against the Quileutes, especially the village of Chief Xawishata. It was assumed he had sent Hoheeshata to raid their village and the Makah code of justice demanded payment for every person murdered, either in material wealth or in blood. And grieving parents wanted their daughters returned as soon as possible.

When Anna and Tatiana heard all the mutterings about killing or kidnapping the wives of Hoheeshata and Chief Xawishata in revenge, they became afraid for Marya and Katya and Keeah.

"We must ask our husbands not to attack their village," Anna said.

"But will they listen to us?" Tatiana questioned doubtfully.

"We can only try."

Nervously, Tatiana agreed and said she would talk to Black Hawk. That evening when she served him his meal, she asked him to reconsider attacking Chief Xawishata's village.

He took a piece of broiled fish and dipped it in the wooden bowl of seal oil, which had an intricately carved bear's head for a handle. As he chewed the food, he looked at her and frowned, then pointed to the platter of fish.

"This is your work, woman. Leave the business of war to men."

She drew back, affronted. Before she could stop herself, she blurted, "How can you say that when I killed your worst enemy right in front of you? That was the work of a woman!"

Black Hawk had heard the whisperings about his wife and her connection to the war spirit, Thunderbird. Although it was not unheard of for a woman to have a spirit guardian, it was not something he wished for in a wife. It hurt his male pride that his pregnant wife had been able to slay the feared Hoheeshata when he, a warrior, could not.

Sometimes he did not know what to think of Daughter of the Sun, except she was unlike any woman of the Makahs.

Then he sighed. But that's what attracted him to her in the first place; her courageous spirit; her defiance of the Quileute *shaman*; her matchless beauty. And lately, she had become even more beautiful, if that were possible in her condition. Whenever she smiled, her face glowed like the sun in her hair and her eyes sparkled like the wild grape hyacinths in the meadows.

"You are right, wife. You are not like other women. There are times I think a man spirit speaks to you."

Tatiana caught her breath. Was he talking about God? Could he tell of the mammoth change inside her soul?

He placed a hand on her arm and gave her a tender look. "Speak your mind, wife."

"I understand the Makah need for revenge, my husband. But I am afraid for the life of my sister and her unborn child and for the daughter of Knows Much and the Tlingit slave."

"Wife, you have my word that no harm shall come to any of them from the Makah."

Tatiana let out her breath. "Thank you, Husband."

"I need to reward Green Eyes for shooting Dark Cloud," he said, changing the subject. "This morning I asked him what he wished in return for saving your life."

"And what was that?" Tatiana immediately thought he might have asked for Anna, as daring as that was.

"He wished to have his own canoe and harpoons, so he and Yellow Hair can go hunt the otter. I do not like the thought, but I granted his wish."

"I don't understand why you disapprove."

Black Hawk gave her a troubled frown. "Unlike my father, I do not like the white man. From what you tell me, there must be more white people in the world than there are grains of sand. Unless they leave the Makah alone, I see a dark time coming for my people. Already, many of the younger men, after seeing all the iron kettles, knives, and thundersticks the Nootkas have traded from the whites for the sea otter, are talking about hunting only for the otter now, not seals or whales or fish. I am afraid the day will come when the Makah will forget how to hunt a whale."

Last year when they sailed on the *Sea Rose*, Tatiana remembered Dmitri saying that sea otter skins were selling for three hundred Yankee dollars a piece in London. A man could become rich with one voyage.

Black Hawk was right. The white men would never go away.

* * *

At the same time in the chief's compartment when Utramaka was finished with his meal and smoking contentedly on his pipe, Anna nervously approached him.

"Husband," she said, "is there another way to take revenge on the Quileutes without raiding their village?"

The chief looked at her in surprise. Then he thought he understood. "You are worried about your daughter. I promise she will come to no harm. I will bring her to you when we return. This will make you happy?"

Anna smiled. "Yes, it is my deepest wish to have her with me again, but--"

"There is nothing more to talk about, Wife," he said abruptly. "We leave in one moon's time, after our warriors have time to heal, our houses rebuilt, and we've made the proper sacrifices and preparations for war."

Her heart sank. But she had to try once more. "Hasn't there been enough bloodshed already?"

An angry frown creased his wrinkled face. "The Quileutes must be punished for what they did. If not, they will come again and again. Now, we speak no more of this!"

Gray Cloud had been listening to their conversation and she said, "Perhaps Knows Much speaks out of fear for your own life, Husband."

Utramaka shot her a puzzled glance. "What do you mean?"

The older woman knelt down in front of him and took one of his hands in hers, in a rare gesture of affection in front of Anna. "You remember my dreams of seeing you in danger in your canoe?"

"Now is not the time to remind me," he said in irritation. "The two of you must put aside your fears and show me and the village your support as the chief's wives."

Gray Cloud nodded then cast a sly look at Anna. "Your mother also had dreams."

Utramaka lifted his head and narrowed his eyes. "Old woman always have dreams. You, too," he added a bit unkindly.

A hurt expression passed over Gray Cloud's face then she said, "Your mother dreamt that our grandson came to her very unhappy because his killer is still free. She told me and Lightning Eagle of this when you were on the whale hunt."

The chief shifted uneasily and took another puff on his pipe. "We have done all we can to find the slave. The spirits in the forest must have eaten him by now."

"Your mother said our grandson told her the slave is not his murderer."

"What?" Chief Utramaka was so startled, he dropped his pipe. "Who could it be then?"

During this conversation Anna was rolling a wooden ball that John made, across the floor to She-Who-Never-Sleeps. The child had recently learned to sit up and crawl, and she squealed with joy each time the ball came to her, batting at it with her tiny hands. But now Anna turned to look at Gray Cloud.

The older woman pursed her thin lips and said, "Your mother didn't say who killed our grandson, but she did say the murderer might not be a man at all, but a woman. And then," she hesitated with a meaningful look at Anna, "she said that Lightning Eagle should ask Knows Much who she thought it could be."

Anna clutched the wooden ball in her hand and felt a tremor of alarm. What had Laughing Gull found out? Did she know about her and Lightning Eagle in the woods that day, and that Red Hawk had spied on them?

The chief swung his attention to her. "What do you know about this, Wife?"

Anna was paralyzed with indecision. She couldn't say she knew nothing, because she suspected Lightning Eagle had somehow poisoned the boy. But she had no evidence, and she couldn't accuse him without revealing her own part in the entire situation.

The chief and Gray Cloud were waiting for her answer. As Anna looked at the cold expression in the older woman's face, she suddenly realized why the woman had been so hostile to her lately.

Gray Cloud thought that she poisoned Red Hawk!

"I--I can only say that I never believed Little Man With Big Stories was responsible for your grandson's death."

"Then do you have any idea who is?" the chief asked in a stern voice.

Anna closed her eyes briefly and prayed, but she already knew what her answer had to be. "Yes," she said quietly, "but I cannot accuse him, because I have no proof."

"Or," said Gray Cloud with a triumphant look, "you dare not say because it is not a he, but a she, namely yourself!"

The chief looked as shocked as Anna, who gasped, "I never harmed Red---your grandson! You must believe me!"

"You have killed once before," Gray Cloud commented dryly. "The *shaman*."

"No!" Anna protested. "I never wished or did him any harm."

Gray Cloud barked a short sarcastic laugh. "We all saw how he collapsed after you set a curse upon him. And you were there when our grandson fell sick and died."

Anna opened her mouth to protest again, when the chief cut her off with a short chop of his hand. "Enough! I have heard enough! I will speak to Lightning Eagle, and then I will call a council to discuss this further." He glared at Anna. "And you will stay in your compartment until it is decided if you are guilty or innocent."

He slowly rose to his feet. "Wife," he said to Gray Cloud, "bring my daughter to bed with us. She is not to stay with Knows Much for now."

Later, in her compartment, Anna realized that this was the first time the chief had not referred to her as his wife.

* * *

The next night there was a feast given in honor of Sean and Robby, who were both praised for saving the lives of Daughter of the Sun and

Small Fawn. After everyone had eaten well of the food and smoked a few pipes, Chief Utramaka announced that the two men would now have new names.

Strong Elk stood up to present Robby with a gift of his own bow and arrows, a thick robe made of brown bear fur, and his own compartment in his house.

"The spirit of the whale welcomed you and my daughter to hide inside him, and protected you both from the enemy. From now on, your name is not Hollow Stomach, but Gray Whale."

After the whoops and cheers from the villagers had died down, Black Hawk rose and gestured to Sean.

"As a gift for saving my wife from the Quileutes, I give Green Eyes his own canoe and harpoons to hunt the otter and the seal. From now on, his name is Running Wolf, for his cunning, stealth, and courage of that night will never be forgotten."

When the feast was over, Sean pulled John aside and said worriedly, "Anna was not with the other women tonight. Have ye heard anything, that she might be ill?"

Samuel and his wife Starlight were standing near them, and Samuel said, "The chief, he not be happy with her."

"Do ye know the reason why?"

Samuel turned to his wife and haltingly asked her in Makah, but she shook her head. At that moment Robby strutted over to them, parading his new brown bear fur robe.

"Hey, Running Wolf," he said jovially, then seeing the brooding scowl on Sean's face, added more respectfully, "I mean, Cap'n, sir."

"Do ye know where Anna is?"

"Aye, Small Fawn says she can't go outta her room. The chief is angry with her." Then Robby remembered something else. "I hate to be the one to tell ya, Cap'n, but she might be in big trouble. She might be accused of killing the chief's grandson, Red Hawk."

"What?" Sean, Samuel, and John all exploded the question at the same time.

* * *

Lightning Eagle was deeply disturbed. His worst fears had become true. When Chief Utramaka had visited him that morning and told him of Laughing Gull's accusations against Knows Much, he had been stunned.

A good man, a man obedient to the Great Spirit, the Creator, would have confessed to the chief at once, rather than allowing an innocent woman, the woman he loved, take the blame for his own crime. But Lightning Eagle was afraid he was not a good man, that he had become as evil as Utilla. Lies, treachery, lust, and murder. He was guilty of all of them.

So, when the chief asked him if he thought she could be guilty, instead of vehemently saying no, he had said, "Bring her to me and I will discover the truth."

The chief hadn't liked the idea. "No, her power can be greater than any *shaman*. It is best if we accuse her in front of the council. Come tonight at dusk to my house and we will settle this one way or another."

Frog had been listening in the corner while she quietly mended a pair of Lightning Eagle's moccasins. After the chief was gone she said, "The old *shaman* was right that you should beware of Knows Much."

Lightning Eagle whirled on her. "What do you mean by that?"

She stared at him, unafraid. "It is because of her that you have done things that you shouldn't, and if you aren't careful, you will do them again."

He stomped over to her and yanked her upright, not caring how she winced in pain at his hard grasp. "What do you know, Frog?"

"Nothing. I know nothing."

"I don't believe you."

But he let her go and considered, then turned to her. "Did you kill the old *shaman*?"

His question startled her and she blurted out, "No, of course not."

But he'd seen the flicker of fear cross her face and he pressed on, "You were alone with him when he died. And I know how much you hated him. It would've been easy for you to pinch his nose and mouth shut until he suffocated."

"No," she protested weakly, "I didn't do such an evil thing."

"I believe you did. And if I tell the chief of my accusations, you are a dead woman, Frog."

She hung her head, not daring to meet his knowing gaze. He chuckled a hollow laugh. "So, you have your secrets and I have mine. What do you say now?"

She stared at the neatly swept, hard earthen floor. "I say I should keep my thoughts to myself from now on," she mumbled.

Lightning Eagle gave her a triumphant smile then left the hut. The ugly slave woman had to go, he decided. She had outlived her usefulness. It was then he thought of a way to save Knows Much from being accused a murderess without incriminating himself.

* * *

Tatiana was anxious to see Anna, but no one was allowed to see her except Gray Cloud and Chief Utramaka. The rumor that she poisoned Red Hawk was all over the village and Tatiana was worried sick. It was the most ridiculous thing she'd ever heard, but more alarming was how eagerly people believed Anna was guilty.

Even Black Hawk had his doubts of her innocence. "I know she is like a sister to you," he'd told her that morning, "but my father must have good reasons to suspect her. From what he told me, my own grandmother was the one who first said Knows Much might be guilty."

"She believed that from a dream," said Tatiana with scorn. "How reliable can that be?"

"We Makah take our dreams and our visions very seriously," he answered with a frown of disapproval. "Especially now that my grandmother has joined my son in the land of the dead. I believe he spoke to her, because he knew she was coming soon, but first, he wanted us to know that the real murderer was not Little Man With Big Stories."

"But did your son actually name Knows Much as the one?"

Black Hawk thought carefully. "No, he did not. So, it is possible that she is innocent. My father has called a council tonight to sit in judgment. Except for the accused, no women allowed," he added before she could ask him if she could be there.

The council was made up of the chief, several elders, Lightning Eagle, Black Hawk, Strong Elk, and Brave Spear. As an afterthought, Chief Utramaka granted permission for Black Crow, Running Wolf, Yellow Hair, and Gray Whale to also attend. He thought it would be good for the white men to see that the Makah were fair in their judgments.

During the meeting, Tatiana and the other women were cloistered in Brown Bird and Swift Deer's compartment. Although they could not watch the proceedings, the wooden partitions were thin and they could hear some of the men's voices.

By this time, most of the visitors had left to return to their own villages, including the ones from Ozette. Tatiana had not had the chance to talk to Anton again, although she had seen him about the village. It was just as well he was gone, she decided. If Black Hawk ever saw her speaking to him, he would be livid with rage, putting Anton in danger, if not herself.

As she tried to amuse a cranky She-Who-Never-Sleeps with her wooden ball, Tatiana found herself praying for a miracle for Anna. Brown Bird, Gray Cloud, Swift Deer, and even Soft Fawn thought she was guilty. If the men decided the same thing tonight, it would be Black Hawk who would exact payment for his son's death. If it came to that, she would beg her husband to spare Anna, and instead ask the chief to give him many skins and blankets for Red Hawk.

But deep in her heart, she feared Black Hawk's thirst for vengeance would demand the ultimate price, Anna's life for his son's life. Even her position as chief's wife would not save her. It was the Makah code.

Sean was also full of fear for Anna. He and John sat cross-legged on the floor in the outside circle of the council. They were invited to listen, not to partake of the discussion, but Sean knew he would not keep silent if Anna was found guilty.

She was the only woman there, and the chief had her stand in front of all the men as they discussed her. Her face was ashen in color and her legs trembled occasionally, but otherwise, she met the gaze of each man, clearly and steadily. She wore a headband and had undone her braids, so her honey colored hair flowed past her shoulders. Sean thought she looked thinner, more fragile and he fought the impulse to charge over to her and snatch her away from all those dark accusing eyes.

Everyone was there but Lightning Eagle. Chief Utramaka was irritated at the *shaman*'s tardiness, but eventually, he became tired of waiting and ordered the council to begin. Questions shot out quickly, about Laughing Gull's dream, what exactly did she say that Red Hawk told her about his killer, did anyone actually see Knows Much put foxglove in his food, and also put the cascara bark into the vegetable stew?

It soon became apparent that no one had any satisfactory answers to these questions. So, the chief said, "Did any of you ever see my grandson and Knows Much argue?"

Most of the men muttered and shook their heads then Strong Elk said, "A couple days before my nephew died, he and I went hunting. I noticed how quiet the boy was and he seemed troubled. At night when we camped, I asked him if something was wrong. At first he said no then he said, 'Yes, Uncle, but I cannot tell you.'

"I said nothing, but the next day, I asked him again. This time he said, 'Uncle, I saw a powerful person do a wrong thing. And if I tell, I am afraid something bad will happen to me.'"

Black Hawk looked at him with surprise. "Brother, why did you not speak of this before?"

"I did not think of it until yesterday when I heard about Knows Much."

"Did you ask my son who this person was?"

"Yes, but he would not tell me. We did not speak of it again."

The chief puffed on his pipe, then passed it to the elder on his right. "So, we know someone in a powerful position was threatening my grandson if he told on him, or her."

"Someone who knew about herbs," Brave Spear pointed out.

"Sounds like the *shaman* to me," Sean suddenly interjected.

A silence fell in the room while everyone turned to stare at him. He knew he wasn't supposed to talk unless asked to, but it was becoming obvious to him who the real murderer was. And the way Anna was looking at him at the moment, with a growing fear in her face, he realized he was probably correct. But how did she know this? What hold did Lightning Eagle have on her that she would meekly take the blame for a hideous crime she did not commit?

"Running Wolf speaks without permission," scowled Brave Spear as the all the men began to argue at once.

The chief raised his hand for silence. "Running Wolf," he said loudly, "are you accusing Lightning Eagle of poisoning my grandson?"

Before Sean could reply, the *shaman* himself marched into the room, pulling along a cowering Frog.

"Here is the real killer, Chief," he announced. "My slave has confessed not only to killing your grandson, but to killing your cousin, the old *shaman*."

Frog shook her head in protest as a collective gasp of shock went around the room. Anna stared at Lightning Eagle with disbelief. How despicable he had become to blame his own crime upon poor Frog.

Chief Utramaka told the *shaman* to bring the slave forward. The woman's face was streaked with tears and sweat and her thick lips trembled. Saliva drooled from one corner of her mouth and her tongue kept flicking out.

"Frog," he said, staring intently into her eyes, "is this true?"

She could not meet his gaze and her eyes darted everywhere, up towards the rafters and around the room until they settled upon on Anna. The two women looked at each other. Anna could see the terror in her expression, and she felt a deep pity for her. She also thought Frog appeared to be ill, noticing how she clutched her stomach as if in pain.

"Answer me, woman," Utramaka said sharply. "Did you kill the old *shaman*?"

She shuddered, then raised her head and said simply, "Yes."

The room erupted in a babble of astonished voices and the chief motioned everyone to quiet down. "Why did you do this?" Utramaka demanded.

"I hated him!" she cried out. "He was an evil man and he did terrible things to me. One night when I was alone with him in the hut, I smothered him in his bed while he slept. But he opened his eyes at the last minute, and he knew it was me." She put a hand across her chest then gasped out, "I'm glad he knew I killed him."

Everyone began talking again. Frog twisted her head around to look at Lightning Eagle at her side. "What was in that tea you gave me?" she asked in a low voice. "Poison?"

He pretended not to hear her in the loud tumult of the room. As it was, he was highly agitated. The timing was critical in his plan. If the foxglove didn't stop her heart soon, it would all be for naught.

A half hour earlier he had told Frog that she was summoned by the council to give witness to Laughing Gull's statements about her dreams. She hadn't wanted to go.

"I'm too nervous," she'd said. "If they start questioning me, I might say something I shouldn't."

"I have made some tea for you that will calm you down," Lightning Eagle said with solicitous concern. "I mixed in a little crushed root of the purple flower."

Frog had taken it with reluctance, for she knew the medicine to be a diuretic that stimulated the kidneys as much as a soothing tonic to tranquilize her nerves. But she drank every drop, then said, "Thank you. It will help me."

Now she knew it was a deadly mistake to have trusted her master. He was as evil as Utilla. He mustn't be allowed to get away with murdering her and Red Hawk. Before it was too late, she had to speak and tell the truth about Lightning Eagle.

Utramaka scowled at all the council members and they fell silent. "I understand why you killed my cousin," he said, "but I don't understand why you hated my grandson, too."

"He was only a boy," Black Hawk blurted out, sorrow heavy in his face.

Frog visibly winced. "I--I--did not---" she began then stopped as her heart jumped in an erratic rhythm, flashing pain throughout her body. She gasped for her next breath and found it to be excruciatingly agonizing. With shock she realized she was losing her sense of hearing and sight. The light from the fire was growing dimmer and the men's voices in the room were becoming a low rumble of nonsense. She felt like she was being pulled away from everyone by a gigantic force she could not stop.

Without warning, she crumpled to the floor, the back of her head smashing onto the wooden planks. Her eyelids fluttered and her large rounded eyeballs rolled upwards as she stared sightlessly ahead at nothing.

She was dead.

Anna and Sean exchanged glances of horror then they both looked at Lightning Eagle. He was acting as distressed as anyone there, bending over Frog and trying to rouse her.

"She must have taken poison," he was saying to the chief and Black Hawk. "She drank some tea before we left."

"She killed my son," said Black Hawk, aiming a hard kick at the woman's body. "And she knew she would be sentenced to death. She took the coward's way out. Get her out of my sight!"

"Throw her off the cliffs!" Utramaka ordered. "And never speak her cursed name again!"

"What about Knows Much?" Lightning Eagle asked, as he gathered Frog into his arms, feeling relieved that she was dead.

The chief glanced at Anna and smiled. "She is innocent. She is still my wife."

"No!" Anna said in a loud voice. "I am not your wife any longer!"

Utramaka's mouth fell open in shock, revealing his few remaining teeth. "What do you mean?"

"I would like to divorce you. You believed I was guilty of murder. How can I remain your wife after that?" Anna's heart was beating rapidly at her audacity in challenging the chief in front of the council. But she couldn't stand the thought of living with him or any of the women of the house again. She decided she would rather be a slave to someone else, than stay in this farce of a marriage to Chief Utramaka.

His face darkened in humiliation. He turned to the council members. "All you men heard what this woman dared to say to me. What should I do with her?"

"Banish her from the village!" said one of the elders.

"Make her a slave!" said Brave Spear.

"Trade her away!" said Strong Elk. "The Nootkas would take her for much shell money."

"What about your daughter?" Lightning Eagle questioned, suddenly fearing that he would lose Knows Much after all. "Her heart will break if she loses another mother."

Utramaka silenced everyone with a loud shout. "Enough! The *shaman* is right. My daughter still needs a mother. She will stay in the village. Does anyone here wish to have her as their slave or wife?"

"I do!" Sean said swiftly.

"I do!" Lightning Eagle echoed.

The two men glared at each other in surprised anger. Utramaka began to chuckle as a crafty expression crossed his weathered face.

"I will offer the woman in trade. In one moon's time, she will be given as slave or wife to the man who gives me the most skins of the otter."

Lightning Eagle's face blanched in sudden fear as he remembered the warning given him years ago. He would die if he ever went in a canoe again. What was he going to do?

"I'll help you get the skins," John whispered to Sean. He glanced at Anna and gave her a quick confident smile, thinking how brave she was to stand up to the chief.

Utramaka smiled with satisfaction. The next time one of the big canoes of the white man came near the village, he would have many pelts to trade for their goods. He would become richer then ever. And he wouldn't miss Knows Much. She was more trouble than she was worth. It was time he found his daughter another mother.

He thought of the upcoming raid on the Quileute village. He and Black Hawk both intended to revenge themselves on the losses of his mother and his son's First Wife by taking the wives of Chief Xawishata and Hoheeshata. His wife was getting old and his son's white wife was going to have a child soon. The household needed more young wives to help.

He smiled again. What a great future he had!

CHAPTER FORTY SIX

For the next few weeks Anna became a slave in the chief's household. At night she was banished to the far corner of the chief's house, sleeping on the floor wrapped in a thin moth eaten fur robe. All her possessions and clothing were given to Gray Cloud. Each day she hauled water and firewood, gutted and cleaned fish, and performed any other dirty exhausting chore the Indian women didn't want to do. Except for giving Anna orders, they all shunned her until evening when she was allowed to see She-who-Never-Sleeps. The child was confused and fretful, and once again lived up to her name now that she couldn't spend the nights with her adoptive mother. Anna bore all the work with good cheer. She focused her thoughts on Sean, who was gone most of the time hunting the sea otter in his canoe. John often went with him. Anna prayed daily for their safety and success in the treacherous waters around the rocky inlets of Cape Flattery. It was her fervent hope that soon she would be living in his hut with him as his wife.

She couldn't face the fact that Sean might fail. The thought of being Lightning Eagle's slave filled her with terrible dread. She was afraid the *shaman* would take advantage of her helpless position in his hut, perhaps in the same manner that Frog was abused by Utilla.

Her disappointment in Lightning Eagle's character was acute. Once she had thought he was close to accepting Christianity, but after she'd spurned him in the forest, he'd changed dramatically for the worse. She had no doubt he poisoned poor Frog in the same manner he murdered Red Hawk. Obviously the power of being the village *shaman* had gone to his head, turning him towards evil instead of good.

Tatiana kept Anna informed on the contest to win her. The chief's price of otter skins had put Lightning Eagle at a distinct disadvantage. Although he had trained to be a seal hunter as a boy, it was many years since he'd stepped foot in a canoe, much less clubbed a seal or an otter. But the *shaman* was clever and rich. He soon hired other young men of the village to hunt for him, paying them in charms, amulets, shell money, amber, silver, copper, blankets, and fur robes, all coming from Utilla's horde of wealth that he'd accumulated over the years.

Soon the many experienced hunters were bringing in more otter pelts than the two inexperienced white men. After two weeks of hunting, Tatiana told Anna that Running Wolf had accumulated forty skins, while Lightning Eagle had more than sixty.

Then the weather turned against the hunters. Late spring thunderstorms and choppy seas kept them idle for days in the village. Sean became increasingly worried he would run out of time before he could get more pelts.

Early one morning he approached Anna by the stream as she filled tightly woven cedar boxes with water. She looked tired with dark circles under her eyes and he could tell she wasn't eating enough. It made him even more anxious and determined to free her from being a slave.

He greeted her then bent down to help her with her chore, but she shook her head.

"No, Sean, if Brown Bird or Gray Cloud find out you are helping me, they will punish me, either by denying me food the rest of the day, or hitting me a few times with their sticks."

Sean was appalled. In an angry voice he said, "How dare they treat ye like a common slave?"

"Because that's what I am," she said simply. She gazed into his darkly tanned face, burnt brown by the hours in his canoe at sea. If it wasn't for the green of his eyes, she would think he was an Indian, dressed only in a loincloth with his long black hair flowing about his shoulders.

"It drives me crazy to see ye workin' so hard, Anna."

"My papa used to say, what doesn't kill you, only makes you stronger."

He raised his eyebrows at that and gave a short laugh. "I don't think he was talking about his daughter slaving away for savages."

She smiled wearily. "No, he wasn't. It was his way of telling my brothers, especially Jack, to quit complaining about their chores." A look of pain flashed across her face. "Oh, how I miss them!"

"I promise to take ye home someday, Anna. But first we have to get away from this blasted village and back to civilization."

"Have you seen any ships yet?"

"Me and John saw one last week sailin' north when we were hunting otters. But she was too far out at sea for them to see us. And even if they did, they'd just think we were Indians."

"How many pelts do you have by now?"

"Not enough." He glanced around to make sure no one was nearby then lowered his voice, "John said that we mustn't worry. The chief wants all the young men of the village to begin their war preparations for the raid on the Hoh river village before the Quileutes scatter in family groups for the summer to fish, hunt, and gather berries and such. Some of the Makah split up into different camps too in the warmer months, so the chief wants to return quickly. Do ye know what that means, Anna? All of Lightning Eagle's hired hunters will have to stop hunting and get ready for the raid. The *shaman* will have to go out hunting himself or admit defeat."

"So, they really are going to attack Marya's village," Anna said worriedly. "If they do, the chief promised me he would bring Katya back. But that was when I was still his wife. Oh, Sean, did I make a terrible mistake in telling him I wanted a divorce?"

"Nay!" he said vehemently. "I'm glad you did it! Now we have a chance to be together."

Anna heard the laughter of a group of women coming to the stream and she hastily picked up her two boxes of water, sloshing some liquid over the sides. "I must go now."

As she turned to leave, Sean said, "Anna, keep believing and keep praying. God is still taking care of us. He will bring us all through this hard time safely. Don't forget to read your Bible."

She nodded wordlessly, feeling tears stinging her eyes. Her Bible was the only possession Gray Cloud let her keep and Anna poured over its pages whenever she had the chance. God's promise to never forsake her was the only thing that was keeping her at peace in these days of uncertainty.

John was right. The very next day Chief Utramaka instructed his warriors to prepare for war. Immediately, all the young men ceased fishing, hunting, and sleeping with their wives, and began to fast, pray to the spirits, and sharpen their weapons. The chief also announced that when they returned, he would make his decision concerning Knows Much.

Inside his hut Lightning Eagle gnashed his teeth in frustration. The pile of otter skin pelts in the corner of the room had grown to a hefty seven tens of fingers, but he wasn't sure if that was enough. Now that the weather had calmed, Running Wolf and Yellow Hair were back out hunting from dawn to dusk. By the time the war party came back, they could easily have that many pelts and more.

He had two choices. Either to go out hunting himself and hope no disaster would strike him, or find a way to stop Running Wolf from acquiring any more pelts. At times Lightning Eagle had been tempted to steal his skins out of his hut, but if he was caught, he would be dishonored by the whole village.

The thought of paddling out in a canoe both frightened and tantalized him. During all these past years he'd never forgotten the bliss of being on the water. He had missed gliding across the waves, away from land and all its responsibilities and problems, and becoming one with the sea, sky, wind, birds, and fish. Was it really true that something bad would happen to him if he ever rode a canoe again?

Perhaps it was time to seek his spirit guardian, and ask him what he should do. One night he left his hut and headed towards the sacred cedar tree deep in the forest. He would fast and pray for however long it took until he found his answer. He knew some would say he was wasting precious time, but they would not understand that as a *shaman*, he must have the spirits to guide him or he would fail.

Before he entered the woods he glanced upwards at the night sky where countless stars winked at him. He cringed. Everyone knew the stars to be the spirits of the dead and he was afraid that Utilla, Red Hawk, and Frog might be watching him. Quickly he sped deeper into the trees where the thick canopies overhead blocked out the twinkling stars.

The dark forest was alive with hooting owls and bats flying through the air, and thousands of branches rustled in the wind, whispering words of welcome. When he reached the cedar tree, he felt a moment's peace until he remembered the last time he'd been there, when he'd brought Knows Much.

Her face danced before him in the pitch blackness of the night, her hazel eyes gleaming softly, her lips parted in a slight smile. This was where the darkness had entered his soul, he thought. When she had rebuffed his advances, he realized she would never love him like he loved her. All her love was for Running Wolf, a man that he had come to loathe.

A bat flew by his head and Lightning Eagle felt the soft brush of its wings. It reminded him of the night the old *shaman* died, when he sensed a dark winged creature following him out of the hut. Frog had killed the old man right after he left. Had it been his soul reaching out for him? Was the evil spirit of the old *shaman* inside him now? Was that why he was able to kill both Red Hawk and Frog without remorse? And even now, if he was honest with himself, he was contemplating ways to kill Running Wolf.

He had turned evil. He knew that. He had disobeyed the Great Spirit and he didn't know how to change back to the good man he had once been.

"What can I do to save myself?" he cried out to the tree.

There was no answer. The tree stood, solid, silent, and ancient.

Then he remembered the words of Knows Much, "Jesus, the son of the Great Spirit Father, died to save us from our bad deeds. All you have to do is believe in Him and confess and He will save your soul. Your life will be changed."

How could it be that simple? He wondered, feeling tempted to try it.

Then he heard another voice, a deep guttural voice booming all around him, "Don't do it, Lightning Eagle! It is the white man's religion. It is not for you. Not for you...not for you..."

The repeated words had a hypnotic affect and he spoke them out loud. Each time he did, the black despair in his soul grew darker and darker. He fell to the ground at the base of the tree and wept.

* * *

One week later the war party departed in four of the largest canoes belonging to Chief Utramaka, Black Hawk, Strong Elk, and Brave Spear. Each canoe held twenty men and all their weapons and supplies for the two day trip down the coast.

The village was at its most vulnerable with all the warriors gone. Only the elderly and women and children remained. The chief told Lightning Eagle, Running Wolf, Yellow Hair, Black Crow, and Gray Whale that he expected them to take care of the people during his absence. Black Crow had wished to go on the raid, but Brave Spear told him to stay home and take care of his daughter Starlight who was expecting his first grandchild.

After the last canoe disappeared into the west, Lightning Eagle surprised everyone by saying he was going hunting for the otter. He asked to borrow Black Crow's canoe.

"You're going hunting all by yourself?" Samuel asked in surprise.

"I can handle a small canoe and hunt, too. Otter are tricky to spot, but they are small, and once I find them, I'll have no trouble clubbing them over the head."

Lightning Eagle knew he sounded more confident than he felt, but he'd heard that Running Wolf had skins of almost seven tens of fingers now, and he had little choice but to go hunting. After spending three days fasting and praying in the forest, he'd had no guidance from the Eagle. The only voice he'd heard was the one telling him to beware of the white man's religion. So, he made up his own mind. He would gather his courage and hunt until the war party returned.

To his surprise and that of the village, he came back the first day with five sleek pelts. On the second day he had similar success, and also the third day. That night as he counted his skins, he knew he should be rejoicing, yet his spirit felt sad. Killing sea otters was a dreadful business. They were such delightful little creatures as they floated on their backs, their little paws folded across their chests, sometimes nibbling on a clam.

As a boy on seal hunts he'd enjoyed watching the otter families. His father had told him otters have only one pup at a time. If the pup dies, the parents will grieve, hugging each other and starving themselves. The only time a mother will leave a pup, is to dive underwater for food. Whenever Lightning Eagle saw a pup alone, he speared it, making the poor thing cry like a baby. The parents heard its cries and when they came to save the pup, he speared them as well.

Lightning Eagle found himself weeping for every otter he killed and apologizing to their spirits. He was afraid that someday if the white man didn't stop his greed for their skins, the otter would be no more.

On the fourth day, purple clouds were building to the west when he left. He felt some apprehension, especially when he noted that Running Wolf and Yellow Hair had seen the clouds and decided not to go hunting.

But he believed luck was with him, and soon he would have won Knows Much as his slave. He had pelts that totaled almost nine tens of fingers now, and he knew that Running Wolf had a few less.

He's a fool, he thought, as he paddled towards the cape, *he'll never have her now*. Today the warriors are due back, and I'll have the most otter skins for the chief.

As the hours progressed, the clouds moved closer and the waves grew steeper. The small canoe pitched and rolled. Lightning Eagle struggled to keep away from the sharp rocks along the coves and inlets where the otter liked to play, eat, and sleep. Finally, he realized the ocean was too rough and the otters were all waiting out the bad weather. He decided they were wiser than he, and turned the canoe around to head for the village.

Without warning thunder rumbled overhead and lightning flashed. As the wind blew with sudden strength rain fell in horizontal sheets. Icy drops of hail knifed his face under his cone-shaped hat, stinging his cheeks, lips, and eyes. He paddled harder, fighting to keep the canoe in control through the increasing swells that towered on each side of him. He aimed the bow into each wave and rode it out, but soon saw with dismay, that the canoe was acting sluggish. It was taking on water from the heavy rain and seas, and he had no partner to act as bailer.

Suddenly he realized he was the foolish one in going out, and not Running Wolf. Fear clutched him as he tried to see the shore, but the heavy curtain of rain and clouds hid the land from his view. He was lost in a never-ending gray world of swirling and crashing water.

A bolt of lightning lit up the sky and he glanced up and saw to his amazement what looked like an eagle. How could it fly in such a wind without breaking a wing? The bird circled closer and closer to him until Lightning Eagle could see its black fierce eyes and proud yellow beak. A feeling of awe swept through him as he realized he was looking at his spirit guardian.

Then the bird flew off in a straight direction, uttering one loud cry. Lightning Eagle paddled after him as fast as he could. *It must be showing me the way home*, he thought with relief.

The occasional flash of lightning helped him keep the eagle in view. "Who needs a white woman's religion?" he yelled out triumphantly. "I already know the true one, the only one. The lightning and the eagle have come to save me, for I am Lightning Eagle!"

Using all his strength, he propelled the canoe through the snarling ocean swells. Soon the eagle became only a dot in the gray sky then he vanished altogether. But Lightning Eagle was not worried. At any moment he expected to see the cove where his village was.

After some time he noticed that it was getting darker. Could it be evening already? He should be home by now. Suddenly his arms felt as weak as a child's and his body was turning numb from the cold and constant wetness. His legs and knees ached with fatigue, and his eyes burned from the salt water.

Had he been mistaken? Had Eagle led him in the wrong direction? With an effort he tried to control the increasing feeling of panic as the canoe sank lower and lower. Finally, he abandoned paddling altogether, and grabbed the bailing box to ship water out of the canoe. But his arms would hardly obey him and his legs didn't want to move.

Lightning struck again and the sea and sky brightened up. Frantically, he looked around for any sign of land, but saw nothing. He was lost, hopelessly lost in the middle of the ocean in a tiny half sunk canoe, abandoned and deceived by his own spirit guardian, the Eagle.

He thought of Knows Much and sighed. Would what she think if she saw him now? He could almost hear her saying, "I told you so. You trust the wrong spirits. Only the Great Spirit and His son Jesus is the true one."

He gazed up at the gray clouds. "If you are real, Jesus Spirit," he spoke out loud. "Save me from death and I will follow you the rest of my life."

He would wait to see what happened, if anything. Otherwise, Eagle was right. His life would end in a canoe.

* * *

On the fifth day the war party returned, but only three canoes were sighted. The women waiting on the rooftops let out a long wailing sound, knowing at once that another disaster had struck. The first came the day before when the *shaman* did not return from hunting otters. It was hoped he'd made it to shore somewhere and was waiting out the storm. But today the sun was shining and he still was missing. The villagers were afraid something bad happened to him.

Their *shaman* had become too greedy for a woman, many thought. And many more panicked at the bad omen of the possible death of another *shaman*. What terrible thing would happen next?

They soon found out. Chief Utramaka's canoe was missing. Gray Cloud swooned in a heap on the ground when she realized her dreaded dreams had come true, and her husband was dead.

Ironically, the raid had been successfully carried out without one Makah warrior killed or even badly wounded. When the war party had neared the Hoh River late at night, they waited while the Quileutes were celebrating a wedding feast. They struck in the darkest hour, right before dawn when everyone was fast asleep. The fires they set threw the people into a panic. Many of the women and children fled into the forest, and the warriors who remained were ill prepared to fight.

On the way home the Makahs encountered the storm. Sturdy and heavy, the canoes rode up and down the swells as the warriors continually bailed out the excess water. All the Quileute captives, about twenty women and girls, moaned in fright and were wretchedly seasick. The warriors laughed at them, showing no fear as the thunder roared and the lightning flashed around them. They had all been at sea many times in such precarious conditions and never lost a man. It didn't occur to them this time would be different.

They were in a jubilant mood, singing their songs of victory. Fifteen freshly severed heads were piled in Utramaka's canoe, one of whom belonged to Chief Xawishata. His first wife, Many Baskets and her daughter, was also riding in the chief's canoe. Unfortunately, the Quileute chief's second wife, Talks A Lot, and her four daughters had managed to escape into the forest. But Black Hawk had Xawishata's third wife, the beautiful Whispering Doe, in his canoe, along with Hoheeshata's two young wives, Buttercup and Hummingbird.

In Brave Spear's canoe were all the rescued Makah young women except for two that had been traded away. The remaining captives rode with Strong Elk. And these were the unhappiest, knowing their fate was to be a slave for the rest of their lives.

They were just rounding Cape Flattery near the Fuca Pillar, which the Makah called the *Tsar-tsar-dark*, when a rogue wave appeared out of nowhere. It was a gigantic wall of gray-green water thundering towards them from their left side, as tall as an old cedar tree. Chief Utramaka was in the lead canoe and he didn't have time to react properly, to aim his bow straight into the wave. The wave struck the chief's canoe broadside and flipped it over. People and severed heads and weapons and supplies all tumbled out into the swirling frothing water.

The other three canoes managed to ride up the monstrous swell and safely down the other side. Immediately they turned around to retrieve everyone they could. The first person spotted was Many Baskets, who was struggling to keep her head and her infant daughter's head above the water. They were instantly plucked out, sopping wet, freezing cold, but alive. The child screamed non stop with fright.

By the time all the others had been rescued, they realized there was not a trace of Chief Utramaka. One of the warriors claimed he'd seen the canoe strike the chief on the head when it turned over, and it was feared he was knocked unconscious and drowned.

Horrified and sobered by the loss of their chief, they continued on towards the village. That night instead of a celebration feast the village was plunged into mourning.

Also that night Whispering Doe's child decided to be born.

* * *

John paced around his and Sean's hut as they listened to the shrieking and keening of the village women for the chief. While he waited to hear word about Marya, he remembered his joy and excitement at seeing her for the first time in many months. Then when she first stepped foot on shore, he was dismayed to see her appearance, bedraggled from the trip, looking ill, exhausted and swollen with child.

His gaze had met hers and she brightened momentarily, then her face paled and she'd clutched her abdomen and cried out. When John rushed to help her he realized the child was coming. She obviously had been having labor pains in the canoe for many hours.

"Marya, is your Tlingit maid, Keeah, here to help you?" he'd asked, glancing at the captives.

"No," she gasped, "a seal hunter from another Quileute village wanted her for a wife. I knew it was her only chance at happiness, so I let her go. She left with him last winter. The last I heard she was expecting a child." She uttered a moan as another pain knifed through her.

As John reached out to comfort her, Chief Black Hawk stepped in between them, looking fierce with his war paint still on his face. "I will help the woman. She is to be my second wife."

The news had hit John like a punch in the face.

Now he stood in the hut, still angry, his fists clenched in fury. "Why, when I'm so close to getting her back, did that savage have to claim her for his wife?" His hair was a wild mass of tangled blonde locks, tied back by a strip of cedar twig twine. With his vivid blue eyes and his bronzed skin, he could have his pick of the Indian women, but his heart firmly belonged to Marya.

"I don't know," Sean said, "but we have to find a way to get us all out of here as soon as possible. Life in this village is spinning out of control. Now that Black Hawk is chief, I feel the stability is threatened. Black Hawk does not like white men. We have to find a way to signal a passing ship before the trading season is done when fall comes."

John grimaced. "Right now all I can think of is Marya coming through the childbirth safely."

Sean nodded sympathetically, remembering how he felt when Anna birthed Katya. He stumbled over the remains of their dinner, pieces of broiled salmon laying on a platter with flies crawling all over it. Sean picked up the dish and threw the food out the door for the village dogs. Neither of them had any appetite.

He glanced at the tall pile of thick velvety otter skins in the corner of the hut. Now that Lightning Eagle was missing, and the chief was dead, they probably were worthless. He wondered what happened to the *shaman*. Did his canoe sink in the storm? Had he drowned like Chief Utramaka? Or was he marooned on some shore and in time, would find his way back to the village to try and claim Anna again?

But his biggest torment was the worry that Black Hawk would not recognize his father's offer of trade for Anna. While the new chief was in deep mourning for Utramaka, Sean knew he dared not approach him. Already Black Hawk and his brother, Strong Elk, and their mother, Gray Cloud, had slashed their arms and legs and hacked their hair to show their grief.

"John," said a voice in the doorway.

Both men turned to see Anna standing there. “Marya has just been delivered of her son,” she said with a weary smile. “She is doing well and so is the child.”

A look of deep relief passed over John’s face. His eyes grew moist and he said, “Oh, Anna, I’m so glad she came through it. Thank you for telling me.”

“And you do know that Black Hawk has claimed her for his second wife.”

“Yes,” he said, bowing his head, so she wouldn’t see the gleam of hatred he felt.

“But that’s not all he’s claimed,” she said, shaking her head. “He has also taken Hoheeshata’s two wives, Buttercup and Hummingbird.”

"And has he taken ye for his wife, too?" Sean asked, worry churning in his gut along with his dinner.

"Thank God he has not. He wishes me to remain as a slave in the household with my primary duties to take care of She-Who-Never-Sleeps."

"It's almost unheard of for an Indian to have so many wives," mused John.

“He says having four wives is payment for the four deaths he’s recently suffered, his son, his first wife, his grandmother, and now his father. Strong Elk is unhappy about it. He wanted at least one of Hoheeshata’s wives for his own. But I’m afraid the power of being chief has gone to Black Hawk’s head. And without a *shaman* in the village to counteract him, he is the supreme leader."

“No one dares defy Black Hawk,” said Sean grimly. “'Tis a shame he's nothing like old Chief Utramaka. I respected him. He was tough, but he had a soft heart, especially where white people were concerned. Black Hawk is a hardened, brutal man.”

“You’d think Black Hawk would honor his father’s trade agreement with you and Lightning Eagle,” John said. “Perhaps he’s so full of grief about his father, he’s forgotten it.”

“I think I’ll go and remind him then,” Sean snapped.

“It would be wise to wait until after the village is done with mourning their chief.”

“John’s right, “said Anna. “It will be some time yet before Black Hawk officially recognizes any of the women as his wives. He will have to give a great feast and *potlatch*, and that will take time to prepare and to invite guests from other villages.”

“And how is Katya?”

Her expression drooped in sadness. “She clings to Many Baskets and stares at us as if we are strange monsters, especially me and Tatiana with our golden hair. Many Baskets refuses to allow me near her. And Black Hawk said to let her have the child for now.” Her voice shook slightly. “I must go. The house is in a total uproar with all the new women and the new babe and the others wailing their grief."

* * *

Marya held her one week old son in her arms as he slept, satiated after eating. He was finely formed, strong limbed and with a thick patch of straight black hair on his head. She often thought she would resent this child, but she could not. Warm feelings of love bubbled inside her every time she saw his tiny face, so adorable, so helpless, so much a part of her. Then she thought of Xawishata. He had a son, finally, after all the years of only having daughters. How joyful he would be if he knew.

A tear slipped from her eye as she remembered the terrible night when the Makah attacked the village. She had tried to run away with the rest of the women, but her heavy body was so slow, she was caught almost immediately by Black Hawk. While he was taking her to his canoe, Chief Xawishata ran after them, swinging his war club. Strong Elk took his bow and shot an arrow into his heart. Her husband had died instantly, trying to protect her and his unborn child.

More tears sprang into her dark eyes. He'd been a kind and generous man, and in his own way, he'd loved her. She had never loved him, but she mourned his loss. It was such a waste and a tragedy for the Quileutes. What were Talks A Lot and her four young daughters to do now without their husband and father? She had become fond of the little family and her heart ached for their loss. Each day she prayed that God would watch over them.

"You are crying, Sister," said Tatiana suddenly appearing at her side. "Are you in pain?"

Marya rubbed her eyes. "No, I was only thinking of my husband and how sad it is that he is dead." She gave Tatiana a speculative look. "I want you to know that I do not wish to become Black Hawk's second wife."

She recalled a conversation with him the morning after her son was born. "You and my First Wife are sisters," he said. "It is good for me to have both of you. I will raise your son as a Makah, and he will grow up to be a brave whaler like me. Then you will give me more sons."

"He has become greedy for sons, wealth, and power," said Tatiana flatly.

Days before when Black Hawk announced his intention to have three more wives, she'd confronted him. "Why do you want all these women, my husband? Have I displeased you in any way, so that you feel a need for more wives?"

She stood in front of him with her fists clenched together to keep from striking him. He saw her anger and laughed. "I am happy with you. You are my First Wife, the woman of my heart. You will give me a fine son, like Whispering Doe. But I wish for more sons, as many as I can have.

Whispering Doe, Hummingbird, and Buttercup, all will give them to me."

"Why does he want so many?" Marya now asked.

"He lost his only son last winter, and now he realizes how fragile children are. He wants a brood of sons to make sure some of them survive to carry on his family, and become the next chief after him. If he has no sons, then when he dies, Strong Elk will become chief. As much as the two brothers care for each other, there is a rivalry between them. Strong Elk is furious that our husband will have so many wives when he has only two."

"I feel troubled for poor Anna," said Marya. "To think that she went from being a chief's wife to a mere slave. How did that happen?"

Tatiana explained quickly about Red Hawk's death and the suspicion of his murder first upon Wang Li, then upon Anna, and finally the blame falling on the *shaman*'s slave woman. "After that, Anna refused to stay married to Black Hawk's father and he offered her in trade. The *shaman* and the captain both wanted her. The chief devised a contest between the two men. Whoever brought him the most otter skins by the time he returned from the raid would have Anna. Then the *shaman* disappeared hunting the otters in the same storm that drowned the chief."

"There is as much intrigue and gossip in an Indian village as there was in New Archangel," said Marya with a slight smile.

"I think people are the same the world over, no matter what their race," agreed Tatiana. She gave Marya a hesitant smile. "Do you know whatever happened to my little cat, Otter?"

"I think she's still alive and has adapted to the forest environment. Every once in awhile, someone would claim they'd seen the cat, but no one could come near her. She has become a legend of the forest among the Quileutes," Marya laughed, then added more seriously, "I used to pray for Otter, so I know God watched over her."

Tatiana broke into a huge smile. "That reminds me, Marya. I have become a Christian."

"You have?" A look of joy crossed her face and she cried out, "Oh, sister, that makes me wonderfully happy!"

"I knew you would be surprised and pleased."

"Oh, I am very surprised, but both Anna and I have been praying for a long time that you would discover how much God loves you."

"I never believed He really existed, or if He did, that He cared about me at all. Then I saw Him perform a miracle. He healed a sick baby after Anna prayed. I realized then that He was real, and that everything Anna has been preaching to me was true. But still, I stubbornly resisted. Finally, it took me killing a man and being so consumed by guilt afterwards, that I reached out to God to take it all away."

"Who did you kill?" Marya's eyes were wide with shocked curiosity.

"Hoheeshata."

At her sister's gasp, Tatiana described the night of the raid on the Makah village, and the death of Soft Fern and Laughing Gull.

"So that's why they came to take revenge," Marya said thoughtfully. "It never stops then, does it? One night the Quileutes might come here to avenge this last raid."

"By then I pray we've all been rescued."

"Are there ships passing by?"

"Yes, we see them occasionally sailing north to trade for furs. The Indians say every couple years one stops in the Strait. If that happens, John is trying to find a way to catch their attention. The old chief once said we would be allowed to leave, but I don't know if Black Hawk will keep the promises of his father."

Outside the chief's lodge Sean roamed throughout the village seeking Black Hawk to ask him that very question. He found the new chief on the beach, talking to a couple of Makah men from Neah Bay. Sean overheard him tell the two about the *potlatch* he was giving in one moon's time to celebrate his new wives. All the nobles from their village were invited.

Sean waited politely until the discussion was finished and the two men departed in their canoe. Black Hawk turned to him. "You wish to speak with me, Running Wolf?"

"Yes, Chief. I would like to show you something in my hut. Will you come?"

Black Hawk inclined his head and the two made their way back into the village. John was squatting outside the entrance, using his knife to carve a wooden doll for She-Who-Never-Sleeps. The chief paused to watch for a few minutes then smiled in approval.

Inside the dim dank hut, Sean gestured at his pile of otter pelts and said, "Do you remember the trade your father offered for Knows Much?"

Black Hawk looked startled. "I had forgotten."

"He said when he returned he would give her to me or the *shaman* for the greatest number of otter skins. I hope that as his son, you will honor his promise. I would like to give all these to you for the woman."

The chief narrowed his eyes thoughtfully. He was quiet for a few moments, a time that made Sean feel the sweat gathering under his arms and behind his neck. Then he nodded.

"You are right. I will honor my father's promise. I will trade Knows Much to you for all those skins, but," he paused, staring sternly at Sean, "only if you have more pelts than the *shaman*."

"But he is gone," Sean protested.

"His otter skins are not," Black Hawk pointed out. "They are still in his hut. We will go there and count them. If he has less skins than you, I will give her to you."

"And if there are more?"

"Then I will keep her as my slave."

Feeling frustrated, Sean counted his pelts as Black Hawk watched keenly. There were a total of ninety. The two men went outside and walked through the village to the forest edge where Lightning Eagle's hut stood. No one had gone near it since the *shaman* vanished.

Black Hawk hesitated at the entrance as the musty odors of strange herbs and old blood from ancient creatures in boxes assailed his nostrils. Peeking inside through the gloom, he could see many of the frightening masks hanging on the walls, along with assorted charms, amulets, and medicine bags. From the dark corners came scuttling noises and it felt as if many pairs of eyes were watching him, spirit eyes.

He nervously backed out and said, "I will have a slave bring the skins to my house where we can count them."

When all of Lightning Eagle's pelts were carried to the chief's house and stacked in a pile, Sean thought the number looked about the same as his. It would be close.

The news of the trade spread quickly. A group of curious villagers came to watch, among them Robby and Samuel and John. Some of the women came out of the house, Brown Bird, Swift Deer, Small Fawn, and Anna. She and Sean exchanged looks of hope mixed with apprehension.

Black Hawk began to count Lightning Eagle's pelts, taking a skin from one pile and making another. Ten, twenty, thirty, forty, fifty, sixty, seventy, eighty, then eight-nine, and one more. It looked to be a tie. But as Black Hawk picked up the ninetieth skin, there was another stuck to it, a very tiny pelt of a baby otter.

People murmured with surprised disapproval. It was considered offensive to the spirit of an animal to kill its offspring unless one was very hungry. The survival of a species depended upon the young, growing up, mating, and reproducing. Lightning Eagle must have become desperate to have slaughtered a pup.

Sean hoped Black Hawk would not count the last skin. Due to its small size, it was practically worthless in trade.

But the chief gave him a triumphant smile and said, "Nine tens of fingers plus one for the *shaman*. Nine tens of fingers for Running Wolf. The woman is mine."

Sudden anger made Sean feel reckless. "You will regret your decision, Chief. She is a woman who brings trouble as your father discovered."

"My father spoiled Knows Much. I will make sure she works so hard each day she will not have the strength or time to stir up trouble."

With frustration Sean looked at Anna. He could see the disappointment and despair in her eyes.

In English she said, "Find us a ship, Sean. Until then, at least I can be near Katya. Don't give up hope. God will take care of us."

In bitterness he turned away and stumbled back to his hut. Right now he felt like God had forsaken all of them.

***

On the northernmost tip of Vancouver Island, a battered half sunk canoe washed ashore in a small inlet. Two young brothers from the nearby village of Nahwitti of the Kwakiutl Indians were looking for sea urchins at low tide among the tidal pools when they spotted the red and black canoe stuck between two rocks. Creeping closer, they peered over the edge and saw a corpse of a man crumpled inside.

He had long legs and arms, bent in a fetal position. His emaciated body was sun burnt and blistered to an angry reddish brown and was covered with fascinating tattoos and oozing sores. His lips were swollen and cracked and caked with dried blood. His salt encrusted eyelids were closed over his sunken eye sockets.

Without warning his chest rose and fell and he groaned. The two boys looked at each other in startled fright. He was not dead!

“Come,” said the elder brother, “we must tell our father at once. Grandmother will know how to make him well again.”

CHAPTER FORTY SEVEN

John and Sean stood at the tip of Cape Flattery, looking out at the grand scene in front of them. It was an endless world of blue, the darker sapphire hues of the ocean rolling endlessly to the horizon where the sea met the lighter turquoise sky shimmering with the golden rays of the sun. Ancient cliffs fell away from their feet to the water where the ocean swells broke in a thunderous mass of roaring, snarling, hissing green water and white foam. Some of the water trickled into the caves and hollows below the cape, creating mysterious liquid echoes and great booming sounds that frightened the Makah into thinking demons lived there.

The moss and lichen covered cliffs below were pierced with a network of deep caverns and arches where in calmer seas canoes could meander unseen by the seals. The creatures nested in hiding places on the sandy bottoms of caves which the Makah believed mysterious beings inhabited. Only the bravest hunters dared venture inside these dark rocky labyrinths. When hunting the Makah used torches to find the seals, but if they angered the beings whose secret lairs were invaded, their torches blew out and only the lucky ones found their way out again.

In the distance the flat top of rocky Tatoosh Island stood guard, and nearer, were the savage rocks the Makah called the *Kwat'utal's Jaws*, jagged black pinnacles jutting out majestically from their circles of white frothing spindrift. Seabirds by the thousands swooped and circled around them, calling to one another while seals and sea lions sunned themselves on the flatter rocks, the only residents of this wild spot at the edge of the continent.

"This is the perfect place to fly the kite," said John, unrolling the wad of string he'd made from twisting seal guts.

The kite was his ingenious idea, made of the thinnest cloth stretched out over a wooden frame. When the wind caught it, the kite would rise well above any fog bank and catch the attention of a passing ship. They hoped the crew would see it and realize only a white man could have made such a thing. Then it was their fervent prayer the ship would stop to investigate the kite and they would be rescued.

"We can take turns flyin' the kite," said Sean, "in between working on Black Hawk's new canoe."

It was early September or as the Makah said, *kars-put'hl*, the Moon of Work, especially that of cutting wood, splitting out boards, and making canoes. A few days ago the chief had announced his wish to have the largest, most impressive whaling canoe of all the Makahs. Constructed from a huge cedar tree, the canoe was to be over forty feet long and six feet wide when completed. It was to be a canoe fit for a king.

But Sean was more impressed by his friend's clever plan, and he believed the kite might signal a passing vessel. So far nothing else had. Since spring they'd watched ship after ship sail by Cape Flattery, never veering from their northerly course. In a few more weeks, the trading season would be over and the ships returning south. Flying the kite was their final hope before the fall weather set in and they were trapped in Classet for another dismal winter.

As things stood in the village, he dreaded even one more day there. Black Hawk had become ruthless and power mad. No one dared oppose him, especially since a string of good luck had come since he became chief.

First a large flock of ducks flew so low over the village every bird was an easy shot. Then a huge elk wandered out of the forest and ran onto the beach near the village. All the women chased it into the water while the men leaped into their canoes, weapons in hand, and surrounded the poor beast, clubbing and shooting it to death. There was fresh meat that night.

The next day whales were spotted off the cape in numbers larger than ever seen before so late in their migration north. Black Hawk and Brave Spear and Black Crow went whale hunting and successfully caught a huge mammal.

The day after they returned, a huge run of silvery smelts were sighted in the surf on the ocean beaches south of the cape. The arrival of the fish was signaled by the frenzied feeding of seagulls and seals. The six inch fish did not come every spring, and no one knew whenever they would appear. In five days the breakers were black with them and all a man had to do was stand in the water with his long-handled wood framed net and the waves would pour the smelts into it. The tasty little fish were a welcome addition to their diets and Sean thought they smelled slightly like cucumbers when freshly caught.

The chief's only weakness was his wives, all four of them. He bragged constantly about his prowess as a husband, and how Buttercup and Hummingbird were already with child. Sean knew the thought of Marya and Black Hawk together drove John into creating the kite as a last desperate attempt to find a ship and free the women.

Muddy Feet and many of the Makah children had followed them, including a few curious adults. When John lifted the kite up into the wind, slowly letting out the string, the Indians gasped in awe as the breezes caught the kite and carried it out over the sea, higher and higher. The kite grew smaller as it rose until it was only a tiny speck in the sky.

"Yellow Hair and Running Wolf have found a way to reach the sun," some of the men murmured.

"Chief Black Hawk should make them our *shamans*. They must have much power to send messages to the sun spirit," said another.

But when Muddy Feet ran back to the village to tell his uncle what the white men were doing, Black Hawk barely listened to him. The chief had another more pressing concern on his mind. His favorite wife Daughter of the Sun was in the birthing hut laboring to have his child.

A group of women were in attendance, Anna, Marya, Gray Cloud and Brown Bird. The healthy delivery of the chief's child was of the utmost importance. Small Fawn, Swift Deer, Hummingbird, and Buttercup also fluttered around nearby, offering their support if needed. The youngest wives of Black Hawk were excited at the prospect of the birth, especially since both were facing the same experience in seven months time.

The two girls were hardly the same defeated creatures once captured by the white men the year before. They had blossomed since their marriage to Black Hawk who gave gifts to them, the best foods, and surrounded them with the warmth of his family. In turn, they worked hard to please him, his mother, and the other women of the household.

But no one toiled as hard as Anna. She was up each morning before daybreak, hauling water and rekindling the cooking fires. Then she fed She-Who-Never-Sleeps and her daughter, Katya, before starting a long day of drudgery and never ending chores.

The only bright spot in Anna's life were the two little girls. To her deep relief and gratitude, many weeks ago Tatiana had asked Black Hawk to return Katya to Anna. He had agreed and soon traded Many Baskets to his friend Brave Spear as a slave. For the first few days Katya cried and whimpered without Many Baskets, then suddenly one morning, she started babbling happily at Anna and had been fine since. She-Who-Never-Sleeps was fascinated by her "little sister." And seeing the two heads together, one dark as a raven's wing, the other the color of the sunrise, brought Anna the only joy she knew in these difficult days.

Many Baskets took the separation from her adopted daughter stoically, but whenever she and Anna chanced to meet, the Quileute woman flashed her a look of such hatred, she made Anna uneasy. As a result, she rarely let her daughter out of her sight.

"It's a boy, a strong handsome boy!" Gray Cloud announced proudly, as the newly born infant let out a high wail. "Buttercup, tell the chief he has a new son, my grandson!"

The death of her husband, the old chief, had been hard on Gray Cloud, but she was slowly recovering. Because she had prophesied his death before it happened, she now was known as a Dreamer. The villagers not only respected her as the matriarch of the village, but also trusted her to attend the sick. With Lightning Eagle and Laughing Gull both gone, she had become a midwife and medicine woman.

Tatiana saw Buttercup run out of the hut and she smiled weakly with relief, feeling like she had survived the most painful experience of her life. During most of the birth she was forced to stand up, clutching a post in agony, until the baby fell out, caught swiftly by Gray Cloud. Now that it was all over with, she was finally allowed to rest while the women washed her clean.

"Never again," was her thought as she held her son in her arms. She took one glance at the infant, noting his straight black hair and light coppery skin, and felt disappointment. He looked nothing like her. He was a miniature replica of Black Hawk.

Then he opened his eyes and stared at her. She stifled a gasp of pleasure. His eyes were the color of dark blue violets exactly like her own. A rush of maternal affection for him overwhelmed her. *My son, my own darling son.*

That night the chief was overjoyed and ordered a feast to celebrate the birth of his new son. He gave out gifts of venison, saying proudly in the Makah way, that the baby had killed the deer. He also plied Tatiana with more gifts of necklaces and silver bracelets, and told her she was the most special of all his wives.

As the days passed Tatiana recovered her strength rapidly. The child was healthy, alert, and quite perfect. She was delighted with him, but found herself to be a clumsy mother and unable to keep him happy for long. She often wished she had a nanny or a wet nurse for him. As hard as she tried to care for him as any loving mother, humming to him, feeding him, washing him, changing the shredded cedarbark in his cradleboard whenever it was soiled, he didn't seem to like her. The instant he finished nursing, instead of falling asleep contentedly in her arms like Marya's son did with her, he would turn his face away almost angrily and fuss until she put him back in his cradleboard, or until someone else picked him up.

That someone was either Hummingbird or Buttercup, whose magic touch quieted him down immediately. Nine times out of ten they could get him to fall asleep faster than Tatiana. Whenever she tried rocking or singing to him, he would remain awake, gazing at her with a faint frown on his tiny mouth, as if he disapproved of her as his mother.

Sometimes she thought Black Hawk had enough love for his son for the both of them. She had never seen such a proud, protective father. He spent every spare moment holding and talking to the child, often singing him to sleep with an old Makah lullaby for a boy, "Everybody will be afraid to look upon his little face, because on his little round cheek, will be the sign of the Thunderbird."

Whenever he noticed his son's extra fussiness around her, he would smile and say, "Look, wife, my son is so anxious to grow up and become a great whaler, warrior, and chief like me, he wishes he didn't need a mother anymore."

It was as good a reason as any for the odd relationship between mother and son, and Tatiana would smile at him in agreement.

Earlier in the summer much of the village had scattered into family groups to hunt, fish, and pick berries. Now that Tatiana was safely delivered of her child, Gray Cloud announced it was time for all the women of the house to go on a final food gathering expedition for the coming winter.

"It will be a fun few days," Swift Deer told Tatiana and Anna and Marya. "We women get to sit around the fire in the best places and eat without having to serve the men first." She giggled. "No men are allowed in our camp, but sometimes a young man might sneak into the camp, supposedly on a hunting trip. But we all know he's looking for a certain girl. Then we get to tease him endlessly until he leaves."

Anna soon found it was an idyllic time she wished would never end. Although she still had plenty of responsibilities, she reveled in the freedom of the all female camping party. Sometimes cousins and sisters from other villages met up with them, gossiping in the berry patches, while the older women watched the children and tended to the drying of the food.

One afternoon she left She-Who-Never-Sleeps with Gray Cloud and took Katya with her to find food. They followed Tatiana and Marya, both with their infants strapped to their backs in their cradleboards. The three women spent hours searching the riverbanks and the forest trails for cow parsnip, horsetail rush, clover, green thistle, fern, black cap, rose hips, crab apples, camas roots, and wild onion. Dazzling their eyes with bright colors, wild flowers of purple fireweed, purple asters, and lupine of yellow, blue, and red grew in abundance, along with bushes of ripened blackberry, blueberry, and huckleberry, gooseberry, Oregon grape, and salal berries.

Most of the berry bushes were thorny, including the wild rose bushes. Earlier in the summer Anna loved smelling the sweet fragrance of the wild roses, small pink flowers that after blooming turned into rose hips, which could be brewed into tea for medicinal purposes. The sight of the small hard red berries reminded her of the shipwrecked *Sea Rose* and all the troubles since. As she collected and placed all the various food items in her basket, Anna hoped she and Katya would not be in the village this winter to eat any of it. Ever since Robby had told her that Sean and John were flying a kite at Cape Flattery nearly every day to signal a passing ship, she felt a new sense of hope for the future.

Her daughter was now eighteen months old, a bundle of non stop energy from her first waking moment to her last at the end of the day. Instead of walking, she ran and if Anna didn't keep a close eye on her, she would disappear into the bushes or behind a tree.

"You should've left her with the older women," said Tatiana as they picked big juicy blackberries from a thorny patch of bushes growing in a sunny clearing in the woods.

To keep Katya occupied, Anna fed her the ripest sweetest berries, and the child had smeared the purple juice all over herself. She was naked like the other Indian children and her tiny body was tanned to a light golden brown. With her red gold curls, bright blue eyes, and messy freckled face, she looked like a mischievous Scottish elf. Finally, after all the excitement, she was getting cranky, and she soon curled up near a stump at the edge of the clearing and fell asleep.

Anna felt her heart swell with maternal pride and love whenever she glanced at her. Lately, She-Who-Never-Sleeps had sensed this, and the little Indian girl clamored jealously for her attention whenever Anna was holding Katya.

"I know I should have left her, but I'm always afraid Many Baskets might come while I'm gone, and steal her away."

"If she tried to take Katya, Black Hawk would have Brave Spear punish her," said Tatiana.

"Aren't you ever afraid of him?" Marya questioned.

"I have at times," Tatiana admitted. "He has a savage side, but so far, it has never been directed at me. But to tell you girls the truth, ever since Black Hawk took all these wives, I don't feel the same about him anymore. He used to make me feel as if I was the most special woman in the world, but lately, when he's with me, I sense his thoughts elsewhere and then I wonder which wife he'd rather be with. He certainly seems to favor Hummingbird and Buttercup."

"I wish he would leave me alone," muttered Marya. "Every time Black Hawk touches me, my skin crawls. If I wasn't a Christian, I'd ask Gray Cloud for an anti-love potion that would make me unattractive to him. I remember hearing about such things among my people, the Aleuts. I imagine a Makah medicine woman can do the same."

She frowned. "Once I believed John might marry me. If we are rescued will he ever wish me for his wife, especially with an Indian child?"

"I never thought I'd say this, but I am thankful to be only a slave," Anna said then suddenly stiffened when she noticed Katya was not sleeping by the stump anymore. Nor did she see her anywhere about. Fear shot through her.

"Katya," she blurted, "where is Katya?"

With alarm all three women dropped their baskets on the ground and began calling for her. Anna peered through the thorny bushes and saw only sun dappled green leaves hanging over clusters of berries, but no flash of reddish gold hair. Frantically she began looking around the patch and the clearing while Tatiana and Marya checked behind the nearby trees and bushes.

Anna's heart hammered with dread and fear as she realized Katya must have woken up and wandered away when her back was turned. Or had someone or something taken her?

No, she screamed silently, *I can't lose her again when I just got her back.*

A sob tore out of her throat. "What can we do?" she cried out, "How can we find her?"

"She can't have gotten far," said Marya. "Her legs are so tiny."

Tatiana immediately thought of bears, cougars, or coyotes. She was sure Anna was thinking the same. If only they hadn't left the rest of the young women, who could now help them look for Katya. But Hummingbird, Buttercup, Small Fawn, and Swift Deer said they didn't wish to penetrate too deeply into the thick forest to pick berries. Tatiana knew they were spooked by the dark woods because of their superstitions about the evil forest spirits.

At the moment, she wondered if they were right. It was as if something had just snatched the little child away. She had vanished without a trace.

Chills ran down her neck as she suddenly heard a heavy crunching sound coming towards them in the trees and saw the bushes rustling at the edge of the clearing. Anna and Marya noticed it too, and froze. The commotion was much too large for a small child.

Anna let out a cry of welcomed relief when she saw a grim-faced Sean march into the clearing holding Katya in his arms.

John followed them, pulling a resisting Many Baskets behind him. She was snarling, her face distorted with rage.

Anna ran over to Sean and flung her arms around him and Katya, kissing and hugging them both with obvious love and happiness.

"Thank you, Sean, thank you," she kept murmuring. "I thought she was lost. Or that a bear got her, or that--" she broke off and turned to look at the Quileute woman with shock. "Many Baskets must have taken Katya while we were picking berries!"

"We found her running through the forest with Katya in her arms," said Sean, balancing one arm around Katya and sliding the other around Anna's waist.

"I'll take her to Black Hawk, and he can deal with her," said John, all the while trying not to stare at Marya, looking very pretty in her cedar bark garments with her shiny black hair cascading down to her tiny waist. His gaze slid away from the sleeping infant on her back.

Tightening his grip on Many Basket's arm, he spoke to her in the harsh guttural tones of the Quileute. Her pitted face creased into a frightened expression as she realized what she had done. She tried to twist away, saying, "No, no...Black Hawk."

"Ask her what she intended to do with my daughter," said Anna, still holding onto Sean and Katya. She saw how he was smiling tenderly at Katya, who was returning his smile as if she remembered him from somewhere. The little girl began to pat the dark stubble under his chin with her tiny hands and giggled at the coarse feel.

Sean was surprised Katya was not afraid of him. It was the closest he'd been to her in a year. The sweetness of her little body trustingly placed in his arms and the feel of Anna's slim form pressing against him gave him a jolt of unexpected happiness as if he had a family again.

John spoke to Many Baskets and listened to her explanation. "She says she found the child wandering in the trees alone and crying. She said she was trying to find Knows Much and return Little Dawn, but she didn't know where you were."

"She lies," said Tatiana. "She must have followed us here and waited until our backs were turned and then she grabbed Katya, who was sleeping at the edge of the clearing."

"What should I do with her?" John questioned.

Sean looked at Anna. "It's up to you."

"What would Black Hawk do to her?" she asked Tatiana.

"For trying to steal the child of one of his slaves, probably beat her soundly and return her to his friend Brave Spear, who would then make her work even harder."

Many Baskets shot her a defiant scowl. Anna could feel the hate emanating from her and she knew the woman needed to be taught a lesson. Then her glance fell on Sean's upper torso and the ugly puckers of scarred tissue that crisscrossed his back, a hideous reminder of the *knout*.

She remembered how the sight of his ravaged back had filled Chief Utramaka and many of the Makah with awe when they'd first seen it. The chief had told her they all respected the bravery and courage Running Wolf must have shown to survive such a terrible whipping. Then with a troubled expression, the chief said it also was evidence of the brutality of the white man towards each other.

She looked at Many Basket's face. The woman was already so scarred from smallpox, Anna winced as she realized a whipping would do even more damage to her fragile skin. Yet, Many Baskets was her mortal enemy and deserved to be punished.

Just as she opened her mouth to speak those harsh words, she heard a voice inside her head say, *Anna, forgive her as I have forgiven you. Bless your enemies. Do not curse them.*

She took a deep breath and said, "Let her go, John. Just let her go."

"Are you certain?" John asked with surprise.

"Yes," she said. "The woman has suffered enough in her life without me adding to it. And perhaps I owe her something."

"Owe her what?" Sean said, looking down at her. "She took Katya away from you."

"Yes, she did, but she also took excellent care of her. Katya is a very healthy child. I owe her that, the good care of my daughter."

John shrugged and released his grip on Many Baskets' arm. "You may go," he told her, "but stay away from the child if you wish to keep the skin on your back."

Many Baskets nodded and without another word, fled into the forest. But she didn't go far. As soon as she was out of sight, she stopped and circled back, creeping closer to watch the white people. She had been shocked when the chief's slave had greeted Running Wolf with such obvious affection.

Then, as she hid behind a tangle of vines and bushes, she saw something else just as shocking. Whispering Doe walked over to Yellow Hair and attempted to embrace him. He caught her arms and murmured something to her. Whispering Doe's face crumpled with tears.

Her gaze swung back to Running Wolf and Knows Much. She was still standing close to him, talking in low intimate tones, when she stood up on her tiptoes and the two kissed right over Little Dawn's red gold curls.

It was obvious to Many Baskets that both couples were lovers. Her master Brave Spear would be interested to know that two of his best friend's women, one a wife, the other a slave, were deceiving him with the white men. She chuckled softly. Finally, she would have her revenge on the hated Knows Much!

* * *

"No, wife, I forbid it!" yelled Black Hawk.

He andTatiana were arguing, something that happened more and more often lately. This time it started because she wished to visit Anna and Marya.

It had been ten days since Black Hawk had divorced Whispering Doe for being an unfaithful wife. Since then she and Knows Much had been confined to a slave hut while he decided what to do with them. Whispering Doe was allowed to keep her infant son, but Little Dawn had been given back to Many Baskets as a reward for her valuable information about his wife's and her slave's immoral behavior with Running Wolf and Yellow Hair. Brave Spear had also granted Many Baskets her freedom from slavery, and she had moved into the empty *shaman*'s hut, which no one else wanted.

The two white men were now banished from the village for an undetermined amount of time. Since the old chief had given them their freedom months ago, they were not slaves Black Hawk could trade away. He had been tempted to kill them, but their skills in woodcarving and metal working made them too valuable in the village. Eventually, it was believed they would return after Black Hawk's temper cooled off.

Robby kept Tatiana informed of their whereabouts. The Captain and Mister Hill were spending their time hunting in the forest, fishing, and flying kites off Cape Flattery. It was her most fervent prayer they would soon signal a ship.

"But I haven't seen them for so long," she protested to Black Hawk. "And Whispering Doe is my sister. Her son is my nephew."

"You will get used to not seeing any of them," he said, a stubborn look crossing his handsome face. "I am thinking of trading them to the

Nootkas soon. I will get much shell money for two white women and a Quileute infant."

"What?" Tatiana's mouth fell open in horror. "How can you consider doing such a terrible thing?"

"It is Knows Much and Whispering Doe who have done the bad thing, wife. Something you would be wise to remember. They are fortunate I have not punished them in the way of the Makah by slicing off the tips of their nose and ears, so they will be ugly to every man the rest of their days."

Her face paled at the thought. He noticed her fear and gave a small grunt of amusement, then took a large bite of the broiled salmon she'd cooked for his breakfast.

Tatiana fought the urge to pick up the bowl of whale oil and dump it over his head. He was so greedy, so vain, and so cruel. He had no qualms about separating a mother from her child. By now, Anna must be heartbroken without Katya. How she wished that day in the forest, Anna had let John take Many Baskets back to the village to be punished, instead of forgiving her and allowing her to leave unharmed. But that was Anna, a kind Christian woman.

When Many Baskets accused Anna and Marya of betraying the chief, Black Hawk gave them the chance to deny it. But neither one would. They both admitted they loved the white men, and Marya said she didn't want to be married to Black Hawk any longer.

Neither did she. Tatiana didn't think she could stand being around him anymore. Any feelings she'd had for him had turned sour. Lately she almost envied Anna and Marya being free of him.

"I never understood why you didn't give Knows Much to Running Wolf in the first place," she said. "You would've had his ninety otter skins to add to the *shaman*'s skins. Think how many trade goods from the white men you could buy with so much."

Black Hawk scowled. "I do not wish to trade with the white men."

"Your brother does and so do many of the people."

"My brother wants the metal knives and smoking weapons and his women are greedy for the iron cooking pots, the glass beads, and the bright cloths. The children long for the sweet taste of what you call 'molasses,' and some of the young men crave the fire water which makes them crazy."

"Some of those things can help the people, my husband. Change is not always bad."

"If what you tell me is true, the white man is as countless as the stars. I am afraid that once we begin to trade with them, nothing will be the same for the Makah again. I have heard of the white man's sickness that can kill a whole village. It happened to Many Baskets' Quileute village years ago. Yet, my people do not listen to me when I tell them we should stay with the old way of life, that the white man will only bring us trouble."

"Your father promised Knows Much if a ship comes to trade, he would release all the captives. Will you do the same?"

He was silent for a few minutes then said, "I will gladly free the Makah of all the white men who live among us, but not the women, and not you. I will never let you go. You are the mother of my son."

Her heart sank in utter disappointment at his words. As if on cue, her son began to cry in his cradleboard. He was hungry. She sighed and went to pick him up. The argument was over, and Black Hawk had won, as usual.

* * *

Another two weeks passed and the late summer days of sunshine soon became cooler and wetter then turned into the warm days and cold nights of early autumn. One chilly morning Anna woke up out of a fitful sleep to the sounds of harsh squawking ravens and a baby's whimpering. Talons made a scuttling sound as the birds ran across the roof overhead looking for insects. She sighed with depression at the thought of another day cooped up inside this dingy dank place; another day without Katya.

At least Marya had her son, thought Anna, as black despair gripped her soul. Why had God allowed her to have Katya back, only to lose her again? And was it forever this time? What if Black Hawk traded them away to another tribe such as the Nootkas? All these worries tormented her day and night. Many times she cried out to God, begging Him for help, but after all these weeks, nothing changed.

Reading her Bible gave them both some comfort and sanity. Black Hawk had sent it with Anna, saying he didn't want her holy object in his house in case it had power over him. Marya was grateful for it since her Bible had been left behind in Chief Xawishata's village when she was captured.

Every other morning the two women, accompanied by a stern-faced Brown Bird, were permitted to bathe in the stream, otherwise, they were forbidden to step foot outside the hut. This morning was not one of those. Anna rose from her bed, a thin fur robe thrown on the dirt floor, and washed her face and hands from the small amount of water inside a watertight basket.

"I hope someone comes soon with more water so we can boil some dried fish for breakfast," said Marya, rocking her child gently in her arms. "And I hope they bring more shredded cedar bark for my son. He needs to be changed before he gets a rash on his bottom."

Anna sighed. "I wish we were allowed fresh meat instead of this dry fish that tastes like the leftovers from last winter. But I guess we should be thankful they're feeding us at all."

"And I am thankful I don't have to put up with Black Hawk anymore," Marya said, then added sadly, "although I wonder if John will ever want me again after being a wife to two Indian men." She tried not to think about the cold expression on John's face the last time she'd seen him in the forest.

"If he truly loves you, he will not hold your two forced marriages against you," said Anna.

Marya sighed dejectedly. "I don't know if John does love me anymore."

Shaking her head in sympathy, Anna swept the sandy soil around the fireplace with a cedar branch, then broke up a few pieces of cedar bark and placed them on the few coals left from the night before. Flames flared up and she carefully put several cooking stones in the fire. "When these are hot enough I can put them in the cooking box to boil the fish, if only we had enough water."

"We could fetch it ourselves if they hadn't tied the door flap shut on the outside. It makes me feel so trapped."

Feeling discouraged and slightly hungry, Anna sat down on her fur robe and listened to the sounds of the people going about their morning work. The village smokehouses and drying racks were in continual use in preparing fish for the coming winter. The men were busy adding fresh game, seal, birds, and fish to the food supplies, and some of the younger women and children were picking the last of the berries.

Another hour went by, then two. She and Marya were feeling very thirsty and the child was fussing from his filthy cradleboard. Soon the fire was a mound of cold ashes and stones. Anna took a piece of dried cod and chewed the tough sinewy strands slowly. Marya did the same.

"If no one comes soon, we should start yelling for attention," she said.

"Perhaps this is Black Hawk's final punishment, to have us die slowly from dehydration. During this spell of warm weather, it shouldn't take any more than three days."

"Oh, don't say such a thing," Marya protested. "Already I feel my milk drying up."

"I'm sorry, Marya. Instead of complaining and predicting our demise, we should be praying that God will send someone to help us."

"I agree." She bowed her head and prayed simply, "Heavenly Father, you know our needs and you know how helpless we are. Please have someone bring us water and more food soon."

She smiled at Anna. "Once I never would've dreamed I could pray to God directly and he would hear me. How thankful I am that I met you, Anna."

She returned Marya's smile, and thought how strange it was that she had come half way around the world from her tiny village of Furstenau to this place in the wilderness. Had God brought her here so she could help others find Him?

Then she remembered Wang Li and Lightning Eagle. She had tried to explain God's love to them, but she had no idea if they had understood her words. And now both men had disappeared and were probably dead. How long ago had that happened? Was it October, yet? If so, she would soon be turning twenty-one years old. As a child, she always imagined by this age she would be a happily married woman, living on a farm with several children. Instead, she'd been widowed, had fallen in love again, and now her betrothed and her daughter were taken away from her.

Tears sprang into her eyes. It was easy to feel full of self pity when one was terribly thirsty, hungry, and tired.

A fumbling at the door startled her and Marya. *At last. Water*. Anna jumped to her feet, swaying dizzily.

"What has taken you so long, you wretched girl?" Marya demanded, thinking it was a slave entering. But it was Tatiana with Strong Elk, Black Hawk's brother, following right behind her. With a grunt he shoved her and knocked her to the ground. Tatiana smacked her bare knees onto the dirt floor and she gave a short cry of pain.

Strong Elk laughed then said, "Either you women will soon bring me much wealth, or all of you will be my wives." His black eyes surveyed them cruelly with a gleam of added lust before he swung out the door.

Anna and Marya gaped at Tatiana. "What did he mean by those awful words?" Anna demanded.

Tatiana rose stiffly to her feet, brushing the dirt off her bruised kneecaps and said, "Three days ago a British ship entered the Strait and anchored off what the Makah call Deeah, or Neah Bay. The captain and Mr. Hill caught the crew's attention with their kite. Both of them have already escaped and are on board the ship.

"Captain O'Connell convinced the British captain to negotiate with all the tribes who have the crew and passengers of the *Sea Rose* to release them for ransom. Yesterday conferences were held aboard the ship with the chiefs of the Makah villages. A price was agreed upon for each captive, five blankets, twelve yards of cloth, a locksmith's saw, a mirror, two steel knives, one musket, five bags of powder, and five bags of shot. The message has gone out everywhere, up and down the coast. There's a good chance everyone will be ransomed."

She paused, then said bitterly, "Everyone but us, that is."

"What do you mean?" Anna asked in alarm.

Tatiana flushed in anger. "At the meeting Black Hawk refused to ransom any of us women. Captain O'Connell became so enraged, he persuaded the British captain to order his men to seize Black Hawk and put him in irons. They will not release him until we are safely aboard. The only problem is, Strong Elk refuses to let us go. He says if the white men kill his brother, then he is chief. The thought of that powerful position is so tempting to him he actually is willing to sacrifice his own brother."

"Where is your son?" Marya questioned.

Tatiana was silent for a moment. "Strong Elk gave him to Swift Deer. He said if he trades me away, she will be his mother."

CHAPTER FORTY EIGHT

Gray Cloud sat in her compartment weaving another cattail mat. She was furious with her youngest son, Strong Elk. She couldn't believe he'd refused to ransom Black Hawk from the white man. As boys, she remembered there had been a measure of sibling rivalry between them, but no more than in other families. Whatever possessed Strong Elk now to become so greedy he would endanger the life of his older brother so he could be chief?

She chastised herself for not seeing this coming. Everyone believed she could see into the future, yet she had failed to see the storm brewing between her sons. She knew Strong Elk was jealous of Black Hawk and all his new wives and added wealth since their father died. But she had dismissed his feelings as trivial, as a part of his grief.

No more. Her youngest son had become dangerous, not only to Black Hawk, but to the entire village. His desire for power was undermining the stability of the village. Already, people were taking sides. Brave Spear and Black Crow and the elders for Black Hawk, and the younger men for Strong Elk.

There had been much grumbling against Black Hawk for his stand against trading with the white men. Many would prefer Strong Elk as chief, who was eager for the trade goods they brought.

Brown Bird and Swift Deer were humiliated by their husband's actions and could barely look Gray Cloud in the face this morning. They knew what he was doing was not right, that it could tear apart their family and the village like a speared fish.

And the babies....all of them were so unhappy without their mothers. For weeks She-Who-Never-Sleeps had been having daily tantrums without Knows Much, and her newest grandson had developed a colicky stomach now that Swift Deer was feeding him instead of his mother, Daughter of the Sun. She'd even heard that Little Dawn, the white daughter of Knows Much, was still fussing for her at times.

Something had to be done. And no one knew quite what to do. She'd gone to Brave Spear and begged him to try and make Strong Elk see some sense. But that had only provoked a quarrel between the two men which might have come to blows if Black Crow hadn't stepped in and calmed them down.

The big black man was such a gift to the village. It made her relieved to hear that he had no intention of returning to the white man's world. He said he was happy being married to Starlight and was looking forward to their child's birth this coming winter.

Her granddaughter, Small Fern, was heartbroken about losing her brother, Gray Whale. Strong Elk had accepted the ransom for him even though the young white man said he would like to stay with the Makah. She suspected he loved her granddaughter and didn't want to leave her. But Strong Elk wanted the musket and knives and other things and told him to go.

Gray Cloud threw down her half finished mat in frustration just as Brown Bird and Swift Deer walked in.

"Where are all the children?" she asked them.

"With Buttercup and Hummingbird. They are so worried about their husband and long for his return."

"So do I," said Gray Cloud.

"Mother, we have an idea," said Swift Deer. She gave Brown Bird a shy look. "You tell her."

Her older sister took a deep breath then said, "We believe our husband, your son, is bewitched by the three white women in the hut. He wants his brother's wives as his own. That is one of the main reasons he refuses to let them go to ransom our chief. My sister and I do not wish our husband to have these women as wives. They have been nothing but trouble since they came. We would like them to go back to the white man. If you will help us, we would like to set them free tonight after dark, and send them to Deeah to the white man's big canoe."

Gray Cloud considered. Then she said slowly, "Yes, it might work if we are quiet and careful. I'll ask Brave Spear and Black Crow to take them there after my son is asleep. It will make him very angry when he finds out, but I will tell him it was my decision, not yours. There will be nothing he can do then." She looked at Swift Deer. "And what about the child of Daughter of the Sun?"

"Our husband was right to give him to me," she said. "I have watched Daughter of the Sun. She is not a good mother. He belongs here with the Makah and his father."

"What should be done with Little Dawn, the white child of Knows Much?" Brown Bird asked.

Gray Cloud shrugged. "After Black Hawk is free, he can decide."

* * *

Captain Matthew Hunter of the British trader named *Elizabeth Ann*, tugged at his blonde mustache and frowned. He was immaculately dressed in a brass buttoned black coat and wool trousers, with well groomed fair hair tied back neatly in a queue under his captain's hat. About thirty years old, he was a dignified looking man with the thin lips and long nose of an English aristocrat. His sharp eyes surveyed the men sitting in his cabin having tea and biscuits.

"Gentlemen," he said, "we've been here a week and I can't wait much longer. It's October and the sooner we've passed these godforsaken shores and their unpredictable gales, the better. As seafaring men yourselves, you do understand my predicament."

"Aye, we do," said Sean, taking a gulp of hot tea and savoring the smooth taste of the expensive blend from Ceylon, a far cry from the Indian herbal swill he'd been drinking the past year. "We know more than anyone how treacherous this Pacific coast is. Yet, in all good conscience, how can we leave Mistress Campbell, Miss Bolkonsky, and the Baroness Volodin with the Makah?"

Hunter sighed in exasperation. "I don't like the idea of helpless white women left in the hands of merciless savages either, but if it comes down to their safety or that of my ship, my ship comes first. I will wait another day, no more."

"You'd think the Makah would be so eager to free their chief, they would've traded the women for him days ago," said Anton, warming his hands around his mug.

He and Jake O'Riley had already been ransomed, along with ten of the American crew and four of the Russians. The rest could not be found, scattered too far among the Quileutes, the Quinault, and even as far south as the Chinook tribe on the Columbia River.

"Someone in the village doesn't want to let the women go," said John in a worried voice. "And if I can make a guess, it might be Strong Elk. I've watched him for a long time, and I've seen the envy in his face whenever he looks at his brother and his many wives. Now that we have Black Hawk imprisoned in the brig, it's Strong Elk's chance to seize the power in his village."

"And the lasses," said Sean with a ferocious scowl. He looked at Hunter. "Cap'n, I suppose 'tis foolish of me to ask if I can have a number of men with muskets to storm the village to free them."

"I can't risk the safety of my crew over a few women. I'm truly sorry, Captain O'Connell," he added, seeing the quick look of fury cross over Sean's face.

There came a knock on the cabin door and the second mate, Mr. Benjamin Todd, poked his head into the room. "Another captive just arrived by canoe, Captain. Not a white man, a Chinaman. Do you want me to pay off the Clallam Indians who brought him?"

Sean and John looked at each other in amazement. "He's our missing cook," laughed Sean. "We all thought he was dead!"

"Certainly, Mr. Todd," said Hunter. "Give them the agreed upon ransom."

Minutes later a grinning Wang Li burst through the doorway, halting immediately and bowing to Sean and Captain Hunter. "Ye wee rascal!" Sean cried, jumping up from his chair and thumping Wang Li on his back. "Where have ye been all this time?"

"With Clallam tribe. They find me in forest and take me to village. They hate Makah. Both tribes enemies. I work hard for them, but they treat me well. Then they hear about ship and want to trade me. They bring me here at night so Makah don't see Clallam canoe."

"And how did ye escape, Wang Li?" Sean questioned. "Who was the person who freed ye? And how did ye manage to survive the forest?"

"Old woman cut the ropes. Chief's mother."

"Laughing Gull?" John asked in surprise. "Who would ever have thought of her?"

"She say she know I am innocent. She say the *shaman* killed her great grandson. She give me pouch of dried fish and tell me to go. I run through forest many days. I eat all the fish. Storms come. I get cold and wet. I never get dry. I get so weak I get sick. One night I fall down and hurt ankle. Next morning I hear something in bushes. Afraid of bear or cougar. I afraid I will die. I pray again ."

"Ye prayed?" Sean echoed in disbelief.

Wang Li bowed his head briefly. "Always I listen to Missy and her Jesus talk. When I tied up with ropes I pray to Jesus, not Buddha. Laughing Gull comes and frees me. I pray in forest and then Clallam come. Not bear. They see hurt ankle and carry me to village. I speak Makah to chief who understands. I tell them Makah think I kill grandson of Chief Utramaka. He laughs, say he is glad to rescue me who kills the Makah. I decide to let them think that. Women take good care of me. Give me much food. Now I am well. Thanks to Jesus. Not Buddha," he added again.

"A Christian Chinaman," muttered Hunter, incredulous. "Never thought I'd see the day!"

"Where is Missy?"

"Strong Elk has her and the Baroness Volodin and her sister confined in the village. We have Black Hawk imprisoned below in exchange for them. He's now the chief since Utramaka drowned in his canoe last spring when they raided the Quileute village."

"Mercy!" Wang Li blinked several times in dismay. "We pray to Jesus. He will rescue Missy and the others."

Captain Hunter and John and Anton glanced at each other, trying to hide their smiles at the naivety of the little man. Sean stared at him, impressed by his childlike faith.

If only it was that simple, he thought. It would take a miracle to free Anna and Katya. Then he realized the *Elizabeth Ann* herself was a miracle, a real Godsend. Why not another?

Six days ago he and John were in deep despair. For weeks they'd been living in a crude shelter they'd built in the forest near the edge of Cape Flattery, worrying incessantly over the fate of Anna and Marya and their own future. They knew the fur trading season was almost over. The last of the ships heading south from Alaska had probably passed by without any of them seeing the kite.

That morning there was a thick fog bank cloaking the entrance of the Strait, but they decided to fly the kite one more day. Near noon the ghostly outlines of a ship had materialized suddenly out of the mist. Sean and John almost fainted in shock.

Immediately they climbed down the nearest rocky cliff to a beach where they shouted and waved at the ship. The lookout in the crow's nest of the *Elizabeth Ann* had seen the strange sight of a kite soaring above the fog bank. He'd notified Captain Hunter immediately. An intelligent man, he knew at once what it meant, white men were stranded on the shores. When they spotted Sean and John on the beach, he sent his longboat to pick them up and bring them on board.

"Well, gentlemen," said Hunter, "it's late and time to retire. Tomorrow will be a busy day. I intend to sail on the noon tide. If the Makah do not bring the women by then, I will release their chief. There's no point in detaining him any longer." He glanced at Wang Li with interest. "Say, Captain O'Connell, is the Chinaman a good cook?"

"The very best," Sean said, remembering how much the Makah hated his cooking.

"Well, then, in the morning send him to the galley. Our regular cook took a fever in the tropics and died. Our cook now is just a lad who doesn't know the difference between a scone and a hardtack biscuit. It's a miracle his cooking hasn't killed anyone yet. He'll be glad to have the Chinaman take his place, so he can go back to regular duties."

"Aye, Captain Hunter, he'll be there first thing."

Looking as glum as they felt, Sean, John, and Anton left the captain's cabin with Wang Li. When the three reached their quarters below in the deck beneath the great aft cabin, Robby and Jake were astounded to see Wang Li.

After hearing his amazing and story and his constant references to Jesus saving him, Jake finally rolled his eyes and groaned, "How did the little bloke get religion, then?"

"Missus Campbell, I reckon," said Robby, smiling broadly. "If she coulda done it, she woulda saved all the Injuns, too. She's a good, what do ya call it, missionary?"

"I know she tried to tell Lightning Eagle about God," said Sean, curling up on his bunk. "Not much good that did. He was the one who killed Red Hawk."

"I think he also poisoned poor Frog, the slave woman," said John. "I think it was God's justice that the scoundrel drowned at sea."

"Where is Samuel?" Wang Li asked, looking concerned. "He okay?"

"He refused to be ransomed," said Sean. "He said he likes the Makah and their way of life. It reminds him of his childhood village in Africa. And more importantly, he's happily married with a child on the way. He said the Makah treat him with respect and honor, something white people never have. Still, I tried to get him to change his mind. I reminded him of his sister, but he said he didn't believe she was still alive. Or if she was, there was any way to find and free her. I promised him I'd keep looking for her, though."

"I'll be yer steward, Cap'n," said Robby eagerly. "I can look after ya like he did."

"First, I have to find me another ship, lad," Sean smiled. "And that will be up to Thomas Hill. He may never give me another command after this disastrous voyage."

"My uncle knows you're the best captain around," said John, yawning. "After we get back to Boston, I bet you'll be back at sea within a year or less."

"We'll see," he said with a hint of doubt. "But now, men, we better get some sleep."

Anton gave Wang Li a blanket. The Chinaman would have to sleep on the floor along with Robby. There were only four bunks in the cabin, which was used to quarter the first and second officers of the *Elizabeth Ann* and the ship's carpenter and sail maker. The mates were bunking with Hunter and the others elsewhere. The American crew and the Russians were squeezed in with the British crew forward. Hopefully, everyone would get along.

There was a long voyage ahead, first to the Sandwich Islands for a cargo of sandalwood, then to Canton to trade the wood and furs for a fortune worth of precious spices, porcelain, teak, and exotic oriental furnishings, then off to London, the home port of the *Elizabeth Ann.*

Somewhere along the way, Hunter hoped to unload all his extra passengers. Before crossing the Pacific he planned to leave the Russians at Fort Ross, California. And if he sighted a Yankee ship sailing back to the United States, the Americans could transfer over to her. Otherwise, he would have to stop in Boston before returning to London.

The ship had spent the past several months dodging the Russian warships in the waters of Russian America. But Hunter was as crafty and knowledgeable as they, and he managed to evade them all summer. Still, the extra precautions had made it more difficult to trade with the coastal Indians and it had taken him longer than expected.

For the stranded crew and passengers of the *Sea Rose*, Sean thought, closing his eyes, the delay had been most fortunate, as the *Elizabeth Ann* was probably the last of the ships passing by Cape Flattery this year. Somehow he fell asleep, after praying in his heart for God to help them bring back Anna and the other women before the ship sailed on the morrow.

Sometime later, in the wee hours before dawn's first light, all the men in the cabin were rudely awakened by a pounding on the door and a shout, "Cap'n O'Connell! Cap'n Hunter says to come topside at once! All of you!"

With a bunch of muttering and groaning, everyone donned their new clothes, shirts, pants, coats, and boots, which had been given to them, and wearily stumbled their way up a ladder and aft to a passageway to the ship's great after cabin or main salon. Sean was the first to reach the door, wondering what was so important. He shoved it open and grinned in delighted surprise.

Anna, Tatiana, and Marya and her infant son, were all sitting on the sofas, wrapped in blankets and sipping hot tea out of mugs. Seeing him, Anna sprang to her feet, the blanket falling onto the polished wooden floor, and rushed towards him. Automatically, he opened his arms and held her, feeling tears of joy prick his eyelids.

Marya let out a soft cry when she saw John and he greeted her with a swift kiss on her cheek. She smiled in relief that he had not rebuffed her, but she sensed a stiffness in his manner. She hoped he was only acting distantly because he felt self-conscious in front of their audience. If they could ever get away by themselves, surely he would be warmer towards her.

Robby, Jake, and Wang Li stood watching the tearful reunions of the two couples, but were even more amazed when Baroness Volodin and Lieutenant Dohktorov embraced as well.

Over Sean's shoulder Anna spied the small Chinaman. "Wang Li!" she exclaimed in surprise, "I can't believe it's you! Where did you come from?"

Wang Li grinned, showing his brown opium-stained teeth. "Missy, I was with the Clallam tribe all this time. They take good care of me. You will be happy to know I pray to your Jesus now."

Anna was instantly full of curiosity, and she couldn't wait to ask him questions. She smiled. "You must tell me all about your experiences very soon."

As Wang Li gave her a slight bow Captain Hunter and his two officers, Mr. Lennon and Mr. Todd, tried not to stare at the beautiful scantily clad ladies, but the cedar bark Indian garments left little to the imagination.

The women needed civilized clothing as quickly as possible, Hunter thought, before the female-starved crew had time to ogle them. There would be an uproar for certain.

And they were already having problems enough from that miserable Yankee they'd rescued from the hurricane in the Caribbean a year ago. How he regretted ever taking on that troublemaker! The man carried out orders with barely concealed hostility and had been heard badmouthing Mr. Lennon to the other seamen and stating that he should be the chief officer.

If they hadn't been so shorthanded this voyage with too many men sickening from scurvy, he'd have put the fellow off on an island with the natives long ago. What was his name?

Oh, yes, Horn, Arthur Horn.

"Mr. Todd," he said to his second mate, a tall wiry man with thick auburn hair and intense brown eyes. "Have a man fetch several bolts of cloth from the hold, and find needles and thread. The ladies will spend the morrow stitching more proper, er, gowns before we can allow them on deck."

His two officers exchanged barely suppressed looks of mirth then Mr. Todd departed the cabin. After he was gone Hunter turned to the first officer. "Mr. Lennon, now all we have to do is release the chief and we can be on our way by noon."

Anna heard his words and stiffened like a stick of wood in Sean's arms. "Katya," she said to him, "what about Katya? We can't leave her there."

He brushed the top of her head with his lips and said, "Go wrap yourself up in your blanket and I'll talk to the captain."

With a worried frown she did as he asked, then sat down on the long sofa built under the square windows of the stern. She had forgotten how soft and comfortable furniture was, and her weak and shaky legs collapsed gratefully underneath her. Beside her, Marya's son began to whimper and Marya returned to pick him up, crooning softly to him as she rewrapped herself in her blanket. Tatiana left Anton's side, also feeling self conscious in her skimpy clothes, and grabbed a blanket.

"Captain Hunter," said Sean, "Mistress Campbell has a daughter, a child of nineteen months, who is still a captive in the village."

The captain looked at Anna. "Why didn't you bring your daughter with you tonight?"

"She was taken from me several weeks ago and given to another Indian woman. I didn't want to leave her, but I had no choice." Anna looked at Sean. "The three of us were asleep earlier tonight when Gray Cloud came to our hut, and told us to follow her. We crept through the village, trying not to wake anyone, especially the dogs. She took us to the beach where Brave Spear and Samuel waited in a canoe to bring us to the ship. Before I joined them I told her I couldn't leave without Katya. But Gray Cloud said she didn't have the authority to take her away from Many Baskets. She said when Black Hawk is released today I should ask him for my child."

Anna turned pleading eyes upon Hunter. "So, please, Captain, if you can wait until Black Hawk is freed, I know he'll free my daughter, too."

"I'll try to trade for her, Mistress, but I can't make any promises."

"Tatiana," said Anton, "why was your child left behind?"

"He was given to Swift Deer, Strong Elk's wife, who also has an infant." Tears moistened her lovely violet eyes. "I know I will never see him again."

"It's likely just as well," muttered John, glancing at Marya's tiny son with a slight frown. "He would have a difficult time trying to adjust to white society as he grows up."

Marya pretended not to have heard, yet Anna saw her face flush darkly as she held her child. Anna wondered if Marya's own babe would become a source of irritation if she married John. And how would his family, the prominent Hills of Boston, react if John came home, bringing not only a half Aleut wife, but also her Indian son?

* * *

The next morning in the gray light of early dawn, Black Hawk stood on the deck next to Captain Hunter and his two officers, along with Sean, John and Anton. The three women stayed in the background along with many of the crew who were armed with muskets.

Arthur Horn was among them. But his gaze was not centered on the Makah chief. Instead he stared at Sean O'Connell and John Hill. He couldn't believe his good luck in encountering the two men he hated most in the world right here on this ship, practically in his lap. As yet, they didn't know he was on board, but the ship was too small for him to go unnoticed for long. When they did spot him, they would go straight to Captain Hunter and tell him that he was wanted by the Boston police for the attack on Abigail Simpson. Just the thought of being locked up in the brig again made him sweat. Before anything like that happened, he had to find a way to eliminate both men.

He thought of the women. It was obvious both Hill and O'Connell were deeply attached to two of them. This made both men extremely vulnerable. Perhaps there was a way to use their women for his revenge. A glimmer of a smile touched his chapped lips as he remembered what he did to John Hill's betrothed back in Boston.

Then his eyes fastened on the Russian baroness. She was the most beautiful woman he'd ever seen in all his voyages around the world. He'd taken one look at her and realized she was a treasure to be prized almost as highly as a chest of gold.

However, a woman like her would never look twice at a man like him, unless he was very rich and powerful. He was planning on becoming both as soon as the *Elizabeth Ann* reached the United States. As the sole survivor of the sinking of the privateer, the *Jupiter*, he was the only man alive who knew exactly which island off the Carolina coast hid the bulk of the captain's fortune. It was a shame some of the money and gold were now at the bottom of the sea inside the ship's hold, but he was certain there was enough left for him to be able to become a wealthy ship owner, build himself a fine mansion, and marry a beautiful woman like the Baroness.

Too bad she once was a white squaw, but he could forgive it. He chuckled to himself as he clutched his musket, imagining how he would command respect in civilized society with such a lovely and aristocratic wife on his arm.

Black Hawk's ankles and wrists were fettered in irons and his skin was chafed and swollen from where the metal was clamped too tightly. Filthy and rank smelling with matted black hair and his eyes darting wildly around, he looked more like a savage beast in chains than a proud dignified chief of the Makahs.

He glared at every white man in sight then turned his hostile gaze upon Sean and John. In Makah he said harshly, “Running Wolf, Yellow Hair, you have betrayed me over and over. I can never forgive you.”

“We weren't the ones who betrayed you, Chief,” said Sean. “Twas your own brother Strong Elk. He refused to trade our women for you. He intended to let you die here on this ship, so he could be chief.”

“No!” Black Hawk exploded, straining against his irons. “That can’t be true! My brother would never betray me!”

“Yes, husband, it is true,” said Tatiana, suddenly, shoving her way through the maze of men standing around Black Hawk. She clutched her blanket tightly around her as Anna and Marya followed closely behind.

Sean saw them and his face tensed in disapproval. Captain Hunter motioned to his men to stand back, but to keep their muskets primed and aimed on the chief. Below on the water next to the ship Brave Spear and a canoe full of warriors waited for Black Hawk. He glanced over the rail and noticed Strong Elk was not among them.

He looked at Tatiana. “Have you betrayed me, too, wife?”

“No, my husband,” she said in a steady voice. “After you were taken prisoner here, your brother came and took me to the slave hut with Whispering Doe and Knows Much. He said we all were to stay there until he became chief. Then he was either going to trade us away to the Nootkas, or keep us as his wives.”

Black Hawk was silent, his black hooded eyes growing darker with his inner rage. “And where is my son?”

“He is with Swift Deer.”

“How did you escape Strong Elk?”

“Last night your mother came to free us. She took us to Brave Spear and Black Crow. They brought us here in their canoe.”

“My mother is a brave woman like you, Daughter of the Sun. She did the right thing even though she has broken my heart in letting you go. I will never forget you. Someday when my son is older, I will tell him about his beautiful mother, who came to me across the sea and went back again.”

With those words he looked at the captain and said in English, “Please take off the metal ropes. I will go back to my people now.”

His polite request in English startled Captain Hunter. Quickly recovering, he nodded to Mr. Lennon, who produced a set of keys, and gingerly approached Black Hawk as if he was a rabid dog, only temporarily restrained. Swiftly, he unlocked all the irons, and they rattled to the deck with a loud clank.

Black Hawk stepped over to the rail and was poised to climb over to the rope ladder when Anna rushed towards him. "Chief," she said in Makah, "Many Baskets still has my child. The captain here will give you trade goods if you will return her to me."

"I promised Many Baskets she could keep the girl as her daughter forever," he said. "I cannot go back on my word as chief."

"But she is my daughter, not hers," Anna protested. She began to tremble from fear as she saw that Black Hawk remained unmoved.

"You can have all my otter skins for her," said Sean, coming up beside Anna. "They are in my hut."

Black Hawk gave him a scornful laugh. "I took those long ago. You have nothing here I want except Daughter of the Sun. I'll trade the girl for her, but nothing else."

Sean and Anna looked at Tatiana, who gasped. "He can't mean that."

Black Hawk gazed at her with such longing and desire, she blushed. "I will give you the chance to return, wife. If you do, I will give Knows Much back her child."

"What is happening here?" Captain Hunter asked, looking puzzled.

Sean briefly explained and by the time he'd finished, Anton had reached Tatiana's side. He put his arm around Tatiana's shoulders and said in English. "This woman is mine. You will not take her back, not even for a child."

Black Hawk's face darkened. "Is this true, wife?"

Tatiana felt trapped in a nightmare. Everyone was looking at her, especially Anna. Her friend's face was a picture of anguished fear. Tatiana felt confused and guilty as she realized she didn't feel the same anguish at the loss of her own infant son. How could she have such a hard heart that she could give him up so easily without nary a tear? Or would the tears and pain come later when she had more time to think about it?

What would God want her to do? The last thing she wished was to return to the Makahs. She had loved Black Hawk once, but not anymore. Her heart belonged to Anton, and the thought of spending the rest of her life with him in civilization seemed like a dream come true. But if she did, Katya would never have a chance at a normal life with her real mother.

And how could Tatiana ever look Anna in the face again knowing she was the one person who could give her back her child, but didn't do it? Wouldn't God want her to be unselfish for the first time in her life and sacrifice herself for someone else?

She took a deep breath and said in English so everyone could hear, "No, husband, this white man is wrong. I am still your wife. I will return with you."

The British crew erupted in a babble of protests as everyone stared at her in shock. The words, “white squaw” were said more than once. A terrible look of pain crossed Anton's face and he stepped hastily away from her as if she had just contracted a deadly disease.

Black Hawk held out his hand to her. “Come, wife,” he said, “let us go home.”

Anna was stunned. She couldn’t believe what Tatiana intended to do. How brave her friend was, she marveled. The old Tatiana would never have offered to make such a noble sacrifice. Anna was amazed at how much God had changed her friend, from the most self-centered vain creature she’d ever met, to this wonderful woman willing to ruin the rest of her life to make her happy. But no matter how much she longed to have her child, it wasn’t right. She could not allow Tatiana to throw away her only chance at rescue.

Looking dazed, Tatiana moved to follow Black Hawk. Without warning, Anna blocked her path. “Tatiana, don’t go with him,” she said in a strong voice.

“But Anna, it’s the only way you’ll ever have Katya again.” She lifted her chin in a brave gesture. “Black Hawk will give me a good life. And I will be with my own son.”

“Is it your son who calls you back then?”

Tatiana shook her head. “To be honest, Anna, no.”

“Then why?”

“Because I love you, Anna. You are the sister of my heart. You deserve to be happy for all you’ve suffered.”

Before Anna could say anything more to change her mind, Tatiana turned to Black Hawk and stretched out her hand.

In that moment she heard a man shout, "Nay! Yer my woman!" then a shot thundered across the deck.

Tatiana felt something hard slam into her chest and she spun around into Black Hawk's arms. His face seemed to shimmer as he stared down at her and she thought he opened his mouth to speak. But she could not hear him. Instead she heard the sound of a thousand voices singing somewhere above her. As she lifted her head up towards the heavens, the last thing she saw with her earthly eyes was his incredulous expression.

A shocked hush settled over the ship, but only for a moment before the shouting erupted all around. Immediate suspicion fell on Anton as he cried out in anguish, but it was quickly apparent that he had no weapon in hand.

As Black Hawk continued to hold a blood spattered Tatiana, Anna and Marya ran over to them, both women hoping she was still alive. Anna reached her friend first, choking back a scream of horror as she saw Tatiana's lovely violet eyes staring sightlessly up at the sky. With a tenderness belaying his savage appearance, Black Hawk gently closed her eyelids.

He looked at Anna and said in a wooden voice, "I will honor the sacrifice my wife has made for you. Before the sun goes down your daughter will be returned."

They exchanged one pain filled glance then Black Hawk released Tatiana into Anna's and Marya's arms. He turned and leaped gracefully over the rail to the ladder. After climbing into the canoe he was greeted with subdued joy by the Makah warriors. Immediately Brave Spear steered the canoe away from the ship's hull and with firm strong stokes, the warriors paddled west along the shore back to Classet.

At that moment a scream of rage resounded as Arthur Horn was seized, still holding his smoking musket.

"I was aimin' for the Injun, not--not the baroness," he spat then cursed at the sailors holding him.

As he had watched the drama playing out in front of him, he had only a moment's thought that if he saved the baroness from leaving with the savage, he would be hailed as a hero. Then it wouldn't matter what accusations John Hill and Sean O'Connell told about him. But he'd made a dreadful mistake. He'd killed the only woman he ever truly wanted.

"Why 'tis the devil himself, Arthur Horn, alive and well," said John, shaking his head in disbelief. He and Sean couldn't believe their eyes.

"Do you know that man?" asked Captain Hunter.

"He's wanted back in Boston for attacking and almost killing a woman," said Sean. "The last we heard he was on a privateer called the *Jupiter*."

"The *Jupiter* sank last year in the Caribbean in a hurricane. We found Horn floating on a raft. The men thought he'd be a good luck charm on the voyage after cheating death. But his luck has run out now."

His expression turned grim. "The punishment for murder on my ship is being hung from the yardarm and cast into the sea.

“Mr. Todd, place Mr. Horn in the Makah chief's chains and then take him below to await justice. The hanging will commence as soon as the child is returned and we've sailed away from shore."

EPILOGUE

Russia, July 1826

The endless sea of rippling golden wheat stretched to the horizon as the horse-drawn carriage reached the village of Furstenau and halted in front of the thatch-roofed home of Herman Teichroew. Sean was the first to alight, dressed smartly in a black frock coat and dark gray trousers, wearing a gray top hat and polished black boots. He offered his hand to Anna, who slipped her gloved hand inside his and stepped out with her other arm holding their one-year-old daughter, Rose Tatiana O'Connell. In the next second little Katya scampered out.

Mother and daughters made a charming picture. Anna wore a light silk shawl and gown of soft green with a rose pink sash. Katya and her sister were both attired in white cambric dresses with pink lace. Katya's mop of unruly curls was tucked into a white bonnet and Baby Rose's dark hair was covered by a cap with pink ribbons. Anna had a green silk bonnet on her head and held a matching parasol to shield both her and Rose from the relentless sun of the open steppes.

It had taken many months to arrive here. First was the voyage from Boston to London on one of Thomas Hill's ships. Then they sailed to Saint Petersburg, where they'd hired the carriage and horses and spent several exhausting weeks traveling south to Furstenau.

This journey through the wide expanse of Russia was made possible because of the new treaty with the United States, signed the year before. Relations between the two countries had eased, thanks to the diligent work of John Quincey Adams, who had once served as the American minister to Saint Petersburg. After President Monroe declared his doctrine in 1823, stating that the United States would do no meddling in the Old World, as long as they similarly respected the boundaries of the New World, Adams pursued negotiations with the Duke of Wellington from England, in jointly persuading Czar Alexander into seeing how imprudent the *Ukase* of 1821 had been.

Count Karl Nesselrode, the Russian foreign minister, tried his best to disrupt the negotiations by telling the British that the *ukase* was directed only at United States citizens. He knew that if the two governments agreed together to fight the ban on foreigners in Russian America, the Czar would have to listen. In 1824, thanks to John Adams, the boundary was drawn back north of the Queen Charlotte Islands. Russia agreed not to establish any more posts outside of their colony, and freedom of navigation, fishing, and trading with the natives was reassured inside the interior seas of Alaska. The United States promised to prohibit liquor and arms, but gave Russia no right to punish Americans, or search and seize their ships.

In the following year of 1825, the British negotiated a similar treaty with Russia. They wanted an eastern boundary for Russian America to separate it from Canada and the right to navigate all the rivers, so the British could reach their own territory inland by passing through the Russian territory. These two treaties had now opened the doors to the Americans and British in the fur trade in Alaska.

When last December Czar Alexander had taken ill and died his twenty-nine-year-old brother Nikolas became the heir to the throne. The new czar soon learned of a revolutionary plot to assassinate him. The ringleader was an office manager at the headquarters of the Russian American Fur Company. Czar Nikolas's secret police arrested him and three others, a board member of the Company and two naval officers, one of whom was Lieutenant Mikael Vasilyich Bolkonsky. Eventually, these men were found guilty and hanged.

Now Anna stared at her old family house, feeling apprehensive and nervous. How was her papa going to react when they knocked on the door?

I can only hope and pray he welcomes us in the same way Uncle Heinrich and Tante *Sarah did,* she thought.

A few days before on their journey to Furstenau, they'd stopped in Silberfeld. To Anna's immense relief her uncle, aunt and cousins were overjoyed to see her again and to meet her husband and daughters.

It had been six years since she'd seen any of them. The twins, Judith and Maria, were now both married matrons, one to a miller, another to a farmer, each with a child and more on the way. Helena at age seventeen was a lovely young woman, betrothed to the son of a wealthy Mennonite farmer. The wedding was to take place in one month and Helena was full of excitement.

Then to Anna's great surprise and happiness, her brother Jack, now twenty two, came with his young wife. He lived nearby and raised horses for Uncle Heinrich. Jack was a stocky broad shouldered young man who took one look at Anna, and with a big grin swung her up into his arms, exclaiming with joy at seeing his older sister safe and sound. His wife Lena was shy, but soon warmed up to Anna, although she seemed dazzled and in awe of Sean, as did the rest of the women. Helena laughingly whispered in her ear that the captain was the handsomest man she'd ever seen, which included her betrothed.

Anna was relieved to find that none of them were disturbed by her marrying a man who was not a Mennonite. That first evening in the parlor the stories of her and Sean's adventures with the Russians and the natives of the Pacific Northwest kept the family spellbound for hours.

Eventually their curiosity turned towards Marya. "Did Count Vasily Bolkonsky ever acknowledge Marya Nikolayevna as his niece?" Helena inquired with interest. She and her sisters were fascinated with the romantic story of the dashing John Hill marrying a half Indian girl from the wilds of Alaska. "And how did she adjust to life in Boston?"

Anna explained how Thomas Hill and his wife Priscilla had been shocked by the arrival of their nephew's *Creole* wife and Indian son. The couple had never lost hope that someday John would marry their good friends' daughter, Abigail Simpson. Her parents wished for that, too, especially since Abigail was deeply involved in the Quaker abolitionist movement to end slavery in the United States, a most unfeminine occupation.

But Arthur Horn had left his mark upon her. Even though Abigail's physical injuries had healed to a few facial scars, her inner scars were still raw. She disliked men in general and was adamant about never marrying. Most of Boston society expected her to treat the new Mrs. Hill with bitter antagonism. Yet, she surprised them all, especially her parents and John, by accepting Marya as a friend and fellow abolitionist.

"Two years went by after the Hills notified Count Bolkonsky of Marya's existence and that of her son Nikolas," said Anna. "Then just before we left Boston a letter came from her uncle welcoming her into the family. Perhaps after losing both his son Mikael and his niece Tatiana, he realized how few real Bolkonskys were left."

"John Hill has built Marya and Nikolas a fine house in Boston," Sean said, "an' the last we heard, they are expectin' a bairn of their own soon."

"Like us," said Jack, smiling at Lena, who blushed with embarrassment.

Anna was glad her brother had married someone who obviously adored him, but what about the rest of her family? Were they as content and happy as Jack? She turned to him and immediately began to ask questions about Papa, Jacob, Peter, Katarina, and even her stepmother Agatha.

Jack smiled and said, "First of all, the family has grown so much, you wouldn't know half of them. Papa and Agatha have quite a brood. There is Heinrich, almost six years old now, and Helena age five, then Elizabeth who is four, and the twins Susan and Anya who are one years old like your Rose."

Anna paled, feeling overwhelmed. "Goodness gracious! How is Papa's health with having to take care of such a large family?"

"He is well, but a bit more gray haired and complains about moving slower in the mornings than he used to. Agatha is still," he hesitated, then shrugged, "Agatha. She rules the house with an iron fist. As soon as Jacob and Peter turned eighteen earlier this year, Jacob left home to study medicine at the university in Moscow, and hopes to be a doctor someday. Peter wanted to run off to sea, but he is Papa's right hand man on the farm. He sure will be excited to find out his sister has married a sea captain." Jack smiled at Sean. "He still is fascinated by anything nautical and might ask to join your crew, sir."

Anna had told them the exciting news that when they returned to Boston, a new ship awaited Sean to command. He chuckled. "The lad can ask, but I don't wish to anger my father-in-law before I even have the chance to know him."

"Will Papa be glad to see me?" Anna asked Jack in a nervous voice.

"I don't know," her brother answered honestly. "When you left with the Bolkonsky family Agatha spoke ill of you to everyone in the village, until Papa became angry with her and said if she couldn't say a good thing about you, she wasn't to ever mention your name again. Since then, he never talks about you either."

He must think of me as the prodigal daughter, she thought sadly. Then she sighed. "And little Tina, how is she?"

"Not so little anymore. Katarina is eleven, almost a young lady."

"Agatha works her much too hard," sniffed *Tante* Sarah. "Heinrich and I are thinking about asking Herman if she can come stay with us. After Helena is married, this big house will be so empty. It would be nice to have a young girl here again to learn how to play the piano, speak French, and dress properly."

Anna hoped her father would agree. It sounded like her younger sister needed to be rescued from Agatha in the same way she had six years before.

So, here they were in front of her old home. It was evening and Anna knew most families were eating supper after a hard day of work, including her own family. At first she thought their arrival had gone unnoticed in the village then she heard the Yoder dogs barking fiercely next door.

Suddenly to Anna's dismay, Gerhard himself strode outside, gigantic and sweaty from his day at the smithy. He took one blank look at her and as recognition dawned upon him, he blurted, "Anna?"

His mother *Frau* Yoder pushed by him and stared at them. She appeared more shrunken than ever, but still wore her usual expression of sharp disdain, now tempered with avid curiosity. A young plump woman with a weary frown on her face followed her. Two chubby boys the image of Gerhard clung wide-eyed to her skirts, one on each side. With a start Anna realized their mother was none other than Esther Klassen, one of Agatha's younger sisters.

"Nosy neighbors," Sean muttered, keeping one wary eye on the salivating Yoder dogs while he took Anna's elbow and firmly guided her towards the front door.

"It is Gerhard Yoder and his family," said Anna. "He's the man I once was betrothed to marry."

"The brute who threatened to kill ye?" Sean turned and gave Gerhard a hard unblinking stare until the big man lowered his gaze. He said something to his mother, who scowled and muttered in response.

"He's the reason I ran away to Saint Petersburg with Tatiana."

"And if ye hadn't done that, I'd never known ye, Anna. I must say God does work in mysterious ways. Oh, look out!"

He broke off as two whining dogs, one golden-haired, the other spotted black and white, ran around the house charging straight at Anna. Sean reached for his knife in his boot, a weapon he never went without, but before he could pull it out, Anna laughed and exclaimed, "Gerda! Alexi!" She handed a startled Rose to her equally startled husband as she dropped her parasol and hugged each deliriously happy dog.

Then the Teichroew front door whipped open and Papa stood there, gazing at them with a shocked expression. Agatha's bulk loomed behind him and she held a baby on each ample hip. He appeared just as Jack described with his hair and mustache totally gray, his face weathered and lined, his shoulders more stooped than wide, but his eyes were as clear blue and penetrating as always. Speechless he stared at Anna, then looked at Sean holding baby Rose in his arms with Katya standing shyly at his side. Finally his gaze slid back to Anna.

For one brief second, the longest in her life, she waited for his reaction. Would he become angry and tell her to leave? Nervous fear clutched her heart as she absently stroked the dogs and smiled at her Papa.

"Anna! My darling Anna!"

Instantly the joy booming out of his voice silenced all her doubts, her fears, and the painful memories of the past. As he opened up his arms in a gesture of love and forgiveness, she rushed towards him. Moments later she was in her Papa's embrace while her younger sister, Katarina, bounced around them with cries of happiness, and her brother Peter stood nearby, a look of surprised pleasure on his face. She couldn't believe how grown-up Tina looked or how tall Peter was!

"I didn't think I'd ever see you again, Anna," Papa cried, tears streaming down his leathery cheeks. "You look so much like your mama."

"Papa," she choked, "this is my husband Captain Sean O'Connell and our daughters, Katya and Rose."

She held her breath while he glanced at Sean and the two girls. "Pleased to meet you, Captain," he said then patted her shoulder awkwardly.

"Yah, yah, it's goot to be a grandpapa," he chuckled, wiping his eyes. "Come, you must all be hungry. We have supper waiting, *twaback* and ham and *keelke* and *pluma moos*."

Anna's mouth watered at the thought of the familiar food. She took a tentative step forwards then halted. Agatha barred her way. Anna glanced up to see her glaring down at her with unconcealed dismay. The twin babies balancing on her hips stared at her with saucer eyes and the three younger children, a boy and two girls, looked at her in awe.

They made her feel like a stranger in what was once her own home.

"And this lovely lady must be *Frau* Teichroew," Sean said, smiling his handsomest grin while giving Agatha an exaggerated bow.

Agatha blushed, a hot pink color sweeping across her cheeks. A bit of sparkle lit up her normally flat gray eyes and she smiled at him before turning to Anna.

She hesitated, then with a grudging nod of respect, she said, "Anna, I bid you and your family welcome. Please come and sit at our table and meet your new sisters and brother."

THE END

BIBLIOGRAPHY

Bleeker, Sonia. THE SEA HUNTERS, INDIANS OF THE NORTHWEST COAST. New York: William Morrow & Company, 1951.

Braun-Ronsdorf, Margarete. MIRROR OF FASHION, A HISTORY OF EUROPEAN COSTUME 1789-1929. New York: Macgraw-Hill Book Company, 1964.

Cheneviere, Antoine. RUSSIAN FURNITURE THE GOLDEN AGE 1780-1840. New York: The Vendome Press, 1988.

Chevigny, Hector. LORD OF ALASKA The story of Baranov and the Russian Adventure. Portland, OR: Binfords & Mort, 1971.

Chevigny, Hector. RUSSIAN AMERICA, The Great Alaskan Venture 1741-1867. New York: The Viking Press, 1965.

Cochran, George M. INDIAN PORTRAITS OF THE PACIFIC NORTHWEST. Portland, Oregon: Binfords & Mort, 1959.

Cohlene, Terri. CLAMSHELL BOY, A Makah Legend. Vero Beach, Florida: The Rourke Corporation, Inc. 1990.

Conly, Arlyn. NEVER TRUST A WHITE MAN. Rochester, WA: Gorham Printing, 1998.

Cooper, Bryan. ALASKA THE LAST FRONTIER. New York: William Morrow & Company, 1973.

Cross, Anthony. RUSSIA UNDER WESTERN EYES 1517-1825. New York: st. Martin's Press, 1971.

Depauw, Linda Grant. SEAFARING WOMEN. Boston: Houghton Mifflin Company, 1982.

Drake, Samuel Adams. OLD LANDMARKS and HISTORIC PERSONAGES of BOSTON. New and Revised edition. Detroit: Singing Tree Press, 1970.

Drimmer, Frederick. SCALPS AND TOMAHAWKS. New York: Coward-McCann, Inc., 1961.

Dziewanowski, M.K. ALEXANDER I, RUSSIA'S MYSTERIOUS TSAR. New York:
Hippocrene Books, 1990.

Epp, Margaret. CHARIOTS IN THE SMOKE. Winnipeg, Manitoba: Kindred Press, 1990.

Fair, Susan W. ALASKA NATIVE ARTS AND CRAFTS. Anchorage: The Alaska Geographic Society, 1985.

Figes, Orlando. NATASHA'S DANCE, A CULTURAL HISTORY OF RUSSIA. New York: Metropolitan Books, 2002.

Foster, Wanda. A VISUAL HISTORY OF COSTUME THE NINETEENTH CENTURY. New York: Drama Book Publishers, 1984.

Gaynor, Elizabeth and Haavisto, Kari. RUSSIAN HOUSES. New York: stewart, Tabori & Chang, 1991.

Gibbs, James Atwood. SHIPWRECKS OFF JUAN DE FUCA. Portland, Oregon: Binfords & Mort, 1968.

Gibbs, James Atwood. SHIPWRECKS OF THE PACIFIC OCEAN. Portland, Oregon: Binfords & Mort, 1957.

Gunther, Erna. INDIAN LIFE ON THE NORTHWEST COAST OF NORTH AMERICA. Chicago: The University of Chicago Press, 1972.

Hardwick, Susan Wiley. RUSSIAN REFUGE, Religion, Migration and Settlement on the North American Pacific Rim. Chicago: University of Chicago Press, 1993.

Hope, Andrew III. RAVEN'S BONES. Sitka, Alaska: Sitka Community Association, 1982.

Hunt, William R. ALASKA A BICENTENNIAL HISTORY. New York: W.W.Norton & Company, Inc., 1976.

Karamanki, Theodore J. FUR TRADE AND EXPLORATION. Norman: University of Oklahoma Press, 1953.

Kashevaroff, Sasha. FAMOUS RUSSIAN RECIPES. Sitka: Old Harbor Press, 1988.

Krause, Aurel. THE TLINGIT INDIANS. Seattle: University of Washington Press, 1956.

Kybalova, Ludmila. THE PICTORIAL ENCYCLOPEDIA OF FASHION. New York: Crown Publishers, Inc., 1968.

Lawrence, John. A HISTORY OF RUSSIA. New York: Farra, straus and Cudahy, 1957.

Loewen, Harry and Nolt, steven. THROUGH FIRE AND WATER, An Overview of Mennonite History. Scottsdale, PA: Herald Press, 1996.

Malloy, Mary. 'BOSTON MEN' ON THE NORTHWEST COAST: THE AMERICAN MARITIME FUR TRADE 1788-1844. Kingston, Ontario: The Limestone Press, 1998.

Maroon, Fred J. THE ENGLISH COUNTRY HOUSE, A Tapestry of Ages. Charlottsville, VA: Thomasson-Grant, 1987.

May, Allan. THE SEA PEOPLE OF OZETTE. Everett, Wash: B & E Enterprises, 1975.

McCune, Don. MAKAH INDIAN HISTORY. Video. Woodinville, WA: The Don McCune Library, Inc. 1993.

McMillan, Alan D. SINCE THE TIME OF THE TRANSFORMERS, The Ancient Heritage of the Nuu-chah-nulth, Ditidaht, and Makah. Vancouver B.C.: UBC Press, 1999.

Morgan, Lael. ALASKA'S NATIVE PEOPLE. Anchorage: The Alaska Geographic Society, 1979.

Powell, J.V. QUILEUTE, An Introduction to the Indians of La Push. Seattle; University of Washington Press, 1976.

Quiring, Walter, Dr. and Bartel, Helen. IN THE FULLNESS OF TIME, 150 Years of Mennonite Sojourn in Russia. Waterloo, Ontario: Reeve Bean Limited, 1974.

Reece, Daphne. HISTORIC HOUSES OF THE PACIFIC NORTHWEST. San Francisco, CA: Chronicle Books, 1985.

Rennick, Penny and Campbell, L.J. SITKA. Anchorage: The Alaska Geographic Society, 1995.

Schuyler, Sackett. RUSSIAN ORTHODOX ALASKA. (videorecording), Thousand Oaks, CA: Goldhill Video, 1998.

Seebaum, Caroline and Sykes, Christopher Simon. ENGLISH COUNTRY, Living in England's Private Houses. New York: C.N. Potter, Crown Publishers, 1987.

Shiels, Archie W. THE PURCHASE OF ALASKA. College, Alaska: The University of Alaska Press, 1967.

Svensson, Sam. SAILS THROUGH THE CENTURIES. New York: The Macmillan Company, 1965.

Swan, James G. INDIANS OF CAPE FLATTERY, at the entrance to the Strait of Fuca, Washington Territory. Seattle: Shorey Publications, 1982.

Tikhmenev, P.A. A HISTORY OF THE RUSSIAN-AMERICAN COMPANY. Seattle: University of Washington Press, 1978.

Tolstoy, Nikolai. THE TOLSTOYS, Twenty-Four Generations of Russian History 1353-1983. New York: William Morrow & Company, Inc., 1983.

Tweedie, Ann M. DRAWING BACK CULTURE, The Makah struggle for Repatriation. Seattle: University of Washington Press, 2002.

Underhill, Ruth Murray. INDIANS OF THE PACIFIC NORTHWEST. Lawrence, Kansas: Publications Service, Haskell Institute, 1945.

Villiers, Alan. THE WAY OF A SHIP. New York: Charles Scribner's Sons, 1953.

Williams, Harold. ONE WHALING FAMILY. Boston, Massachusetts: Houghton Mifflin Company, 1964.

Yarwood, Doreen. EUROPEAN COSTUME, 4000 Years of Fashion. New York: Bonanza Books, 1982.

ACKNOWLEDGMENTS

I wish to thank my husband, Rob, and my two sons, Matthew and Todd, for all their love and support throughout the years I spent in creating this novel. I offer a special thank you to my friends, Alaskan sea captain Jeff Boddington and his wife Leona, for taking me to Alaska on the *Pacific Enterprise* on a fishing expedition. The experiences were invaluable for me in understanding the entire coasts of Washington, British Columbia, and southeast Alaska. I am also grateful to Joyce Du Val and Peggy Coverdale for reading my first draft and helping me correct errors. Many thanks to librarian Susan Murphy for being my "editor" in polishing up the manuscript, so I could eventually submit it to author Eileen Pinkerton, who formatted and finalized the publishing details.

Of course, this novel would be nothing without the two main characters, my great-grandmother Anna Teichroew and Anna Petrovna, whose name I changed to "Tatiana Nikolayevna" to erase the confusion of two characters named "Anna." Besides the journal of my great-grandmother, I am grateful to my grandmother Kate for her own journal of Mennonite life and my mother Marjorie's unpublished book, *From the Steppes to the Plains,* the family memoir of my ancestors from their lives in Russia to the plains of North America.

In reality neither Anna knew each other, but both of their stories so intrigued me that I took the liberty of bringing them together into this novel. Although this is a work of fiction much of the book's events are based on true happenings. My great-grandmother did flee Furstenau, Russia to her relatives in Silberfeld after her father remarried a harsh young woman and attempted to marry Anna to the village "idiot," who then threatened to kill her when she refused his proposal. My great-grandfather came to her rescue and took her to America to Minnesota.

The story of Anna Petrovna can be read further in the book *Russian America* by Hector Chevigny. He wrote a chapter called, "The Tragedy of Anna Petrovna," which tells of the shipwreck of the Russian naval ship *Saint Nicholas* on the Washington Coast and the capture of Captain Bulygin, his wife Anna, and the crew by natives. I tried to portray their experiences as accurately as possible. Unfortunately, not all of them survived their captivity among the Makah tribe of Cape Flattery.

16250199R40442

Made in the USA
San Bernardino, CA
26 October 2014